STEPHEN KING

YOU LIKE IT DARKER

STORIES

SCRIBNER

NEW YORK   LONDON   TORONTO   SYDNEY   NEW DELHI

For the twins, Thomas and Edward

CONTENTS

TWO TALENTED BASTIDS

1

My father—my *famous* father—died in 2023, at the age of ninety. Two years before he passed, he got an email from a freelance writer named Ruth Crawford asking him for an interview. I read it to him, as I did all his personal and business correspondence, because by then he'd given up his electronic devices—first his desktop computer, then his laptop, and finally his beloved phone. His eyesight stayed good right up to the end, but he said that looking at the iPhone's screen gave him a headache. At the reception following the funeral, Doc Goodwin told me that Pop might have suffered a series of mini-strokes leading up to the big one.

Around the time he gave up his phone—this would have been five or six years before he died—I took early retirement from my position as Castle County School Superintendent, and went to work for my dad full-time. There was plenty to do. He had a housekeeper, but those duties fell to me at night and on the weekends. I helped him dress in the morning and undress at night. I did most of the cooking, and cleaned up the occasional mess when Pop couldn't make it to the bathroom in the middle of the night.

He had a handyman as well, but by then Jimmy Griggs was pushing eighty himself, and so I found myself doing the chores Jimmy didn't get around to—everything from mulching Pop's treasured flowerbeds to plunging out the drains when they got clogged. Assisted living was never discussed, although God knows Pop could have afforded it; a dozen mega-bestselling novels over forty years had left him very well off.

The last of his "engaging doorstoppers" (Donna Tartt, *New York Times*) was published when Pop was eighty-two. He did the obligatory round of interviews, sat for the obligatory photos, and then announced his retirement. To the press, he did so graciously, with his "trademark humor" (Ron Charles, *Washington Post*). To me he said, "Thank God the bullshit's finished." With the exception of the informal picket-fence interview he gave Ruth Crawford, he never spoke for the record again. He was asked many times and always refused; claimed he'd said all he had to say, including some things he probably should have kept to himself.

"You give enough interviews," he told me once, "and you are bound to stick your foot in your mouth a time or two. Those are the quotes that last, and the older you are, the more likely it becomes."

Yet his books continued to sell, so his business affairs continued. I went over the contract renewals, cover concepts, and the occasional movie or TV option with him, and I dutifully read every interview proposal once he was incapable of reading them himself. He always said no, and that included Ruth Crawford's proposal.

"Give her the standard response, Mark—flattered to be asked, but no thanks." He hesitated, though, because this one was a little different.

Crawford wanted to write a piece about my father and his long-time friend, David "Butch" LaVerdiere, who died in 2019. Pop and I went to his funeral on the West Coast in a chartered Gulfstream. Pop was always close with his money—not stingy, but close—and the whopping expense of that roundtrip said a lot about his feeling for the man I grew up calling Uncle Butch. That feeling held strong, although the two men hadn't seen each other face to face in ten years or more.

Pop was asked to speak at the funeral. I didn't think he would—his rejection of the public spotlight spread in all directions, not just interviews—but he did it. He didn't go to the podium, only stood up where he was with the help of his cane. He was always a good speaker, and that didn't change with age.

"Butch and I were kids going to a one-room schoolhouse before the Second World War. We grew up in a no-stoplight dirt-road town fixing cars, patching them up, playing sports and then coaching them. As men we took part in town politics and maintained the town dump—very similar jobs, now that I think about it. We hunted, we fished, we put out grassfires in the summer and plowed the town roads in the winter. Knocked over a right smart of mailboxes doing it, too. I knew him when no one knew his name—or mine—outside of a twenty-mile radius. I should have come to see him these last years, but I was busy with my own affairs. I thought to myself, there's time. We always think that, I guess. Then time runs out. Butch was a fine artist, but he was also a good man. I think that's more important. Maybe some here don't and that's all right, that's all right. Thing is, I always had his back and he always had mine."

He paused, head down, thinking.

"In my little Maine town there's a saying for friends like that. We kep' close."

Yes they did, and that included their secrets.

Ruth Crawford had a solid clip-file—I checked. She had published articles, mostly personality profiles, in a dozen places, many local or regional (*Yankee, Downeast, New England Life*), but a few national, including a piece on the benighted town of Derry in the *New Yorker*. When it came to Laird Carmody and Dave LaVerdiere, I thought she had a good hook to hang her proposed story on. Her thesis had come up glancingly in pieces about either Pop or Uncle Butch, but she wanted to drill down on it: two men from the same small town in Maine who had become famous in two different fields of cultural endeavor. Not only that, either; both Carmody and LaVerdiere had achieved fame in their mid-forties, at a time when most men and women have given over the ambitions of their youth. Who have, as Pop once put it, dug themselves a rut and begun furnishing it. Ruth wanted to explore how such an unlikely coincidence had happened . . . assuming it *was* coincidence.

"Has to be a reason?" Pop asked when I finished reading him Ms. Crawford's letter. "Is that what she's suggesting? I guess she never heard about the twin brothers who won large sums of money in their respective state lotteries on the same day."

"Well, that might not have been a *complete* coincidence," I said. "Assuming, that is, that you didn't just make the story up on the spur of the moment."

I gave him space to comment, but he only offered a smile that could have meant anything. Or nothing. So I pressed on.

"I mean, those twins might have grown up in a house where gambling was a big thing. Which would make it a little less unlikely, right? Plus, what about all the lottery tickets they bought that were losers?"

"I'm not getting your point, Mark," Pop said. Still with the little smile. "Do you even have one?"

"Just that I can understand this woman's interest in exploring the fact of you and Dave both coming from Nowheresville and blossoming in the middle of your lives." I raised my hands beside my head as if framing a headline. "Could it be . . . *fate?*"

Pop considered this, rubbing one hand up the white stubble on the side of his deeply lined face. I actually thought he might be about to change his mind and say yes. Then he shook his head. "Just write her one of your nice letters, tell her I'm going to pass, and wish her well on her future endeavors."

So that was what I did, although something about the way Pop looked just then stuck with me. It was the look of a man who could say quite a lot on the subject of how he and his friend Butch had achieved fame and fortune . . . but who chose not to. Who chose, in fact, to keep it close.

Ruth Crawford might have been disappointed in Pop's refusal to be interviewed, but she didn't drop the project. Nor did she drop it when I also refused to be interviewed, saying my father wouldn't want me to after he'd said no, and besides, all I knew was that my father had always enjoyed stories. He read a lot, went nowhere without a paperback jammed in his back pocket. He told me wonderful tales at bedtime, and he sometimes wrote them down in spiral notebooks. As for Uncle Butch? He painted a mural in my bedroom—boys playing ball, boys catching fireflies, boys with fishing poles. Ruth wanted to see it, of course, but it had been painted over long ago, when I outgrew such childish things. When first Pop and then Uncle Butch took off like a couple of rockets, I was at the University of Maine, getting a degree in advanced education. Because, according to the old canard, those who can't do teach, and those who can't teach, teach teachers. The success of my father and his best friend was, I said, as much a surprise to me as to anyone else in town. There's another old canard about how no good can come out of Nazareth.

I put that in a letter to Ms. Crawford, because I did feel bad—a little—about not giving her the interview. In it I said they surely had dreams, most men do, and like most men, they kept those dreams to themselves. I had assumed Pop's stories and Uncle Butch's cheerful paintings were just hobbies, like whittling or guitar-picking, until the money started rolling in. I typed that, then handwrote a postscript: *And good for them!*

There are twenty-seven incorporated towns in Castle County. Castle Rock is the largest; Gates Falls is the second largest. Harlow, where I grew up, the son of Laird and Sheila Carmody, isn't even in the top ten. It's grown considerably since I was a kid, though, and sometimes my pop—who also spent his whole life in Harlow—said he could hardly recognize it. He went to a one-room school; I went to a four-roomer (two grades in each room); now there's an eight-room school with geothermal heating and cooling.

When Pop was a kid, all the town roads were unpaved except for Route 9, the Portland Road. When I came along, only Deep Cut and Methodist Road were dirt. These days, all of them are paved. In the sixties there was only one store, Brownie's, where old men sat around an actual pickle barrel. Now there are two or three, and a kind of downtown (if you want to call it that) on the Quaker Hill Road. We have a pizza joint, two beauty parlors, and—hard to believe but true—a nail salon that seems to be a going concern. No high school, though; that hasn't changed. Harlow kids have three choices: Castle Rock High, Gates Falls High, or Mountain View Secondary, most commonly known as the Christer Academy. We're a bunch of country bumpkins out here: pickup-driving, country-music-listening, coffee-brandy-drinking,

Republican-leaning hicks from the sticks. There's nothing much to recommend us, except for two men who came from here: my pop and his friend Butch LaVerdiere. Two talented bastids, as Pop put it during his brief over-the-fence conversation with Ruth Crawford.

Your mom and pop spent their whole lives there? a city person might ask. *And then YOU spent your whole life there? What are you, crazy?*

Nope.

Robert Frost said home is the place that, when you go there, they have to take you in. It's also the place you start from, and if you're one of the lucky ones, it's where you finish up. Butch died in Seattle, a stranger in a strange land. Maybe that was okay with him, but I have to wonder if in the end he wouldn't have preferred a little dirt road and the lakeside forest known as the 30-Mile Wood.

Although most of Ruth Crawford's research—her *investigation*—was centered in Harlow, where her subjects grew up, there are no motels there, not even a bed and breakfast, so her base of operations was the Gateway Motel, in Castle Rock. There actually *is* a senior living facility in Harlow, and there Ruth interviewed a fellow named Alden Toothaker, who went to school with my pop and his friend. It was Alden who told her how Dave got his nickname. He always carried a tube of Lucky Tiger Butch Wax in his hip pocket and used it frequently so his flattop would stand up straight in front. He wore his hair (what there was of it) that way his whole life. It became his trademark. As to whether he still carried Butch Wax once he got famous, your guess is as good as mine. I don't know if they even still make it.

"They used to pal around together back in grade school," Alden told her. "Just a couple of boys who liked to fish or go hunting with their daddies. They grew up around hard work and didn't expect nothing different. You might talk to folks my age who'll tellya those boys were going to amount to something, but I'm not one of em. They were ordinary fellas right up until they weren't."

Laird and Butch went to Gates Falls High. They were placed in what was then called "the general education" courses, which were for kids who had no plans to go to college. No one came out and said they weren't bright enough; it was just assumed. They took something called Daily Math and Business English, where several pages of their textbook explained how to correctly fold a business letter, complete with diagrams. They spent a lot of time in woodshop and auto shop. Both played football and basketball, although my pop spent most of his time riding the bench. They both finished with B averages and graduated together on June 8th, 1951.

Dave LaVerdiere went to work with his father, a plumber. Laird Carmody and his dad fixed cars out on the family farm and sold them on to Peewee's Car Mart in Gates Falls. They also kept a vegetable stand on the Portland Road that brought in good money.

Uncle Butch and his father didn't get along so well and Dave eventually struck out on his own, fixing drains, laying pipe, and sometimes digging wells in Gates and Castle Rock. (His father had all the business in Harlow, and wasn't about to share.) In 1954 the two friends formed L&D Haulage, which mostly meant dragging the summer people's crappie to the dump. In 1955 they *bought* the dump and the town was happy to be rid of it. They cleaned it up, did controlled burns, instituted a primitive recycling program, and kept it vermin-free. The town paid them a stipend that made a nice addition to their regular jobs. Scrap metal, especially copper wire, brought in more cash. Folks in town called them the Garbage Twins, but Ruth Crawford was assured by Alden Toothaker (and other oldies with intact memories) that this was harmless ribbing, and taken as such.

The dump was maybe five acres, and surrounded by a high board fence. Dave painted it with murals of town life, adding to it each year. Although that fence is long gone (and the dump is now a landfill), photographs remain. Those murals remind people of Dave's later work. There were quilting bees that merged into baseball games, baseball games that merged into cartoon caricatures of long-gone Harlow residents, scenes of spring planting and fall reaping. Every aspect of smalltown life was represented, but Uncle Butch also added Jesus followed by the apostles (last in line came Judas, with a shit-eating grin on his face). There was nothing really remarkable about any of these scenes, but they were exuberant and good-humored. They were, you might say, *harbingers*.

Shortly after Uncle Butch died, a LaVerdiere painting of Elvis Presley and Marilyn Monroe strolling hand-in-hand down the sawdust-floored midway of a smalltown carnival sold for three million dollars. It was a thousand times better than Uncle Butch's dump murals, but it would have looked at home there: the same screwy sense of humor, set off by an undercurrent of despair and—maybe—contempt. Dave's dump murals were the bud; *Elvis & Marilyn* was the bloom.

Uncle Butch never married, but Pop did. He'd had a high school sweetheart named Sheila Wise, who went away to Vermont State Teachers College after graduation. When she came back to teach the fifth and sixth grades at Harlow Elementary, my father was delighted to find she was still single. He wooed and won her. They were married in August of 1957. Dave LaVerdiere was Pop's best man. I came along a year later, and Pop's best friend became my Uncle Butch.

I read a review of Pop's first book, *The Lightning Storm*, and the reviewer said this: "Not much happens in the first hundred or so pages of Mr. Carmody's suspenseful yarn, but the reader is drawn on anyway, because there are violins."

I thought that was a clever way to put it. There were few violins for Ruth Crawford to hear; the background picture she got from Alden and others around town was of two men, decent and upstanding and pretty much on the dead level when it came to honesty. They were country men living country lives. One married and the other was what was called "a confirmed bachelor" in those days, but with not a whiff of scandal concerning his private life.

Dave's younger sister, Vicky, did agree to be interviewed. She told Ruth that sometimes Dave went "up the city"—meaning Lewiston—to visit the beer-and-boogie clubs on lower Lisbon Street. "He'd be jolly at the Holly," she said, meaning the Holiday Lounge (now long gone). "He was most apt to go if Little Jonna Jaye was playing there. Oh my, such a crush he had on her. He never brought *her* home—no such luck!—but he didn't always come home alone, either."

Vicky paused there, Ruth told me later, and then added, "I know what you might be thinking, *Miz* Crawford, most everyone does these days when a man spends his life without a long-time woman, but it's not so. My brother may have turned out to be a famous artist, but he sure as hell wasn't *gay*."

The two men were well liked; everyone said so. And they *neighbored*. When Philly Loubird had a heart attack with his field half-hayed and thunderstorms in the offing, Pop took him to the hospital in Castle Rock while Butch marshaled a few of his dump-picking buddies and they finished the job before the first drops hit. They fought grassfires and the occasional housefire with the local volunteer fire department. Pop went around with my mother collecting for what was then called the Poor Fund, if he didn't have too many cars to fix or work to do at the dump. They coached youth sports. They cooked side by side at the VFD pork roast supper in the spring and the chicken barbecue that marked the end of summer.

Just country men living country lives.

No violins.

Until there was a whole orchestra.

I knew a lot of this. I learned more from Ruth Crawford herself at the Korner Koffee Kup, across the street from the Gateway Motel and just about a block down from the post office. That's where Pop got his mail, and there was usually a pretty damn good budget of it. I always stopped at the Koffee Kup after grabbing the post. The Kup's java is strictly okay, no more than that, but the blueberry muffins? You never had a better one.

I was going through the mail, sorting out the trash from the treasure, when someone said, "May I sit down?"

It was Ruth Crawford, looking slim and trim in white slacks, a pink shell top, and a matching mask—that was the second year of Covid. She was already sliding into the other side of the booth, which made me laugh. "You don't give up, do you?"

"Timidity never won a fair maiden the Nobel Prize," she said, and took off her mask. "How's the coffee here?"

"Not bad. As you must know, since you're staying right across the street. The muffins are better. But still no interview. Sorry, Ms. Crawford, can't do it."

"No interview, check. Anything we say is strictly off the record, okay?"

"Which means you can't use it."

"That's what it means."

The waitress came—Suzie McDonald. I asked her if she was keeping up with her night classes. She smiled behind her own mask and said she was. Ruth and I ordered coffee and muffins.

"Do you know *everyone* in the three towns?" Ruth asked when Suzie was gone.

"Not everyone, no. I used to know more, and a lot more people, when I was still Superintendent of Schools. Off the record, right?"

"Absolutely."

"Suzie had a baby when she was seventeen and her parents kicked her out. Holy rollers, Church of Christ the Redeemer. Went to live with her aunt in Gates. Since then she's finished high school and is taking classes at the County Extension, associated with Bates College. Eventually she wants to be a vet. I think she'll make it, and her little girl is doing fine. What about you? Having a good time? Learning a lot about Pop and Uncle Butch?"

She smiled. "I learned your father was quite the hot-rodder before he married your mother—sorry for your loss, by the way."

"Thanks." Although in that summer of 2021, my mother had been gone five years.

"Your dad rolled some old farmer's Dodge and lost his license for a year, did you know that?"

I hadn't, and told her so.

"I found out Dave LaVerdiere liked the bars in Lewiston, and had a crush on a local singer who called herself Little Jonna Jaye. I found out he bolted the Republican Party after the Watergate thing, but your father never did."

"No, Pop will vote Republican until the day he dies. But . . ." I leaned forward. "Still off the record?"

"Totally!" Smiling, but her eyes were bright with curiosity.

I lowered my voice to a near whisper. "He didn't vote for Trump the second time. Couldn't bring himself to vote for Biden, but he had a bellyful of the Donald. I expect you to take that to your grave."

"I swear. I found out that Dave won the annual town fair pie-eating contest from 1960 to 1966, when he retired from competition. I learned that your father sat on the ducking stool at Old Home Days until 1972. There are amusing pictures of him in one of those old-fashioned bathing suits and a derby hat . . . waterproof, I assume."

"I was totally embarrassed," I said. "Such a ribbing I took at school."

"I learned that when Dave went west, he packed everything he felt he needed into the saddlebags of his Harley-Davidson motorcycle and just took off. Your father and mother sold everything else he owned at a yard sale and sent him the money. Your dad also sold his house for him."

"At a pretty nice profit," I said. "Which was good. By then Uncle Butch was painting full-time, and he used that money until he started selling his work."

"And by then your father was writing full-time."

"Yes, and still ran the dump. Did until he sold it back to the town in the early nineties. That's when it became a landfill."

"He also bought Peewee's Car Mart and sold that. Gave the proceeds to the town."

"Seriously? He never told me." Although I was sure my mom knew.

"He did, and why not? He didn't need the money, did he? By then writing was his job and all the town stuff was just a hobby."

"Good works," I said, "are never a hobby."

"Your father taught you that?"

"My mother."

"What did *she* think of the sudden change in your fortunes? Not to mention your Uncle Butch's change in his?"

I considered her question while Suzie brought our muffins and coffee. Then I said, "I don't really want to go there, Ms. Crawford."

"Call me Ruth."

"Ruth, then . . . but I still don't want to go there."

She buttered her muffin. She was looking at me with a kind of sharp-eyed bewilderment—I don't know what else to call it—that made me uncomfortable.

"With what I've got I can write a good piece and sell it to *Yankee* magazine," she said. "Ten thousand words, full of local color and amusing anecdotes. All the Maine shit people like, lots of *ayuh* and *I sh'd smile and kiss a pig*. I've got pictures of Dave LaVerdiere's dump murals. I've got pictures of your father—the famous author—wearing a 1920s-style bathing suit while townies try to dump him into a tank of water."

"Two bucks for three throws at the big Ducking Lever. All profits to various town charities. They cheered every time he went kersplash."

"I have photos of them serving chicken dinners to tourists and summer people, the two of them wearing aprons and joke toques that said YOU MAY KISS THE COOK."

"Plenty of women did."

"I've got fishing stories, hunting stories, good deeds done—like getting in the hay for the man who had the heart attack. I've got the story of Laird joyriding and losing his license. I've got all of that, and I've got *nothing*. Which is to say nothing of real substance. People love to tell stories about them—I knew Laird Carmody *when*, I knew Butchie LaVerdiere *when*, but none of them explain what they *became*. Do you see what I'm getting at?"

I said I did.

"You must know some of those things, Mark. What the fuck *happened*? Won't you tell me?"

"There's nothing to tell," I said. I was lying, and I think she knew it.

I remember a call I got in the fall of 1978, the dormitory mom (there actually were such things back then) puffing up to the third floor of Roberts Hall and telling me my mother was on the phone and sounded upset. I hurried down to Mrs. Hathaway's little suite, afraid of what I might hear.

"Mom? Everything okay?"

"Yes. No. I don't know. Something happened to your father while they were on their hunting trip in the 30-Mile Wood." Then, as if an afterthought: "And to Butch."

My stomach dropped; my testicles seemed to rise up to meet it. "Was there an accident? Are they hurt? Is someone . . ." I couldn't finish, as if to ask if someone was dead would make it so.

"They're all right. Physically all right. But something happened. Your father looks like he saw a ghost. And Butch . . . the same. They told me they got lost, but that's hogwash. Those two men know the 30-Mile like the back of their hand. I wish you'd come home, Mark. Not right now, this weekend. Maybe you can get it out of him."

But when I asked, Pop insisted that they'd just gotten lost, finally found their way back to Jilasi Creek (a slurred, Americanized version of the Micmac word for hello), and came out behind the Harlow Cemetery, pretty as you please.

I didn't believe that crap story any more than Mom did. I went back to school, and before Christmas break, a terrible idea surfaced in my mind: that one of them had shot another hunter—which happens several times a year during hunting season—and killed him, and buried him in the woods.

On Christmas Eve, after Mom had gone to bed, I finally summoned the nerve to ask him about that idea. We were sitting in the living room, looking at the tree. Pop looked startled . . . then he laughed. "God, no! If something like that had happened, we would have reported it and taken our medicine. We just got lost. It happens to the best of us, kiddo."

My mother's word came to me, and I almost said it: hogwash.

My father had a dry sense of humor, and it was never on better display than when his accountant came up from New York—this was around the time Pop's last novel was published—and told Pop his net worth was just over ten million dollars. Not J.K. Rowling numbers (or even James Patterson's), but considerable. Pop thought it over and then said, "I guess books do a lot more than furnish a room."

The accountant looked puzzled, but I got the reference and laughed.

"I won't be leaving you broke, Markey," Pop said.

He must have seen me wince, or maybe just realized the implication of what he'd said. He leaned over and patted my hand, as he had when I was a child and something was troubling me.

I wasn't a child any longer, but I was alone. In 1988 I married Susan Wiggins, a lawyer in the county attorney's office. She said she wanted kids but kept putting it off. Shortly before our twelfth wedding anniversary (for which I'd purchased a string of pearls), she told me she was leaving me for another man. There's a lot more to the story, I suppose there always is, but that's all you need to know, because this story isn't about me—not really. But when my father said that thing about not leaving me broke, what I thought of—what I believe we both thought of—is to whom *I* would leave that ten million, or whatever remained of it, when my time came?

Probably Maine School Administrative District 19. Schools always need money.

"You must know," Ruth said to me that day in the Koffee Kup. "You *must*. Off the record, remember?"

"Off the record or on it, I really don't," I said. All I knew was something happened to Pop and Uncle Butch in November of 1978, on their annual hunting trip. After that Pop became a bestselling writer of thick novels, the kind critics used to call three-deckers, and Dave LaVerdiere gained fame first as an illustrator and then as a painter "who combines the surrealism of Frida Kahlo with the American romance of Norman Rockwell" (*ArtReview*).

"Maybe they went down to the crossroads," she said. "You know, like Robert Johnson was supposed to have done. Made a deal with the devil."

I laughed, although I would be lying if I hadn't had the same idea cross my mind, mostly on stormy summer nights when the rolls of thunder kept me awake. "If they did, the contract must have been for a lot more than seven years. Pop's first book was published in 1980, the same year Uncle Butch's portrait of John Lennon was on the cover of *Time*."

"Almost forty years for LaVerdiere," she mused, "and your father's retired but still going strong."

"Strong might be too strong a word for it," I said, thinking about the pissy sheets I'd changed just that morning before setting sail for the Rock. "But he *is* still going. What about you? How much longer are you going to spend in our neck of the woods, ferreting out dirt on Carmody and LaVerdiere?"

"That's kind of a shitty way of putting it."

"I'm sorry. Bad joke."

She had eaten her muffin (I told you they were good) and was mashing up the few remaining crumbs with a forefinger. "Another day or two. I want to go back to the elder care place in Harlow, and maybe talk to LaVerdiere's sis again, if she's willing. I'll come out of this with a very salable piece, but no way is it the piece I wanted."

"Maybe what you wanted is something that can't be found. Maybe creativity is supposed to remain a mystery."

She wrinkled her nose and said, "Save your metaphysics to cool your porridge. Can I pick up the check?"

"No."

Everyone in Harlow knows our house on Benson Street. Sometimes fans of Pop's books from away stop by for a peek if they happen to be on vacation, although they tend to be disappointed by it; just your typical New England saltbox in a town that's full of them. A little bigger than most, set back from a good-sized lawn dotted with flowerbeds. My mother planted those and tended them until she died. Now Jimmy Griggs, our handyman, keeps them watered and pruned. Except for the daylilies growing along the picket fence out front, that is. Pop likes to see to them himself, because Mom loved them best. When Pop waters them, or just walks their length, limping slowly along on his cane, I think he does it to remember the woman he always called "my dear Sheila." Sometimes he bends to caress one of the blossoms—crowns that form on leafless stems called scapes. The blooms are yellow, pink, and orange, but he particularly likes the red ones, which he says remind him of her cheeks when she blushed. His public persona was crusty and a bit cynical—plus there was that dry sense of humor—but at heart he was always a romantic and could be a bit corny. He told me once that he kept that part hidden, because it bruised easily.

Ruth knew where the house was, of course. I'd seen her cruise past in her little Corolla several times, and once she stopped to snap pictures. I'm sure she also knew that Pop was most apt to walk our picket fence, looking at the daylilies, at midmorning, and if you don't know by this point that she was a very determined lady, I haven't done my job.

Two days after our off-the-record talk in the Koffee Kup, she came slow-rolling down Benson Street, and instead of driving past, she pulled over and stopped right next to the little signs on either side of the gate. One says PLEASE RESPECT OUR PRIVACY. The other says MR. CARMODY DOES NOT GIVE AUTOGRAPHS. I was walking with Pop as I usually did when he inspected the daylilies; he turned eighty-eight in that summer of 2021, and even with the cane he sometimes tottered.

Ruth got out and approached the fence, although she made no effort to try the gate. Persistent, but also mindful of boundaries. I liked her for that. Hell, I liked her, period. She was wearing a flower-printed mask. Pop wasn't, claimed they made it hard to breathe, but he'd had no objections to the vaccinations.

Pop looked at her with curiosity, but also with a faint smile. She was good-looking, especially in the light of a summer morning. Checked shirt, denim skirt, white socks and sneakers, hair pulled back in a teenager's ponytail.

"As the sign says, Miss, I don't give autographs."

"Oh, I don't think that's what she wants," I said. I was amused by her chutzpah.

"My name is Ruth Crawford, sir. I wrote and asked for an interview. You turned me down, but I thought I'd try one more time in person before getting on the road to Boston."

"Ah," Pop said. "Me and Butch, right? And is serendipity still your angle?"

"Yes. Although I don't feel I ever really got to the heart of the matter."

"The heart of darkness," he said, and laughed. "Literary joke. I've got a bunch of them, although they have been gathering dust since I retired from giving interviews. A vow I intend to keep even though you seem like a nice woman, and Mark here tells me you're well about it."

I was both surprised and pleased to see him extend a hand over the fence. She seemed surprised, too, but she shook it, being careful not to squeeze too hard.

"Thank you, sir. I felt I had to try. Your flowers are beautiful, by the way. I love daylilies."

"Do you really, or are you just saying that?"

"I do really."

"My wife did, as well. And since you've been kind enough to compliment what my dear Sheila loved, I'm going to offer you a fairy tale deal." His eyes were sparkling. Her good looks—and maybe her chutzpah—had perked him up the way a splash of water seemed to perk up his dear Sheila's blooms.

She smiled. "What would that be, Mr. Carmody?"

"You get three questions, and you can put my answers in your article. How is that?"

I was delighted, and Ruth Crawford looked the same. "Totally excellent," she said.

"Ask away, young lady."

"Give me a second. You're putting me under pressure."

"True, but pressure creates diamonds from coal."

She didn't ask if she could record him, which I thought was smart. She tapped her lips with a forefinger, maintaining eye contact with Pop as she did it. "Okay, question one. What did you like best about Mr. LaVerdiere?"

He didn't stop to consider. "Loyalty. Trustworthiness. They come to the same, I suppose, or almost. Men are lucky to have even one good friend. Women, I suspect, have more . . . but you would know better than I."

She considered. "I think I have two friends I'd trust with my deepest secrets. No . . . three."

"Then you're lucky. Next question."

She hesitated, because she probably had at least a hundred of them and this short interview over our picket fence, for which she hadn't prepared, was going to be her only shot. And Pop's smile—not entirely kind—said he knew the position he'd put her in.

"Time is ticking away, Miss Crawford. Soon I'll have to go inside and rest my tired old pins."

"All right. What's your best memory of time you spent with your friend? I'd like to know the worst time, too, but I want to save my last question."

Pop laughed. "I'll give you that one for free, because I like your persistence, and because you are easy on the eyes. The worst time was out in Seattle, the last cross-country trip I imagine I'll ever make, looking at a coffin and knowing my old friend was inside. His talented right hand stilled forever."

"And the best?"

"Hunting in the 30-Mile," he said promptly. "We went the second week of November from the time we were teenagers right up until Butch mounted his steel pony and set sail for the golden west. We stayed at a little cabin in the woods that my grandfather built. Butch claimed that *his* grandfather pitched in when it came to the roofing, which might or might not have been true. It was a quarter-mile or so beyond Jilasi Creek. We had an old Willys jeep, and until '54 or '55, we drove it across the plank bridge, parked on the other side, and humped it to the cabin with our packs and our rifles. Then we got so we didn't trust the Willys on the bridge because floods had undercut it some, so we'd park on the town side and walk across."

He sighed, looking off into the distance.

"What with all the clear-cutting by Diamond Match, and that housing development on Dark Score Lake where the Noonan place used to be, 30-Mile Wood is more like 20-Mile Wood now. But back then there was plenty of forest for two boys . . . then two young men . . . to ramble around in. We sometimes shot a deer, and once we shot a turkey that turned out tough and sour, but the hunting was the least of it. We just liked being on our own for those five or six or seven days. I guess a lot of men take to the woods so they can drink and smoke, maybe go out to the bars and bring back a night's worth of poontang, but we never did those things. Oh well, yes, we did drink a little, but if we brought a bottle of Jack it'd last us the whole week with some left over, which we pitched into the fire to watch the flames shoot up. We talked about God and the Red Sox and politics and how the world might end in nuclear fire.

"I remember once we were sitting on a log, and a buck, biggest one I ever saw, an eighteen-pointer, maybe the biggest one *anybody* ever saw, at least in these parts . . . it came walking through the marsh below us, as delicate as you please. I raised my rifle and Butch put his hand on my arm. 'Don't,' he said. 'Please don't. Not that one.' And so I didn't.

"Nights we'd lay a fire in the fireplace and have us a knock or two of Jack. Butch brought a pad and he'd draw. Sometimes while he did, he'd ask me to tell him a story, and I did. One of those stories eventually became my first book, *The Lightning Storm*."

I could see her trying to remember it all. It was like gold to her, and it was like gold to me. Pop never talked about the cabin.

"I don't suppose you've read an essay called 'Come Back to the Raft Ag'in, Huck Honey!,' have you?"

Ruth shook her head.

"No? No, of course not. Nobody reads Leslie Fiedler anymore, which is a shame. He was outrageous, a slayer of sacred cows, and that made him fun. He argued in the essay that homoeroticism was the great engine of American literature—that stories of male bonding were actually stories of suppressed sexual desire. Bullshit, of course, probably says more about Fiedler than it does male sexuality. Because . . . why? Can either of you tell me?"

Ruth looked like she was afraid to break the spell (the one he'd cast over himself as well as her), so I spoke up. "It's shallow. Turns male friendship into a dirty joke."

"Oversimplified but not wrong," Pop said. "Butch and I were friends, not lovers, and during those weeks in the woods we enjoyed that friendship in its purest state. Which is a kind of love. It wasn't that I loved Sheila less, or that Butch didn't enjoy his trips up the city less—he was so crazy about rock and roll music, which he called bop—but in the 30-Mile, all the bump, bustle, and roar of the world fell away."

"You kep' close," I said.

"We did indeed. Time for your last question, Miss."

She didn't hesitate. "What happened? How was it that you stopped being men of the town and became men of the world? Cultural icons?"

Something in his face changed, and I remembered my mother's distress call when I was in college: *Your father looks like he saw a ghost.* If so, I thought he was seeing it again. Then he smiled, and the ghost was gone.

"We were just two talented bastids," he said. "Leave it at that. Now I need to get inside and out of this bright sun."

"But—"

"No." He spoke curtly, and she recoiled a little. "We're done."

"I think you got more than you expected," I told her. "Be content with that."

"I guess I'll have to. Thank you, Mr. Carmody."

Pop lifted one arthritic hand in acknowledgement. I guided him back to the house and helped him up the porch steps. Ruth Crawford stood there for a bit, then got in her car and drove away. I never saw her again, but of course I read the article she wrote about Pop and Uncle Butch. It was lively and full of amusing anecdotes, if short on real insight. It was in *Yankee* magazine, and twice the length they usually allowed for their articles. I'm sure she really did get more than she expected when she stopped by the house on her way out of town, and that included the title: "Two Talented Bastids."

My mother—Sheila Wise Carmody, Our Lady of the Daylilies—died in 2016, at the age of seventy-eight. It came as a shock to everyone who knew her. She didn't smoke, she only drank the rare glass of wine on special occasions, she was neither over nor underweight. Her mother lived to ninety-seven, her grandmother to ninety-nine, but Mom suffered a massive heart attack while driving home from the Castle Rock IGA with a load of groceries in the trunk of her car. She pulled over on the shoulder of Sirois Hill, set the emergency brake, turned off the engine, folded her hands in her lap, and went into the darkness that surrounds this bright flash we call life. My father was shaken by the death of his old friend Dave LaVerdiere, but his wife's death left him inconsolable.

"She should have lived," he said at her funeral. "Someone in the clerical department has made a terrible mistake." Not very eloquent, not his best, but he was in shock.

For six months, Pop slept downstairs on the pullout couch. Finally, at my urging, we cleaned out the bedroom where they had spent over 21,000 nights. Most of her clothes went to the Goodwill in Lewiston, which was a favorite charity. He shared her jewelry out among her friends, with the exception of her engagement ring and her wedding ring, which he carried in the watch pocket of his jeans until the day he died.

The cleaning out was a hard job for him (for both of us), but when it came to clearing her little study, hardly more than a closet adjacent to the mudroom, he flat refused.

"I can't, Mark," he said. "I just can't. It would break me. You'll have to do it. Box up her papers and put them in the basement. I'll look at them eventually, and decide what needs to be kept."

But so far as I know, he never did look. Those boxes are still where I put them, under the Ping-Pong table that nobody has used since Mom and I used to have spirited games down there, Mom swearing colorfully every time I hit a smash she couldn't handle. Cleaning out her little "think room," as she called it, was hard. Looking at the dusty Ping-Pong table with its sagging green net was even harder.

A day or two after Pop's extraordinary picket-fence interview with Ruth Crawford, I found myself remembering how I'd fortified myself with a Valium before going into her think room with a couple of empty banker's boxes. When I got to the bottom drawer of her desk, I found a stack of spiral notebooks, and when I opened one, I'd seen my father's unmistakable backslanted printing. They predated his breakthrough, after which every book, even the first, became a bestseller.

His first three novels, written before word processors and computers became commonplace, were composed on an IBM Selectric, which he lugged home each afternoon from the Harlow Town Office. He gave me those typed manuscripts to read and I remembered them well. There were places where he'd scratched out words and added different ones between the lines, and he'd make a pen-slash through a paragraph or two if they went long—that's how it was done before the delete button was invented. Sometimes he used the *x* key, where *A beautiful lovely day* might become *A xxxxxxxxx lovely day*.

I'm going on about this because there were few strike-outs or strike-overs in the finished manuscripts of *The Lightning Storm*, *The Terrible Generation*, and *Highway 19*. The spiral notebooks, on the other hand, were full of cross-outs, some so heavy they had torn the pages. Other pages had been entirely scribbled over, as if in a fury. There were marginal notes, like *What happens to Tommy?* and *Remember the bureau!!!* There were a dozen of those notebooks in all, and the one at the bottom was pretty clearly a trial run at *The Lightning Storm*. It wasn't terrible . . . but it wasn't very good, either.

Thinking of Ruth's final question—also of my mother's distress call in 1978—I found the banker's box containing those old notebooks. I dug out the one I wanted and read some of it sitting crosslegged beneath a naked lightbulb.

A storm was coming!

~~Jason~~ Jack stood on the porch watching black clouds form in the west. Thunder rolled! Lightning ~~hit everywhere!~~ smashed the ground like battering rams of fire! The wind began to ~~blow~~ howl. Jack was wicked scared but he couldn't stop looking. Fire before rain, he thought. FIRE BEFORE RAIN!

There was a picture in those words, and there was narration, but it was hackneyed at best. On that page and the ones that followed, I could see Pop straining to say what he saw. As if he knew what he was doing wasn't very good and kept trying, trying, trying to make it better. It was painful because it *wanted* to be good . . . and wasn't.

I went downstairs and got a copy of *The Lightning Storm* from the shelf of proofs in Pop's office. I turned to the first page and read this:

A storm was on the way.

Jack Elway stood on the porch, hands in his pockets, watching as black clouds rose in the west like smoke, blotting out the stars as they came. Thunder muttered. Lightning lit the clouds, making them look like brains, or so he thought. The wind began to pick up. *Fire before rain*, the boy thought. *Fire before rain*. The idea terrified him, but he couldn't stop looking.

Comparing the bad (but trying so hard to be good) handwritten copy to the version in the finished book, I found myself thinking first of Butch LaVerdiere's dump murals, then of his painting of Elvis and

Marilyn on the midway, which had sold for three million dollars. I thought again that one was the bud and one was the bloom.

All over this country—all over the *world*—men and women are painting pictures, writing stories, playing instruments. Some of these wannabes go to seminars and workshops and art classes. Some hire teachers. The fruit of their labors is dutifully admired by friends and relatives, who say things like *Wow, really good!* and then forget it. I always enjoyed my father's stories when I was a kid. They enthralled me and I thought *Wow, really good, Pop!* As I'm sure people passing on Dump Road saw Uncle Butch's brash and busy murals of town life and thought *Wow, really good!* and then went on their way. Because someone is always painting pictures, someone is always telling stories, someone is always playing "Call Me the Breeze" on the guitar. Most are forgettable. Some are competent. A very few are indelible. Why that should be I don't know. And how those two country men made the leap from good to good enough to great—I didn't know that, either.

But I found out.

Two years after his brief interview with Ruth Crawford, Pop was once more inspecting the daylilies growing along the picket fence. He was showing me how outliers had begun to pop up on the other side of the fence, even on the other side of Benson Street, when I heard a muffled crack. I thought he might have stepped on a fallen branch. He looked at me with wide eyes, his mouth open, and I thought (I remember this clearly) *This is what Pop looked like when he was a kid.* Then he tilted to the side. He grabbed for the fence. I grabbed his arm. We both missed our holds. He fell to the grass and began screaming.

I didn't always carry my cell—I'm not of the generation that would no more go without a phone than without underwear—but that day I had it. I called 911 and told them I needed an ambulance at 29 Benson because my father had had an accident.

I knelt next to Pop and tried to straighten his leg. He shrieked and said no-no-no, it hurts, Markey, it hurts. His face was as white as fresh snow, as Moby-Dick's underbelly, as amnesia. I didn't often feel old, probably because the man I lived with was so much older, but I felt plenty old then. I told myself not to pass out. I told myself not to have a heart attack. And I hoped the Harlow EMT wagon (which my father and Butch had paid for) was in the area, because an ambulance from Gates Falls would take half an hour and one from the Rock might take even longer.

I can still hear my father's screams. Just before the Harlow EMT vehicle showed up, he passed out. That was a relief. They got him in the back with a power lift and took him to St. Stephen's, where he was stabilized—supposing a ninety-year-old man *can* be stabilized—and took X-rays. His left hip had snapped. There was no attributable cause; it just happened. Nor was it a mere break, the orthopedist told me. It had exploded.

"I'm not sure how to proceed," Dr. Patel said. "If he was your age, I would of course recommend a hip replacement, but Mr. Carmody is suffering from advanced osteoporosis. His bones are like glass. All of them. And he is, of course, of an advanced age." He spread his hands above the X-rays. "You must advise me."

"Is he awake?"

Patel made a call. Asked. Listened. Hung up. "He's soupy from the pain medication but conscious and able to respond to questions. He wants to speak to you."

Even with Covid on the decline, space was at a premium in St. Stevie's. Still, my father was given a single room. This was because he could pay, but also because he was a celebrity. And loved in Castle County. I once gave him a tee-shirt that said ROCK STAR WRITER, and he wore it.

He was no longer as white as Moby-Dick's belly, but he looked shrunken. His face was haggard and shiny with sweat. His hair was every whichway. "Broke my goddam hip, Markey." His voice was little more than a whisper. "That Pakistani doc says it's a wonder it didn't happen, when we went to Butchie's funeral. Remember that?"

"Of course I do." I sat down beside him and took my comb out of my pocket.

He held up a hand in his old imperious *stop* gesture. "Don't do that, I'm not a baby."

"I know, but you look like a crazy person."

The hand dropped to the sheet. "All right. But only because I once changed your shitty diapers."

I guessed that had probably been Mom's job, but I didn't argue, just put his hair as right as I could. "Pop, the doc is trying to decide if you should have a hip repla—"

"Hush up," he said. "My pants are in the closet."

"Dad, you're not going anywh—"

He rolled his eyes. "Jesus Christ, I know that. Bring me my key-ring."

I found it in his left front pocket beneath a little jingle of change. He held it close to his eyes with a trembling hand (I hated to see that tremble) and picked through the keys until he found a small silver one.

"This opens the bottom drawer of my desk. If I don't pull through this clusterfuck—"

"Pop, you'll be fi—"

He held up the hand with the keys in it, his old gesture. "If I don't pull through, you'll find the explanation for my success—and Butch's—in that drawer. Everything that woman . . . I can't recall her name just now . . . was curious about. She wouldn't have believed it, and you won't, but it's the truth. Call it my last epistle to the world."

"Fine. I understand. Now what about the operation?"

"Well, let's see. Let's think this through. If I don't have it, what? A wheelchair? And a nurse, I suppose. Not a pretty one, a big hairy fullback of a fellow with a shaved head who wears English Leather. You certainly won't be capable of horsing my freight around, not at your age."

I supposed that was true.

"I think I'm going to go for it. I may die on the operating table. I may pull through, do six weeks of physical therapy, and then break the other hip. Or my arm. Or my shoulder. God has a vile sense of humor."

His bones were fragile, but his brains were still in good working order, even doped to the gills. I was glad he hadn't put the responsibility for the decision—and its consequences—on me.

"I'll tell Dr. Patel."

"You do that," he said, "and tell him to get the painkiller train ready to roll. I love you, son."

"I love you, too, Pop."

"Bring my keys back if I come through. Look in the drawer if I don't."

"You've got it."

"What was that woman's name? Crockett?"

"Crawford. Ruth Crawford."

"She wanted an answer. An explanation. The Unified Field Theory of Creativity, God save the Queen. And in the end, all I could have given her was a bigger mystery." His eyes slipped closed. "Whatever they gave me must have been strong. No pain just now. It'll be back, but right now I think I can sleep."

He did, and never woke up. Sleep became a coma. He had signed a DNR years before. I was sitting at his bedside and holding his hand when his heart stopped at 9:19 the following evening. He didn't even get the lead obituary in the *New York Times*, because an ex–Secretary of State died in a car accident that same night. Pop would have said it's an old story: in death as in life, politics almost always trumps art.

Just about everyone in Harlow came to the funeral at Grace Baptist Church, along with a good contingent of press. Ruth Crawford didn't come, she was in California, but she sent flowers and a nice condolence note. Luckily the funeral director knew what to expect, and put speakers on the church lawn for the overflow. He offered to add video screens; I refused on the grounds that it was a funeral, not a rock concert. The graveside service was shorter and less well attended, and when I showed up a week later with flowers (daylilies, of course), I was alone—the last leaf on the Carmody family tree, and now turning an autumnal brown. *Sic transit gloria mundi.*

I knelt to prop the vase against his headstone. "Hey, Pop—I've got the key you gave me. I'm going to respect your dying wish and open that drawer, but if there's anything in there that explains anything, I'll be . . . what did you always used to say? . . . a monkey's testicle."

*　　*　　*

The first thing I found in it was a manila folder. Either the sly dog hadn't completely given up his laptop after all, or he'd gotten someone at the library to do a printout for him, because the page on top was an article from *Time* magazine, dated May 23, 2022. The headline read CONGRESS IS FINALLY TAKING UFOs SERIOUSLY.

I scanned it and learned that these days UFOs are actually called UAPs—unidentified aerial phenomena. The Congressional hearings, chaired by Adam Schiff, were the first to take place on the subject since Project Blue Book, fifty years before, and everyone who testified was eager to point out that the focus wasn't on little green men from Mars or anywhere else. All witnesses said that while craft of extraterrestrial origin couldn't be ruled out, they were considered highly unlikely. What they were worried about was the possibility that some other country—Russia, China—had developed hypersonic technology far greater than our own.

Below the printout were clippings, yellowed and slightly brittle, from September and October of 1978. One from the *Press Herald* was headlined MYSTERIOUS LIGHTS SPOTTED OVER MARGINAL WAY. The one in the *Castle Rock Call* read CIGAR-SHAPED "UFO" SPOTTED OVER CASTLE VIEW. There was a photo of the View, with the rusty Suicide Stairs (as long gone as my Uncle Butch's dump murals) zig-zagging up the side. No sign of the flying White Owl, though.

Below the folder of clippings was a spiral notebook. I flipped back the cover, expecting to see another of Pop's early efforts—a stab at *The Terrible Generation*, perhaps, or *Highway 19*. It was his backslanted printing, unmistakable, but there were no cross-outs, scribbles, or doodles while he struggled for a way to express what he was thinking. It wasn't a bit like the early notebooks I'd found after my mother died. This was Laird Carmody in total command of his writing ability, although some of the letters looked shaky. I couldn't be sure, but I thought the narrative had been written at some point after he claimed retirement.

Pop was a novelist in full, usually respected for his storytelling abilities, and it only took me three pages to decide this was another story, albeit one with real people—Laird Carmody and Dave LaVerdiere—as made-up characters. Metafiction, in other words. Not uncommon; any number of fine writers have dabbled in the concept (or maybe you call that sort of thing a conceit). Dave certainly couldn't object, Pop would have thought, because his old friend was dead. If Pop had claimed it as true in his hospital room, it was only because he was addled with dope and pain. Such things happened. At the end of his life, hadn't Nathaniel Hawthorne confused himself with the Reverend Dimmesdale? Didn't Emily Dickinson leave the world saying "I must go in, the fog is rising"?

My father had never written fantasy *or* metafiction, and this was both, but he was up to his good old tricks nevertheless. I was caught up immediately and read through the pages in that notebook without stopping. Not just because I knew the people and the Harlow landscape, either. Laird Carmody could always tell a story, even his harshest critics admitted that, and this was a good one. But true?

I called bullshit on that.

2

In the old days, when Butch and I ran the town dump, we had Picker Tuesday. It was Butch's idea. (We also had Rat Saturday, but that's a different story.)

"If they're gonna pick," Butch said, "we should give em a day to do it when we can watch out for em and make sure some juicer or pothead doesn't gash a leg and get gangrene."

One old alkie who showed up more Tuesdays than not was Rennie Lacasse. He was what Maine folks call a ratchet-jaw, probably even talked in his sleep. Whenever he got talking about the old days, he'd always begin by saying "That pitcher never excaped my memory."

That's how I feel about the hunting trip in 1978 that changed our lives. Those pitchers have never excaped my memory.

We left on November 11th of that year, a Saturday, and the plan was to be back on the 17th or 18th, maybe earlier if one or both of us got our deer. If we did, we'd have plenty of time to get them dressed out at Ordway's Butcher Shop in Gates Falls. Everyone enjoyed venison at Thanksgiving, especially Mark, who was due home from college on the 21st.

Butch and I clubbed together to buy an Army surplus Willys jeep back in the early fifties. By 1978 she was an old lady, but still perfect for loading up our gear and groceries and bucketing off into the woods. Sheila used to tell me every year that NellyBelle was going to throw a rod or drop her transmission somewhere in the 30-Mile, but she never did. We drove that Willys out there until Butch headed west. Only we didn't do much hunting after 1978. We even avoided the subject. Although we thought about it, of course. Hard not to. By then I'd sold my first book, and Butch was making money doing comics and graphic novels. Nothing like the money he made later, but a-country fair, as Rennie Lacasse might have said.

I kissed Sheila, Butch gave her a hug, and off we went. Chapel Road took us to Cemetery Road, then to three woods roads, each more overgrown than the last. By then we were deep into the 30-Mile and pretty soon we could hear Jilasi Creek. Some years it wasn't much more than a chuckle, but that summer and fall we'd had buckets of rain and old Jilasi was roaring.

"I hope the bridge is still there," Butch said.

It was, but listing a bit to starboard. There was a yellow sign nailed to a stanchion with one word on it: UNSAFE. When the spring runoff came the next year, the bridge washed out entirely. After that you'd have to go twenty miles downstream to cross the Jilasi. Damn near to Bethel.

We didn't need the sign. It had been years since we'd dared to drive across that bridge, and that day we weren't sure we even dared walk across it.

"Well," Butch said, "I'll be damned if I'm going to drive twenty miles down Route 119 and then twenty miles back."

"You'd be pulled over by a cop for sure if you tried," I said, and slapped the side of the Willys. "NellyBelle hasn't had an inspection sticker on her since 1964."

He grabbed his pack and his sleeping bag and walked to the edge of that clattery old wooden bridge. There he stopped and looked back. "You coming?"

"I think I'll wait and see if you make it across," I said. "If the bridge goes, I'll fish you out. And if the current takes you before I can, I'll wave you goodbye." I actually didn't want both of us on it at once. That would have been tempting fate.

Butch started across. I could hear the hollow clonk of his bootheels over the sound of the creek. When he got to the other side he put down his gear, dropped his pants, and mooned me.

As I went across I could feel the bridge trembling like it was alive, and in pain. We went back—one at a time—and got the cartons with our food in them. They were full of things men eat in the woods: Dinty Moore, canned soup, sardines, eggs, bacon, pudding cups, coffee, plenty of Wonder Bread, two sixpacks of beer, and our annual bottle of Jack Daniel's. Also a couple of T-bone steaks. We were big eaters in those days, although far from healthy ones. On the last trip we brought our rifles and the first aid kit. It was a big one. Both of us were members of the Harlow Volunteer Fire Department, and the EMT first aid training course was a requirement. Sheila insisted we drag the VFD kit with us for our hunting week, because accidents can happen in the woods. Sometimes bad ones.

As we tarped NellyBelle to keep her from filling up with rain, Butch said, "This is the time one of us will go in the drink, you wait and see."

We didn't, although that last trip we had to make together, one holding each end of the first aid kit, which weighed thirty pounds and was the size of a footlocker. We talked about leaving it in the jeep, but in the end we didn't.

On the far side of the bridge there was a little clearing. It would have been a nice place to fish, except the Jilasi ran through Mexico and Rumford before it got to us, and any fish we caught would be toxic because of the runoff from the textile mills. Beyond the clearing was an overgrown path that led a quarter of a mile to our cabin. It was neat enough then, with two bedrooms, a wood-fired cookstove in the kitchen half of the main room, and a composting toilet out back. No electricity, of course, but there was a little pumphouse for water. All a couple of mighty hunters could possibly want.

By the time we got our gear bucked up to the cabin, it was almost dark. I made a meal (Butch was always willing to do his share, but that man would burn water, Sheila used to say) and Butch built a fire in the fireplace. I settled down with a book—there's nothing like an Agatha Christie when you're out in the woods—and Butch had a Strathmore drawing pad, which he would fill with cartoons, caricatures, and forest scenes. His Nikon was on the table beside him. Our rifles were propped in the corner, unloaded.

We talked a little, as we always did up there, some about the past and some about our hopes for the future. Those hopes were fading by then—we were in our early middle age—but they always seemed a little more realistic, a little more attainable, out in the woods, where it was always so quiet and life seemed less . . . busy? That's not exactly right. Less cluttered. No phones to ring and no fires—literal as well as metaphorical—to put out. I don't think we ever went into the woods to hunt, not really, although if a deer walked into our sights, who were we to say no? I think we went out there to be our best selves. Well . . . our honest selves, maybe. I always tried to be my best self with Sheila.

I remember going to bed that night, pulling the covers up to my chin and listening to the wind sigh through the trees. I remember thinking that the fading of hopes and ambitions was mostly painless. That was good, but it was also rather horrible. I wanted to be a writer, but I was beginning to think being a good one was beyond me. If it was, the world would continue to spin. You relaxed your hand . . . opened your fingers . . . and something flew away. I remember thinking *maybe that's all right.*

Out the window, through the swaying branches, I could see some stars.

That pitcher has never excaped my memory.

On the 12th we put on our orange vests and orange hats and into the woods we went. In the morning we separated, getting together again for lunch and to compare notes—what we'd seen and what we hadn't. That first day we met back at the cabin and I made a big pot of pasta with cheese and half a pound of bacon. (I called this Hungarian goulash, but any self-respecting Hungarian would have taken one look and covered his eyes.) That afternoon we hunted together.

The next day we ate a picnic lunch in the clearing, looking across the creek—which was more like a river that day—at NellyBelle. Butch made sandwiches, which he could be trusted to do. There was sweet water from our well to drink, and Hostess Fruit Pies for afters: blueberry for me, apple for Butch.

"Did you see any deer?" Butch asked, licking frosting from his fingers. Well . . . those fruit pies aren't exactly *frosted*, but they have a glaze that's quite tasty.

"Nope. Not today, not yesterday. But you know what the oldtimers say—the deer know when November comes, and they hide."

"I actually think that could be true," Butch said. "They do have a tendency to disappear after Halloween. But what about gunshots? Heard any?"

I thought it over. "A couple yesterday. None today."

"Are you going to tell me we're the only hunters in the 30-Mile?"

"Christ, no. The woods between here and Dark Score Lake are probably the best hunting in the county, you know that. I saw a couple of guys this morning not long after I started out, although they didn't see me. I think one of them might have been that nummie Freddy Skillins. The one who likes to call himself a carpenter."

He nodded. "I was over on that humpback ridge, and I saw three men on the other side. Dressed like models from L.L.Bean's and carrying scoped rifles. Just about had to be out-of-staters. And for every one we see, there's probably five or ten more. There should be plenty of bang-bang, because not *all* the deer decided to up stakes and head for Canada, did they?"

"Seems unlikely," I said. "The deer are out there, Butchie."

"Then why haven't we seen them? And listen!"

"What am I supposed to be listening f—"

"Just shut up a minute and you'll hear it. By which I mean you won't."

I shut up. I heard the Jilasi roaring away, no doubt undercutting the bridge supports even as we sat there on the grass munching the last of our fruit pies. I heard the far-off drone of an airplane, probably bound for the Portland Jetport. Otherwise, nothing.

I looked at Butch. He was looking at me and not smiling. Solemn.

"No birds," I said.

"No. And the woods should be full of them."

Just then a crow gave out a single loud caw.

"There you go," I said, and actually felt relieved.

"One crow," he said. "Big deal. Where are the robins?"

"Flown south?"

"Not yet, not all of them. We should be hearing nuthatches and cardinals. Maybe a goldfinch, and chickadees galore. But there's not even a fucking woodpecker."

I usually ignore the soundtrack of the woods—you get used to it—but now that he mentioned it, where *were* the birds? And something else.

"The squirrels," I said. "They should be running around everywhere, getting ready for winter. I think I've seen a couple . . ." I trailed off because I wasn't even sure of that.

"It's aliens," Butch said in a low, joke-spooky voice. "They could be creeping toward us through the woods right now. With their disintegrator rayguns."

"You saw that story in the *Call*," I said. "The one about the flying saucer."

"Wasn't a saucer, it was a cigar," Butch said. "A flying see-gar."

"The Tiparillo that came from Planet X," I said.

"With a lust for Earth women!"

We looked at each other and snickered.

I had an idea for a story that afternoon—much later it became a novel called *The Terrible Generation*—and I was making some notes in one of my spiral notebooks that evening. I was trying to think of a good name for the villainous young man at the heart of the story when the cabin door banged open and Butch ran in. "Come here, Lare. You have to see this." He grabbed his camera.

"See what?"

"Just come!"

I looked at his wide eyes, put aside my notebook, and followed him out the door. While we walked the quarter-mile to the clearing and the creek, he told me he'd come out to check if the bridge's tilt had increased (we would have heard it if it had collapsed entirely). Then he saw what was in the sky and forgot all about the bridge.

"Look," he said when we got to the clearing, and pointed up.

It had started to rain, just a gentle mist. It was full dark and I shouldn't have been able to see the lowering clouds, but I could, because they were lit by slowly moving circles of bright light. Five, then seven, then nine. They were different sizes. The smallest was maybe thirty feet across. The biggest could have been a hundred. They weren't shining off the clouds, the way a bright spotlight or a powerful flashlight will; they were *in* the clouds.

"What are they?" I asked, almost whispering.

"I don't know, but they sure as shit aren't Tiparillos."

"Or White Owls," I said, and we began to laugh. Not the way you do when something is funny; the way you do when you're absolutely gobsmacked with amazement.

Butch took pictures. This was years before chip technology allowed for instant gratification, but I saw the prints later, after he developed them in his own little darkroom. They were disappointing. Just big circles of light above the dark jig-jags of the treetops. I have seen pictures of UFOs since then (or UAPs, if you prefer), and they are usually disappointing: blurry shapes that could be anything, including the trick photography of hoaxers. You had to be there to understand how wonderful it was, and how weird: great soundless lights moving in the clouds, seeming almost to waltz.

What I remember most clearly—other than a sense of awe—was how divided my mind was during the five or ten minutes it went on. I wanted to see what was making those lights . . . yet I didn't. I was afraid, you see, that we were close to artifacts—maybe even intelligent beings—from another world. That exalted me but it also terrified me. Looking back on that first contact (for surely it was that), I think our only two choices were to laugh or to scream. If I'd been alone, I almost certainly would have screamed. And run away, probably to hide under my bed like a child and deny I'd seen anything. Because we were together, and grown men, we laughed.

I say five or ten minutes, but it might have been fifteen. I don't know. It was long enough for the drizzle to thicken into real rain.

Two of the bright circles grew smaller and disappeared. Then two or three more went. The biggest stayed the longest, then it also began to dwindle. It didn't move from side to side; simply shrank to the size of a plate, then a fifty-cent piece, then a penny, then a brilliant dot . . . then gone. As if it had shot straight up.

We stood there in the rain, waiting for something else to happen. Nothing did. After a little while Butch grabbed my shoulder. I gave a squawk.

"Sorry, sorry," he muttered. "Let's go in. Lightshow's over and we're getting soaked."

That was what we did. I hadn't bothered to put on a jacket, so I built up the fire, which had been down to coals, and stripped off my wet shirt. I was rubbing my arms and shivering.

"We can tell people what we saw, but they won't believe it," Butch said. "Or they'll shrug and say it was some crazy weather phenomenon."

"Maybe it was. Or . . . how far away is the Castle Rock Airport?"

He shrugged. "Has to be twenty or thirty miles east of here."

"The runway lights . . . maybe with the clouds . . . the moisture . . . it could, you know . . . some prismatic effect . . ."

He was sitting on the couch, camera in his lap, looking at me. Smiling just a little. Saying nothing. He didn't have to.

"That's bullshit, isn't it?" I said.

"Yes. I don't know what that was, but it wasn't lights from the airport and it wasn't a fucking weather balloon. There were eight or ten of those things, maybe a dozen, and they were *big*."

"There are other hunters in the woods. I saw Freddy Skillins and you saw three guys who were probably flatlanders. They could have seen it."

"Maybe they did, but I doubt it. I just happened to be in the right place—that clearing on the edge of the creek—at the right time. In any case, it's over. I'm going to bed."

It rained all the next day—the 14th, that would have been. Neither of us wanted to go out and get soaked looking for deer we probably wouldn't find. I read and worked a little bit on the idea for my story. I kept trying to come up with a good name for the bad kid and didn't have any luck—maybe because I didn't have a clear fix on why the bad kid was bad. Butch spent most of the morning with his pad. He drew three different pictures of the lights in the clouds, then gave up in disgust.

"I hope the photos come out, because these suck," he said.

I looked them over and told him they were good, but they weren't. They didn't suck, but they didn't convey the strangeness of what we'd seen. The *enormity*.

I looked at all the crossed-out names of my proposed bad guy. *Trig Adams*. No. *Vic Ellenby*. No. *Jack Claggart*. Too on-the-nose. *Carter Cantwell*. Oh, puke. The story I had in mind seemed amorphous: I had an idea but no specifics. Nothing to hold onto. It reminded me of what we'd seen the previous night. Something was there, but it was impossible to tell what, because it was in the clouds.

"What are you doing?" Butch asked me.

"Fucking off. I think I'll take a nap."

"What about lunch?"

"Don't want any."

He considered this, then looked out the window at the steady rain. Nothing is colder than cold November rain. It crossed my mind that someone should write a song about it . . . and eventually, someone did.

"A nap sounds like just the ticket," Butch said. He put his pad aside and stood up. "Tell you something, Lare. I'm going to draw all my life, but I'll never be an artist."

The rain stopped around four o'clock that afternoon. By six the clouds had unraveled and we could see stars and a sliver of moon—God's fingernail, the oldtimers say. We ate our steaks for dinner (along with plenty of Wonder Bread to sop up the juice), then went out to the clearing. We didn't talk about it, just went. We stood there for maybe half an hour, craning our necks. There were no lights, no saucers, no flying cigars. We went back inside, Butch found a pack of Bicycles in the living room cabinet, and we played cribbage until almost ten o'clock.

"I can hear the Jilasi even in here," I said as we finished the last hand.

"I know. That rain didn't do the bridge any help. Why is there a fucking bridge there, anyway? Did you ever ask yourself that?"

"I think someone had an idea for a development back in the sixties. Or pulpers. They must have clear-cut these woods back before World War I."

"What would you think about hunting one more day and going back?"

I had an idea he was thinking of more than going home, most likely empty-handed. Seeing those lights in the clouds had done something to him. Could have done something to both of us. I'm not going to call it a come-to-Jesus moment. It's just that maybe you see something, lights in the sky or a certain shadow at a certain time of day, how it lies across your path. You take it as a sign and decide to move along. You say to yourself that when I was a child I spoke as a child, understood as a child, thought as a child, but there comes a time to put away childish things.

Or it could have been nothing.

"Lare?"

"Sure. One more day, then we go back. I have to clean the gutters before the snow flies, and I keep putting it off."

The next day was cool and clear and perfect for hunting, but neither of us saw so much as a single flick of a single whitetail. I heard no birdsong, just the occasional crow-call. I kept an eye out for squirrels, but didn't see any. I didn't even see a chipmunk, and the woods should have been full of their scurry. I heard some gunshots, but they were far away, near the lake, and hunters shooting didn't mean they were shooting at deer. Sometimes guys get bored and just want to let off a round or two, especially if they've decided there's no game to scare away.

We met back at the cabin for lunch, then went out together. We no longer expected to see deer, and we didn't, but it was a fine day to be outdoors. We walked along the creek for a mile or so, then sat on a fallen log and opened cans of Bud.

"This just isn't natural," Butch said, "and I don't care for it much. I'd say drive out this afternoon, but by the time we got loaded up it'd be dark, and I don't trust NellyBelle's headlights on those woods roads."

A sudden breeze kicked up, rattling leaves off the trees. The sound made me startle and look over my shoulder. Butch did, too. Then we looked at each other and laughed.

"Jumpy much?" I asked.

"Just a little. Remember when we went in the old Spier place on a dare? 1946 or so, wasn't it?"

I remembered. Old Man Spier came back from Okinawa missing an eye and blew his head off in his parlor with a shotgun. It was the talk of the town.

"The house was supposed to be haunted," I said. "We were . . . what? Thirteen?"

"I guess. We went in and picked up some stuff to show our friends we'd been there."

"I got a picture. Some old landscape I grabbed off the wall. What'd you get?"

"A fucking sofa cushion," he said, and laughed. "Talk about stupid! I thought of the Spier house because the way I felt then is how I feel now. No deer, no birds, no squirrels. Maybe that house wasn't haunted, but these woods . . ." He shrugged and drank some of his beer.

"We could leave today. Those headlights will probably be okay."

"Nope. Tomorrow. We'll pack up tonight, go to bed early, and leave at first light. If it suits you."

"Suits me fine."

Things would have been very different for us if we'd trusted Nelly-Belle's headlights. Sometimes I think we did. Sometimes I think there's a Shadow Laird and a Shadow Butch who led shadow lives. Shadow Butch never went to Seattle. Shadow Laird never wrote a novel, let alone a dozen of them. Those shadows were decent men who lived unremarkable Harlow lives. They ran the dump, they owned a hauling company, they did the town's business the way it should be done—which means so the books balance at Town Meeting in March and there's less bitching from mossbacks who'd be happy to bring back the Poor Farm. Shadow Butch got married to some girl he met in a Lewiston bop joint and had a litter of shadow young'uns.

I tell myself now it was good none of that happened. Butch told himself the same thing. I know, because we told each other when we talked on the phone or, later, via Skype or FaceTime. It was all good. Of course it was. We became famous. We became rich. Our dreams came true. Nothing wrong with those things, and if I ever have doubts about the shape of my life, doesn't everybody?

Don't you?

That night Butch threw a bunch of leftovers into a pot and called the result stew. We ate it with Wonder Bread and washed it down with well-water, which was really the best part of the meal.

"I'll never let you cook again," I told Butch as we did our few dishes.

"After that mess, I'll hold you to it," he said.

We packed up what we had and put it by the door. Butch dealt the big first aid kit a sideways kick with one sneaker. "Why do we always bring this thing?"

"Because Sheila insists. She's convinced one of us is going to fall in a sinkhole and break a leg or one of us will get shot. Probably by a flatlander with a scoped rifle."

"Bullshit. I think she's just superstitious. Believes the one time we don't haul it out here is the one time we'd need it. You want to go take another look?"

I didn't have to ask what he meant. "Might as well."

We went down to the clearing to look at the sky.

There were no lights up there, but there was something on the bridge. Or rather, someone. A woman, lying facedown on the planks.

"What the fuck?" Butch said, and ran onto the bridge. I followed. I didn't like the idea of three of us on it at the same time, and close together, but we weren't going to leave her lying there unconscious, maybe even dead. She had long black hair. It was a breezy night and I noticed that when the wind gusted her hair blew in a clump, as if the strands had been glued together. There were no gauzy flyaways, just that clump.

"Grab her feet," Butch said. "We have to get her off before the fucking bridge falls into the fucking creek." He was right. I could hear the supports groaning and the Jilasi thundering, in full spate thanks to all the rain.

I got her feet. She was wearing boots and corduroy pants, and there was something funny about them, too. But it was dark and I was scared and all I wanted right then was some solid ground under my feet. Butch lifted her by the shoulders and gave a cry of disgust.

"What?" I asked.

"Ne'mind, come on, hurry!"

We got her off the bridge and into the clearing. Only sixty feet, but it seemed to take forever.

"Put her down, put her down. Jesus! Jesus Christ!"

Butch dropped the top half of her and she face-planted, but he paid no attention. He crossed his arms and started rubbing his hands in his armpits, as if to get rid of something nasty.

I started to put her legs down and froze, not able to believe what I thought I was seeing. My fingers appeared to have sunk into her boots, as if they were made of clay instead of leather. I pulled free and stared stupidly at the marks of my fingers as they smoothed out. "My God!"

"It's like . . . fuck, like she's made out of Play-Doh, or something."

"Butch."

"What? For Chrissakes, *what?*"

"Her clothes aren't clothes. It's like . . . body-paint. Or camouflage. Or some damn thing."

He bent toward her. "It's too dark. Have you got—?"

"A flashlight? No. Didn't bring it. Her hair—"

I touched it, then pulled away. It wasn't hair. It was something solid but pliable. Not a wig, more like a carving. I didn't know what it was.

"Is she dead?" I asked. "She is, isn't sh—"

But just then the woman took a long, rasping breath. One of her legs twitched.

"Help me turn her over," Butch said.

I took one of her legs, trying to ignore that weird pliability. A thought—*Gumby*—shot through my head like a meteor and was gone. Butch grabbed her shoulder. We rolled her. Even in the dark we could see she was young, pretty, and ghastly white. We could see something else, as well. It was the face of a department store mannequin, smooth and unlined. The eyes were shut. Only her lids had color; they looked bruised.

This is not a human being, I thought.

She took another rasping breath. It seemed to catch in her throat as if on hooks, when she exhaled. She didn't take another one.

I think I would have stayed where I was, frozen, and let her die. It was Butch who saved her. He dropped to his knees, used two fingers to yank down her jaw, and put his mouth on hers. He pinched her nose shut and breathed into her. Her chest rose. Butch turned his head to one side, spat, and took another deep breath. He blew into her again and her chest rose again. He lifted his head and stared at me, bug-eyed. "It's like kissing plastic," he said, then did it again.

While he was bent over her, the woman's eyes opened. She looked at me through the bristles of Butch's buzzcut. When Butch pulled back she took another of those rasping, guttural breaths.

"The kit," Butch said. "EpiPen. Inogen, too. Hurry! Fucking run!"

I swayed on my feet and for a moment thought I was going to faint. I slapped myself to clear my head, then ran for the cabin. *She, it, whatever it is, will be dead when I get back*, I thought (I told you, none of this ever excaped my memory). *That's probably good.*

The first aid kit was just inside the door, with our packs on top of it. I shoved them aside and opened it. There were two fold-out drawers. Three EpiPens in the top one. I took two of them and rammed the drawers shut, pinching my right index finger in the process. That nail turned black and fell off, but at the time I didn't even feel it. My head was throbbing. I felt like I had a fever.

The Inogen oxygen bottle with the attached mask and the controller was in the bottom, along with flares, rolls of bandage, gauze pads, a plastic splint, an ankle brace, various tubes and ointments. There was also a Penlite. I took that as well and sprinted back down the path with the light swinging back and forth in front of me.

Butch was still on his knees. The woman was still giving intermittent gasps for breath. Her eyes were still open. As I dropped to my knees beside Butch, she stopped breathing again.

He bent, sealed his mouth over hers, and pushed breath into her. Raised his head and said, "Thigh, thigh!"

"I know, I took the course."

"Then do it!"

He gulped another breath and went at her again. I popped the cap on the Epi, put it against her thigh—it looked like corduroy pants but it wasn't, it was her thigh—and listened for the click. Then I counted to ten. At five she gave a hard jerk.

"Hold on, Lare, hold it!"

"I'm holding it. Do you think I should use the other one?"

"Save it, she's breathing again. Whatever she is. Christ, the taste of her is so *weird*. Like one of those see-through slipcovers you put on furniture. Have you got the oxygen?"

"Right here."

I gave him the mask and bottle. He held the mask over her mouth and nose. I hit the power switch on the controller and saw the green light. "High flow?"

"Yeah, yeah, shoot the works." I saw a drop of sweat from his forehead hit the plastic mask and run down the side like a tear.

I pushed the slider all the way to HIGH FLOW. Oxygen began to hiss. On high, the oxy would last for no more than five minutes. And while there were backups of almost everything in the kit (there was a reason it was so heavy), this was the only Inogen. We stared at each other across her.

"This is not a human being," I said. "I don't know what it is, maybe some top secret cyborg, but it's not human."

"It's not a cyborg."

He jerked his thumb at the sky.

When the oxy ran out, Butch removed the mask and she—might as well call her that—kept breathing on her own. The rasp quieted. I shone the light on her face and she closed her eyes against the glare.

"Look," I said. "Look at her face, Butchie."

He looked, then looked at me. "It's different now."

"It's more human now, is what you mean. And look at her clothes. They look better, too. More . . . jeepers, more realistic."

"What do we do with her?"

I snapped off the light. Her eyes opened. I said, "Do you hear me?"
She nodded.

"Who are you?"

She closed her eyes. I shook her shoulder, and my fingers no longer
sank in.

"*What* are you?"

Nothing. I looked at Butch.

"Let's take her to the cabin," he said. "I'll carry her. Keep that other
EpiPen ready if she starts to choke and rasp for breath again."

He got her in his arms. I helped him to his feet, but he carried
her easily enough once he was upright. Her dark hair hung down,
and when the breeze gusted, it blew the way normal hair does. The
clumping was gone.

I had left the cabin door open. He carried her in, put her on the
sofa, then bent over with his hands on his knees, getting his breath
back. "I want my camera. It's in my pack. Will you get it?"

I found it wrapped in a couple of tee-shirts and gave it to him. The
woman—now she almost *did* look like a woman—was looking up at
him. Her eyes were a washed-out blue, like the knees of old denim
pants.

"Smile pretty," Butch said.

She didn't smile. He took her picture anyway.

"What's your name?" I asked.

No response.

Butch took another picture. I leaned forward and put my hand on
her neck. I thought she might pull away, but she didn't. It looked
like skin (unless you looked closely), but it didn't quite feel like skin.
I held my hand there for maybe twenty seconds, then took it away.
"She has no pulse."

"No?" He didn't sound surprised and I didn't feel surprised. We
were in shock, our processing equipment overloaded.

Butch tried to slide his hand into the right front pocket of her
corduroy pants and couldn't. "Not a real pocket," he said. "None of it
is. It's like . . . a costume. I think *she's* a costume."

"What do we do with her, Butch?"

"Fucked if I know."

43

"Call the police?"

He lifted his hands and then dropped them, a very un-Butchlike gesture of indecision. "The closest phone is Brownie's Store. That's miles from here. And Brownie closes at seven. I'd have to carry her across the bridge to the jeep . . ."

"I'd take a turn." I said this stoutly enough, but I kept thinking of how my fingers had sunk into what looked like boots and weren't.

"It would mean testing the bridge again," he said. "As for moving her, she's stable now, but . . . what? What are you smiling about?"

I gestured to the woman—what looked like a woman—on the couch. "She has no pulse, Butchie. She's clinically dead. You can't get much more stable than that."

"But she's breathing! And she's . . ." He checked to make sure. "She's looking at us. Listen, Laird—are you prepared to be on the front page of every newspaper and the lead story on every TV station not just in Maine or the U.S., but in the whole round world? Because if we take her out, that's what it'll come to. She's an *alien*. She came from outer fucking *space*. And not with a lust for Earth women, either."

"Unless she's a lesbian," I said. "Then she might, you know, lust for Earth women."

We started laughing the way you do when you're trying not to go crazy. She was still looking at us. No smile, no frown, no expression of any kind. A woman who wasn't a woman, who had no pulse but was breathing, who was wearing clothes that weren't clothes but looked more like clothes all the time. I had an idea that if Butch tried her pocket now, his hand would go in. He might even find some change or a half-used roll of Life Savers.

"Why did she end up on the bridge? What do you suppose happened to her?"

"I don't know. I think—"

I never heard what he thought. That was when light flooded in the east-facing window of our cabin's main room. Thoughts came to me, knocking each other over like dominoes. The first was that time had slipped somehow and the sun was coming up. The second was that sunrise was never that bright in our cabin, because there were too many trees on that side. My third was that some government organization had

come for the woman and those were searchlights. The fourth was that
someone had come for her, all right . . . but it wasn't the government.

The light grew brighter still. Butch squinted and raised a hand to
shield his eyes. I did the same. I wondered if we were taking a hard
dose of radioactivity. Just before the room grew so bright that my vision
whited out, I looked at the woman on the couch. Remember me saying
that, like old Rennie Lacasse, these pitchers never excaped my memory? There's one exception to that. I can't remember what I saw when I
looked at her in that awful brilliance. Or maybe I blocked it out. Either
way, I don't think I was looking *at* her at all. I think I was looking *into*
her. As to what I saw, I can remember thinking just one word: *ganglia*.

I covered my eyes. No good. The light shone straight through my
hands and through my closed lids. There was no heat, but it was going
to burn my brains to a cinder just the same. I heard Butch scream.
That was when I lost consciousness, and I was glad to go.

When I came to, the awful brilliance was gone. So was the woman.
Sitting on the couch where she'd been was a young man—maybe
thirty, probably younger—with neatly combed blond hair, the part
as straight as a ruler. He was wearing khaki pants and a quilted vest.
A small shoulder bag hung at his side from a strap across his chest.
My first thought was he was an out-of-state hunter, a flatlander with
ammo in his bag and a scoped rifle nearby.

Probably not was my second one.

We had half a dozen battery-powered lamps and he'd turned them
all on. They gave plenty of light, but nothing like that unearthly
(literally) glare that had invaded our cabin earlier. How much earlier
was a question I couldn't answer. I wasn't even sure it was the same
night. I looked at my watch but it had stopped.

Butch sat up, looked around, saw me, saw the newcomer. He
asked a question that was both mad and—under the circumstances—
completely logical. "Are you her?"

"No," the young man said. "That one is gone."

I tried for my feet and made it okay. I didn't feel hungover or dazed.
If anything, invigorated. And while I'd seen a dozen movies about evil

invaders from space, I didn't feel that this young man meant us any harm. Nor did I believe he was actually a young man any more than the woman from the bridge had been a young woman.

There was a pitcher of water and three leftover cans of beer in our little coldbox. I debated and took a beer.

"Give me one," Butch said.

I tossed it and he caught it one-handed. "What about you, sir?" I asked.

"Why not?"

I gave him the last can. Our visitor looked normal—like any young man on a hunting trip with his friends or his dad—but I was still careful not to touch his fingers. I can write what happened, but as to how I felt . . . much more complicated. All I can do is reiterate that I didn't feel threatened, and later on Butch said the same. Of course we were in shock.

"You're not human, are you?" Butch said.

The young man opened his beer. "No."

"But you're in better shape than she was."

"That one was badly hurt. You saved her life. I think it was what you call 'luck.' You could just as easily have injected her with something that would have killed her."

"But the EpiPen worked," I said.

"Is that what you call it? Epi? EpiPen?"

"Short for epinephrine. So I guess it was an allergy that knocked her down."

"Could have been a bee sting," Butch said, and shrugged. "Do you know what bees are?"

"Yes. You also gave her your breath. *That* was the actual saving. Breath is life. *More* than life."

"I did what we were taught. Laird would have done the same."

I like to think that was true.

The young man took a sip of beer. "May I take the can when I go?"

Butch sat on the arm of one of our two old easy chairs. "Well, old man, you'll be robbing me of the nickel deposit, but under the circumstances, sure. Only because you're from another planet, you understand."

Our visitor smiled the way people do when they understand it's a joke but don't get the point of it. He had no accent, certainly not a Downeast twang, but I got the clear sense of a man who was speaking a learned language. He opened his bag. There was no zipper. He just ran his finger down its length and it opened. He popped the Bud can inside.

"Most people wouldn't have done what you did. Most would have run away."

Butch shrugged. "Instinct. And a little training, I guess. Laird and me are in the local volunteer fire department. Do you get that?"

"You halt combustion before it can spread."

"I guess that's one way of putting it."

The young man dipped into his bag and brought out something that looked like a spectacle case. It was gray, with a silver shape like a sine wave embossed on the lid. He held it in his lap. He repeated, "Most people wouldn't have done what you did. We owe you. For Ylla."

I knew that name, and although he pronounced it *Yella*, I knew the correct spelling. And I could see by his eyes that he knew I knew.

"That's from *The Martian Chronicles*. But you're not from Mars, sir, are you?"

He smiled. "Not at all. Nor are we here because we lust for Earth women."

Butch put his beer down carefully, as if a hard bump might shatter the can. "You're reading our minds."

"Sometimes. Not always. It's like this." With one finger he traced the wave shape on the gray case. "Thoughts don't matter to us. They come, they pass, they are replaced by others. Ephemera. We are more interested in the engine that drives them. To intelligent creatures that is what's . . . central? Powerful? Meaningful? I don't know the correct word. Perhaps you don't have one."

"Primal?" I said.

He nodded, smiled, and sipped his beer. "Yes. Primal. Good."

"Where do you come from?" Butch asked.

"It doesn't matter."

"Why?" I asked. "Why do you come?"

"That's a more interesting question, and because you saved Ylla, I will answer it. We gather."

"Gather what?" I asked, and thought of stories I'd read (and seen on TV) about aliens kidnapping folks and sticking probes up their asses. "People?"

"No. Other things. Items. But not like this." He reached into his bag and showed us his empty beer can. "This is special to me and means nothing. There's a good word for it, perhaps French. A *venir*?"

"Souvenir," I said.

"Yes. It is my souvenir of this remarkable night. We visit yard sales."

"You're joking," I said.

"They are called different things in different places. In Italy, *vendita in cantiere*. Samoan, *fanua fa'tau*. We take some of these things to remember, some to study. We have film of your Kennedy's death from rifleshot. We have an autographed picture of Juhjudi."

"Wait." Butch was frowning. "Are you talking about Judge Judy?"

"Yes, Juhjudi. We have a picture of Emmett Till, a young man with his face gone. Mickey Mouse and his Club. We have a jet engine. That came from a repository of discarded objects."

They're dump pickers, I thought. *Not much different from Rennie Lacasse.*

"We take these things to remember your world, which will be gone soon. We do the same on other worlds, but there aren't many. The universe is cold. Intelligent life is rare."

I didn't care how rare it was. "How soon will ours be gone? Do you know, or are you only guessing?" And before he could reply: "You *can't* know. Not for sure."

"It may be what you call a century, if you are, as you say, 'lucky.' Which is only an eyeblink in the sweep of time."

"I don't believe that," Butch said flatly. "We've got our problems, but we're not suicidal." Then, perhaps thinking of Buddhist monks who had been setting themselves on fire in Vietnam not so long ago: "Not most of us."

"It's inevitable," the young man said. He looked regretful. Maybe he was thinking of the *Mona Lisa*, or the pyramids. Or maybe just of no more beer cans, no more autographed pictures of Juhjudi. "When intelligence outraces emotional stability, it's always just a matter of time." He pointed to the corner of the cabin. "You're children, playing with weapons." He stood up. "I must go. This is for you. A gift. Our way of saying thank you for saving Ylla."

He held out the gray case. Butch took it and looked it over. "I don't see how to open it."

I took it. He was right. There was no hinge and no lid.

"Breathe on the wave," the young man said. "Not now, after I've gone. We give you a key of breath because you gave Ylla yours. You gave her part of your life."

"This is for both of us?" I asked. Only Butch had given the woman mouth-to-mouth, after all.

"Yes."

"What does it actually do?"

"There is no word for what it does except *primal*. A way to use what you are not using, because of . . ." He bent forward, brow furrowed, then looked up. "Because of the *noise* in your *lives*. Because of your *thoughts*. Thoughts are pointless. Worse, dangerous."

I was bemused. "Does it grant wishes? Like in a fairy tale?"

He laughed, then looked surprised . . . as if he hadn't known he *could* laugh. "Nothing can give you what isn't already there. This is axiomatic."

He went to the door, then looked back.

"I'm sorry for you. Your world is a living breath in a universe that is mostly filled with deadlights."

He left. I waited for the light to flood in, but it didn't. Except for the gray case Butch was now holding, the whole interlude might never have occurred.

"Lare, did that actually happen?"

I pointed to the case.

He smiled, the reckless one that went right back to when we were kids, racing up and down the Suicide Stairs in Castle Rock, feeling them shake beneath our pounding sneakers. "Want to try it?"

"There's an old saying, beware of Greeks bearing gifts . . ."

"Yeah, but?"

"What the hell, I'm game. Blow your precious primal breath, Butchie."

He smiled, shook his head, and held the case out. "After you. And if it kills you I promise to take care of Sheila and Mark."

"Mark's almost old enough to take care of himself," I said. "Okay, open sesame."

I blew gently on the wave. The case opened. It was empty. But when I breathed in, I caught a faint whiff of peppermint. I think that was it.

The case closed by itself. There was no line where the lid met the body, and indeed no hinges. It looked completely solid.

"Nothing?" Butch said.

"Nothing. You try." I held it out to him.

He took it and breathed gently on the wave. The case popped open. He bent down, took a timid sniff, then a deep breath. The case shut. "Wintergreen?"

"I thought peppermint, but I guess they're about the same."

"So much for Greeks bearing gifts," he said. "Lare . . . it wasn't some kind of a hoax, was it? You know, like some girl and some guy pretending to be . . . you know, a trick . . ." He stopped. "No, huh?"

"No."

He put the gray case on the end table next to his drawing pad. "What are you going to tell Sheila?"

"Nothing, I guess. I'd prefer it if my wife didn't think I've gone crazy."

He laughed. "Good luck with that. She can read you like a book."

He was right, of course. And when Sheila pushed—which she did—I told her no, we hadn't gotten lost, we'd had a close call in the woods. Some hunter had fired at what he thought was a deer and the bullet went between us. We never saw who it was, I told her . . . and when she asked Butch, he backed me up. He said it had probably been some out-of-state flatlander. Butch had seen a couple, so that much was true.

Butch yawned. "I'm going to bed."

"You can *sleep*?" Then I yawned, too. "What time is it, anyway?"

Butch looked at his watch and shook his head. "Stopped. Yours?"

"Yes, and . . ." I yawned again. " . . . it's a wind-up. Should be fine, but it's not."

"Lare? What we breathed in . . . I think it was some kind of sedative. What if it's poisonous?"

"Then we'll die," I said. "I'm going to bed."

That was what we did.

I had a dream of fire.

It was full daylight when I woke up. Butch was in the kitchen part of the main room. The coffee pot was on the stove, huffing away. He asked how I felt.

"Okay," I said. "You?"

"Fine as paint . . . whatever that means. Coffee?"

"Yes. Then we ought to go see if the bridge is still there. If it is, we'll get going. Show up earlier than planned."

"Which we do some years anyway," he said, and poured. Black coffee, rich and strong. Just the thing after an encounter with creatures from another world. By daylight it all should have seemed hallucinatory, but it didn't. Not to me, and when I asked Butch, he said the same.

The Wonder Bread was gone, but there were a couple of fruit pies left. I imagined Sheila shaking her head and saying that only men in the woods would eat Hostess Fruit Pies for breakfast.

"Good," Butch said, munching.

"Yes. Excellent. Did you have dreams from that stuff we breathed in, Butchie?"

"Nope." He considered. "At least not that I remember. But look at this."

He picked up his pad and flipped past the pictures he'd drawn during our evenings—the usual sketches and caricatures, including one of me with a big grin on my balloon head, flipping flapjacks in a skillet. Near the back he stopped and held the pad up to me. It was our young visitor from the previous night: blond hair, vest, khaki pants, shoulder bag. It was no caricature; it was that man (might as well call him that) to the life . . . with one exception. Butch had filled his eyes with stars.

"Holy shit, that's terrific," I said. "How long have you been up, anyway?"

"About an hour. I did that in twenty minutes. I just knew what to do. Like it was already there. Never changed a single line. Crazy, right?"

"Crazy," I agreed.

I thought of telling him I'd dreamed about a burning barn. It had been incredibly vivid. I had tried several different ways to get into a story about a freak storm I'd been playing with for quite awhile. Years, actually; it had originally occurred to me when I'd been about the age my son was now. I'd try this character, then that character, then some overview of the town where I wanted to set the thing; once I even tried kicking things off with a weather bulletin.

Nothing worked. I felt like a guy trying to open a safe when he's forgotten the combination. Then, this morning, courtesy of my dream, I saw a bolt of lightning hitting a barn. I saw the weathervane—a rooster—turn red with the heat as fingers of fire spread down the barn's roof. I thought everything else would follow. No; I knew it.

I picked up the thing that looked like a spectacle case from where we'd left it the previous night and tossed it from hand to hand. "This did it," I said, then tossed it to Butch.

He caught it and said, "Sure. What else?"

All that was over forty years ago, but the passage of time has never caused me to believe my recollection of that night is faulty. Doubt has never crept in and the pitchers have never excaped my memory.

Butch remembered it as well as I did: Ylla, the light, passing out, the young man, the spectacle case. That case, so far as I know, is still in the cabin. We went out there a few more Novembers before Butch headed west, and each took a turn blowing on the embossed wave, but the case never opened for us again. Nor will it open for anyone else, I'm sure. Unless someone has stolen it—and why would they?—it's still on the mantel of the fireplace, where Butch put it the last time we were there.

The final thing Butch said to me before we left the cabin that day was that he didn't want to draw in his pad anymore, at least not for awhile. "I want to paint," he said. "I have a thousand ideas."

I had only one—the burning barn that became the first scene in *The Lightning Storm*—but I felt sure others would follow. The door was open. All I had to do was walk through it.

*   *   *

Sometimes I'm haunted by the idea that I'm a fake. Before he died, Butch said the same in several interviews.

Is that surprising? I don't think so. We were one thing when we went into the woods in the fall of 1978; we were something else ever after. We became what we became. I suppose the question has to do with talent—was it in us, or was it something given to us like a box of candy, because we saved Ylla's life? Could we be proud of what we accomplished, kind of a lifting-up-by-the-bootstraps deal, or were we just a pair of poseurs, taking credit for what we never would have had if not for that night?

What the fuck *is* talent, anyway? I ask myself that question sometimes while I'm shaving, or—in the old book-promotion days—while waiting to go on television and sell my latest glut of make-believe, or when I'm watering my late wife's daylilies. Especially then. What is it, really? Why would I be chosen when so many others try so hard and would give anything to be chosen? Why are there so few at the top of the pyramid? Talent is supposed to be the answer, but where does it come from and how does it grow? *Why* does it grow?

Well, I tell myself, *we call it a gift and we call ourselves gifted, but gifts are never really earned, are they? Only given. Talent is grace made visible.*

The young man said *nothing can give you what isn't already there. This is axiomatic.* I hold onto that.

Of course, he also said he felt sorry for us.

3

Pop's story ended there. Maybe he lost interest in his fantasy version of that hunting trip in 1978, but I don't think so. Those last few lines felt like a climax to me.

I pulled a proof copy of *The Lightning Storm* from the shelf over his desk, maybe the same one I'd looked at not long after my mother's death.

A ragged bolt of lightning struck the barn. It hit with a hollow bang, like the report of a shotgun muffled in a blanket. Jack barely had time to register it before the follow-thunder bellowed. He saw the weathervane—an iron rooster—turn red with the heat and begin spinning even as it sagged and runnels of fire spread down the barn's roof.

It didn't match the copy in the hand-written document exactly, but it was close. And better, I thought.

Which means nothing, I told myself. *He held onto those lines, that* image, *because it was good . . . or good enough. That's all it means.*

I thought of my mother's call that day in November of '78. That was a lot of years ago, but I was clear on the first thing she said: *Something happened to your father while they were on their hunting trip . . . and to Butch.* She didn't want me to come home right away, she said, because both of them were all right. But that weekend, for sure. She said they claimed to have gotten lost, although both of them knew the 30-Mile too well for that to happen.

"Like the back of their hand," I murmured. "That's what she said. But . . ."

I went back to Pop's manuscript.

I told her . . . we'd had a close call in the woods. Some hunter had fired at what he thought was a deer . . . the bullet went between us.

Which version was true? According to the manuscript, neither of them. I think that was when I started to believe Pop's story. Or . . . no, that's not quite right, because it was still too fantastic. But that's where the door opened to belief.

Did he ever tell her what he thought was the real story? Was that possible? I thought it was. Marriage is honesty; it's also a repository of shared secrets.

He'd only filled half of the spiral notebook; the rest of the pages were blank. I picked it up, meaning to put it back in the bottom drawer, and a sheet of paper fluttered out from between the last page and the back cover. I picked it up and saw it was a receipt from the

Incorporated Town of Harlow, made out to L&D Haulage, a company I'd thought defunct for at least fifty years and maybe longer. L&D had paid property taxes for the years 2010 to 2050 ("at current 2010 rate") for a tract of land bordering on Jilasi Creek in the unincorporated township of TR-90. Paid it in a lump sum.

I sat back in Pop's chair, staring at the amount tendered. I think I said *holy fuck*. Paying in advance at 2010 rates was probably a terrific deal, but to pay *forty years* in advance—in a town where most people were *behind* on their taxes—was unheard-of. According to this sheet, L&D Haulage—Laird Carmody and Dave LaVerdiere, in other words—had forked over 110,000 dollars. Of course by then they could afford it, but why?

Only one answer seemed to fit: they had wanted to protect their little hunting cabin from development. Why? Because that other-worldly glasses case was still out there? It seemed unlikely; my guess was scavengers had long since stripped the cabin of anything even remotely valuable. What *did* seem likely—and now it was a little easier to believe—was that my father and his friend had decided to preserve the location where they had met beings from another world.

I decided to go out there.

The network of woods roads Pop and Uncle Butch used to get to Jilasi Creek was long gone. There's a housing development and a trailer park there now, both called Hemlock Run. Nor does TR-90 exist. These days it's the incorporated town of Pritchard, named for a local hero who died in Vietnam. It's still the 30-Mile Wood on maps and GPS, but now it's just ten miles of forest, if that. Maybe only five. The rickety bridge is long gone, but there's another one—narrow but sturdy—a bit further downstream. Its *raison d'etre* is Grace of Jesus Baptist Church, which sits on the Pritchard bank of the creek. I drove across it and parked in the church lot, although that day the Jilasi was so low I could almost have walked across it, had I thought to wear my waders.

I made my way back upstream and found the broken stubs of the old bridge sunk deep into weeds and ferns. I turned and saw the path to the cabin, now badly overgrown with bushes and brambles. It was marked by a sign that read NO HUNTING NO TRESPASSING BY ORDER OF GAME WARDEN. I went (carefully, fearing poison ivy or poison oak) through the bushes. A quarter of a mile, Pop had written, and I knew from my own trips out here (only a few; I had little interest in shooting creatures that couldn't shoot back) that was about right.

I came to a locked gate I didn't remember. There was another sign on it, this one showing a frog over the words HIPPITY HOPPITY GET OFF MY PROPERTY. One of Pop's keys opened the gate. I walked around a curve, and there was the cabin. No one had maintained it. The roof hadn't caved in from years of snowfall, probably because it was partially protected by the interlaced branches of old-growth pine and spruce, but it was swaybacked and wouldn't last much longer. The board sides, once painted brown, were now a faded no-color. The windows were bleared with dirt and pollen. The place was the very picture of desertion, but it apparently hadn't been vandalized, which I thought was sort of a miracle. Lines of some old poem, probably read in high school, occurred to me: *Weave a circle round him thrice, and close your eyes with holy dread.*

I found the right key on Pop's ring and went inside to must and dust and heat. Also to the scribble-scrabble of the current tenants: mice or chipmunks. Probably both. A deck of Bicycle playing cards had been scattered across the eating table and on the floor, likely tossed by gusts of wind down the chimney. Once my father and his friend had played cribbage with those very cards. A fan of ash lay in front of the fireplace, but there was no graffiti and no empty cans or liquor bottles.

A circle was woven around this place, I thought.

I told myself—*scolded* myself—that I was being ridiculous, but maybe I wasn't. Hemlock Run, both parts of it, was close. Surely kids would have explored this far into the woods, and surely HIPPITY HOPPITY GET OFF MY PROPERTY wouldn't have kept them away. But it seemed they *had* kept away.

I looked at the sofa. If I sat on it now, dust would puff up in a cloud and mice might flee from beneath, but I could imagine a young man with blond hair sitting there, a stranger my Uncle Butch had drawn with stars for eyes. It was easier to believe it had actually happened now that I was out here, in a cabin Pop and Uncle Butch had paid to keep safe (if not sound) until the middle of the century.

Much easier.

Had either of them come out here again, possibly to retrieve a case that looked like it might contain spectacles? Not Butch, at least not once he went off to the West Coast . . . but I don't think my father had, either. They were done with it, and although I was Pop's heir, I felt like an intruder.

I crossed the room and looked on the mantel, expecting nothing, but the gray case was there, covered by a scrim of dust. I reached for it and winced as I closed my hand around it, as if afraid it might give me an electric shock. It didn't. I wiped away the dust from the top and saw the wave, bright gold embossed on what might have been gray suede. Except it didn't feel like suede, nor did it precisely feel like metal. There was no seam in the case. It was perfectly blank.

This has been waiting for me, I thought. *It was all true, every word, and this is now part of my inheritance.*

Did I believe my father's story then? I almost did. And had he left the case for me? The answer to that is more difficult. I couldn't ask the two talented bastids who'd come out here to hunt in November of 1978, because they were both dead. They had made their mark on the world—paintings, stories—and then left it.

The young man who wasn't a man said the gift was for them, because Pop had shot the not-woman up with the EpiPen and Uncle Butch had given her his—I quote—"precious breath." He didn't say it was *just* for them, though, did he? And if Pop's breath had opened it, might not mine do it as well? Same blood, same DNA. Would it open-sesame for me? Did I dare try it?

What have I told you about myself? Let me see. You know that I was Castle County School Superintendent for many years, before I retired to become my father's amanuensis . . . not to mention the one who changed his bedding if he wet himself during the night. You know that I was married and my wife left me. You know that on the day when I stood in that decaying cabin, looking at a gray case from another world,

I was alone: parents dead, wife gone, no kids. Those are the things you know, but there's a universe of things you don't know. I suppose that's true of every man jack and woman jill on earth. I'm not going to tell you much, not just because it would take too long but because it would bore you. If I told you I drank too much after Susan left me, would you care? That I had a brief romance with Internet pornography? That I thought of suicide, but never seriously?

I will tell you two things, even though both of them embarrass me almost—but not quite!—to the point of shame. They are sad things. The daydreams of men and women "of a certain age" are always sad, I think, because they run so counter to the plain-vanilla futures we have to look forward to.

I have some writing talent (as I hope this memoir will show), and I dreamed of writing a great novel, one for the ages. I loved my father and love him still, but living in his shadow became tiresome. I daydreamed of critics saying, "The depth of Mark Carmody's novel makes his father's work look shabby. The pupil has truly outshone the teacher." I don't want to feel that way, and mostly I don't, yet part of me does and always will. That part of me is a cave-dweller who grins a lot but never smiles.

I can play the piano, but not well. I am asked to accompany the hymns at the Congo church only if Mrs. Stanhope is out of town or under the weather. I'm a plodder and a thumper of keys. My ability to read music is on the third-grade level. I have polish only on the three or four pieces that I have memorized, and people get tired of hearing those.

I daydream about writing that great novel, but it's not the most powerful daydream I have. Shall I tell you what is? Having come this far, why not?

I'm in a nightclub, and all my friends are there. My father is, too. The band has left the stand, and I ask if I can play a tune on the piano. The bandleader of course says yes. My pop groans, *Oh God, Markey, not "Bring It On Home to Me" again!* I say (with appropriate modesty) *No, I learned something new,* and start to play the Albert Ammons classic, "Boogie Woogie Stomp." My fingers are flying! Conversation ceases! They stare at me, amazed and admiring! The drummer resumes his seat and picks up the beat. The horn guy starts blowing a dirty alto sax, like the one in "Tequila." The audience starts to clap along. Some of them jitterbug. And when I finish, standing for the final right-hand glissando like Jerry Lee Lewis, they get up on their feet and yell for more.

You can't see me, but I'm blushing as I write this.

Not just because it's my most treasured fantasy, but because it's so common. All over the world, even now, women are playing air guitar like Joan Jett and men are pretending to conduct Beethoven's Fifth in their rec rooms. These are the ordinary fantasies of those who would give anything to be chosen, and are not.

In that dusty, ready-to-fall-down cabin where two men once met a being from another world, I thought I would love to play "Boogie Woogie Stomp" like Albert Ammons just once. Once would be enough, I told myself, knowing it would not be; it never is.

I blew on the wave. A line appeared in the middle of the case . . . held for a moment . . . and then disappeared. I stood there for awhile, holding the case, then put it back on the mantel.

I remembered the young man saying *nothing can give you what isn't already there.*

"It's all right," I said, and laughed a little.

It wasn't all right, it stung, but I understood the sting would go away. I'd go back to my life and the sting would go away. I had my famous father's affairs to tie up, that would keep me busy, and I'd have plenty of money. Maybe I'd go to Aruba. It's all right to want what you can't have. You learn to live with it.

I tell myself that, and mostly I believe it.

THE FIFTH STEP

Harold Jamieson, once Chief Engineer of New York City's Sanitation Department, enjoyed retirement. He knew from his small circle of friends that some didn't, so he considered himself lucky. He had an acre of garden in upper Manhattan that he shared with several like-minded horticulturalists, he had discovered Netflix, and he was making inroads in the books he'd always meant to read. He still missed his wife—a victim of breast cancer five years previous—but aside from that persistent ache, his life was quite full. Before rising every morning, he reminded himself to enjoy the day. At sixty-eight he liked to think he had a fair amount of road left, but there was no denying it had begun to narrow.

The best part of those days—assuming it wasn't raining, snowing, or too cold—was the nine-block walk to Central Park after breakfast. Although he carried a cell phone and used an electronic tablet (had grown dependent on it, in fact), he still preferred the print version of the *Times*. In the park he would settle on his favorite bench and spend an hour with it, reading the sections back to front, telling himself he was progressing from the sublime to the ridiculous.

One morning in mid-May, the weather coolish but perfectly adequate for bench-sitting and newspaper-reading, he was annoyed to look up from his paper to see a middle-aged man sitting down on the other end of his bench, although there were plenty of empty ones in the vicinity. This invader of Jamieson's morning space looked to be in his mid to late forties, neither handsome nor ugly, in fact perfectly nondescript. The same was true of his attire: New Balance walking shoes, jeans, a Yankee cap, and a Yankee hoodie with the hood tossed back. Jamieson gave him an impatient side-glance and prepared to move to another bench.

"Don't go," the man said. "Please. I sat down here because I need a favor. It's not a big one, but I'll pay." He reached into the kangaroo pouch of the hoodie and held out a twenty-dollar bill.

"I don't do favors for strange men," Jamieson said, and got up.

"But that's exactly the point—the two of us being strangers. Hear me out. If you say no, that's fine. But please hear me out. You could . . ." He cleared his throat, and Jamieson realized the guy was nervous. Maybe more, maybe scared. "You could be saving my life."

Jamieson considered, then sat down. But as far from the other man as he could, while still keeping both butt-cheeks on the bench. "I'll give you a minute, but if you sound crazy to me, I'm leaving. And put your money away. I don't need it and I don't want it."

The man looked at the bill as if surprised to find it still in his hand, then put it back in the kangaroo pouch. He put his hands on his thighs and looked down at them instead of at Jamieson. "I'm an alcoholic. Four months sober. Four months and twelve days, to be exact."

"Congratulations," Jamieson said. He guessed he meant it, but he was even more ready to get up. To leave the park, if necessary. The guy seemed sane, but Jamieson was old enough to know that sometimes the woo-woo didn't come out right away.

"I've tried three times before and once got almost a year. I think this might be my last chance to grab the brass ring. I'm in AA. That's—"

"I know what it is. What's your name, Mr. Four Months Sober?"

"You can call me Jack, that's good enough. We don't use last names in the program."

Jamieson knew that, too. Lots of people on the Netflix shows had alcohol problems. "So what can I do for you, Jack?"

"The first three times I tried, I didn't get a sponsor in the program—somebody who listens to you, answers your questions, sometimes tells you what to do. This time I did. Met a guy at the Bowery Sundown meeting and really liked the stuff he said. And, you know, how he carried himself. Twelve years sober, feet on the ground, works in sales, like me."

He had turned to look at Jamieson, but now he returned his gaze to his hands.

"I used to be a hell of a salesman, for five years I headed the sales department of . . . well, it doesn't matter, but it was a big deal, you'd know the company. That was in San Diego. Now I'm down to peddling greeting cards and energy drinks to convenience stores and bodegas in the five boroughs. Last rung on the ladder, man."

"Get to the point," Jamieson said, but not harshly; he had become a little interested in spite of himself. It was not every day that a stranger sat down on your bench and started spilling his shit. Especially not in New York. "I was just going to check on the Mets. They're off to a good start."

Jack rubbed a palm across his mouth. "I liked this guy I met at the Sundown, so I got up my courage after a meeting and asked him to be my sponsor. In March, this was. He looked me over and said he'd take me on, but only on two conditions. That I do everything he said and call him if I felt like drinking. 'Then I'll be calling you every fucking night,' I said, and he said 'So call me every fucking night, and if I don't answer talk to the machine.' Then he asked me if I worked the Steps. Do you know what those are?"

"Vaguely."

"I said I hadn't gotten around to them. He said that if I wanted him to be my sponsor, I'd have to start. He said the first three were both the hardest and the easiest. They boil down to 'I can't stop on my own, but with God's help I can, so I'm going to let him help.'"

Jamieson grunted.

"I said I didn't believe in God. This guy—Randy's his name—said he didn't give a shit. He told me to get down on my knees every morning and ask this God I didn't believe in to help me stay sober another day. And if I didn't drink, he said for me to get down on my knees before I turned in and thank God for my sober day. Randy asked if I was willing to do that, and I said I was. Because I'd lose him otherwise. You see?"

"Sure. You were desperate."

"Exactly! 'The gift of desperation,' that's what AAs call it. Randy said if I didn't do those prayers and *said* I was doing them, he'd know. Because he spent thirty years lying his ass off about everything."

"So you did it? Even though you don't believe in God?"

"I did it and it's been working. As for my belief that there's no God . . . the longer I stay sober, the more that wavers."

"If you're going to ask me to pray with you, forget it."

Jack smiled down at his hands. "Nope. I still feel self-conscious about the on-my-knees thing even when I'm by myself. Last month—April—Randy told me to do the Fourth Step. That's when you make a moral inventory—supposedly searching and fearless—of your character."

"Did you?"

"Yes. Randy said I was supposed to put down the bad stuff, then turn the page and list the good stuff. It took me ten minutes for the bad stuff. Over an hour for the good stuff. At first I couldn't think of anything good, but finally I wrote 'At least I've got a sense of humor.' Which I do. Once I got that, I was able to think of a few other things. When I told Randy I had trouble thinking of character strengths, he said that was normal. 'You drank for almost thirty years,' he said. 'That puts a lot of scars and bruises on a man's self-image. But if you stay sober, the bruises will heal.' Then he told me to burn the lists. He said it would make me feel better."

"Did it?"

"Strangely enough, it did. Anyway, that brings us to this month's request from Randy."

"More of a demand, I'm guessing," Jamieson said, smiling a little. He folded his newspaper and laid it aside.

Jack also smiled. "I think you're catching the sponsor-sponsee dynamic. Randy told me it was time to do my Fifth Step."

"Which is?"

"'Admitted to God, to ourselves, and to another human being the exact nature of our wrongs,'" Jack said, making quote marks with his fingers. "I told him okay, I'd make a list and read it to him. God could listen in. Two birds with one stone deal."

"I'm thinking he said no."

"He said no. He told me to approach a complete stranger. His first suggestion was a priest or a minister, but I haven't set foot in a church since I was twelve, and I have no urge to go back. Whatever I'm coming to believe—and I don't know yet what that is—I don't need to sit in a church pew to help it along."

Jamieson, no churchgoer himself, nodded.

"Randy said, 'Just walk up to somebody in Grant Park or Washington Square Park or Central Park and ask him to hear you list your wrongs. Offer a few bucks to sweeten the deal if that's what it takes. Keep asking until someone agrees to listen.' He said the hard part would be the asking part, and he was right."

"Am I . . ." *Your first victim* was the phrase that came to mind, but Jamieson decided it wasn't exactly fair. "Am I the first person you've approached?"

"The second. I tried an off-duty cab driver yesterday and he told me to get lost."

Jamieson thought of an old New York joke: Out-of-towner approaches a guy on Lexington Avenue and says, "Can you tell me how to get to City Hall or should I just go fuck myself?" He decided he wasn't going to tell the guy in the Yankee gear to go fuck himself. He would listen, and the next time he met his friend Alex (another retiree) for lunch, he'd have something interesting to talk about.

"Okay, go for it."

Jack reached into the pouch of his hoodie, took out a piece of paper, and unfolded it. "When I was in fourth grade—"

"If this is going to be your life story, maybe you better give me that twenty after all."

Jack reached into his hoodie with the hand not holding his list of wrongdoings, but Jamieson waved him off. "Joking."

"Sure?"

"Yes. But let's not take too long. I've got an appointment at eight-thirty." This wasn't true, and Jamieson reflected that it was good he didn't have the alcohol problem, because according to the TV meetings he'd attended, honesty was a big deal if you did.

"Keep it speedy, got it. Here goes. In fourth grade I got into a fight with another kid. Gave him a bloody lip and nose. When we got to the office, I said it was because he'd called my mother a dirty name. He denied it, of course, but we both got sent home with a note for our parents. Or just my mom in my case, because my dad left us when I was two."

"And the dirty name thing?"

"A lie. I was having a bad day and thought I'd feel better if I got into a fight with this kid I didn't like. I don't know why I didn't like him, I guess there was a reason, but I don't remember what it was. Only that set a pattern of lying.

"I started drinking in junior high. My mother had a bottle of vodka she kept in the freezer. I'd swig from it, then add water. She finally caught me, and the vodka disappeared from the freezer. I knew where she put it—on a high shelf over the stove—but I left it alone after that. By then it was probably mostly water, anyway. I saved my allowance and chore money and got some old wino to buy me nips. He'd buy four and keep one. I enabled his drinking. That's what my sponsor would say."

Jack shook his head.

"I don't know what happened to that guy. Ralph, his name was, only I thought of him as Wretched Ralph. Kids can be cruel. For all I know, he's dead and I helped kill him."

"Don't get carried away," Jamieson said. "I'm sure you have stuff to feel guilty about without having to invent a bunch of might-have-beens."

Jack looked up and grinned. When he did, Jamieson saw the man actually had tears in his eyes. Not falling, but brimming. "Now you sound like Randy."

"Is that a good thing?"

"I think so. I think I'm lucky I found you."

Jamieson discovered he actually felt lucky to have been found. "What else have you got on that list? Because time's passing."

"I went to Brown and graduated *cum laude*, but mostly I lied and cheated my way through. I was good at it. And—here's a big one— the student advisor I had my senior year was a coke addict. I won't go into how I found that out, like you said, time's passing, but I did, and I made a deal with him. Good recommends in exchange for a key of coke. Plus, of course, he'd pay for the dope. I wasn't into charity."

"Key as in kilo?" Jamieson asked. His eyebrows went up most of the way to his hairline.

"Right. I brought it in through the Canadian border, tucked into the spare tire of my old Ford. Trying to look like any other college kid who'd spent his semester break having fun and getting laid in Toronto, but my heart was beating like crazy and I bet my blood pressure was red-lining. The car in front of me at the checkpoint got tossed completely, but I got waved right through after showing my driver's license. Of course things were much looser back then." He paused, then said, "I overcharged him for the key, too. Pocketed the difference."

"But you didn't use any of the cocaine yourself?"

"No, that was never my scene. I blew a little dope once in a while, but what I really wanted—still want—is grain alcohol. I lied to my bosses, but eventually that gave out. It wasn't like college, and there was nobody to mule coke for. Not that I found, anyway."

"What did you do, exactly?"

"Massaged my sell-sheets. Made up appointments that didn't exist to explain days when I was too hungover to come in. Jiggered expense sheets. That first job was a good one. The sky was the limit. And I blew it.

"After they let me go, I decided what I really needed was a change of location. In AA that's called a geographic cure. Never works, but I didn't know that. Seems simple enough now; if you put an asshole on a plane in Boston, an asshole gets off in LA. Or Denver. Or Des Moines. I fucked up a second job, not as good as the first one, but good. That was in San Diego. And what I decided then was that I needed to get married and settle down. *That* would solve the problem. So I got married to a nice girl who deserved better than me. It lasted two years, me lying right down the line about my drinking. Inventing non-existent business appointments to explain why I was home late, inventing non-existent flu symptoms to explain why I was going in late or not at all. I could have bought stock in one of those breath mint companies—Altoids, Breath Savers—but was she fooled?"

"I'm guessing not," Jamieson said. "Listen, are we approaching the end here?"

"Yes. Five more minutes. Promise."

"Okay."

"There were arguments that kept getting worse. Stuff got thrown occasionally, and not just by her. There was a night when I came home around midnight, stinking drunk, and she started in on me. You know, all the usual jabber, and all of it was true. I felt like she was throwing poison darts at me and never missing."

Jack was looking at his hands again. His mouth was turned down at the corners so severely that for a moment he looked to Jamieson like Emmett Kelly, that famous sad-faced clown.

"You know what came into my mind while she was yelling at me? Glenn Ferguson, that boy I beat up in the fourth grade. How good it felt, like squeezing the pus out of an infected boil. I thought it would be good to beat *her* up, and for sure no one would send me home with a note for my mother, because my mom died the year after I graduated from Brown."

"Whoa," Jamieson said. Feeling good about this uninvited confession took a hike. Unease replaced it. He wasn't sure he wanted to hear what came next.

"I left," Jack said. "But I was scared enough to know I had to do something about my drinking. That was the first time I tried AA, out there in San Diego. I was sober when I came back to New York, but that didn't last. Tried again and *that* didn't last, either. Neither did the third. But now I've got Randy, and this time I might make it. Partly thanks to you." He held out his hand.

"Well, you're welcome," Jamieson said, and took it.

"There is one more thing," Jack said. His grip was very strong. He was looking into Jamieson's eyes and smiling. "I did leave, but I cut that bitch's throat before I did. I didn't stop drinking, but it made me feel better. The way beating up Glenn Ferguson made me feel better. And that wino I told you about? Kicking him around made me feel better, too. Don't know if I killed him, but I sure did bust him up."

Jamieson tried to pull back, but the grip was too strong. The other hand was once more inside the pocket of the Yankee hoodie.

"I really want to stop drinking, and I can't do a complete Fifth Step without admitting that I seem to really enjoy . . ."

What felt like a streak of hot white light slid between Jamieson's ribs, and when Jack pulled the dripping icepick away, once more tucking it into the pocket of his hoodie, Jamieson realized he couldn't breathe.

". . . killing people. It's a character defect, I know, and probably the chief of my wrongs."

He got to his feet.

"Thank you, sir. I don't know what your name is, but you've helped me so much."

He started away toward Central Park West, then turned back to Jamieson, who was grasping blindly for his *Times* . . . as if, perhaps, a quick scan of the Arts and Leisure section would put everything right.

"You'll be in my prayers tonight," Jack said.

WILLIE THE WEIRDO

Willie's mom and dad thought their son was strange, with his careful study of dead birds and his collections of dead bugs and the way he might look at drifting clouds for an hour or more, but only Roxie would say it out loud. "Willie the Weirdo," she called him one night at the dinner table while Willie was making (trying to, anyway) a clown face in his mashed potatoes with gravy for eyes. Willie was ten. Roxie was twelve and getting breasts, of which she was very proud. Except when Willie stared at them, which made her feel creepy.

"Don't call him that," Mother said. She was Sharon.

"But it's true," Roxie said.

Father said, "I'm sure he gets enough of that at school." He was Richard.

Sometimes—often—the family talked about Willie as if he wasn't there. Except for the old man at the foot of the table.

"*Do* you get that at school?" Grandfather asked. He rubbed a finger between his nose and upper lip, his habit after asking a question (or answering one). Grandfather was James. Ordinarily during family meals he was a silent man. Partly because it was his nature and partly because eating had become a chore. He was making slow work of his roast beef. Most of his teeth were gone.

"I don't know," Willie said. "I guess sometimes." He was studying his mashed potatoes. The clown was now grinning a shiny brown grin with small globules of fat for teeth.

*   *   *

Sharon and Roxie cleaned up after dinner. Roxie enjoyed doing the dishes with her mother. It was a sexist division of labor to be sure, but they could have undisturbed conversations about important matters. Such as Willie.

Roxie said, "He *is* weird. Admit it. That's why he's in the Remedial."

Sharon looked around to make sure they were alone. Richard had gone for a walk and Willie had retired to Grandfather's room with the man Rich sometimes called the old boy and sometimes the roomer. Never Dad or my father.

"Willie isn't like other boys," Sharon said, "but we love him anyway. Don't we?"

Roxie gave it some thought. "I guess I love him, but I don't exactly *like* him. He's got a bottle filled with fireflies in Grampa's room. He says he likes to watch them go out when they die. *That's* weird. He's like a case history in a book called *Serial Killers as Children*."

"Don't you ever say that," Sharon told her. "He can be very sweet."

Roxie had never experienced what she'd call sweetness but thought it better not to say so. Besides, she was still thinking of the fireflies, their little lights going out one by one. "And Grampa watches right along with him. They're in there all the time, talking. Grampa doesn't talk to anyone else, hardly."

"Your grandfather has had a hard life."

"He's really not my grampa, anyway. Not by blood, I mean."

"He might as well be. Grampa James and Gramma Elise adopted your father when he was just a baby. It's not like Dad grew up in an orphanage and got adopted at twelve, or something."

"Dad says Grampa hardly ever talked to him after Gramma Elise died. He says there were nights when they hardly said six words to each other. But since he came to live with us, he and Willie go in there and talk up a storm."

"It's good they have a connection," Sharon said, but she was frowning down at the soapy water. "It keeps your grandfather tethered to the world, I think. He's very old. Richard came to them late, when James and Elise were already in their fifties."

"I didn't think they let people that old adopt," Roxie said.

"I don't know how that stuff works," Mother said. She pulled the plug and the soapy water began to gurgle down the drain. There was a dishwasher, but it was broken and Father—Richard—kept not getting it fixed. Money had been tight since Grandfather came to live with them, because he only had his pittance of a pension to contribute. Also, Roxie knew, Mom and Dad had already begun saving for her college education. Probably not for Willie's, though, with him being in the Remedial and all. He liked clouds, and dead birds, and dying fireflies, but he wasn't much of a scholar.

"I don't think Dad likes Grampa very much," Roxie said in a low voice.

Mother lowered hers even further, so it was hard to hear over the last few chuckles from the sink. "He doesn't. But Rox?"

"What?"

"This is how families do. Remember when you have one of your own."

Roxie never intended to have children, but if she did, and one of them turned out like Willie, she thought she'd be tempted to drive him into the deepest darkest woods, let him out of the car, and just leave him there. Like a wicked stepmother in a fairy tale. She briefly wondered if that made *her* weird and decided it didn't. Once she heard her father tell Mother that Willie's career might turn out to be bagging groceries at Kroger's.

James Jonas Fiedler—aka Grandfather, aka Grampa, aka the old boy— came out of his room (called his den by Sharon, his lair by Richard) for meals, and sometimes he would sit on the back porch and smoke a cigarette (three a day), but mostly he stayed in the small back bedroom that had been Mother's study until last year. Sometimes he watched the little TV on top of his dresser (three channels, no cable). Mostly he either slept or sat quietly in one of the two wicker chairs, looking out of the window.

But when Willie came in, he would close the door and talk. Willie would listen, and when he asked questions Grampa would always answer them. Willie knew most of the answers were untruthful and he was aware that most of Grandfather's advice was bad advice—Willie was in the Remedial because it allowed him time to think about more important things, not because he was stupid—but Willie enjoyed the answers and advice just the same. If it was crazy, so much the better.

That night, while his mother and sister were discussing the two of them in the kitchen, Willie asked Grandfather again—just to see if it jibed with earlier stories—what the weather had been like at Gettysburg.

Grandfather rubbed a finger beneath his nose, as if feeling for stubble, and ruminated. "Day One, cloudy and mid-70s. Not bad. Day Two, partly cloudy and 81. Still not bad. Day Three, the day of Pickett's Charge, 87 degrees with the sun beating down on us like a hammer. And remember, we were in wool uniforms. We all stank of sweat."

The weather report matched. So far so good. "Were you really there, Grampa?"

"Yes," said Grandfather with no hesitation. He passed his finger below his nose and above his lip, then began to pick his remaining teeth with a yellow fingernail, extracting a few filaments of roast beef. "And lived to tell the tale. Many did not. Want to know about July 4th, Independence Day? People tend to forget that one because the battle was over." He didn't wait for Willie to answer. "Pouring rain, boot-sucking mud, men crying like babies. Lee on his horse—"

"Traveler."

"Yes, Traveler. His back was to us. He had blood on his hat and the seat of his britches. But not his blood. He was unwounded. That man was the devil."

Willie picked up the bottle on the windowsill (Heinz Relish on the fading label) and tilted it from side to side, enjoying the dry rustle of the dead fireflies. He imagined it was like the sound of the wind in graveyard grass on a hot July day.

"Tell me about the flag boy."

Grandfather passed his finger between nose and lip. "You've heard that story twenty times."

"Just the ending. That's the part I like."

"He was twelve. Going up the hill beside me, Stars and Bars flying high. The end of the pole was socked into a little tin cup on his belt. My mate Micah Leblanc made that cup. We were halfway up Cemetery Hill when the boy got hit spang in the throat."

"Tell about the blood!"

"His lips parted. His teeth were clenched. In pain, I suppose. Blood squirted out between them."

"And it gleamed—"

"That's right." The finger took a quick swipe beneath his nose, then returned to his teeth, where one pesky filament remained. "It gleamed like—"

"Like rubies in the sun. And you were really there."

"Didn't I say so? I was the one who picked up the Dixie flag when that boy went down. I carried it twenty more running steps before we were turned back not a stone's throw from the rock wall the bluebellies were hiding behind. When we skedaddled, I carried it back down the hill again. Tried to step over the bodies, but I couldn't step over all of them because there were so many."

"Tell about the fat one."

Grandfather rubbed his cheek—*scritch*—then under his nose again—*scratch*. "When I stepped on his back he farted."

Willie's face twisted in a silent laugh and he clutched himself. It was what he did when he was amused, and whenever Roxie observed that knotted face and self-hug, she *knew* he was weird.

"There!" Grampa said, and finally dislodged a long strand of beef. "Feed it to the fireflies."

He gave the strand to Willie, who dropped it on top of the dead fireflies in the Heinz jar. "Now tell me about Cleopatra."

"Which part?"

"The barge."

"Ah-ha, the barge, is it?" Grandfather caressed his philtrum, this time with his fingernail—*scritch*! "Well, I don't mind. The Nile was so broad we could hardly see across it, but that day it was as smooth as a baby's belly. I had the rudder . . ."

Willie leaned forward, rapt.

*   *   *

On a day not long after the roast beef and the mashed potatoes that made a clown face, Willie was sitting on a curb after a rainstorm. He had missed the bus going home again, but that was all right. He was watching a dead mole in the gutter, waiting to see if the rushing water would wash it into a sewer grate. A couple of big boys came along, trading arm punches and various profane witticisms. They stopped when they saw Willie.

"Look at that kid huggin' himself," one said.

"Because no girl in her right mind ever would," said the other.

"It's the freako," said the first. "Check out those little pink eyes."

"And the haircut," said the second. "Looks like somebody sculped him. Hey short bus kid!"

Willie stopped hugging himself and looked up at them.

"Your face looks suspiciously like my ass," said the first, and accepted a high five from his companion.

Willie looked back down at the dead mole. It was moving toward the sewer grate, but very slowly. He didn't believe it was going to make it. At least not unless it started raining again.

Number One kicked him in the hip and proposed beating him up.

"Let him alone," Number Two said. "I like his sister. She got a hot bod."

They went on their way. Willie waited until they were out of sight, then got up, pulled the damp seat of his pants away from his butt, and walked home. His mother and father were still at work. Roxie was somewhere, probably with one of her friends. Grampa was in his room, looking at a game show on his TV. When Willie came in, he snapped it off.

"You've got a bit of a hitch in your gitalong," Grampa said.

"What?"

"A limp, a limp. Let's go out on the back porch. I want to smoke. What happened to you?"

"Kid kicked me," Willie said. "I was watching a mole. It was dead. I wanted to see if it would go into the sewer or not."

"Did it?"

"No. Unless it did after I left, but I don't think so."

"Kicked you, did he?"

"Yes."

"Ah-ha," Grampa said, and that closed the subject. They went out on the porch. They sat down. Grampa lit a cigarette and coughed out the first drag in several puffs.

"Tell me about the volcano under Yellowstone," Willie proposed.

"Again?"

"Yes, please."

"Well, it's a big one. Maybe the biggest. And someday it's going to blow. It'll take the whole state of Wyoming when it does, plus some of Idaho and most of Montana."

"But that isn't all," Willie said.

"Not at all." Grampa smoked and coughed. "It'll throw a billion tons of ash into the atmosphere. The crops will die worldwide. *People* will die worldwide. The Internet everyone is so proud of will go kerblooey."

"The ones who don't starve will choke to death," Willie said. His eyes were shining. He clutched his throat and went *grrrahh*. "It could be an extinction event, like what killed the dinosaurs. Only it would be *us* this time."

"Correct," Grandfather said. "That boy who kicked you won't be thinking about kicking anybody then. He'll be crying for his mommy."

"But his mommy will be dead."

"Correct," said Grandfather.

That winter, a disease in China that had been just another item on the nightly news turned into a plague that started killing people all over the world. Hospitals and morgues were overflowing. People in Europe were mostly staying inside and when they went out they put on masks. Some people in America also put on masks, mostly if they were going to the supermarket. It wasn't as good as a massive volcanic eruption in Yellowstone National Park, but Willie thought it was pretty good. He kept track of the dead-numbers on his phone. Schools were shut down early. Roxie cried because she was missing the end-of-year dance, but Willie didn't mind. You didn't get a dance at the end of the year when you were Remedial.

In March of that year, Grandfather began to cough a lot more, and sometimes he coughed up blood. Father took him to the doctor, where they had to sit in the parking lot until they were called because of the virus that was killing people. Mother and Father were both pretty sure Grampa had the virus, probably brought into the house by either Roxie or Willie. Most kids didn't get sick, it seemed, or at least not *very* sick, but they could pass it on and when old people caught it, they usually died. According to the news, in New York the hospitals were using refrigerated trucks to store the bodies. Mostly the bodies of old people like Grampa. Willie wondered what the insides of those trucks looked like. Were the dead people wrapped in sheets, or were they in body bags? What if one of them was still alive but froze to death? Willie thought that would make a good TV show.

It turned out Grampa didn't have the virus. He had cancer. The doctor said it started in his pancreas and then spread to his lungs. Mother told Roxie everything while they were doing dishes, and Roxie told Willie. Ordinarily she wouldn't have done that, usually the kitchen after supper was like Vegas, what got said there stayed there, but Roxie couldn't wait to tell Willie the Weirdo that his beloved grampa was circling the drain.

"Daddy asked if he should go in the hospital," she told Willie, "and the doctor said if you don't want him to die in two weeks instead of in six months or a year, take him home. The doctor said the hospital is a germ-pit and everybody who works there has to dress like in a sci-fi movie. So that's why he's still here."

"Ah-ha," Willie said.

Roxie elbowed him. "Aren't you sad? I mean, he's the only friend you've got, right? Unless you're friends with some of your fellow weirdos at that school. Which—" Roxie made a sad *wah-wahh* trumpet sound. "—is now closed, just like mine."

"What will happen when he can't go to the bathroom anymore?" Willie asked.

"Oh, he'll keep going poop and pee until he dies. He'll just do it in bed. He'll have to wear *diapers*. Mom said they'd put him in a hospice, only they can't afford it."

"Ah-ha," Willie said.

"You should be *crying*," Roxie said. "You really are a fucking weirdo."

"Grampa was a cop in a place called Selma back in the olden days," Willie told her. "He beat on Black people. He said he didn't really want to, but he had to. Because orders is orders."

"Sure," Roxie said. "And back in the *really* olden days, he had pointy ears and shoes with curly toes and worked in Santa's workshop."

"Not true," Willie said. "Santa Claus isn't real."

Roxie clutched her head.

Grandfather didn't last a year, or six months, or even four. He went down fast. By the middle of that spring he was bedridden and wearing Adult Pampers under a nightgown. Changing the Pampers was Sharon's job, of course. Richard said he couldn't stand the stink.

When Willie offered to help if she showed him how, she looked at him as if he were crazy. She wore her mask when she went in to change his diapers or give him his little meals, which were now pureed in the blender. It wasn't the virus she was worried about, because he didn't have it. Just the smell. Which she called the stench.

Willie kind of liked the stench. He didn't *love* it, that would be going too far, but he did like it—that mixture of pee, and Vicks, and slowly decaying Grampa was interesting the way looking at dead birds was interesting, or watching the dead mole make its final journey down the gutter—a kind of slow-motion funeral.

Although there were two wicker chairs in Grampa's room, now only one of them got used. Willie would pull it up beside the bed and talk to Grandfather.

"How close are you now?" he asked one day.

"Pretty close," Grandfather said. He swiped a trembling finger under his nose. His finger was yellow now. His skin was yellow all over because he was suffering from something called jaundice as well as cancer. He had to give up the cigarettes.

"Does it hurt?"

"When I cough," Grampa said. His voice had grown low and harsh, like a dog's growl. "The pills are pretty good, but when I cough it feels like it's ripping me up."

"And when you cough you can taste your own shit," Willie said matter-of-factly.

"Correct."

"Are you sad?"

"Nope. All set."

Outside, Sharon and Roxie were in the garden, bent over so all Willie could see was their sticking-up asses. Which was fine.

"When you die, will you know?"

"I will if I'm awake."

"What do you want your last thought to be?"

"Not sure. Maybe the flag boy at Gettysburg."

Willie was a little disappointed that it wouldn't be of him, but not too. "Can I watch?"

"If you're here," Grampa said.

"Because I want to see it."

Grampa said nothing.

"Will there be a white light, do you think?"

Grampa massaged his upper lip as he considered the question. "Probably. It's a chemical reaction as the brain shuts down. People who think it's a door opening on some glorious afterlife are just fooling themselves."

"But there *is* an afterlife. Isn't there, Grampa?"

James Jonas Fiedler ran that long yellow finger along the scant skin beneath his nose again, then showed his few remaining teeth in a smile. "You'd be surprised."

"Tell me about how you saw Cleopatra's tits."

"No. I'm too tired."

One night a week later, Sharon served pork chops and told her family to enjoy them—*savor every bite* was how she put it. "There won't be any more chops for awhile. Bacon, either. The pork processing plants are closing down because almost all of the workers have the virus. The price is going to go through the roof."

"*A Day No Pigs Would Die!*" Roxie exclaimed, cutting into her chop.

"What?" Father asked.

"It's a book. I did a book report on it. Got a B-plus." She popped a bite into her mouth and turned to Willie with a smile. "Read any good first-grade primers lately?"

"What's a primer?" Willie asked.

"Leave him alone," Mother said.

Father was on a birdhouse kick. A local gift shop took them on consignment and actually sold a few. After dinner he went out to his little garage workshop to build another one. Mother and Roxie went into the kitchen to do the dishes and jabber. Willie's job was clearing the table. When it was done, he went into Grampa's room. James Fiedler was now only a skeleton with a skin-covered skull face. Willie thought that if the bugs got into his coffin they wouldn't find much to eat. The sickroom smell was still there, but the smell of decaying Grampa seemed to be almost gone.

Grampa raised a hand and motioned Willie over. When Willie sat down beside the bed, Grampa beckoned him closer. "This is it," he whispered. "My big day."

Willie pulled his chair closer. He looked into Grampa's eyes. "What's it like?"

"Good," Grampa breathed. Willie wondered if he looked to Grampa like he was retreating and getting dim. He saw that in a movie once.

"Come closer."

Willie couldn't pull his chair any closer, so he bent down almost near enough to kiss Grampa's withered lips. "I want to watch you go. I want to be the last thing you see."

"I want to watch you go," Grampa repeated. "I want to be the last thing you see."

His hand came up and grasped the nape of Willie's neck with surprising strength. His nails dug in. He pulled. "You want death? Get a mouthful."

A few minutes later Willie paused outside the kitchen door to listen. "We're taking him to the hospital tomorrow," Sharon said. She sounded on the verge of tears. "I don't care what it costs, I can't do this anymore."

Roxie murmured something sympathetic.

Willie went into the kitchen. "You won't have to take him to the hospital," he said. "He just died."

They turned to him, staring at him with identical expressions of shock and dawning hope.

Mother said, "Are you sure?"

"Yes," Willie said, and stroked the skin between his lip and nose with one finger.

DANNY COUGHLIN'S
BAD DREAM

1

It's a bad dream. Danny's had a few before, everyone has a nightmare from time to time, but this is the worst one ever. Nothing bad is happening at first, but that doesn't help; the sense of impending doom is so strong it's an actual taste in his mouth, like sucking on a clump of pennies.

He's walking along the shoulder of a dirt road that's been packed and oiled to keep the dust down. It's night. A quarter moon has just risen. To Danny it looks like a sideways grin. Or a sneer. He passes a sign reading COUNTY ROAD F, only the O and the Y have been spraypainted over, and UCK has been crammed in to the right of the F, so the sign now reads CUNT ROAD FUCK. There are a couple of bullet holes for good measure.

There's corn on both sides of the road, not as high as an elephant's eye but maybe four feet, suggesting it's early summer. County Road F runs dead straight up a mild rise (in Kansas most rises are mild). At the top is a black bulk of a building that fills Danny with unreasoning horror. Some tin thing is going tinka-tinka-tinka. He wants to stop, wants nothing to do with that square black bulk, but his legs carry him on. There's no stopping them. He's not in control. A breeze gives the corn a bonelike rattle. It's chilly on his cheeks and forehead and he realizes he's sweating. Sweating in a dream!

When he gets to the top of the rise (calling it "a crest" would just be stupid), there's enough light to see the sign on the cinderblock building reads HILLTOP TEXACO. In front are two cracked concrete islands where gasoline pumps once stood. The tinka-tinka-tinka *sound is coming from rusty signs on a pole out front. One reads* REG $1.99, *one reads* MID $2.19, *and the one on the bottom reads* HI-TEST $2.49.

Nothing here to worry about, *Danny thinks,* nothing here to be afraid of. *And he's not worried. He's not afraid. Terrified is what he is.*

Tinka-tinka-tinka *go the signs advertising long-gone gas prices. The big office window is broken, ditto the glass in the door, but Danny can see weeds growing up around the shards reflecting the moonlight and knows that it's been awhile since they were broken. The vandals—bored country kids, most likely—have had their fun and moved on.*

Danny moves on, too. Around the side of the abandoned station. Doesn't want to; has to. He's not in control. Now he hears something else: scratching and panting.

I don't want to see this, *he thinks. If spoken aloud, the thought would have come out as a moan.*

He goes around the side, kicking a couple of empty motor oil cans (Havoline, the Texaco brand) out of his way. There's a rusty metal trash barrel, overturned and spilling more cans and Coors bottles and whatever paper trash hasn't blown away. Behind the station there's a mangy mongrel dog digging at the oil-stained earth. It hears Danny and looks around, its eyes silver circles in the moonlight. It wrinkles back its snout and gives a growl that can mean only one thing: mine, mine.

"That's not for you," Danny says, *thinking* I wish it wasn't for me, either, but I think it is.

The dog lowers its haunches as if to spring, but Danny's not afraid (not of the mutt, anyway). He's a town man these days, but he grew up in rural Colorado where there were dogs everywhere and he knows an empty threat when he faces one. He bends and picks up an empty oil can, the dream so real, so detailed, *he can feel the scrim of leftover grease down the side. He doesn't even have to throw it; raising it is enough. The dog turns tail and leaves at a limping run—either something wrong with one of its back legs or a split pad on one of its paws.*

Danny's feet carry him forward. He sees that the dog has scratched a hand and part of a forearm out of the ground. Two of the fingers have been stripped to the bone. The fleshy part of the palm is also gone, now in the dog's belly. Around the wrist—inedible, and thus of no use to a hungry dog—is a charm bracelet.

Danny draws in a breath and opens his mouth and

2

screams himself awake sitting bolt upright in bed, a thing he's never done before. Thank God he lives alone so there's no one to hear it. At first he doesn't even know where he is—that derelict gas station seems like the reality, the morning light coming in through the curtains the dream. He's even rubbing his hand on the Royals tee-shirt he went to bed still wearing, to wipe off the oil that was on the side of the Havoline can he picked up. There's gooseflesh from one end of his body to the other. His balls are drawn up, tight as walnuts. Then he registers his bedroom, and realizes none of that was real, no matter how real it seemed.

He strips off the tee-shirt, drops his boxers, and heads into the trailer's tiny bathroom to shave and shower off the dream. The good thing about the bad ones, he thinks as he lathers his face, is that they never last long. Dreams are like cotton candy: they just melt away.

3

Only this one doesn't melt. It retains its clarity in the shower, and while he dresses in a clean set of Dickies and attaches his keyring to his belt loop, and while he drives to the high school in his old Toyota pickup, which still runs good even though it's going to turn back to all zeroes again pretty soon. Maybe by this fall.

The student and faculty parking lots of Wilder High are almost completely empty because school let out some weeks earlier. Danny goes around back and parks in the usual place, at the end of the school bus line. There's no sign saying it's reserved for the head custodian, but everyone knows it's his.

This is his favorite time of year, when you can do work and it stays done . . . at least for awhile. A waxed hallway floor will still shine a week from now, even two weeks. You can scrape the gum off the floors in the boys' and girls' locker rooms (the girls are the worst offenders when it comes to gum, he doesn't know why) and not have to do it again until

August. Freshly washed windows don't pick up adolescent fingerprints. As far as Danny's concerned, summer vacation is a beautiful thing.

There are summer classes at Hinkle High one county over, where there are three full-time janitors. They can have it, as far as Danny's concerned. He has a couple of summer employment kids. The good one, Jesse Jackson, is just punching in when Danny enters the supply room. There's no sign of the other one—who, in Danny's opinion, isn't worth a hill of beans.

Hill, he thinks. *Hilltop Texaco*.

"Where's Pat?"

Jesse shrugs. He's a Black kid, tall and slim, moves well. Built for baseball and basketball, not football. "Dunno. His car's not here yet. Maybe he decided to start the weekend a day early."

That would be a bad idea, Danny thinks, but guesses Pat Grady's the kind of boy who might have all sorts of bad ideas.

"We're going to wax the rooms in the new wing. Start with Room 12. Move all the desks to one side. Stack em up two by two. Then go to 10 and repeat. I'll follow along with the buffer. If Pat decides to show up, have him help you."

"Yes, Mr. Coughlin."

"No mister needed, kiddo. I'm just Danny. Think you can remember that?"

Jesse grins. "Yes, sir."

"No sir, either. Off you go. Unless you want a coffee first to get you cranking."

"Had one at the Total coming in."

"Good for you. I need to check something in the library and then I'll get going, too."

"Want me to get the buffer out?"

Danny grins. He could get to like this kid. "Are you bucking for a raise?"

Jesse laughs. "Not likely."

"Good. Here in Wilder County it's RR, Republicans rule, and they keep a tight grip on the purse strings. Sure, get the buffer and roll it on down to 12. Keep meaning to ask if you're by any chance named after the other Jesse Jackson. The famous one."

"Yes, sir. I mean Danny."

"You'll get there, kid. I have faith in you."

Danny takes his Thermos of coffee down to the library—another benefit of summer vacation.

4

He turns on one of the computers and uses the librarian's code to unlock it. The passcode the kids use blocks anything resembling porn, also access to social media. With Mrs. Golden's you can go anywhere, not that Danny is planning on visiting Pornhub. He opens Firefox and types in *Hilltop Texaco*. His finger hovers over the enter button, then he adds *County Road F* for good measure. The dream is just as clear now as it was when he woke up, it's bugging him (actually scaring him just a little, even with morning sunlight streaming in through the windows), and finding nothing will, he hopes, put paid to it.

He pushes the button, and a second later he's looking at a gray cinderblock building. In this photo it's new instead of old and the Texaco sign is spandy clean. The glass in the office window and door is intact. The gas pumps sparkle. The prices on the signs say it's $1.09 for regular and $1.21 for mid-grade. There was apparently no hi-test to be had at Hilltop Texaco when the picture was taken, which must have been a long time ago. The car at the pumps is a boat of a Buick and the road out front is two-lane blacktop instead of oiled dirt. Danny thinks the Buick must have rolled off the line in Detroit around 1980.

County Road F is in the town of Gunnel. Danny has never heard of it, but that's not surprising; Kansas is big and there must be hundreds of tiny towns he's never heard of. For all he knows, Gunnel might be across the state line in Nebraska. The hours of operation are 6 AM to 10 PM. Pretty standard for a gas-em-up out in the country. Below the hours, in red, is one word: CLOSED.

Danny looks at this dream-made-real with a dismay so deep it's almost fear. Hell, maybe it *is* fear. All he wanted was to make sure Hilltop Texaco (and the hand sticking out of the ground, don't forget the hand) was just some bullshit his sleeping mind created, and now look at this. Just look at it.

Well, I've been by it at some time or other, he reasons. *That's it, gotta be. Didn't I read somewhere that the brain never forgets anything, just stores the old trivia away on the back shelves?*

He searches for more info about the Hilltop Texaco and finds none. Only Hilltop Bakery (in Des Moines), Hilltop Subaru (in Danvers, Massachusetts), and forty-eleven other Hilltops, including a petting zoo in New Hampshire. In each of these, a line has been drawn through *Texaco County Road F*, showing that part of his search parameter hasn't been met. Why would there be more info, anyway? It's just a gas station somewhere out in the williwags—what his dad used to call East Overshoe. A Texaco franchise that went broke, maybe back in the nineties.

Above his main selection are a few other options: NEWS, VIDEOS, SHOPPING . . . and IMAGES. He clicks on images and sits back in his chair, more dismayed than ever by what comes up. There are plenty of photos showing various Hilltops, including four of the Texaco. The first is a duplicate of the one on the main page, but in another the gas station stands deserted: pumps gone, windows busted, trash scattered around. This is the one he visited in his dream, the very one. There can be no doubt about it. The only question is whether or not there's a body buried in the oil-soaked earth behind it.

"I'll be dipped in shit."

It's all Danny can think of to say. He's a thirty-six-year-old man, high school graduate but no college diploma, divorced, no kids, steady worker, Royals fan, Chiefs fan, keeps out of the bars after a spell of bad drinking that led—partially, at least—to his split with Marjorie. He drives an old pickem-up, works his hours, collects his pay, enjoys the occasional binge-out on Netflix, visits his brother Stevie every now and then, doesn't follow the news, has no politics, has no interest in psychic phenomena. He's never seen a ghost, finds movies about demons and curses a waste of time, and wouldn't hesitate to stroll through a graveyard after dark if it provided a shortcut to where he's going. He doesn't attend church, doesn't think about God, doesn't think about the afterlife, takes this life as it comes, has never questioned reality.

He's questioning it this morning. Plenty.

The blat of a car with a bad muffler (or none at all) startles him out of a state that's close to hypnosis. He looks up from the screen and sees an old Mustang pulling into the student parking lot. Pat Grady, his other summer helper, has finally decided to grace the Wilder High custodial staff with his presence. Danny looks at his watch and sees it's quarter to eight.

Keep your temper, he thinks, getting up. This is good Advice to Self, because his temper has gotten him in trouble before. It's why he spent a night in jail and why he quit the drinking. As for the marriage, that would have ended anyway . . . although it might have limped along for another year or two.

He goes to the door at the end of the new wing. Jesse has indeed brought down the buffer, and is busy moving and stacking desks in Room 12. Danny tips him a wave and Jesse tips him one right back.

Pat is ambling toward the door—no worries, no problem—in jeans, a cut-off tee, and a Wilder Wildcats hat turned around backward. Danny is there to greet him. He's got a firm grip on his temper, but the boy's who-gives-a-fuck attitude bugs him. And those motorcycle boots he's wearing are apt to leave scuff marks.

"Hey, Dan, what up?"

"You're late," Danny says, "that's what's up. Punch-in's seven-thirty. It's now pushing eight o'clock."

"Sorry 'bout that." Pat gives him a *my bad* shrug and glides past him, jeans riding low on his hips.

"This is the third time."

Pat turns back. His lazy little smile is gone. "Overslept, forgot to set my phone alarm, what can I say?"

"Here's what *I* say. Punch in late again and you're all done. Got it?"

"Are you shitting me? For being twenty minutes late?"

"Last Wednesday it was half an hour. And no, I shit you not. Punch in and help Jesse move desks in the new wing."

"The teacher's pet," Pat says, rolling his eyes.

Danny doesn't reply, knowing anything he says at this point will be the wrong thing. His summer work kids are being paid by the school department. Danny doesn't want to say or do something that will allow Pat Grady (or his folks) to go to the superintendent with a grievance about how he was hassled on the job. So he's not going to call Pat a lazy little twerp. Probably he doesn't have to. Pat sees it on his face and turns toward the supply room to punch in, hitching at his jeans with one hand. Danny doesn't know if Pat is holding the other hand to his chest with the middle finger stuck out, but wouldn't be surprised.

That kid will be gone by July, Danny thinks. *And I've got other things to worry about. Don't I?*

Jesse is standing in the doorway of Room 12. Danny gives him a shrug. Jesse gives a cautious grin and goes back to moving desks. Danny plugs in the buffer. When Pat comes back from punching in—at that same lazy amble—Danny tells him to get busy moving desks in Room 10. He thinks if Pat says a single wiseass thing, he'll fire him on the spot. But Pat keeps his mouth shut.

Maybe not entirely stupid, after all.

Danny keeps his phone in the glovebox of his Tundra so he won't be tempted to look at it during working hours (he's seen both Pat and Jesse doing exactly that—Jesse only once, Pat several times). When they knock off for lunch, he goes out to his truck long enough to look up the town of Gunnel. It's in Dart County, ninety miles north. Not over the Nebraska line, but butting up against it. He could swear he's never been in Dart County his whole life, not even as far north as Republic County, but he must have been at some point. He tosses his phone back in the glovebox and heads to where Jesse is eating his lunch—phone in hand—at one of the picnic tables in the shade of the gymnasium.

"Forgot to lock your truck. No beep."

Danny grins. "Anyone who steals from it, good luck and welcome to what they get. Plus the truck itself has eaten her share of road. Got almost two hundred thousand miles on the clock."

"Bet you love it, though. My dad loves his old Ford quarter-ton."

"I sort of do. Seen Pat?"

Jesse shrugs. "Prob'ly eating in his car. He loves that old Mustie. I think he should take better care of it, but that's just me. We gonna finish the new wing?"

"Gonna give it a try," Danny says. "If we don't, there's always Monday."

5

That night he calls his ex, a thing he does from time to time. He even went down to Wichita for her birthday in April, brought her a scarf—blue, to match her eyes—and stayed for cake and ice cream with her new guy. He and Margie get along a lot better since they split. Sometimes Danny thinks that's a shame. Sometimes he thinks it's just the way it should be.

They talk a little bit, this and that, people they know, her mother's glaucoma and how Danny's brother is doing at his job (fabulous), and then he asks if they ever drove north, maybe over into Nebraska, maybe to Franklin or Beaver City. Didn't they have lunch one time in Beaver City?

She laughs—not quite her old mean laugh, the one that used to drive him crazy, but close. "I never would have gone to Nebraska with you, Danno. Ain't Kansas borin enough?"

"You're sure?"

"Posi-lute," Margie says, then tells him she thinks Hal—her new guy—is going to pop the question pretty soon. Would he come to the wedding?

Danny says he would. She asks if he's taking care of himself, meaning is he still off the booze. Danny says he is, tells her to look both ways before crossing the street (an old joke between them), and hangs up.

Never would have gone to Nebraska with you, Danno, she said.

Danny has been to Lincoln a couple of times and Omaha once, but those towns are east of Wilder, and Gunnel is dead north. Yet he must have been there and just forgot it. Maybe back in his drinking days? Except he never drove when he was out-and-out shitfaced, afraid of losing his license or maybe hurting somebody.

I was there. Must have been, back when that county road was still tarvy instead of packed dirt.

He stays up later than usual and tosses around quite a bit before finally dropping off, afraid the dream will come back. It doesn't, but the next morning it's as clear as ever: deserted gas station, half-moon, stray dog, hand, charm bracelet.

6

Unlike many men of his age and station, Danny doesn't drink (not now, anyway), doesn't smoke, doesn't chew. He likes pro sports and might put five bucks down on the Super Bowl just to make it interesting, but otherwise he doesn't gamble—not even two-buck scratch tickets on payday. Nor does he chase after women. There's a lady in his trailer park he visits from time to time, Becky's what used to be called a grass widow, but that's more of a casual friendship than what the afternoon talk shows call "a relationship." Sometimes he stays over at Becky's place. Sometimes he brings her a bag of groceries or babysits her daughter if Beck has errands to run or an early evening hair appointment. There's plenty of get-along between them, but love ain't in it.

On Saturday morning he packs his dinnerbucket with a couple of sandwiches and a piece of the cake Becky brought over after he wired up the tailpipe of her old Honda Civic. He fills his Thermos with black coffee and heads north. He thinks he'll feel like eating if he takes a look behind that deserted gas station and finds nothing. If he sees what he saw in his dream, probably not.

The GPS on his phone gets him to Gunnel by ten-thirty. The day is all Kansas, hot and bright and clear and not very interesting. The town is nothing but a grocery store, a farm supply store, a café, and a rusty water tower with GUNNEL on the side. Ten minutes after leaving it, he comes to County Road F and turns onto it. It's tar, not packed dirt. Nevertheless his stomach is tight and his heart is beating hard enough so he can feel it in his neck and his temples.

Corn closes in on both sides. Feed corn, not eating corn. As in his dream, it's not yet as high as an elephant's eye, but it looks good for late June and will be six feet by the time August rolls around.

The road is tarvy and that's different from the goddam dream, he thinks, but only two miles along the tar quits and then it's packed dirt. A mile after that he stops dead in the road (which is no problem since there's no traffic). Just ahead on his right is a county road sign, which has been defaced with spraypaint so it reads CUNT ROAD FUCK. There's no way he saw that in his dream, but he did. The road is rising now. When he goes another quarter of a mile, maybe even less, he will see the squat shape of the abandoned gas station.

Turn around, he thinks. *You don't want to go there and nobody's making you, so just turn around and go home.*

Except he can't. His curiosity is too strong. Also, there's the dog. If it's there it will eventually disinter the body, visiting further violation on a girl or woman who has already suffered the ultimate violation of being murdered. Letting that happen would haunt him worse—and longer—than the dream itself.

Does he know for a fact that the hand belongs to a female? Yes, because of the charm bracelet. Does he know for a fact that she was murdered? Why else would someone have buried her behind a deserted gas station somewhere north of hoot and south of holler?

He drives on. The gas station is there. The rusty tin signs out front read $1.99 for regular, $2.19 for mid-grade, and $2.49 for high octane, just as they did in his dream. There's a light breeze here at the top of the rise, and the signs go *tinka-tinka-tinka* against the steel pole on which they are mounted.

Danny pulls onto the cracked and weed-sprouting tarmac, careful to stay clear of the busted glass. His tires aren't new, and the spare is so bald it's showing cord in a couple of places. The last thing he wants—the last thing in the world—is to be stranded out here.

He gets out of his truck, slams the door, and jumps at the sound it makes. Stupid, but he can't help it. He's pretty well scared to death. Somewhere in the distance, a tractor is blatting. It might as well be on another planet, as far as Danny's concerned. He can't remember ever feeling this utterly alone.

Walking around the station is like re-entering his dream; his legs seem to be moving on their own, with no directions from the control room. He kicks aside a deserted oil can. Havoline, of course. He wants to pause at the corner of the cinderblock building long enough to visualize seeing nothing, nothing at all, but his legs carry him around without a pause. They are relentless. The rusty trash barrel is there, overturned and spilling its crap. The dog is there, too. It's standing at the edge of the corn, looking at him.

Damn mutt was waiting for me, Danny thinks. *It knew I was coming.*

This should be a stupid idea, but it's not. Standing here, miles from the nearest human being (*living* human being, that is), he knows it's not. He dreamed of the dog, and the dog dreamed of him. Simple.

"Fuck off!" Danny yells, and claps his hands. The dog gives him a baleful look and limps away into the corn.

Danny turns to his left and sees the hand, or what's left of it. And more. The stray has been busy. It has exhumed part of a forearm. Bone glimmers through the flesh, and there are bugs, but there's enough left for him to see that the person buried here is white, and there's a tattoo above the charm bracelet. It looks like either rope or a circlet of barbed wire. He could tell which if he went closer, but he has no urge to go closer. What he wants is to get the hell out of here.

But if he leaves, the dog will come back. Danny can't see it, but he knows it's close. Watching. Waiting to be left alone with its early lunch.

He goes back to his truck, gets his phone out of the glove compartment, and just looks at it. If he uses it, he's going to look guilty as shit. But that goddam dog!

An idea comes to him. The trash barrel is on its side. He tips it all the way over, sliding out a pile of crap (but no rats, thank God). Under the rust it's solid steel, has to go thirty, thirty-five pounds. He clasps it against his midsection, sweat rolling down his cheeks, and walks it to the hand and forearm. He lowers it and steps back, brushing rust off his shirt. Will that be enough, or will the dog be able to tip it over? Hard to say.

Danny goes around to the front of the station and pries up two good-sized chunks of the crumbling concrete. He takes them around back and stacks them on top of the overturned barrel. Good enough? He thinks so. For awhile, anyway. If the dog decides to batter at the barrel to get what's beneath, one of those chunks is apt to fall off and bonk it on the head.

Good so far. Now what?

7

By the time he gets to his truck, his head is a little clearer and he has an idea of how he should go. He starts the engine and backs around to head south, once more being careful not to roll over any of the broken glass. A farm truck goes by headed north. It's hauling a small open trailer filled with lumber. The driver, gimme cap yanked down to the tops of his ears, stares grimly ahead, taking no notice of Danny. Which is good. When the farm truck is over the rise, Danny pulls out and heads back the way he came.

On the outskirts of Thompson he stops in at a Dollar General and asks if they sell prepaid cell phones—what are called burners in some of the TV programs he watches. He's never bought such an item, and thinks the clerk will probably direct him elsewhere, maybe to the Walmart in Belleville, but the clerk points him to aisle five. There are lots of them, but the Tracfone seems to be the cheapest, there's no activation fee, and it comes with instructions.

Danny takes his wallet out of his hip pocket, ready to pay with his Visa, and then asks himself if he was born dumb or just grew that way. He puts it back and takes his folding money out of his left front pocket instead. He pays with that.

The clerk is a young guy with acne and a scruffy soul patch. He gives Danny a grin and asks him if he's going to kick some dickens on Tinder. He calls Danny "bro."

Danny has no idea what he's talking about, so just tells the clerk he doesn't need a bag.

The young guy says no more, only rings Danny up and gives him his receipt. Outside the door, Danny drops the receipt in a handy trashcan. He wants no record of this transaction. All he wants is to report the body. The rest is up to people who investigate things for a living. The sooner he can get this business behind him, the better. The idea of letting it go entirely never crosses his mind. Sooner or later that dog—maybe with others—will tip the barrel over to get at the meat beneath. He can't let that happen. Someone's wife or daughter is buried behind that abandoned station.

8

Two miles down the road he parks in a little rest area. There are two picnic tables and a Porta-John. That's the whole deal. Danny pulls in, opens the blister pack the Tracfone came in, and scans the instructions. They are simple enough, and the phone comes with a fifty per cent charge. Three minutes later it's live and ready to go. Danny considers writing down what he wants to say and decides there's no need. He's going to keep this brief so nobody can trace the call.

His first thought was the Belleville PD, but that's in a different county, and he knows the emergency number for the Kansas Highway Patrol—it's posted in the Wilder High School office and in the halls of both the old and the new wing. In schools all across the state, Danny supposes. Nobody says it's in case of an active shooter because no one has to.

He touches *47. It rings just a single time.

"Kansas Highway Patrol. Do you have an emergency?"

"I want to report a buried body. I think it must be a murder victim."

"What is your name, sir?"

He almost gives it. Stupid. "The body's located behind an abandoned Texaco station in the town of Gunnel."

"Sir, may I please have your name?"

"You go up County Road F. You'll come to a rise. The gas station is at the top."

"Sir—"

"Just listen. The body is behind the station, all right? A dog was chewing on the hand of whoever's buried there. It's a woman or maybe a girl. I covered her hand with a trash barrel, but the dog'll get that off pretty soon."

"Sir, I need your name and the location you're calling fr—"

"Gunnel. County Road F, about three miles in from the highway. Behind the Texaco station. Get her out of there. Please. Someone'll be missing her."

He ends the call. His heart is triphammering in his chest. His face is wet with sweat and his shirt is damp with it. He feels like he's just run a marathon, and the burner phone feels radioactive in his hand. He takes it to the trash barrel between the picnic tables, dumps it in, thinks better of it, fishes it out, wipes it all over on his shirt, and tosses it in again. He's five miles down the road before recalling—also from some TV show or other—that he maybe should have taken out the SIM card. Whatever *that* is. But he's not going back now. He doesn't think the police can trace calls made from burner phones anyway, but he's not going to risk going back to the scene of the crime.

What crime? You reported *a crime, for God's sake!*

Nevertheless, all he wants is to go home and sit in front of the television and forget this ever happened. He thinks about eating the lunch he packed, but has no appetite.

9

Now that his drinking days are over, Danny doesn't sleep in even on the weekends. Sunday morning he's up at six-thirty, eats a bowl of cereal, and turns on the KSNB Morning Report at seven. The big story is a nine-car pileup on I-70 west of Wilson. Nothing about a body being discovered behind an abandoned gas station. He's about to turn the TV off when the Sunday morning anchor, who probably needs to show ID to get a beer in a bar, says, "This just in. We have a report that a body has been discovered buried behind an empty building in the small town of Gunnel, not far from the Nebraska state line. Police have closed off a county road just north of town and the site is under investigation. We'll update this story on our website and on the evening news."

Danny goes to the station's website several times as the morning progresses, also the website of KAAS out of Salina. At quarter of noon the KAAS website adds a forty-second clip of police cars blocking the entrance to County Road F. There's one other addition to the story he saw on the morning newscast: the body is said to be that of a woman. Which isn't news to Danny.

He goes across the trailer park to see Becky. He gets a nice hug from her daughter, a nine-year-old cutie named Darla Jean. Becky asks if he wants to go out and get a bag of burgers at Snack Shack. "You can take my car," she says.

"I want to go, too!" Darla Jean says.

"All right," Becky says, "but you go and change your shirt first. That one's all smutty."

"She doesn't need to change," Danny says. "I'll just drive through."

They get the burgers, plus fries and limeades, and eat in the shade behind Becky's trailer. It's nice there. Becky has a jacaranda tree that she has to water all the time. Because, she says, "This kind of flora don't belong in Kansas." She asks if there's something on his mind, because she twice has to repeat things she's told him. "Either that or you're going senile."

"Just thinking about what I've got on for next week," he says.

"You sure you're not thinking about Margie?"

"Talked to her yesterday," Danny says. "She thinks her boyfriend's gonna pop the question."

"Are you still carrying a torch for her? Is that it?"

Danny laughs. "Not likely."

"Danny!" Darla Jean shouts. "Watch me do a double somersault!"

So he does.

10

That night KSNB has a reporter on the scene. She looks unsure of herself—definitely weekend help. She's standing in front of the police cars blocking County Road F from the turnout.

"Following an anonymous tip, KHP troopers were called to a deserted gas station in the town of Gunnel late yesterday afternoon. They discovered the body of an unidentified female buried behind the station, which . . ." She consults her notes and brushes hair out of her eyes. ". . . which closed in 2012 when Route 119 was widened to four lanes. If the woman has been identified, KHP isn't saying. Certainly her identity won't be released to the press pending notification of next-of-kin. Police are not saying if she was murdered, either, but given this isolated location . . ." She shrugs, as if to say *what else?* "Back to you, Pete."

She'll be identified soon enough, Danny thinks. The important thing is *he* hasn't been ID'd. He is just "an anonymous tipster."

My good deed for the year, he thinks. *And who says no good deed goes unpunished?*

But then, just to be safe, he knocks on wood.

11

Pat Grady shows up on time for work every day of the following week. Danny dares to hope Pat's learned his lesson, but he'll never be the worker Jesse Jackson is. As the oldtimers used to say, that young man knows how to squat and lean.

Meanwhile, information about Danny's dream girl begins to accrete. Although not named, she's reported to be twenty-four and a resident of Oklahoma City. According to a friend, this unnamed girl had had enough of both her parents and community college and intended to hitchhike out to Los Angeles and go to hairdressing school, maybe get work as an extra in the movies or TV shows. She made it as far as Kansas. The body had been there for awhile—KHP detectives weren't saying how long, but long enough to be "badly decomposed."

Dog might have had something to do with that, Danny thinks.

She had been "repeatedly stabbed," according to a police source. Also sexually assaulted, which was a semi-polite way of saying raped.

It was the end of the Thursday night story on the local news that made Danny uncomfortable. The stand-up reporter was older than the weekend woman, male, obviously part of the A Team. He was standing in front of the gas station, where the tarmac was blocked with yellow police tape. "Kansas Bureau of Investigation detectives are actively seeking the man who phoned in the original tip giving the location of the body. If anyone knows his identity, detectives hope they will come forward. Or if anyone recognizes his voice. Listen."

The screen showed the sort of silhouette some people used to hide their faces on social media. Then Danny heard his own voice. It was awesomely clear, hardly distorted at all: *The body's located behind an abandoned Texaco station in the town of Gunnel . . . County Road F, about three miles in from the highway. Behind the Texaco station. Get her out of there. Please. Someone'll be missing her.*

He was starting to wish he'd left well enough alone. Except when he thought of that chewed hand and forearm sticking out of the ground, he knew there was nothing well enough about it. He snapped off the television and spoke to the empty trailer. "What I really wish is I'd never had that fucking dream." He paused, then added: "And I hope I never have another one."

12

On Friday afternoon Danny is using a longneck mop to clean the tops of the hanging fluorescents in the main office when a dark blue sedan pulls into the faculty parking lot. A woman in a white shirt and blue slacks gets out from behind the wheel. She hangs a satchel-sized purse over one shoulder. A man in a black sportcoat and saggy-ass dad jeans gets out from the passenger side. Danny takes one look at them as they walk toward the high school's front doors and thinks, *I'm caught.*

He leans the mop in the corner and goes to meet them. The only thing that surprises him about this arrival is his lack of surprise. It's as if he was expecting it.

He can hear faint rock music playing through the speakers in the gym. Jesse and Pat are down there, cleaning up the crap that always appears when the bleachers are rolled back and collapsed against the walls. The plan is to revarnish the hardwood next week, a job that always gives Danny a headache. Now he wonders if he'll even be here next week. Telling himself that's ridiculous, telling himself that he's done nothing wrong, doesn't help much. The catchphrase from some old sitcom comes to him: *You got some 'splainin to do.*

The woman opens the outside door and holds it for the man. Danny leaves the office and walks down the front hall. The newcomers are in the lobby, standing by the trophy case with the blue and gold WILDCAT PRIDE banner above it. The woman looks to be in her thirties, dark hair pulled back in a tight bun. She's got a pistol on the left side of her belt, the butt turned outward. On the right side is a badge. It's blue and yellow with the letters KBI in the middle. She's good-looking in a severe way, but it's the man who draws Danny's attention, although he can't initially say why. Later it will occur to him that you instinctively recognize a nemesis when one appears in your life. He'll try to dismiss the idea as bullshit, but he's clear on what went through his mind, even as he approached them: *Watch out for this guy*.

The male half of the team is older than the woman, but how much is a question. Danny is usually good at guessing ages within a few years one way or the other, but he can't get a handle on this guy. He could be forty-five. He could be pushing retirement. He could be sick, or just tired. A peninsula of coarse, wavy hair in which red and gray are equally mixed comes down almost to the top line on his forehead. It's combed back into what looks to Danny like a jumbo widow's peak. His skull gleams creamy unblemished white on either side of it. His eyes are dark and deepset with bags beneath. The black sportcoat is fading at the elbows, like it's been dry-cleaned dozens of times. He also has a KBI badge on his belt, but isn't carrying a gun. If he were, Danny thinks the weight of it might pull those dad jeans right down to his ankles, exposing a pair of billowy old-fella boxers. He has no belly in front, no hips on the sides, and if he turned around, Danny thinks those jeans would sag on a no-ass that is the particular property of so many skinny-built white men from the Midwest. All he's lacking is a Skoal pouch pushing out his lower lip.

The cop steps forward, holding out his hand. "Daniel Coughlin? I'm Inspector Franklin Jalbert, Kansas Bureau of Investigation. This is my partner, Inspector Ella Davis."

Jalbert's hand is hard and his grip is hot, almost as if he's running a fever. Danny gives it a token shake and lets go. The woman doesn't offer her hand, just gives him an assessing stare. It's as if she can already see him doing that sad dance known as the perp walk, but this doesn't bother Danny the way Jalbert's gaze does. There's something dusty about it, as if he's seen versions of Danny a thousand times before.

"Do you know why we're here?" Ella Davis asks.

Danny recognizes the sort of question—like asking a guy if he's still beating his wife—to which there's no right answer. "Why don't you tell me?"

Before either of them can reply, the door at the end of the old wing screeks open and booms shut. It's Jesse. "We finished sweeping where the bleachers were, Danny. You should have seen all the—" He sees the man in the fading black sportcoat and the woman in the blue pants and stops.

"Jesse, why don't you—"

The door screeks and booms again before Danny can finish. This time it's Pat, jeans low-riding, hat turned around backward, totally down widdit. He stands just behind Jesse, looking at Danny's company with his head cocked to one side. He sees the woman's gun, he clocks the badges, and a slight smile starts to form.

Danny tries again. "Why don't you two get an early start on the weekend? I'll punch you out at four."

"For reals?" Pat asks.

Jesse asks if he's sure. Pat gives him a *don't fuck this up* thump on the shoulder. He's still smiling, and not because the weekend's starting an hour early. He likes the idea that his boss might be in trouble with the po-po.

"I'm sure. If you left any of your stuff in the supply room, pick it up on your way out."

They leave. Jesse throws a quick look over his shoulder, and Danny is touched by the concern he sees in it. When the door booms shut, he turns back to Jalbert and Davis and repeats his question. "Why don't you tell me?"

Davis skirts that. "We just have a few questions for you, Mr. Coughlin. Why don't you take a little ride with us? The Manitou PD has kindly set aside their break room for us. We can be there in twenty."

Danny shakes his head. "I promised those young men I'd punch them out at four. Let's talk in the library."

Ella Davis shoots a quick look at Jalbert, who shrugs and gives a smile that momentarily exposes teeth that are white—*so no Skoal*, Danny thinks—but so small they're no more than pegs. *He grinds them*, Danny thinks. *That's what does that.*

"I think the library sounds just about fine," Jalbert says.

"It's this way."

Danny sets off down the hall, but not leading them; Jalbert is on his left side, Davis on his right. When they're seated at one of the library tables, Davis asks if Danny minds having their little talk recorded. Danny says he doesn't mind. She dips into her purse, brings out her phone, and sets it on the table in front of Danny.

"Just so you know," she says, "you don't *have* to talk to us. You have the right to remain silent. Anything you say—"

Jalbert flips two fingers up from the table and she stops at once. "I don't think we have to give Mr. Coughlin . . . say, can I call you Danny?"

Danny shrugs. "Either way."

"I don't think we have to give him the Miranda as of now. He's heard it before, haven't you, Danny?"

"I have." He wants to add *the charge was dismissed, Margie agreed, by then I'd quit drinking and hassling her.* But he thinks Jalbert already knows that. He thinks these two may have known who made that tip call for awhile. Long enough to dig into his past, long enough to know about Margie taking out a restraining order on him.

They are waiting for him to say more. When Danny doesn't, Davis rummages in her almost-a-satchel and brings out her electronic tablet. She shows him a photograph. It's of a Tracfone in a plastic bag, which has been tagged with the date it was discovered and the name of the officer—*G.S. Laing, KBI Forensics*—who found it.

"Did you buy this phone at a Dollar General store on the Byfield Road in the town of Thompson?" Davis asks.

There is no point in lying. This pair will have shown the Dollar General clerk his mug shot from when he was arrested for violating the restraining order. He sighs. "Yes. I guess I should have taken out that card thing from the back."

"Wouldn't have mattered," Jalbert says. He's not looking at Danny. He's looking out the window at Jesse and at Pat, who is laughing his ass off. He gives Jesse a whack on the shoulder and heads for his car.

"The officer who took your call had the phone's number on her screen, and the cell tower it pinged on."

"Ah. I didn't think it through, did I?"

"No, Danny, you really didn't." Davis gives him an earnest look, not smiling but letting him know she *could* smile, if he gives her more. "Almost like you wanted to be found out. Is that what you wanted?"

Danny considers the question and decides it's idiotic. "Nope. Just didn't think it through."

"But you admit you made the call, right? The one about the location of Yvonne Wicker? That was her name. The dead woman."

"Yes."

He's in for it now and knows it. He doesn't believe they can arrest him for the murder, the idea is absurd, the worst thing he ever did in his life was to stand outside his soon-to-be ex-wife's house and yell at her until she called Wichita PD. The first two times they just made him leave. The third time—this was after she'd taken out the restraining order—they arrested him and he spent a night in County.

They are waiting for him to go on. Danny crosses his arms and says nothing. He'll have to do some 'splainin, no doubt about it, but dreads it.

"So you were at the Texaco in Gunnel?" Jalbert asks.

"Yes."

"How many times?"

Twice, Danny thinks. *Once when I was asleep and once when I was awake.* "Once."

"Did you put a trash barrel over that poor girl's remains to protect it from animal depredation?" Jalbert's voice is low and gentle, inviting confidences.

Danny doesn't know the word *depredation*, but the context is clear. "Yes. There was a dog. Do you know what happened to it?"

"It was destroyed," Ella Davis says. "The responding officers couldn't discourage it, and they didn't want to wait for Animal Control from Belleville, so—"

Jalbert puts a hand on her arm, a *gentle* hand, and she stills at once, even coloring a little. *You don't give information to a suspect*, Danny thinks. *He knows that even if she doesn't.* And he thinks again, *watch out for this guy.*

Davis swipes her tablet, presumably to another photo. "Do you own a white 2010 Toyota Tundra pickup truck?"

"It's a 2011. I park around back by the school buses." Where they haven't seen it, but they know the make and model. And *he* knows what the picture will show even before she shows it to him. It's his truck, in the lot of the Dollar General where he bought the phone. The license plate is clear.

"Security camera?"

"Yes. I have others with you in them. Want to see?"

Danny shakes his head.

"Okay, but here's one that might interest you." This time it's a high-rez black-and-white photo of tire tracks on the cracked tarmac of the Texaco. "When we compare these to the tires on your truck, will they match?"

"I guess they will." He never thought he might've left tracks, but should have. Because beyond the tarvy, County Road F is dirt. It occurs to him that you can be damn careless about covering your tracks—literally—if you haven't committed a crime.

Davis nods. "Also, a farmer named Delroy Ferguson saw a white truck parked in front of that gas station. Same day you made that call from Thompson. He called the Highway Patrol, said he thought it might be someone scavenging. Or a dope meet."

Danny sighs. He could have sworn that farmer never took his eyes off the road as he hauled his trailer of barnboards north along the otherwise deserted county road. He thinks again, *I'm caught.*

"It was my truck, I was there, I bought the phone, I made the call. So why don't we cut through the bullshit? Ask me why I was there. I'll tell you." He thinks about adding *you won't believe it*, but wouldn't that be stating the obvious?

He thinks Davis is going to ask just that, but the man in the black coat cuts in. "Funny thing about that phone. It was wiped clean of fingerprints."

"Yes, I did that. Although from what you're telling me, you would have found it anyway."

"Yup, yup. On the other hand, you paid cash for it," Jalbert says, as if just passing the time. "That was smart. Without the security camera video, we might have taken quite awhile to find you. Might not have found you at all."

"I didn't think it through. I told you that." The library is cool, but he's starting to sweat. Color is rising in his cheeks. He feels like a fool. No good deed goes unpunished is exactly right.

Jalbert watches Pat Grady pull out, engine blatting and bad-valve oil shooting from the tailpipe. Then he trains his somehow dusty gaze on Danny. "You wanted to be caught, am I right?"

"No," Danny says, although in his heart he wonders. Jalbert's gaze is powerful. *I know what I know*, it says. *I've been doing this a long time, Sunny Jim, and I know what I know.* "I just didn't want to explain how I knew that woman was there. I didn't think anyone would believe me. If I had it to do over again, I would have written an anonymous letter."

He pauses, looking down at his hands and biting his lip. Then he looks up again and says the truth.

"No. I'd do it the same. Because of the dog. It got at her. It would have gotten at her some more. And maybe other dogs would have come, once it had the hand and arm out of the ground. They would have scented the . . ."

He stops. Jalbert helps him. "The body. Poor Miss Yvonne's body."

"I didn't want that to happen." He is still getting used to her name. Yvonne. Pretty name.

Ella Davis is looking at him like he has a disease, but Jalbert's somehow dusty eyes never change. He says, "So tell us. You knew it was there how?"

So then Danny tells them about the dream. About the sign defaced to read CUNT ROAD FUCK, the moon, the *tinka-tinka-tinka* of the price signs tapping on their pole. He tells them about how his legs carried him forward of their own accord. He tells them about the hand, the charm bracelet, the dog. He tells them everything, but he can't convey the *clarity* of the dream, how it felt like reality.

"I thought it would just fade away like most dreams do after you wake up. But it didn't. So finally I went out there because I wanted to see for myself that it was just some crazy movie in my own head. Only . . . she was there. The dog was there. So I made the call."

They are silent, looking at him. Considering him. Ella Davis doesn't say *Do you really expect us to swallow that?* She doesn't have to. Her face says it for her.

The silence spins out. Danny knows he's supposed to break it, supposed to try and convince them by giving more details. He's supposed to stumble over his words, start to babble. He keeps silent. It's an effort.

Jalbert smiles. It's startling, because it's a good one. Warm. Except for the eyes. They stay the same. Like a man uttering a great truth, he says, "You're a psychic! Like Miss Cleo!"

Davis rolls her eyes.

Danny shakes his head. "I'm not."

"Yes! Yes, you are! By God! Three! I bet you have helped the police in other investigations, like that Nancy Weber or Peter Hurkos. You might even know what people are thinking!" He taps one sunken temple, where a snarl of little blue veins pulse.

Danny smiles and points at Ella Davis. "I don't know Nancy Weber or Peter Hurkos from a hole in the ground, but I know what *she's* thinking. That I'm full of shit."

Davis smiles back without humor. "Got that right."

Danny turns to Jalbert. "I haven't ever helped the police. Before this, I mean."

"No?"

"I never had a dream like that before, either."

"No psychic flashes at all? Maybe telling a friend there's stuff on the cellar stairs so watch out or someone's going to take a header?"

"No."

"For gosh sakes don't leave the house on the 12th of May? Twelve?"

"No."

"The missing ring is on top of the bathroom medicine cabinet?"

"No."

"Just this one time!" Jalbert is trying to sound amazed. His eyes aren't amazed. They crawl back and forth across Danny's face. They almost have weight. "One!"

"Yes."

Jalbert shakes his head—more amazement—and looks to his partner. "What are we going to do with this guy?"

"How about arresting him for the murder of Yvonne Wicker, does that sound like a plan?"

107

"Oh, come on! I told you guys where the body was. If I killed her, why would I do that?"

"Publicity?" She almost spits the word. "How about that? Arsonists do it all the time. Set the fire, report the fire, fight the fire, get their pictures in the paper."

Jalbert suddenly leans forward and grasps Danny's hand. His touch is unpleasant—so dry and so hot. Danny tries to pull away, but Jalbert's grip is strong. "Do you swear?" he asks in a confidential whisper. "Do you swear, swear, *swear*—three times, one and two more—that you didn't kill Miss Yvonne Wicker?"

"Yes!" Danny yanks his hand back. He was embarrassed and scared to start with; now he's freaked out. It crosses his mind that Franklin Jalbert might be mental. It's probably an act, but what if it's not? "I dreamed where her body was, and that's all!"

"Tell you what," Ella Davis says, "I've heard some terrible alibis in my time, but this one takes the prize. It's way better than the dog ate my homework."

Jalbert, meanwhile, is shaking his head and looking sorrowful . . . but the eyes don't change. They keep crawling over Danny's face. Back and forth they go. "Ella, I think we need to clear this man."

"But he knew where the body was!"

They're working off a script, Danny thinks. *Damned if they're not.*

Jalbert continues to shake his head. "No . . . no . . . we need to clear him. We need to clear this one-time-only psychic janitor."

"I'm a *custodian*!" Danny says, and immediately feels foolish.

"I'm sorry, this one-time-only psychic custodian. We can do that because the man who raped Miss Yvonne didn't wear a prophylactic, and that left a goldmine of DNA. Would you mind giving us a swab, Danny? So we can eliminate you from our investigation? No strain, no pain, just a Q-tip inside your cheek. Does that sound all right?"

Danny doesn't realize how ramrod straight he's been sitting until he settles in his seat. "Yes! Do it!"

Davis immediately dips into her bag again. She's a good Girl Scout who comes prepared. She brings out a packet of swabs. Danny is looking at Jalbert, and what he sees—maybe—is the briefest flicker of disappointment. Danny's not positive, but he thinks Jalbert was bluffing, that the rapist-killer actually did wear a rubber.

"Open wide, Mr. Psychic Custodian," Davis says.

Danny opens wide and Davis swabs the inside of his cheek. She looks approvingly at the Q-tip before popping it into the container. "Cells tell," she says. "They always do."

"Carrier's here," Jalbert says.

Danny looks out the window and sees a flatbed pulling into the parking lot. Ella Davis is looking at Jalbert. He gives her a nod and she delves into her bag again. She comes out with two thin bundles of paper held together with paper clips. "Search warrants. One for your truck and one for your home at . . ." She consults one of them. "919 Oak Drive. Would you care to read them over?"

Danny shakes his head. What else should he have expected?

Jalbert says, "Go out and tell them his pickup's around back. Video them putting the truck on the flatbed so our custodian can't claim later that we planted anything."

She takes her phone and stands up but looks doubtful. Jalbert gives her a smile, showing those tiny pegs that serve him as teeth, and flaps a hand at the door. "We'll be fine, won't we, Danny?"

"If you say so."

"Keys?" she asks.

"Under the seat." He flicks the keyring hanging on his belt loop. "I've got enough keys for this place, I don't need to add more. Truck's not locked." And for once he has his phone with him.

She nods and goes out. When the door closes, Jalbert says, "That flatbed is going to take your pickup to Great Bend, where it will be gone over from bumper to tailpipe. Will we find anything belonging to Miss Yvonne?"

"Not unless you plant it."

"One of her hairs? One single blond hair?"

"Not unless—"

"Not unless we plant it, yes. Danny, we'll be taking a ride after all, but not to the Manitou PD. To your place. Just out of curiosity, are there any oaks in Oak Grove Trailer Park? Four or five? Maybe only three?"

"No."

"I didn't think so. There will be some cops and a forensic unit there. Is your housekey on the ring with the keys to your truck?"

"Yes, but the door is unlocked."

Jalbert raises eyebrows that are the same red mixed with gray as his jumbo widow's peak. "Aren't you the trusting soul?"

"I lock up at night. In the daytime . . ." Danny shrugs. "I've got nothing worth stealing."

"Travel light, do you? Not just psychic but an acolyte of Thoreau!"

Danny doesn't know who that is any more than he knows what Tinder is. He guesses Jalbert knows that. His eyes crawl and crawl. Danny realizes why he felt the man's gaze was dusty. His eyes have no shine, no sparkle, just a certain avidity. *He's like room tone*, he thinks. Odd idea, but it's right somehow. He wonders if Jalbert dreams.

"I've got a question for you, Danny, one I've already asked and you've answered, but this time I'll give you your rights first. You have the right to remain silent. If you choose to speak to me—you don't have to, but if you do—anything you say can be used against you in a court of law. You have a right to have an attorney present. If you can't afford an attorney, one will be provided for you." He pauses. The small white pegs make an appearance. "I'm sure that has a familiar ring."

"It does." What Danny's thinking is that when he and Jalbert arrive at his trailer, there will be cops there already. Those residents not at work will see and pass it on—*police were searching Danny Coughlin's trailer*. By dark the news will be all over Oak Grove.

"You understand your rights?"

"I do. But you're not recording. She took her phone."

"Doesn't matter. This is just between us." Jalbert stands and leans forward, his fingers tented on the library table, his eyes searching Danny's face. "So, one more time. Did you kill Yvonne Wicker?"

"No."

For the first time Jalbert's smile looks real. In a low, almost caressing voice, he says, "I think you did. I *know* you did. Sure you don't want to talk about it?"

Danny looks at his watch. "What I want is to clock out those two kids. And myself."

13

It's what Danny expected at Oak Grove. Two police cars and a white forensics van are parked in front of his trailer. Half a dozen of his neighbors are standing around watching. Ella Davis is there, along with four uniformed cops and two forensics guys who are wearing white pullover suits, gloves, and booties. Danny assumes she caught a ride to the trailer park with the flatbed hauling his truck, so the neighbors will have seen that, too. Nice. At least Becky's not here, which is a relief. On Mondays, Wednesdays, and Fridays she has a part-time job at Freddy's Washateria. Darla Jean colors or reads a book while Becky empties washers and driers and makes change and folds clothes.

But she'll find out, Danny thinks. *Someone will be eager to tell her. Probably that motormouth Cynthia Babson.*

Although his trailer is unlocked, they've waited for Jalbert. Davis walks over to the car. When Danny gets out of the front seat instead of the back, she frowns at Jalbert, who only shrugs.

She says, "Are we going to find any weapons in there, Mr. Coughlin?"

So no more Danny, and she's speaking loud enough for the lookie-loos to hear. Does she want them to understand Danny Coughlin is a suspect of something serious? Of course she does.

".38 semi-auto in the bedside table. Colt Commander." He wants to add he has a perfect right to a home defense weapon, he's never been convicted of a felony, but keeps his mouth shut. He can see Bill Dumfries standing by his trailer, beefy arms crossed over his chest, face neutral. Danny decides he wants to talk to Bill when he gets a chance.

"Loaded?"

"Yes."

"Are we going to find any drugs, syringes, or other drug parapher-nalia?"

"Just aspirin."

She nods to the forensics guys. They go inside, carrying their cases. A cop with a videocam follows behind. He's wearing booties and nitrile gloves, but no all-over suit.

"Can I go in?" Danny asks.

Davis shakes her head.

"Let him stand in the doorway and watch," Jalbert says. "No harm in that."

Davis gives Jalbert another frown, but Danny is pretty sure they have done this dance before. Not good-cop bad-cop, but aggressive-cop neutral-cop. Only he doubts if Jalbert is neutral. Davis either.

Danny goes up the steps. They're concrete block, even after three years he keeps thinking his Oak Grove trailer is temporary, but there are flowers on either side. He gave Becky money to buy the seeds. He and Darla Jean planted them.

He stands in the doorway and watches the forensics guys go through his private space, opening drawers and cupboards. They look in the fridge, his oven, the countertop microwave. It's infuriating. He keeps thinking, *This is what you get for trying to help, this is what you get.*

From behind him, soft, Jalbert says, "They'll give you receipts for what they take for testing."

Danny jumps a little. He never heard Jalbert coming. He's a quiet son of a bitch.

In the end, all they take are his gun and a butcher knife. One of the forensics guys bags them and the other forensics guy photographs them—video isn't enough, apparently. Danny has three steak knives, but they don't take those. He surmises that their serrated blades don't match the wounds they found on Yvonne Wicker's body.

Danny goes down the steps. Davis and Jalbert have their heads together. She's murmuring something to Jalbert, who listens without taking his eyes off Danny. Jalbert nods, murmurs something in return, and then they walk back to Danny. Curious eyes are watching them. Police visits aren't uncommon in the trailer park, but this is the first time Danny has been visited by them.

Ella Davis says in a casual tone, as if just passing the time of day: "Have you killed others, Danny? And it just got to be too much for you? Was it guilt instead of publicity? Was the Wicker girl the straw that broke the camel's back?"

Looking her dead in the eye, Danny says, "I haven't killed anybody."

Davis smiles. "You need to come on down to the Manitou cop shop tomorrow. We have more questions. How does ten o'clock sound?"

Just the way I wanted to spend my Saturday morning, Danny thinks. "What if I refuse?"

She makes her eyes round. "Well, that would be your choice. For now, anyway. But if you didn't do anything but report the body, I'd think you would want to get this cleared up."

"Done and dusted," Jalbert says, and brushes his hands together to demonstrate. "Ten o'clock, okay?"

"In case you didn't notice, your guys took my truck."

"We'll send a car for you," Jalbert says.

"Maybe I should rent one from Budget and send you guys the bill."

"Good luck getting someone to okay paying that," Jalbert says. "Bureaucracy." The pegs of his teeth wink, then disappear. "But you can try."

Davis says, "Stay close tonight. You can leave town but don't leave the county." She smiles. "We'll be watching."

"I have no doubt." Danny hesitates a moment, then says, "If this is how you guys act when someone does you a solid, I'd hate to see how you act when someone does you dirt."

"We *know*—"

Danny has had enough. "You know nothing, Inspector Davis. Now get out. Both of you."

She's unperturbed, just unzips the side pocket of her satchel purse and hands him a card. "This is my cell. It will get me day or night. Give me a call if you decide against a further interview tomorrow morning. But I don't advise it."

She and Jalbert get into the dark blue sedan. They drive toward the trailer park entrance, past the sign reading SLOW WE LOVE OUR CHILDREN.

Danny walks over to Bill Dumfries. "What in the hell was *that* about?" Bill asks.

"Long story short, I found the body of a murdered girl in a little town north of here. Gunnel. Tried to call it in anonymously. They found out. Now they think I did it."

"Jesus," Bill says, and shakes his head. "Cops!"

It sounds good, and maybe the doubt Danny thinks he sees in Bill's eyes is his imagination. Danny doesn't care. Bill retired from Dumfries

Contracting three years ago, and if anyone in Oak Grove knows of a lawyer in the area, it's Bill. He asks, Bill checks his phone, and Danny has a name and number even before the dark blue sedan turns onto the highway. He types the info into his contacts.

"I'm surprised they didn't take my phone, too," Danny says. "If I'd left it in the glove compartment of my truck like I usually do, they'd have it."

Bill says he's pretty sure they would have needed a separate warrant for that, then says: "They might ask you to turn it over tomorrow. If you've got something on it you don't want them to see, I'd trash it."

"I don't," Danny says, a little too loudly. People are still looking at him and his trailer door has been left open. He feels violated and tells himself that's stupid, but the feeling doesn't go away. Because it's not stupid.

"Billy!" It's Mrs. Dumfries, standing in the door of their trailer, a doublewide that's the fanciest one in the park. "Come in here, your dinner's getting cold!"

Bill doesn't look back, but he gives Danny a quick thumbs-up. Which is better than nothing, Danny supposes.

14

In the trailer with the door shut, Danny has a sudden fit of the shakes and has to sit down. It's the first one since his drinking days, when he used to get the shakes on mornings-after until he got his first cup of coffee into him. Also some aspirin. And of course he had them when he woke up in that Wichita jail cell, and there was no coffee or aspirin to banish them. That was when he decided he had to quit the booze or he was going to get into even more serious trouble. So he quit, and look at the mess he's in now. No good deed, et cetera.

He doesn't bother making coffee, but there's a sixpack of Pepsi in the fridge. He chugs one down, lets out a ringing belch, and the shakes start to subside. The lawyer's name is Edgar Ball and he's local. He doesn't expect to get Ball—it's past 5 PM on a Friday evening—but the recorded message gives him a number to call if it's urgent. Danny calls it.

"Hello?"

"Is this Edgar Ball? The lawyer?"

"It is, and I'm just about to take my wife out to dinner at Happy Jack's. Tell me why you're calling and make it brief."

"My name is Daniel Coughlin. I think the police believe I murdered a girl." He rethinks that. "I know they believe it. I didn't do it, I just told them where the body was. I'm supposed to go in for questioning tomorrow at the Manitou police station."

"Manitou PD wants to—"

"Not them, KBI. They're just going to use a room at the Manitou station to question me. They're giving me tonight to stew, but I think they might arrest me in the morning. I need a lawyer. I got your name from Bill Dumfries."

A woman calls something in the background. Ball says he'll be there in two shakes of a lamb's tail. Then, to Danny: "I'm a real estate lawyer, did Bill tell you that? I haven't handled a criminal case since the first year I hung out my shingle, and back then it was mostly DUIs and petty larceny."

"I don't know any other—"

"What time is your interview?"

"They want me at ten."

"At Manitou PD on Rampart Street."

"If you say so."

"I'll represent you at the interview, I can do that much."

"Thank y—"

"Then, if they don't just drop this, I'll recommend a lawyer who deals with criminal matters."

Danny starts to say thank you again, and maybe ask Ball if he could give him a ride to the police station, but Ball has hung up.

It isn't much, but it's something. He calls Becky.

"Hey, Beck," he says when she answers. "I've got a little problem here, and I wondered—"

"I know about your little problem," Becky says, "and it doesn't sound so little to me. I just got off the phone with Cynthia Babson."

Of course you did, Danny thinks.

"She says the cops think you killed that girl they found up north."

She stops there, waiting for him to say he didn't do it, that it's ridiculous, but he shouldn't have to do that. She's known him for three years, they have sex once a week, sometimes twice, he's picked her daughter up from school, and he shouldn't have to do that, end of story.

He says, "I'm supposed to talk to them tomorrow, these two investigators from KBI, and I wondered if I could borrow your car. They took my truck to Great Bend and I'm not sure when I'll get it back."

There's a long pause, then Becky says, "I was going to take DJ to the High Banks Hall of Fame tomorrow. You know she loves those funny cars."

Danny knows the place, although he's never been there. He also knows Darla Jean has never expressed the slightest interest in seeing a bunch of midget racing cars, at least not to him. If it was a doll museum, that would be different.

"All right. No problem."

"You didn't have anything to do with that girl, did you, Danny?"

He sighs. "No, Beck. I knew where she was, is all."

"How? How did you know that?"

"I had a dream."

She kindles. "Like Letitia in *Inside View*?"

"Yes. Just like her. I have to go, Becky."

"You take care of yourself, Danny."

"You too, Beck."

At least she believed me about the dream, he thinks. On the other hand, Becky seems to believe everything she reads in her favorite supermarket tabloid, including how the ghost of Queen Elizabeth is haunting Balmoral Castle and about the intelligent ant-people living deep in the Amazon rainforest.

15

Ella Davis takes her partner to his hotel in Lyons and parks under the canopy. Jalbert grabs his battered old briefcase—companion of twenty-plus years of investigations covering Kansas from side to side and top to bottom—and tells her he'll be at the Manitou PD by nine tomorrow. No need to pick him up, he'll drive his personal. They can go over their plan of attack one more time before Coughlin arrives at ten. Davis herself is going on to Great Bend, where she's staying with her sister. There's a big birthday party coming up. Ella's daughter is turning eight.

"Do we have enough to arrest him, Frank?"

"Let's see what forensics finds in his truck."

"No doubt in your mind that he did it?"

"None. Drive safe, Ella."

She heads out. Jalbert gives her a wave and then heads to his room, giving his Chevy Caprice a pat on the way by. Like his briefcase, the Caprice has been with him on many cases from Kansas City on one side of the state to Scott City on the other.

The two-room suite, far from fancy, is what's known as "Kansas plain." There's a smell of disinfectant and a fainter smell of mold. The toilet has a tendency to chuckle after flushing unless you flap the handle a few times. The air conditioner has a slight rattle. He's been in better places, but he's been in far worse. Jalbert drops his briefcase on the bed and runs the combination lock. He takes out a file with WICKER written on the tab. He makes sure the curtains are pulled tight. He puts the chain on the door and turns the thumb lock. Then he undresses down to the skin, folding each item of clothing on top of the briefcase as he goes. He sits in the chair by the door.

"One."

He moves to the chair by the tiny (almost useless) desk and sits down. "One plus two, add three: six."

He goes to the bed and sits beside his briefcase and folded clothes. "One, two, three, four, five, and six make twenty-one."

He goes into the bathroom and sits on the closed lid of the toilet. The plastic is cold on his skinny buttocks.

"One, two, three, four, five, six, seven, eight, nine, and ten make fifty-five."

He goes back to the first chair, skinny penis swinging like a pendulum, and sits down. "Now add eleven, twelve, thirteen, fourteen, and fifteen, makes a hundred and twenty."

He makes another full round, which satisfies him. Sometimes he has to go to ten or twenty rounds before his mind tells him it's enough. He allows himself a piss that he's been holding a long time, then washes his hands while he counts to seventeen. He doesn't know why seventeen is perfect for hand-washing, it just is. It works for teeth-brushing, too. Hair washing is a twenty-five count, has been since he was a teenager.

He pulls his suitcase from under the bed and puts on fresh clothes. Those he took off and folded go into the suitcase. The suitcase goes back under the bed. On his knees he says, "Lord, by Your will I serve the people of Kansas. Tomorrow if it's Your will, I'll arrest the man who killed poor Miss Yvonne."

He takes the folder to the chair by the useless desk and opens the file. He looks at the pictures of Miss Yvonne, leafing through them five times (one to five added together make fifteen). She is terrible to look at; terrible, terrible. These pictures would break the stoniest heart. What he keeps coming back to is the charm bracelet—some of the charms missing, from the look of it—and the dirt in her hair. Poor Miss Yvonne! Twenty years old, raped and murdered! The pain she must have felt! The fear! Jalbert's pastor claims that all earthly terrors and pains are wiped away in the joys of heaven. It's a beautiful idea, but Jalbert isn't so sure. Jalbert thinks that some traumas may transcend even death. A terrible thought, but it feels true to him.

He looks at the pathologist's report, which is a problem. It states that Miss Yvonne was in the oil-soaked ground at least ten days, plus or minus, before her body was exhumed by the Highway Patrol, and there is no way of telling when she was actually murdered. Coughlin could have buried her behind the deserted gas station immediately, or he could have held onto the body for awhile, possibly because he couldn't decide where to dispose of it, possibly for some psycho reason of his own. Without a more precise time of death, Coughlin really doesn't have to have an alibi; he's a moving target.

"On the other hand," Jalbert says, "he wants to be caught. That's why he came forward. He's like a girl saying no-no with her mouth and yes-yes with her eyes." Not that he could make such a comparison to anyone else—most of all Ella Davis. Not in this era of #BelievetheWoman.

I believe in Miss Yvonne, he thinks.

He's unhappy that they don't have more and thinks about doing the chairs again, but doesn't. He walks down to the Snack Shack for a cheeseburger and a shake instead. He counts his steps and adds them. Not as good as doing the chairs, but quite soothing. He sits in his Kansas plain suite, which he will forget as soon as he leaves it, as he has forgotten so many other temporary accommodations. He eats his burger. He drinks his shake until the straw crackles in the bottom. He thinks about Coughlin saying he dreamed Miss Yvonne's location. That's the part of him that wants to confess. He'll admit it and then he's done.

16

Danny is watching something on Netflix without really seeing it when his phone rings. He looks at the screen, sees it's Becky, and thinks she's had time to change her mind about loaning him her car. Only that's not it. She tells him they better cool it for awhile, keep their distance. Just until the cops clear him of the Wicker thing, as of course they will.

"But see, here's the thing, Danny. Andy's talking about going back to court and suing me . . . or whatever they call it . . . for custody of Darla Jean. And if his lawyer can say I've been spending time with someone under suspicion for . . . you know, that girl . . . he might be able to convince a judge."

"Really, Beck? Didn't you tell me he's six months behind on his child support payments? I don't think a judge would be very eager to turn DJ over to a deadbeat dad, do you?"

"I know, but . . . Danny, please try to understand . . . if he had Darla Jean, he wouldn't *have* to pay child support. In fact . . . I don't know exactly how these things work, but *I* might have to pay *him*."

"When was the last time he even took DJ for the weekend?"

She has an answer for that, too, more weak bullshit, and he doesn't know why he's pressing the issue. It's never been true love, just an arrangement between two single people who are living in a trailer park and edging into middle age. She doesn't want to be involved? Fine. But he'll miss Darla Jean, who helped him plant flowers to dress up his cement block steps a little. DJ is a sweetie, and—

An idea strikes him. It's unpleasant, it's plausible, it's unpleasantly plausible.

"Are you afraid I might do something to DJ, Becky? Molest her, or something? Is that what this is about?"

"No, of course not!"

But he hears it in her voice, or thinks he does, and it comes to the same.

"Take care of yourself, Beck."

"Danny—"

He ends the call, sits down, and looks at the TV, where some male doofus is telling some female doofus that it's complicated.

"Ain't it just?" Danny says, and zaps the show into oblivion. He sits and looks at the blank television screen and thinks, *I will not pity myself. I just screwed up reporting what I found, and I won't pity myself.*

Then he thinks of Jalbert's eyes, crawling over his face.

"Watch out for that one," he says. For the first time in two years he finds himself wishing for a beer.

17

Jalbert lies in his bed, ramrod straight, listening to a prairie wind blowing outside, thinking about the next day's interrogation. He doesn't want to think about it, he needs his sleep so he can be fresh in the morning. *Coughlin* is the one who should lie sleepless tonight, tossing and turning.

But sometimes you can't turn off the machine.

He swings his legs out of bed, grabs his phone, and calls George Gibson, who's been heading the KBI forensics unit for the last seven years. Gibson flew in from Wichita as soon as the judge signed off on the search warrants, and was ready to start work as soon as Coughlin's truck was delivered. Calling him is a mistake, Gibson will call *him* if he has something, but Jalbert can't help himself. Sometimes—like now, for instance—he knows how junkies feel.

"George, it's Frank. Have you got anything? Any sign at all that the girl was in his truck?"

"Nothing yet," Gibson says, "but we're still working."

"I'm going to leave my phone on. Call me if you get something definitive. It doesn't matter how late."

"I will. Now may I go back to work?"

"Yes. Sorry. It's just . . . we're working for the girl, George. For Miss Yvonne. We're her—"

"Advocates. Thanks for reminding me."

"Sorry. Sorry. Go back to work."

Jalbert ends the call and lies down. He begins counting and adding. One and two makes three, three more is six, four more is ten, five more is fifteen. By the time he gets to seventeen is a hundred and fifty-three, he has finally begun to relax. By the time he gets to twenty-eight is four hundred and six, he's drifting into sleep.

18

At two o'clock his phone wakes him. It's Gibson.

"Give me some good news, George."

"I would if I could." Gibson sounds beat. "The truck is clean. I'm going home while I can still keep my eyes open."

Jalbert is sitting bolt upright in bed. "*Nothing?* Are you kidding?"

"I never kid after midnight."

"Did you put it on the lift? Did you check the undercarriage?"

"Don't tell your granny how to suck eggs, Frank."

Gibson sounds on the verge of losing his temper. Jalbert should stop. He can't stop.

"He washed it, didn't he? Son of a bitch washed it and probably had it detailed."

"Not lately, he didn't. There's still plenty of dirt on it from his trip out to Gunnel. No traces of bleach in the cab or the truck bed, either."

Jalbert expected more. He expected something. He really did.

Gibson says, "Finding fingerprints, hair, an item of her clothing . . . that would've been ideal, the gold standard, but it doesn't mean he didn't have her. He either did an ace cleaning job inside or—"

"Or she was never in the truck at all." Jalbert is hatching a headache and getting back to sleep is probably going to be out of the question. "He could have used some other vehicle to transport her. He's got a girlfriend in that trailer park. Maybe he used her car. If he doesn't confess, we may have to—"

"There's a third possibility," Gibson says.

"What?" Jalbert snaps.

"He could be innocent."

Jalbert is amazed to silence for a few seconds. Then he laughs.

19

When Jalbert arrives at the Manitou police station the next morning—fresh pair of dad jeans, fresh shirt, same lucky black coat—he sees Ella Davis waiting for him on the front step, smoking a cigarette. When she sees him coming, she drops it and steps on the butt. She thinks of telling him he looks tired, rejects the idea, and instead asks him what he knows about Coughlin's truck.

"Clean," Jalbert says, and sets his briefcase down between his sensible black shoes. "Which means we've got a little more work to do."

"It could also mean Yvonne Wicker wasn't his first. Have you thought of that?"

Of course he has. Serials often botch their first one, but if they're not caught they learn from their mistakes. He could tell Davis there was no bleach residue in the truck, meaning Coughlin didn't use it to clean up blood, other fluid, or touch DNA, but the idea doesn't cross his mind because it doesn't matter. Coughlin did her. The dream story was either a half-assed effort to show off—like an arsonist showing up to help fight the fire he started, as Davis said—or because the guilt has gotten too much for him and he wants to confess. Jalbert thinks the latter, and will be happy to help him in that regard.

"Miss Yvonne stayed at a shelter in Arkansas City on the night of May 31st," Jalbert says. "Her signature is in their ledger. Next morning she buys coffee and a sausage biscuit at a Gas-n-Go near the intersection of I-35 and . . . help me."

"State Road 166," Davis says. "She's on the security video. Big as life. Clerk saw her picture in the *Oklahoman* and called it in. Gold star for him."

Jalbert nods. "June 1st, just past eight AM. Off she goes to hitch a ride on 35. And that's the last time anyone saw Miss Yvonne until Coughlin drives out to Gunnel and reports the body. We together so far?"

Davis nods.

"So when we question Coughlin, we have to ask him where he was and what he was doing between the 1st of June and the 24th, when he made that call."

"He'll say he doesn't remember. Which is reasonable. It's only on TV that people remember where they were. If you asked me where I was on June 5th . . . or the 10th . . . I couldn't tell you. Not for sure."

"He punches a clock at the high school where he works, that takes care of some of the time."

She starts to say something and he raises those two fingers to cut her off.

"I know what you're thinking, a time-clock doesn't know what you do after you punch in, but he's got those two boys working for him. We'll talk to them. See if he left them on their own for a few hours, or even a whole day."

Davis takes a notebook out of her big bag and begins to scribble in it. Without looking up she says, "School was still in the first week of June. I checked the calendar online. Plenty of people will have seen him, if he was there."

"We're going to talk to everyone," Jalbert says. "Just you and me, Ella. Find out as much as we can about where he was during those three weeks. Find out where the holes are. The inconsistencies. Are you up for that?"

"Yes."

"That's if he doesn't confess this morning, which I have a feeling he might do."

"Only one thing bothers me," Davis says. "How he looked when you told him the perp left semen. What I saw on his face—and his body, that too—was relief. Gladness, almost. He couldn't wait to give me a cheek swab."

Jalbert raises his hands, palms out, as if to physically push the idea away. "Why would he worry about DNA? He knew it was a bluff because he put on a prophylactic before he raped her."

She says nothing, but there's a look on her face that makes him frown. "What?"

"It was relief," she repeats. "Like he *didn't* know about the rubber. Like he thought a DNA compare might really let him off the hook."

Jalbert laughs. "Some of these bad boys are exceptional actors. Ted Bundy had a girlfriend. Dennis Rader fooled his own wife. For *years*."

"I suppose, but he wasn't very clever about the burner he used, was he?"

The frown reappears. "Come on, Ella, he wanted us to find him. Now are we going to get justice for Miss Yvonne this morning?"

She considers this. Jalbert has been an investigator with KBI for twenty years. She's been an inspector for five. She trusts his instincts. Plus the story of the dream is such obvious bullshit.

"We are."

He pats her on the shoulder. "That's it, partner. You hold that thought."

20

The last thing Danny wants is another cop car showing up at his trailer, so at nine-thirty he's standing at the entrance to Oak Grove, hands in his pockets, waiting for his ride. He's thinking about how badly he fucked up the anonymous call, succeeding in only making things look worse for himself. And he's thinking about Jalbert. The woman doesn't scare him. Jalbert does. Because Jalbert has made up his mind and all Danny has is a story about a dream that only a few people (such as *Inside View* readers like Becky) would believe.

Well, he does have one other thing going for him: he didn't kill the girl.

As it turns out, he could have waited at his trailer, because the cop who picks him up is driving an unmarked. He's wearing his uniform, but sitting behind the wheel with his hat on the seat and the top button of his shirt undone, he could be any John Q. Citizen.

He powers down the passenger window. "Are you Coughlin?"

"Yes. Can I sit up front with you?"

"Well, I don't know," the cop says. He's young, surely no more than twenty-five. This is Kansas, but he gives off a laid-back surfer-dude vibe. "Are you going to launch an attack on me?"

Danny smiles. "I don't launch attacks on anyone until at least mid-afternoon."

"Okay, you can sit up front just like a big boy, but do me a favor and keep your hands where I can see them."

Danny gets in. He clicks his seatbelt. The cop's dashboard computer is off but his police radio mutters constantly, too low to hear.

"So," the cop says. "Getting questioned by KBI in our little police station. What a thrill, right?"

"Not for me," Danny says.

"Did you kill that girl? The one they found in Gunnel? Just between us, you know."

"No."

"Well, what else *would* you say?" the cop asks, and laughs. Danny surprises himself by laughing with him. "How'd you know she was there if you didn't kill her?"

Danny sighs. It's out there now; as Elvis used to say, it's your baby, you have to rock it. "I saw it in a dream. Went out to see for myself, and she was there."

He expects the cop to say that's the most ridiculous story he's ever heard, but he doesn't. "Weird shit happens," he says. "You know Red Bluff, about sixty miles west of here?"

"Heard of it, never been there."

"An old lady went to the cops and said she'd had a vision of a little boy falling down an old well. This was six or eight years ago. And you know what? That kid was there. Still alive. Made national news.

Tell those KBIers to google it. Red Bluff, kid down the well. They'll find it. *But*."

"But what?"

"Stick to your story if you didn't do that girl in. Don't go changing it, or they'll hang you."

"You sound like you're no fan of the KBI."

The cop shrugs. "They're all right for the most part. Treat us like hicks, mostly, but ain't that what we are, when you get right down to it? Six-man force, little speed trap outside of town, that's us. Our OOD told those two they can have the break room to question you. We use it for interrogations when we have to, so it's got a camera and a mike."

He pulls up in front. The station door opens and Jalbert comes out. He stands on the top step in his black coat with the faded elbows, looking down.

"One other thing, Mr. Coughlin. We all know about Frank Jalbert. He don't quit. Highway Patrol worships him, think he's a fucking legend. And my guess is he don't believe in dreams."

"I know that much already," Danny says.

21

Danny mounts the steps. Jalbert holds out his hand. Danny hesitates but shakes it. The hand is as dry and feverish as it was yesterday.

"Thank you for coming, Danny. Let's go inside and straighten this thing out, what do you say? The officer in charge just put on a fresh pot of coffee."

"Not just yet."

Jalbert frowns.

"It's only five to ten," Danny says. "I'm expecting someone."

"Oh?"

"A lawyer."

Jalbert raises his eyebrows. "As a rule, folks who feel the need to lawyer up are guilty folks."

"Or smart folks."

To this Jalbert says nothing.

Edgar Ball shows up at ten on the dot. He's riding a ginormous Honda Gold Wing motorcycle. The motor is so quiet that Danny can hear an easy-listening oldie—REO Speedwagon's "Take It On the Run"—from the in-dash radio. Ball parks, kickstands his ride, and dismounts. Danny likes him immediately, partly for the huge bike, partly because he's middle-aged, dressed in a golf shirt that makes no secret of his man-boobs, and big old khaki shorts that flap down to his knees. Never did a real estate lawyer look less like a real estate lawyer.

"I take it you are Daniel Coughlin," he says, and sticks out a pudgy hand.

"I am," Danny says, shaking with him. "Thank you for coming."

Ball switches his attention to the man in the black coat. "I'm Eddie Ball, Counselor at Law. And you, sir, are—?"

"Inspector Franklin Jalbert, Kansas Bureau of Investigation." He's gazing across the mostly deserted Manitou Main Street, seeming not to see Ball's outstretched hand. "Let's go inside. We have questions for Danny."

"*You* go inside," Ball says, "and we'll join you shortly. I'd like to have a private word with my client."

Jalbert frowns. "We don't have all day. I'd like to get this done, and I'm sure Danny would, too."

"Of course, but this is a serious matter," Ball says, still pleasant. "If it takes all day, that's what it will take. I have a right to speak with my client before you question him. If you're with KBI, you know this. Be grateful, Inspector, that I'm willing to do it out here on the police station steps instead of taking him to my office on the backseat of my sled."

"Five minutes," Jalbert says. Then, to Danny: "You're making it worse for yourself, son."

"Oh, please," Ball says, pleasant as ever, "spare us the movie music."

Jalbert shows the pegs of his teeth in a momentary grin. *That's how he looks like inside all the time*, Danny thinks.

Once Jalbert's gone, Ball says, "He's quite the Tatar, isn't he?"

Danny doesn't know the word and wonders briefly if Ball called Jalbert a tater, as in Tater Tot. "Well, he's something. Truth is, he scares me. Mostly because I didn't kill that girl and he's sure I did."

Ball holds up his hand. "Whoa, no primary declarations. I called you my client, but you're not, at least as yet. My fee for this morning is four hundred dollars. I should charge only two, because I've forgotten most of what I once knew about criminal law, but it's Saturday morning and I'd really prefer to be on the golf course. Is the amount agreeable?"

"Fine, but I don't have my checkb—"

"Do you have a dollar?"

"Yes."

"Good enough for a retainer. Fork it over." And when Danny has done so: "Now you're my client. Tell me exactly what happened and why Inspector Jalbert has it in for you, as he clearly does. Add nothing extraneous and leave nothing out that's going to come back to haunt you later."

Danny tells him about the dream. He tells him about going to Gunnel and finding the Texaco station. He tells him about the dog. He tells him about the hand and the trash barrel. This is all crazy-time stuff, but the color doesn't rise in his cheeks until he tells Ball how stupid he was about the anonymous tip.

"The way I look at it, that's actually in your favor," Ball says. "You didn't know what you were doing. And wishing for anonymity, given how you came by your information, is completely understandable."

"I should have studied it a little more," Danny says. "I assumed, and you know what they say about—"

"Yes, yes, makes an ass out of *u* and *me*. An oldie but a goodie. Daniel, have you ever had a previous experience of a psychic nature?"

"No."

"Think carefully. It certainly wouldn't hurt if there were prior—"

"No. Just this."

Ball sighs and rocks back and forth. He's wearing motorcycle boots and knee-high compression socks with his XL shorts, which Danny finds amusing.

"All right," he says. "It is what it is, another oldie but goodie."

Ella Davis comes out. "Danny, if you don't want to make the two-hour ride to Great Bend and answer our questions there, let's get this show on the road."

Ball smiles at her. "You are?"

"Inspector Davis, KBI, and I'm losing my patience. So is Frank."

"Well, we certainly don't want *that*, do we?" Ball says. "And since your valuable time is also my client's valuable time, I'm sure Daniel will be happy to help you with your enquiries, so he can get back to his Saturday."

22

There's a rattling soft drink machine in the Manitou PD's break room. There's a counter with a coffee maker and a few pastries on it. The sign over the pastries says KICK A BUCK. On one wall is a plaque reading WE SERVE AND PROTECT. On another is a poster showing O.J. Simpson and Johnnie Cochran. The caption reads, IT DON'T MEAN SHIT IF THE GLOVE DOESN'T FIT. In the middle of the room there's a table with two chairs on either side and a microphone in the middle. Between the drink machine and the pastry counter, a camera on a tripod blinks its red eye.

Jalbert spreads his hands at two of the chairs. Danny and his new lawyer take them. Ella Davis sits across from them and takes out a notebook. Jalbert stands, for the time being at least. He gives the date, the time, and the names of those present. Then he gives Danny the Miranda warning again, asking if he understands his rights.

"I do," Danny says.

"Spoiler alert, Inspectors, I'm mostly a real estate lawyer," Ball says. "I do land, I work with a number of local banks, I coordinate buyers and sellers, I write contracts, I write the occasional will. I'm no Perry Mason or Saul Goodman. Just here to make sure you are respectful and open-minded."

"Who is Saul Goodman?" Jalbert asks. He sounds suspicious.

Ball sighs. "TV show. Fictional character. Forget it. Ask your questions."

Jalbert says, "Speaking of respect, I want to tell you who deserved some—Yvonne Wicker. What she got instead was raped, stabbed repeatedly, and murdered."

Ball frowns for the first time. "You are not prosecuting this case, sir. You are investigating it. Save the speeches and ask your questions so we can get out of here."

Jalbert shows his pegs again in what he may assume is a smile. "Just so you understand, Mr. Ball. Understand and remember. We're talking about the cold-blooded murder of a defenseless young woman."

"Understood." Ball doesn't look cowed—at least Danny doesn't think so—but the pleasant smile is gone.

Jalbert nods to his partner. Ella Davis says, "How are you this morning, Danny? Doing okay?"

Danny thinks, *So it's good cop and bad cop after all*.

"Other than everyone in Oak Grove thinking I'm in police trouble, I'm doing all right. You?"

"I'm fine."

"They'll know what kind of trouble this is soon enough, won't they?"

"Not from us," she says. "We don't talk about our cases until they're made."

But Becky will, Danny thinks. *And once she tells Cynthia Babson, it'll go viral.*

"We'd like to have a peek at your phone," Davis says. "Just a matter of routine. Would that be okay?" She's giving him direct eye contact and a smile. "Just a look at your locations could eliminate you from our enquiries. Save time for us and trouble for you."

"Bad idea," Ball says to Danny. "I think they need a special search warrant for your phone, or they would have taken it already."

Ignoring him, still wearing her best *trust me* smile, Davis says, "And you'd have to unlock it for us, of course. Apple is very touchy about the privacy issue."

Jalbert has retreated to the pastry counter, content to let the good cop carry the ball, at least for now. As he pours himself some coffee he says, "It would go a long way toward establishing trust, Danny."

Danny almost says *You trust me about as far as you could throw this table*, but keeps it to himself. He doesn't need Ball—likeable, but clearly out of his depth—to tell him the less he says, the better. Hostile comments won't help, no matter how much he'd like to make them.

He can tell the truth; that won't get him in trouble. Trying to *explain* the truth might.

Danny takes his phone out of his pocket and looks at it. 10:23 already. *How the time flies when you're having fun*, he thinks, and puts it away again. "I'm going to wait on that until we see how this goes."

"We don't actually need a warrant," Jalbert says. Now that he has his coffee, he's retreated to the poster of O.J. and his lawyer.

"Pretty sure that's bogus," Ball says, "but I could phone a colleague to make sure. Want me to do that, Inspectors?"

"I'm sure Danny will make the right call," Davis says. The flint-eyed woman who came to Wilder High with Jalbert is gone. This woman is younger and prettier, projecting an I'm-on-your-side vibe.

At least trying to, Danny thinks.

"There's no event data recorder on your truck," she says. "Do you know what that is?"

Danny nods. "Darn thing doesn't even have a backup camera. When you put it in reverse you actually have to turn around and look out the back window."

She nods. "So you'll have to help us with your travels over the last few weeks, can you do that?"

"There's not much. I did go to see my brother in Boulder the weekend after school let out. I flew."

"That would be the weekend of—?"

Jalbert is looking at his phone. "June 3rd and 4th?"

"That sounds right. He works at the Table Mesa King Soopers." He feels like saying more, he's very proud of Stevie, but he leaves it at that.

Earnest, wide-eyed, still smiling, Ella Davis says, "Let's try to be exact, Danny. This is important."

Don't you think I know that? he wants to say. *You're playing with my life here.*

"I went on Friday afternoon. Flew United. Came back on Sunday, my flight to Great Bend left late and I didn't get home until after midnight. So actually it was Monday morning by the time I was back in my own bed."

"Thank you, we'll check on that. Other trips?"

Danny thinks it over. "Drove up to Wichita to see my ex on a Sunday. That was before the dream."

Jalbert snorts.

Ball, looking at his own phone, says, "Could it have been the 11th of June?"

Danny thinks. "Must have been. Otherwise, I've just been here. Back and forth to school, trips to the store, picked up DJ at school a couple of times—"

"DJ?" Davis asks.

"Darla Jean. She's my friend Becky's daughter. Good kid." And he can't resist adding: "Thanks to you guys, I don't think I'll be seeing much of her for awhile."

Davis ignores this. "Just to be clear, you went to Wichita to visit your ex-wife, Marjorie Coughlin, on the 11th of June?"

"Eleven," Jalbert says, then says it again, as if to be sure of it.

"Margie, yeah. But she's gone back to her birth name. Gervais." *Said she got tired of cough-cough-Coughlin*, he doesn't add. Once you tell yourself not to spill your guts, it gets easier.

"Hey, you were arrested for stalking her, weren't you?" Davis says, as if just passing the time.

Ball stirs, but Danny puts a hand on his arm before he can say anything. "No. I was arrested for violating the restraining order she took out. And disturbing the peace. The charges were dropped. By her."

"Okay, good, and now you get along!" Davis says this warmly, as if it's an accomplishment on the level of peace between Russia and Ukraine.

Danny shrugs. "Better than the last year we were married. We had lunch that day and I fixed her turn signals. Fuse blew. So yes, we get along."

"Okay, this is good, this is good," Davis says, still warm and wide-eyed. "Now can you explain how Yvonne Wicker's fingerprints happened to be on the dashboard of your truck?"

Danny ponders the question and considers the fact that he's in an interrogation room instead of a jail cell. He gives Davis a smile and says, "Your nose is growing."

"You think you're very smart, don't you?" Jalbert says from in front of the poster.

Davis gives him a look. Jalbert shrugs and flicks his two fingers at her, meaning she should carry on. He says, apropos of nothing (at least that Danny can figure out), "One, three, six."

"What?"

"Nothing. Go on and tell your tale." Slight emphasis on *tale*.

Davis says, "You have a little bit of a temper problem, don't you, Danny?"

"I used to drink. I stopped."

"That isn't a very responsive answer." She says it reproachfully. "If we ask your ex—and we will—what will she say about your temper?"

"She'll say I had what you just called it, a temper problem. Past tense."

"Oh, all gone? Is that right?"

She waits. Danny says nothing.

"Did you ever knock her around?"

"No." Then forces himself to add, because it's the truth: "I grabbed her by the arm once. Left a bruise. That was just before she kicked me out."

"Never by the neck?" She smiles and leans forward, inviting confidence. "Tell the truth and shame the devil."

"No."

"And you never raped her?"

"Hey, come on," Ball says. "Respect, remember?"

"I have to ask," Davis says. "The Wicker girl was raped."

"I never raped my wife," Danny says. Not for the first time he's struck by a feeling of unreality and thinks, *I helped you guys. If not for me, that girl would still be a stray dog's snack bar.*

"When's the last time you went to Arkansas City?"

The change of direction feels like whiplash. "What? I've never been to Arkansas in my life."

"Arkansas City, *Kansas*. Near the Oklahoma border."

"Never been there."

"No? Well, we can't check the EDR in your truck, can we? Because they weren't installed in Toyota Tundras for another year. But we *could* check on your phone, isn't that right?"

Danny repeats, "Let's see how this goes."

"How about Hunnewell? That's also in Kan—"

Danny shakes his head. "I've heard of it but never been there."

"What about the Gas-n-Go where I-35 and SR 166 intersect? Ever been there?"

"I guess not to that particular one, but they're all pretty much the same, aren't they?"

"You *guess*? Come on, Danny. This is serious."

"If that Gas-n-Go is in Hunnewell, I've never been there."

She makes a note, then gives him a reproachful look. "If we could just check your phone—"

Danny's had enough of this. He takes it out of his pocket and slides it across the table. Jalbert steps forward and pounces on it, as if afraid Danny will change his mind.

"The passcode is 7813. And I'll have my IT guy check it when I get it back, just to make sure you haven't added anything." This is pure bluff. Danny doesn't have an IT guy.

"We don't roll that way," Davis says.

"Uh-huh, and you don't lie about fingerprints, either." He pauses. "Or DNA from semen."

For a moment Davis looks off her game. Then she leans forward again and gives him her *you can tell me anything* smile. "Let's talk about your dream, okay?"

Danny says nothing.

"Do you have these fantasies often?"

Ball says, "Come on, now. It wasn't a fantasy if the woman's body actually turned out to be there."

Another snort from Jalbert.

"Well, you have to admit it's awfully convenient," Davis says.

"Not for me," Danny says. "Look where I am, woman."

"Do you mind telling us about this . . . *dream* again, Danny?"

He tells them the dream. It's easy because it hasn't faded a bit, and although his trip out there was similar, there's no cross-contamination between the dream and the reality. The dream is its own thing, as real as the KICK A BUCK sign above the pastries. As real as Jalbert's peculiar wooly widow's peak and avid yet lusterless eyes.

134

When he's finished, Davis asks—for the official record, Danny assumes, since it's been asked before—if he's had previous psychic flashes. Danny says he has not.

Jalbert sits down next to his partner. He drops Danny's phone in the pocket of his black coat. "Would you be willing to take a polygraph?"

"I guess so. I'd have to go to Great Bend for that, wouldn't I? So it would have to be after I finish work. And I'd have to get my truck back, of course."

"Right now cleaning windows and sweeping floors is the least of your worries," Jalbert says.

"Are we done here?" Ball says. "I believe Mr. Coughlin has answered all your questions, and more politely than I would have done in his position. And he'll need his phone back ASAP."

"Just a few more," Davis says. "We can check on your trip to Colorado and your trip to Wichita, Danny, but that leaves a lot of time between the first and the twenty-third. Doesn't it?"

Danny says, "Look at the locations on my phone. When I'm not home, it's usually in the glove compartment of my truck. The two boys I work with at the high school can tell you I was there every day from seven-thirty to four. That's a good amount of the time you want to know about."

Edgar Ball isn't a criminal lawyer, but he's not stupid. To Jalbert he says, "Oh my. You don't know when she was killed, do you? Or even when she was grabbed."

Jalbert gives him a stony look. Color creeps into Ella's cheeks. She says, "That's not relevant to what we're discussing. We are trying to eliminate Danny as a suspect."

"No, you're not," Ball says. "You're trying to nail him, but you don't have a whole lot, do you? Not without a time of death."

Jalbert wanders back to the poster of O.J. and Johnnie Cochran. Davis asks for the names of the boys Danny works with.

"Pat Grady and Jesse Jackson. Like the political guy from the seventies."

Davis scribbles in her notebook. "Maybe your girlfriend can help us to nail down some of the times when—"

"She's my friend, not my girlfriend." *At least she was.* "And stay away from DJ. She's just a kid."

Jalbert chuckles. "You're in no position to give us orders."

"Danny, listen to me," Davis says.

He points at her. "You know what, I'm starting to hate the sound of my first name coming out of your mouth. We're not friends, *Ella.*"

This time it's Ball putting his hand on Danny's arm.

Davis carries on as if Danny has said nothing. She's looking at him earnestly, the smile gone. "You're carrying a weight. I can almost see it. That's why you're telling this story about a dream."

He says nothing.

"It's awfully far-out, you have to admit that. I mean, look at it from our point of view. I don't even think your lawyer believes it, not for a minute."

"Don't be so sure," Ball says. "More things in heaven and earth that are dreamed of in your philosophy. Shakespeare."

"Bullcrap," Jalbert says from the poster. "Me."

Danny just holds the woman's gaze. Jalbert is a lost cause. Davis might not be, in spite of her hard shell.

"You feel remorse, I know you do. Putting that barrel over Yvonne's hand and arm so the dog couldn't get at her anymore, that was remorse."

He says nothing, but if she really believes that, she might be a lost cause, too. It was compassion, not remorse. Compassion for a dead woman with a charm bracelet on her mutilated wrist. But Davis is on a roll, so let her roll.

"We can help you take that weight off. It will be easy once you start. And there's a bonus. If you make a clean breast of it, we may be able to help you. Kansas has the death penalty, and—"

"Hasn't been used in over forty years," Ball says. "Hickock and Smith, the ones Truman Capote wrote the book about, they were the last."

"They might use it for the Wicker girl," Davis persists. Danny thinks it's interesting that *young woman* has become *girl.* But of course that's what the prosecutor would call her: the girl. The defenseless girl. "But if you own up to what you did, the death penalty would almost certainly be off the table. Make it easier for us and for yourself. Tell us what really happened."

"I did," Danny says. "I had a dream. I went out to prove to myself a dream was all it was, but the girl was there. I called it in. You don't believe me. I understand that, but I'm telling the truth. Now let's cut the crap. Are you going to arrest me?"

Silence. Davis continues looking at him for a moment with that same warm earnestness. Then her face changes, becomes not cold but blank. Professional. She sits back and looks at Jalbert.

"Not at this time," Jalbert says. His dusty eyes say *But soon, Danny. Soon.*

Danny stands up. His legs are like the legs in his dream—as if he doesn't own them and they might carry him anywhere. Ball stands up with him. They go to the door together. Danny thinks he must be a little unsteady on his feet, or too pale, because Ball still has his hand on his arm. All Danny wants is to get out of this room, but he turns back and looks at Davis.

"The man who killed that woman is still out there," he says. "I'm talking to you, Inspector Davis, because it's no good talking to him. He's made his mind up. You talk a good game, but I'm not sure you've made up yours. Catch him, all right? Stop looking at me and look for the man who killed her. Before he does it again."

He might see something on her face. He might not.

Ball tugs his arm. "Come on, Danny. Let's go."

23

When they're gone, Jalbert turns off the camera and the recorder. "That was interesting."

She nods.

He peers into her face. "Any doubts?"

"No."

"Because a couple of times you looked like he might actually be convincing you."

"No doubts. He knew where she was because he put her there. That's the logic. The dream story is TV bullshit."

Jalbert takes Danny's phone from the pocket of his coat. He punches in the passcode, swipes through the various apps, then turns it off again. "We'll get this to forensics ASAP and they'll go through the whole schmear, not just his locations going back to June 1st. Emails, texts, photos, search history. Clone it, get it back to him tomorrow or Monday."

"Given the way he turned it over to us, I don't think we'll find much," Davis says. "I didn't expect that."

"He's a confident son-of-a-buck, but he may have forgotten something. Just one single text could be enough."

Davis remembers Jalbert saying that same thing, or close to it, about one single hair in the cab of Coughlin's truck being enough. But they found nothing. She says, "We'll just find the one trip out to Gunnel. You know that, right? His phone was back at his trailer when he killed her and when he buried her, both at the same time or separately. Count on it."

Jalbert says, "Four."

"Pardon me?"

"Nothing. Just thinking out loud. We'll get him, Ella. That confidence of his . . . the arrogance . . . will bring him down."

"How serious were you about the polygraph?"

Jalbert gives a humorless laugh. "He's either a sociopath or an outright psychopath. Did you feel that?"

She considers, then says, "Actually I'm not sure I did."

"I *am* sure. Seen his kind before. And nine times out of ten they can beat the poly. Which would make it pointless."

They leave the room and walk down the hall. The young cop who brought Coughlin in asks them how it went.

"Turning the screws," Davis says. Jalbert likes that and gives her a pat on the arm.

When they're outside, Davis digs her cigarettes out of her bag and offers them to Jalbert, who shakes his head but tells her to go ahead, the smoking lamp is lit. She flicks her Bic and takes a deep drag. "The lawyer was right. We don't have much, do we?"

Jalbert looks out over Main Street where not much is happening—par for the course in Manitou. "We will, Ella. Count on it. All else aside, he really does want to confess. You almost had him. He was wavering."

Davis doesn't think he was wavering at all, but doesn't say so. Jalbert has been doing this for a long time and she trusts his instincts over her own.

"Two things continue to bother me," she says.

"What?"

"How relieved he looked when you told him you had DNA from the doer and how he smiled when I told him we had her fingerprints on the dashboard of his truck. He knew I was lying."

Jalbert runs a hand through what remains of his red and gray hair. "He knew you were *bluffing*."

"But the DNA thing, it was just so . . ."

"So what?"

"So *immediate*. Like he thought he was off the hook."

He turns to her. "Think about the dream, Ella. Did you believe that for even a single second?"

She answers without hesitation. "No. He was lying. There was no dream."

He nods. "Keep that centered in your thoughts, and you'll be fine."

24

Jalbert has a five-room bachelor ranchette in Lawrence, almost within shouting distance of the home office in Kansas City, but he won't be going back there until Coughlin has been arrested, indicted, and bound over for trial. His boxy two-bedroom suite in Lyons is close to both Manitou and Great Bend. Well . . . in Kansas terms they're close. It's a big state, the thirteenth largest. Jalbert likes to keep track of such things.

He stands at the window on Saturday evening, watching dusk turn to dark and thinking about the interrogation of Coughlin that morning. Ella did a fine job, Jalbert couldn't have done better himself, but it was unsatisfying just the same. He didn't expect Coughlin to lawyer up; he expected him to confess.

Next time, he thinks. *Just have to keep grinding.*

He's good at grinding, but tonight he has nothing to grind on. Nothing to do. He doesn't watch TV and he's run the chairs twice. He got a couple of Hot Pockets at the convenience store across the street and zapped them in the microwave. Three minutes, 180 seconds, 1 to 18 added inclusively with 9 left over. Jalbert doesn't like leftover numbers, but sometimes you have to live with them. The Hot Pockets aren't particularly tasty, and Jalbert has an expense account, but he never even considers ordering from room service. What would be the point? Food is just body gasoline.

He's never been married, he has no friends (he likes Davis, but she is and always will be an associate), he has no pets. Once, as a child, he had a parakeet but it died. He has no vices unless masturbation counts, which he does once a week. The problem of Coughlin nags at him. He's like a fly that keeps avoiding the rolled-up newspaper.

Jalbert decides to go to bed. He'll be up at four, but that's all right. He likes the early hours, and he may wake with more clarity on the Coughlin problem. He undresses slowly, counting to 11 each time he takes off an item of clothing. Two shoes, two socks, pants, underpants, shirt, undershirt. That makes 88. Not a good number; it's one favored by neo-Fascists. He takes his suitcase out from under the bed, removes the gym shorts he sleeps in, and puts them on. That takes him up to 99. He sits in the desk chair to add one more, which takes him to a hundred. A good number, one you can depend on. He goes into the bathroom. There's no scale. He'll ask for one tomorrow. He brushes his teeth counting strokes down from 17. He urinates, washes his hands, and kneels at the foot of his bed. He asks God to help him get justice for poor Miss Yvonne. Then he lies in the dark with his hands clasped on his narrow chest, waiting for sleep.

We don't have much, Ella said, and she was right. They know he did it, but the truck was clean, the trailer was clean, and he showed up with a lawyer. Not a very good one, but a lawyer is a lawyer. The phone may give them something, but given the way Coughlin handed it over . . .

"Not at first," Jalbert says. "He took time to think about it, didn't he? Making sure it was safe."

Why the lawyer? Is it possible that Coughlin doesn't want to confess until he's had his fifteen minutes of fame as the psychic who dreamed where the body was buried? That he wants publicity?

"If that's what he wants, I'll see that he gets some," Jalbert says, and not long after that sleep takes him.

25

For Danny, the week of the 4th of July is the week from hell.

Pat Grady doesn't show up for work on Monday. Danny asks Jesse if Pat is sick.

"No clue," Jesse says. "I work with him here, otherwise we don't hang. Maybe he thought because the 4th is tomorrow, we had today off, too."

This doesn't surprise Danny. Jesse Jackson is a young man on his way to somewhere. Pat Grady is a young man on his way to nowhere. Except maybe to the Manitou bars, once he's old enough to drink. There are quite a few. Danny visited all of them back in the day.

Pat strolls in around ten, starts some story about having to help his dad, and Danny tells him he's fired.

Pat stares at him, shocked. "You can't do that!"

Danny says, "I just did."

Pat gives him an unbelieving look, cheeks flushing, the acne on his forehead flaring. Then he heads for the door. When he gets there, he whirls around and shouts, "Fuck you!"

"Back atcha," Danny says.

Pat slams out. Danny turns and sees Jesse down by the doors to the gym, rolling a mop bucket. He pauses long enough to give Danny a thumbs-up, which makes Danny grin. Pat leaves the parking lot with the motor of his poor old abused Mustang screaming. He lays forty feet of rubber. *That won't do your tires any good*, Danny thinks. But at least Pat Grady is one stone out of his shoe.

When he gets home that evening (Jesse gives him a ride), his truck is parked outside his trailer. There are smears of fingerprint powder all over the cab and a lingering smell like ether, probably from the stuff they use to look for bloodstains. The keys are in the cupholder and his phone is on the passenger seat.

On Tuesday—the Glorious Fourth—Danny sleeps in. While he's eating a late breakfast he remembers he took his keys but his phone is still in the truck. He gets it, mostly to see if he's gotten a text from Margie, something with fireworks, maybe. There's no Happy Fourth from her, and no emails, but he's got a voicemail from his lawyer, asking Danny to call. Danny has a good idea what that's about. He wishes Ball a happy holiday. Ball wishes him one right back.

"You're probably calling about your fee, but they didn't bring my truck back until yesterday." He's wryly aware that he sounds quite a lot like Pat. "I'll bring a check around to your office this afternoon."

"That's not why I called. You made the paper."

Danny frowns. "What are you talking about? The Belleville paper?"

"Not the *Telescope*. *Plains Truth*."

Danny pushes away his cereal bowl. "You mean that free handout? The one that's full of coupons? I never bother with it."

"The very one. Sarah, my assistant, called me about it so I picked one up with my morning doughnut. It's strictly advertiser-supported so they can give it away free. Those ads must pay pretty well, because you can pick one up at every market, convenience store, feed store, and gas station across four counties. The content—such as it is—features local sports, right-wing editorials, and two or three pages of reader letters, mostly of the rant and rave variety. As far as news goes, they don't care what they print. Which in the latest issue includes the dead woman's name."

"They printed it?"

"Yup, Yvonne Wicker of Oklahoma City. And listen to this: 'Police received an anonymous tip which led them to the unfortunate young woman's shallow grave behind an abandoned building in Gunnel, a small town near the Nebraska border. A reliable source tells *Plains Truth* that the tipster has been identified as Daniel M. Coughlin, currently employed as a janitor at Wilder High School. He is said to be aiding KBI detectives with their hunt for the killer.'"

Danny is astounded. "Can they do that? Release my name when I haven't been charged with anything?"

"It's not accepted newspaper practice, but *Plains Truth* ain't really a newspaper, just toilet reading. There's more. It goes on to say 'When asked how Mr. Coughlin knew the location of the body, our source was mum.' It doesn't tell readers to connect the dots, but it really doesn't have to, does it?"

"Jalbert," Danny says. The hand not holding his phone is curled into a fist.

"Let's say I agree, either him or Davis—"

"Not her, him."

"—but try proving it. Half a dozen cops in the Manitou station knew; they saw us come in. Plus the one who gave you a ride to the interrogation from your trailer park. Then there's the people *in* your trailer park. They could have made a pretty good guess why the cops were there."

Sure, and Becky knew. He even told her about the dream. But still . . .

"He doesn't have enough to arrest me, so he does this."

"Jumping to conclusions really won't help—"

"Come on, man. Did you see him? Hear him?"

Ball sighs. "Danny, you need a lawyer who can advise you better than I can. A criminal lawyer."

"I'll stick with you for the time being. Maybe this will blow over."

"It might, I suppose." Only four words, but they are enough to tell Danny that Ball thinks that is unlikely. Maybe even absurd.

26

On Wednesday of the week from hell, Danny finds out he's going to lose his job.

At noon he goes out to his truck, planning to grab his dinnerbucket and join Jesse at one of the picnic tables out back. He takes his phone out of the glove compartment, checks his emails, and immediately loses his appetite. He has three. One is from the Belleville *Telescope* and one is from *Plains Truth*, both asking for comment about his connection to the murder of Yvonne Wicker. The one from *Plains Truth* also asks him to confirm or deny "reports that you were led to Ms. Wicker's burial site in a dream."

He deletes both. The third is from the Wilder County Superintendent of Schools. It informs him that due to budget cuts, his position as head custodian at Wilder High School has been eliminated. He's instructed to finish the week, but come Monday he'll be out of a job.

"Due to the regrettable suddenness of this reorganization," the email continues, "your salary will continue to be paid through the month of July and the first week of August."

If he has questions, he should get in touch with the assistant superintendent and county schools comptroller, Susan Eggers. There's a phone number and also a Zoom link.

Danny reads this boilerplate fuck-you over several times to make sure he understands. Then he tosses the phone back into the glove compartment and cuts through the gym to the picnic table.

"Want some chili?" Jesse asks. "My ma always gives me too much. I heated it up in the mike."

"I'll pass. I've got liverwurst and cheese."

Jesse wrinkles his nose, as if at a bad smell.

"Also," Danny continues, "I seem to have been fired."

Jesse puts down his plastic spoon. "Say *what*?"

"You heard me. Friday is my last day."

"*Why?*" He pauses, then says: "Is it about the girl?"

"You know about that, huh?"

"Everybody knows about it."

Of course they do, Danny thinks. "Well, they're not saying that, but they couldn't, could they? Since I didn't do anything but report a body. They're saying budget cuts."

He expects more questions from Jesse about the body and how he found it, but Jesse may be the only person in Wilder or Republic County who isn't eager to know about his bad dream. Jesse has other concerns. *And God bless him for it*, Danny thinks.

"Oh, man! We're supposed to put a coat of varnish on the gym floor! I can't do that by myself, I don't know how!"

"It's not rocket science. We'll do it tomorrow. The important thing is once you start, you have to keep going. And wear a bandanna or a Covid mask. We'll open all the windows but it's still going to stink."

"They can't leave me here alone!" Jesse almost bleats this. "I don't have any *keys*! And I don't want em! Jeez, Danny, I'm *Black*! Something happens—cleaning supplies disappear or stuff from the canteen—who's gonna get blamed?"

"I hear you, and I'll find out what the plan is," Danny says. "I have a number to call. I'm going to take care of you if I can."

"Can they do it? Can't you, like, sue their asses?"

"I don't think so," Danny says. "Kansas is an at-will state. What that means is that my employer doesn't need to provide just cause for my termination."

"That's so unfair!"

Danny smiles. "For which of us?"

"Both of us, man! I mean *shit*!"

Danny says, "Could I still have some of that chili?"

27

He doesn't call Susan Eggers that afternoon, he Zooms her. He wants to look her in the face. But first he checks the Wilder County budget for last year and the current one. He finds what he expected.

Eggers is a middle-aged woman with a helmet of gray hair, round gold-rimmed glasses, and a narrow face. An accountant's face, Danny thinks. She's at her desk. Behind her is a framed, jumbo-sized version of the *Little House on the Prairie* book jacket, little girls in the back of a Conestoga wagon, both of them looking scared to death.

"Mr. Coughlin," she says.

"That's right. The man you just fired."

Eggers folds her hands and looks directly into her computer's camera lens. "Terminated, Mr. Coughlin. And although we didn't have to, we even gave you a valid reason—"

"Budget cuts. Yes. But the county's school budget isn't smaller this year, it's actually ten per cent larger. I checked to be sure."

She gives him a tight little smile that says *Oh ye of little knowledge.* "Inflation has outpaced our budget."

Danny says, "Why don't we cut through this, Ms. Eggers? You didn't terminate me, you fired me. And the reason wasn't budgetary. It was because of rumors about a crime I didn't commit and haven't been charged with. Tell the goddam truth."

Susan Eggers clearly isn't used to being talked to this way. Her cheeks flush and a vertical line grooves her previously smooth forehead. "Do you really want to go there? All right. I have been given some rather unpleasant information about you, Mr. Coughlin. Aside from your current situation, you were arrested for violating a restraining order after stalking your ex-wife. You were jailed in Wichita, I understand."

The jail part is true, but he was only in the cooler for a night and it was for being drunk and obstreperous. Saying this, however, won't help his case . . . not that he has a case to make.

"You've been talking to a man named Jalbert, haven't you? You or the superintendent? Inspector with KBI? Wears a black coat and baggy jeans?"

She doesn't answer, but she blinks. That's answer enough. "Mr. Coughlin, the school department has been more than generous with you, in my view. We are paying you through July for work—"

"And the first week of August, don't forget that."

"Yes, through July and the first week of August for work you won't be doing." She hesitates, clearly debating the wisdom of going forward, but he's stung her. If he wants the goddam truth, he can have it. "Let us say, for the sake of discussion, that your current . . . situation . . . has played a part. Your name is in print, in connection with a terrible crime. What would *you* do if it came to your attention that a high school custodian in your district, a man who is around teenage girls every school day, was an accused wife abuser and is now being questioned by the police about a rape and murder?"

He could tell her that Margie never accused him of abuse, she just wanted him to stop yelling on her lawn at two in the morning—*come on back, Margie, I'll change.* He could tell her that he has no idea who killed Yvonne Wicker. He could tell her that he's morally sure the freebie rag got his name from Inspector Jalbert, because Jalbert knew they'd have no qualms about publishing it. None of that is going to make a dime's worth of difference to this woman.

"Are we done, Mr. Coughlin? Because I have work to do."

"Not quite, because you don't seem to have thought about what's going to happen at WHS once I'm gone. The whatdoyoucallit, ramifications. Who's going to replace me? I have one summer hire, a kid named Jesse Jackson. He's a good kid and an excellent worker, but he can't do the job by himself. For one thing, he doesn't know how. For another, he's only seventeen. Too young to take on the responsibility. For a third, he'll be back in class full-time come September."

"He will be let go as well," Eggers says. "When you lock up on Friday, the keys should be returned to the school principal, Mr. Coates. He lives right there in Manitou, I believe."

"Does Jesse also get paid for July and the first week of August?" Danny knows the answer to this question, but he wants to hear her say it.

If he was hoping for embarrassment, he doesn't get it. What he gets is an indulgent smile. "I'm afraid not."

"He needs that money. He's helping out at home."

"I'm sure he'll find another job." Like they're just lying around in Wilder County. She picks up a paper on her desk, studies it, puts it down. "I believe you had another boy, Patrick Grady. His parents have lodged a complaint. They called Mr. Coates and told him the boy quit because you threatened him."

For a moment Danny is so amazed and infuriated he can't even speak. Then he says, "Pat Grady was fired for chronic tardiness and sloppy work. He wasn't threatened, he's just a common garden-variety slacker. Jesse would tell you the same thing, if you were to ask him. Which I doubt you'll do."

"There's hardly any need for that. It's just one more part of a picture that's less than handsome. A picture of your character, Mr. Coughlin. Be happy that we're letting you go for budgetary reasons. It will look better on your resume when you seek further employment. And now, as I'm rather busy—"

"The school is just going to stand empty for the rest of the summer?" All else aside, Danny hates to think of that. WHS is a good old lady, and there's so much wear and tear in the course of a school year. It's July and he's barely gotten started. "And what about in the fall?"

"Not your concern," Eggers says. "Thank you for calling, Mr. Coughlin. I hope your current problems work out. Goodbye."

"Wait just a damn—"

But there's no point, because Susan Eggers is gone.

28

Early on Thursday evening of the week from hell, Danny is in the Manitou IGA, doing his weekly shopping. He likes to do this chore on Thursdays because for most working people the eagle screams on Friday and the market isn't very busy. His own paycheck—one of his last five or six—will go into Citizens National via direct deposit the following day. He also has a little over three thousand put aside, combined savings and checking, which won't stretch very far. He doesn't pay hellimony to his ex, but he sends her fifty or sixty bucks every week or two. He owes her that just for the trouble he's caused her. He won't be able to do it much longer and he dreads the call to her he'll have to make, explaining his situation. Although she probably knows already. Good news goes Pony Express, bad news takes a jet. And he no longer has to support Stevie. Danny's younger brother is still living in the group home in Melody Heights, but he's probably bringing home more than Danny's weekly wage.

Maybe he'll end up supporting me, Danny thinks. *That would be a hoot.*

He's at the meat counter, trying to decide between a one- or two-pound package of ground chuck (it's the cheapest) when a loud voice behind him says, "Daniel Coughlin? Need to ask you a few questions."

It's Jalbert. Of course it is. This evening he's exchanged his baggy black coat for a blue windbreaker with KBI on the left breast. Although Danny can't see the back of the windbreaker, he knows the same letters will be there, only bigger. Jalbert could have come up beside him and spoken in a normal tone, but he also could have chosen the parking lot. Other browsers along the meat counter are looking around, which is what Jalbert wants.

"I've already answered your questions." Danny drops a package of meat into his cart—one pound instead of two, it's time to start economizing. "If you want to ask more, I'll want my lawyer present."

"You have that right," Jalbert says in that same loud voice. Danny thinks the man's reddish wooly hair looks almost like an arrowhead, or the business end of a rusty spear. The deepset eyes stare at Danny the way they might stare at a new species of bug. "The right to an attorney. You'll have to wait at the police station until he gets there, though."

Same overloud voice. People have begun to congregate at the head and foot of the meat aisle, some pushing their carts, some just gawking. "Or we can do it here. Your choice."

With everyone listening, Danny thinks. *You'd like that, wouldn't you?*

"Split the difference. Let's step outside."

Danny doesn't give Jalbert a chance to object, just walks past him (restraining the urge to bump his shoulder on the way by) and heads for the door. It isn't as if the inspector can restrain him; Danny outweighs him by fifty or sixty pounds, and Jalbert once again isn't wearing a gun, just his badge clipped to his belt. Also his ID on a lanyard hung around his neck. Danny doesn't look to see if Jalbert is following him.

The checkout women have stopped working their registers. Two of them he knows from the high school. He knows a lot of people from the high school, because he's worked at WHS since leaving Wichita. As the OUT doors slide apart to let him emerge into the warm Kansas night, it occurs to him that nobody he passed in the aisles said hello to him, although he recognized several of them, including a couple of teachers.

Past the white light falling on the sidewalk from the front windows of the market, he turns to face Jalbert. "You're hounding me."

"I am pursuing my case. If anyone got hounded, it was poor Miss Yvonne. You hounded her to death. Didn't you?"

Recalling some TV show, Danny responds, "Asked and answered."

"We've been through your phone. There are a great many gaps in the location log. I'll need you to explain each one. If you can."

"No."

Jalbert's brows—as wooly and tangled as his receding flow of hair—fly up. An odd thought comes to Danny: *He may be hounding me, but maybe I'm returning the favor. Those circles under his eyes are deeper and darker, I think.*

"No? *No?* Don't you want to be eliminated as a suspect, Danny?"

"You don't want that. It's the last thing you want." He points at the bright yellow KBI on the breast of Jalbert's windbreaker. "You might as well be wearing a billboard. Hey, have you lost weight?"

Jalbert does his best not to look surprised at this unexpected question, but Danny thinks he is. Wishful thinking? Maybe.

"I need you to fill in those blank spots, Danny. As many as possi—"

"No."

"Then you'll be seeing a lot of me. You know that, don't you?"

"How about a polygraph? I've got my truck back, and I'll be able to go just about any day next week, since you saw to it I lost my job."

Jalbert shows the pegs that pass for his teeth. *He must eat a lot of soft food*, Danny thinks. "It's interesting how people such as yourself— sociopaths—are able to blame all their misfortunes on others."

"The polygraph, Inspector. What about the polygraph?"

Jalbert waves one hand in front of his face, as if shooing away a troublesome fly. "Sociopaths almost always beat the poly. It's a proven fact."

"Or it could be you're afraid it would show I'm telling the truth."

"Twenty-one," Jalbert says.

"What?"

"Nothing."

"Are you all right?" It gives Danny great pleasure to ask this question. That's low, and it's mean, but he's just been embarrassed in front of his town. What used to be his town, anyway.

Jalbert says, "You killed her."

"I did not."

"Come on. Own up to it. Take the weight, Danny. You'll feel better. It's just you and me here. I'm not wearing a wire, and you can deny it later. Do it for me, and do it for yourself. Get it off your chest."

"There's nothing to confess. I had a dream. I went to where she was buried. I told the police. That's all there is."

Jalbert laughs. "You're persistent, Danny. I'll give you that. But I am, too."

"Here's an idea. If you think I did it, charge me. Arrest me."

Jalbert says nothing.

"You can't, can you? I bet you've talked to the county attorney up in Wilder City and he's told you that you don't have enough. No forensic evidence, no video evidence, no witnesses. You've got an old man who saw me at that Texaco, but it was the same day I reported the body, so he can't help you. Basically, Inspector, you're fucked."

Which is funny, Danny reflects, because he is also fucked. Jalbert has seen to that.

Jalbert grins and points a finger at Danny. The grin reminds him of the quarter moon in his dream. "You did it. I know it, you know it, twenty-eight."

Danny says, "I'm going in and finishing my shopping. You can follow me if you want. I can't stop you and the damage is done. It was done when you leaked my name to that rag."

Jalbert doesn't deny it, and he doesn't follow Danny back into the IGA. His job is finished. Everyone looks at Danny as he shops. Some actually swerve their carts out of the way when they see him coming.

29

He goes home to his trailer in Oak Grove. He puts away his groceries. He allowed himself a box of Nabisco Pinwheels—his favorite cookie—and intended to eat a couple while watching TV. Now he doesn't want to watch TV, and he certainly doesn't want any cookies. If he tried to eat one, he thinks he'd choke on it. He's never felt so angry since being bullied by a bigger boy in middle school, and he's certainly never felt so . . . so . . .

"So cornered," he murmurs.

Will he sleep tonight? Not unless he can calm down. And he wants to calm down, wants to get hold of himself. Jalbert looks like he hasn't been sleeping and he'd like Danny to join him in that. *Get a little ragged, Danny, do something stupid. Like to take a swing at me? Think how good it would make you feel! Try it!*

Is there something he can do to take some of the pressure off? There might be.

He gets out his wallet and thumbs through it. Each of the investigators has given him a card with their KBI numbers and extensions on the front and their cell numbers on the back. Just in case he gets tired of his unbelievable dream story and decides to tell them what really happened. He puts Jalbert's card back in his wallet and calls Davis's cell. She answers on the first ring, her hello almost drowned out by what's going on near her, or possibly around her. It's an off-key rendition of "Happy Birthday" sung by young voices.

"Hello, Inspector Davis. It's Danny Coughlin."

There's a moment of silence from her end, as if she doesn't know how to respond to this 7 PM call from her prime suspect. He thinks he has blindsided her as he was blindsided by Jalbert, which seems fair . . . at least in his current red-assed mood. The pause is long enough for Danny to hear *happy birthday dear Laurie, happy birthday to you*, and then Davis is back. "Give me a second." Then, to the partygoers (Danny assumes it's a party), "I have to take this."

The singing fades as she carries her unexpected call to somewhere quieter. It's time enough for him to consider verbs. *Talked?* No. *Interviewed?* No, that's totally wrong. *Questioned?* Right . . . but also wrong. Then he has it.

"How can I help you, Danny?"

"Half an hour ago your partner ambushed me in the supermarket while I was doing my shopping."

Another pause. Then, "We still have questions about your locations during those three weeks we're concerned with. I did speak to your brother and confirmed you were there on the first weekend in June. Is he on the spectrum?"

Danny wants to ask if she upset Stevie—he's easily upset when he's out of his comfort zone—but he's not going to let her swerve him away from what he wants to tell her.

"Instead of that black sport jacket of his he was wearing a windbreaker with KBI on the front and back. He didn't have a bullhorn and didn't need one, he was plenty loud. Not too many people shop on Thursday evening, but everyone who was there had a good listen. And a good look."

"Danny, you sound a bit paranoid."

"Nothing paranoid about thirty people watching while you get rousted. I got him to follow me outside when I realized what he was up to. And you know what? There were no questions. Once we were on the sidewalk it was the same refrain—confess, you did it, you'll feel better."

"You will," she says earnestly. "You really will."

"I called to ask *you* a couple of questions."

"It's not my job to answer your questions, Danny. It's your job to answer mine."

"But see, these aren't about the case. At least not directly. They're more of what I'd call a procedural nature. The first is this. Would *you* have come up to me in the IGA wearing your cop windbreaker and making sure everyone heard what you were asking?"

She doesn't reply.

"Come on, it's a simple question. Would you have embarrassed me in front of my neighbors?"

This time her reply is immediate, low, and furious. "You did a lot more than embarrass Yvonne Wicker. You *raped* her. You *killed* her!"

"What the hell happened to innocent until proven guilty, Inspector Davis? I only found her. But we've already been around that mulberry bush and it has nothing to do with what I'm asking. Would you have done it the way Jalbert did, especially when he had absolutely nothing new to question me about?"

Danny can hear party people, very faint. The pause is quite long before she says, "Each investigator has his own techniques."

"That's your answer?"

She gives a short, exasperated laugh. "I'm not on the stand. You don't get to cross-examine me. Since you have nothing substantive, I'm going to end this c—"

"Does the name Peter Andersson mean anything to you? That's Andersson with two esses."

"Why would it?"

"He's a writer for a freebie newspaper called *Plains Truth*. They printed Ms. Wicker's name. Is *that* usual procedure? Giving out the names of murder victims when their next of kin hasn't been notified?"

"I . . . they *were* notified!" At last Ella Davis sounds flustered. "Last week!"

"But the *Telescope* didn't have it. Or if they did, they didn't print it. *Plains Truth* did. And what about my name? They printed that, too. Is giving out the names of people who haven't been charged with a crime part of KBI procedure?"

More silence. Danny hears a faint pop. He thinks it might have been a birthday balloon.

"Your name was printed? You're actually claiming that?"

"Pick up a copy and see for yourself. We know who leaked it, don't we? And we know why. He has nothing concrete, only a story he refuses to believe. Can't believe. Doesn't have enough imagination to believe. The same is true of you, but at least you didn't give my name to the only rag that would have run it. That's why I called you."

"Danny, I—" She stops there before she can maybe say *apologize*. Danny doesn't know that was the word on the tip of her tongue, but he's pretty sure.

She rewinds. "Your name could have been leaked to that paper by any number of people. Very likely by one of your neighbors at the trailer park. Your idea that Frank Jalbert is persecuting you is absurd."

"Is it?"

"Yes."

"Let me tell you what I know about *Plains Truth*," Danny says. "I picked one up on my way home from work. It's my second to last day. I've been let go. I have that to thank you for, too."

She makes no reply.

"It's mostly ads with a few local news stories thrown in . . . plus the crime stories, they love those. Anything from cow tipping to arson. It gets people to pick the damn thing up."

"Danny, I really think this conversation has gone on long enough."

He plows ahead. "There are no crusading reporters on the *Plains Truth* staff. They don't do investigations. Andersson and a couple of others sit on their asses and let the news come to them. In this case, Wicker's name and mine. Somebody picked up the phone and gave it to them."

"If you're going to ask me to find out who did that, you're dreaming. Reporters protect their sources."

Danny laughs. "Calling the guys who work for that rag *reporters* is like calling a remedial math kid Einstein. I think Peter Andersson will give you a name, if he got one. Just push him a little. The way you pushed me."

Silence, but she hasn't ended the call. He can still hear the party, very faint. Is Laurie her daughter? A niece?

"A name, not *the* name," Danny says. "If Andersson even asked for one, Jalbert would have said he's with the Manitou PD or the Highway Patrol and hung up. A reputable paper wouldn't have published an anonymous tip without another source, but they did, and happy to do it. It was him, Inspector. I know it and I think you know it, too."

"Goodbye, Danny. Don't call me again. Unless you'd like to confess, that is."

Shot in the dark time. "Has he been spouting random numbers? Not having to do with anything, just off the cuff?"

Nothing.

"Don't want to talk about that? Okay. Wish the birthday girl—" he begins, but she's gone.

He immediately calls Stevie in Boulder. His brother answers as he always does, sounding like a recorded voicemail message. "You have reached Steven Albert Coughlin."

"Hi, Stevie, it's—"

"I know, I know," Stevie says, laughing. "Danny-Danny-bo-banny, banana-fanna-fo-fanny. How you doin, brother-man?"

That says everything Danny called to find out. Ella Davis didn't tell Stevie that his big brother was under suspicion of murder. She was . . . careful? Maybe more. Maybe the word he's looking for is *diplomatic*. Danny doesn't want to like her, but he does a little bit, for that. Stevie has his special ability, and he's developed—slowly—some social skills, but he's emotionally fragile.

"I'm in good shape, Stevie. Did my friend Ella Davis call you?"

"Yes, the lady. She said she was a police inspector and you were helping them with a case. Are you helping them with a case, Danny-bo-banny?"

"Trying," he says, then guides the conversation away. They talk about Nederland, where Stevie goes hiking on the weekends. They talk about a dance Stevie went to with his friend Janet and how they kissed three times after it was over, while they were walking home. Someone is playing music loud and Stevie shouts at them to turn it down, which he never could have done as a teenager; back then he would have simply struck himself in the side of the head until someone made him stop.

Danny says he has to go. His anger is mostly gone. Talking to Stevie does that. Stevie says okay, then says the usual: "Ask me one!"

Danny is ready. "Folgers Special Roast."

Stevie laughs. It's a beautiful, joyful sound. When he's happy, he's really happy. "Aisle 5, top shelf on the right as you go toward the meat counter, price twelve dollars and nine cents. It's actually Classic Roast." He lowers his voice confidentially. "Folgers Special Roast has been discontinued."

"Good one, Stevie. I have to go."

"Okay, Danny-bo-banny. I love you."

"I love you, too."

He's glad it was Davis who talked to Stevie. The thought of Jalbert doing it—of coming anywhere near his brother—makes Danny feel cold to the bone.

30

Ella Davis puts her phone in the pocket of her slacks and goes back to the party. Her sister is doling out cake and ice cream to half a dozen little girls wearing party hats. Davis's daughter, birthday girl and star of tonight's show, keeps casting greedy eyes at the pile of presents on the sideboard. Laurie is eight today. The gifts will be opened soon and soon forgotten—except maybe for Adora, a doll that cost Davis forty hard-earned bucks. The little girls, fueled by sugar and primed to party hearty, will play games in the living room and their shrieks will fill her sister's house. By eight o'clock they'll be ready to fall asleep while the umpteenth showing of *Frozen* plays on the TV.

"Who was that?" her sister asks. "Was it your case?"

"Yes." One dish of ice cream has already been spilled. Mitzi, Regina's beagle, gets on that right away.

"It wasn't *him*, was it?" Regina asks, whispering. "Coughlin?" Then: "Use your fork, Olivia!"

"No," Davis lies.

"When are you going to arrest him?"

"I don't kn—"

"*Arrest WHO?*" a little girl bugles. Her name is Mary or Megan, Ella can't remember which. *"Arrest WHO?"*

"Nobody," Regina says. "Mind your beeswax, Marin."

"I don't know, Reg. That's above my pay grade."

When the cake and ice cream have been served and the girls are eating, Davis excuses herself and goes out on the back porch for a cigarette. She's troubled by the idea that Frank approached Coughlin in the market, deliberately marking him out, saying to the witnesses to the confrontation *this is him, this is the guy who did it, get a good look.*

She's more troubled by the idea that Jalbert may have given Coughlin's name to the only publication that would run it. She doesn't want to believe he'd do that, and mostly she doesn't, but there can be no doubt that Frank has homed in on Coughlin. He's fixated.

Wrong word, she tells herself. *The right one is* dedicated.

She's most troubled by Coughlin himself. He *did* seem relieved when Frank said they had DNA, and was happy to give a sample for comparison. He *did* know Davis was lying about the girl's fingerprints on the dashboard of his truck. But that could have been because he wiped them. It could also have been because Wicker—poor Miss Yvonne to Jalbert—was never in the cab at all; he could have wrapped her dead body in a tarpaulin and put it in back. If he got rid of the tarp, it would also explain why they found no hair, prints, or DNA in the truck bed. But why wouldn't he have buried her *in* the tarpaulin?

Or it could have been because Yvonne Wicker was never in the truck at all.

No. I don't accept that.

Coughlin also offered to take a polygraph, almost begged to take one. Frank had shot that one down, and for good reasons, but—

Her sister comes out. "Laurie's opening her presents," she says, with the faintest etch of acid. "Do you care to join?"

What the hell happened to innocent until proven guilty, Inspector Davis?

"Yes," Ella says, putting out her cigarette. "Absolutely."

Reggie takes her by the shoulders. "You look troubled, hon. *Was* it him?"

Davis sighs. "Yes."

"Proclaiming his innocence?"

"Yes."

"You'll feel better once he's locked up, won't you?"

"Yes."

Later, with the girls in their jammies and clustered on the living room floor, entranced as always when Elsa and Anna sing "For the First Time in Forever," Ella asks Reggie if she's ever had a psychic experience. Like a dream that came true.

"Not me, but my friend Ida dreamed Horst was going to have a heart attack, and two weeks later he *did*."

"Really?"

"Yes!"

"So you believe such things are possible."

Reggie considers this. "Well, I don't think Ida is a liar, but I'd believe it more if she'd told me about that dream *before* Horst had his heart attack. And it's not like he wasn't asking for one, fat as he is. Look at your kiddo, Els! She loves that doll!"

Laurie is cradling auburn-haired Adora to her chest and Davis suddenly has her own vision: Danny Coughlin stabbing Yvonne Wicker again and again, then climbing on top of her in a cornfield and raping her even as she bled to death. They know it was a cornfield because there was cornsilk in her hair.

If he did that, he deserves everything Frank throws at him, she thinks. Then, standing in the doorway next to her sister, she realizes it's the first time that deadly (and disloyal, that too) two-letter word has entered her thinking.

There's something else, too, and she's willing to admit—to herself, only to herself—that it was what really shook her. *Has he been spouting random numbers? Not having to do with anything, just off the cuff?* She's heard Frank do that several times, more since they've been investigating the Wicker murder, and it probably means nothing, but he's lost weight and he's so fixated on Coughlin . . .

Don't use that word! Not fixated, dedicated. *He's Wicker's advocate, he wants to give her justice.*

Only what if *if* is the right word?

31

Halfway back to Lyons, Jalbert pulls into the cracked and potholed parking lot of an abandoned strip mall. He feels if he doesn't get out of this car and do some counting, he will explode. It's still daylight, and will be until nine o'clock. Not too far away, a giggle of girls is watching *Frozen*.

"He's running it out," Jalbert whispers. "That son of a bitch is trying to run out the clock on me."

Oh, his head! Throbbing! He runs both hands through his arrow-head swoop of hair. On either side of the widow's peak, he can feel tiny beads of sweat. He needs to count. Counting will soothe him. It always does, and when he gets back to his two-room Celebration Centre suite, he can run the chairs. He won't be able to sleep until he does. What was once a game to pass the time has become a necessity.

He walks from his car to the front of an abandoned pawnshop. Thirty-three steps, which is seventeen and sixteen. He walks back, fifteen and fourteen. He walks back to the pawnshop again: thirteen, twelve, eleven—the last three baby steps because that trio totals thirty-six and it must come out right. He's starting to feel better. Ten, nine, eight, and seven takes him back to his car. He makes a fist and raps it on the hood twenty-one times, counting the numbers off under his breath.

He can't arrest Coughlin yet. Never mind the county attorney; the KBI Director put the kibosh on that. And, Jalbert is forced to admit, the director is right. The story of the dream is absurd, but without anything else, even that smalltown lawyer Edgar Ball could get the case dismissed.

Or maybe he *wouldn't* get it dismissed. If the county attorney was stupid enough to take such a dumb case to trial, Coughlin would be found innocent and couldn't be re-tried: double jeopardy, case closed. Jalbert needs something that will pry Coughlin open so the world can see the psycho beneath those wide-eyed proclamations of innocence. He has to grind. He has to turn the screws.

Jalbert decides to walk around the strip mall, counting carefully from one. He's made it to twenty-six (351 total) when he returns to the front and sees a Highway Patrol car, misery lights flashing, parked beside his unmarked Ford. A trooper is using his shoulder mike to call in his license plate. He hears Jalbert coming and turns, hand going to the butt of his Glock. Then he sees Jalbert's KBI windbreaker and relaxes.

"Hello, sir. I saw you parked here and——"

"And you did your duty. Your due diligence. Twenty-six. Good for you. I'm going to reach into my pocket and show you some ID."

The trooper shakes his head and grins. "Not necessary. Frank Jalbert, isn't it?"

"Yes." He holds out his hand. The trooper shakes it three times, just right for a handshake. "What's your name, Trooper?"

"Henry Calten, sir. Are you investigating the dead girl?"

"Miss Yvonne, yes." Jalbert shakes his head. "Poor Miss Yvonne. I stopped to stretch my legs and think about my next move."

"The guy who reported the body looks good for it," Trooper Calten says. "Just my opinion."

"Mine, too, Troop, but he's hunkered down." Jalbert shakes his head. "Kind of laughing at us, to tell you the truth."

"I hate to hear that."

"We have to grind. Find a way to turn the screws."

"I'll let you do your thinking," Calten says, "but listen—if I could do anything to help, I know it's unlikely . . ."

"Not that unlikely," Jalbert says. "In this world, anything is possible. Sixteen."

Calten frowns. "Pardon?"

"It's a sweet number, that's all. Speaking of numbers, give me yours."

Calten, eagerly: "You bet, sure." He takes a KHP card from his breast pocket and scribbles the number of his personal on the back. "You know, I was thinking about applying to KBI myself."

"How old are you?" Jalbert takes the card.

"Twenty-four."

"Eight tripled, good. Want some advice? Don't wait too long. Don't put it off. And have a good night."

"You do the same. And if I can, you know, help in any way . . ."

"I'm going to keep that in mind. Might give you a call."

Trooper Calten pauses getting into his car and looks back with a grim little smile. "Get him, Inspector."

"That's the plan."

32

At his hotel Jalbert stops at the front desk and asks if they have folding chairs. The clerk says he believes they do, in the hotel's business center. Jalbert asks the clerk to send three up to 521.

"On second thought, I'll get them myself," Jalbert says, and does just that. There's a dozen or more leaning against the wall, so he takes four. Four is a good number, better than three. Hard to say why, but even always beats the dickens out of odd. He takes two in each hand and carries them to the elevator, ignoring the clerk's questioning look.

He unfolds two in the small sitting room and two in the bedroom. He now has eight chairs (the bed and the toilet seat count). One to eight inclusive makes thirty-six, one to twenty-four inclusive makes three hundred, one to forty inclusive makes eight hundred twenty. People wouldn't understand (*most* people), but it's really a beautiful thing, a kind of from-the-top-down pyramid scheme that pays dividends not in money but in clarity.

As he nears the end of his fifth round of chairs, he knows what his next step must be. He folds up the chairs he's brought from the conference room and stacks them next to the little desk. They may come in handy. He takes his suitcase out from under the bed and opens it. From the elastic pouch he takes a pair of thin rubber gloves and puts them on. Time to grind. Then he calls Trooper Calten. Time to turn the screws a little more.

33

Early on Friday morning of the week from hell, Danny is awakened by a loud metallic thud followed by the rev of a car engine with either a bad muffler or no muffler at all. The clock on his nightstand says it's 2:19 AM. He gets up, grabs the flashlight he keeps in case of power outages, and goes to the front window of his sitting room. Nothing is stirring out there except for a cloud of moths circling a pole light standing tall between the park's office and laundry. Oak Grove (where there are no oaks) is fast asleep. That loud thud has awakened nobody but him, because it was *meant* for him.

Danny opens the door. He sometimes forgets to lock up at night, but he supposes that after *Plains Truth* and Jalbert's little show in the IGA last night, that will have to change. He goes down the concrete steps and clicks on the flashlight, searching for the source of the thud. It doesn't take long. There's a divot in the trailer's aluminum shell, just below the frosted bathroom window. Danny surmises it was the window his nighttime visitor was aiming for.

There's a smear of red in the deepest part of the divot. Danny runs his light down the side of his trailer, and there on the gravel is a brick. Wrapped around it and secured with a twist of wire is a note. Danny knows what it's going to say, but squats and pulls it free anyway. The message is short, written in either black crayon or a felt-tip pen.

GET OUT YOU FUCKING MURDERER. OR ELSE.

Danny's first thought on reading this is *Not on your life.* His next is *Oh really? Is this a movie? Are you Clint Eastwood?*

Standing here at two in the morning with a threat in one hand and the brick that delivered it at his feet, getting out of Manitou seems not only reasonable but attractive. His friend Becky—a friend with benefits—is through with him, she'll keep sweet little DJ away from him as if he has the bubonic plague, and he's lost his job. Bonus attraction, it seems like half the town has Covid. He doesn't much like the idea of being driven out like Cain after he murdered his brother, but this trailer park is nobody's idea of Eden. It might be time to give Colorado a try. He thinks Stevie would like that.

He wonders if that noisy car he heard going away was Pat Grady's Mustang. It might well have been, but what does it matter?

Danny goes inside and back to bed, but first he locks the trailer's door.

34

On his last day as an employee of the Wilder County School Department, Danny is moving books from the storage room to the teacher's lounge, which serves as the *de facto* History and English Departments. The books will be stacked there, ready to be passed out to students when school recommences in September . . . by which time Danny Coughlin hopes to be far away from Wilder County.

Jesse comes jogging up the hall from where he's been scrubbing baseboards in the new wing. He meets Danny outside the library and says, "Just a heads-up, that cop from the other day is coming to see you. The one with the funny . . . ?" Jesse rubs two fingers on his forehead, indicating Jalbert's widow's peak. "He parked around back."

"Is the woman with him?"

"Nuh, by himself."

"Thanks, Jesse."

"Guy's really got a hardon for you, doesn't he?"

"I'll come down and help you as soon as I get these books offloaded."

Jesse persists. "He's not going to arrest you, is he?"

Danny cracks a smile at that. "I don't think he can, and it's driving him crazy. Go on, now. Let's make our last day a good one."

Jesse goes. Jalbert is in the lobby, once more examining the trophy case. He has what appears to be a rolled-up newspaper in one hand.

Maybe he means to spank my nose with it, Danny thinks. That's a welcome ray of amusement in the dread he feels at seeing Jalbert again. He knows dread is exactly what Jalbert wants him to feel. Danny would change it if he could, but he can't. He starts down the hall just as Jalbert comes through the door. "Did you have a nice Fourth?" he asks.

Danny doesn't bother with that. "What are you doing here on your own?"

To his surprise, Jalbert actually answers the question. "My partner's daughter is sick. Too much cake and ice cream, she thinks. I need you to come to Great Bend this afternoon."

"Am I under arrest?"

Jalbert shows his pegs. "Not just yet. I need you to give an official statement. For the record. All about the *dream* you had. Once your *dream* becomes public knowledge, I'll bet you can get on TV. All the publicity you ever *dreamed* of. Too bad Jerry Springer is dead, you'd fit right in with the whores and deadbeats."

"Accusing me of being a publicity hound when you're the one who leaked my name? That's pretty fucked up even for you."

"It wasn't me," Jalbert says, still smiling. "I'd never do such a thing. Must have been one of your neighbors."

Danny could tell Jalbert one of his neighbors (or maybe it was Pat Grady) threw a brick at his trailer last night, could even show him the note—it's in his pocket—but that would be fruitless.

Instead Danny asks Jalbert why he waited so long to ask him to make a report. "Because you were hoping for something better, right? Not a statement but a confession. Only your bosses wouldn't find my confession very satisfactory. Think about it, Inspector Jalbert. I don't know where she was stabbed, or how many times, or what with."

"You were in a kill frenzy," Jalbert says. He believes in Danny's guilt as fervently as Danny's late mother believed in Christ the Redeemer. "It's common with homicidal maniacs. That's an old term, probably not politically correct, but I like it. It describes you perfectly."

"I didn't kill her. Just found her."

Jalbert shows what's left of his teeth. "Tell me about Santa Claus, Danny. I love that story."

"I don't punch out until four. Which means I can't be in Great Bend until six-thirty if I keep to the speed limit. Which I intend to do."

"I'll wait for you. Ella Davis, too. Or you could punch out a little early, it being your last day and all."

Danny is so tired of this man.

"I thought you might also like to see this." Jalbert unrolls the newspaper. It's the *Oklahoman*. Jalbert turns to an inside page and hands it to Danny. The story is headlined MURDERED GIRL COMES HOME. There's a photograph. It's what Jalbert wanted him to see. Danny thinks it's the real reason Jalbert came.

The picture shows all anyone needs to know about human grief in a single image. Yvonne Wicker's father is holding his wife, whose face is buried in his shirt. His head is cocked skyward. His mouth is pulled down in a grimace. The cords stand out on his neck. His eyes are squeezed shut. Standing behind them, next to a long black Cadillac with HEARST MORTUARY on the side, is a young man in what appears to be a high school letter jacket. He's wearing a baseball cap. The brim obscures his lowered face. Danny guesses it's Yvonne's kid brother.

Danny thinks he's looking at something the movies and TV dramas rarely express, or even comprehend: the human toll. The hammer of grief and the stupidity of loss. The wreckage.

His eyes fill with tears. He looks down at the picture and the headline, MURDERED GIRL COMES HOME, then up into Jalbert's face. He's astounded to see the man is *smiling*.

"Oh, look! The murderer cries! It's like one of those Italian operas!"

Danny almost hits him. In his mind he *does* hit him, smashing Jalbert's nose to one side and sending blood down on either side of his mouth in a red Fu Manchu mustache. The only thing that holds him back is the knowledge that Jalbert wants that. He wipes a hand across his eyes instead.

"At least tell me her folks don't know about the dog. At least tell me that much."

"No idea," Jalbert says, almost cheerfully. "I was not the informing party, that was a detective from Oklahoma City. My job is working the case, Danny. Which means working *you*."

Danny is still holding the newspaper. It's crumpled. He smooths it out and holds it up for Jalbert to see. "Do you want to see another mom and dad in a picture like this? Because whoever killed her may not be done. He could get two or three more while you're fixated on me."

Jalbert recoils as if Danny has waved a hand in his face. "I'm not fixated, I'm dedicated. I know you did it, Danny. There was no dream. You didn't need a dream to go where she was buried, because you buried her. But let's agree to disagree. Be in Great Bend by six-thirty or I'll put your name and plate number out to KHP. Bring your lawyer if you want. And you can keep the newspaper. You might like to gloat over what you did to her family. Four vics for the price of one."

He turns, the tail of his black coat flying, and walks back toward the lobby.

"Inspector Jalbert!"

He turns, eyebrows raised, smooth skull on either side of that weird widow's peak as pale as cream.

"Do you grind your teeth?"

Jalbert's brow furrows. "What?"

"Your teeth. They're all worn down. Maybe you should get one of those rubber dams. They sell them in Walgreens."

"My teeth are hardly the subject under discus—"

"Does it help when you count?"

For the first time, Jalbert looks really rocked back on his heels.

"I looked that up this morning before I came to work," Danny says. "It's called arithmomania. Do you do that? Do you do it when you wake up in the night because you're grinding your teeth?"

Also for the first time, Danny sees a vein pulsing in Jalbert's right temple: ticka-ticka-ticka. "You killed her, smart boy. We both know it and you're going down for it."

He leaves. Danny stands where he is, crumpled newspaper in hand, trying to get himself under control. Each encounter with Jalbert is worse than the last. He wipes his eyes with the arm of his work shirt. Then he goes back to moving books. Last day, do it right.

35

At lunch he goes out to his truck for his phone. He owes Margie a call, needs to tell her that he's lost his job and Kansas has lost its charm, at least for him. He's thinking about Boulder. She'll understand that, she likes Stevie. If she needs money, he supposes he can part with a little . . . but not too much. Until he gets a job, he'll be living on what he's got. Besides, she's getting married, right?

He opens the passenger door, reminding himself he also needs to pay Edgar Ball, and gets his phone out of the glove compartment. He starts back to the school, head down, checking for text messages, then stops. He's thinking about something Jesse said: *He parked around back.* Why would Jalbert do that, when the faculty parking lot is the one closest to the school? Danny can think of one reason.

He goes back to the Tundra. He gives the truck bed only a cursory glance. It's empty except for his toolbox, which he keeps padlocked. The cab, on the other hand, is unlocked. He always leaves it unlocked, and Jalbert would have seen that. Danny might have even told him and his partner himself. He can't remember.

He goes through the accumulated crap in the glove compartment—weird how it piles up—expecting to find nothing and nothing is what he finds. Jalbert wouldn't have put anything in there. Not once he saw it was where Danny kept his phone. The center console strikes him as more likely, but there's nothing there, either . . . although he does find a bag of M&M's he meant to give Darla Jean the next time she showed him an A paper. DJ gets lots of As, she's a smart little thing.

He looks in the side pockets. Nothing. He looks under the passenger seat and finds nothing. He looks under the driver's seat and there it is, a glassine envelope containing white powder that can only be cocaine, heroin, or fentanyl. Kansas is hard on hard drugs, Danny knows; the kids get lectured on it at assemblies all the time. This is too small an amount to be considered "with intent to distribute," but in Kansas even possession is a Class 5 felony which can get you two years in jail.

Does Jalbert want him in prison for two years—ninety days in county, more likely—on a drug charge? No, but he does want him in jail. Because then he can work him. And work him. And work him. The guards might work him, too. If Jalbert asked.

Behind the seat is a space where all sorts of crap accumulates, including a crumpled McDonald's bag. Inside the bag is a hamburger wrapper and one of those cardboard sleeves that once contained a fast-food fried apple pie. It's just the right size. Danny picks up the envelope of dope by the sides and slides it in, bending the sleeve so the envelope won't rub, blurring any fingerprints that might be on it. Prints are unlikely but possible. He puts the cardboard sleeve back in the McDonald's bag and puts the bag in his dinnerbucket. When he goes back to the school, Jesse is at the picnic table.

"Be with you in a bit," Danny says, and goes inside. He puts the bag on a high shelf in the storage room, behind some cleaning supplies. Then he phones Edgar Ball.

"Are you still my lawyer?"

"I am until you need a pro," Ball answers. "This is interesting."

They talk for awhile. Edgar Ball promises to drop by the high school around two, and to meet Danny at the KBI station in Great Bend at six-fifteen that evening. Danny promises to give him a check for four hundred dollars.

"Better make it five, considering what you're asking me to do," Ball says.

Danny says okay. It's fair, but it will take a big bite out of his nest egg. He calls Margie and says he may not be able to help out very much for awhile because he lost his job. She tells him she gets it.

"Have those cops talk to me," she says. "I'll tell em you're a shouter, not a stabber. The idea of you killing anyone is flat crazy."

Danny says she's a peach. Margie—Margie-Margie-bo-bargie to Stevie—says you're goddam right I am. He takes his sandwich and Thermos out to the picnic table and has a nice lunch with Jesse.

"I'm gonna miss this place," Jesse says. "Weird but true. And I'm gonna miss working with you. You're a good boss, Danny."

"You'll catch on somewhere," Danny says. "I'd write you a reference, but you know . . . under the circumstances . . ."

"Yeah," Jesse says, and laughs. "I feel you."

Edgar Ball shows up at two-fifteen. Danny gives him the check and the McDonald's bag. "Sure you want to do it this way?" Ball asks. "You'll be going out on a limb."

"I'm already out on a limb," Danny says. "Getting further out all the time."

36

They punch out at three-thirty, half an hour before their usual quitting time. Danny locks up the school for the last time, all seven doors. Jesse gives Danny a man-hug and Danny returns it along with a couple of slaps on the back. Danny tells Jesse to take care of himself and stay in touch. Jesse says for Danny to do the same.

Danny drives to Oak Grove, keeping an eye on the rearview mirror, looking for cops. He sees none. When he gets home, he finds a note taped to his door. It's short and to the point: *Move Out. We Don't Want You Here.* He pulls it off the door, tosses it in the kitchen trash, takes a quick shower, and puts on fresh clothes. Then he calls Ella Davis.

"Danny Coughlin again, Inspector."

"How can I help you?"

"By trusting me just a little." Danny tells her what he wants her to do. She doesn't say yes . . . but she doesn't say no, either.

He sets out for Great Bend and has covered about thirty miles when a KHP cruiser pulls out of a farm road and comes after him, lights flashing. The trooper gives him a blurp of the siren, totally unnecessary because Danny is already pulling over and powering down his window. Once it's open, he puts both hands on top of the steering wheel where they can be seen.

The trooper's name is H. Calten. He comes up to Danny with one hand on his Glock. The strap has been unsnapped.

"License and registration, please."

"My license is in my wallet," Danny says. "I'm going to reach into my hip pocket and get it." He does so, moving very slowly. Once he's handed his DL to Trooper Calten, he says, "Now I'm going to reach into my glove compartment and take out my registration."

"Do you have a weapon in the glove compartment?"

"No."

"In the center console?"

"No."

"Go ahead."

Once again in slo-mo, Danny opens the glove compartment and takes out his registration.

"Do you have proof of insurance?"

"Yes." He starts to reach for the glove compartment again.

"Never mind the insurance card. Sit still, Mr. Coughlin."

Calten goes back to his cruiser and gets on his radio. Danny sits still. Five minutes pass. He is going to be late getting to Great Bend, but that's all right. Jalbert doesn't think he'll be there at all.

Having verified that the 2011 Tundra he's pulled over does indeed belong to Daniel Coughlin—a thing Calten already knew, Danny is quite sure—the trooper returns to the driver's side with Danny's paperwork. But he doesn't hand it over. "Do you know why I stopped you, Mr. Coughlin?"

Danny says he doesn't.

"You were weaving all over the road."

Danny knows that isn't true but keeps quiet.

"Have you had anything to drink today, Mr. Coughlin?"

"If you're asking about alcohol, the answer is no."

"How would you feel about a Breathalyzer test? Willing to take one?"

"Yes."

"How about drugs? Been using any of those? Pot? Ecstasy? Cocaine?"

"No."

"Would you consent to a search of your truck?"

"Don't you need a search warrant or something for that?"

"Not if I have observed you driving in a dangerous manner. You can consent to a search or I can impound your vehicle."

"Okay," Danny says, opening the door. "I have an appointment, so I guess you better search."

Trooper Calten makes a show of searching the cab, saving the underside of the driver's seat for last. He spends a long time looking under there, even getting his flashlight from his cruiser. Then he slams the door and gives Danny a flat look.

"What about that Breathalyzer?" Danny asks.

"Sir, are you being smart with me?" Danny can't tell if the cop's cheeks are flushed or if it's sunburn.

"No. But I wasn't weaving and we both know it."

"I'm going to write you up for reckless driving, Mr. Coughlin."

"I wouldn't do that," Danny says. "If you do, I'll see you in court. Where my lawyer will ask if you spoke to Inspector Jalbert of the KBI prior to pulling me over. Then you'll have to decide whether you want to tell the truth or commit perjury. Which might or might not come back to bite you in the ass. Do you want that?"

Calten takes a minute while trying to decide if he wants to push this. It's not sunburn; definitely a flush. Danny thinks it's nice not to be playing defense for once. Calten hands him back his license and registration. "Try to keep on your side of the road from now on, sir."

Danny almost pushes it a little farther, almost asks if Calten doesn't at least want to give him a warning, and decides enough is enough. Calten is armed, and he still hasn't snapped the strap over the butt of his service weapon.

"I will, Officer."

"Get out of here."

Calten follows him for five miles, almost riding Danny's bumper, then turns off. The rest of Danny's trip to Great Bend is without incident.

37

Edgar Ball is waiting for him at the far end of the KBI station's parking lot. He asks Danny how his trip was. Danny tells him about Trooper Calten.

"Unbelievable," Ball says. "Are you sure you want to take that dope back?"

"It should be safe enough now, Jalbert took his shot." Danny hopes he's right about that, and also hopes he won't be arrested later by Inspector Davis.

Ball opens the trunk of his car and hands Danny the McDonald's bag. Danny puts it in the center console, and this time he locks his truck.

"Let's go in," Danny says. "Watch Jalbert when he sees me. That'll be interesting."

But it's not. What they see is the barest flicker of surprise, there and gone. The room, equipped with audio-visual recording equipment, is crowded. In addition to Jalbert and Davis, there's a tubby bald guy named Albert Heller and a suit-wearing beefcake named Vernon Ramsey. Heller is the Wilder County Attorney. Ramsey is a detective from Oklahoma City. With six people crowded in, the feel is downright claustrophobic. Somewhere in this facility there's probably a more spacious conference room, but conferencing isn't what Jalbert and Heller have in mind. What they have in mind is breaking Danny down. Now that he's here.

Introductions are made. Hands are shaken (Danny and Jalbert forgo this). The Miranda warning is given, this time by the county attorney. Heller finishes by announcing for the record that "Mr. Coughlin has brought his counselor at law."

Heller takes the lead, covering the same ground that was covered at Danny's last interview. They sit facing each other, with Edgar Ball on Danny's side of the table and Ella Davis on Heller's. Ramsey leans against the wall, face impassive. Jalbert stands in the corner with his arms crossed.

Under questioning, Danny recounts his dream. He recounts his trip out to the abandoned gas station in Dart County. He recounts his clumsy attempt to make an anonymous report. When Heller asks why he called, Danny tells him about the dog. "It was digging her up. Chewing on her. I'm sure you saw the photographs."

Heller tells him they need to know much more about where Danny was during the first three weeks of June. Danny says he'll help all he can, but he doesn't keep a diary or anything.

When Heller runs out of questions, Vernon Ramsey, the Oklahoma City cop, steps forward. "Did you kill Yvonne Wicker?"

"No."

Ramsey steps back. He has no follow-up questions. Jalbert whispers something in his ear and Ramsey nods, face impassive.

Heller winds things up by telling Danny not to leave the county.

Danny shakes his head. "I'm actually planning to leave the county *and* the state. My name was printed in a free handout newspaper. I'm the prime suspect, and somebody wanted to make sure everyone in central Kansas knew it." Danny's eyes flick to Jalbert. Jalbert looks blandly back.

"I can assure you no one involved in the murder investigation gave your name to the press," Heller says. "That was unfortunate, but nevertheless it would be a very bad idea for you to leave the town of Manitou, let alone Kansas. It would have conse—"

"Arrest me," Danny says. "If you want to keep me in Kansas, arrest me."

Heller stares at him. Ella Davis looks down at her hands, which are folded on the table. Ramsey appears to be studying the ceiling. Jalbert is openly glaring.

"You can't," Danny says. "You have no proof that I killed Yvonne Wicker, because I didn't. I only reported the body. So don't tell me there would be consequences."

"Actually, there would be," Ball says, almost apologetically. "A suit for false arrest. Filed by me."

"I strongly advise you to stay where you are," Heller says. "Leaving would only make you look more guilty."

From the corner, in a mild voice, Jalbert says, "He *is* guilty."

Danny takes a folded piece of paper from his back pocket and hands it across the table, not to Heller but to Davis. "It says, 'Get out you fucking murderer. Or else.' It was wrapped around a brick. The brick was thrown at the side of my trailer in the middle of the night. *That's* a consequence of getting my name in the paper, Mr. Heller. The well has been poisoned." He again flicks his eyes to Jalbert. "The next brick could be at my head."

Ramsey says, "Where are you going?"

"I'm thinking Colorado. I have a brother there and I don't see him enough."

"It won't matter where you go," Jalbert says. "Miss Wicker will follow you like a bad stink. One that won't wash off."

Danny knows this is probably true. He looks at Ramsey. "Are you pursuing any other suspects? Any at all? Maybe a boyfriend she dropped and wasn't happy about it? A bad home situation?"

Ramsey says, "The OHP Investigative Division isn't in the habit of sharing information with suspects."

Danny didn't expect any better. He has an idea that OHP isn't pursuing any suspects in Oklahoma, and for good reason. He thinks that there is no connection between Yvonne Wicker and her killer. She was hitchhiking, got picked up by the wrong person, and it cost her her life.

He stands up. "I'm leaving."

No one stops him, but Jalbert says, "You'll be back."

38

In the parking lot, Danny shakes hands with his lawyer, who drove his big honker of a Honda from Manitou. He said very little . . . except for that zinger about suing for false arrest. That was a good one. Otherwise, what was there to say?

"Are you sure you want to take a chance on Davis?" Ball asks.

Danny shrugs. "You're thinking she'll arrest me for possession when I show her the coke? Compared to what's hanging over me, that's a minor risk."

Ball rocks back and forth on his feet. "If you didn't kill her, you're the most divine liar I've ever come across. Even better than my Uncle Red, which I would have thought impossible."

"I didn't," Danny says. He's getting tired of saying it.

39

It's only a couple of miles from the KBI station to where he's supposed to meet Ella Davis, but Danny goes the long way through Great Bend's paltry downtown, checking his rearview mirror, doing his best to make sure no one is following him. When he finally arrives at the Coffee Hut, it's eight-thirty. There's a paved parking area in front, dirt in the back. That's where Danny parks, pulling up next to a RAV4 sport utility. He's pretty sure it belongs to Davis. There's an action figure on the passenger seat that he recognizes, thanks to Darla Jean. It's Elsa Oldenburg from *Frozen*.

He goes inside. Davis is in a booth around the corner from the counter, where she can't be seen from the main parking lot.

"I didn't think you were coming," she says. "I was getting ready to leave."

"I wanted to make sure I wasn't followed. Sure as I could, anyway."

She raises her eyebrows. "You really are paranoid, aren't you?"

"It was for your benefit as well as mine. I don't think Jalbert would like you meeting me behind his back."

She's spared a response by the arrival of a waitress. Danny, who hasn't had anything to eat since his sandwich at lunch, orders country ham with gravy and a Coke.

"That will clog your arteries," Davis says when she's gone.

"Beats a brick in the head."

"Frank Jalbert thinks you wrote that note yourself."

"He would."

"Why are we here, Danny? I've got a babysitter and her meter's running."

Danny tells her about Jalbert's visit to the school, ostensibly to inform Danny he needed to make an official statement. Also to show him the picture of the grieving Wicker family in the *Oklahoman*.

"But he had another reason. I wouldn't have known if Jesse—the kid I work with—hadn't mentioned that Jalbert parked out back when it's only steps to the front door from the faculty parking lot, which is empty in the summer. That made me suspicious. I checked, and found a little envelope under the driver's seat of my truck." He slides the fried pie sleeve across to her. "It's in here. Might be heroin, but I think it's coke."

For the first time since he's met her, Davis's professional veneer cracks. She lifts one of the sleeve's end flaps and peeks inside.

"I handled the envelope just by the sides. I doubt if he left any fingerprints, he's too smart for that, but on the off chance he slipped up, you might want to check."

She recovers smartly. "Let me get this straight. You're accusing Frank Jalbert, twenty-plus years a KBI inspector, half a dozen citations, including two for bravery, of planting drugs in your truck."

"I'm sure he's a hell of a cop, but he's convinced I killed that woman." Only that's not right, not enough. "He's obsessed, and if you haven't seen it, I'd be very surprised."

"You could have planted this on yourself, Danny."

"I'm not done." He tells her about the bogus highway stop and how Trooper Calten spent most of his time looking under the driver's seat. "He skimped everything else, because he knew where it was supposed to be. And as far as planting it on myself . . . ask Jesse Jackson about Jalbert parking around back. He'll tell you."

The waitress is coming with Danny's food. Davis sweeps the fried pie sleeve into her purse with the side of her hand. When the waitress is gone, Ella points at his plate and says, "That looks like something the dog sicked up."

Danny laughs and digs in. "There! Now you sound like a human being."

"I *am* a human being. I also work for the Kansas Bureau of Investigation, and that makes me a Doubting Thomas."

"Jalbert gave my name out to that rag. *Plains Truth*."

"*You* say. You're as obsessed with him as he is with you."

"I have to be, he's trying to nail me for a crime I didn't commit. And what can I do to fight back? Let out the air in his tires? Slap a KICK ME HARD Post-it on the back of that black coat he wears? Only talk to you, and that's a risk. My lawyer said you might arrest me for possession."

"I'm not going to do that."

She watches him eat and twiddles at the small gold cross she wears around her neck. "Let's say, for the sake of argument, that Frank gave out your name to the one outfit that would publish it, and that he planted cocaine in your truck. Assuming it's not talcum powder or Mannitol. Just for the sake of argument let's say that. Do either of those things prove you didn't rape and murder Yvonne Wicker? Not in my book."

Danny can't argue that.

"I will get what's in your little envelope tested, and I'll talk to that guy at *Plains Truth*, Andersson. Text me your young assistant janitor's number and I'll also get in touch with him. Now I have to go." She starts to get up.

"That little gold cross—is it just for show, or are you a believer?"

"I go to Mass," she says warily.

"So you can believe in God but not that I had a dream about where Wicker's body was. Have I got that right?"

She touches the little gold cross briefly. "Jesus performed thirty miracles, Danny. You had one dream. Or so you say. The check's yours. I just had coffee."

Danny says, "Lady, you don't know how much I wish I'd never had that fucking—no, that *motherfucking*—dream."

Ella Davis pauses. She's almost smiling. "You're an engaging guy, Danny. Reasonable. Friendly. At least that's the face you show the world. What's underneath I don't know. But I'll tell you a secret."

She bends over him, fingers splayed on the table, little gold cross swinging. "I'd *like* to believe you. Maybe I even could, except *this is the only goddam psychic dream you've ever had.* Why you, I ask myself?"

"Great question," he says. "Guys who win the lottery probably ask themselves the same thing. Only this is the opposite. I don't know why me. It's easier for you to believe I killed her, isn't it?"

"By far."

"Do me one favor. Be careful of Jalbert. I think he might be dangerous. It isn't just planting drugs or giving out my name. That counting thing is bizarre. I looked it up. It's called—"

"Arithmomania," she says, then looks like she wishes she could unsay it. She leaves without looking back, that big purse of hers swinging. The waitress comes by and says, "Save room for blueberry buckle, hon."

"I'll try," Danny says.

40

On his way back to his hotel, Jalbert uses a burner phone to make a call.

"There were no drugs in his truck," Calten tells him. "Not under the seat, not anywhere."

"That's all right," Jalbert says, although it's not. "He found them and got rid of them, that's all. Like a wolf smelling a trap. As for you, Troop, you know nothing, right? You just stopped him because he was weaving."

"That's right," Calten says.

"It might be smart to delete this call."

"Roger that, Inspector. Sorry it didn't work out."

"I appreciate the effort."

Jalbert ends the call and puts his burner back under the seat. He'll hold onto it for awhile, maybe another ten days or so (five plus five, four plus six, etc.), then trash it and swap it out for another one.

Does Coughlin know he planted the drugs? Of course. Can he do anything about it? No. The police would say he planted the blow on himself. But finding it . . . Jalbert didn't expect that. Coughlin

177

really is like a wolf, one that can scent a trap no matter how well it's concealed. He'll kill again if he isn't stopped. He *must* be stopped, not just for poor Miss Yvonne, but for other girls who might be unlucky enough to cross his path.

And if he goes to Colorado, Jalbert thinks, *we could lose sight of him. Animals know how to hide. How to fade into the brush.*

He has to be stopped here in Kansas.

"Arrest me," Jalbert whispers, and brings a fist down on the steering wheel—*bang*. "The arrogance. The insolence. But you know what, Mr. Coughlin? We're not done. A long way from done." He thinks of Coughlin's face. His constant open-faced denials. His *gall*.

Arrest me.

Jalbert needs to settle himself so he can think about his next move. He needs to count.

41

The clerk at the Celebration Centre is browsing a weird-ass catalogue called What On Earth. He's currently considering a tee-shirt that says FOR BEARS, PEOPLE IN SLEEPING BAGS ARE SOFT TACOS. He's interrupted by a guest striding up to the desk . . . and not just any guest, that KBI inspector. He looks mad, too—really mad. Face all red right up to both sides of his shaggy widow's peak, which has been disarranged in a way that's almost comic . . . not that the clerk feels much like laughing. The inspector's eyes are wide and bulgy, sort of bloodshot. The clerk shoves the retail porn catalogue under the desk's overhang in a hurry and asks how he can help.

"The chairs are gone."

"What chairs, sir?"

"The *folding* chairs. I had four folding chairs from the conference room, or business center, or whatever you call it. I had them set up just where I wanted them, and they're gone!"

"Housekeeping must have—"

"*I had the Do Not Disturb sign on my door!*" Jalbert shouts. A woman on her way to the gift shop gives him a startled look.

"Those signs're pretty old," the clerk says, wondering if the inspector is armed. "Sometimes they fall off and the chambermaids don't see—"

"The sign didn't fall off!" Jalbert doesn't actually know if it did or not; he is too upset. He was looking forward to those chairs.

"I'll have someone get—"

"Don't bother, I'll do it myself." Jalbert makes an effort to lower his voice, aware that he's gone a little over the top, but still, to come into his little suite and find those chairs gone! It was a shock.

He goes down to the business center and takes five chairs. Only two in one hand and three in the other feels wrong. Unbalanced. He debates taking a sixth, or putting one back. It's a hard choice, because he keeps thinking of Coughlin, how insolent he looked when he said *If you want to keep me in Kansas, arrest me.* Then the crowning, infuriating touch: *You can't.* Infuriating because true.

Only for now, he thinks.

Jalbert decides on four chairs, and counts steps back to the elevator by fours, under his breath: *"One* two three four, *two* two three four, *three* two three four." He knows the counting thing is peculiar, but it's also harmless. A way to soothe counterproductive thoughts and clear the mind. He's up to *nine* two three four when he reaches the desk, a total of thirty-six. To the clerk he says, "I was out of line. I apologize."

"No problem," the clerk says, and watches Inspector Jalbert walk to the elevators. He seems to be muttering under his breath. The clerk thinks that it takes all kinds to make a world. To him this is an original thought. He thinks it would look good on a tee-shirt.

42

In his boxy Kansas plain suite, Jalbert sets up the chairs and runs them. He knows he's been doing it a lot lately, maybe too much, but it helps. It really does. And maybe he was doing it a lot even before Coughlin, maybe it's a problem—the chairs and the counting. He's aware that numbers rarely leave his mind these days—adding them, dividing them—and it may be an addiction. Sometimes when he's counting, a number will pop out of his mouth, like a Jack from its box. It happened with Calten, and although he can't remember for sure, it could have happened with the clerk downstairs. Certainly the clerk thought he was being peculiar about the folding chairs. He ought to do something about it before it gets out of hand—maybe hypnosis?—and he will as soon as Coughlin has been charged with the murder of Miss Yvonne, but in the meantime he needs to plan his next move. Counting helps. Running the chairs helps.

He goes from a folding chair to the bed, which is four steps. From the bed to the closed seat of the toilet, which is eleven more. That's a total of fifteen, 1 to 5 added sequentially. Next, to the chair by the desk in the sitting room. That's fourteen more. Which makes . . .

For a moment he has no idea what it makes and a kind of panic sets in. Poor Miss Yvonne is depending on him, her family is depending on him, and if he can't remember a simple arithmetical total, how can he possibly . . .

Twenty-nine, he thinks, and relief floods him.

His upset is all Coughlin's fault. "Arrest me," Jalbert murmurs, sitting bolt upright in one of the folding chairs. "You can't. You can't."

Coughlin leaving the state? Jalbert can count all he wants, but he didn't count on that. How can he, Inspector Frank Jalbert, keep the pressure on if Coughlin simply folds his tent and leaves?

He counts. He adds. Occasionally he divides. The idea of killing Coughlin comes to him, and not for the first time; he's sure he could get away with it if he was careful and it would save the girls who might suffer poor Miss Yvonne's fate. But without hard evidence of Coughlin's guilt—or a confession, even better—the son of a bitch would die an innocent man.

Unacceptable.

Jalbert goes from one room chair to the next, to the bed, to a folding chair, to the toilet seat, to another folding chair. He lies down for awhile, hoping to sleep, at least to get some rest, but when he closes his eyes he sees Coughlin's insolent face. *Arrest me. You can't, can you?*

He springs up and begins running the chairs again.

Last time, he tells himself. *Then I'll be able to sleep. When I wake up I'll know what comes next.*

On the toilet seat, he covers his face with his hands and whispers, "I'm doing it for you, Miss Yvonne. All for you."

Which is a lie, and he knows it. Miss Yvonne is beyond help. Danny Coughlin is alive. And free.

43

On Saturday morning, Ella Davis drives to Manitou. Her daughter is strapped in the backseat, absorbed with the iPad Mini she got for her birthday. Ella told Danny Coughlin that she had a babysitter and the meter was running. That was a lie, but she doesn't feel bad about it. He is lying about Yvonne Wicker, after all, and his lie is bigger than hers.

Are you sure he's lying? Totally sure?

Ella and Laurie are staying with Regina in Great Bend. Reggie has a daughter just Laurie's age, and the birthday party was actually Reggie's idea. She's crazy about Laurie and is delighted to keep her when Davis has to work.

One hundred per cent sure?

She tells herself she is. She's less sure that he called in the location of the girl's body out of remorse and a desire to be punished for his horrific crime. He would have confessed already if that were the case. She thinks now that it's a kind of arrogance.

"He's playing chicken with us," she murmurs.

"What, Mommy?"

"Nothing, hon."

"Are we almost there?"

"Three or four more miles."

"Good. I'm beating Beer Pong."

"*What* Pong?"

"I use my finger to throw the little balls into the cups of beer. When they go in, there's a ker-sploosh and I get points."

"That's nice, Laurie."

She thinks: *Beer Pong. My eight-year-old is playing Beer Pong.* She thinks: *What if he's telling the truth? What if there really was a dream?*

It's the same story each time, without significant variations and without the liar's tells that she's been trained to look for: a shifting of the eyes to the left, a wetting of the lips, a raising of the voice, as if being loud would convince her of the truth. He doesn't over-explain, either, and risk getting tripped up by his own lies. Is it possible he's even convinced himself? That his rational mind, horrified by what the alligator deep inside did, has constructed its own alternate reality?

Is it possible he's telling the truth?

This morning she called the Jacksons in Manitou and asked Jesse if he would be willing to talk to her. He said yes without hesitation, and here she is, turning into the Jacksons' driveway. She isn't here because she believes Danny about the dream. She's here because she *almost* believes him about Jalbert. If Frank's been doing what Danny says he's been doing, it could very well screw up any chance they have of making a case. More than that, it's wrong. It's bad policing. Her unease about her partner is growing. She's almost ready to be angry at him.

Bullshit, you're angry at him already.

"True," she says.

"What, Mommy?"

"Nothing, Lore."

Mrs. Jackson is hanging out clothes. A little boy who looks to be Laurie's age is on a swing set nearby, singing that awful "Baby Shark" song. When Davis opens the back door and lets Laurie get out, the little boy hops off his swing and runs over, examining the newcomers. Laurie stands close to Ella, putting one hand on her mother's leg. Mrs. Jackson turns to Ella and says hello.

"Hi. I'm Inspector Davis, here to see Jesse?"

"He's just in the house. *Jesse! Your company's here!*"

The little boy says, "I'm Luke. Is that an iPad Mini?"

"Yes," Laurie says. "I got it for my birthday."

"Radical!"

"My name is Laurie Rose Davis. I'm eight."

"Me too," Luke says. "Want to go on the swing?"

Laurie looks at Davis. "Can I, Mommy?"

"Yes, but be careful. Don't break your iPad."

"I won't!"

They run for the swing set.

"Pretty girl," Mrs. Jackson says. "I'm the mother of boys. I'd pay to get one of those."

"She can be a handful," Ella says.

"Try Luke, you want a handful." She goes back to hanging clothes.

Jesse comes out of the house, dressed in jeans and a plain white tee. He walks to Davis without hesitation and shakes her hand. "Happy to talk to you if it's about Danny. Tell you up front, though, I don't think he did what the cops say he did. He's a good man."

Davis has heard this several times now, even from Becky Richardson, Danny's sometime girlfriend. Richardson wants nothing to do with him now, of course, but continues to say that "he seems like the nicest guy you'd ever want to meet." And Richardson believes the dream story.

"It isn't Danny Coughlin I want to talk about, at least not directly," Davis says. "Is it true that Inspector Frank Jalbert came by to see him at the school yesterday?"

"Yeah. I didn't like him."

"Oh? Why?"

"He's made up his mind. I could tell just by the way he looked at Danny."

Well, she thinks, *I have, too. Right?*

"Danny says you saw Inspector Jalbert park around back."

"That's right. Why?"

"Did he park near Danny's truck?"

"No, by the school buses, but that's pretty close. Hey, did he put something in Danny's truck? Try to set him up? I wouldn't put it past him. He looked totally locked and loaded."

"Did you *see* him put anything in Danny's truck?"

"No . . ."

"Did you see him go to Danny's truck? Kind of looking it over? You know, the way some guys look at trucks?"

"No, soon as I saw him get out of his car I told Danny. Then I went back to work. Danny said just because it was our last day, that was no reason to be slacking off."

"I'm sorry you lost your job because of Coughlin."

Jesse's face darkens. "Wasn't him. Chickenshit school administration said Danny had to go and I had to go with him. They made up a lot of bullshit reasons—"

"Jesse, watch your mouth," his mother says. "This is an officer of the law you're talking to."

"It just makes me mad. They probably made up some stupid stuff on account of they couldn't fire him because of that girl. Whatever happened to innocent until proven guilty?"

I keep hearing that, Ella thinks.

"He went, so I had to go," Jesse says. "I get that, I'm just a kid. But I needed that money for college."

"You'll get another job," Davis says.

"Already did. At the sawmill." Jesse makes a face. "The pay is better, so long as I don't cut off a hand."

"You better not," his mom says. "You need that hand."

Laurie and Luke have abandoned the swings. They are sitting in the shade of the small yard's only tree, heads together, looking at the iPad Mini. As Davis glances their way, the two kids start giggling at whatever's on the screen. Davis is suddenly very glad she came. After spending so much time with Jalbert, it's like coming out of a stale room into fresh air.

"Let me get this straight," Davis says, taking out her notebook. "You saw Inspector Jalbert park in back—"

"Yeah, even though out front is a lot closer to the building."

"But you didn't see him approach Danny Coughlin's truck, or touch it in any way."

"I told you, I had to go back to work."

"Okay, understood." She smiles and gives him her card. "If anything else occurs to you—"

"You should have seen him!" Jesse bursts out. "Waving that newspaper in Danny's face. Low class! After Danny did the cops a favor! I don't think that guy even cares who did it, he just wants to put Danny in jail."

"Enough, Jesse," his mother says. "Show some manners."

"That guy Jalbert didn't show any," Jesse says, and Davis guesses that was true. But excusable. When you've got a rapist-murderer standing in front of you, manners have a way of going out the window.

"Thank you for your time. Come on, Laurie, we have to go."

"We just *got* here!" Laurie groans. "Me'n Luke are playing Corgi Hop! It's so funny!"

"Five minutes," Ella says. Her ex claims she spoils the girl, and Ella supposes he's right. But Laurie is what she's got, *all* she's got, and how she loves her. The thought of Coughlin putting his dirty bloodstained hands on her—on any girl—makes Ella cold.

"Mrs. Jackson, can I help you hang those clothes while I wait for them to finish their game?"

"If you want to," Mrs. Jackson says, sounding both surprised and pleased. "The pins are in that mesh bag."

The two women finish up fast, hanging the last two sheets as a team. Davis thinks about Jalbert parking near Coughlin's truck. She doesn't—can't—believe that Danny Coughlin dreamed the location where a murdered girl was buried, but she is closer than ever to believing that Frank Jalbert, a decorated inspector, planted drugs and then got some cop to stop Danny on the road to Great Bend. She just can't prove it, any more than they can prove Danny Coughlin killed Yvonne Wicker.

Let it alone, she tells herself as she puts the last pin on the last sheet.

Probably good advice, but she won't do it. If Jalbert is over the line, she can't just stand by. And she has someone else to question. It will probably come to nothing, but at least she'll be able to tell herself she tried.

"You want a glass of iced tea?" Mrs. Jackson asks as she picks up her laundry basket.

"You know, that sounds good," Ella says, and follows her toward the house.

One thing she's sure of: This is going to be her last case with Frank. All else aside, Danny is absolutely correct about one thing— that counting business, the arithmomania, is spooky. And it's getting worse.

44

At ten-thirty on Sunday morning someone knocks on the door of Danny's trailer. He expects to see Jalbert or Davis, but it's Bill Dumfries, the retired contractor who put him in touch with Edgar Ball. He looks uncomfortable, arms crossed over his meaty chest, not making eye contact. Danny has a pretty good idea that he hasn't come to invite him to dinner.

"Hey, Danny."

"Hey. What can I do for you?"

Dumfries sighs. "There's no easy way to say this, so I'm just gonna come right out with it. Most of the people in the park think it'd be good if you left."

Danny is already planning to leave, which should make this all right—*sort* of all right—but it doesn't. "You want to come in and have a cup of coffee? Talk about it a little?"

"Better not." Dumfries glances toward his trailer and Danny sees Althea Dumfries standing on the top step, watching them. Probably wanting to make sure Danny doesn't whip out his murder-knife and start stabbing on her husband. Which is funny, in a way; Danny thinks if he made a move on Bill, the guy would break him in half.

"There was a kind of meeting last night," Dumfries says. A flush is creeping up his neck and infecting his cheeks. "People were talking about getting up a petition, but I said screw that, I'll talk to him. Tell him which way the wind's blowing."

Danny thinks of his mother, who had a saying for every occasion. One of them was *it's an ill wind that blows no good*. Here was that wind, and he knew the name of the evil sorcerer who had ginned it up. Angry as he was at Jalbert, Danny didn't want to do the man harm. That would make his situation even worse. All he wanted was to get away from his zone of influence. The sooner the better.

"You tell people not to worry." Danny gives Althea Dumfries a wave, restraining the urge to flip her the bird. She doesn't wave back. "I'll be gone soon. You don't want me here and I don't want to stay. My mother would say this just proves that no good deed goes unpunished."

"You really didn't kill her."

"No, Bill. I really didn't kill her. And the only one who's close to believing me is the lawyer you recommended. I don't know if you'd call that irony or not."

"Where are you going?"

Bill Dumfries doesn't need to know that Danny still hasn't nailed that down, but because Bill at least had the guts to face him (without eye contact, it's true), Danny closes the door of his trailer gently instead of slamming it in Bill's face.

Back in his living area, he makes a FaceTime call to his brother, knowing Stevie will be on break. Stevie keeps to a regular schedule and gets upset if something happens to knock him off it. *In that way,* Danny thinks, *he's kind of like a sunnyside version of Jalbert.*

Stevie is sitting on a box of Charmin and eating a Twinkie. He brightens when he sees Danny's face.

"What's up, Danny-bo-banny?"

"I'm thinking I might move to Colorado," Danny says. "What would you think about that?"

Stevie looks both pleased and worried. "Well . . . mayyy-be. But why? Why would you?"

"Tired of Kansas," Danny says. Which is the absolute truth. Then he understands why Stevie looks worried, and has stopped munching his snack. He's a creature of routine, is Stevie Coughlin; routine keeps him safe. His motto is: keep the shiny side up, keep the rubber side down. He is the Chief Information Officer at King Soopers, even has a plaque that says so, and he loves his room and his friends in the group home.

"I'm not talking about us moving in together," Danny says. "I might not even live in Boulder. I looked at some places in Longmont, you know, online . . ."

Stevie breaks out a relieved grin. "Longmont's nice!"

Danny doubts if Stevie has even been there. "That's what I've heard, and rents are cheap. Well . . . chea*per*. We could have supper together sometimes . . . maybe hit a movie . . . you could take me on one of your hikes . . ."

"West Magnolia! Mud Lake! I could show you those! Great hikes! Wildlife! I take so many pictures you wouldn't even believe it. Mud Lake, I know it's an ugly name, but it's really pretty!"

"I think it sounds great," Danny says, then adds something else that's nothing but the truth: "I miss you, Stevie."

Now that Stevie knows he won't have to forego the group home—and maybe Janet—he looks almost ecstatic. "I miss you, too, Danny-bo-banny. You should come! Rocky Mountain High, in Col-o-*raaado*."

"Sounds good. I'll tell you what's going on when I know more."

"Good. That's good. Give me one. But quick, my break's almost over."

Once more Danny is ready. "King Oscar sardines."

Stevie laughs. "End of Aisle 6, top shelf on the left, just before the end-cap. Four-pack, nine dollars and ninety-nine cents."

"You're the best, Stevie. They are lucky to have you."

"I know," Stevie says. And chortles.

45

On Monday, Jalbert is called to Wichita to make a report on the Yvonne Wicker case. Top brass will be present, also the county attorney from Wilder County. Dart County doesn't even *have* a county attorney, Jalbert tells Davis.

"Do you want me to go with you?" Ella asks.

"No. What I *want* is for you to press Coughlin on where he was during those blanks in the first three weeks of June. And you need to knock on doors in that trailer park. Talk to Becky Richardson—"

"I did—"

He makes a chopping gesture with one hand, a gesture that's very unlike him. "Talk to her again. And talk to her daughter. Ask if Coughlin ever made her uncomfortable. You know, touching."

"Jesus, Frank!"

"Jesus *what*? You think what he did to Miss Yvonne just came out of nowhere? There will have been signs. Now are you with me on this or not?"

"Yes, sure."

"Good. Nineteen."

"What?"

"It's the only good prime number," Jalbert says, then makes the chopping gesture again. "Never mind. Knock on doors. Find *something*. We can't let him leave Wilder County, let alone the state. I'll take care of Wichita."

"Can you convince them to arrest Coughlin?"

"I'm going to try," Jalbert says, "but don't hold your breath."

He leaves. Davis goes to Oak Grove and starts knocking on doors, although not on Danny Coughlin's; after their conversation at the Coffee Hut, she's not ready to talk with him again. Becky Richardson is home but on her way out, telling Davis she has to do a favor for a friend. She has nothing new to add anyway, only that she and Coughlin had a relationship but now are quits. The daughter, Darla Jean, stares at Davis from in front of the TV with big eyes. Ella makes no attempt to interview her.

At eleven o'clock, after a series of fruitless interviews that have told her nothing new except Danny has agreed to leave the park, she calls *Plains Truth*. She half-expects voicemail, but the phone is answered by a young man. "*Yell*-o."

"I'd like to speak to Peter Andersson, please."

"That's me."

"Mr. Andersson, I'm Inspector Ella Davis of the Kansas Bureau of Investigation. I'd like to talk to you about Daniel Coughlin."

There's a long pause. Davis is about to ask if Andersson is still there when he speaks again, sounding younger than ever. "I was given a good tip and I published it, okay? If there was something wrong with giving out his name, I didn't know."

Ignorance of the law is no excuse, Davis thinks, but in this case there's no law anyway—just accepted practice.

"But if there's something wrong with the follow-up, I guess I could print a retraction. If it's not true, that is."

What follow-up? she thinks, and makes a mental note to pick up the latest issue of *Plains Truth*.

"What I want to know, Mr. Andersson, is who gave you your information?"

"A cop." Andersson pauses for a moment, then blurts, "At least he *said* he was a cop, and I believed him because he really had the inside

189

track on the investigation. He said printing the guy's name would put pressure on him to, you know, come clean."

"This mystery cop didn't give you a name?"

"No—"

"But you ran the story anyway."

"Well, isn't it true?" Andersson is trying to sound pugnacious. "Isn't this Coughlin the guy you're looking at for the murder of the girl?"

"Mr. Andersson, I think I'd better come see you in person," Davis says.

"Oh God," he says, sounding younger than ever.

"What time would be convenient?"

"I guess I could be at the office. There now. Have you got the address? We're in Cathcart."

"I have it."

"*Truth* is pretty much a one-man operation. Just tell me one thing, ma'am. Did I break the law when I printed his name?"

"Not to my knowledge," Davis says. "It wasn't illegal, just shitty. I'll be by this afternoon."

46

Danny doesn't know what his next stop will be—maybe Denver, maybe Longmont, maybe Arvada—but after nearly three years in Oak Grove, his two small suitcases won't be enough for the belongings he means to take. He decides to go to Manitou Fine Liquors and see if he can get some empty boxes for his clothes. They might not know his face there because even in his drinking days he stuck mostly to beer.

He opens his trailer door shortly after noon and stops on the top step. Darla Jean Richardson has set up her dollhouse on the asphalt in the shade of the Oak Grove office building. It's a big one, damn near a mansion. Carrying it from her trailer must have been a chore. Becky ordered it from Amazon for DJ's seventh birthday, then threw up her hands in despair when she realized it had to be assembled. Danny put it together with DJ handing him the various components, both of them singing along with the radio. That was a good day.

She's nine now, and he hasn't seen Marigold's DreemHouse for almost a year. He supposes she plays with it in her bedroom. Or has outgrown it. But if she lugged it all the way out here from her trailer, it can only have been for one reason.

"Hey, DJ, what do you say?"

That's always been good for a smile, but not today. She gives him a solemn look. "She's gone, if that's why you were staying inside."

Danny doesn't have to ask who DJ's talking about. Ella Davis was in the park earlier, knocking on doors and talking to anyone who was home. He expected her to make a visit to his trailer, but she never did; just took off her Covid mask and left.

"Where's your mom?"

"She hadda take Marielle's shift at the diner. Marielle's got impetigo." DJ says the word very carefully, syllable by syllable. "She said I could stay on my own and she'd bring me back a slice of cake. I don't want cake, I don't care if I ever have cake again. She told me I couldn't knock on your door, so I came here. So I'd see you when you came out."

Danny goes down the steps, walks half the distance to DJ, then stops. The dollhouse is open on its hinges and he can see Barbie and Ken inside, sitting at the kitchen table. Barbie sits with her legs stuck awkwardly out because her knees don't bend very well. There was a time when DJ and Danny discussed this, and other unrealistic attributes of various dolls—plastic skin, creepy hair—at some length.

"Why are you just standing there?" DJ asks.

Because he can feel eyes, of course. The accused killer and the defenseless little girl. Most people are at work, but some are at home— the ones Inspector Davis talked to—and they will be watching. Maybe he shouldn't care, but he does.

Before he can think of a reply, she says, "Ma ast if you ever *molested* me. I know what that means, it means stranger danger, and I said Danny would never *molest* me because he's my *friend*."

Darla Jean starts to cry.

"DJ, Jesus, don't—"

"You didn't kill that girl. *Did* you." Not a question.

Fuck the watchers. He goes to where she's sitting and squats down beside her. "No. They think I did because I had a dream of where she was buried, but I didn't kill her."

DJ swipes an arm across her eyes. "Ma says I can't come over your trailer anymore and you can't pick me up at school anymore. She says they'll either arrest you or you'll go away. Are they going to arrest you?"

"They can't because I didn't do anything wrong."

"Are you going away?"

"I have to. I don't have a job and most people don't want me here anymore."

"*I* want you! What if Ma decides she wants Bobby for a boyfriend again? *He* can't fix the car if it busts! I hate him, he sent me to my room once without my supper and Ma didn't stop him!"

She begins to sob, and double fuck the watchers, Danny puts an arm around her and pulls her to him. Her face against his shirt is hot and wet but okay. More than okay.

"She won't have Bob back," he says. "She knows better."

He has no idea if this is true, but hopes it is. He's never met his predecessor, for all Danny knows he could be a skinny bespectacled accountant who gets a kick out of sending little girls to their rooms, but he imagines a big hulk with a crewcut and lots of tattoos. Someone a little girl could really be scared of.

"Take me with you," DJ says against his shirt.

Danny laughs and gives her dark blond hair a scruff. "Then they'd arrest me for sure."

She looks up at him and gives him a tentative smile. That's when Althea Dumfries comes out of her trailer. "Let loose of that child!" she shouts. "Let loose of that child this minute or I'm calling the police!"

DJ shoots to her feet, tears still streaming down her face. *"Go fuck yourself! GO FUCK YOURSELF, YOU FAT BITCH!"*

Danny is horrified but also admiring. And even though he's sure Darla Jean just bought herself a whole boatload of trouble, he can't help thinking that he couldn't have said it better himself.

47

Ella Davis didn't think they made burgs like Cathcart anymore, even in dead-red central Kansas. It's a dusty one-stoplight town about forty miles north of Manitou. There's a Kwik Shop across from the rusty water tower (WELCOME TO CATHCART WHERE ALL LIVES MATTER is printed on the side). Davis buys herself an RC, and grabs a *Plains Truth* from the rack by the cash register. Danny Coughlin has made the front page, sandwiched between an ad for Royal Tires and one for the Discount Furniture Warehouse Where Every Day Is Sale Day. The headline reads SUSPECT CLAIMS "IT WAS ALL A DREAM."

Davis cranks up the AC in her car and reads the story before heading down Main Street. It's Peter Andersson's byline (excepting local sports, Andersson seems to write all the *Plains Truth* stories), and Davis doesn't think the *New York Times* will be calling him anytime soon. If Andersson's intent was irony, he fell far short, achieving only a kind of lumbering skepticism. Perversely, it makes her want to believe Danny's version. She tosses the miserable excuse for a newspaper behind her.

Plains Truth is on the street-level floor of a white-frame building halfway down Main Street. It's squeezed between a Dollar Tree and a long defunct Western Auto. It needs paint. The boards are loose, the nails bleeding streaks of red rust. The door is locked. She cups her hands to peer through the window and sees one large cluttered room with an old desktop computer presiding over it like an ancient god. The chair in front of the computer looks new, but the rest of the furniture looks like it was picked up either at a yard sale or on a dump-picking safari. A long bulletin board is drifted deep with ad mock-ups and old copy, some of it yellowed and curling with age.

"Hello, hello, hello, are you Davis?"

She turns to behold a very tall young man, perhaps six-seven or -eight. He's as skinny as a playing card. He's also strikingly pale at a time of year when most Kansans have at least a touch of tan. A Hitlerian forelock of black hair hangs over one eye. He brushes it back and it flops back down.

"I am," she says.

"Hold on, hold on, I'll unlock." He does so and they step in. She smells air freshener and beneath it, a ghost aroma of pot. "I was downstreet to see Ma. She's got the diabetes. Lost a foot last year. Would you like a cold drink? I think there's some in the——"

She holds up her bottle of RC.

"Oh. Right, right, okay, great. As for snacks, I'm afraid the cupboard is bare." He laughs—titters, actually—and brushes away the forelock. It promptly falls back. "I'm sorry it's so warm in here. The air conditioning's on the fritz. Always something, isn't it? We roll the rock, Sisyphus and all that."

Davis has no idea what he's talking about, but she realizes he's scared to death. Good.

"I didn't come here for snacks."

"No, of course not. Coughlin, the story about Coughlin."

"*Two* stories, it turns out."

"Two, yes, right, okay. As I said on the phone, I thought I was getting information from someone on the inside of the investigation. A policeman. In fact he said that. KHP, he said."

"Not KBI? The Kansas Bureau of Inves——"

"No, no, he was from the Highway Patrol, I'm sure, totally sure, positive." The forelock flops. Andersson brushes it back.

"He also gave you the information about the dream?"

"Yes, sure did, absolutely, even suggested I withhold that for my next issue. He said I'd still be scooping the regular newspapers. I thought that was a very good idea."

"Do you usually take advice from anonymous tipsters, Mr. Andersson?"

He gives the unsettling titter. Davis could more easily envision this man killing Yvonne than Coughlin; in a TV show he would turn out to be a serial killer with some strange alias, like The Reporter.

"I rarely *get* tips, Ms. Davis. We're basically an ad-based——"

"*Inspector* Davis," she corrects, not because she's in love with her title, but because she wants him to remember who has the hammer here.

"Asking again, did I print anything that wasn't true, Inspector Davis?"

"I'm not at liberty to say, and it's not the point. Although what you did was so irresponsible that I'd have trouble believing it if I hadn't read it myself."

"Now, now, that's a little—"

"I don't suppose you have a recording of this mystery call, do you?" She doesn't hold out much hope of that.

He gives her a wide-eyed look and another unsettling titter. "I record *everything*."

She thinks she must have misheard. "Everything? Really? Every phone-in?"

"I have to. This is a shoestring operation, Ms. . . . Inspector. I also work part-time at the lumberyard outside of town. You must have passed it on your way in. Wolf Lumber?"

She can't remember if she did or not. She was thinking about Jalbert. She gestures for Andersson to go on.

"While I'm out at the yard or seeing to Ma—she takes a lot of seeing to—every call I get, most of them are about ads but some are from Hurd Conway, he does the sports, are recorded and zip directly up to the Cloud."

"You don't erase them?"

He titters. "Why would I bother? Plenty of room on the Cloud. Many mansions, as the Good Book says. My soul hath elbow-room. Shakespeare. Our set-up might not work for a big city newspaper, but it's fine for us. Here, I'll show you."

Andersson wakes up his computer and types in a password. Davis is far from a compulsive neatnik, but the desktop's screen is so littered with icons that looking at it makes her eyes hurt. Andersson mouses to the phone icon and pushes it. A message blares from speakers on either side of the room. He winces and turns down the volume.

"You have reached *Plains Truth*, the voice of central Kansas and the best buy for your ad dollar. We are a free news and sports weekly, sometimes bi-weekly, that is given out *free of charge* in over six thousand locations in six counties."

If that's true, I'll eat my shorts, Ella thinks.

"If you have news, press 5. If you have a sports score, press 4. If you want to report an accident, press 3. If you want to place an ad, press 2. If you have a question about rates, push 1. That's 5 for news, 4 for sports, 3 for an accident report, 2 to place an ad, 1 for rates. And don't worry about getting cut off!" There's the titter she's coming to know all too well. "This is *Plaaaiiiins Truth*, where the truth matters!"

Andersson turns to her. "It's good, don't you think? All the bells and whistles. Bases covered."

Under other circumstances Davis—curious by nature—might ask Andersson how much ad revenue *Plains Truth* generates. But not under these. "Can you find that anonymous call?"

"Yes, sure. Tell me the date I'm searching for."

She doesn't know. "Try between June 30th and July 4th."

Andersson brings up a file. "That's a lot of incoming, but maybe . . ." He frowns. The forelock flops. "Some guy called in about a chimney fire, I think it was after that. Pretty sure."

Andersson clicks, listens, shakes his head, clicks some more. At last he gets a drawly farmer type who says he seen a chimbly fahr out on Farm Road 17. Andersson gives Davis a thumbs-up and goes to the next message. She has drawn up a chair next to him.

"It sounds funny, because—"

"*Shhh!*"

Andersson draws a finger across his lips, zipping them shut.

It does sound funny, because the caller was using a voice-altering device, maybe a vocoder. It sounds like a man, then a woman, then a man again.

"Hello, *Plains Truth*. I'm with the Kansas Highway Patrol. I'm not investigating the Yvonne Wicker murder but I've seen the reports. Your readers might like to know the man who discovered the body is Daniel M. Coughlin. He's a janitor at Wilder High School. He lives in the Oak Grove Trailer Park—"

"I never printed the address," Andersson says. "I thought that would be—"

"*Shhh!* Go back."

Andersson flinches and does something with his mouse.

"—Wilder High School. He lives in the Oak Grove Trailer Park in the town of Manitou. You should print that right away." There's a pause. "He is KBI's prime suspect because he claims he had a dream of where the body was. The investigators don't believe him. You might want to save that for a follow-up. Just a suggestion." There's another pause. Then the vocoder voice says, "Fifteen. Goodbye."

There's a click, followed by someone who wants *Plains Truth* to know the July 4th festivities in Wilder County have been postponed until the 8th, very sorry. Andersson kills the sound and looks at Davis. "Are you okay, ma'am?"

"Yes," she says. She's not. She's sick to her stomach. "Play it again."

She takes out her phone and hits record.

48

Back in her car, with the air conditioning on high, Davis listens to it again. Then she turns off her phone and stares through the windshield at Cathcart's dusty Main Street. She's thinking of an arson case she worked with Jalbert in the spring. It was in a rural town called Lindsborg. On their way to the site, they passed a field where a few cows were grazing. Ella, riding shotgun that day, counted them aloud, just for something to do.

"Seven," she said.

"Twenty-eight," Jalbert replied, with no pause.

She gave him a questioning look and he told her one to seven added up to twenty-eight. He said adding inclusively passed the time and also kept him mentally sharp. She thought her partner might have a little touch of OCD. She'd even looked up the name of that particular compulsion on her phone, then dismissed it. Everyone had their little tics, didn't they? She herself couldn't go to sleep until all the dishes were washed and put away . . . but she had never considered *counting* them.

Now, sitting in her car, she thinks of Peter Andersson's outgoing message. Five choices, and when you added one two three four five, the total was . . .

"Fifteen," she says. "It *was* him. Fuck. *Fuck!*"

She sits awhile longer, trying to convince herself that she's wrong. She can't do it. Absolutely can't. So she calls Troop C of the Kansas

Highway Patrol, identifies herself, and asks for a callback from Trooper Calten, as soon as possible.

While she waits for the callback—which she dreads—she asks herself what she's going to do with what she now knows.

49

Danny gets all the empty boxes he wants at Manitou Fine Liquors. He also gets a fifth of Jim Beam. At four o'clock that afternoon the boxes are piled up in his bedroom and the bottle of Beam is on the kitchen table. He sits there looking at it with his hands folded in front of him. He's trying to think of the last time he drank whiskey. Not on the night he got arrested for standing on Margie's lawn and shouting at her house; that night he'd been beered up. He'd downed almost a case of Coors between Manitou and Wichita. He could still remember vomiting it up into the stainless steel toilet of the cell they put him in, then going to sleep not on the bunk but underneath it, as if sleeping on concrete was some kind of penance.

He decides the last time he got into the high-tension stuff was fishing with Deke Mathers. The two of them were so loaded they didn't find their way out to Route 327 until it was almost dark, by then both of them badly hungover and promising never again, never again. He didn't know how that had worked out with Deke, Danny had lost touch with him since moving to Oak Grove, but he hadn't touched brown liquor since. Not any beer for the last couple of years, either.

Jim Beam won't solve his problems, he knows that. They'll still be there when he gets up on Tuesday morning, only with a hangover to add to his misery. But what it would do is to blot out DJ's sad face, at least for awhile. She said *What if Ma decides she wants Bobby for a boyfriend again?* She said *He can't fix the car if it busts!* She said (and somehow this was the worst of all, God knew why) *I don't want cake, I don't care if I ever have cake again.*

"That dream," he says. "That fucking goddam dream."

Only the dream isn't really the problem. Jalbert is the problem. Jalbert has sprayed his goddam life with his version of Agent Orange.

198

He's trying to poison everything, including a little girl who thought her life was pretty much okey-dokey: her mom finally had a boyfriend Darla Jean liked, who didn't shout and send her from the table without her supper.

Jalbert.

All Jalbert.

Danny unscrews the cap, tips the bottle toward himself, takes a good long sniff. He remembers how he and Deke Mathers laughed there on the riverbank, everything fine. Then he remembers how they cursed as they shoved through that final blackberry tangle to the road, getting all scratched up and sweating into those scratches, making the sting even worse.

Jalbert would love you to get drunk, he thinks. *Get drunk and do something stupid.*

He goes into the bathroom, pours the whiskey into the toilet, and flushes it away. Then he starts packing his clothes into boxes. He can't beat Jalbert except by leaving, so that's what he's going to do. He'll get to spend time with Stevie, who knows where everything is in the Table Mesa King Soopers. As for Darla Jean . . . she'll have to find her way. In the end, most kids do. So he tells himself.

50

I'm not angry, Jalbert thinks as he drives back to his hotel in Lyons. *Just upset.*

The meeting in Wichita didn't go well. He argued for taking Coughlin in. Forty-eight hours, he said. We can call it protective custody. Just let me sweat him. I'll break him down. He's ready. I know it.

Protective custody from who? That was Tishman, the Director in Charge. Neville, the Assistant Director, sat next to him nodding like a puppet. *The killer? Coughlin doesn't claim to know him. He only claims to know where the body was because of the dream he had.*

Jalbert asked those in attendance—including Ramsey, the stolid, close-mouthed detective from Oklahoma—if any of them believed Coughlin's dream story. The unanimous belief was that no one did.

Coughlin was the killer. But with no confession and no physical evidence tying him to the crime . . .

And so on.

Jalbert needs to do some counting. That would settle him. With a clear head he'll be able to decide on his next move. When he gets back to the hotel he'll run the chairs, take a shower, and call Ella. Maybe she's picked up a lead at the trailer park. Or possibly Coughlin has given something away, but probably not. He's a sly one—got rid of the drugs, didn't he?—but he's paying a price. He's out of a job and his neighbors have turned against him. He's got to be angry, and angry people make mistakes.

But I'm not angry. Just upset, and why? Because he did it, and he'll do it again.

"Don't they see that?" he asks, and bangs on the steering wheel. "Are they really that blind?"

Answer: they are not.

Every video feed between Arkansas City, where Miss Yvonne spent her last night, and the Gas-n-Go where she was last seen has been checked. Several Tundras were spotted, but none were white and all were newer than Danny's.

He used a different vehicle when he took her, Jalbert thinks. *That's why we didn't find any DNA or other evidence in his truck. Clever, so clever.*

Jalbert began—Ella did, too—by believing that Danny wanted either to be a media star or to confess. Ella may still believe those things, but Jalbert no longer does. *It's a game to him. He's sticking it in our faces and saying prove it, prove it, arrest me, arrest me, ha-ha, you can't, can you? You know my story is bullshit and there's not a damn thing you can do about it.*

Jalbert bangs the steering wheel again.

Fifteen years ago, even ten, it was a different playing field with different rules. Coughlin would have been in a little room with Jalbert and Davis and they'd sweat him until he gave it up. Ten hours, twelve, it wouldn't matter. Turn and turn about, whap-whap-whap. They were advocates for poor Miss Yvonne and all the girls that might follow her, they'd go at him tirelessly in a room with no clock.

You have to be hungry. Give us something and we'll send someone out for chow. You like Burger King? There's one right up the street. Whopper, fries, chocolate shake, how does that sound? At least tell us when you buried her. Day or night? No? Okay, let's start again, from the beginning.

Like that.

Jalbert begins counting barns and silos and farmhouses to pass the time. He's up to twenty-three (which, added in arithmetical progression, totals 276) when his phone rings. It's Ella. He expects her to ask how it went in Wichita, but she doesn't. Instead she asks when he expects to get back to his hotel. Her voice is clipped and tight, she hardly sounds like herself. Could it be excitement because she has something?

Just a thread, that's all I ask. We'll follow it. We'll follow it all the way through hell, if that's what it takes.

"I should be there in forty minutes. What have you got?"

"I'm on the road from Manitou now. I'll meet you there."

"Come on, give." He runs his hand through the peninsula of his hair. "Did Coughlin tell you something?"

"Not on the phone."

"Make that half an hour," Jalbert says, and speeds up.

51

Ella is waiting in the lobby when Frank comes in. She dreads the impending conversation, but will do what has to be done. It would be worse if she liked Frank. She's tried to do that and failed, but until the last couple of days she respected him. In a way she respects him still. He is fiercely dedicated to the job, to getting justice for the woman he calls "poor Miss Yvonne." It's just that his dedication has crossed a line and when it did, it turned into something else.

He gives her a smile, showing those eroded teeth that really need caps. The thick triangle of his widow's peak is disarranged, as if he's been running a hand through it. Perhaps pulling at it. "Let's go to my so-called suite. It's not great—the only view is of the parking lot—but it fits the expense account."

Ella follows. She doesn't know why he's formed such a fierce connection with the Wicker girl—or is it Coughlin he's made a connection with?—but she knows it's put pressure on some fundamental crack in his personality. What was once a hairline is now a fissure.

He unlocks the door. She goes in ahead of him and stops, looking around the suite's boxy little living room. "What's up with the folding chairs?"

"Nothing. I just . . . nothing."

He goes to the two in the living room and claps them shut. He goes into the bedroom and comes back with two more. He leans them against the wall beside the TV. "I have to take those back to the business center. Been meaning to. Want a soft drink? There's plenty in the minibar."

"No, thank you."

"Is it Coughlin? Did he let something slip?"

"I didn't talk to him."

Jalbert frowns. "I specifically asked you to re-interview him, Ella." Then the frown lightens. "Was it Becky? The girlfriend? Or the daughter! Did she—"

"Listen, Frank. There's no easy way to say this. You have to step away from the case. That's for starters."

He's giving her a quizzical little smile. He has no idea what she's talking about.

"Then it's time for you to retire. You've got your twenty years. Twenty and more."

"I don't—"

"And get some professional help."

The little smile is still there. "You're talking nonsense, Ella. I'm not going to retire. Not even thinking about it. What I'm going to do—what *we're* going to do—is collar Danny Coughlin and put him behind bars for the rest of his life."

She's surprised by fury, but later she'll think it was there all along. "What you're *doing* is risking any chance we have of making a case against him! You outed him to *Plains Truth*, Frank!"

The smile is fading. "What gave you that crazy idea?"

"It's not crazy, it's a fact. You outed him and you outed yourself with your counting thing. At the end of the message you left, you said fifteen. It had nothing to do with anything . . . except when you add the number of choices on the menu together, one to five, you get fifteen."

Now the smile is gone. "On the basis of *one number* you jump to the conclusion that I—"

"Sometimes a random number pops out of your mouth—half the time you don't even know you're doing it. That's what happened on the recording Peter Andersson played for me. I heard it. You can hear it, too, if you want to. I've got it on my phone."

His lips part in a grin, showing those eroded teeth. *He grinds them,* she thinks. *Of course he does.*

"I wouldn't want to report you for these false accusations, Ella. You've been a good partner, couldn't ask for a better one. But if you persist, I'll have to. There's no way you could have recognized the voice that made that call—that *anybody* could recognize it—because it was disguised by some gadget."

"Yes. It was. But how do *you* know that?"

He blinks and there's the briefest of hesitations. Then he says, "Because I asked him. Andersson. I interviewed him."

"Not at any time when I was with you."

"No, from here. On the phone."

"Will he confirm that?"

"I'm confirming it to you right now."

"Nevertheless, I'll ask him. If I have to. And we both know what he'll say, don't we?"

Jalbert doesn't reply. He's looking at her as if she were a stranger. *And probably right now that's just how he feels.*

She points to the chairs. "Do you count those? Or maybe set them up and count the steps between them?"

"I think you better leave."

"I see your lips moving sometimes when you're counting. There's even a name for it. Arithmomania."

"Get out. Think about what you're saying and we'll talk when you're not . . . not all wound up."

Davis is suddenly too tired to stand. Who knew how exhausting confrontations of this sort could be? She sits and puts her open purse on the little desk. Her phone is inside, recording.

"You also planted drugs in Coughlin's truck. At the high school."

He recoils as if she had struck at him with her fist. "That's an out-rageous accusation!"

"It was outrageous that you did it. Coughlin got suspicious when the kid who works with him saw you park in back instead of in the faculty lot. Coughlin searched his truck, found the dope, and turned it over to me."

"*What?* When?"

"I met him at a coffee shop in Great Bend after the meeting where he challenged us to arrest him. Which we could not do then and can't now, as I'm sure you found out in Wichita."

"He's a liar! And you went behind my back! Thanks, *partner*!"

She flushes. She can't help it.

Jalbert is running his hands through his thick mat of receding hair. "If there were drugs in his truck, he planted them himself. He's sly, oh boy, is he ever. And you actually believed his story?" Jalbert shakes his head. His tone is pitying, but what she sees in his eyes is bare unvarnished fury. *Be careful of this man*, she thinks, *Danny was right about that.*

"I had no idea you were so credulous, Ella. Has he convinced you of his dream story, too? Are you on his side now?"

"I've spoken to Trooper Calten."

That stops him.

"Coughlin saw his name tag. I called Calten and told him I knew who set up the plant and the search. I said I'd keep his participation quiet if he told me what his role was. He did."

Jalbert goes to the window, looks out, then comes back to her. "I didn't want him for the dope. I wanted him for Miss Yvonne. I wanted him locked up so I could turn the screws. Where's the dope now?"

"In a safe place." That last question is a tiny bit frightening. She doesn't really believe Frank would hurt her, but he's not right. There's no question of that.

He goes to the window again and comes back again. His lips are moving. He's counting. Does he even know he's doing it? She doesn't think so.

"He killed her. Raped her and killed her. Coughlin. You know he did."

She thinks of Coughlin asking her about her cross—did she wear it just for show, or was she a believer? Then he asked her if she could believe in God but not his dream.

"Frank, listen carefully. In this context it no longer matters whether he killed her or not. Here in this room all that matters is you telling me you're going to write an email to Don Tishman saying you need to take a leave of absence for personal reasons and you're planning to retire."

"Never!" He's clenching and unclenching his fists.

"Either that or I go to Tishman and tell him what you've done. The call to Andersson might not get you fired, but the dope thing certainly will. More, it will muddy up any case we might be able to make against Danny Coughlin so completely that even that smalltown lawyer Ball could get him off."

"You'd do that?"

"*You* did it!" Davis cries, standing up. "You screwed the case, you screwed yourself, and you screwed me, as well! Look at the mess you made!"

"We can't let him get away," Jalbert says. He's looking around the room, eyes not settling anywhere. "He did it."

"If you believe that, don't fuck up any chance we have of nailing him. I'm leaving now. It's a big decision, I know. Sleep on it."

"Sleep?" he says, and laughs. "Sleep!"

"I'll call you tomorrow morning. See how you feel. But the choice is pretty clear, it seems to me. Step down and we still have a chance of making a case against Coughlin. There'll be no nasty mess about planted evidence and you get to keep your pension."

"*Do you think I care about my pension?*" he shouts. Cords stand out on his neck. Ella keeps her eyes locked on his. She's afraid to take them away.

"You might not care about it now, in the heat of the moment, but you will later. And I know you still care about Yvonne Wicker. Think carefully, Frank. I'll let this slide if you step away, but it all comes out if you don't, and oy vey, the stench."

She walks to the door. It's one of the longest walks of her life because she keeps expecting him to come after her. He doesn't. In the hallway, with the door closed, she lets out a breath she didn't know she was holding. She starts to zip her purse closed when from behind her comes a crash. Something just broke. Does she want to know what? She doesn't. Ella walks slowly and steadily down the hall.

In her car, she lowers her head and cries. There was a moment there, just a moment, when she really thought he might kill her.

52

Franklin Jalbert has stayed in hundreds of motel rooms during his career as an investigator, crisscrossing Kansas from north to south and east to west. Almost all of those rooms come with plastic glasses in little baggies, mostly printed with slogans like SANITIZED FOR YOUR SAFETY. The glasses on top of the minibar of his little suite in the Celebration Centre just happen to be real glass. He registers the weight of the one he's picked up before it's too late to stop—and he probably wouldn't have stopped, anyway. He hurls it against the door Davis has just left, and it shatters.

Better the glass than her, he thinks. *Not that I would ever hurt her.*

Of course not. She may be a traitor, but they put in some good time together. Caught some bad boys and bad girls. He taught Ella, and she was eager to learn. Only she hasn't learned enough, it seems. She doesn't understand how dangerous Coughlin is. He wonders if perhaps after their traitorous meeting at the coffee shop, they might have gone somewhere else. Maybe to a motel?

No, no, she'd never. Not with the prime suspect in a murder case.

Never? Really? *Never?*

Coughlin's not a bad-looking man, and he has a wide-eyed *I'm telling the truth* look about him. Some might find that appealing. Is it really beyond the realm of possibility that she . . . and he . . . maybe kind of a weird twist on the Stockholm Syndrome . . . ?

In spite of her backstabbing, he can't believe it of her. And never mind Ella. She's out of the picture. The question is what he's going to do about Coughlin.

The answer seems to be . . . nothing. She's put him in a box. *That damned spineless trooper had to spill his guts, didn't he?*

The idea of retiring, as she suggested, is awful. Like being marched toward the edge of a cliff. He can't imagine stepping off into the void. He has no hobbies except for the daily newspaper crossword and the occasional jigsaw puzzle. His vacations have consisted of aimless wanderings in a rented camper, seeing sights he doesn't care about and snapping pictures he rarely looks at later. Each hour feels three hours long. Retirement would multiply those long hours by a thousand, then two thousand, then ten thousand. Each hour haunted by thoughts of Danny Coughlin looking at him across the table with that wide-eyed wouldn't-hurt-a-fly gaze, saying *Arrest me. You can't, can you?* Thoughts of Danny Coughlin stopping in some other state for another young girl with her thumb out and a pack on her back.

And what can I do?

Well, he can do one thing; pick up the broken glass. He brings over a wastebasket, kneels down, and starts doing that. Pretty soon he's up to 57 shards, 1,653 when added in progression.

I wouldn't have hurt her, absolutely not. But there was one second—

Sharp pain needles the ball of his thumb. A bead of blood appears. Jalbert realizes he's lost count. He debates starting again from one.

53

Danny Coughlin's last week in Manitou, Kansas, is both sad and a relief.

On Tuesday he finds a big pile of dogshit in his mailbox. He dons a pair of his rubber work gloves, removes it, and washes the inner surface clean. Someone will want to use that mailbox after he's gone.

On Wednesday he goes to Food Town to pick up a few final supplies, including a steak he plans to eat on Friday night as a goodbye dinner. He's not in the market for long, but when he comes out the two back tires of his truck are flat.

At least they're not punctured, he thinks, but probably just because whoever did it wasn't carrying a knife. He calls Jesse because Jesse's number is in his contacts and he can't think of anyone else who might give him a help. Jesse says his dad left a lot of stuff when he ran out on his family, and one of those things was a Hausbell tire inflator. "Give me twenty minutes," he says.

While Danny waits, he stands beside his truck and collects dirty looks. Jesse arrives in his beat-up Caprice and the Tundra's back tires are good to go in no time. Danny thanks him, alarmed to feel tears threatening.

"No problem," Jesse says, and holds out his hand. "Listen, man, I gotta say it again. I know you didn't kill that girl."

"Thanks for that, too. How's the sawmill? I was driving by and saw you hauling lumber in a shortbox."

Jesse shrugs. "It's a paycheck. What's up with you, Danny? What's next?"

"Getting out of town this weekend. I'm thinking Nederland to start with. I'll camp out, I've got some gear, and look for a job. And a place."

Jesse sighs. "Probably for the best, the way things are. Shoot me a text when you get someplace." He gives Danny a shy look that's all seventeen. "You know, stay in touch."

"I'll do that," Danny says. "Don't cut off any fingers at that mill."

Jesse flashes a grin. "Got the same advice from my moms. She says I'm the man of the house now."

On Thursday, most of his stuff packed and ready to go, the trailer looking nude somehow, he gets a call from Edgar Ball while he's drinking his first cup of coffee. Ball says, "I have bad news, good news, and really good news. At least I think it is. Which do you want first?"

Danny sets his cup down with a bang. "Did they catch him? The guy who killed her?"

"Not that good, I'm afraid," Ball says. "The bad news is that it's not just *Plains Truth* anymore. You're in the *Telescope*, the *Wichita Eagle*, the *Kansas City Star*, and the *Oklahoman*. Along with your picture."

"Fuck," Danny says.

"The good news is the picture they're running has got to be ten years old. You've got hair down to your shoulders and a biker 'stash. Looks like you're standing in front of a bar, but I might only think that because you're holding up a bottle of beer in each hand."

"Probably the Golden Rope in Kingman. Before I married Margie I used to do a lot of drinking there. I think it burned down."

"Don't know about that," Ball says cheerfully, "but that photo doesn't look anything like you now. You ready for the best news?"

"Lay it on me."

"It came from a friend who's a clerk in Troop F of the Highway Patrol. That's in Kechi, near Wichita. I used to date the lady in question, but that was in another life. She knows you retained me. She called last night and said Frank Jalbert is taking a leave of absence. Rumor is he's going to retire."

Danny feels a big grin break over his face. It's the first real one since he woke up after that fucking dream. Jalbert has haunted his thoughts. Not even talking to Stevie can get the inspector entirely out of his mind. He reminds Danny of some animal—maybe a wolverine?—that supposedly won't unclamp its jaws from whatever it's bitten even after it's dead.

"That really is good news."

"Want to go out to Dabney's to celebrate? Big breakfast, I'm buying."

Dabney's is two towns over and should be safe enough, especially if the picture the newspapers are running is from the days when Danny wanted to look like Lonesome Dave Peverett from Foghat.

"Sounds good. I might bring a friend. The kid I used to work with."

But Jesse says he can't, as much as he'd like to. He punches in at eight. "Also, my mom was pretty mad that I went out to help you yesterday. I told her you didn't do what they were saying and she said that didn't matter, because I was a young Black man and you were . . . you know."

"A white man accused of murder," Danny says. "I get it."

"Well, yeah. But I'd go anyway if I didn't have to work."

"I appreciate that, Jess, but your mom is probably right."

He goes out to Dabney's. Ball is there. They order huge breakfasts and eat every bite. Danny offers to split the check but Ball won't hear of it. He asks Danny what comes next for him. Danny tells him about his plan to go to Colorado to be near his brother, who's on the spectrum but has a gift a psychologist who examined him in his late teens called "global recognition." Basically, he sees where everything is. They talk about that for awhile.

"Got something in mind," Ball says as they leave the restaurant. "I've been thinking about it ever since our first go-round with that hairball Jalbert, but then I got reading the comments in the *Eagle* and the *Telescope* and I thought yeah, maybe, might work."

"I have no idea what you're talking about. What comments?"

"I guess you don't read them. It's the equivalent of letters to the editor in the old days. After you finish reading the story, you can comment on it. There are lots of comments on the stories about you."

"Hang him fast and hang him high," Danny says.

"There are some like that, sure, but you'd be surprised how many people believe you actually did dream where the body was. Everyone— those that believe you, I mean—has a story about how their grammaw knew the propane was going to explode and got everyone out of the house, or that the plane was going to crash so they took a later flight—"

"Those are premonitory dreams," Danny says. He's done some reading. "Not the same."

"Yes, but there are also comments from people who dreamed the location of a lost ring or a lost dog or in one case a missing kid. This woman claims she dreamed a neighbor boy fell down an old well, and there he was. It's not just you, Danny. And people love stuff like that, because it gives them the idea that there's more to the world than we know." He pauses. "Of course, there are also people who think you're so full of shit you squeak."

That makes Danny laugh.

At Danny's truck Ball says, "Okay, so here's what I'm thinking. It might be a way to get a little money, but that's really secondary. It would be a way to fight back."

"You're thinking . . . what? Filing a lawsuit?"

"Exactly. For harassment. Someone hucked a brick at your trailer, right?"

"Right . . ."

"Dogshit in your mailbox, let the air out of your tires . . ."

"Pretty thin," Danny says. "And I thought cops were protected from that sort of thing. Jalbert may retire, but he was a cop in good standing when he came after me."

"Ah, but he planted drugs on you," Ball says, "and if we can get the cop who rousted you in court, and under oath . . . can we go back to your trailer and talk about it? I mean, what else have you got to do?"

"Not much," Danny admits. "Sure, I guess we could talk about it."

He drives back to Oak Grove with Ball behind him on his Honda. Danny pulls up at his trailer and sees someone sitting on the concrete block steps, head down, hands dangling between his knees. Danny gets out of his truck, closes the door, and for a moment just stands there, struck by *déjà vu*. Almost overwhelmed by it. His visitor is wearing a high school letter jacket—where has he seen that before? Ball's Honda Gold Wing pulls up behind his truck. The kid stands up and raises his head. Then Danny knows. It's the kid from the newspaper photo, the one standing in front of the hearse and behind his grief-stricken parents.

"Bastard, you killed my sis," the kid says. He reaches into the right pocket of his letter jacket and brings out a revolver.

Behind Danny, the Gold Wing shuts off and Ball dismounts, but that's in another universe.

"Whoa, son. I didn't—"

That's as far as he gets before the kid fires. A fist hits Danny in the midsection. He takes a step back and then the pain comes, like the worst acid indigestion attack he ever had. The pain goes up to his throat and down to his thighs. He gropes behind him for the door-handle of his Tundra and can barely feel it when he finds it. His legs are getting loopy. He tells them not to buckle. Warmth is running down his stomach. His shirt and jeans are turning red.

"Hey!" Ball shouts from that other universe. "Hey, *gun*!"

No shit, Danny thinks. With his weight to pull it, the driver's door of the Tundra swings open. Danny doesn't fall where he stands only because he opened his window on the way back from Dabney's. The morning air was so cool and fresh. That seems like another lifetime. He hooks his elbow through the window and around the doorpost and pivots like a stripper on a pole. The kid fires again and there's a *plung* sound as the bullet hits the door below the open window.

"*Gun! GUN!*" Edgar Ball is shouting.

The next bullet goes through the open window and buzzes past Danny's right ear. He sees the kid's cheeks are wet with tears. He sees Althea Dumfries standing on the top step of her trailer—*fanciest one in the park*, Danny thinks, crazy what goes through your head when you're shot. She appears to be holding a piece of toast with a bite out of it.

Danny goes to his knees. The pain in his abdomen is excruciating. He hears another *plung* as another bullet strikes the Tundra's open door. Then he's all the way down. He can see the kid's feet. He's wearing Converse sneakers. Danny sees the gun when the kid drops it on the ground. Ball is still yelling. *Ball is bawling*, he thinks, and then the world slides into darkness.

54

He comes to on a stretcher. Edgar Ball is looking down at him, eyes wide. There's dirt smeared on his cheeks and forehead. He's saying something, it might be *hang in there buddy*, and then the stretcher bumps something and the pain explodes, the pain becomes the world. Danny tries to scream and can only moan. For a moment there's sky, then a roof above him and he thinks *it might be an ambulance, how'd it get here so fast, how long was I out*.

Someone says "Little pinch and then you'll feel better."

There's a pinch. Darkness follows.

55

When it goes away he sees lights sliding by above him. It's like a shot in a movie. A loudspeaker calls for Dr. Broder. *Doctor Broder, stat*, it says. Danny tries to speak, tries to say *is it the Good Doctor, the one on TV*, just as a joke, he knows better, but all that comes out are a few muffled sounds because he's got some kind of a mask over his mouth and nose. Doors bang open. There are brighter lights and green tile walls. He supposes it's an operating room and he wants to say he doesn't know

212

if he can afford an operation because he lost his job. Hands hoist him and oh Jesus Savior it hurts.

There's a pinch. Darkness follows.

56

Now he's in a bed. Has to be a hospital bed. There's light, but not the cruel we're-going-to-cut-you-open lights shining down in that green room. No, this is daylight. Margie, his ex, is sitting by his bed. She's all dolled up and Danny knows that if she dressed up for him he's probably going to die. His midsection is stiff. Stiff as a plank. Bandages, maybe, and there's an IV hanging on a hook and he thinks *if they're putting stuff into me maybe I'm not going to die.* Margie asks, "How do you feel, Danno," like in the old days when they still got along, like *book 'em, Danno*, and he tries to answer but can't.

Darkness.

57

He opens his eyes and Edgar Ball is sitting by his bed. No dirt on his face, so he must have cleaned up. How much time has passed? Danny has no idea. "Close call but you're going to pull through," Ball tells him, and Danny thinks *that's what they all say.* On the other hand maybe it's the truth.

"Good thing you got behind the truck door. If he'd been shooting a larger caliber gun the bullets would have gone right through. But it was a .32."

"Kid," he manages.

"Albert Wicker," Ball says. "Yvonne Wicker's brother."

I knew that, Danny tries to say.

"Fired three or four times, dropped the gun, walked right past me. Went out to the street and sat down on the curb and waited for the cops. In a movie I would have tackled him, but the truth is I face-planted beside my motorcycle at the first gunshot. Sorry."

"Okay," Danny says. "You . . . okay."

"Thanks for saying that. We've got a *real* suit now, Danny. Soon as you get better."

Danny tries to smile. He closes his eyes.

Darkness.

58

Is it Jesse next time? Or a dream? They're giving him a lot of dope, so he can't be sure. But he's positive (*almost* positive) that he sees a dark brown hand over his white one.

59

Next time he surfaces it's Ella Davis. He's a little stronger and she looks a little younger in faded jeans and a boatneck tee. Her hair is down. And she is smiling.

"Danny? Are you awake?"

"Yes." A bare croak. "Water. Is there—"

She holds a glass for him. There's a bendy straw sticking out of it. He drinks and it's heaven on his throat.

"Danny, we got him."

"The kid?" His voice is a little stronger. "I think Edgar told the cops—"

"Not the kid, *him*. The man who killed Yvonne Wicker. He . . . are you getting this? Do you understand what I'm telling you?"

"Yes." Does he feel relieved? Vindicated? He can't tell. He's not even sure how badly he's hurt, or if he'll ever be really well again. What if he has to spend the rest of his life shitting into a bag?

"He's confessed, Danny. Confessed to Wicker and two others. Cops in Illinois and Missouri are looking for the bodies."

"All right," Danny says. He's very tired. He wants her to go.

"I went to Mass and prayed for you."

"It helps if you believe," Danny says.

He feels her take his hand, her skin cool on his. He thinks he should tell her he doesn't blame her, but the very idea of blame seems pointless right now. He turns his head. Floats away.

Darkness.

60

By the third day he hurts bad but he's back in the world. He understands he's at Regional Hospital in Great Bend, and he's going to be here at least a week, maybe ten days. The bullet perforated his stomach. He's been repaired and sewed up, but Broder, the doctor in charge of his case, says if he tries to walk, even to the bathroom, he's apt to open it up again. "Be grateful it wasn't a soft-nosed slug and a bigger caliber. That would have done a *lot* of damage. You'll be on soft food for awhile. I hope you like scrambled eggs and yogurt."

Being in bed means the bedpan, but the indignity of that is mitigated by the fact that he's been spared the catheter and colostomy bag. He learns that Margie was allowed to see him early on because she claimed to be his wife, which wasn't true. Edgar Ball was allowed to see him because he claimed to be his lawyer, which was. Ella Davis was also allowed in, because she was a KBI officer and because she said she had good news to share—very good. And Jesse? That might have been a drug-induced hallucination, but Danny doesn't believe it. He thinks Jesse slipped in somehow, and took his hand. At some point he'll have to ask him.

Stevie doesn't know, and that's good. It would upset him. Danny will have to tell him at some point, but that's for later.

Late in the afternoon of his fourth day at the hospital, he's allowed to sit by the window in his room—two steps, supported by a pair of orderlies. While he's enjoying the feel of the sun on his face, Edgar Ball comes to see him again. He sits on the bed and asks Danny how he feels.

"Not bad. The dope is primo."

"What do you want to know?"

"Everything."

"That will strain my powers of condensation. They're only giving me twenty minutes. Then they have to put you back to bed and irrigate you." Ball grimaces. "I don't even want to know what that entails."

"Davis told me they caught the guy who killed Yvonne Wicker, but I passed out before she could give me any details. Start there."

"His name is Andrew Iverson, no fixed address. An itinerant Mr. Fixit. He was heading west, driving a little blue panel truck with ANDY I., PLUMBING AND HEATING on the side. It showed up on video both in Arkansas City where Wicker last stayed and at the Gas-n-Go where she was last spotted. He's also on video in Great Bend, Manitou, and Cawker City."

"Cawker's close to Dart County, isn't it?"

"Yes. Wicker was probably dead in the back of his truck when he drove through there. He was looking for a lonely spot to bury her."

"And found one."

"Iverson's picture should be in the encyclopedia next to the entry for serial killers. He drives, stops for awhile, does some business—cash only, he told the cops, because, he says, cash don't tell."

"You got this from Davis?"

"Yes. We had a long talk. She feels terrible about this whole business."

She's not the only one, Danny thinks.

"Iverson killed a girl in Illinois and another in Missouri. Buried them in rural locations. The cops have found one, they're still looking for the other. He picked up a fourth girl hitchhiking in Wyoming, outside a little town called Glenrock. He pulled over on some country road and tried to rape her. She had a knife in her boot. While he was getting his pants down, she stabbed him four times."

"Good for her," Danny says. He thinks of the dog that was chewing on Yvonne Wicker's arm. "Goddam good for her."

"Davis says this was one tough chick. She tumbled him out of the van, drove toward Casper until she had a cell signal, and called the police. He wasn't where the girl said he was, but they followed a blood trail to a nearby barn. He was in a horse stall, passed out from blood loss. Davis says he's going to recover."

"He confessed? She told me he confessed. Unless I dreamed that part."

"You didn't. Wounds hurt, as I think you know. You got shot once. Iverson got stabbed four times, once in the cheek, once in the shoulder, once in the side, and once in the leg. He wanted painkillers. The cops wanted information. They both got what they wanted."

"Davis told you all that?"

"She did, and asked me to tell you. I think she's afraid to face you again."

"I get that, but I guess in the end she did her job."

"She stood up to Jalbert, if that's what you mean, but that's a story for another day. My twenty minutes are almost up. Do you remember the charm bracelet the Wicker girl was wearing?"

Danny remembers. He saw it twice, once in his dream and once in real life.

"Iverson had two of the charms in his kill-sack. As trophies. There was more stuff in there. From the other two."

"Where's the kid that shot me?"

"Albert Wicker is in a Manitou motel with his folks. He made bail. Or rather, his parents did. I know the lawyer who represented him at his arraignment. He says the Wickers mortgaged their house to come up with the money."

Danny thinks about that. Daughter dead, son facing attempted murder charges, parents probably facing bankruptcy. *And I'm in the hospital with a hole in my stomach*, Danny thinks. The wandering plumber did a lot of damage, and that's just the spreading circle of pain around the young woman Jalbert insisted on calling "poor Miss Yvonne." Danny wishes the girl who got away, the fabled Last Girl, had stabbed Iverson in the balls for good measure.

"I don't want to press charges," Danny says.

Edgar Ball smiles. "Am I surprised? I am not. But it's not entirely up to you. Wicker will do some time, but considering the mitigating circumstances, it may not be much."

A nurse pokes her head in the door. "Sir, you need to let my good pal Danny rest. Plus, he needs some services you won't want to be around for."

"Irrigation," Danny says glumly. "This doesn't happen when someone gets shot on TV."

"Five more minutes," Ball says. "Please."

"You can have three," the nurse says, and leaves.

"I had a meeting with Don Tishman, who was technically in charge of the KBI investigation. I laid out the facts of the matter concerning Jalbert, but felt it would be smart to withhold the name of the trooper who stopped you and looked for drugs."

"For a smalltown lawyer who specializes in real estate contracts, you've been pretty busy."

Danny means it lightly, almost as a joke, but Ball flushes and looks down at his hands. "I should have tackled that kid. I could have, he was totally focused on you. Instead I went facedown in the dirt."

Danny repeats that it's not like TV.

Ball raises his head. "Understood, but I don't have to like it. No man wants to think he's a coward, especially one that rides a badass bike."

"I wouldn't call a Honda Gold Wing badass, Edgar. A Harley Softail, that's badass."

"Be that as it may, we've reached an accommodation. I think. A few details still to be worked out, but . . . yes, it looks good. In exchange for keeping quiet about Jalbert—who has indeed put in his retirement papers—you're going to have your medical bills paid by the Sunflower State, and with a certain sum left over. Not huge, but tidy. Five figures. It will get you relocated in Colorado, if you still decide to go."

The nurse doesn't just poke her head in this time. She points at Ball. "Not asking. Telling."

"Going," Ball says, and gets up. "You could have your job back, you know. Once you're well enough to do it."

"Good to know," Danny says.

He has no intention of staying. Someone threw a brick at his trailer. Someone put shit in his mailbox. Bill Dumfries basically told him, on behalf of the good people of Oak Grove, to get out of Dodge. What weighs against those things is Darla Jean sitting in the dirt next to her dollhouse with tears rolling down her cheeks. But he doesn't think it weighs enough to tip the scales. He has a brother in Colorado, and if getting shot does nothing else, it gives you insight into how short the time is you have to spend with your loved ones.

"All because of one dream," he says bitterly. "It didn't even help catch the guy."

"But think of the adventure you had."

Danny shows him a middle finger.

"On that note," Ball says, and takes his leave.

61

While Albert Wicker is spending his first afternoon in the Wilder County jail, hardly aware of what he did—the last few days are a blur, that morning hardly there at all—Franklin Jalbert is sitting in his dining room in his bathrobe doing a thousand-piece jigsaw puzzle.

When completed, it will show a collage of movie posters—classics like *Casablanca, It's a Wonderful Life, Jaws*, two dozen in all. Jalbert keeps track of how many pieces he's put in. After 10 pieces, he takes one step (in place, as if marching, so he can sit down again). After 20, he takes two, one out from his chair and one back. He's up to 800 pieces, almost done, when his phone rings. He looks at the screen and sees H. Allard. Hank Allard is a friend of his, a captain in the Kansas Highway Patrol. Jalbert is torn between answering and doing the next set of steps, which would be one to eighty, inclusive.

He decides on the steps. 3,240—quite a lot! He starts at 80 and counts in reverse. The steps take him outside to the small backyard of his ranchette and back again. He sees that previous trips have made a path in the grass: a rut, in fact. He's aware that the step-counting thing—and running the chairs, that too—has gotten even more out of control since his failure to arrest Danny Coughlin. Davis called it arithmomania. While doing the steps associated with his jigsaw puzzle, Jalbert often thinks he's like a hamster running on a wheel, going and going, shitting on the run and never getting anywhere. But that's all right. What Davis couldn't realize is that this minor craziness keeps him from the greater craziness of contemplating a future from which his job has been subtracted. How many jigsaw puzzles can he do before facing the pointlessness of his life going forward and slides his service weapon deep into his mouth? Boom, gone. God knows he wouldn't be the first. God knows he's thought about it. Is thinking.

He comes back to the steps when he's down to five. By the time he gets to zero, he's in the kitchen. Time for another 10 pieces and then he'll count down from 81. Possibly first by odd numbers, then doing the even ones. After that it will be time for lunch, and a nap. He loves his naps. Such smooth oblivion!

His phone is beside the mostly completed jigsaw puzzle (he's currently assembling *The Ten Commandments*, which he most definitely doesn't consider a classic). Hank Allard has left a voicemail, and he sounds excited.

"Call me, I've got news. You'll want to hear."

Jalbert can't imagine any news he wants to hear, but he returns the call. Allard answers on the first ring and wastes no time. "Your boy Coughlin has been shot."

"What?" Jalbert stands up, giving the table a hard bump and sliding the nearly completed puzzle almost to the edge. Several pieces patter to the floor.

Allard laughs. "The Wicker girl's brother shot the motherfucker. You want to talk about justice? Whoomp, there it is."

"Is he dead?"

"We can hope. The first trooper to respond to the scene said there was a lot of blood and several bullet holes in the bastard's truck. They took him to Regional in an ambulance instead of treating him at that little excuse for a hospital in Manitou, so it was bad. Maybe he died on the way."

Jalbert shakes a fist at the ceiling, thinking *closure, sweet closure.* "God did what I couldn't." His voice isn't quite steady.

"I wouldn't disagree," Allard says.

"Keep me informed. You know I'm out of the loop."

"Which is one more fucked-up thing in a fucked-up world," Allard says. "You bet I will."

That night Jalbert goes out to Bullwinkles and gets drunk for the first time in twenty years. He does not count steps, which is a relief. Counting steps and running chairs is hard work. So many numbers to keep track of, so easy to lose count. He supposes nobody would believe that, but it's the truth. If you lose count, you have to start over.

While Jalbert is drinking his second whiskey and soda, Allard calls again. Jalbert has to shout because of the combined roar of the TV, the jukebox, and a bunch of unwinding KU summer students. *"Is he dead?"*

"No! Serious condition! Shot in the stomach!"

Jalbert first feels disappointed, then happy. Isn't that better than life in prison, where Coughlin would get three meals a day, a TV in his cell, and time in the exercise yard? It hurts to get shot in the gut. The pain is excruciating, so Jalbert has heard, and it's the sort of wound that Coughlin might not—depending on the caliber of the slug—ever come back from.

"*Maybe that's good!*" he shouts.

"I get where you're coming from, buddy," Allard says. "And from the sound of it, I get where you are. Have one for me."

"I'll have two," Jalbert says, and laughs. It's the first real laugh to come out of him in a long time, and the hangover he wakes up with the next day feels entirely justified. He takes a long walk without counting his steps, simply hoping—almost praying—that Coughlin will live, but get some sort of serious infection. Possibly need to have his stomach removed. Was it possible to live if that happened? Would you have to be fed through a tube? If so, wouldn't that be an even greater punishment?

Jalbert thinks yes.

By noon his hangover is gone. He eats a hearty lunch and doesn't even think about going into the dining room to work on his Classic Movie Posters puzzle. He is contemplating the idea of sending Coughlin flowers (with a card reading *Don't get well soon*) when his phone rings. It's his ex-partner.

"Frank, I have some fantastic news."

"I already know. Our boy Coughlin took one in the belly. He's in the hosp—"

"They caught him!"

Jalbert shakes his head, not sure he's following her. "Do you mean Yvonne Wicker's brother, or did you uncover some evidence about Coughlin? Did you? Is that it?" He could hope. Gutshot *and* going to prison, how beautiful that would b—

"The man who killed her! They caught him in Iowa! His name is Andrew Iverson!"

Jalbert frowns. His headache is creeping back. "I have no idea what you're talking about. *Coughlin* killed poor Miss—"

"Iverson was trying to take another one! She stabbed him and got away!" Davis pours out the whole story, saving the best for last: two of the charms from Yvonne Wicker's bracelet in Iverson's kill-bag.

"We hounded an innocent man for nothing," she finishes. "Because we couldn't believe."

Jalbert sits up straight. His headache is worse than ever. He will have to do something about it. Take some aspirin. Then run the chairs. "We didn't *hound* him, Ella. We *pursued* him. Given what we knew, we had every right. Every duty."

"Stop with the *we* stuff, Frank." Now she just sounds weary. "I didn't give his name to that free newspaper and I didn't plant dope in his truck. You did those things on your own. And I didn't get him shot."

"You're not thinking clearly."

"That's you, not me. I told him I went to Mass and prayed for him, and do you know what he said? 'It helps if you believe.' I'm going to keep that in mind going forward."

"Then you better quit police work and get a job as a . . . a voodoo priestess or something."

"Do you not feel the slightest shred of guilt, Frank?"

"No. I'm going to hang up now, Ella. Don't call me again."

He ends the call. He runs the chairs. He puts ten pieces in his jigsaw puzzle and then counts steps in his backyard: 81 down to 1. A total of 3,321. A good number, but his head still aches.

62

Danny's supper following Edgar Ball's visit is green gluck that looks like liquified snot and tastes a little like V8. If, that is, V8 tasted nasty. He gets it all down anyway, because for the first time since waking up in the hospital he's actually hungry. In truth for the first time since his trip to Gunnel, in Dart County. Things have changed. He feels saved.

At nine o'clock a nurse comes in with a couple of pain pills. He tells her he doesn't need them, at least not yet. She raises her eyebrows. "Really? Will you be able to sleep?"

"I think so. Leave them on the night table, in case I want them later."

222

She does that, checks his bandages for seepage, finds none, and wishes him a good night. Danny wishes her the same. His stomach hurts, but the pain is down to a dull throb unless he makes a sudden move. He grabs the TV controller, switches around through a few channels, then turns it off. He thinks about Edgar Ball saying he could probably have his old job back if he wants it. The idea actually hurts. There are people in Manitou who are always going to believe he's guilty of *something*. Gossip is like radioactive waste. It has a long and toxic half-life.

Stevie sent him an email with attachments to several rentals in Nederland and Longmont. They would have been far out of his reach a week ago, but if Edgar's right about how he, Danny, might get a little payday . . .

He's still thinking about that when he drifts into the first good sleep he's had since the night before he dreamed that inexplicable dream.

That lasts until 1:20 AM, when the second dream begins.

63

Unless he's working a case—and thanks to Ella Davis, all of that is done—Jalbert goes to bed every night at nine-thirty. That's supposed to be the healthiest time, according to what he's read on the Internet, but tonight he's not able to get down.

Just tonight? If only. He hasn't managed more than a few light dozes since finding out a wandering plumber named Andrew Iverson has been arrested for the murder of Yvonne Wicker and two others.

Who is the bad guy in all of this? Frank Jalbert! And who is the loser in all of this? Frank Jalbert!

Twenty good years, half a dozen commendations, all flushed down the commode. Everything he dedicated his life to is gone. His name is mud. While Danny is having a good sleep in Great Bend, Jalbert is wide awake in Lawrence. His mind has turned on itself, gnawing and biting like a mangy dog snapping at its own flanks until the blood flows.

After ninety minutes or so of tossing and turning, he throws back the covers and gets up. He has to walk, and he has to count. If he doesn't, he'll go crazy. The thought of sticking his gun in his mouth comes, and it's attractive, but if he does that, will he not be giving Coughlin the ultimate victory? And Ella! Ella saying *We hounded an innocent man for nothing . . . because we couldn't believe*. That was nonsense, not to mention Monday morning quarterbacking. Were they supposed to throw out years of fact-based police work because a high school janitor said he'd had a *dream*? When Covid was burning across America, they said to follow the science. When you were a policeman, you followed the logic. Did that not make sense, or had the world gone crazy?

"Ella believed he killed her," he says as he leaves the house on this hot summer night. "She believed it as much as I did."

He walks on West 6th Street in his bedroom slippers, past the Walgreens and the Hy-Vee, past Dillons and Starbucks and the Big Biscuit, now closed and dark. He walks past the Six Mile Chop House and the Alvadora Apartments, where he once arrested a murderer who is now doing his just time in El Dorado. He walks all the way to the Highway 40 interchange. He counts his steps. He's up to 154, a total of 11,935 when added sequentially. Then a sudden burst of insight— of *logic*—lights up his mind.

Did the girl in Wyoming escape Andrew Iverson? Andrew Iverson in his little plumbing and heating van?

Yes. Jalbert accepts that.

Did Andrew Iverson kill two other girls, one in Illinois and the other in Missouri?

He accepts that, too.

Did Andrew Iverson have two of the charms from poor Miss Yvonne's bracelet in his kill-sack?

All right, say he did. *And say Danny Coughlin put them there.*

It makes perfect sense once you throw out the new age bullshit. Ella may believe that crap now, but Jalbert never did and never will. Follow the science, follow the logic.

Coughlin and Iverson knew each other. He's sure of it. It stands to reason. Jalbert is also sure that the good police work necessary to uncover that connection will never be done. Why would any KBI investigator even try, when everything is tied up in a neat bow? When

Danny Coughlin will probably come out of this looking like a hero who just tried to do his civic duty? A *psychic* hero!

The only question in Jalbert's mind as he stands looking at late-night cars passing on Highway 40 is whether Iverson held poor Miss Yvonne down while Coughlin raped her, or if Coughlin held her down while Iverson did his dirt.

Would they be the first kill-team? No, of course not. There have been others. Ian Brady and Myra Hindley. Kenneth Bianchi and Angelo Buono. Dick Hickock and Perry Smith, those two right here in Kansas.

A car goes by on 6th and a young voice sings out, "Hey Pop, you're in your *pajaaamas*!"

There's diminishing laughter. Jalbert doesn't notice. He's putting the pieces together just as he put the pieces of his Classic Movie Posters puzzle together and they all fit.

Iverson called Coughlin from wherever he picked up poor Miss Yvonne—somewhere near that Gas-n-Go down south—and asked if he, Coughlin, wanted to have a little fun. And when they were done, Coughlin stripped a couple of charms from poor Miss Yvonne's charm bracelet and told Iverson . . . told him . . .

"Here, you take these," Jalbert mutters. "Something to look at when you whack off."

No bullshit about dreams, just cold logic.

Coughlin thought, I'll not only get the fun of raping her and killing her, I'll get the glory of being the one to find her.

It makes perfect sense. *Divine* sense. Because Coughlin always knew they'd trace the source of that ridiculous anonymous call, didn't he? How could he not?

It occurs to Jalbert—he's walking home now, counting forgotten—that he might be able to investigate on his own. Do some digging. Find out where the lives of Coughlin and Iverson intersected. At school, maybe. After that, emails and texts. Iverson killed others; it seems likely that Coughlin has, as well.

Likely? Try *certain*.

But be real: he hasn't the resources to mount that kind of an investigation, and if he did, he'd draw attention to himself and they—KBI, the newspapers—would shut him down. They have their story, complete with gosh-wow dream information; no one would believe his. *Take your pension and shut up*, they'd say. *You're lucky we let you have one after what you did.*

Which left what? Where was justice for poor Miss Yvonne? Who would be her advocate?

That, too, seems perfectly clear to Jalbert.

He will have to take care of Danny Coughlin himself. This very night. Tomorrow morning the hospital where Coughlin is currently recuperating will fill with people, but in the small hours ahead it will be at its lowest ebb. Coughlin isn't being guarded; why would he be, when the blind idiots at KBI think poor Miss Yvonne's killer is handcuffed to his own hospital bed in Wyoming? Coughlin is the psychic *hero*!

At home, Jalbert dresses in jeans and his black suit coat, the one he always wore when he was on the job. He puts his badge on his belt, technically against the law now that he's retired, but it will help him get in if any late shift person asks questions.

To this he adds his service weapon.

64

At quarter of two in the morning, Charles Beeson, an orderly on the third floor of Regional Hospital, is playing Fruit Ninja on his phone.

"Chuck? Chuck!"

He turns and is startled to see Danny Coughlin limping toward him. Danny's johnny flaps around his knees. He's barefoot. One hand is pressed against his abdomen. Tears are running down his cheeks. They are tears of pain, but they are also tears of horror.

"Mr. Coughlin, you're not supposed to get out of bed until the doctor gives you permiss—"

"My phone," Danny says. He's hoarse, panting. "It's in my drawer, but the battery's dead. Please, I have to charge it up. I have to make a call."

The pain wasn't bad when he fell asleep, but walking down the hall has awakened it. He grimaces and almost falls. Chuck gets an arm around him, but that's not good enough. He hoists Danny into his arms and carries him back to his room. Once he's in bed, Chuck holds out his own phone. "Here. If it's important, use mine."

Danny shakes his head. His hair is sticking to his forehead. Sweat runs down his cheeks. "I need my contacts. I put her number in my contacts. Even two per cent will be enough. I have to make that call."

65

While Danny's phone is on a charger in the nurses' station, Jalbert is on Route 56, heading for Great Bend. The Interstate would be shorter, but he's less likely to run into the Highway Patrol on 56 and he's running hot. According to his GPS, the trip from Lawrence should take about three and a half hours if he kept to the speed limit, but with the highway almost completely deserted at this small hour, he's doing 85. It was almost twelve-thirty in the morning before he got rolling. He expects to be there by 3 AM at the latest. 150 minutes, which is 1 to 17 when added sequentially. With three left over, of course, but who is counting?

It's vital that he should give Coughlin the justice he will otherwise escape; nothing must stand in his way. It will be his ultimate sacrifice, to save all the girls and women Coughlin might otherwise encounter.

The burner he used to call Andersson is in the center console of his car. He pre-programmed the number for the Great Bend Police Department before he left home for what will be the last time. He makes the call at 2:15 AM, never taking his eyes off the cone of his headlights. He doesn't have the voice-altering device he used with Andersson, so when the night dispatcher answers—"Great Bend Police, how may I help?"—Jalbert just makes his voice a little higher. He hopes he sounds like an adolescent, but it doesn't really matter; they will respond. On calls like this they *must* respond.

"There's going to be an explosion at the high school. A big one. It's going to happen around the time the kids start arriving." And then, it just pops out: "Three."

"Sir, where are you calling fr—"

"Three bombs," he says, improvising on the fly. "Three. They want to take out the whole school."

"Sir—"

Jalbert ends the call. He throws the phone out the driver's side window without slowing down. They may find the phone and if they do, they'll find his prints when they dust it, but it doesn't matter. He won't be coming back from this, and that will be a relief.

66

When Chuck the orderly brings Danny his phone, it's five per cent charged. That should be enough.

"Listen to me, Chuck. I want you to get the night nurses—Karen and the other one, the blond, I can't remember her name—and go down to the second floor."

"What? Why?"

"Just trust me. There isn't much time." Danny glances at the clock on his nightstand. 2:10 AM. Chuck is still standing in the door, frowning at him. "Go. It's life and death. Not kidding."

"You're not having a pain med reaction, are you?"

Belief, Danny thinks. *It's all about belief. Isn't it?*

"*No*. Second floor. All of you. This will be over one way or the other in an hour. Until then, get out. Get safe."

He goes to his contacts. For a moment he's terrified that Davis isn't in them, that he only *thought* he added her number from the card she gave him. But it's there and he makes the call, praying her phone isn't shut off.

It rings four times, then five. Just as he's despairing, she answers. Sleepy, she sounds more human than ever. "H'lo? Who—"

"Danny Coughlin," he says. "Wake up, Inspector Davis. Listen to me. I had another dream. This time it was premonitory. Do you understand?"

A moment's silence. When she replies, she sounds more awake. "Do you mean—"

"He's coming for me. Unless something changes it, there's going to be shooting down the hall, I think at the nurses' station. Screaming.

Then he's here. Dressed like he was when you first came to the school. Black coat, blue jeans. Only that time he wasn't armed. This time he is."

"I'll call the police," she says, "but if this is some kind of weird joke—"

"Do I sound like I'm joking?" He almost screams it. "The police won't come, he's sent them off on some kind of wild goose-chase, don't ask me how I know that, it wasn't in the dream, but I—"

"It's what he'd do," she says. "If he really means to come after you . . . yes, it's what he'd do." She sounds fully awake now. "I'll call the cops in Dundee and Pawnee Rock and then I'll come myself. I'm at my sister's, only six miles from Regional."

This second dream is as clear in his memory as the dream of County Road F, the Texaco station, and the constant *tinka-tinka-tinka* of those price signs against the rusty pole. As real as the dog and the unearthed arm. There were—*will* be—shots at the nurses' station followed by a single scream. A man's scream, so probably Chuck the orderly. And then the man in the black coat and the dad jeans was—*will* be— standing in his doorway. *Looming* in his doorway. That strange peninsular widow's peak surrounded by white skin, those deepset, tired eyes.

For poor Miss Yvonne, he'll say as he raises the gun. And just as he fires Danny turns his head on the pillow. He looks at the clock on his night table.

"I told the orderly to send everyone down to the second floor, but they're not going. I can hear them down there. They don't believe me. Just like him. Just like you."

He looked at the clock in his dream; he looks at it now.

"Forget about Dundee and Pawnee Rock, Inspector. They're too far away. He's going to start shooting at a minute to three. You've got thirty-nine minutes to do something about it."

67

Ella's sister Regina is alone in the master bedroom. Her husband is away on one of his many business trips. Davis has her suspicions about those trips, and she supposes Regina does, too, but that is a matter for another time. The digital clock beside Regina's bed reads 2:24.

"Reg! Reggie! Wake up!"

Regina stirs and opens her eyes. Davis is wearing jeans, sneakers without socks, and a KU tee-shirt, clearly without a bra. But it's the sight of the gun on her hip and the ID laminate her sister is slipping over her head that wakes her all the way up.

"What—"

"I have to go. Right now. I'll be back before Laurie wakes up." She hopes so, at least. "There's a problem."

"What problem?"

"I can't explain, Reg. I hope it's nothing." She doesn't believe that, not anymore. She believes Coughlin. About everything. She can only hope it's not too late. "I'll call when it's taken care of."

Reggie is still asking questions when her sister leaves. Ella runs down the stairs two at a time and snatches her keys from the basket by the door. Her personal car is parked in the driveway and goddam, Regina parked hers directly behind it. Davis pulls forward until the collision monitor hollers and her bumper thumps the porch. She cranks the wheel and backs around Reggie's Subaru, hitting the Subaru's bumper hard enough to rock it on its springs. She misses the mailbox by inches when she reverses into the street. She looks at the dashboard clock. It's 2:28.

The streets are deserted, and she ignores the stop signs, only slowing to look for headlights coming in either direction. She takes 7th, which proves to be a mistake. There's construction, a line of smudge pots in front of a hole in the road probably meant for a culvert. The pots glow smoky orange in the night. She wheels into someone's driveway, turns back, and takes 8th, hating the delay. She works her phone out of her pocket, and when she comes to a blinker flashing red at the McKinley Street intersection, she tells Siri to call the Great Bend PD.

Davis identifies herself and tells Dispatch there's a possible shooter approaching Regional Hospital, send any and all available officers. Dispatch tells her she has no one to send. Someone has phoned in a bomb threat at the high school—*three* bombs, in fact—and the few officers working the night shift have gone there to close off the streets leading to the building. The Bomb Squad is on its way from Wichita.

"There's no bomb," Davis says. "This guy wants to draw your cops off until he finishes what he's coming to do."

"Ma'am . . . Inspector . . . you know this how?"

The clock on her dashboard reads 2:39. It occurs to Ella that lack of belief is the curse of intelligence. She throws her phone on the passenger seat without ending the call and turns onto McKinley. She floors it, then stamps both feet on the brake as a late-night shambler pushes a shopping cart into the street. She lays both hands on the horn. The shambler gives her a lazy middle finger, tick-tocking it from side to side as he continues on his way. Davis veers around him and tromps the gas, laying fifty feet of rubber.

Here, at last, is Cleveland Street and the bulk of the hospital. The red EMERGENCY sign over the portico is her beacon. It's 2:46. *Beat him*, Davis thinks. *If Danny was right about the time, I beat h—*

A red SUV looms up in her rearview. It swings beside her, almost sideswipes her, then bolts ahead. Davis gets just a glimpse of the driver, but a glimpse is enough. That thick widow's peak is all the ID she needs. Taillights flash as the SUV pulls up in front of the main entrance. Jalbert gets out: black coat, baggy dad jeans. In spite of her terror and the sense that she's having her own dream—it's hardly been an hour since she was called from a sound sleep by her phone, after all—there's a feeling of almost miraculous wonder. Because Danny was right about everything, and now she knows how he must have felt at that Texaco station, seeing his dream made real.

She doesn't slow, simply rear-ends Jalbert's vehicle. He wheels around, eyes wide, going for his gun. Ella lays on the horn with her right hand—*wake up, you people, wake up*—and opens the door with her left.

She draws her own gun as she gets out, hoping two things—that she won't have to shoot her ex-partner, and that her ex-partner won't shoot her. She has a little girl to go back to.

"Frank! Stop! Do not go in!"

"Ella? What are you doing here?"

He looks so haggard, she thinks. *So lost.* And so dangerous.

"Put your gun away, Frank."

People are coming out now. Nurses in pink and blue rayon, a couple of orderlies in white, a doctor in green scrubs, a couple of patients from 24 Hour Care, one with his arm in a sling.

"He's lying, Ella. Of course he is, are you blind?"

They are pointing Glocks at each other like a pair of gunfighters at the end of a Western movie. The .40 S&W ammo those guns fire will be lethal at this short range. If the shooting starts, one or both of them will almost certainly be killed.

"No, Frank. They caught the doer in Wyoming. His name is Andrew—"

"Iverson, yes." Jalbert is nodding. "I believe that, but they were in it together. Can't you see that? Follow the logic, Ella, they were a kill-team! Use your brain. How can you believe his story? You're too smart! Sixteen times too smart! Eighteen times too smart!"

More people have come out. They cluster on the steps. Davis wants to tell them to go back in, but she doesn't dare take her eyes off Jalbert. Now she can hear a siren. It's approaching, but it's too far, too far.

"Frank, why do you think I'm here? How do you think I *got* here?"

For the first time he looks unsure. "I don't . . . know."

"Danny called me. He knew you were coming. He dreamed it."

"That's ridiculous! A lie! A fable for children!"

"But here I am. How else can you explain it?"

A nurse—a large woman in a blue smock—has come out of Urgent Care and is now sneaking up on Jalbert from behind. Ella wants to tell her that's a bad idea, the *worst* idea, but doesn't dare. Jalbert will think she's trying to distract him, and he'll shoot.

"I can't," Jalbert says. "You shouldn't be here. I don't think you *are* here. You're a hallucin—"

The big woman throws her arms around Jalbert, pinning his arms. She must outweigh him by sixty pounds, but his reaction is immediate. He stamps down on one of her feet. She screams. Her grip loosens. He frees one arm and drives an elbow backward into her throat. The nurse stumbles away, gagging. He turns toward her and away from Davis.

"Frank, put it down! DROP IT DROP IT DROP IT!"

He doesn't seem to hear her. The nurse is bent over, hands to her throat. Jalbert raises the gun. He does it very slowly. Ella has time to think about all the miles they've driven on Kansas roads and all the meals they've eaten in Kansas diners. Prepping each other before testifying. Sitting through endless briefings. There's time to shoot him, but she doesn't. Can't. She can only watch as Jalbert continues to raise the gun, but he's not pointing it at the nurse. He puts it to his own head.

"Frank, don't. Please don't."

"I did it all for poor Miss Yvonne." Then he says "Three, two, one." And pulls the trigger.

68

It's almost an hour later when Ella is finally allowed into Danny Coughlin's room. Two cops are standing guard outside his door. She thinks this is a perfect example of locking the barn after the horse has been stolen. Chuck the orderly is there, and a doctor. Ella thinks it's the one she saw on the steps during the final confrontation, but she might be wrong. They all look the same in their green scrubs. In his hospital johnny, Danny looks like he's lost forty pounds. He's as haggard as Jalbert was at the end, but there's a clarity in his face that's different.

Ella doesn't hesitate. She goes to him and hugs him. "I'm sorry. I'm sorry about everything."

"It's all right," Danny tells her. He strokes her hair. That seems like the wrong thing to do. It also seems right.

She pulls back from him.

"Ma'am," the doctor says, "this man has had enough excitement for one night. He needs his rest."

"I know. I'll go. But Danny . . . why did you have that dream? *Why?* Do you have any idea at all?"

He laughs. It's a sorry laugh. "Why does a man get hit by lightning twice?"

She shakes her head. "I don't know."

"Neither do I." He points. "I see you're wearing your cross."

233

She touches it. "I always wear it."

"Sure. But belief is hard, isn't it?" He lies down on his pillow, puts his hands over his eyes—as if to blot out both worlds, the one seen and the one behind it, so rarely revealed—and says it again. "Belief is hard."

He drops his hands. They look at each other without speaking. There's nothing to say.

FINN

Finn had a hard go of it from the very beginning. He slipped through the hands of a midwife who had delivered hundreds of babies and gave his birthday cry when he hit the floor. When he was five, there was a house party next door. He was allowed out to listen to the music (The Pogues blasting from pole-mounted portable speakers) on his side of the street. It was summer, he was barefoot, and a cherry bomb thrown by an exuberant partygoer flew up, arced down with the stub of its fuse fizzing, and blew off the baby toe on his left foot.

Wouldn't have happened again in a thousand years, his grandma said.

At seven he and his sisters were playing in Pettingill Park while Grandma sat on a nearby bench, alternately knitting and doing one of her word-search puzzles. Finn didn't care for the swings, had no use for the seesaws, could have cared less about the roundy-round. What he liked was the Twisty, an entrancing curlicue of blue plastic twenty feet high. There were steps, but Finn preferred to climb the slide itself on his hands and knees, up and around, up and around. At the top he would sit and glide to the packed dirt at the bottom. He never had an accident on the Twisty.

"Stop that awhile, why don't ya," Grandma said one day. "You're always on that old Twisty. Try something new. Try the monkeybars. Show me a trick."

His sisters, Colleen and Marie, were on them, climbing and swinging like . . . well, like monkeys. So, to please Grandma, he went on the monkeybars and slipped while hanging upside down and fell and broke his arm.

His teacher that year, pretty Miss Monahan, liked to end each day by saying, *What have we learned today, kiddos?* At the Urgent Care, while having his arm set (the lollipop he was given afterward hardly seemed adequate compensation for the pain), Finn thought what he'd learned that day was *Stick to the Twisty*.

At fourteen, running home from his friend Patrick's house in a driving thunderstorm, a stroke of lightning hit the street directly behind him, close enough to frizz his hair and char a line down the back of his jacket. Finn fell forward, hit his head on the curb, suffered a concussion, and lay unconscious in his bed for two days before waking up and asking what happened. It was Deirdre Hanlon from across the street (one of the partygoers on that long-ago Pogues day, although not the cherry bomb thrower) who saw him and fished the unconscious boy out of the gutter. "I thought poor old Finn was dead for sure," she said.

His late father said Finn was born under a bad sign. Grandma (who never apologized for the monkeybars day) held a different view. She told Finn that for every stroke of bad luck God dealt out, he gave two strokes of the good. Finn thought that over and said he'd had no good luck to speak of, unless it wasn't being hit dead center by the lightning-bolt.

"You should be *glad* your luck's out," Grandma said. "Maybe it will come in all at once and you'll win the Lotto. Or a rich relative will die and leave you everything."

"I don't have any rich relatives."

"That you *know* of," Grandma said. She was the kind of woman who always got the last word. "When things go wrong, just remind yourself 'God *owes* me.' And God always pays His debts."

Not soon enough to suit Finn, however. Worse luck awaited.

One evening in his nineteenth year, Finn came running home from his girlfriend's house, not because it was raining but because even with a case of blue balls, all that hugging and touching and smooching had left him exhilarated. He felt he had to run or explode. He was wearing a leather jacket, jeans, a Cabinteely cap, and a vintage tee-shirt with the logo of an old band—Nazareth—on the front. He rounded the corner onto Peeke Street and ran into a young man running the other way. They both fell down. Finn picked himself up and started to apologize, but the young man was already legging it again, looking back over his shoulder. He was also wearing jeans, a bill cap, and a tee-shirt, which didn't strike Finn as particularly coincidental; in this city, it was the uniform of the young, men and women both.

Finn carried on running down Peeke, rubbing a scraped elbow as he went. A black tradesman's van came toward him, lights off. Finn thought nothing of it until it pulled up beside him and some men—at least four—came rushing out of the back even before the van had rolled completely to a stop.

Two of them grabbed him by the arms. Finn managed "Hey!"

A third man said "Hey yourself!" and pulled a bag over his head.

There was a sting in his upper arm just above his scraped elbow. He was aware of being hustled, feet not touching the pavement, and then the world flew away.

When Finn came to, he was lying on a cot in a small room with a high ceiling. In one corner was a table lamp with no table beneath it. In another was a commode. The commode was blue plastic, exactly the same shade as the Twisty in Pettingill Park. There was no other furniture. There was a skylight, but it had been painted black in slopping, careless strokes.

Finn sat up and winced. He didn't have a headache, exactly, but his neck was terribly stiff and his arm hurt the way it had after he'd gotten his Covid shot. He looked at it and saw someone had put a sticking plaster above his scraped elbow. He peeled it back and saw a tiny hole with a red corona around it.

Finn tried the door and found it locked. He knocked, then pounded on it. As if in answer, AC/DC blasted at him: "Dirty Deeds Done Dirt Cheap" at what sounded like two thousand decibels. Finn clapped his hands over his ears. It went on for twenty or thirty seconds, then stopped. He looked up and saw three speakers mounted high up. To him they looked like Bose models, which meant expensive. In the corner above the table lamp without a table, the lens of a camera stared down at him.

Unlike the time when he had almost been struck by lightning, Finn remembered what had happened before he temporarily lost the plot, and guessed what it meant. It was absurd but not amazing. Being kidnapped was just another example of Finn Murrie luck.

He went back to pounding on the door and yelling for someone to come. When no one did, he stepped back and looked up at the camera.

"Is someone there? Like, monitoring this? If you are, please come and let me out. I believe you've dropped a bollock. You want the other fella."

There was no response for almost a full minute. Finn was walking back to the cot, having decided to lie down until someone came to rectify what was obviously a mistake, when the speakers blared again. Finn liked the Ramones, but not at such apocalyptic volume in a closed room. This time the sonic assault went on for about two minutes before cutting out just as abruptly.

He lay on the cot and had just begun to drift when Cheap Trick roared down. Twenty minutes later it was Dexys Midnight Runners.

It went on that way for quite some time. Probably hours. There was no way Finn could tell for sure. His captors had taken his watch while he was unconscious.

He was dozing when the door opened. Two men came in. Finn wasn't sure they were the ones who had grabbed him by the arms, but pretty sure. One of them had a droopy eye. He said, "Are you going to be troublesome, Bobby-O?"

"Not if you're going to make this right," Finn said. He took little notice of being called Bobby-O, thought it was just some kind of nickname, like Daddy-O, or how if his father had seen a drunk staggering up the street, he'd always say, "There goes Paddy O'Reilly."

"That's up to you," the other said. He had a narrow face and black eyes, like a weasel.

They went out the door, Finn between the two men, who were both wearing chinos and white shirts. Neither of them had a gun, which was a bit of a comfort, although Finn had no doubt they could handle him easily if he decided to make trouble for them. They looked fit. Finn was tall but weedy.

The room they came out in was lined with shelves, all of them empty. To Finn it looked like a pantry, or maybe, given the size, what his grandma would have called a larder. As a young woman, she'd been "in service."

From the pantry they entered the biggest kitchen Finn had ever seen. There were a couple of empty bowls on the counter with spoons in them. Judging by the scum inside, he guessed they had contained soup. His belly rumbled. He didn't know how long it had been since he'd eaten. Ellie had made him some scrambled eggs before the necking started, but Finn had an idea that was long since digested. If digestion continued when you were unconscious, that was. He thought it must. A person's body just went about its business.

Next came a dining room with a shining mahogany table that looked long enough to play shuffleboard on. Heavy plum-colored drapes had been pulled all the way closed. Finn strained his ears for the sound of passing traffic and heard nothing.

They went down a hall and the droopy-eye man opened a door on the right. The weasel gave Finn a light shove. There was a fancy desk in the room. The walls were lined with books and folders. More drapes, a deep dull red, had been drawn over the window behind the desk. A man with white hair combed back like the early Cliff Richard sat behind the desk. His tanned face was scored with lines. He looked not much older than Finn's father had been when he died.

"Sit down."

Finn sat down across from the white-haired man. Mr. Droopy Eye stood in one corner. Mr. Weasel stood in the other corner. They clasped their hands in front of their belt buckles.

There was a folder in front of the white-haired man, thinner than the ones crammed in helter-skelter on the shelves. He opened it, lifted a sheet of paper, looked at it, and sighed.

"This can be easy or hard, Mr. Feeney. That's entirely up to you."

Finn leaned forward. "See, that's not my name. You have the wrong person."

The white-haired man looked interested. He put the sheet of paper back in the thin folder and closed it. "Not Bobby Feeney? Is that so?"

"My name is Finn Murrie. That's Murrie with an *ie* at the end, not *ay*." He felt that this detail alone should be enough to convince the white-haired man. It was so specific.

"Is it now?" the white-haired man said. "Will wonders never cease!"

"I'll tell you what happened. What I *think* happened. When I came round the corner into Peeke Street I ran into a fella running the other way. We knocked each other down. He got up and ran on. *I* got up and ran on. These fellas . . ." He pointed at the men in the corners. " . . . must have wanted that other fella, Bobby Feeney. He was dressed the same as me."

"Dressed the same, was he? Cabinteely cap? Nazareth tee-shirt? Leather jacket?"

"Well, I don't know what was on the shirt, but I remember the cap. It all happened fast, but it's sure that's who you wanted. This happens to me all the time."

The white-haired man leaned forward, his hands (scarred, Finn saw, or maybe burned) clasped on his thin folder. He looked more interested than ever. "You are taken into custody all the time, are you?"

"No, bad luck. Bad luck happens to me all the time." He told the white-haired man about being dropped at birth, and the cherry bomb, the broken arm because he let his grandma coax him off the Twisty, the lightning strike. There were other things he could have added, but he thought the lightning strike and resulting concussion made a good place to stop. Like the climax of a storybook story. "So you see, I'm not the boyo you're looking for."

"Huh." The white-haired man sat back, pressed a hand to his belly as if it pained him, and sighed.

Inspiration struck Finn. "Just think about it, sir. If I was running away from these fellas of yours, I'd run away. But I didn't, did I? I ran right into their outstretched arms, so to speak. It was the other fella, this Bobby Feeney, who ran away."

"You're not Bobby Feeney?"

"No, sir."

"You're Finn Donovan."

"Finn *Murrie*. With an *ie*." This should have been settled by now. That it apparently was not gave Finn a bad feeling.

"Do you have any identification? Because if you had a wallet, it must be crammed up your arse. That's the only place we didn't look."

Finn actually reached for his back pocket before remembering.

"I left it at my girlfriend's house. We were sitting on the couch . . ." Lying on it, actually, Ellie on top. " . . . and it was digging into my butt, so I took it out and put it on this little table, with our cans of lager. I must have forgotten it."

"Forgot it," said Mr. Weasel, grinning.

"Stands to reason," said Mr. Droopy Eye. He was grinning, too.

"You see, we have a problem here already," the white-haired man said.

Finn had another inspo. The unpleasant situation he was in—the unbelievable situation, really, although he had no choice but to believe it—seemed to be bringing inspirations on thick and fast. "I had my Odeon card in my pocket, I kept it separate in case Ellie wanted to go out to the Royale . . ."

He felt for the card. It wasn't there.

The white-haired man opened his folder, riffled through the few papers inside, and brought out an orange card. "This card?"

"Yes, that's it. See my name?" He reached for it. The white-haired man leaned back. Mr. Weasel and Mr. Droopy Eye unclasped their hands, ready to pounce should pouncing be called for.

The white-haired man held the card close to his face, as if he were nearsighted. "Finn Murray, it says here. With an *ay*."

Finn felt heat rising in his cheeks, as if he had been caught in a lie. He hadn't been, but that was how it felt. "People misspell names all the time. My father's name was Stephen and people were always for spelling it with a *v* or even an *f*, like Stefan."

The white-haired man slipped the Odeon card back into his folder. "Did you enjoy the music we had piped into your room?"

"I know why you do that. I've seen it on telly. It's a tactic, like. To keep people on edge."

"Ah, is *that* why we do it? Pando, did you know that's why we do it?"

"Hard to say," Mr. Weasel replied with a shrug. "I have heard it said that music soothes the savage beast, although I'm not sure that speaks to your question."

"We can arrange some Nazareth, if you like," said the white-haired man. "You being a fan and all." And with what sounded grotesquely like pride: "We have Spotify!"

"I want to go home." Finn didn't like the tremble he heard in his voice but couldn't help it. "You made a mistake and I want to go home. I won't say nuffink." He was sorry as soon as it came out. Kidnap victims were always saying it and it never worked. He'd seen that on telly, too.

"Going home might also be arranged, and very easily. But first you must answer one question. What did you do with the briefcase, Bobby? The one with the papers in it. For you surely didn't have it when you were brought here."

Finn felt tears sting at the corners of his eyes. "Sir—"

"Call me Mr. Ludlum, if you like. I used to call myself Mr. Deighton, but I got tired of it."

"Mr. Ludlum, I'm not Bobby Feeney and I didn't have any briefcase. I never did. I'm not who you're looking for, and while you're gassing at me the fella you *are* looking for is getting away."

"So your name is Bobby Murrie. With an *ie*."

"Yes. I mean no. I'm Finn Murrie. *Finn*."

"Doc." The white-haired man—Mr. Ludlum—nodded to the one with the droopy eye. "Help this fine young man to remember his name."

Doc stepped forward. Pando, aka Mr. Weasel, grabbed Finn by the shoulders. Doc removed a heavy ring, put it in the pocket of his chinos, and slapped Finn across the face, good and hard. Then he went the other way, even harder. Spit flew from the side of Finn's mouth. It hurt plenty, but what he felt most in that moment was astonishment. And shame. He had nothing to be ashamed of, but ashamed he was.

"Now," Mr. Ludlum said, leaning back and clasping his hands on his midsection, "what is your name?"

"Finn! Finn Mur—"

Mr. Ludlum nodded to Doc, who administered two more brisk slaps. Finn's ears rang. His cheeks burned. The tears came. "You can't do that! *Why* would you do that? *You made a mistake!*"

"I *can* do it." Mr. Ludlum opened his folder and tossed a pamphlet across the desk. "Open-handed slaps are a world-approved technique for advanced interrogation. I think you should read that carefully before we talk again. See what other techniques we might decide to employ. Take him back, you two. Mr. Bobby Donovan has some homework to do."

"You don't even know who you're—"

He was jerked to his feet, Pando on one side and Doc on the other. Pando picked up the pamphlet and stuffed it into the waistband of Finn's jeans. "Come along, Bobby-O," he said.

"Ta-ta," said Mr. Ludlum. "Be a friend to all and all will be a friend to you."

With that Finn was hustled from the study with his cheeks burning and tears streaming from his eyes.

Back in his room—his *cell*—Finn pulled the pamphlet free of his jeans and looked at it. There was no binding, not even a staple. It was just a few sheets of paper folded together. On the front, smearily printed and slightly askew, was this: WORLD-APPROVED TECHNEEKS FOR ADVANCED INTEROGATION.

"Are you shitting me?" Finn asked. He spoke in a whisper, so the mikes—surely there were mikes as well as the camera staring down—wouldn't pick it up. His first thought was that the "pamphlet" was a joke. But the slaps hadn't been a joke. His face still burned.

The first page of the pamphlet: OPEN-HANDED SLAPS, **OKAY!**

The second page: SLEEP DEPERVATION TECHNEEKS (LOUD MUSIC, SOUND FX, ETC.), **OKAY!**

Third page: THREATS (TO FAMILY MEMBERS, FUCK-BUDDIES, ETC.), **OKAY!**

Fourth: ENEMAS, **OKAY!**

Fifth: STRESS POSITIONS, **OKAY!**

Sixth: WATERBORDING, **OKAY!**

Seventh: FIST HITTING, FOOT PADDLING, BURNING (WITH CIGARETTES OR LITERS), RAPE & SEXUAL ABUSE, **NOT OKAY!**

Eighth: IF NOT SPECIFICALLY MENTIONED, **PROBABLY OKAY!**

The rest of the pages were blank.

"They can't even fucking spell," Finn whispered. But if it wasn't a mistake, or someone's macabre idea of a joke, it could mean he was in the hands of psychopaths. The idea was more terrifying than believing it was a case of mistaken identity. *That* could be resolved.

One of his grandma's aphorisms (she had many) came to mind: *Most people will be reasonable if you speak soft and give them a chance.*

Because he had no better idea, he dropped the pamphlet on the floor, got up, and faced the camera. He spoke soft. "My name is Finn Murrie. I live at 19 Rowan Tree Road with my grandma and my two sisters, Colleen and Marie. My mother is away on business, but she can be reached on her mobile at . . ." Finn reeled off the number. "All of them will tell you I am who I say I am. Then . . ."

Then what?

Inspiration came. Or logic. Maybe both.

"Then you can put a bag over my head, even knock me out again if you feel like you need to, and drop me off on some random streetcorner. You can do that because I don't know who you are and I don't know where this is. I don't have no briefcase and I don't have no papers. Just, you know, be reasonable. Please."

He'd lost track of how many times he'd said please. Quite a few, for sure.

Finn went back to the cot and lay down. He began to drift. Just as he was slipping away, Anthrax came ripping out of the speakers: "Madhouse."

He almost fell off the cot. He covered his ears. After two minutes that seemed much longer, the music stopped. He no longer felt sleepy, but he felt plenty hungry. Would they feed him? Maybe not. Starving a prisoner wasn't specifically mentioned, so it was **PROBABLY OKAY!**

He slept.

They gave him four hours.

Then they came for him.

Finn didn't see if it was Doc and Pando or some of the other ones. Before he realized what was happening, he was hauled to his feet, still mostly asleep. A bag came down over his head. It smelled vaguely of chickendirt. He was propelled forward and slammed into the side of the door.

"Whoops, sorry!" someone said. "Little off course there, Bobby."

He was yanked back and propelled forward again. His nose was bleeding, maybe broken. He snuffled up blood, choked, began to cough. They were moving him at suicidal speed, his paddling feet barely touching the floor. They came to stairs and he was driven down them like a hog in a chute. Near the bottom they let go and one of the men gave him a hearty push. Finn screamed into the bag, imagining a drop of a hundred, two hundred, three hundred feet, with broken-bodied death awaiting him upon touchdown.

It was only two or three steps. His foot caught on the bottom one and he went sprawling. He was grabbed again. Every time he pulled in a breath the bag went into his mouth and he tasted his own blood, fresh and still warm, set off by a soupcon of chickenshit.

"Stop it!" he screamed. *"Stop it, I can't breathe!"*

"Pull the other one, Bobby," one of them said. "The not-breathing part comes later."

His knees hit something hard. He was whacked open-handed across the back of the neck and he fell forward onto what felt like a bench.

"Gotta flip the omelet so it won't burn," someone said cheerily, and he was turned over. One of his flailing hands hit something soft.

"Off my crotch, faggot," a new voice said, and he was slapped through the bag. "That's strictly my girlfriend's proppity."

"Please," Finn said. He was crying, trying not to choke on the blood now running down his throat. His nose throbbed like an infected tooth. "Please don't, please stop, I'm not the guy, I'm not Bobby Donovan—"

Someone fetched the side of his face a tremendous whack. "Bobby *Feeney*, you stupid git."

245

A cloth was draped over the bag. The first voice said, "Here it comes, Bobby! *Bwoosh!*"

Warm water soaked the cloth, then the bag, then Finn's face. He sucked water in and spluttered it out again. He held his breath. The water continued to pour down. At last he had to breathe. Instead of air, he sucked in water. He gargled it, choked on it, spit it out, swallowed more. There was no air. Air was gone. Air was a golden oldie, a blast from the past. He was drowning.

Finn thrashed. The water continued to pour through the hood. There was no sense of drifting away, no peace, only the horror of the constant water. He reached for unconsciousness and couldn't find it. Only more water.

At last it stopped. They rolled him on his side. He vomited into the bag. One of the men patted it gently all around. "A puke facial!" he exclaimed. "And we don't even charge!"

They rolled him on his back and yanked the hood off. He was allowed a hand free to wipe his face. He coughed and coughed while he did it. At last his vision cleared enough for him to see Mr. Ludlum peering down at him. Because he was at the head of the bench, he looked upside down.

"Are you Bobby Feeney or Finn Murrie?" Mr. Ludlum asked.

Finn was at first coughing too hard to answer. When it eased a little he said, "Whichever you want. I'll swear to it. Just don't do it again. Please, no more."

"Let's say investigation has proved to our satisfaction that you are Murrie, rather than Feeney. Where is he?"

"Who?"

Mr. Ludlum nodded. One of the men—not Doc, not Pando, they weren't here—fetched him a terrific open-handed wallop. A mixture of vomit and water flew.

"Feeney, Feeney, *Feeney*! Where is he?"

"I don't know!"

"Where is the bomb factory? Last chance, my boy, before you enjoy another baptism."

Finn coughed, choked, turned his head to the side, heaved, spat. "You said . . . papers. Papers in a briefcase."

"Papers be damned. Where is the bomb factory?"

"I don't know anything about—"

Mr. Ludlum nodded. The wet cloth went over Finn's face. The water began to flow. Soon he wanted to die. He wanted that more than anything. But he didn't. At last, semiconscious with the puke-stained bag once more over his head, he was brought back to his cell. He was no longer hungry. There was that, at least.

The last thing Mr. Ludlum said before closing the door was, "It doesn't have to be this way, Finn. Tell us what Feeney did with the blueprints and this can end."

There were no blasts of music, but Finn was still unable to sleep for a long time. Every time he started to drift, a new coughing fit would shake him awake. The last one was so furious he thought he might pass out, which would be welcome. Anything to escape this nightmare. The skylight high above him sent a few slices of subdued light through the slopped-over black paint. Outside, in a world that was no longer his, it was daytime. Maybe early, maybe late. Whichever it was, there were people out there going about their business with no idea that in this cell, a young man with no luck but bad luck was trying to cough water out of his lungs.

For every stroke of bad luck God deals out, his grandma had said, *he gives two strokes of the good.*

"I don't believe it," Finn croaked, and finally fell asleep.

He dreamed of Pettingill Park. Colleen was on the roundy-round. Marie was on the monkeybars, hanging upside down and picking her nose—a habit of which she could not be broken. Grandma said Marie would pick her nose on her deathbed. That elderly lady sat on a nearby bench with her knitting in her lap as she frowned over her latest word search. Finn climbed the spiral curves of the Twisty on his hands and knees, then sat and slid down again and again and again.

There were no musical interludes to interrupt this pleasant dream, which finally slipped away unnoticed, as dreams mostly do. He was awakened by Doc and another man, much older than the others, some unknown time later. They yanked him off the cot and hustled him back through the kitchen and dining room to the study, where white-haired Mr. Ludlum awaited. White-haired Mr. Ludlum seemed a bit grizzled this morning (it was morning to Finn, at least), his eyes were rimmed with red, and there was what looked like a mustard stain on his shirt. His hands were folded on the desk again, and Finn observed his scarred knuckles looked swollen. Stained, too. Was that blood?

Mr. Ludlum stared at him. Finn stared back, thinking of something else he'd seen on the telly. One of the boring and endless panel discussions on BBC that Finn's mother seemed to enjoy for reasons he and his sisters and Grandma (who liked *Coronation Street*, *EastEnders*, and *Doctor Who*) could never understand. This panel had been talking about enhanced interrogation techniques (aka torture), and one of the panelists—a jowly man who looked like Prince Andrew might after a year in a dark room drinking milkshakes and eating double burgers—said that it never worked.

"Because if the poor fellow don't know what his . . . *hum* . . . his *interlocutors* want to find out, he'll . . . *hum* . . . make something up. Stands to reason!"

It did stand to reason, and Finn was an inventive lad—inventive enough to have gotten out of any number of minor scrapes at home, in school, and around the neighborhood. But inventive or not, he couldn't think of a story that would satisfy Mr. Ludlum and keep him from another near drowning. Finn could have made up a tale about the missing briefcase, could even have added in the blueprints, but was he supposed to say that the missing blueprints were stashed in a briefcase in the bomb factory? It sounded like something from that Cluedo board game. And what might come next? Stolen submarine parts? Hacked passwords to the bank accounts of Russian oligarchs?

Meanwhile, Mr. Ludlum went on staring.

"I'm hungry," Finn blurted. "Could I possibly have something to eat, sir?"

Mr. Ludlum went on staring. Just when Finn decided he wasn't going to speak, that he was in some kind of trance, Mr. Ludlum said, "How does the full Irish sound to you, Mr. Herlihy?"

Finn gaped. Mr. Ludlum laughed.

"Just yanking your lower extremity, Finn. Finn now, Finn forever. What do you say to the whole shooting match? Eggs, bacon, mush-roomies, and a nice plump banger. With a tomato for good looks!"

Finn's stomach gurgled. That made Mr. Ludlum laugh again. "Asked and answered, I'd say—by the hair of my chinny-chin-chin. Not to mention my Finny-Finn-Finn. Eh? Eh?"

"Are you all right, Mr. Ludlum?" This was a strange question for Finn to ask, given the circumstances, but the man seemed to have *lost some of his sangy-froidy*, as Grandma said when someone on a quiz program couldn't come up with the proper answer and the time ticked away to nothing.

"I am *swell*," Mr. Ludlum said. "A swell fella is what I am. You shall have breakfast, Finn, if you can tell me the names of three songs by the late Elvis Presley."

Finn didn't bother asking why—the man was clearly crazy—but instead thought back to his grandma's extensive record collection. One of her favorites, played until the grooves had a strange whitish look, as if dusted with chalk, was called *50,000,000 Elvis Fans Can't Be Wrong*. Colleen and Marie thought those millions of fans *could* be wrong. They made faces and clapped their hands over their ears when she put it on, but did Grandma mind? She did not.

He said, "You'll really give me breakfast?"

Mr. Ludlum put his hand over his heart and yes, those were almost surely bloodstains grimed into his knuckles. "My word on it."

Finn said, "All right. 'I Got Stung.' That's one. 'One Night of Sin.' That's two. And 'A Bigga-Bigga-Hunka Love.' That's three."

"Very good!" The oldish man was standing in the corner, hands clasped in front of his chinos. Mr. Ludlum turned to him and said, "Breakfast for our friend Finn, Marm! He has rung the bell!"

Marm left. Doc stayed. Finn thought Doc looked tired and—maybe—sad.

"You know your Elvis songs," Mr. Ludlum said. He leaned for-ward, gazing at Finn from eyes that were bloodshot as well as red-rimmed. "But do you know *Elvis*? Do you know the King of Rock and Roll?"

Finn shook his head. All he knew about Elvis was that he was some old-time bugger who died on the toilet. And that Grandma loved him. She had probably screamed for him in the days of her youth.

"He was a *twin*," Mr. Ludlum breathed, and the smell of alcohol—maybe Scotch, maybe whiskey—drifted to Finn from across the desk. "A twin but also a single birth. How do you explain that paradox?"

"I don't know."

"Then I'll tell you. The future King of Rock and Roll absorbed his twin brother *in utero*. Ate him in an act of fetal cannibalism!"

Finn was momentarily shocked out of his own troubles. He was sure (*fairly* sure) that Elvis's twin brother was as mythical as the briefcase full of stolen papers or the supposed bomb factory, but the idea of fetal cannibalism was strangely fascinating.

"Can that actually happen?"

"Can and did," Mr. Ludlum said. "My dear old mother was very prim and proper, but she had a coarse joke about Mr. Presley. She said he was Elvis the Pelvis and his twin brother would have been Enos the Penis. Do you get it, Finn?"

Finn nodded, thinking, *I am being held prisoner and tortured by a man who believes I know where there's a bomb factory and that Elvis Presley gobbled up his twin brother while still in his mother's belly.*

"I always found Elvis a trifle *gay*," Mr. Ludlum said in a ruminative tone. "There are songs . . . 'Teddy Bear' is one, 'Wooden Heart' is another . . . where he sings in a kind of whispery falsetto. One can almost envision him *prancing* in the studio as he warbled, arms outstretched, fingers gently waving, perhaps in patent leather shoes. I never believed that story about Elvis and Nick Adams, total rot, but the rhinestone outfits he wore toward the end . . . and the scarves . . . there were rumors of a *girdle* . . . yes, there was something there, something we might call *latent*, and . . ." He stopped, sighed, and briefly covered his face. When he lowered his hands he said, "Two of my men have left me, Finn. Scarpered. Did a bunk. Buggered off. I tried to persuade them to stay, but they feel our enemies are closing in. The *putain de bougnoule*, so to speak."

He drooped one bloodshot eye in a wink.

250

"So our time has grown short. I'll send you back to your quarters now to eat your breakfast, but think very carefully. I'm sure you don't want to suffer any more discomfort. All we need to know is where you put the translation. And the key to the code itself, of course. We'll want that. Doc, will you escort our young friend?"

Doc went to the door and gestured for Finn, who got up and joined him. "Are you going to be good?" Doc asked.

Finn, who was thinking of bacon and eggs with mushroomies and a plump banger as well, nodded that he would be good. Absolutely. He walked beside Doc to the kitchen, where the oldish man—Marm—was using tongs to put what looked like a perfectly fried sausage on a plate that already held two eggs (fried hard, just the way Finn liked them), four strips of bacon, mushrooms still sizzling in butter, and a slice of tomato. Finn veered toward the plate like a compass needle swinging to magnetic north. Doc pulled him back.

"Wait," he said. "No grabbing, my son." And to Marm: "I'll take it from here. He'll want you."

Marm nodded, gave Finn a wink, and headed for Mr. Ludlum's study.

Doc picked up the plate with its freight of cholesterol-loaded goodies, but as soon as Marm was gone, he put it down again and pulled Finn to the right, away from the pantry and the room beyond.

"Hey!" Finn said. "My breakfast!"

Doc's hand clamped Finn's elbow hard enough to hurt. He dragged Finn to a door between the sink and the refrigerator. They emerged in an alley. Finn smelled fresh air tanged with gasoline. The black tradesman's van was there, the engine running. Mr. Weasel was behind the wheel. When he saw them, he went between the seats into the back. The rear doors flew open.

"Hurry the fuck up," Pando said.

"No fear, he'll be in the jakes," Doc said.

"Yeah, but he don't stay in there long these days, and he ain't entirely stupid, even yet. Get in here, son."

Finn had time for one amazed look at the thin slice of blue sky above the alley, then stumbled into the back of the van. His legs were stiff and he went sprawling, half in and half out. Pando grabbed him and hauled him the rest of the way. From his back pocket he pulled a black hood.

"Put this over your head. No argument. This ain't the time."

Finn pulled the bag over his head. His hands were trembling. One of them—Doc, he thought—shouldered into him and he went down on his arse, head banging the side of the van hard enough to see stars inside the bag. The doors slammed shut.

"Go," Doc snarled. "And mind you don't get us into a haxcident."

Finn heard Pando return to the driver's seat and the squeak of springs as he sat down. The van started to move. There was a pause at the end of the alley, and then a hard right turn.

Doc thumped down beside Finn with a sigh. "Fuck me for a criminal," he said.

Well, Finn thought, *what else would you call yourself?*

"Are you taking me somewhere to kill me?" The idea actually didn't seem so bad. Not compared to being faceup on the drowning board with a sopping towel across his face.

Doc gave a brief grunt of what might have been laughter. "If I'd wanted you dead, I would have let you eat breakfast. The mushrooms were poisoned."

"What—"

"Poison, poison! You never heard of it, you thick prat?"

"Where are you—"

"Shut up."

There was a left turn, a right, then some of both as they circled at least two roundabouts. There was a long pause—at a traffic light, Finn assumed—and Pando laid on the horn when the queue didn't move quick enough to suit him.

"Belay that, you numpty," Doc called.

On they went. More lefts and rights. Then the van picked up speed, so they were on a faster road, but Finn didn't hear enough noise to make him believe it was a motorway. Time passed. There was the click of a lighter, then the smell of cigarette smoke.

"He doesn't let us smoke when we're on a job," Doc said.

Finn kept quiet. He was thinking about the poisoned mushrooms. If they *had* been poisoned.

Sometime later—maybe fifteen minutes, maybe twenty—Doc helped himself to another cigarette and said, "He thinks he's only lost two, but the rest slipped away last night. Me 'n Pando were the last. Except for Marm. Marm won't leave him."

From up front Pando said, "Marm's as crazy as he is."

"We risked our lives to bring you out, Finn," Doc said. "I don't expect thanks, but we did."

Finn thanked him anyway. His voice was trembling and his legs were shaking. *Shake, shake, sugar, but you'll never shake me*, he thought. That was Elvis, "Stuck on You." Finn wondered if his grandma knew Elvis had gobbled up his twin brother, Enos.

"Thank you so much."

"I don't know if you're worth a shite to anyone, but you don't deserve to die just because he is the way he is now. Did you see that pamphlet he's so proud of? Wrote it himself, didn't he? But he wasn't always that way. No. We did good work once upon a time, didn't we, Pando?"

"Saved the fucking world in '17," Pando said, "and not more than a dozen people ever knew. But *we* knew, kid. We did."

"Feeney's up to something," Doc said. "That much I never doubted. You weren't a part of it, but he wouldn't let it go. Even though he don't remember *squat*."

"Is it—"

"Shut up," Doc said. "Just be a good little laddie and keep your goddamned mouth shut. Unless you want to get into worse trouble."

From the front Pando said, "No, he wasn't always this way. I remember . . . ah, never mind. For half a crown I'd put a bullet in your goddamned head myself."

Two hours later—at least two—they came into another town, a biggish one from the sound of the cars and lorries and the voices Finn heard at stoplights. Voices and laughter, the sound foreign to him.

At last the van pulled up and Doc yanked the bag from Finn's head. "This is your stop, son. And this is for your trouble." He stuffed something into the front pocket of Finn's jeans. Then, suddenly—Doc didn't seem to know he was going to do it until it was done—he kissed

Finn on the forehead. "Keep me in your prayers. I'll need a fucking lot of them."

He opened the back doors. Finn step-stumbled out. The van pulled away while Doc was still yanking the doors shut. Finn looked around like a man waking from a vivid dream. A bicyclist rang a bell and called, "Left, on your left!"

Finn stepped up onto the curb to keep from being hit broadside by an old buffer with a white mustache and a nose like the prow of a destroyer. To his right was the Randolph Street newsagent's, where he bought Grandma's word-search books, and sometimes—if he was feeling generous—an *OK!* or a *Heat* for his sisters. Next to it was the Yor Best chippie. Finn hadn't spent half a fortune in there over the last ten years. He was less than a mile from home.

He walked that way slowly, looking around, meeting the eyes of other pedestrians (most looked away at once, surely believing they were crossing gazes with a crazy street person), looking at the sky, looking in every window. *I'm alive*, he thought. *Alive, alive, alive.* He also looked over his shoulder several times, making sure there was no sign of the black tradesman's van.

He stopped at the corner of Peeke Street and peered around to make sure Bobby Feeney wasn't running toward him on a collision course, bearing away the secret papers, or the blueprints, or heading for the bomb factory. No one was there. He reached into his pocket and brought out a wad of banknotes: green euros, forty or more. He stuffed the wad back into his pocket.

For every stroke of bad luck, two strokes of the good, Grandma had said. Well, he had at least four thousand, that was one stroke. And he had his life, that was another.

Home was only two blocks down and one street over. They would be worried about him, for all he knew his mother had flown home early from her big business thingy, but they could wait a little longer. He turned back along Peeke Street to Emberly, then from Emberly to Jane Street. Halfway down Jane was Pettingill Park. It must have been early afternoon of a school day because the playground was empty except for two toddlers on the roundy-round who were circling slowly, pushed by either their mother or their minder. Finn sat on a bench.

He looked at the Twisty and a terrible memory came to him. In his last year of school, Mr. Edgerton assigned them a story by Ambrose Bierce. After they had all read it (presumably; not all of Finn's classmates were of the reading class), Mr. Edgerton showed them a short film based on the story, which was about the hanging of a slave-owner in the American Civil War. The slave-owner is pushed off a bridge, but the rope breaks and he swims to safety. The twist is this: the fortuitous escape was all in his mind, a kind of mini-dream before he's *actually* pushed from the bridge and executed.

That could be happening to me, Finn thought. *They went too far with the waterboarding and I'm drowning. Only instead of my whole life flashing in front of my eyes, as it's supposed to do, I'm imagining that Doc took me out, Pando drove us away, and here I am, in the park I enjoyed so much as a wee lad. Because really, is my escape likely? Is it realistic? You might believe it in a story, but in real life?*

Was it real life, though? Was it?

Finn seized one of his cheeks, still tender from slaps administered by Doc before Doc's (unlikely) change of heart. He twisted it hard. It hurt, and for a moment Pettingill Park seemed to waver like a mirage. That was caused by tears of pain, though.

Wasn't it?

Nor was it just Doc's change of heart that was bizarre. Mr. Ludlum who used to be Mr. Deighton . . . the badly printed pamphlet (and badly spelled, don't forget that) . . . the business about Elvis's twin brother . . . wasn't that all the stuff of dreams? What if Bobby Feeney hadn't just knocked him on his arse but on his noggin? What if Finn had hit said noggin on the exact same place where it had once been cracked on the memorable (not that he actually *did* remember) day when he had been brushed by lightning? Wouldn't that just be Finn Murrie's luck? What if he was lying in a hospital bed somewhere, deep in a coma, his damaged brain creating some crackpot alternate reality?

Finn got up and walked slowly to the Twisty. He hadn't climbed its curves in years, not since he was *knee-high to a grasshopper*, as Grandma would say. He climbed it now, pulling himself along by the raised sides. It was a tight fit, but he managed.

The mom or child minder had stopped pushing the kids on the roundy-round. She shaded her eyes with her hands and said, "What in heaven's name are you about? You'll break it, you great galoot!"

Finn didn't reply, and he didn't break it. He reached the top, turned himself around, and sat with his legs on the first curve. He thought, *Either I'll still be here when I get to the bottom, or I won't be. Simple as that.*

He looked at the woman and said, "Elvis has left the building." Then he pushed off.

ON SLIDE INN ROAD

Granpop's dinosaur of a Buick creeps along the dirt road at twenty miles an hour. Frank Brown is driving with his eyes slitted and his mouth compressed to a fine white line. Corinne, his missus, is riding shotgun with her iPad open in her lap, and when Frank asks her if she's sure this is right, she tells him everything is fine, steady as she goes, they'll rejoin the main road in another six miles, eight at most, and from there it's just a hop, skip, and a jump to the turnpike. She doesn't want to say that the blinking blue dot marking their location disappeared five minutes ago and the map is frozen in place. They've been married fourteen years and Corinne knows the mouth her husband is currently wearing. It means he's close to blowing his stack.

In the spacious backseat, Billy Brown and Mary Brown sit flanking Granpop, who has his big old black shoes planted on either side of the driveshaft hump. Billy is eleven. Mary is nine. Granpop is seventy-five, a giant pain in the ass as far as his son is concerned, and too old to have such young grandchildren, but there it is.

When they set out from Falmouth to see Granpop's dying sister up in Derry, Granpop talked nonstop, mostly about the zipper bag in the backseat. It contains Nan's baseball souvenirs. Mad about baseball she was, he tells them. There are baseball cards that he says are worth a fortune (Frank Brown fucking doubts this), her college softball glove signed by Dom DiMaggio, and the prize of all prizes, a Louisville

Slugger signed by Ted Williams. She won it in a Jimmy Fund charity raffle the year before the Splendid Splinter called it quits.

"Teddy Ballgame flew in Korea, you know," Granpop tells the kids. "Bombed hell out of the gooks."

"Not a word the children need to know," Corinne said from the front seat—but without much thought of success. Her father-in-law grew up in a politically incorrect age, and he's carried it with him. She also thought of asking him what a dying, semi-comatose octogenarian was supposed to do with a bat and glove, but kept still on that point, too. Donald Brown has never had much to say about his sister, good or bad, but he must feel something for her or he wouldn't have insisted they make this trip. He insisted on his old Buick, too. Because it's roomy, and because he said he knew a shortcut that might be a little rough. He's right on both counts.

He also tucked a pile of his old comic books into the bag. "Reading material for the youngsters on the trip," he said. Billy doesn't give shit one for old comic books, he's playing a game on his phone, but Mary got on her knees, unzipped Granpop's bag, and grabbed a stack. Most are cruddy, but some are pretty good. In the one she's reading now, Betty and Veronica are fighting over Archie, pulling each other's hair and such.

"You know what, back in the old days you could go down to Fenway on three dollars' gas," Granpop says. "And you could go to the game, snag a hotdog and a beer . . ."

"And still get change back from a five-spot," Frank mutters from behind the wheel.

"That's right!" Granpop shouts. "Damn straight you could! First game I ever saw with my sis, Ellis Kinder was pitching and Hoot Evers was in center field. My, that boy could hit! He knocked one over the right field fence and Nan spilled her popcorn she was cheering so hard!"

Billy Brown also gives shit one about baseball. "Granpop, why do you like to sit in the middle like that? You have to spread your legs."

"I'm giving my balls an airing," Granpop says.

"What balls?" Mary asks, and frowns when Billy sniggers.

Corinne looks back over her shoulder. "That's enough of that, Gran-pop," she says. "We're taking you to see your sister and we're going in your old car as you requested, so—"

258

"And it gobbles gas like you wouldn't believe," Frank says.

Corinne ignores this; she has her eyes on the prize. "It's a favor. So do me one and keep the nasty talk to yourself."

Granpop says he will, sorry, then bares his dentures at her in a leer that says he'll do just about whatever the fuck he wants.

"What balls?" Mary persists.

"Baseballs," Billy says. "Granpop's got baseball on the brain. Just read your funnybook and shut up. Don't distract me. I've made it to level five."

"If Nan had been born with balls, she could have played pro," Granpop says. "That bitch was good."

"Donald!" Corinne Brown nearly shouts. "Enough!"

"Well, she was," the old man says sulkily. "Played varsity softball on the University of Maine team that went to the Women's World Series. All the way to Oklahoma City, and almost got sucked up by a tornado!"

Frank doesn't contribute to the conversation, only peers ahead at the road he never should have gone down and thanks God he didn't overrule his father and take the Volvo. Is the road getting narrower? He believes it is. Is it getting rougher? He knows it is. Even the name strikes Frank as ominous. Who calls a road, even a piece of shit like this one, Slide Inn Road? Granpop said it was a shortcut to Highway 196, and Corinne agreed after consulting her iPad, and although Frank is no fan of shortcuts (as a banker he knows they usually lead to trouble), he is initially seduced by the smooth black tar. Soon enough, however, tar gave way to dirt, and a mile or two later the dirt gave way to rutted hardpan lined on both sides by high weeds, goldenrod, and staring sunflowers. They go over a washboard that causes the Buick to shake like a dog after a bath. He wouldn't care if the high-mileage, gas-guzzling, overweening piece of Detroit stupidity shook itself to death, were it not for the possibility of being broken down out here in East Jesus.

And now, dear God, a plugged culvert has washed out half the road, and Mr. Brown has to creep around it on the left, the tires on his side barely skirting the ditch. If there had been room to turn around he would have said the hell with this and gone back, but there is no room.

They make it. Barely.

"How far now?" he asks Corinne.

"About five miles." With MapQuest frozen she has no idea, but she has a hopeful heart. Which is a good thing. She discovered years ago that marriage to Frank and motherhood to Billy and Mary weren't what she had expected, and now, as a shitty bonus, they have this unpleasant old man living with them because they can't afford to put him in a retirement home. Hope is getting her through.

They are going to see an old lady dying of cancer but Corinne Brown hopes someday to go on a Carnival cruise and drink something with a paper umbrella in it. She hopes to have a richer, fuller life when the kids finally grow up and go out on their own. She would also like to fuck a lifeguard with muscles, a tan, and a dazzling grin full of white teeth, but understands the difference between hope and fantasy.

"Granpop," Mary says, "why do they call it the Slide In Road? Who slid in?"

"It's Inn with two *n*'s," Granpop says. "There used to be a fine one out here, even had a golf course, but it burned flat. Road's gotten bad since the last time I drove it. Used to be as smooth as a baby's bottom."

"When was that, Dad?" Frank asks. "When Ted Williams was still playing for the Red Sox? Because it sure isn't up to much now." They hit a big pothole. The Buick jounces. Frank grits his teeth.

"Whoops-my-dear!" Granpop cries, and when Billy asks him what that means, Granpop tells him it's what you say when you go over a bump like that. "Isn't it, Frank? We used to say that all the time, didn't we?"

Mr. Brown doesn't answer.

"Didn't we?"

Frank doesn't answer. His knuckles are white on the steering wheel.

"Didn't we?"

"Yeah, Dad. Whoops-my-fucking-dear."

"Frank," Corinne says in a chiding tone.

Mary giggles. Billy snickers. Granpop bares his dentures in another leer.

We're having such fun, Frank thinks. *Gee, if this trip could only last longer. If only it could last forever.*

The trouble with the old bastard, Corinne thinks, is that he still gets a kick out of life, and people who get a kick out of life take a long time kicking the bucket. They like that old bucket.

Billy returns to his game. He's reached level six. He has yet to make it to level seven.

"Billy," Frank says, "have you got bars on your phone?"

Billy pauses the game and checks. "One, but it keeps flickering on and off."

"Great. Terrific."

Another washboard shivers through the Buick and Frank slows to fifteen. He wonders if he could change his name, ditch his family, and get a job at some little bank in an Australian town. Learn to call people mate and say g'day.

"Lookit, kids!" Granpop bawls.

He's leaning forward, and from this position is able to overload both his son's right ear and his daughter-in-law's left. They wince away in opposite directions, not just from the noise but from his breath. It smells like a small animal died in his mouth, shitting as it expired. He starts most mornings burping up bile and smacking his lips afterward, as if it's tasty. Whatever's going on inside him can't be good and yet he exudes that horrible vitality. Sometimes, Corinne thinks, *I believe I could kill him. I really do. Only I think the kids love him. Christ knows why, but they do.*

"Lookit there, right over there!" One arthritis-bunched finger stabs out between Mr. and Mrs. Brown. The horny talon at the tip almost rips into Mrs. Brown's cheek. "That's the old Slide Inn, what's left of it! Right there! I been there once, you know. Me and my sister Nan and our folks. We had breakfast in our rooms!"

The kids look dutifully at what remains of the Slide Inn: a few charred beams and a cellar hole. Mrs. Brown sees an old panel truck up there, parked in the weeds and sunflowers. It looks even older than Granpop's Buick, the sides caked with rust.

"Cool, Granpop," Billy says, and once more returns to his game.

"Cool, Granpop," Mary says, and goes back to her funnybook.

The ruin of the hotel slips behind them. Frank wonders if perhaps the owners burned it down on purpose. For the insurance money.

Because, really, who would want to come out here to spend a weekend or, God forbid, a honeymoon? Maine has plenty of beauty spots, but this isn't one of them. This isn't even a place you go through to get to somewhere else unless you can't avoid it. And they could have. That's the hair across his ass.

"What if Great-Aunt Nan dies before we get there, Granpop?" Mary asks. She's finished her comic book. The next one is *Little Lulu*, and she has no interest. Little Lulu looks like a turd in a dress.

"Well, then we'll turn around and go back," Granpop says. "After the funeral, accourse."

The funeral. Oh God, the funeral. Frank hasn't even thought about how she could be dead already. She might even pop off while they're visiting, and then they would have to stay for the old bird's funeral. He's only brought a single change of clothes, and—

"Look out!" Corinne shouts. "Stop!"

Frank does, and just in time. There's another plugged culvert and another washout at the top of the hill. Only this washout goes all the way across. The crevasse looks at least three feet wide. God knows how deep it is.

"What's wrong, Dad?" Billy asks, pausing his game again.

"What's wrong, Dad?" Mary asks, stopping her search for another Archie funnybook.

"What's wrong, Frankie?" Granpop asks.

For a moment Frank Brown only sits with his hands at ten and two on the Buick's steering wheel, staring over the Buick's long hood. They knew how to make 'em back in the old days, his father sometimes likes to opine. Those, of course, being the same old days when a self-respecting woman wouldn't go shopping without first cinching on a girdle and hooking up her stockings to a garter belt, the days when gay people went in fear of their lives and there was a penny candy called niggerbabies available at every five-and-dime. Nothing like the old days, yessir!

"Well fuck your fucking shortcut," he says. "You see where it's gotten us."

"Frank," Corinne starts, but he gets out before she can finish and stands staring at the place where the road has cracked open.

Billy leans over Granpop's lap to whisper in his sister's ear: "Fuck your fucking shortcut." She puts her hands over her mouth and snickers. That's good. Granpop chuckles, which is even better. There are reasons why they love him.

Corinne gets out and joins her husband in front of the Buick's sneery grille. She looks into the deep crack in the road and sees nothing good. "What do you think we should do?"

The kids join them, Mary on her mother's side and Billy on his father's. Then Granpop comes shuffling along in his big black shoes, looking cheerful.

"I don't know," Frank says, "but we're sure not going this way."

"Got to back up," Granpop says. "Back all the way down to the good old Slide Inn. You can turn around in the driveway. No chain."

"Jesus," Frank says, and runs his hands through his thinning hair. "All right. When we get to the main road, we can decide whether to keep going to Derry or just head home."

Granpop looks outraged at the idea of retreat, but after scanning his son's face—especially the red spots on his cheeks and the red line dashed across his forehead—he keeps his trap shut.

"Everybody back in," Frank says, "but this time you sit on one side or the other, Dad. So I can see where I'm going without your head in the way."

If we had the Volvo, he thinks, I could use the backup camera. Instead we've got this oversized piece of stupidity.

"I'll walk," Granpop says. "It's not but two hundred yards."

"Me too," Mary says, and Billy seconds that.

"Fine," Frank says. "Try not to fall down and break your leg, Dad. That would be the final touch to an absolutely wonderful day."

Granpop and the kids start back down the hill to the burned-out inn's driveway, Mary and Billy holding the old man's hands. Frank thinks it could be a Norman Rockwell painting: *And a Stinky Old Bastard Shall Lead Them.*

He gets behind the Buick's steering wheel. Corinne gets in the passenger seat. She puts a hand on his arm and gives him her sweetest smile, the one that says *I love you, you big strong man.* Frank isn't big, he's not particularly strong, and there's not much bloom left on the

263

rose of their marriage (a bit wilted, that rose, petals going brown at the edges), but she needs to soothe him out of the red zone, and long experience has taught her how to do it.

He sighs and puts the Buick in reverse.

"Try not to run them down," she says, looking back over her shoulder.

"Don't tempt me," Frank says, and begins to creep the Buick backward. The ditches are deep on either side of this narrow track, and if he drops the rear end into one of them, it will be Katie bar the door.

Granpop and the kids reach the driveway before Frank is even halfway down the hill. The old man can see tracks pressed into the weeds. That panel truck looks like it's been there for years, but Granpop guesses that's not the case. Maybe someone decided to camp for a few days. It's the only thing he can think of. There sure can't be anything up there left to scavenge, any fool could see that.

Donald Brown loves his son, and there are many things Frankie can do well (although Granpop can't think of any right off the top of his head), but when it comes to backing up that Buick Estate Wagon, he isn't worth a dry popcorn fart. The rear end is wagging from side to side like the tail of an old tired dog. He almost dumps it in the left ditch, overcorrects, almost dumps it in the right one, and overcorrects again.

"Boy, he's not doing that very good," Billy says.

"Hush up," Granpop says. "He's doing fine."

"Can me and Mary go up and look at the old Slip Inn?"

"Slide Inn," Granpop says. "Sure, go on up for a minute. Run, and be ready to come back down. Your dad's not in a very good temper."

The kids run up the overgrown drive.

"Don't fall in the cellar hole!" Granpop bawls after them, and is about to add that they should stay in sight, but before he can do it there's a crunch, an abbreviated honk of the horn, and then his son cursing a blue streak. There. That's one of the things he's good at.

Granpop turns from the scampering kids to see that, after managing to back all the way down the hill without going off the road, Frank's ditched the wagon while trying to make a three-point turn.

"Shut up, Frankie!" Granpop shouts. "Quit that cussing and turn off the motor before you stall it out!" He's probably torn off half the tailpipe anyway, but there's no point telling him that.

Frank shuts off the motor and gets out. Corinne gets out too, but it's a struggle. She tears an arc of weeds ahead of the door and finally manages. The car's rear end is bumper-deep on the right side and the front is angled upward on the left.

Frank walks to his father. "The ground gave way while I was turning!"

"You cut it too tight," the old man says. "That's why only your rightside back wheel went in."

"The ground gave way, I'm telling you!"

"Cut it too tight."

"It gave way, goddammit!"

Standing side by side as they are, Corinne sees how much they look alike, and although she's seen the resemblance many times before, on this beshitted summer morning it comes as a revelation. She realizes that her husband is on time's conveyor belt, and before it dumps him off into the boneyard, he will actually *become* his father, only without Granpop's sour but occasionally engaging sense of humor. Sometimes she gets so tired. Of Frank, yes, but also of herself. Because is she any better? She'd like to think so but really doesn't believe it.

She looks around where Billy and Mary were, then at Granpop. "Donald? Where are the kids?"

The kids are inspecting the panel truck at the top of the hill, close to where the Slide Inn once stood. The tire on the driver's side is flat. While Mary goes around the front to look at the license plate (she's always on the lookout for new ones, a game Granpop taught her), Billy walks to the edge of the long hole in the ground where the inn once stood. He looks down and sees it's full of dark water. Charred beams stick up. And a woman's leg. The foot is clad in a bright blue sneaker. He stares, at first frozen, then backs away.

"Billy!" Mary calls. "It's a Delaware! My first Delaware!"

"That's right, sweetie," someone says. "Delaware it is."

Billy looks up. Two men are walking around the far end of the foundation hole. They are young. One is tall, with red hair that's all oily and clumpy. He has a lot of pimples. The other one is short and fat. He's got a bag in one hand that looks like Granpop's old bowling bag, the one with ROLLING THUNDER on the side in fading blue letters. This one has no writing on it. Both men are smiling.

Billy tries to smile back. He doesn't know if it really looks like a smile or more like a kid trying not to scream, but he hopes it's a smile. He doesn't want these two men to know he was looking into the cellar hole.

Mary comes around the side of the little white truck with its flat shoe. Her smile looks completely natural. Sure, why not? She's a little girl, and as far as she knows, everybody likes little girls.

"Hi," she says. "I'm Mary. That's my brother Billy. Our car went in the ditch." She points down the hill, at where her father and Granpop are looking at the back end of the Buick and her mother is looking up at them.

"Well hi there, Mary," says the redhead. "Good to meet you."

"You too, Billy." The fat young man drops a hand on Billy's shoulder. The touch is startling, but Billy is too scared to jump. He holds onto his smile with all his might.

"Yup, yup, little problem there," the fat young man says, peering down, and when Corinne raises one hand—tentatively—the fat one raises his in return. "Think we could help, Galen?"

"I bet we could," says the redhead. "We've got our own problem, as you see." And he points to the flat tire. "No spare." He bends down to Billy. His eyes are bright blue. There doesn't seem to be anything in them. "Did you check out that hole, Billy? Mighty big one."

"No," Billy says. He's trying to sound natural, unconcerned by the question, but doesn't know if he's getting that in his voice or not. He thinks he might faint. He wishes, God he wishes that he'd never looked down there. Blue sneaker. "I was afraid I might fall in."

"Smart kid," Galen says. "Isn't he, Pete?"

"Smart," the fat one agrees, and tosses Corinne another wave. Granpop is now looking up the hill, too. Frank is still staring at the Buick's ditched rear end, shoulders slumped.

"That skinny one your dad?" redheaded Galen asks Mary.

"Yup, and that's our granpop. He's old."

"No shit Sherlock," Pete says. His hand is still on Billy's shoulder. Billy looks down at it and sees what might be blood under the nail of Pete's second finger.

"Well, you know what?" Galen says—he's leaning down, speaking to Mary, who's smiling up at him. "I bet we could push that big old sumbitch right out of there. Then maybe your dad could give us a ride to someplace where there's a garage. Get a new tire for our little truck."

"Are you from Delaware?" Mary asks.

"Well, we been through there," Pete says. Then he and Galen exchange a look and they laugh.

"Let's take a look at that car of yours," Galen says. "Want me to carry you down, sweetie?"

"No, that's okay," Mary says, her smile growing slightly tentative. "I can walk."

"Your bro don't talk much, does he?" Pete says. His hand, the one not holding the bowling bag (if that's what it is), is still on Billy's shoulder.

"Usually you can't keep him quiet," Mary says. "His tongue is hung in the middle and runs at both ends, that's what Granpop says."

"Maybe he saw something that scared him quiet," Galen says. "Woodchuck or fox. Or something else."

"I didn't see anything," Billy says. He thinks he might start crying and tells himself he can't, he can't.

"Well, come on," Galen says. He takes Mary's hand—this she allows—and they start down the overgrown driveway. Pete walks beside Billy with his hand still on Billy's shoulder. It's not gripping, but Billy has an idea it would grip if he tried to run. He's pretty sure the men saw him looking into that water-filled cellar hole. He has an idea they are in bad trouble here.

"Hey, guys! Hello, ma'am!" Galen sounds as cheerful as a day in July. "Looks like you got a little trouble here. Want a hand?"

"Oh, that would be wonderful," Corinne says.

"Terrific," Frank says. "Damn road went out from under the car while I was turning around."

"Cut it too tight," Granpop says.

Frank gives him an ugly look, then turns back to the newcomers and gets up a grin. "I bet with you two men, we could push it right out of there."

"No doubt," says Pete.

Frank holds out his hand. "Frank Brown. This is my wife, Corinne, and my father, Donald."

"Pete Smith," says the fat young man.

"Galen Prentice," says the redhead.

There are handshakes all around. Granpop mutters "Meetcha," but hardly gives them a glance. He's looking at Billy.

"Ma'am," Galen says, "why don't you take the wheel? Me and Pete and your handsome hubby here can push while you steer."

"Oh, I don't know," Corinne says.

"I could do it," Granpop says. "It's my car. From back in the old days. They really knew how to make em back then." He sounds sulky, and Billy's heart, which had risen a little, now sinks. He thought Granpop might have an idea about these men, but now guesses he doesn't.

"Gramps, I need you to do the heavy looking-on. I'm sure Frank's missus can do the driving. Can't you?"

"I suppose . . ." Corinne trails off.

Galen gives her a thumbs-up. "Sure you can! Kids, you stand aside with your gramps."

"He's Granpop," Mary says. "Not Gramps."

Galen grins. "Why sure," he says. "Granpop it is. Granpop goes the weasel."

Corinne gets behind the wheel of the Buick and adjusts the seat forward. Billy can't stop thinking of that leg sticking up out of the murky water in the cellar hole. The blue sneaker.

Galen and Pete take spots on the left and right of the Buick's canted rear deck. Frank is in the middle.

"Start her up, missus!" Galen calls, and when she does, the three men lean forward, brace their feet, and place their hands on the station wagon's flat back. "Okay! Give it some gas! Not a lot, just easy!"

The motor revs. Granpop bends toward Billy. His breath is as sour as ever, but it's Granpop's breath and Billy doesn't mind. "What's wrong, kiddo?"

"Dead lady," Billy whispers back, and now the tears come. "Dead lady in that hole up there."

"Little more!" Fat Pete yells. "Goose the bitch!"

Corinne gives it more gas and the men push. The Buick's rear tires start to spin, then take hold. The Estate Wagon comes up onto the road.

"Whoa, whoa, whoa!" Galen shouts.

Billy has a sudden confused wish that his mother would just drive away and leave them, that she would go and be safe. But she stops, puts the Buick in park, and gets out, holding down the hem of her dress with the heel of her palm.

"Easy-peasy-Japaneezy!" Galen cries. "Back on the road and good as new! Only we've still got a little problem. Don't we, Pete?"

"Sure do," Pete says. "Flat tire on our truck and no spare. Picked up a nail when we druv up there, I guess." He puffs out his stubbled cheeks, now shiny with sweat, and makes a flat-tire sound: *Pwsshhh!* He put his bag down to push, but now he picks it up. And unzips it.

"Damn," Frank says. "No spare, huh?"

"Don't that suck?" Galen says.

"What were you doing up there?" Corinne asks. She's left the Buick running, the door open. She looks at her husband, who's smiling his big banker's smile, then at her two children. Her girl looks okay, but Billy's face is white as wax.

"Campin," Pete says. His hand has disappeared into his bag that isn't a bowling bag.

"Huh," Frank says. "That's . . ."

He doesn't finish, maybe doesn't know how, and no one seems to know how to start the conversation going again. Birds sing in the trees. Crickets rub their reedy legs in the high weeds, which is the universe they know. The seven people stand in a loose circle behind the idling Buick. Frank and Corinne exchange a look that asks *what's going on here?*

Granpop knows. He saw men like these in Vietnam. Scavengers and skedaddlers. One got stood up against a board fence and was shot by one of his own men after the Tet Offensive wound down, a clusterfuck the grandchildren he's too old to have will probably never read about in their history books.

Frank, meanwhile, jerks to life like a wind-up toy. His your-loan-is-approved smile reappears. He takes his wallet from his back pocket.

269

"I wish we could take you to a garage or something, but I've got a full car, as you see—"

"Your missus could sit on my lap," Pete says, and waggles his eyebrows.

Frank chooses to ignore this. "But tell you what, we'll stop and send someone back first place we see. In the meantime, how does ten apiece sound? For helping us out."

He opens the wallet. Very gently, Galen plucks it from his hand. Frank doesn't try to stop him. He just stares at his hands, wide-eyed, as if the wallet is still there. As if he can still feel its weight but now it's invisible.

"Why don't I just take all of it?" Galen says.

"Give that back!" Corinne says. She feels Mary's hand creep into hers and she folds her own fingers over it. "That's not yours!"

"Is now." His voice is as gentle as the hand that took the wallet. "Let's see what we got here."

He opens it. Frank takes a step forward. Pete takes his hand out of his not-a-bowling-bag. There's a revolver in it. Looks like a .38 to Granpop.

"Stand back, Frankie-Wankie," Pete says. "We're doing business here."

Galen removes a small sheaf of bills from the wallet. He folds them over, puts them in the pocket of his jeans, then tosses the wallet to Pete, who puts it in the bag. "Gramps, let's have yours."

"Outlaws," Granpop says. "That's what you are."

"That's right," Galen agrees in his gentle voice, "and if you don't want me to go upside this boy's head, give me your wallet."

That does it for Billy; his bladder lets go and his crotch gets warm. He starts to cry, partly out of shame and partly from fear.

Granpop digs his old scarred Lord Buxton from the front left pocket of his baggy pants and hands it over. It's bulging, but mostly with cards, photos, and receipts going back five or more years. Galen pulls out a twenty and a few ones, stuffs them in his pocket, and tosses the Lord Buxton to Pete. Into the bag it goes.

"Ought to clean it out once in a while, Grampy," Galen says. "That's one slutty billfold."

"Says the man who looks like he warshed his hair last Thanksgiving," Granpop says, and quick as a snake striking out of a bush, Galen slaps him across the face. Mary bursts into tears and puts her face against her mother's hip.

"Stop that!" Frank says, as if the thing is not already done and his father bleeding from lip and nostril. Then, in the same breath: "Shut up, Dad!"

"I don't let folks sass me," Galen says, "not even old men. Old men should especially know better. Now Corinne. Let's get your purse out of the car. Your little girl can come with us." He takes Mary by the arm, the pads of his fingers sinking into her scant flesh.

"Let her alone," Corinne says.

"You're not in charge here," Galen says. "Tell me what to do again and I'll change your face. Pete, make Frank and his father stand together. Shoulders touching. And if either of them moves . . ."

Pete gestures with the revolver. Granpop shuffles next to his son. Frank is breathing through his nose in quick little snorts. Granpop wouldn't be surprised if he passed out.

"You saw, didn't you?" Pete asks Billy. "Fess up."

"I didn't see anything," Billy says through his tears. Blubbing like a baby and can't help it. Blue sneaker.

"Liar liar pants on fire," Pete says. He laughs and ruffles the boy's hair.

Galen comes back, folding more bills into his pocket. He's let go of Mary. The girl is now clinging to her mother. Corinne looks dazed.

Granpop doesn't waste time looking at his people. He's watching Galen rejoin Pete, needing to see what passes between them, and he sees pretty much what he expected and no sense pretending otherwise. They can take the Buick and leave the Brown family, or they can take the Buick and kill the Brown family. If caught, these two will get life in the Shank no matter what kind of score they run up.

"There's more," Granpop says.

"What's that?" Galen asks. He's the talker. His fellow outlaw seems to be the fat silent type.

"More money. Quite a bit. I'll give it to you if you let us be. Just take the wagon and let us be."

"How much more?" Galen asks.

"Can't say for sure, but I put it around thirty-three hundred. It's in my go-bag."

"Why would an old fuck like you be driving around the williwags with three thousand and change?"

"Because of my sister Nan. We were going up to Derry to see her before she passes away. Won't be long, if it hasn't happened already. She's got the cancer. It's all through her."

Pete has put his not-a-bowling-bag down again. Now he rubs two of his fingers together and says, "This is the world's smallest violin playing 'My Heart Pumps Purple Piss For You.'"

Granpop pays no attention. "I cashed out most of my Social Security to pay for the funeral. Nan hasn't got squat, and they give you a discount if you pay cash." He pats Billy's shoulder. "This boy looked it all up for me on the Internet."

Billy did no such thing, but except for another chest-hitching sob or two, he keeps quiet. He wishes he and Mary had never gone up to the Slide Inn, and when he looks at his father through blurry eyes, he feels a moment of bright hate. *It's your fault, Dad,* he thinks. *You ditched the car and these men stole our money and now they're going to kill us. Granpop knows. I can see he does.*

"Where's your go-bag?" Galen asks.

"In back with the rest of the luggage."

"Get it."

Granpop goes to the Buick. He gives a grunt as he raises the trunk lid; that's his back trying to cramp up. Back goes first, pecker goes last, everything else in between, his own father used to say.

The bag is just like Pete's, with a zipper along the top, except it's longer—more like a dufflebag than a bowling bag. He runs the zipper and spreads the bag open.

"No gun in there, Gramps, is there?" Galen asks.

"No, no, that's for boys like you, but looka this." Granpop brings out a battered old softball glove. "The sister I was telling you about? This was hers. I brought it for her to look at if she hasn't passed on yet. Or in a coma. She wore it in the Women's World Series, out in Okie City. Softball, you know. Played shortstop. Before the Second

World War, if you can believe it. And lookit this!" He turns the glove over.

"Gramps," Galen says, "all due respect but I don't give a fuck."

"Yeah, but here on the back," Granpop persists. "See it? Signed by Dom DiMaggio. Joltin' Joe's brother, you know."

He tosses the glove aside and burrows into the bag again. "Got about two hundred baseball cards, some signed and worth money—"

Pete grabs Billy's arm and twists it. Billy screams.

"Don't!" Corinne screams back. "Don't hurt my boy!"

"It's your boy's fault you're in this mess," Pete says. "Snoopy little brat." Then, to Granpop: "We don't want no fuckin baseball cards!"

Mary is crying, Corinne is crying, Billy sees his dad looking ready to pass out, and Granpop doesn't seem to care about any of them. Granpop has retreated into his own world. "What about funnybooks?" he says. He brings out a handful and brandishes them. "The Archies and Caspers wouldn't fetch nothing, but there's a few old Supermans . . . and a Batman or two, one where he fights the Joker . . ."

"I think I'm going to tell Pete to shoot your son, if you don't stop stalling," Galen says. "Is the money there or not?"

"Yeah, yeah," Granpop says, "down at the bottom, but I got something else that might interest you."

"I'm all done being interested," Galen says. He steps forward. "I'll just get the money myself. If it's there at all. Get out of my way."

"Oh, wake up," Granpop says. "This would fetch twice what I got for cash." He brings out the Louisville Slugger. "Signed by Ted Williams, the Splendid Splinter himself. Put it on eBay, it'd fetch seven thousand. Seven at least."

"How'd your sis come by it?" Galen asks, interested at last. He can see the signature, faded but legible, on the barrel.

"Just gave him a smile and a wink when he came down Autograph Alley," Granpop says, and swings the bat. It connects with Galen's temple. His scalp pops open like a windowshade. Blood flies up. His eyes squeeze shut in pain and surprise. He staggers, one hand out and flailing, trying to keep his balance.

"Get the other one, Frankie!" Granpop shouts. "Take him down!"

Frank doesn't move, just stands there with his mouth open.

Pete stares at Galen, for a precious moment completely stunned, but the moment passes. He turns the gun toward Granpop. Billy springs at him.

"No!" Corinne shouts. "Billy, no!"

Billy grabs Pete's arm, bringing it down, and when Pete fires the gun, the slug goes into the ground between his feet. Galen straightens, one hand clutching the station wagon's raised trunk lid. Granpop winds up, ignoring a howl of protest from his back, and hits the redhead in the ribs with 33 ounces of solid Kentucky ash. Galen's knees buckle and his gasp—"Pete, shoot this fucker!"—is hardly more than a whisper. Granpop raises the bat. There's another shot, but he's not hit (at least he doesn't think so), and he brings the bat down on Galen's lowered head. Galen falls face-first into one of the Buick wagon's tire treads.

Pete tries to shake Billy off, but Billy holds on like a ferret, his eyes bulging and his teeth digging into his lower lip. The gun waves here and there and goes off a third time, sending a bullet into the sky.

"Now you, motherhump," Granpop snarls.

Pete at last flings Billy away, but before he can raise the gun, Granpop brings the bat down on his wrist, breaking it. The gun drops onto the ground. Pete turns and runs, leaving his not-a-bowling-bag on the ground.

The two children fling themselves at Granpop, hugging him and almost knocking him over. He pushes them away. His old heart is hammering and if it just gave out, he wouldn't be a bit surprised.

"Billy, get the fat one's bag. Our goods are in it and I don't think I can bend over."

The boy doesn't, maybe the gunshots deafened him a little, but the girl does. She throws the bag into the back of the Buick and then rubs her hands on the front of her unicorn tee.

"Frank," Granpop says, "is that redhaired boy dead?"

Frank doesn't move, but Corinne kneels next to Galen. After several seconds she looks up, her eyes very blue under her pale forehead. "He's not breathing."

"Well, that's no great loss to the world," Granpop says. "Billy, get that gun. Keep your hands away from the trigger."

Billy picks up the fallen revolver. He holds it out to his father, but Frank only looks at it. Granpop takes it and puts it in the pocket where his wallet was. Frank just stands there, looking at Galen, lying facedown in the weeds with the top of his head stove in.

"Granpop, Granpop!" Billy says, tugging the old man's arm. His mouth is trembling, tears are streaming down his cheeks, and snot lathers his upper lip. "What if the fat one has another gun in their little truck?"

"What if we just get the hell out of here?" Granpop says. "Corinne, you drive. I can't. Kids, get in back." He's not even sure he can sit, he's fucked up his back most righteously, but he'll have to do it, no matter how much it hurts.

Corinne closes the trunk. The kids take one more look up the overgrown driveway to see if Pete is coming back, then they run for the wagon.

Granpop goes to his son. "You had a chance and just stood there. You could have got me killed. Got all of us killed." Granpop slaps Frank across the face just as he, Granpop, was slapped by the man who now lies dead at their feet. "Get in, son. Maybe you're too old to help what you are, I don't know."

Frank walks to the front passenger side like a man in a dream and gets in. Granpop opens the door behind him and finds he can't bend down. So he falls backward onto the seat, pulling his legs in after him with little whimpers of pain. Mary crawls over him to close the door and that hurts, too. It's not just his back, feels like he's busted his gut.

"Granpop, are you all right?" Corinne asks. She's looking back. Frank is staring straight ahead through the windshield. His hands are on his knees.

"I'm all right," Granpop says, although he isn't. He'd like to have about six of the painkillers his sister no doubt has from her oncologist, but Nan is a hundred miles from here and he doesn't think they'll be seeing her today. No, not today. "Drive."

"Did you really have that money, Granpop?" Billy asks as his mother starts back the way they came, going much faster than Frank dared to. Wanting to put the Slide Inn behind them. And Slide Inn Road—that, too.

"Course not," Granpop says. He wipes tears from his granddaughter's face and hugs her against him. It hurts, but he does it.

"Granpop," she says. "You left Aunt Nan's special baseball bat."

"That's all right," Granpop says, stroking her hair. It's all sweaty and tangled. "Maybe we'll get it later."

Frank finally speaks. "We passed a little store on 196 just before we turned off. I'll call the police from there." He turns and looks at the old man. There's a red mark on his cheek from the slap. "This is your fault, Dad. It's all on you. We had to bring your fucking car, didn't we? If we'd had the Volvo—"

"Shut up, Frank," Corinne says. "Please. Just this once."

And Frank does.

Thinking of Flannery O'Connor

RED SCREEN

Wilson is having a bad morning. He cuts himself shaving and is using a Kleenex to clean away a rill of blood on his chin when Sandi pops her head in to admonish him about leaving the toilet seat up and the cap off the toothpaste. He spills juice on his tie and has to change it. Before he can escape to work, there are several more admonishments: she found beer bottles in the trash instead of the recycling, and he forgot to rinse his ice cream bowl before putting it in the dishwasher. There's another one, but it goes in one ear and out the other without catching on anything in between. Kind of a bummer, all in all. Has he become forgetful and a little slipshod lately, or has she gotten more prickly in the last six or eight months? He doesn't know and it's too early for such questions.

Yet once in the car and backing down the driveway, he has an idea that elevates his mood. If there's such a thing as bad karma, he may have frontloaded his for the day and from here on . . .

"Clear sailing!" he exclaims, and treats himself to a cigarette out of the pack in the glove compartment.

This optimistic idea holds for fifteen minutes. Then he gets a call redirecting him to 34th Avenue in Queens. He is told to see the officers, which is never good karma.

*   *   *

Five hours later, when he should be thinking about lunch, Wilson is instead looking through oneway glass into a small interview room. There's a table and two chairs. In one of the chairs sits a man named Leonard Crocker. He's handcuffed to a ringbolt on his side of the table. He's wearing a strap-style undershirt on top of khaki work pants. His outer shirt is now in a tagged plastic bag and bound for forensics. When its turn comes (it will be awhile because there's always a backlog), the bloodstains on it will be typed and DNA-matched. This is a formality. Crocker has already confessed to the murder. Soon his undershirt and khakis will be swapped for jailhouse tans.

Wilson puts on his ID lanyard. When he goes into the room, he also puts on a smile. "Hi, Mr. Crocker. Remember me?"

Leonard Crocker seems perfectly at ease, handcuffs and all. "You're the detective."

"Right!" Wilson sits down. "Do you answer to Len, Lennie, or Leonard?"

"Lennie, mostly. That's what the guys down at the plumbing shop call me."

"Lennie it is, then. What we're having here—if you agree—is just sort of a preliminary conversation. You were given your rights, correct?"

Lennie smiles as a man does when seeing through a trick question. "First by the officers at the scene, then by you. I called them, you know. The officers."

"Great! Just to recap, anything you say—"

"Can be used against me."

Wilson's smile widens into a grin. "Bingo! What about legal representation? How's your memory on that? Because we're being recorded, you know."

"I can have a lawyer at any time. If I can't afford one, you'll get me one. It's the law."

"Correctamundo. So do you want one? Just say the word." *And I can get some lunch*, Wilson thinks.

"I'm happy to talk to you, Detective, but I'll need a lawyer at the trial, right?"

"Unless you want to defend yourself. But a man who defends himself—"

Lennie raises a finger and cocks his head, more the gesture of a scholar than a plumber. "—has a fool for a client."

Wilson laughs and nods. "Give the man a Kewpie doll." Then he grows more serious, folding his hands under his chin and looking straight at Lennie. "Why don't we get right to the point? You killed your wife this morning, didn't you? Stabbed her three times in the stomach, after which she bled out. That's what you told the officers, right? And me."

Lennie shakes his head. "If you'll recall, what I actually said was *I did it*."

"Meaning you killed your wife. Arlene Crocker."

"She wasn't my wife."

Wilson takes his notebook from the inside pocket of his jacket and consults it. "Isn't your wife Arlene Crocker?"

"Not today. Not for the last year." He considers. "Maybe longer. It's hard to be sure."

"Are you saying you killed a stranger? One who just happens to look like your wife of nine years?"

"Yes." Lennie is looking at Wilson patiently, his face saying *eventually you'll get to the right questions but I'm not going to help you.*

"So . . . when we type and DNA-test the blood on your kitchen floor and all over your shirt, it won't match that of the deceased woman?"

"Oh, it probably will." Lennie gives a judicious nod. "I'm almost sure it will. Although I hope your science people will look for peculiar . . . mmm . . ." He searches for the right word. "Peculiar *components*. I don't think you'll find any, but it would be wise to check. I expect to go to jail for killing that thing, but I'd certainly prefer not to."

Now Wilson understands. Crocker has already got an insanity plea on his radar.

"What are you telling me, Lennie? That your wife was possessed? Help me understand."

Lennie thinks it over. "I don't think you could call it that, exactly. When a person is possessed—correct me if I'm wrong, Detective—a spirit, or maybe a demon, comes in and takes over, but that person is still there, inside. Being held prisoner. Is that your understanding?"

Wilson has seen *The Exorcist* and a couple of similar movies, so he nods. "Pretty much. But that isn't what happened to your wife?"

"No. She died when it came in. They all do."

"They all? Who all?"

"Not many so far, compared to the population of the earth, which is now eight billion—you can google it—but there's more of them all the time. They take over, Detective. It's the perfect disguise. *We're* the perfect disguise."

Wilson pretends to think this over. What he's really thinking is this interview will be useless to the District Attorney. There's going to be plenty of rigamarole ahead—a couple of prosecution psychiatrists, plus Crocker's own shrink. Wilson wouldn't be surprised if Crocker already had one on speed-dial.

"Aliens?"

Crocker's face says *the penny drops*. "That's right. Aliens. I don't know if they come from space or from some parallel world. The websites are pretty much split on that. I think space. It makes sense, because . . ." He leans forward, earnest. "The speed of light, you know."

"What about it?" Not that Wilson cares. He's losing interest. What interests him is a ham and turkey club from the deli down the street. And a Marlboro chaser.

"Spaceships can't exceed it or they go backwards in time or maybe just disintegrate. That's the science. But pure *mind*, Detective . . . *that* can make the jump. Only once they get here, they need bodies. Would probably die without them. We're in the preliminary stage of the invasion now, but if the world governments don't wise up, they'll be coming in thousands, hundreds of thousands, *millions*."

Crocker has been leaning forward over his cuffed and chained hands, but now he sits back. "It's all on the Internet."

"I bet it is, Lennie. I bet Kamala Harris is one of those invaders, just waiting for Amtrak Joe to croak so she can get her hands on the levers of power." He gets up. "I think you need to go back to your cell and think this over before you get arraigned. And, just my advice, I think you need a good lawyer. Because only a good one could sell that to a jury."

"Sit down," Lennie says quietly. "You'll want to hear this."

Wilson looks at his watch and decides to give Leonard Crocker five more minutes, possibly even ten. Maybe he can decide if the man is really crazy or trying to play him. He should be able to do that; he's a detective, after all.

"Five or six years ago, someone figured out what's going on. It's on the dark web, Detective, and spreading up from there. Like ink in water."

"I'm sure it is." Wilson is no longer smiling. "Along with blood-drinking Democrats, Clorox enemas to cure Covid, animal crush videos, and kiddie porn. You killed your wife, Lennie. You need to cut the shit and think about that a little. You stabbed her with a butcher knife and watched her die."

"They change. They become short-tempered and critical. They're not content with just being here, they want to dominate. But we have a chance because some computer wizard figured out a way to detect them. If we survive, there'll be a statue of him in every country, all over the world. The aliens trigger a deep command, okay? Automatic. Foolproof. Only a few people know about it now, but the information is spreading. That's what the Internet's good for, spreading information."

Not to mention mental illness, Wilson thinks.

"It's going to be a race." Lennie's eyes are wide. "A race against time."

"Whoa, rewind, okay? You killed your wife because she got short-tempered and critical?"

Lennie smiles. "Don't be dense, Detective. Many women nag, I know that. So do men. It's easy to dismiss the preliminary indications." He spreads his hands as far as the cuffs will allow. Which isn't very far.

Wilson says, "I think that married to you, Arlene had a lot to be short-tempered and critical about."

"She started picking," Lennie says. "Picking and picking and picking. At first I just felt depressed—"

"Old self-image took a hit, did it?"

"Then I became suspicious."

"My own wife does some picking," Wilson says. "Likes to tell me my car's a traveling pigpen, gets pissy if I forget to put down the toilet seat. But I'm a long way from using a butcher knife on her."

"I got the red screen. It's only for a second or two, so *they* won't see. But when I saw it, I knew."

"What I know is this interview is over." Wilson turns to the mirror on the wall to his left and runs the side of his hand across his throat: *cut it*.

"It's subtle," Lennie says. He's giving Wilson a look that's both pitying and superior. "Like that story about how you boil a frog by turning up the heat very slowly. They take from you. They take your self-respect, and when you're weak . . ." He jerks his hands upward to the length of the chain and makes a choking gesture. ". . . they take your life."

"Women, right?"

"Women or men. It's not a sexist thing, don't get that idea."

"Not *The Exorcist*, but *The Invasion of the Body Snatchers*."

The wife-killer breaks into a wide grin. *"Exactly!"*

"You stick to that, Lennie. See how it works out for you."

Wilson gets home at quarter of seven. Sandi's in the living room, watching the evening news. One place is set at the kitchen table. It looks lonely.

"Hey, babe," he calls.

"Your dinner's in the oven. The chicken's probably dried out. You said you'd be home by five."

"Things came up."

"They always do with you."

Did he tell Sandi he'd be home by five? Wilson honestly can't remember. But he remembers Crocker—probably now cooling his heels in Metropolitan Detention—saying *It's subtle*.

He gets chicken and potatoes out of the oven and green beans out of the steamer on the stove. He thinks the potatoes will be okay, but the chicken and beans look elderly and unappetizing.

"Did you pick up the dry cleaning?"

He pauses, a slice of chicken breast half-cut. Half-*sawn*, actually. "What dry cleaning?"

She gets up and stands in the doorway. *"Our* dry cleaning. I told you last night, Frank. Jesus!"

"I—" His phone rings. He pulls it off his belt and looks at the screen. If the call was from his partner, he would decline. But it's not. It's from Captain Alvarez. "I have to take this."

"Of course you do," she says and turns back to the living room so as not to miss the latest Coronavirus death count. "Honest to *God*."

He thinks of going after her, trying to smooth this over, but it's his boss, so he pushes accept. He listens to what Alvarez has to say, then sits down. "Are you *shitting* me? *How?*"

His voice brings Sandi back into the doorway. His slumped posture—phone to ear, head bent, one forearm resting on his thigh—brings her to the table.

Wilson listens some more, then hangs up. He takes his plate to the sink and dumps everything into the garbage disposer. "The perfect fucking end to a perfect fucking day."

"What happened?" Sandi puts a hand on his arm. Her touch is light but very welcome to him.

"We had a guy in custody who killed his wife. I was at the scene, a real mess. Blood all over the kitchen, her lying in it. Back at the station, I did the preliminary interrogation. The doer was crazy as a loon. He claimed she was an alien, part of an invasion force."

"Oh my God."

"He killed himself. They were doing intake at MetDet. He picked up a pencil, snapped the chain it was on, and stabbed himself in the jugular vein. Alvarez says maybe it was dumb luck, but the intake sergeant says it looked like he knew right where to put it."

"Maybe he had medical training."

"Sandi, he was a *plumber*."

That makes her laugh, which makes Wilson laugh. He puts his forehead against hers.

"It's not funny," Sandi says, "but the way you said it was. *Plumber*." She laughs again.

"He fought them, Alvarez said. All the time the blood was pumping out—*spurting* out—he fought them. When he passed out they got him to Presbyterian, but it was too late. He'd lost too much blood."

"Turn off the TV for me," Sandi says. "I'll scramble you some eggs."

"And bacon?"

"Bad for your cholesterol, but tonight . . . okay."

*   *   *

They make love that night for the first time in . . . weeks? No, longer. A month at least. It's good. When it's over, Sandi says, "Are you still smoking?"

He thinks about lying. He thinks about the now-deceased plumber saying *She started picking. Picking and picking and picking.* He thinks about how nice this evening was. How different from the last six or eight months.

They change, Lennie said. *They become short-tempered and critical.*

He doesn't lie. He says he still smokes, but not much. Half a pack a day at most, expecting her to say *Even that can kill you.*

She doesn't. She says, "Have you got any handy? If you do, give me one, please."

"You haven't smoked in—"

"There's something I need to tell you. I've been putting it off."

Oh God, Wilson thinks.

He turns on his bedside lamp. His keys, wallet, phone, and a little change are scattered across the top of the table. He's put his service weapon in the drawer. He always does. Behind it is a pack of Marlboros and a Bic lighter. He gives her one, thinking *After all these years without, a single puff will probably knock her flat.*

"Take one for yourself."

"I don't have an ashtray. When I want one, I usually go in the guest bathroom."

"We'll use my water glass."

He lights her up, then his own. Smoking in bed, like when they were first married and thought they'd have a couple of kids and live happily ever after. Twelve years later, there are no kids and Wilson is feeling mighty mortal.

"You're not going to tell me you want a divorce, are you?" He's joking. He's not joking.

"No. I want to tell you why I've been so fucking grumpy and hard to live with since this spring."

"Okay . . ."

She puffs her cigarette but doesn't inhale. "I've been wobbling."

"I don't know what that means, Sandi."

"It means I'm going into menopause, Frank. Pretty soon it'll be meno-*stop*."

"Are you sure?"

She gives him a sour look, but then snorts a laugh. "I think I'd know, don't you?"

"Babe . . . you're only thirty-nine."

"In my family we start early and end early. My sister Pat went into the change when she was thirty-six. My emotions have been all over the place. As you may have noticed."

"Why didn't you tell me?"

"Because then I'd have to admit it to myself." She sighs. "My last period was four months ago, and since then, just spotting. Like the last few drips from a faucet when you turn it off." A tear rolls down her cheek, just the one. She drops the half-smoked cigarette into the water glass and covers her eyes with one hand. "I feel *dry*, Frankie. Old and used up and unlovable. I've been a bitch to you, and I'm sorry."

He douses his own cigarette. He puts the glass on his night table and takes her in his arms. "I love you, Sandi. Always have, always will."

"Thank you, sweetheart."

She reaches past him, her breast pressing his cheek, and turns out the light. For a moment, no more than a second, the screen of his cell phone flashes red.

In the dark, Sandi Wilson smiles.

THE TURBULENCE EXPERT

1

Craig Dixon was sitting in the living room of a Four Seasons junior suite, eating expensive room service chow and watching a movie on pay-per-view, when the phone rang. His previously calm heartbeat lost its mojo and sped up. Dixon was unattached, the perfect definition of a rolling stone, and only one person knew he was here in this fancy hotel across from Boston Common. He considered not answering, but the man he thought of as the facilitator would only call back, and keep calling until he answered. If he refused to answer, there would be consequences.

This isn't hell, he thought, the accommodations are too nice, but it's purgatory. And no prospect of retirement for a long time.

He muted the TV and picked up the phone. He didn't say hello. What he said was, "This isn't fair. I just got in from Seattle two days ago. I'm still in recovery mode."

"Understood and terribly sorry, but this has come up and you're the only one available." *Sorry* came out *thorry*.

The facilitator had the soothing, put-you-to-sleep voice of an FM disc jockey, spoiled only by an occasional light lisp. Dixon had never seen him, but imagined him as tall and slim, with blue eyes and an ageless, unlined face. In reality he was probably fat, bald, and swarthy, but Dixon felt confident his mental picture would never change, because he never expected to see the facilitator. He had known a number of turbulence experts over his years with the firm—if it *was* a firm—and none of them had ever seen the man. Certainly none of the experts who worked for him were unlined; even the ones in their twenties and thirties looked middle-aged. It wasn't the job, where there were sometimes late hours but no heavy lifting. It was what made them capable of *doing* the job.

"Tell me," Dixon said.

"Allied Airlines Flight 19. Nonstop Boston to Sarasota. Leaves at 8:10 tonight. You've just got time to make it."

"There's *nobody* else?" Dixon realized he was nearly bleating. "I'm tired, man. *Tired.* That run from Seattle was a bitch."

"Your usual seat," the facilitator said, pronouncing the last word *theat*. Then he hung up.

Dixon looked at swordfish he no longer wanted. He looked at the Kate Winslet TV series he would never finish, at least not in Boston. He thought—and not for the first time!—of just packing up and renting a car and driving north, first to New Hampshire, then to Maine, then across the border to Canada. But they would catch him. This he knew. And the rumors of what happened to TEs who ran included electrocution, evisceration, even being boiled alive. Dixon did not believe these rumors . . . except he sort of did.

He began to pack. There wasn't much. Turbulence experts traveled light.

2

His ticket was waiting for him at the counter. As always, his assignment placed him in coach, just aft of the starboard wing, in the middle seat. How that particular one could always be available was another mystery, like who the facilitator was, where he was calling from, or what sort of an organization he worked for. Like the ticket, the seat was just always waiting for him.

Dixon placed his bag in the overhead bin and looked at tonight's neighbors and fellow travelers: a businessman with red eyes and gin breath on the aisle, a middle-aged lady who looked like a librarian next to the window. The businessman grunted something unintelligible when Dixon sidled past him with a murmured apology. The guy was reading a paperback charmingly titled *Don't Let the Boss F**k With You*. The librarian type was looking out the window at the various pieces of equipment that were trundling back and forth, as if they were the most fascinating things she had ever seen. There was knitting in her lap. Looked to Dixon like a sweater.

She turned, gave him a smile, and held out her hand. "Hello, I'm Mary Worth. Just like the comic strip chick."

Dixon didn't know any comic strip chick named Mary Worth, but he shook her hand. "Craig Dixon. Nice to meet you."

The businessman grunted and turned a page in his book.

"I'm so looking forward to this," Mary Worth said. "I haven't had a real vacation in twelve years. I'm sharing the rent of a little place on Siesta Key with a couple of chums."

"Chums," the businessman grunted. The grunt seemed to be his default position.

"Yes!" Mary Worth twinkled. "We have it for three weeks. We've never actually met, but they are true chums. We're all widows. We met in a chat room on the Internet. It's so wonderful, the Internet. There was nothing like it when I was young."

"Pedophiles think it's wonderful, too," said the businessman, and turned another page.

Ms. Worth's smile faltered, then came on strong. "It's very nice to meet you, Mr. Dixon. Are you traveling for business or pleasure?"

"Business," he said.

The speakers went ding-dong. "Good evening, ladies and gentle-men, this is Captain Stuart speaking. You'll see that we are pulling away from the gate and beginning our taxi to Runway 3, where we're third in line for takeoff. We estimate a two-hour-and-forty-minute flight down to SRQ, which should put you in the land of palms and sandy beaches just before eleven o'clock. Skies are clear, and we're anticipating a smooth ride all the way. Now I'd like you to fasten your seatbelts, put away any tray tables you may have lowered—"

"Like we had anything to put *on* them," the businessman grunted.

"—and secure any personal possessions you may have been using. Thank you for flying Allied tonight. We know you have many choices."

"My ass," the businessman grunted.

"Never mind your ass, just read your book," Dixon said. The businessman shot him a startled look.

Dixon's heart was already beating hard, his stomach was clenched, his throat dry with anticipation. He could tell himself it was going to be all right, it was *always* all right, but that didn't help. He dreaded the depths that would soon open beneath him.

Allied 19 took off at 8:13 PM, just three minutes behind schedule.

3

Somewhere over Maryland, a flight attendant pushed a drinks-and-snacks cart down the aisle. The businessman put his book aside, waiting impatiently for her to reach him. When she did, he took a can of Schweppes tonic, two little bottles of gin, and a bag of Fritos. His Mastercard didn't work when she ran it and he gave her his American Express card, glaring at her as if the failure of his first offering were her fault. Dixon wondered if the Mastercard was maxed out and Mr. Businessman saved the Amex for break-glass-in-case-of-emergency situations. It could be, his haircut was bad and he looked frayed around the edges. It didn't matter one way or the other to Dixon, but it was something to think about besides the constant low terror. The anticipation. They were cruising at 34,000 feet, and that was a long way down.

Mary Worth asked for some wine, and poured it neatly into her little plastic glass.

"You're not having anything, Mr. Dixon?"

"No. I don't eat or drink on airplanes."

Mr. Businessman grunted. He was already through his first gin and tonic, and starting on the second.

"You're a white-knuckle flier, aren't you?" Mary Worth asked sympathetically.

"Yes." There was no reason not to admit it. "I'm afraid I am."

"Needless," Mr. Businessman said. Refreshed by his drink, he was speaking actual words instead of grunting them out. "Safest form of travel ever invented. Hasn't been a commercial aircraft crash in donkey's years. At least not in this country."

"I don't mind," Mary Worth said. She had gotten halfway into her small bottle, and there were now roses in her cheeks. Her eyes sparkled. "I haven't been on a plane since my husband died five years ago, but the two of us used to fly together three or four times a year. I feel close to God up here."

As if on cue, a baby began to cry.

"If heaven is this crowded and noisy," Mr. Businessman observed, surveying the 737's crowded coach cabin, "I don't want to go."

"They say it's fifty times safer than automobile travel," Mary Worth said. "Perhaps even more. It might have been a hundred."

"Try five hundred times safer." Mr. Businessman leaned past Dixon and held out a hand to Mary Worth. Gin had worked its temporary miracle, turning him from surly to affable. "Frank Freeman."

She shook with him, smiling. Craig Dixon sat between them, upright and miserable, but when Freeman offered his hand, he shook it.

"Wow," Freeman said, and actually laughed. "You *are* scared. But you know what they say, cold hands, warm heart." He tossed off the rest of his drink.

Dixon's own credit cards always worked. He stayed in first class hotels and ate first class meals. Sometimes he spent the night with a good-looking woman, paying extra to indulge in quirks that were not, at least judging by certain Internet sites Mary Worth probably did not visit, very quirky. He had friends among the other turbulence experts. They were a close-knit crew, bound together not only by their occupation but by their fears. The pay was far better than good, there were all those fringe benefits . . . but at times like this, none of it seemed to matter. At times like this, there was only the fear.

It would be all right. It was *always* all right.

But as he waited for the shitstorm to happen, that thought had no power. Which was, of course, what made him good at the job.

34,000 feet. A long way down.

4

CAT, for clear air turbulence.

Dixon knew it well, but was never prepared for it. Allied 19 was somewhere above South Carolina when it hit this time. A woman was making her way to the toilet at the back of the plane. A young man wearing jeans and a fashionable scruff of beard was bending to talk to a woman in an aisle seat on the port side, the two of them laughing about something. Mary Worth was dozing with her head resting against the window. Frank Freeman was halfway through his third drink and his second bag of Fritos.

The jetliner suddenly canted to port and took a gigantic upward leap, thudding and creaking. The woman on her way to the can was flung across the last row of portside seats. The beard-scruffy young man flew into the overhead bulkhead, getting one hand up just in time to cushion the blow. Several people who had unfastened their seatbelts rose above their seatbacks as if levitated. There were screams.

The plane dropped like a stone down a well, thudded, then rose again, now tilting the other way. Freeman had been caught raising his drink, and was now wearing it.

"Fuck!" he cried.

Dixon shut his eyes and waited to die. He knew he would not if he did his job, it was what he was there for, but it was always the same. He always waited to die.

The ding-dong went. "This is the captain speaking." Stuart's voice was—as some sportscaster had popularized the phrase—as cool as the other side of the pillow. "We seem to have run into some unexpected turbulence, folks. I have—"

The plane took another horrifying lift, sixty tons of metal thrown upward like a piece of charred paper in a chimney, then dropped with another of those creaking thuds. There were more screams. The bathroom-bound lady, who had picked herself up, staggered backward, flailed her arms, and fell into the seats on the starboard side. Mr. Beard Scruff was crouched in the aisle, holding onto the armrests on either side. Two or three of the overhead compartments popped open and luggage tumbled out.

"Fuck!" Freeman said again.

"So I have turned on the seatbelt sign," the pilot resumed. "Sorry about this, folks, we'll be back to smooth air—"

The plane began to rise and fall in a series of stuttering jerks, like a stone skipping across a pond.

"—in just a few, so hang in there."

The plane dropped, then booted upward again. The carry-on bags in the aisle rose and fell and tumbled. Craig Dixon's eyes were crammed shut. His heart was now running so fast that there seemed to be no individual beats. His mouth was sour with adrenaline. He felt a hand creep into his and opened his eyes. Mary Worth was staring at him, her face parchment pale. Her eyes were huge.

"Are we going to die, Mr. Dixon?"

Yes, he thought. *This time we are going to die.*

"No," he said. "We're perfectly all r—"

The plane seemed to run into a brick wall, throwing them forward against their belts, and then heeled over to port: thirty degrees, forty, fifty. Just when Dixon was sure it was going to roll over completely, it righted itself. Dixon heard people yelling. The baby was wailing. A man was shouting, "It's okay, Julie, it's normal, it's okay!"

Dixon shut his eyes again and let the terror fully take him. It was horrible; it was the only way.

He saw them rolling back, this time not stopping but going all the way over. He saw the big jet losing its place in the thermodynamic mystery that had formerly held it up. He saw the nose rising fast, then slowing, then heeling downward like a rollercoaster car about to plunge. He saw the plane starting its ultimate dive, the passengers who had been unbelted now plastered to the ceiling, the yellow oxygen masks doing a final frantic tarantella in the air. He saw the baby flying forward and disappearing into business class, still wailing. He saw the plane hit, the nose and the first class compartment nothing but a crumpled steel bouquet blooming its way into coach, sprouting wires and plastic and severed limbs even as fire exploded and Dixon drew a final breath that ignited his lungs like paper bags.

All of this in mere seconds—perhaps thirty, no more than forty— and so real it might actually have been happening. Then, after taking one more antic bounce, the plane steadied and Dixon opened his eyes. Mary Worth was staring at him, her eyes welling with tears.

"I thought we were going to die," she said. "I *knew* we were going to die. I *saw* it."

So did I, Dixon thought.

"Nonsense!" Although he sounded hearty, Freeman looked decidedly green around the gills. "These planes, the way they're built, they could fly into a hurricane. They—"

A liquid belch halted his disquisition. Freeman plucked an airsick bag from the pocket in the back of the seat ahead of him, opened it, and put it over his mouth. There followed a noise that reminded Dixon of a small but efficient coffee grinder. It stopped, then started again.

The ding-dong went. "Sorry about that, folks," Captain Stuart said. Still sounding as cool as the other side of the pillow. "It happens from time to time, a little weather phenomenon we call clear air turbulence. The good news is I've called it in, and other aircraft will be vectored around that particular trouble spot. The better news is that we'll be landing in forty minutes, and I guarantee you a smooth ride the rest of the way."

Mary Worth laughed shakily. "That's what he said before."

Frank Freeman was folding down the top of his airsick bag, doing it like a man with experience. "That wasn't fear, don't get that idea, just plain old motion sickness. I can't even ride in the backseat of a car without getting nauseated."

"I'm going to take the train back to Boston," Mary Worth said. "No more of *that*, thank you very much."

Dixon watched as the flight attendants first made sure that the unbelted passengers were all right, then cleared the aisle of spilled luggage. The cabin was filled with chatter and nervous laughter. Dixon watched and listened, his heartbeat returning to normal. He was tired. He was always tired after saving an aircraft filled with passengers.

The rest of the flight was routine, just as the captain had promised.

5

Mary Worth hurried after her luggage, which would be arriving on Carousel 2 downstairs. Dixon, with just the one small bag, stopped for a drink in Dewar's Clubhouse. He invited Mr. Businessman to join him, but Freeman shook his head. "I puked up tomorrow's hangover somewhere over the South Carolina–Georgia line, and I think I'll quit while I'm ahead. Good luck with your business in Sarasota, Mr. Dixon."

Dixon, whose business had actually been transacted over that same South Carolina–Georgia line, nodded and thanked him. A text came in while he was finishing his whiskey and soda. It was from the facilitator, just two words: **Good job**.

He took the escalator down. A man in a dark suit and a chauffer's cap was standing at the bottom, holding a sign with his name on it. "That's me," Dixon said. "Where am I booked?"

"The Ritz-Carlton," the driver said. "Very nice."

Of course it was, and there would be a fine suite waiting for him, probably with a bay view. There would also be a rental car waiting for him in the hotel garage, should he care to visit a nearby beach or any of the local attractions. In the room he would find an envelope containing a list of various female services, which he had no interest in taking advantage of tonight. All he wanted tonight was sleep.

When he and the driver stepped out onto the curb, he saw Mary Worth standing by herself, looking a bit forlorn. She had a suitcase on either side of her (matching, of course, and tartan). Her phone was in her hand.

"Ms. Worth," Dixon said.

She looked up and smiled. "Hello, Mr. Dixon. We survived, didn't we?"

"We did. Is someone meeting you? One of your chums?"

"Mrs. Yeager—Claudette—was supposed to, but her car won't start. I was just about to call an Uber."

He thought of what she'd said when the turbulence—forty seconds that had seemed like four hours—finally eased: I *knew* we were going to die. I *saw* it.

"You don't need to do that. We can take you to Siesta Key." He pointed to the stretch limo a little way down the curb, then turned to the driver. "Can't we?"

"Of course, sir."

She looked at him doubtfully. "Are you sure? It's awfully late."

"My pleasure," he said. "Let's do this thing."

6

"Ooh, this is nice," Mary Worth said, settling into the leather seat and stretching out her legs. "Whatever your business is, you must be very successful at it, Mr. Dixon."

"Call me Craig. You're Mary, I'm Craig. We should be on a first-name basis, because I want to talk to you." He pressed a button and the privacy glass went up.

Mary Worth watched this rather nervously, then turned to Dixon. "You aren't going to, as they say, put a move on me, are you?"

He smiled. "No, you're safe with me. You said you were going to take the train back. Did you mean that?"

"Absolutely. Do you remember me saying that flying made me feel close to God?"

"Yes."

"I didn't feel close to God while we were being tossed like a salad six or seven miles up in the air. Not at all. I only felt close to death."

"Would you *ever* fly again?"

She considered the question carefully, watching the palms and car dealerships and fast food franchises slide past as they rolled south on the Tamiami Trail. "I suppose I would. If someone was on his deathbed, say, and I had to get there fast. Only I don't know who that someone would be, because I don't have much in the way of family. My late husband and I never had children, my parents are dead, and that just leaves a few cousins that I rarely email with, let alone see."

Better and better, Dixon thought.

"But you'd be afraid."

"Yes." She looked back at him, eyes wide. "I really thought we were going to die. In the sky, if the plane came apart, on the ground if it didn't. Nothing left of us but charred little pieces."

"Let me spin you a hypothetical," Dixon said. "Don't laugh, think about it seriously."

"Okay . . ."

"Suppose there's an organization whose job is to keep airplanes safe."

"There is," Mary Worth said, smiling. "I believe it's called the FAA."

"Never mind them, suppose it was an organization that could predict which airplanes would encounter severe and unexpected turbulence on any given flight."

Mary Worth clapped her hands in soft applause, smiling more widely now. Into it. "No doubt staffed by precognates! Those are people who—"

"People who see the future," Dixon said. And wasn't that possible? Likely, even? How else could the facilitator get his information? "But let's say their ability to see the future is limited to this one thing."

"Why would that be? Why wouldn't they be able to predict elections . . . football scores . . . the Kentucky Derby . . ."

"I don't know," Dixon said, thinking, maybe they can. Maybe they can predict all sorts of things, these facilitator precognates in some hypothetical room. Maybe they do. He didn't care. "Now let's go a little further. Let's suppose Mr. Freeman was wrong, and turbulence of the sort we encountered tonight is a lot more serious than anyone—including the airlines—believes, or is willing to admit. Suppose that kind of turbulence can only be survived if there is at least one talented, terrified passenger on each plane that encounters it." He paused. "And suppose that on tonight's flight, that talented and terrified passenger was me."

She pealed merry laughter and only sobered when she saw he wasn't joining her.

"What about the planes that fly into hurricanes, Craig? I believe Mr. Freeman mentioned something about planes like that just before he needed to use the airsick bag. *Those* planes survive turbulence that's probably even worse than what we experienced this evening."

"But the people flying them know what they're getting into," Dixon said. "They are mentally prepared. The same is true of many commercial flights. The pilot will come on even before takeoff and say, 'Folks, I'm sorry, but we're in for a bit of a rough ride tonight, so keep those seatbelts buckled.'"

"I get it," she said. "Mentally prepared passengers could use . . . I guess you'd call it united telepathic strength to hold the plane up. It's only *unexpected* turbulence that would call for the presence of someone already prepared. A terrified . . . mmm . . . I don't know what you'd call a person like that."

"A turbulence expert," Dixon said quietly. "That's what you'd call them. What you'd call me."

"You're not serious."

"I am. And I'm sure you're thinking right now that you're riding with a man suffering a serious delusion, and you can't wait to get out of this car. But in fact it *is* my job. I'm well paid—"

"By whom?"

"I don't know. A man calls. I and the other turbulence experts—there are a few dozen of us—call him the facilitator. Sometimes weeks go by between calls. Once it was two months. This time it was only two days. I came to Boston from Seattle, and over the Rockies . . ." He wiped a hand over his mouth, not wanting to remember but remembering, anyway. "Let's just say it was bad. There were a couple of broken arms."

They turned. Dixon looked out the window and saw a sign reading SIESTA KEY, 2 MILES.

"If this was true," she said, "why in God's name would you do it?"

"The pay is good. The amenities are good. I like to travel . . . or did, anyway; after five or ten years, all places start to look the same. But mostly . . ." He leaned forward and took one of her hands in both of his. He thought she might pull away, but she didn't. She was looking at him, fascinated. "It's saving lives. There were over a hundred and fifty people on that airplane tonight. Only the airlines don't just call them people, they call them *souls*, and that's the right way to put it. I saved a hundred and fifty souls tonight. And since I've been doing this job I've saved thousands." He shook his head. "No, tens of thousands."

"But you're terrified each time. I saw you tonight, Craig. You were in mortal terror. So was I. Unlike Mr. Freeman, who only threw up because he was airsick."

"Mr. Freeman could never do this job," Dixon said. "You can't do the job unless you're convinced each time the turbulence starts that you are going to die. You're convinced of that even though you know you're the one making sure that won't happen."

The driver spoke quietly from the intercom. "Five minutes, Mr. Dixon."

"I must say this has been a fascinating discussion," Mary Worth said. "May I ask how you got this unique job in the first place?"

"I was recruited," Dixon said. "As I am recruiting you, right now."

She smiled, but this time she didn't laugh. "All right, I'll play. Suppose you did recruit me? What would you get out of it? A bonus?"

"Yes," Dixon said. Two years of his future service forgiven, that was the bonus. Two years closer to retirement. He had told the truth about having altruistic motives—saving lives, saving *souls*—but he had also told the truth about how travel eventually became wearying. The same was true of saving souls, when the price of doing so was endless moments of terror high above the earth.

Should he tell her that once you were in, you couldn't get out? That it was your basic deal with the devil? He should. But he wouldn't.

They swung into the circular drive of a beachfront condo. Two ladies—undoubtedly Mary Worth's chums—were waiting there.

"Would you give me your phone number?" Dixon asked.

"What? So you can call me? Or so you can pass it on to your boss? Your facilitator?"

"The latter," Dixon said.

She paused, thinking. The chums-in-waiting were almost dancing with excitement. Then Mary opened her purse and took out a card. She handed it to Dixon. "This is my cell number. You can also reach me at the Boston Public Library."

Dixon laughed. "I *knew* you were a librarian."

"Everyone does," she said. "It's a bit boring, but it pays the rent, as they say." She opened the door. The chums squealed like rock show groupies when they saw her.

"There are more exciting occupations," Dixon said.

She looked at him gravely. "There's a big difference between temporary excitement and mortal fear, Craig. As I think we both know."

He couldn't argue with her on that score, but it wasn't exactly a no. He got out and helped the driver with her bags while Mary Worth hugged two of the widows she had met in an Internet chat room.

7

Mary was back in Boston, and had almost forgotten Craig Dixon, when her phone rang one night. Her caller was a man with a very slight lisp. They talked for quite awhile.

The following day, Mary Worth was on Jetaway Flight 694, nonstop from Boston to Dallas, sitting in coach, just aft of the starboard wing. Middle seat. She refused anything to eat or drink.

The turbulence struck over Oklahoma.

LAURIE

1

Six months after his wife of forty years died, Lloyd Sunderland's sister drove from Boca Raton to Rattlesnake Key to visit him. She brought with her a dark gray puppy which she said was a Border Collie–Mudi mix. Lloyd had no idea what a Mudi was, and didn't care.

"I don't want a dog, Beth. A dog is the last thing in the world I want. I can barely take care of myself."

"That's obvious," she said, unhooking the puppy's toy-sized leash. "How much weight have you lost?"

"I don't know."

She appraised him. "I'd say fifteen pounds. Which you could afford to give, but not much more. I'm going to make you a sausage scramble. With toast. You've got eggs?"

"I don't want a sausage scramble," Lloyd said, eyeing the dog. It was sitting on the white shag carpet, and he wondered how long it would be before it left a calling card there. The carpet needed a good vacuum and probably a shampoo, but at least it had never been peed on. The dog was looking at him with its amber eyes.

"Do you or do you not have eggs?"

"Yes, but—"

"And sausage? No, of course not. You've probably been living on Eggos and Campbell's soup. I'll get some at the Publix. And I'll inventory your fridge and see what else you need."

She was his older sister by five years, had mostly raised him after their mother died, and as a child he had never been able to stand against her. Now they were old, and he still could not stand against her, especially not with Marian gone. It seemed to Lloyd that since Mare went there was a hole in him where his guts had been. They might come back; they might not. Sixty-five was a little old for regeneration. The dog, though—against that he would stand. What in the name of God had Bethie been thinking?

"I'm not keeping it," he said, speaking to her back as she stalked on her stork legs into the kitchen. "You bought it, you can take it back."

"I didn't buy it. The mother was a pure-bred Border Collie that got out and mated up with a neighbor's dog. That was the Mudi. The owner managed to give the other three pups away, but this one's the runt and nobody wanted her. The owner—he's a small-patch truck farmer—was about to take her to the shelter when I came along and saw a sign tacked to a telephone pole. WHO WANTS A DOG, it said."

"And you thought of me." Still eyeing the puppy, who was eyeing him back. The cocked ears seemed to be the biggest part of her.

"Yes."

"I'm *grieving*, Beth." She was the only person to whom he could state his situation so baldly.

"I know that." Bottles rattled in the open fridge. He could see her shadow on the wall as she bent and rearranged. She really is a stork, he thought, a human stork, and she'll probably live forever. "A grieving person needs something to occupy his mind. Something to take care of. That was what I thought when I saw that sign. It's not a case of who wants a dog, it's a case of who needs a dog. That's you. Jesus Christ, this fridge is a mold farm. A science experiment. I am so grossed out."

The puppy got to her feet, took a tentative step toward Lloyd, then changed her mind (assuming she had one) and sat down again.

"Keep her yourself."

"Absolutely not. Jim's allergic."

"Bethie, you have two cats. He's not allergic to them?"

"Yes. He is. And the cats are enough. If that's the way you feel, I'll just take that puppy to the animal shelter in Pompano Beach. They give them three weeks before they euthanize them. She's a good-looking little thing with that smoky fur. Someone may take her before her time is up."

Lloyd rolled his eyes, even though she couldn't see him do it. He had often done the same thing at the age of eight, when Beth told him that if he didn't clean up his room, she'd give him five on his bottom with her badminton racket. Some things never changed.

"Pack your bags," he said, "we're going on one of Beth Young's all-expenses-paid guilt trips."

She shut the fridge and came back into the living room. The puppy glanced at her, then resumed her inspection of Lloyd. "I'm going to Publix, where I expect to spend well over a hundred dollars. I'll bring you the checkout tape and you can reimburse me."

"And what am I supposed to do in the meantime?"

"Why don't you get to know the defenseless puppy you're going to send to the gas chamber?" She bent to pat the top of the puppy's head. "Look at those hopeful eyes."

What Lloyd saw in those amber eyes was only evaluation.

"What am I supposed to do if she pees on the shag? Marian had this installed just before she got sick."

Beth pointed to the toy-sized leash on the hassock. "Take her out. Introduce her to Marian's overgrown flowerbeds. And by the way, that carpet is filthy."

She grabbed her purse and headed for the door, thin legs scissoring in their old self-important way.

"A pet is the absolute worst present you can give someone," Lloyd said. "I read that on the Internet."

"Where everything is true, I suppose."

She paused to look back at him. The harsh September light of Florida's west coast fell on her face, showing the way her lipstick had bled into the little wrinkles around her mouth, and the way her lower lids had begun to sag away from her eyes, and the fragile clockspring of veins beating in the hollow of her temple. She would be seventy soon. His bouncing, opinionated, athletic, argumentative, take-no-prisoners sister was old. So was he. They were proof that life was basically a short dream on a summer afternoon. Only Bethie still had her husband, two grown children, and four grandchildren—nature's nice multiplication.

He'd had Marian, but Marian was gone and there were no children. Was he supposed to replace his wife with a mongrel puppy? The idea was as corny as a Hallmark card and just as unrealistic.

"I'm not keeping her."

She gave him the same look she'd given him as a girl of thirteen, the one that said the badminton racket would soon make an appearance if he didn't shape up. "You are at least until I get back from Publix. I have some other errands to run, too, and dogs die in hot cars. Especially little ones."

She closed the door. Lloyd Sunderland, retired, six months a widower, these days not very interested in food (or any of life's other pleasures), sat staring at this unwelcome visitor on his shag carpet. The dog stared back at him. "What are you looking at, foolish?" he asked.

The puppy got up and walked toward him. Waddled, actually, as if through high weeds. It sat down again by his left foot, looking up. Lloyd lowered his hand tentatively, expecting a nip. The dog licked him instead. He got the toy leash and attached it to the puppy's small pink collar. "Come on. Let's get you off the damn rug while there's still time."

He tugged the leash. The puppy only sat and looked at him. Lloyd sighed and picked her up. She licked his hand again. He carried her outside and put her down in the grass. It needed mowing, and she almost disappeared. Beth was right about the flowers, too. They looked awful, half of them as dead as Marian. This thought made him smile, although smiling at such a comparison made him feel like a bad person.

The dog's waddle was even more pronounced in the grass. She went a dozen or so steps, then lowered her hind end and peed.

"Good, but I'm still not keeping you."

Already suspecting that when Beth went back to Boca, the dog wouldn't be with her. No, this unwanted visitor would be here with him, in his house half a mile from the drawbridge that connected the Key to the mainland. It wouldn't work, he had never owned a dog in his life, but until he found someone who would take her, she might give him something to do besides watch TV or sit in front of his computer, playing solitaire and surfing sites that had seemed interesting when he first retired and now bored him to death.

When Beth returned almost two hours later, Lloyd was back in his easy chair and the puppy was back on the carpet, sleeping. His sister, whom he loved but who had irritated him his whole life, irritated him further today by coming back with a lot more than he had expected. She had a large bag of puppy chow (organic, of course) and a large container of plain yogurt (which, when added to the puppy's food, was supposed to strengthen the cartilage in those radar dish ears). Beth also brought puppy pads, a dog bed, three chew toys (two of which squeaked annoyingly), and a child's playpen. It would keep the puppy from wandering in the night, she said.

"Jesus, Bethie, how much did that playpen cost?"

"It was on sale at Target," she said, dodging the question in a way he was familiar with. "No charge. My treat. And now that I've bought all this, do you still want me to take her back? If you do, you get to do the returns."

Lloyd was used to being outplayed by his sister. "I'll give it a trial run, but I do *not* appreciate being saddled with the responsibility. You always were high-handed."

"Yes," she said. "With Mother gone and Dad a functional but basically hopeless drunk, I had to be. Now how about the scramble?"

"All right."

"Has she peed on the rug yet?"

"No."

"She will." Beth actually sounded pleased with the idea. "What are you going to name her?"

If I name her she's mine, Lloyd thought, only he suspected she was his already, and had been from that first tentative lick. The way that Marian had been his from the first kiss. Another stupid comparison, but could you control how your mind sorted things? No more than you could control your dreams.

"Laurie."

"Why Laurie?"

"I don't know. It just came to me."

"Well," she said, "that's all right."

Laurie followed them into the kitchen. Waddling.

2

Lloyd papered the white shag carpet with puppy pads and set up the playpen in his bedroom (pinching his fingers in the process), then went into his study, fired up his computer, and began reading an article titled **So You Have a New Puppy!** Halfway through it, he became aware that Laurie was sitting beside his shoe, looking up at him. He decided to feed her and found a puddle of pee in the archway between the kitchen and the living room, not six inches from the nearest puppy pad. He picked Laurie up, set her down next to the pee, and said, "Not here." He then put her down on the pristine pad. "Here."

She looked at him, then did her puppy-waddle back into the kitchen, where she lay down by the stove with her snout on one paw, watching him. Lloyd grabbed a handful of paper towels. He had an idea he was going to be using a lot of them in the next week or so.

Once the puddle was cleaned up (a very small one, there was that), he put a quarter-cup of puppy chow—the recommended dosage, according to **So You Have a New Puppy!**—in a cereal bowl and mixed it with yogurt. The puppy tucked in willingly enough. While he was watching her eat, his phone rang. It was Beth, calling from a rest area somewhere in the wilds of Alligator Alley.

"You should take her to a vet," she said. "I forgot to tell you that."

"I know, Bethie." It was in **So You Have a New Puppy!**

She went on as if he hadn't spoken, another trait he knew well. "She'll need vitamins, I think, and heartworm medicine for sure, plus something for fleas and ticks—I think it's a pill they eat with their food. Also, she'll need to be fixed. Spayed, you know, but probably not for a couple of months."

"Yes," he said. "If I keep her."

Laurie had finished eating and wandered away toward the living room. With a full belly, her waddle was more pronounced. To Lloyd, she looked a little drunk.

"Remember to walk her."

"Right." Every four hours, according to **So You Have a New Puppy!** Which was ridiculous. He had no intention of getting up at two in the morning to take his uninvited guest outside.

Mind reading was another of his sister's specialties. "You're probably thinking that getting up in the middle of the night is going to be a hassle."

"It crossed my mind."

She ignored this, as only Bethie could. "But if you're telling the truth about having insomnia since Marian died, I really don't think it will be a hardship."

"That's very understanding and caring of you."

"See how it goes, that's all I'm saying. Give the little girl a chance." She paused. "I worry about you, Lloyd. I worked in an insurance company for almost forty years, and I can tell you that men your age run a much greater risk of disease after a spouse dies. And death, of course."

To this he said nothing.

"Will you?"

"Will I what?" As if he didn't know.

"Give her a chance."

Beth was pushing for a commitment Lloyd was unwilling to make. He looked around, as if for inspiration, and spied a turd—one single small sausage—exactly where the puddle of pee had been, six inches from the nearest puppy pad.

"Well, the little girl's here now," he said. It was the best he could give her. "You drive safe."

"Sixty-five the whole way. I get passed a lot, and some people honk at me, but any faster and I don't trust my reflexes."

He said goodbye, grabbed some more paper towels, and picked up the sausage. Laurie watched him with her amber eyes. He took her back outside, where she did nothing. When he finished the puppy-rearing article twenty minutes later, he found another puddle of pee in the archway. Six inches from the nearest puppy pad.

He bent over, hands on his knees, his back giving its usual warning twang. "You're on borrowed time, dog."

She looked at him.

3

Late that afternoon—two more puppy-pees, one actually on the pad nearest the kitchen—Lloyd attached the toy-sized leash and took Laurie outside, carrying her in the crook of his arm like a football. He set her down and urged her along the path that ran behind this small development of houses. The path led to a shallow canal that eventually flowed beneath the drawbridge. There car traffic was currently backed up, waiting for someone's motor sloop to pass from Oscar's Bay into the Gulf of Mexico. The puppy walked in her usual side-to-side waddle, pausing every now and then to sniff at clumps of weeds that from her perspective must have looked like impenetrable jungle thickets.

A dilapidated boardwalk known as Six Mile Path (for reasons Lloyd had never understood, since it was a mile long at most) ran along the side of the canal, and his next-door neighbor was standing there now between signs reading NO LITTERING and NO FISHING. Further down was one meant to say WATCH FOR ALLIGATORS, only ALLIGATORS had been spraypainted over and replaced with ALIENS.

Seeing Don Pitcher hunched over his fancy mahogany cane and hauling at his truss always gave Lloyd a small but unmistakable frisson of mean satisfaction. The man was a jukebox of tiresome political opinions, and also an unapologetic gore-crow. If anyone in the neighborhood died, Don knew it first. If anyone in the neighborhood was running into financial headwinds, he knew that, too. Lloyd's back was no longer what it had been, nor were his eyes and ears, but he was still years from the cane and truss. Or so he hoped.

"Look at that yacht," Don said as Lloyd joined him on the boardwalk (Laurie, perhaps frightened of the water, hung back at the end of her leash). "How many poor people do you think that would feed in Africa?"

"I don't think even hungry people could eat a boat, Don."

"You know what I . . . say, what have you got there? New puppy? Ain't he cute?"

"It's a she," Lloyd said. "I'm keeping her for my sister."

"Hey there, sweetie," Don said, leaning forward and holding out his hand. Laurie backed away and barked for the first time since Beth had brought her: two high, sharp yaps, then silence. Don straightened up again. "Not too friendly, is she?"

"She doesn't know you."

"She shit around?"

"Not too bad," Lloyd said, and for awhile they watched the yacht, which was probably owned by one of the Richie Riches at the north end of Rattlesnake Key. Laurie sat at the edge of the splintery board-walk and watched Lloyd.

"My wife won't have a dog," Don said. "Says all they are is mess and trouble. I had one when I was a boy, a nice old collie. She fell down a well. Cover was all rotted and down she went. Had to haul her up with a watchacallit."

"Is that so?"

"Yes. You want to be careful of that one near the road. She runs out in it, there goes your ballgame. Look at the size of that fucking boat! A dime to a dollar she grounds."

The yacht didn't ground.

Once the drawbridge closed and the traffic was moving again, Lloyd looked at the puppy and saw her asleep on her side. He picked her up. Laurie opened her eyes, licked his hand, and went back to sleep.

"Got to get back and burn some supper. Take it easy, Don."

"You do the same. And keep an eye on that puppy, or she'll chew up everything you own."

"I've got some toys for her to chew on."

Don smiled, revealing a set of mismatched teeth that gave Lloyd the chills. "She'll prefer your furniture. Wait and see."

4

While he was watching the TV news that night, Laurie came to the side of his easy chair and gave those same two sharp yaps. Lloyd considered her bright-eyed stare, weighed the pros and cons, then picked her up and set her in his lap.

"Wet on me and die."

She didn't wet on him. She went to sleep with her nose under her tail. Lloyd stroked her absently while he watched cell phone footage of a terrorist attack in Belgium. When the news was over, he took Laurie outside, once more using the football-carry. He attached the leash and let her walk to the edge of Oscar Road, where she squatted and did her business.

"Right idea. Hold that thought."

At nine o'clock, he lined the playpen with a double layer of puppy pads—he could see he'd have to buy more tomorrow, along with more paper towels—and lowered her in. She sat, watching him. When he gave her some water in a teacup, she lapped for awhile, then lay down, still watching him.

Lloyd undressed to his underwear and lay down himself, not bothering to pull back the coverlet. He had learned from experience that if he did that, he would find it on the floor in the morning, a victim of his tossing and turning. Tonight, however, he fell asleep almost immediately and didn't wake up until two o'clock, to the sound of high-pitched cries.

Laurie lay with her snout stuck through the bars of the playpen like a lonely inmate in solitary confinement. There were several sausages on the puppy pads. Judging that at such a late hour there would be few if any passersby on Oscar Road to be offended by the sight of a man in his boxers and a strappy tee-shirt, Lloyd put on his Crocs and carried his visitor (which was how he still thought of Laurie) outside. He put her down on the shell driveway. She waddled around for a bit, sniffed at a splat of birdshit, peed on it. He told her again to hold that thought. She sat down and looked at the empty road. Lloyd looked up at the stars. He thought he'd never seen so many, then decided he must have, just not lately. He tried to remember the last time he had been outside at two in the morning, and couldn't. He looked at the Milky Way, almost mesmerized, until he realized he was falling asleep on his feet. He carried the puppy back inside.

Laurie watched him silently as he changed the puppy pads she had shat upon (there were also small yellow stains on two of them), but the keening began again as soon as he put her in the playpen. He considered taking her into bed with him, but that was a very bad idea, according to **So You Have a New Puppy!** The author (one Suzanne Morris, DVM) stated unequivocally, "Once you start down that road, you will have great difficulty turning back." Also, the idea of waking up to find one of those little brown sausages on the side of the bed where his wife had slept did not please him. Not only would it seem symbolically disrespectful, it would mean changing the bed, a chore that also did not please him.

He went into the room that Marian had called her den. Most of her things were still there, because, in spite of his sister's strong suggestions that he do so, Lloyd hadn't yet had the heart to clean the place out. He had mostly steered clear of this room since Marian's death. Even looking at the pictures on the wall hurt, especially at two in the morning. He thought a person's skin was thinner in the small hours. It didn't start to thicken again until five, when the first light began to show in the east.

Marian had never upgraded to an iPod, but the portable CD player she had taken to her twice-weekly exercise group was on the shelf above her small collection of albums. He opened the battery case and saw no corrosion on the triple-As. He thumbed through her CDs, paused at Hall and Oates, then went on to *Joan Baez's Greatest Hits*. He mounted the CD and it spun satisfactorily when he closed the lid. He took it into the bedroom. Laurie stopped whining when she saw him. He pressed play, and Joan Baez began singing "The Night They Drove Old Dixie Down." He placed the CD player on one of the fresh puppy pads. Laurie sniffed at it, then lay down beside it, her nose almost touching the Dymo Tape label reading PROPERTY OF MARIAN SUNDERLAND.

"Will it do? I goddam hope so."

He went back to bed and lay with his hands under the pillow, where it was cool. He listened to the music. When Baez sang "Forever Young," he cried. So predictable, he thought. Such a cliché. Then he fell asleep.

5

September gave way to October, the best month of the year in upstate New York, where he and Marian had lived until his retirement, and in Lloyd's opinion (IMHO, as they said on Facebook) the best month down here on the west coast of Florida. The worst of the heat was gone, but the days were still warm and the cold nights of January and February were still on the next calendar. Most of the snowbirds were also on the next calendar, and instead of opening and closing fifty times a day, the Oscar Drawbridge only impeded traffic a dozen or so times. And there was so much less traffic to impede.

The Rattler Fish House opened after its three-month hiatus, and dogs were allowed on the so-called Puppy Patio. Lloyd took Laurie there often, the two of them ambling along Six Mile Path beside the canal. Lloyd lifted the dog over the places where the boardwalk was overgrown with sawgrass; she trotted easily beneath the overhanging palmetto that Lloyd had to bull his way through, head bent, arm outstretched to push back the thickest clumps, always afraid a tree-rat might fall into his hair, although none ever did. When they arrived at the restaurant, she sat quietly by his shoe in the sunshine, occasionally rewarded for good manners by a piece of french fry from Lloyd's fish and chips basket. The waitresses all oohed over her, bending to stroke her smoky gray fur.

Bernadette, the hostess, was particularly taken with her. "That *face*," she always said, as if that explained everything. She would kneel beside Laurie, which gave Lloyd an excellent and always appreciated view of her cleavage. "Oooh, that *face!*"

Laurie accepted this attention, but did not seem to crave it. She simply sat, examining her new admirer before returning her attention to Lloyd. Part of that attention might have had to do with the french fries, but not all; she looked at him just as studiously when he was watching TV. Until, that was, she fell asleep.

She toilet trained quickly, and in spite of Don's prediction, she did not chew the furniture. She did chew her toys, which multiplied from three to six to a dozen. He found an old crate to store them in. Laurie would go to this crate in the morning, put her forepaws up on its edge, and examine the contents like a Publix shopper evaluating the produce. At last she would select one, take it into the corner, and chew it until it bored her. Then she would return to the crate and select another. By the end of the day, they would be scattered all over the bedroom, the living room, and the kitchen. Lloyd's final chore before going to bed was picking them up and returning them to the crate. Not because of the clutter, but because the dog seemed to take such satisfaction from surveying her accumulated booty each morning.

Beth called often, asking about his eating habits, reminding him of the birthdays and anniversaries of old friends and older relatives, keeping him up to date on who had died. She always ended by asking if Laurie was still on probation. Lloyd said yes until one day in the middle of October. They had just come back from the Fish House, and Laurie was sleeping on her back in the middle of the living room floor, legs splayed to the four major points of the compass. The breeze from the air conditioner was ruffling her belly fur, and Lloyd realized she was beautiful. It wasn't sentiment, only a fact of nature. He felt the same about the stars when he took her out for her final pee of the evening.

"No, I guess we're past the probation stage. But if she outlives me, Bethie, you're either taking her back—and fuck Jim's allergies—or you're finding a good home for her."

"I copy you, Rubber Duck." The Rubber Duck thing was something she'd picked up from an old trucking song back in the seventies and had hung onto ever since. It was another thing about Beth that Lloyd found simultaneously endearing and as annoying as shit. "I'm pleased it's working out." She lowered her voice. "In truth, I didn't think it would."

"Then why did you bring her?"

"Shot in the dark. I knew you needed *something* more labor-intensive than a goldfish. Has she learned to bark?"

"It's more of a yark. She does it when the postman comes, or UPS, or if Don drops by for a beer. Always just the two. Yark-yark, and done. When are you coming up this way?"

"I came last time. It's your turn to come down here."

"I'll have to bring Laurie. There's no way I'm leaving her with Don and Evelyn Pitcher." Looking at his sleeping puppy, he realized that there was no way he was leaving her with anyone. Even short trips to the supermarket made him nervous about her, and he was always relieved to see her waiting at the door when he came home.

"Then bring her. I'd love to see how much she's grown."

"What about Jim's allergies?"

"Fuck his allergies," she said, and hung up, laughing.

6

After mooning and exclaiming over Laurie—who, other than one stop to relieve her bladder, had slept in the backseat all the way to Boca—Beth reverted to her usual big-sister priorities. Although she could nag him on many subjects (she was a virtuoso that way), her main issue this time was Dr. Albright, and Lloyd's need to see him for an overdue checkup.

"Although you look good," she said. "I have to say it. You actually appear to have a tan. Assuming that's not jaundice."

"Just sun. I walk Laurie three times a day. On the beach when we get up, on Six Mile Path to the Fish House, where I have lunch, and back on the beach in the evening. For the sunset. She doesn't care about it—dogs have no aesthetic sense—but I enjoy it."

"You walk her on the canal boardwalk? Jesus, Lloyd, that thing's a wreck. It's apt to collapse under you someday and dump you into the canal, along with the princess here." She rubbed the top of Laurie's head.

"It's been there for forty years or more. I think it will outlast me."

"Have you made that doctor's appointment yet?"

"No, but I will."

She held up her phone. "Do it now, why don't you? I want to watch you."

He could tell by the look in her eyes that she didn't expect him to take her up on this, which was one reason he did it. But not the only reason. In previous years, he had dreaded going to the doctor; kept expecting that moment (no doubt conditioned by too many TV shows) when the doctor would look at him gravely and say, "I have some bad news."

Now, however, he felt good. His legs were stiff when he got up in the morning, probably from so much walking, and his back was creakier than ever, but when he turned his attention inward, he found nothing worrisome. He knew that bad things could grow unfelt in an old man's body for quite some time—creeping along until it was time to dash—but nothing had progressed to the point where there was an outward manifestation: no bloody stool or sputum, no deep pain in the gut, no trouble swallowing, no painful urination. He reflected that it was much easier to go to the doctor when your body was telling you there was no reason to do so.

"What are you smiling about?" Beth sounded suspicious.

"Nothing. Give me that."

He reached for her phone. She held it away from him. "If you really mean to do it, use your own."

7

Two weeks after his checkup, Dr. Albright asked him to come in to go over the results. They were good.

"Your weight's pretty much where it should be, your blood pressure's fine, ditto reflexes. Your cholesterol numbers are better than the last time you let us take some of your blood . . ."

"I know, it's been awhile," Lloyd said. "Probably too long."

"No probably about it. Anyway, no need to put you on lipids as of now, which you should see as a victory. At least half my patients your age take them."

"I do a lot of walking," Lloyd said. "My sister gave me a dog. A puppy."

"Puppies are God's idea of the perfect workout program. How are you doing otherwise? Are you coping?"

Albright didn't need to be more specific. Marian had also been his patient, and far more conscientious than her husband about her six-month checkups—very proactive in all things, was Marian Sunderland—but the tumor that first robbed her of her intelligence and then killed her had been beyond proactivity. It hatched too deep inside. A glioblastoma, Lloyd thought, was God's idea of a .45 caliber bullet.

"Pretty well," Lloyd said. "Sleeping again. I go to bed tired most nights, and that helps."

"Because of the dog?"

"Yes. Mostly that."

"You should call your sister and thank her," Albright said.

Lloyd thought that was a good idea. He called her that evening and did so. Beth told him he was very, very welcome. Lloyd took Laurie down to the beach and walked her. He watched the sunset. Laurie found a dead fish and peed on it. They both went home satisfied.

8

December 6th of that year began in the normal way, with a walk on the beach followed by breakfast: Gaines-Burger for Laurie, a scrambled egg and a piece of toast for Lloyd. There was no premonition that God was cocking his .45. Lloyd watched the first hour of the *Today* program, then went into Marian's den. He had picked up a little accounting work from the Fish House and a car dealership in Sarasota. It was low-pressure stuff, no stress involved, and although his financial needs were met, it was nice to be working again. And he discovered that he liked Marian's desk better than his own. He liked her music, too. Always had. He thought Marian would be glad to know that her space was being used.

Laurie sat beside his chair, chewing thoughtfully on her toy rabbit, then took a nap. At ten-thirty, Lloyd saved his work and pushed back from the computer. "Snack time, girl."

She followed him into the kitchen and accepted a rawhide chew stick. Lloyd had milk and a couple of cookies that had come in an early gift package from Beth. They were burnt on the bottom (burnt Christmas cookies another of Beth's specialties), but edible.

He read for awhile—he was working his way through John Sandford's hefty *oeuvre*—and was eventually roused by a familiar jingling. It was Laurie, by the front door. Her leash was looped over the knob, and she was brushing the steel clip back and forth with her snout. Lloyd looked at his watch and saw it was quarter to twelve. "Okay, right."

He snapped on her leash, grabbed his left front pocket to make sure he had his wallet, and let Laurie lead him out into the bright light of midday. As they walked down to Six Mile Path, he saw that Don had started to put out his usual collection of horrible plastic holiday decorations: a Nativity scene (sacred), a large plastic Santa (profane), and a collection of lawn gnomes tarted up to look like elves (surreal). Soon Don would risk his life by climbing a ladder and stringing lights that flashed on and off, making the Pitcher bungalow look like the world's smallest, tackiest riverboat casino. In previous years, Don's decorations had made Lloyd feel sad, but on this day he laughed. You had to give the son of a bitch credit. He had arthritis, bad eyes, and a bad back, but he wasn't giving up. For Don it was Christmas or bust.

Evelyn came out on the Pitchers' back deck. She was wearing a misbuttoned pink wrapper, there was some kind of whitish-yellow cream smeared on her cheeks, and her hair was every whichway. Don had confided to Lloyd that his wife had begun to lose the plot a little bit, and today she certainly looked it.

"Have you seen him?" she called.

Laurie looked up and gave her trademark greeting: *Yark, yark.*

"Who? Don?"

"No, John Wayne! Of course Don, who else?"

"I haven't," Lloyd said.

"Well if you do, tell him to stop farting around and finish the damn decorations. The lights are hanging down, and the Wise Men are still out in the garage! That man is *loopy*!"

"I'll pass it along if I see him."

Evelyn leaned over the rail, alarmingly far. "That's a good-looking dog you've got there! What's his name again?"

"Laurie," Lloyd told her, as he had many times before.

"Oh, a bitch, a bitch, a bitch!" Evelyn cried in a kind of Shakespearian fervor, and then uttered a cackle. "I'll be glad when goddamned Christmas is over, you can tell him that, too!"

She straightened up (a relief; Lloyd did not think he could have caught her if she'd fallen) and went back inside. Laurie got to her feet and trotted down to the boardwalk, turning toward the smells of fried food wafting from the Fish House. Lloyd turned with her, looking forward to a piece of broiled salmon on a bed of rice. The fried stuff had begun to disagree with him.

The canal meandered; Six Mile Path meandered with it, lazily turning this way and that, hugging the overgrown bank. Here and there a board was missing. Laurie paused to watch a pelican dive and come up with a fish wriggling in its satchel beak, then they went on. She stopped at a spray of sawgrass poking up between two boards that had warped apart. Lloyd lifted her over it by the belly—she was getting too big for the football-carry now. A little way further down, just ahead of the next curve, palmetto had grown over the boardwalk, forming a low arch. Laurie was small enough to walk under, but she paused, head forward and cocked to the side. Lloyd caught up with her and bent to see what she was looking at. It was Don Pitcher's cane. And although it was made of stout mahogany, a crack ran halfway up its length from the rubber tip.

Lloyd picked it up and examined three or four drops of blood dotting the wood. "This isn't good. I think we better go b—"

But Laurie bolted ahead, jerking the leash out of his hand. She disappeared under the green arch, the handle of the leash clattering and spinning behind her. Then the barking began, not just her usual double yark, but a volley of more urgent sounds. Alarmed, Lloyd ducked through the palmetto, waving the cane this way and that to push bunches of it aside. The branches whipped back, scratching at his cheeks and forehead. On some of them were beads and smears of blood. There was more blood on the boards.

On the other side, Laurie stood with her front legs spread, her back bowed, and her muzzle touching the boards. She was barking at an alligator. It was dark green, a full-grown adult at least ten feet long. It stared at Lloyd's barking dog with its dull dead eyes. It was splayed atop Don Pitcher's body, its blunt shovel nose resting on Don's sunburned neck, its short scaly forepaws possessively cupping Don's bony shoulders. It was the first alligator Lloyd had seen since a trip to Jungle Gardens in Sarasota with Marian, and that had been years ago. The top of Don's head was pretty much gone. Lloyd could see splintered bone through what remained of his neighbor's hair. An ooze of blood, still wet, lay drying on his cheek. There were oatmealy strands in it. Lloyd realized he was looking at some of Don Pitcher's brain. That Don had been thinking with that very stuff perhaps only minutes ago seemed to render the whole world meaningless.

The handle of Laurie's leash had dropped over the side of the board-walk and into the canal. She continued to bark. The alligator regarded her, for the moment not moving. It looked remarkably stupid.

"Laurie! Shut up! Shut the fuck up!"

He thought of Evelyn Pitcher standing on her back deck like an actress on the apron of a stage, crying, *Oh, a bitch, a bitch, a bitch!*

Laurie stopped barking, but continued to growl deep down in her throat. She seemed to have grown to twice her size, because her cloudy dark gray fur was standing out not just on the scruff of her neck, but all over her body. Lloyd dropped to one knee, never taking his eyes off the gator, and plunged his left hand into the canal, feeling for the leash. He found the cord, yanked the handle up, clutched it, and got back to his feet. He tugged the leash. At first it was like pulling on a post stuck in the ground—Laurie was that braced—but then she turned toward him. When she did, the gator raised its tail and brought it down, a flat thwack that sprayed up droplets of water and made the boardwalk tremble. Laurie cringed and jumped onto Lloyd's sneakers. He bent and picked her up, never taking his eyes from the gator. Laurie's body was thrumming, as if an electrical current were passing through it. Her eyes were wide enough to show the whites all around. Lloyd had been too stunned by the sight of the alligator astride his dead neighbor's body to be afraid, and when feeling did return, it wasn't fear but a kind of protective rage. He unclipped the leash from Laurie's collar and dropped it.

"Go home. Do you hear me? Go home. I'll be right behind you."

He bent down, still watching the alligator (which never took its eyes from him). He had carried Laurie like a football many times when she was smaller; now he hiked her like one, through his legs and directly into the palmetto arch.

There was no time to see if she was going. The alligator came at him. It moved with amazing speed, kicking Don's body several feet behind it with its rear legs as it pushed off. Its mouth opened, exposing teeth like a dirty picket fence. On its leathery, pinkish-black tongue, Lloyd could see bits of Don's shirt.

He struck at it with the cane, bringing it around in a sideways sweep. It whacked the side of the gator's head below one of those weirdly expressionless eyes, and broke along the crack in the mahogany. The broken piece twirled away and fell into the canal. The gator stopped for a moment, as if surprised, then came on. Lloyd could hear the clitter of its claws. Its mouth yawned, its lower jaw skidding along the boardwalk.

Lloyd thought of nothing. Some deeper part of him took over. He stabbed out with what remained of Don's cane, plunging the jagged end into the whitish flesh at the side of the alligator's shovel head. Grasping the cane's handle with both hands, he leaned forward, putting his weight into it and pushing as hard as he could. The alligator was momentarily driven sideways. Before it could recover, there came a rapid series of cracking sounds, like blanks from a track-starter's pistol. Part of the old boardwalk slumped, spilling the gator's top half into the canal. Its tail came down, whacking the twisted boards and making Don's body jump. The water boiled. Lloyd struggled for balance and stepped back just as the gator's head surfaced, the jaws snapping. He stabbed at it again, not aiming, but the jagged stub of the cane went into the gator's eye. It reared backward, and if Lloyd hadn't let go of the cane's curved handle, he would have been pulled into the water on top of it.

He turned and bolted through the palmetto with his arms outstretched in front of him, expecting at any moment to be bitten from behind or thrust upward as the gator swam under the boardwalk, planted itself on the mucky bottom, and battered its way after him. He came out on the other side, daubed with Don's blood and bleeding from his own scratches. Laurie had not gone home. She was standing ten feet down, and when she saw him, she raced toward him, bunched her hindquarters, and leaped. Lloyd caught her (like a football, like a Hail Mary pass) and ran, hardly aware that Laurie was wriggling in his arms, and whining, and covering his face with frantic licks. Although he would remember this later and call them kisses.

Once he was off the boardwalk and on the shell path, he looked back, expecting to see the alligator hustling after them along the boardwalk with its eerie, unexpected speed. He made it halfway up the path to his house before his legs gave out and he sat down. He was crying and shaking all over. He kept looking back, watching for the gator. Laurie kept licking his face, but her trembling had begun to subside. When he felt able to walk again, he carried Laurie the rest of the way to his house. Twice he felt faint and had to stop.

Evelyn came back onto her deck as he trudged toward his back door. "You know if you carry a dog around like that, it will start expecting it all the time. Did you see Don? He needs to finish putting up his Christing decorations."

Did she not see the blood, Lloyd wondered, or did she not want to see it? "There's been an accident."

"What kind of accident? Did someone run into the goddam draw-bridge again?"

"Go inside," he said.

He went inside himself without waiting to see if she did so. He got Laurie a fresh bowl of water, and she lapped at it eagerly. While she did that, Lloyd called 911.

9

The police must have gone to the Pitchers' house immediately after retrieving Don's body, because Lloyd heard Evelyn screaming. Those screams probably didn't go on for long, but it seemed long. He wondered if he should go over there, maybe try to comfort her, but he didn't feel that he could. He was more tired than he could ever remember, even after high school football practice on hot August afternoons. All he wanted to do was sit in his easy chair with Laurie in his lap. She had gone to sleep, nose to tail.

The police came and interviewed him. After listening to his story, they told him he had been extremely lucky.

"Luck aside, you did some damn quick thinking," one of the cops said, "using Mr. Pitcher's cane like that."

"It still would have gotten me if the outside part of the boardwalk hadn't collapsed under its weight," Lloyd said. It probably would have gotten Laurie, as well. Because Laurie hadn't gone home. Laurie had waited.

That night he took her to bed with him. She slept on Marian's side. Lloyd himself slept little. Each time he started to drift off, he thought of how the alligator had looked splayed on Don's body, with such possessiveness. Its black eyes. How it had seemed to grin. The unexpected speed when it had come at him. Then he would stroke the dog sleeping beside him.

Beth came from Boca the next day. She scolded him, but not until she had hugged him and kissed him repeatedly, making Lloyd think of how frantically Laurie had licked his face when he emerged from the palmetto tangle.

"I love you, you stupid," Beth said. "Thank God you're alive."

Then she picked up Laurie and hugged her. Laurie bore this patiently, but as soon as Beth put her down, she went off to find her rubber rabbit. She took it into the corner, where she made it squeak repeatedly. Lloyd wondered if she was having a fantasy where she tore the alligator to pieces, and told himself he was being stupid. You didn't make animals into something they were not. He hadn't read that in **So You Have a New Puppy!** It was one of those things you found out on your own.

10

The day after Beth's visit, a game warden from Florida Fish and Wildlife came to see Lloyd. They sat in the kitchen, and the warden, whose name was Gibson, accepted a glass of iced tea. Laurie enjoyed smelling his boots and pants cuffs for awhile, then curled up under the table.

"We caught the gator," Gibson said. "You're lucky to be alive, Mr. Sunderland. It was a damn big one."

"I know that. Has it been euthanized?"

"Not yet, and there's some discussion about whether or not it should be. When it attacked Mr. Pitcher, it was protecting a clutch of eggs."

"A nest?"

"That's right."

Lloyd called Laurie. Laurie came. He picked her up and began to stroke her. "How long was that thing there? I walked that damn boardwalk down to the Fish House with my dog almost every day."

"The normal incubation period is sixty-five days."

"That thing was there all that time?"

Gibson nodded. "Much of it, yes. Deep in the weeds and sawgrass."

"Watching us go by."

"You and everyone else who used that boardwalk. Mr. Pitcher must have done something, quite by accident, that roused her . . . well . . ." Gibson shrugged. "Not maternal instincts, I don't think you could say that, but they're programmed to protect the nest."

"He probably swung the cane in its direction," Lloyd said. "He was always swinging that cane. Might even have hit her. Or hit the nest."

Gibson finished his iced tea and stood up. "I just thought you'd like to know."

"Thank you."

"Sure. That's a nice little dog you've got there. Border Collie and what else?"

"Mudi."

"Okay, yeah, I see that now. And she was with you that day."

"Ahead of me, actually. She saw it first."

"She's lucky to be alive, too."

"Yes." Lloyd stroked her. Laurie looked up at him with her amber eyes. He wondered, as he almost always did, just what it was she saw in the face looking down into hers. Like the stars he saw when he took her out at night, it was a mystery. And that was good. A little mystery was good, especially when the years closed down.

Gibson thanked him for the iced tea and left. Lloyd sat where he was for awhile, stroking his hand through that cloudy gray fur. Then he put his dog down to go about her business.

RATTLESNAKES

July–August 2020

I wasn't surprised when I saw the elderly woman pushing the double stroller with the empty seats; I had been forewarned. This was on Rattlesnake Road, which winds the four-mile length of Rattlesnake Key on the Florida Gulf Coast. Houses and condos to the south; a few McMansions at the north end.

There's a blind curve half a mile from Greg Ackerman's McMansion, where I was staying that summer, bouncing around like the last pea in an oversized can. Tangled undergrowth higher than my head (and I'm six-four) flanked the road, seeming to press in and make what was narrow to begin with even narrower. The curve was marked on either side by fluorescent green plastic kids, each bearing the warning SLOW! CHILDREN AT PLAY. I was walking, and at the age of seventy-two, in the simmering heat of a July morning, I was going plenty slow. My plan was to walk to the swing gate which divides the private part of the road from the part the county maintains, then go back to Greg's house. I was already wondering if I'd bitten off more than I could chew.

I hadn't been entirely sure Greg wasn't putting me on about Mrs. Bell, but here she was, and pushing her oversized stroller toward me. One of the wheels had a squeak and could have used some oil. She was wearing baggy shorts, sandals with knee-length socks, and a big blue sunhat. She stopped, and I remembered Greg asking me if her problem—that's what he called it—would give *me* a problem. I said it wouldn't, but now I wondered.

"Hello. I think you must be Mrs. Bell. My name is Vic Trenton. I'm staying at Greg's house for awhile."

"A friend of Greg's? How nice! An old friend?"

"We worked in the same Boston ad agency. I was a copywriter and he—"

"Pictures and layout, I know. Before he made the big bucks." She pushed the double pram closer, but not too close. "Any friend of Greg's, so on and so forth. It's a pleasure to meet you. Since we're going to be neighbors for as long as you'll be here, please call me Alita. Or Allie, if you like. Are you okay? No sign of this new flu?"

"I'm okay. No cough, no fever. I assume you are, too."

"I am. Which is good, as old as I am, and with a few of the usual old-person medical issues. One of the few nice things about being here in the summer is how most people clear out. I saw on the news this morning that Dr. Fauci is saying there could be a hundred thousand new cases every day. Can you believe that?"

I told her I had seen the same thing.

"Did you come here to get away from it?"

"No. I needed some time off and the place was offered to me, so I took it." That was far from the whole story.

"I think you're a little crazy to be vacationing in this part of the world during the summer, Mr. Trenton."

According to Greg, you're the one who's crazy, I thought. *And judging by the stroller you're wheeling around, he wasn't wrong.*

"Vic, please," I said. "Since we're neighbors."

"Would you like to say hello to the twins?" She gestured to the pram. On the seat of one was a pair of blue shorts, on the other a pair of green ones. Draped over the backs of the seats were joke shirts. One said BAD, the other BADDER. "This one is Jacob," indicating the blue shorts, "and this one is Joseph." She touched the shirt that said BADDER. It was a brief touch, but gentle and loving. Her look was calm but cautious, waiting to see how I'd respond.

Nutty? Yes indeed, but I wasn't terribly uncomfortable. There were two reasons for that. One, Greg had clued me in, saying that Mrs. Bell was otherwise perfectly sane and in touch with reality. Two, when you spend your working life in the advertising business, you meet a lot of crazy people. If they're not that way when they come onboard, they get that way.

Just be pleasant, Greg told me. *She's harmless, and she makes the best oatmeal raisin cookies I've ever tasted.* I wasn't sure I believed him about the cookies—admen are prone to superlatives, even those who have left the job—but I was perfectly willing to be pleasant.

"Hello, boys," I said. "Very nice to meet you."

Not being there, Jacob and Joseph made no reply. And not being there, the heat didn't bother them and they would never have to worry about Covid or skin cancer.

"They've just turned four," Allie Bell said. This woman having four-year-old twin boys would be a good trick, I thought, since she looked to be in her mid-sixties. "Old enough to walk, really, but the lazy things would rather ride. I dress them in different colored shorts because sometimes even I get confused about which is which." She laughed. "I'll let you get on with your walk, Mr. Trenton—"

"Vic. Please."

"Vic, then. By ten it will be ninety in the shade, and the humidity, don't even talk about it. Say goodbye, boys."

Presumably they did so. I wished them a good day and told Allie Bell it was nice to meet her.

"The same," she said. "And the twins think you look like a nice man. Don't you, boys?"

"You're right, I am," I assured the empty seats of the double pram.

Allie Bell beamed. If it was a test, I seemed to have passed. "Do you like cookies, Vic?"

"I do. Greg said oatmeal raisin is your specialty."

"*Spécialitie de la maison, oui, oui,*" she said, and trilled a laugh. There was something faintly worrisome about it. Probably it was the context. You aren't introduced to long-dead twins every day. "I will bring you some in the near future, if you don't mind me stopping by."

"Absolutely not."

"But in the evening. When it cools off a little. I have a tendency to lose my breath in the middle of the day, although it doesn't bother Jake and Joe. And I always bring my pole."

"Pole?"

"For the snakes," she said. "Ta-ta, very nice to meet you." She rolled the pram past me, then turned back. "Although this is no time to enjoy the Gulf Coast. October and November is the time for that."

"Duly noted," I said.

I originally thought the Key was named for its shape, which looks remarkably snakelike from the air, twisting and doubling back on itself as it does, but Greg told me there *were* rattlers, a regular infestation of them, until the early eighties. That was when the building boom hit the Keys south of Siesta and Casey. Up until then those lower keys had been left to doze.

"The snakes were a kind of ecological blip," Greg said. "I guess in the beginning a few of them might have swum across from the mainland . . . *can* snakes swim?"

"They can," I told him.

"Or maybe they hitched a ride in the bilge of a supply boat or something. Hell, maybe even in the hold of some rich guy's cabin cruiser. They bred in the undergrowth, where the birds had a hard job getting at the young. Rattlesnakes don't lay eggs, you know. The mamas squeeze out eight or ten at a time and that's a lot of snakeskin boots, let me tell you. Those fuckers were *everywhere*. Hundreds of them, maybe thousands. They got driven north when the southern part of the Key started being developed. Then, when the rich folks came in—"

"Like you," I said.

"Well, yes," he said with appropriate modesty. "The stock market has been good to this boy, especially Apple."

"And Tesla."

"True. I tipped you on that, but you, being the cautious New Englander that you are—"

"Quit it," I said.

"Then, when the rich folks came in and started building their McMansions—"

"Like yours," I said.

"Please, Vic. Unlike some of the stucco and cement horrors in this part of Florida, mine is architecturally pleasing."

"If you say so."

"When the rich folks started to build, the contractors found the snakes everywhere. They were *teeming*. The builders killed the ones on the lots where they were working—Gulf side and Bay side—but there wasn't an *organized* snake hunt until after the Bell twins. The county wouldn't do anything even then, arguing that the north end of the Key was privately owned and developed, so the contractors put together a posse and had a snake hunt. I was still working at MassAds then and day-trading on the side, so I wasn't around, but I've heard that a hundred men and women—a hundred at least—in gloves and high boots started where the swing gate is now and worked their way north, beating the brush and killing every snake they found. Mostly rattlers, but there were others as well—blacksnakes, grass snakes, a couple of copperheads, and, hard to believe but true, a fucking python."

"They killed the non-poisonous ones as well as the kind that bite?"

"Killed em all," Greg said. "Hasn't been many snakes spotted on the Key since."

He called that night. I was sitting out by his pool, sipping a gin and tonic and looking at the stars. He wanted to know how I was enjoying the house. I said I was enjoying it just fine and thanked him again for letting me stay there.

"Although this is no time to enjoy the Key," he said. "Especially with most of the tourist attractions shut down because of Covid. The best times—"

"October and November. Mrs. Bell told me. Allie."

"You met her."

"Yes indeed. Her and the twins. Jacob and Joseph. At least I met their shorts and shirts."

There was a pause. Then Greg said, "Are you okay with that? I was thinking about Donna when I offered you the place. I never thought about how it might make you remember—"

I didn't want to go there, even after all those years. "It's fine. You were right. Allie Bell seems like a very nice woman, otherwise. Offered me cookies."

"You'll love them."

I thought of the little round spots of color in her cheeks. "She assures me she doesn't have Covid—which she called the new flu—and she wasn't coughing, but she didn't look exactly healthy." I thought of the double stroller with its empty shirts and shorts. "Physically, I mean. She said something about having medical issues."

"Well, she's in her seventies—"

"That old? I guessed sixties."

"She and her husband were the first ones to build on the north end, and that was back when Carter was president. All I'm saying is that when you get into your seventies your equipment is off the warranty."

"I haven't seen anyone else, but I've only been here three days. Not even all unpacked." Not that I'd brought much. Mostly I'd been catching up on my reading, just as I'd promised myself I'd do when I retired. When I watched TV, I muted the commercials. I'd be happy to never see another ad in my life.

"Buddy, it's *summer*. The summer of Covid, no less. Once you're past the swing gate, it's just you and Alita. And—" He stopped.

"And the twins," I finished. "Jake and Joe."

"You're sure it doesn't bother you? I mean, considering what happened to—"

"It doesn't. Bad things happen to kids sometimes. It happened to me and Donna and it happened to Allie Bell. Our son was a long time ago. Tad. I've put it to rest." A lie. Some things you never put to rest. "But I have a question."

"And I have an answer."

That made me laugh. Greg Ackerman, older and richer, but still a smartass. When we had the Brite Company's soft drink account, he once came to a meeting with a bottle of Brite Cola, with the distinctive long neck, sticking out of his unzipped fly.

"Does she know?"

"Not sure I follow."

I was pretty sure he did.

"Does she know that stroller is empty? Does she know her little boys died thirty years ago?"

"Forty," he said. "Maybe a little longer. And yeah, she knows."

"Are you positive or only pretty sure?"

"Positive," he said, then paused. "Almost." That was Greg, too. Always leave yourself an out.

I watched the stars and finished my drink. Thunder bumbled and rumbled on the Gulf and there were unfocused flashes of lightning, but I thought those were empty threats.

I finished unpacking my second suitcase, something that should have been done two days ago. When that was done—it took all of five minutes—I went to bed. It was the 10th of July. In the larger world, Covid cases had passed three million just in the United States. Greg had told me I was welcome to stay in his place all the way through September, if I wanted. I told him I thought six weeks would be enough to clear my head, but now that it had cooled off, I thought I might stay longer. Wait out the dread disease.

The silence—broken only by the sleepy sound of waves hitting Greg's shingle of beach—was exquisite. I could get up with the sun and take my walks earlier than I had today . . . and maybe give Allie Bell a miss by doing so. She was pleasant enough, and I thought Greg was right—she had at least three of her four wheels on the road, but that double pram with the shorts of different colors on the seats . . . that was creepy.

"Bad and Badder," I murmured. The master bedroom's slider was open and a puff of breeze lifted the thin white curtains, turning them into arms.

I got Greg's concern about the phantom twins as they related to me. At least now I did. My understanding came late, but wasn't better late than never the accepted wisdom? I had certainly never made the connection to my life when he first told me about Alita Bell's eccentricity. That connection was to my son, who also died, and at roughly the same age as Jacob and Joseph. But Tad wasn't the reason I felt I had to get away from New England, at least for awhile. That grief was old. In this ridiculously oversized house and during these hot summer weeks, I had a new one to deal with.

I dreamed of Donna, as I often did. In this one we were sitting on the couch in our old living room, holding hands. We were young. We weren't talking. That was all, that was the whole dream, but I woke up with tears on my face. The wind was blowing harder now, a warm wind, but it made the curtains look more like reaching arms than ever. I got up to close the slider, then went out on the balcony instead. In the daytime you could see the entire sweep of the Gulf from the upstairs bedrooms (Greg had told me I was welcome to use the master, so that's what I did), but in the early hours of the morning there was only black. Except for the occasional flashes of lightning, which were closer now. And the thunder was louder, the threat of a storm no longer empty.

I stood at the rail above the flagstone patio and the swimming pool with my tee-shirt and boxers flapping around me. I could tell myself it was the thunder that had awakened me, or the freshening wind, but of course it was the dream. The two of us on the couch, holding hands, unable to talk about what was between us. The loss was too big, too permanent, too *there*.

It wasn't rattlesnakes that killed our son. He died of dehydration in a hot car. I never blamed my wife for it; she almost died with him. I never even blamed the dog, a St. Bernard named Cujo, who circled and circled our dead Ford Pinto for three days under the hammering summer sun.

There's a book by Lemony Snicket, *A Series of Unfortunate Events*, and that perfectly described what happened to my wife and son. The house where our car died—because of a plugged needle valve that would have taken a mechanic five minutes to fix—was far out in the country and deserted. The dog was rabid. If Tad had a guardian angel, he was on vacation that July.

All that happened a long time ago. Decades.

I went back inside, closed the slider, and latched it for good measure. I lay back down and was almost asleep when I heard a faint squeaking sound. I sat bolt upright, listening.

You get crazy ideas sometimes, ones that would seem ridiculous in broad daylight but seem quite plausible in the small hours of the morning. I couldn't remember if I'd locked the house, and it was all too easy to imagine that Allie, a lot crazier than Greg believed, was downstairs. That she was pushing the double stroller with the squeaky wheel across the great room to the kitchen, where she would leave a Tupperware container of oatmeal raisin cookies. Pushing the stroller and believing that her twin sons, forty years dead, were sitting in the seats.

Squeak. Pause. *Squeak*. Pause.

Yes, I could see her. I could even see Jake and Joe . . . because *she* could see them. Only because I wasn't her I could see they were dead. Pale skin. Glazed eyes. Swollen legs and ankles because that was where the snakes had bitten.

It was ridiculous, idiotic. Even then, sitting upright in bed with the sheet puddled in my lap, I knew it. And yet:

Squeak. Pause. *Squeak*.

I turned on the bedside lamp and crossed the room, telling myself I wasn't scared. I turned on the room's overhead light, then reached through the doorway and turned on the upstairs gallery's track lighting, also telling myself no one was going to clutch my groping hand and I wasn't going to scream if someone did.

I went halfway across the gallery and looked over the waist-high rail. No one was in the great room, of course, but I could hear the first spatters of rain hitting the downstairs windows. And I could hear something else, as well.

Squeak. Pause. *Squeak*. Pause.

I had neglected to turn off the overhead paddle fan. That was what was squeaking. In the daytime I hadn't even heard it. The switch was at the head of the stairs. I flipped it. The fan coasted to a stop, giving one more squeak as it did so. I went back to bed but left the table lamp on, turned to its lowest setting. If I had another dream, I didn't remember it in the morning.

I slept in, probably because of my late-night scare, and skipped my walk, but I was up early on the next three mornings, when the air was fresh and even the birds were silent. I took my walk to the swing gate and back, seeing plenty of rabbits but no humans. I passed the Bell mailbox at the head of a driveway enclosed by rhododendrons but could barely glimpse the house, which was on the bay side and screened by trees and more rhododendrons.

During weekday working hours I heard leaf blowers and saw a couple of landscaping trucks parked in Allie's driveway when I went to the grocery store, but I think she was otherwise alone. As was I. Plus, we were both singles who had outlived their mates. It might make a decent romcom (if anyone made romcoms about old people, that is—*The Golden Girls* being the exception that proves the rule), but the thought of putting a move on her held zero appeal. Less than zero, actually. What would we do? Push the invisible twins together, one on each side of the stroller? Pretend to feed them SpaghettiOs?

Greg had a caretaker, but he had asked me to water the flowers in the big pots flanking the doors on the driveway side and poolside. I was doing that one twilit evening ten or twelve days after I moved in. I heard the squeaky wheel and turned off the hose. Allie was pushing the pram down the driveway. She was wearing a kind of shoulder sling. In it was a stainless steel pole with a U-shaped hook at the end. She asked me if I was still feeling all right. I said I was.

"I am, too. I come bearing cookies."

"That's very nice of you," I said, although I wouldn't have minded if she had forgotten. Tonight there were red shorts spread on one stroller seat and white ones on the other. Shirts were again draped over the backs. One said SEE YA LATER ALLIGATOR, the other AFTER AWHILE CROCODILE. If there had been actual kids in those tees, they would have looked cute. As it was . . . no.

Still, she was my neighbor and harmless enough. So I said, "Hello, Jake" and "Hello, Joe, what do you know?"

Allie trilled her laugh. "You are very sweet." Then, looking straight at me, she said, "I know they aren't there."

I didn't know how to respond. Allie didn't seem to mind.

"And yet sometimes they *are*."

I remembered Donna once saying something similar. This was months after Tad died and not long before we divorced. *Sometimes I see him*, she said, and when I told her that was stupid—by then we had recovered enough to say unkind things to each other—she said, *No. It's necessary*.

Allie's sling had a pouch on one side. She reached into it and brought out a Ziploc bag of cookies. I took them and thanked her. "Come in and have one with me." I paused, then added, "And bring the boys, of course."

"Of course," she said, as if to ask, *What else?*

There was a set of inside stairs going from the garage to the first floor. She halted the pram at the foot of them and said, "Get out, boys, hustle on up, it's all right, we're invited." Her eyes actually followed their progress. Then she put her sling on one of the seats.

She saw me looking at the snake pole and smiled. "Try it, if you like. You'll be surprised at how light it is."

I pulled it out and hefted it. It couldn't have been more than three pounds.

"Steel, but hollow. The sharp point on the end of the hook is to stick them with, but they're too fast for me." She held out her hand and I gave her the pole. "Usually you can push them, but if they still won't go . . ." She lowered the prod, then gave it a quick lift. "You can flip them into the brush. But you have to do it fast."

I wanted to ask if she'd ever actually used it and decided I already knew the answer. If there were invisible boys, there were invisible snakes. QED. I settled for saying it looked very useful.

"Very *necessary*," she said.

Halfway up the stairs, Allie stopped, patted her chest, and took a few deep breaths. Those hard red spots were back in her cheeks.

"Are you all right?"

"Just a few missed beats of the old ticker. It's not serious, and I have pills. I suppose I ought to take a couple. Perhaps you'd give me a glass of water?"

"What about milk? Nothing goes better with cookies."

"Milk and cookies sounds like a treat."

We climbed the rest of the stairs. She sat down at the kitchen table with a soft grunt. I poured two small glasses of milk and put half a dozen oatmeal raisin cookies on a plate. Three for her, three for me was what I thought, but I ended up eating four. They really were very good.

At one point she got up and called, "Boys, no trouble and no messes! Mind your manners!"

"I'm sure they will. Are you feeling better?"

"Fine, thanks."

"You have a little . . ." I tapped my upper lip.

"A milk mustache?" She actually giggled. It was sort of charming.

When I handed her a napkin from the caddy on the lazy susan, I saw her looking at my hand. "Is your wife not with you, Vic?"

I touched my ring. "No. She died."

Her eyes widened. "Oh! I'm so sorry. Was it recent?"

"Fairly recent. Would you like another cookie?"

The lady might have been off-kilter about her children, but she knew a Keep Out sign when she saw one . . . or heard one. "Okay, but don't tell my doctor."

We chatted awhile, but not about rattlesnakes, invisible children, or dead wives. She talked about the Coronavirus. She talked about Florida politicians, who she believed were hurting the environment. She said the manatees were dying because of fertilizer runoff in the water, and encouraged me to visit Mote Marine Aquarium on City Island in Sarasota and see some, "if they're still open."

I asked her if she'd like a little more milk. She smiled, shook her head, got to her feet, wavered a little, then stood steady. "I have to get the boys home, it's past their bedtime. Jake! Joe! Come on, you guys!" She paused. "There they are. What have you boys been up to?" Then, to me: "They were in that room at the end of the hall. I hope they didn't disarrange anything."

The room at the end of the hall was Greg's study, where I went to read in the evenings. "I'm sure they didn't."

"Little boys have a tendency to clutter, you know. I may let them push the stroller back. I get tired so easily these days. Would you like that, boys?"

I saw her down the stairs to the garage, ready to grab her arm if she tottered, but the milk and cookies seemed to have pepped her up.

"I'll just get you started," she told the twins, and turned the stroller around. "We wouldn't want you to bump Mr. Trenton's car, would we?"

"Bump away," I said. "It's a rental."

That made her giggle again. "Come along, kiddos. We'll have a bedtime story."

She pushed the pram out of the garage. The first stars were coming out and it was cooling off. July days are harsh on the Gulf Coast, I'd found that out, but the evenings can be gentle. The snowbirds miss that.

I walked with her as far as the mailbox.

"Oh, look at them, they've run ahead." She raised her voice. "Not too far, boys! And watch for snakes!"

"I guess you'll have to push the stroller yourself," I said.

"It looks that way, doesn't it?" She smiled, but I thought her eyes were sad. Maybe it was only the light. "You must think I'm a regular nutbird."

"No," I said. "We all have our ways of coping. My wife . . ."

"What?"

"Never mind." I wasn't going to tell her what my wife had said during the last hard months of our marriage (our *first* marriage): *Sometimes I see him.* That was a can of worms I didn't want to open. I watched her go, and as she disappeared into the gloom of twilight lensing to full dark, I heard that squeaky wheel and thought I should have oiled it for her. It only would have taken a minute.

I went back to the house, locked up, and rinsed off our plates. Then I picked up the book I was reading, one of the Joe Pickett novels, and went down to Greg's office. I had no interest in Greg's workstation, hadn't even turned on the desktop computer, but he's got a hell of a nice easy chair with a standing lamp nearby. The perfect place to read a good novel for a couple of hours before bed.

He's also got a cat named Buttons, now presumably residing in Greg's East Hampton abode with Greg and his current girlfriend (who would no doubt be at least twenty years younger than Greg, perhaps even thirty). Buttons had a little wicker basket of toys. It was now on its side with the lid open. A couple of balls, a well-chewed catnip mouse, and a colorful rubber fish lay on the floor. I looked at these a long time, telling myself I must have kicked the basket over earlier in the day and just not noticed. Because really, what else could it have been? I put the toys back in and closed the lid.

Greg's caretaker was Mr. Ito. He came twice a week. He always wore brown shirts, brown knee-length shorts with sharp creases, brown socks, brown canvas shoes. He also wore a brown pith helmet jammed down to his extremely large ears. His posture was perfect and his age was . . . well, ageless. He reminded me of the sadistic Colonel Saito in *The Bridge on the River Kwai*, and I kept expecting him to pass on Colonel Saito's motto to his less than energetic son: "Be happy in your work."

Except Mr. Ito—first name Peter—was the furthest thing from sadistic, and a native Floridian born in Tampa, raised in Port Charlotte, and living across the bridge in Palm Village. Greg was his only client on Rattlesnake Key, but he had plenty of homes on Pardee, Siesta, and Boca Chita. Printed on the sides of his panel trucks (he drove one, his lackadaisical son the other) was the motto *AH SO GREEN*. I suppose it would have been considered racist if his name had been McSweeney.

It was getting on for August when I spied him taking a break one day, standing in the shade and drinking from his canteen (yes, he had one). He was watching his son circling Greg's tennis court on a riding mower. I came out onto the patio and stood beside him.

"Just taking a break, Mr. Trenton," he said, putting on his mask. "Back at it in a minute. I don't deal with the heat as well as I used to."

"Wait until you get to my age," I said. "I'm curious about something. Do you remember the Bell twins? Jake and Joe?"

"Oh my God, yes. Who could forget? 1982 or '83, I think. Terrible thing. I was as young as that idiot when it happened." He pointed to his son Eddie, who appeared to be communing with his phone as he mowed around the court. I half-expected him to roll across it at any time. That could spell disaster.

"I've met Allie, and . . . well . . ."

He nodded. "Sad lady. Sad, sad lady. Always pushing her stroller. I don't know if she really believes the kiddies are in it or not."

"Maybe it's both," I said.

"Sometimes yes, sometimes no?"

I shrugged.

"What happened to them was a fucking shame, if you'll pardon my French. She was young when it happened. Thirty? Might have been, or a bit older. Her husband was much older. Henry was his name."

"Is it true snakes got the kids?"

He pulled down his mask, took another drink from his canteen, put his mask back in place. I'd left mine in the house.

"Yeah, it was snakes. Rattlers. There was an inquest, and the verdict was death by misadventure. The papers were more discreet back then and there was no social media . . . except people talk, and that's a kind of social media, wouldn't you say?"

I agreed it was.

"Mr. Bell was in his office upstairs, making calls. He was some sort of grand high poobah in the investment business. Like your friend Mr. Ackerman. The missus was taking a shower. The boys were playing in the backyard, where there was a high gate, supposedly locked. Only it really wasn't, only looked that way. The county detective in charge of the investigation said the gate latch had been painted over several times on account of rust, and it didn't catch the way it was supposed to and those boys got out. She used to push em in the stroller—don't know if it's the same one she's got now or not—but they could walk just fine and they must have decided to go to the beach."

"They didn't take the boardwalk?"

Mr. Ito shook his head. "No. I don't know why. No one knows why. The searchers could see where they went in, there were broken branches and a little piece of a shirt hanging from one of them."

SEE YOU LATER, ALLIGATOR, I thought.

"It's about four hundred yards from Rattlesnake Road to the beach, all of it choked with undergrowth. They made it about halfway. One of them was dead when the searchers found them. The other died before they could get him back to the road. My Uncle Devin was in the search party and he said each of those little boys had been bit over a hundred times. I don't believe that, but I guess it was a lot. Most of the bites—the punctures—were on their legs, but there were more on their necks and faces."

"Because they fell down?"

"Yeah. Once the poison started to work, they would have fallen down. There was only one rattler left when the search party found the boys. One of the men killed it with a snake pole. That's a kind of thing, has a hook—"

"I know what they are. Allie carries one when she walks near dark."

Mr. Ito nodded. "Not that there are many snakes now. Certainly no rattlers. There was a hunting party two days later. Plenty of men, a regular posse. Some were building contractors and their crews, the rest were from Palm Village. Uncle Devin was in on that one, too. They went north, beating the bush. Killed over two hundred rattlers on the way is what I heard, not to mention assorted other wrigglies. They finished up on the point of land between Daylight Pass and Duma Key . . . at least where Duma used to be, it's underwater now. Some of the snakes swam away and probably drowned. The rest were killed right there. Uncle Devin said another four or five hundred, which has got to be bullshit, pardon my French. But I guess there were plenty. Henry Bell was part of that group, but he wasn't in at the finish. He fainted from the heat and the excitement. And the sorrow, I guess. Mrs. Bell never saw the little boys where they died, only after they'd been, you know, fixed up in the funeral parlor, but their father was part of the search party that found them. They took him to the hospital. He died of a heart attack not long after. Probably never got over it. I mean, who would?"

I could relate to that. Some things you don't get over.

"How did they kill all those snakes?" I had been to the end of the Key, to that small triangle of shell beach between the pass and the little crown of greenery which is all that remains of Duma Key, and I just couldn't picture such a mass of snakes there.

Before he could answer, there was a loud clattering. Eddie Ito had driven onto the tennis court after all.

"Oy, oy, oy!" Mr. Ito screamed, and ran toward him, waving his arms.

Eddie looked up from his phone, startled, and hauled the riding mower back onto the lawn before it could do major damage to the court surface, although there would be plenty of dirt and clods to clean up. So I never got the end of the story.

*   *   *

Donna and I buried our son's body in Harmony Hill Cemetery, but that was the least part of him. We found that out in the months that followed. He was still there, between us. We tried to find a way around him and back to each other and couldn't do it. Donna was withdrawn, suffering from PTSD, taking pills and drinking too much. I couldn't blame her for getting stranded at the Camber farm, so I blamed her for an affair she'd had with a loser named Steve Kemp. It was brief and meaningless and had nothing to do with the goddam clogged needle valve, but the more I scratched that sore place the more inflamed it became.

Once she said, "You're blaming me because you can't blame the universe."

That could have been true, but it didn't help. The divorce, when it came, was no-fault and not contentious. I could say it was amicable, but it wasn't. By then we were both just too emotionally exhausted to be angry at each other.

That night, after hearing Mr. Ito's version of the twins' deaths—hardly reliable, but maybe in truth's ballpark—I had trouble falling asleep. When I did, it was thin. I dreamed that the double pram was rolling slowly down the driveway from the road. At first I thought it was rolling by itself, a ghost pram, but when the security lights came on I saw the twins were pushing it. They looked exactly alike and I thought, *No wonder she puts them in different shorts and shirts*. Beneath their mops of blond hair, the faces were somehow wrong. Or maybe it wasn't the faces; maybe it was their necks, which looked swollen. As if they were suffering from the mumps. Or Covid. When they got closer I saw their arms were also swollen, and marked with red dots like flakes of red pepper.

Squeak, pause. *Squeak*, pause. *Squeak*, pause.

They came closer still, and I saw there was a rattlesnake in each of the seats, squirming and coiling. They were bringing me the snakes as a gift, maybe. Or as a punishment. I had been away when my son died, after all. My reason for going to Boston, trouble with an advertising account, was partly an excuse. I was angry about Donna's affair. No, furious. I needed to cool down.

I never wished her dead, I tried to tell the little blank-eyed children, but maybe that was only half-true. Love and hate are also twins.

I came to a soupy consciousness but at first thought I was still dreaming because I could still hear that rhythmic squeaking. It was the fan in the great room—had to be—so I got up to turn it off. I hadn't even reached the bedroom door before realizing the squeaking had stopped. I walked down the gallery, still more asleep than awake, and didn't even have to turn on the light to see that the fan blades were motionless.

It was the dream, I thought. *It just followed me into half-waking.*

I went back to bed, fell into real sleep almost at once, and this time there were no dreams.

I overslept because I'd been awake in the middle of the night. At least I thought I had; maybe the walk down the gallery to check on the fan had also been part of the dream. I didn't think so but couldn't be sure.

I wouldn't have walked if the day had been hot, but one of the Gulf Coast's fabled cold fronts had come in overnight. They're never very cold, you have to live through a Maine winter to experience a real cold front, but it was in the seventies, and the breeze was refreshing. I toasted myself an English muffin, buttered it liberally, and set out for the swing gate.

I hadn't gone a quarter of a mile before I saw buzzards circling—both the black ones and the red-headed turkey vultures. They're ugly, awkward birds, so big it's hard for them to fly. Greg told me they show up by the hundreds if there's a red tide, gobbling the dead fish that wash up on the beach. But there had been no red tide that summer—the prickling in your lungs is impossible to mistake for anything else—and these birds appeared to be over the road instead of the beach.

I expected to find a dead rabbit or armadillo squashed in the road. Maybe someone's runaway cat or puppy. But it wasn't an animal. It was Allie. She was lying on her back by her mailbox. The double stroller was overturned at the head of her driveway. The shorts and shirts had spilled out and were lying on the crushed shell. Half a dozen buzzards were squabbling over her, hopping around, jostling each other, pecking at her arms and legs and face. Only *pecking* isn't the right word. They were snatching at her flesh with their big beaks. I saw one of them—a redheaded turkey buzzard that had to weigh five pounds—dig into her exposed bicep and raise her arm, shaking its head and making her hand wiggle. As if she were waving at me.

After a moment of shocked paralysis I charged them, windmilling my arms and yelling. Several took clumsy flight. Most of the others backed off along the road in big clumsy hops. Not the one with its beak in her arm, though; it continued to shake its head, trying to tear a strip of flesh loose. I wished for Allie's snake pole—a baseball bat would have been even better—but you know what they say about wishes, beggars, and horses. I saw a fallen palm frond, picked it up, and began waving it.

"Get away!" I shouted. "Get away, you fucker!"

Those fronds weigh almost nothing, but the dry ones make a loud rattling sound. The buzzard gave one more yank of its head and then launched itself and flew past me with a scrap of Allie's arm in its beak. Those black eyes seemed to mark me, to say *your turn will come.* I punched at it but missed.

There was no question that she was dead, but I knelt beside her to make sure. I'm old now, and they tell me that one's thought processes dim even if you're not struck by Alzheimer's or dementia—the slipp'd pantaloon, and all that—but I think I'll never forget what the carrion birds had done to the nice lady who needed to pretend her long-dead children were still alive. The woman who had brought me oatmeal raisin cookies. Her mouth was open and with the lower lip gone, she appeared to be wearing a terminal snarl. The buzzards had gotten half of her nose and both of her eyes. Blood-rimmed sockets stared at me with terminal shock.

I went to the far side of the road and threw up my English muffin and my morning coffee. Then I returned to her. I didn't want to. What I wanted was to run back to Greg's house as fast as my creaky old-man legs would carry me. But if I did that, the buzzards would return and resume their meal. Some were circling overhead. Most were roosting in the Australian pines and palmettos, like vultures in a horror movie version of a *New Yorker* cartoon. I had my phone and called 911. I reported what had happened and said I would stay with the body until the police arrived. An ambulance would probably also arrive, much good it would do.

I wished I had something to cover her mutilated face and realized I did. I set the stroller upright, moved it to the thick wall of rhododendron and sea grape at the side of the driveway, and took one of the shirts draped on the back. I put it over what was left of her face. Her legs were splayed and her skirt was up to her thighs. I knew from TV that you're not supposed to move a body until the police come, but I decided fuck that. I put her legs together. They had also been pecked, and I thought those red dots looked like snakebites. I took the other shirt and covered her legs from below her knees to her shins. One shirt was black, the other white, but they both said the same thing: I'M A TWINDAVIDUAL!

I sat down beside her, waiting for the police and wishing I'd never come to Rattlesnake Key. Duma was the Key that was supposed to have been haunted—so Mr. Ito had told me—but as far as I was concerned, Rattlesnake was worse. If for no other reason than it, unlike Duma, was still there.

The Bell driveway was bordered with bigger shells. I picked some up and every time one of those buzzards came close, I pegged a shell at it. I only hit one, but it gave out a very satisfying squawk.

I waited for the sirens. I tried not to look at the dead woman with the tee-shirts over her face and legs. I thought about oatmeal raisin cookies and about a trip I made to Providence ten years before. I was sixty-two then and thinking about retirement. I didn't know what I'd do with my so-called golden years, but the joy I'd always felt in the advertising biz—composing just the right slogan to go with just the right idea—had started to grow very thin.

I was there, along with two other hotshots in the Boston agency, to talk to an eloquence of lawyers: Debbin & Debbin, if you please.

Their headquarters was in Providence, but they had offices in all the New England states, specializing in auto accident claims, disabilities, and slip-and-fall injuries. The Debbins' crew wanted an aggressive ad campaign that would blanket all the TV stations from Cranston to Caribou. *Something jazzy*, they said. *Something that will make people call that 800 number.* I wasn't looking forward to the meeting, which was apt to be long and contentious. Lawyers think they know everything.

I was sitting in the lobby of the Hilton Hotel the night before, waiting for my compatriots, Jim Woolsy and Andre Dubose, to come down from their rooms. The plan was to go out to Olive Garden and brainstorm, the ultimate goal being to come up with two good pitches. No more than two. Lawyers think they know everything, but lawyers also get easily confused. I had a notepad on which I'd jotted: WHY GET FUCKED WHEN YOU CAN DO THE FUCKING? CALL DEBBIN & DEBBIN!

Probably a non-starter. I flipped the pad closed, put it in my jacket pocket, and glanced into the bar. That's all I did. I think about that sometimes, how I might have looked out the window, or back at the elevators to see if Jim and Andre were coming. But I didn't. I glanced into the bar.

There was a woman on one of the stools. She was dressed in a dark blue pants suit. Her hair, black and streaked with white, was styled in the kind of cut, maybe what hairdressers call a Dutch bob, that brushed the nape of her neck. Her face was only a quarter turned to me as she raised her glass to sip, but I didn't need to see more. There are things we just know, aren't there? The tilt of a person's head. The way the jaw angles into the chin. The way one shoulder might always be slightly lifted, as if in a humorous shrug. The gesture of a hand brushing back a wing of hair, the first two fingers held out, the other two curled toward the palm. Time always has a tale to tell, wouldn't you say? Time and love.

It's not her, I thought. *It can't be.*

All the time knowing it was. Knowing it could be no one else. I hadn't seen her in over two decades, we'd fallen completely out of touch, not even holiday cards for the last dozen or so years, but I knew her at once.

I got up on legs that felt numb. I walked into the bar. I sat down next to her, a stranger who had once been my closest friend, the object of my lust and my love. The woman who had once killed a rabid dog in defense of her son but too late, too late, too late.

"Hey, you," I said. "Can I buy you a drink?"

She turned, startled, ready to say whatever it was she meant to say, thanks but I'm meeting someone, thanks but I'm not looking for company . . . and saw me. Her mouth made a perfect O. She swayed backward on the stool. I caught her by the shoulders. Her eyes on mine. Her dark blue eyes on mine.

"Vic? Is it really you?"

"Is this seat taken?"

Jim and Andre did the brainstorming session by themselves, and the lawyers ended up greenlighting a really awful advertising campaign featuring a has-been cowboy star. I took my ex to dinner, and not at Olive Garden. Our first meal together since three months after the divorce. The last ended in a bitter argument; she threw her salad plate at me and we got kicked out. "I never want to see you again," she said. "If you need to tell me something, write."

She walked away without looking back. Reagan was president. We thought we were old but we didn't know what old was.

There were no arguments that night in Providence. There was a lot of catching up and a fair amount of drinking. She came back to my room. We spent the night. Three months later—long enough for us to make sure this wasn't just some kind of holding-onto-the-past mirage—we remarried.

The police came in three cruisers—maybe overdoing it for one dead old woman. And yes, there was an ambulance. The shirts were removed from Allie Bell's corpse and after an examination by the EMTs and the sort of *in situ* photographs no one wants to look at, my neighbor was zipped into a body bag.

The county cop who took my statement was P. ZANE. The one who took the photographs and videotaped my statement was D. CANAVAN. Canavan was younger, and curious about the stroller and the child-sized clothing. Before I could explain, Zane said, "She's kinda famous. Loopy but nice enough. Ever heard that song, 'Delta Dawn'?"

Canavan shook his head, but as a country music fan in general and a Tanya Tucker fan in particular, I knew the one he was talking about. The similarity wasn't exact, but it wasn't bad.

I said, "It's a song about a woman who keeps looking for her long-gone lover. Mrs. Bell liked to push around her twins, although they were also long-gone. They died years ago."

Canavan thought it over, then said, "That's fucked up."

I thought, *Maybe you have to have lost a child to understand.*

One of the EMTs joined us. "There'll be an autopsy, but I'm guessing it was a stroke or heart attack."

"I'm betting on heart attack," I said. "She took pills for arrhythmia. They might be in her dress pocket. Or . . ."

I went to the stroller and looked in the twin pouches on the backs of the seats. In one there were two little Tampa Rays baseball caps and a tube of sunblock. In the other was a bottle of pills. The EMT took it and looked at the label. "Sotalol," he said. "For fast or irregular heartbeat."

I thought she might have overturned the stroller while trying to get her medication. What else could it have been? She certainly hadn't seen a rattlesnake.

"I imagine you'll have to testify at the inquest," Officer Zane said. "Are you going to be around for awhile, Mr. Trenton?"

"Yes. This summer it seems like everybody's sticking around."

"True," he said, and self-consciously adjusted his mask. "Walk with us. Let's see if she left the house open. We should lock it up if she did."

I pushed the stroller, mostly because nobody told me not to. Zane had taken the pills and put them in an envelope.

"Jesus," Canavan said. "I'm surprised that squeaky wheel didn't drive her nuts." Then, considering what he'd just said: "Although I guess she sorta was."

"She brought me cookies," I said. "I meant to oil it that night, but I forgot."

The house behind the wall of rhododendron and palmetto wasn't a McMansion. In fact, it looked like the sort of summer place that in the mid-twentieth century, long before the Richie Rich types discovered the Gulf Coast Keys, might have been rented to a couple of fishermen or a vacationing family for fifty or seventy dollars a week.

There was a bigger, newer addition behind it, but not big enough (or vulgar enough) to qualify for McMansion status. The garage was connected to the house by a breezeway. I looked in, cupping my hands against the glass, and saw a plain old Chevy Cruze. There was enough light coming through the side windows for me to make out the two small child seats side by side in the back.

Officer Zane knocked on the door of the house, a formality, then tried the knob. It opened. He told Canavan to come with him and roll videotape, presumably so he could show his bosses, including the county attorney, that they hadn't lightfingered anything. Zane asked if I wanted to come in. I declined, but after they had gone inside, I tried the side door of the garage. It was also unlocked. I wheeled the stroller inside and parked it beside the car. There were thunderstorms forecast for later in the day, and I didn't want it getting wet.

"Be good boys," I said. The words were out before I knew I was going to say them.

Zane and Canavan came out ten minutes later, Canavan still video-taping as Zane worked through a loaded keyring, trying various ones until he got one to fit the front door.

"House was totally open," he said to me. "Windows and all. I locked the back and the patio doors from the inside. Must have been a trusting soul."

Well, I thought, *she had her kids with her, and maybe they were the only things she really cared about.*

After some more hunting on the deceased woman's keyring, Zane locked the garage. By then Canavan had turned off the video camera. The three of us walked back to the road. The cops pulled their masks down around their necks. I had forgotten mine again; I hadn't been expecting to meet anyone.

"Ito works for you, doesn't he?" Zane asked. "Japanese-American guy from the Village?"

I said he did.

"Also for Mrs. Bell?"

"No, just me. She had Plant World for the grounds. I sometimes saw their trucks. Maybe twice a week."

"But no caretaker? No one to fix a clogged drain or patch the roof?"

"Not that I know of. Mr. Ito might."

Zane scratched his chin. "She must have been handy. Some women are. Just because you think your kids are still alive forty years later doesn't mean you can't replace a washer or a windowpane."

"Not handy enough to oil the wheel on that squeaky stroller," Canavan said.

"Maybe she liked it," I said. "Or . . ."

"Or nothing," Canavan said, and laughed. "Nobody likes a squeaky wheel. Don't they say that's the one that gets the grease?"

Zane didn't reply. I didn't, either, but I thought maybe the *kids* had liked it. Maybe it had even lulled them off to sleep after a big day of playing and swimming. *Squeak* . . . pause . . . *squeak* . . . pause . . . *squeak* . . .

The ambulance and two of the police cars were gone when we got back to where I'd found her body. Before departing, the other cops had strung yellow DO NOT CROSS tape from palms on either side of the driveway. We ducked under it. I asked Officer Zane what was going to happen with the house, and who was going to take care of her final expenses.

He said he had no idea. "She probably had a will. Somebody'll have to go through the place and find it, plus her phone and any other paperwork. Her children and husband are dead, but there must be relatives somewhere. Until we get this straightened out, you could lend us a hand, Mr. Trenton. You and Ito keep an eye on the house, would you mind doing that? This could take awhile. Partly it's the paperwork, but mostly it's because we've only got three detectives. Two are on vacation and one's sick."

"Covid," Canavan said. "Tris had got it bad, I'm hearing."

"I can do that," I said. "I guess you want to make sure nobody finds out the place is empty and takes advantage."

"That's it. Although hyenas who rob a deceased person's house usually do it because they read the obituary, and who's going to write an obituary for Mrs. Bell? She was alone."

"Why don't I put her name and what I know about her on Facebook?"

"Okay, good. And we'll get it on the news."

"What about Super Gramp?" Canavan said. "Could he go through the house? Look for a will and maybe an address book?"

"You know what, that's a good idea," Zane said.

"Who's Super Gramp?" I asked.

"Andy Pelley," Zane said. "Semi-retired. Refuses to go all the way to full retired. He helps out when we need a hand."

"Charter member of the 10-42 Club," Canavan said. He snickered, which earned him a frown from Zane.

"What's that?"

"Cops who can't quite bring themselves to pull the pin," Zane said. "But Pelley's good police, got a lot of experience, and he's fishing buddies with one of the local judges. I bet he could get a Writ of Exigent Circumstances, or whatever it's called."

"So I wouldn't have to actually go inside the house—"

"Nope, nope, you can't," Zane said. "That'll be Pelley's job, if he agrees to do it. But thanks for calling it in. And for keeping the fucking buzzards off her. They messed her up, but it could have been a lot worse. Sorry your morning walk got ruined."

"Shit happens. I think Confucius said that."

Canavan looked puzzled, but Zane laughed. "Ask Mr. Ito if he knows anything about Mrs. Bell's relatives when you see him."

"I will."

I watched them get into their cruiser and waved as they went around the next bend. Then I walked back home. I thought about Donna. I thought about Tad, our lost boy, who would now—if not for a plugged needle valve—be in his forties and starting to go gray. I thought about Allie Bell, who made good oatmeal cookies and who said *I know they aren't there. And yet sometimes they* are.

I thought about the double pram parked in the dark garage, next to the Chevy Cruze with its no-nonsense blackwall tires. I thought about saying *be good boys* . . . even though the pram was empty.

It wasn't fair. True of the Bell twins, true of my son, true of my twice-married wife. The world is full of rattlesnakes. Sometimes you step on them and they don't bite. Sometimes you step over them and they bite anyway.

By the time I got back to the house, I was hungry. No, ravenous. I scrambled up four eggs and toasted another English muffin. Donna would have said my hunger was healthy, life-affirming, a spit in the eye of death, but maybe I was just hungry. Finding a dead woman at the head of her driveway and waving away the buzzards who wanted to eat her must have burned a lot of calories. I couldn't get her ruined face out of my mind, but I ate everything on my plate anyway, and this time held it down.

Because the day was pleasant instead of oppressively hot ("Hotter than dog-snot" was how Mr. Ito liked to put it), I decided to walk after all . . . but not down to the swing gate, which would mean passing the spot where I'd found Allie. I took Greg's boardwalk to the beach instead. The first part of it was hemmed in by palmettos and junk palms, which turned it into a green tunnel. The raccoons seemed to like that part, and I was careful to avoid the little clumps of their scat. There was a gazebo at the end of the boardwalk. After that the trees fell away to a wide sweep of beach grass and dune reeds. The sound of the waves was mild and soothing. Gulls and terns circled, loafing on the Gulf breeze. There were other birds, too—big 'uns and little 'uns. Greg was an amateur ornithologist and would have known them all. I did not.

I looked south where there were great tangles of underbrush. A few palms poked above them, but they looked tattered and unhealthy, probably because the trash growth was sucking up most of the nutrient-rich groundwater. It was there that Jake and Joe must have come to grief. I could see the Bell boardwalk, and if they had only taken that instead of trying to play jungle explorers they would also be in their forties, maybe pushing their own youngsters in that old stroller. *If onlies* are also rattlesnakes, I think. They are full of poison.

I left the gazebo behind and headed north along the beach, which was wide and wet and shining in the sun. There would be a lot less beach that afternoon, and almost none by evening, when the tide was high. Mr. Ito said it didn't used to be that way; he said it was global warming, and by the time Eddie was his age, the beach would be gone.

It was a pleasant walk with the Gulf on my left and the dunes on my right. Greg Ackerman's was the last house on the Key; north of his property, county land took over and the tangled undergrowth reappeared, growing so close to the beach that I occasionally had to brush away palmetto branches and step over big clumps of beach naupaka. Then the foliage ended and the beach widened into a lopsided triangle deep in shells. Here and there I spotted shark's teeth, some as big as my index finger. I picked a few up and put them in my pocket, thinking I'd give them to Donna. Then I remembered, oh snap, that my wife was dead.

Bitten again, I thought.

The triangle was lopsided because Daylight Pass had cut off the beach. Water ran against the tide from Calypso Bay, first fighting the mild Gulf waves and swirling in a whirlpool before joining them. It was a hurricane that opened Daylight, which had been closed ninety years before. So I'd read in *A Pictorial History of the South Keys*, which had been on Greg's coffee table when I took up residence. Across the way was a floating patch of greenery, all that remained of Duma Key, which had been inundated in the same hurricane that opened the pass.

I lost interest in picking up shark's teeth—remembering your wife is dead will do that, I guess—so just put my hands in my pockets and looked at the shell beach where Rattlesnake Key ended. It was to this dead end that the hunting party had driven the infestation of snakes. A group of lawyers is an eloquence; a group of rattlesnakes is a rhumba. I didn't know how I knew that, but I did. The mind isn't just a venomous reptile that sometimes bites itself; it's also an enthusiastic garbage picker. Freddy Cannon released his 45s on the Swan label, which bore the message DON'T DROP OUT. James Garfield's middle name was Abram. Those are also things I know but don't know how I know.

I stood there with the breeze rippling my shirt and the birds circling overhead and the green mop of foliage that marks what's left of Duma Key rising and falling with the waves, as if it were breathing. How had they driven the snakes here? That was a thing I *didn't* know. And once they got them here, how had they killed those that didn't try to escape by swimming away? I didn't know that, either.

I heard a squeak from behind me. Then another. The sweat on the nape of my neck turned cold. I didn't want to turn my head because I was sure I'd see that double stroller with the dead twins inside it, swollen from snakebites. But because I had nowhere to go (like the rattlers), and didn't believe in ghosts, I did. There were a couple of gulls standing there—white heads, black bodies, beady eyes asking what the hell I was doing trespassing on their spot.

Because I was scared, I threw a couple of shark's teeth at them. They weren't as big as the shells I'd thrown at the buzzards, but they did the job. The gulls flew off, squawking indignantly.

Squawking.

What I'd heard behind me had been *squeaking*—like the wheel that needs some grease. I told myself that was bullshit and could almost believe it. The breeze brought the smell of something that might have been kerosene or gasoline. It didn't surprise me; Florida politicians, from the governor right down to the city and town councils, are more interested in business than they are in preserving the Gulf Coast's fragile ecosystem. They abuse it and eventually they will lose it.

I looked for the telltale rainbow of gas or oil on the surface, or turning at the edges of that constant whirlpool, and saw nothing. Breathed deep and smelled nothing. Went back home . . . which was how I was now thinking of Greg Ackerman's house.

I don't know if remarriages work, as a rule. If there are statistics, I haven't seen them. Ours did. Was it because of the long gap? Those years when we didn't see each other, then fell out of touch completely? The shock of reconnection? That might have been part of it. Or was it because the terrible wound of our son's death had had time to heal? Maybe, but I wonder if couples ever get over a thing like that.

Speaking just for myself, I thought of Tad less often, but when I did, the hurt was nearly as strong as ever. One day at the office I remembered how I used to read him the Monster Words before bedtime—a catechism that was intended to banish his fear of the dark—and had to sit down on a toilet in the office bathroom and cry. That wasn't a year or two or even ten after it happened; that was when I was in my fifties. Now I'm in my seventies, and I still don't look at pictures of him, although there was a time when I stored many on my phone. Donna said she did, but only on what would have been his birthday—a kind of ritual. But she was always stronger than I was. She was a soldier.

I think most first marriages are about romance. I'm sure there are exceptions, people who marry for money or to improve their station in life some other way, but the majority are powered by the giddy, gliding feeling pop songs are written about. "The Wind Beneath My Wings" is a good example, both because of the feeling it evokes and because of the corollary the song doesn't go into: eventually the wind dies. Then you have to flap those wings if you don't want to crash land. Some couples find a tougher love that endures after the romance thins away. Some couples discover that tougher love just isn't in their repertoire. Instead of discussing money, they argue about it. Suspicion replaces trust. Secrets blossom in the shadows.

And some marriages break up because a child dies. Allie Bell's didn't, but might have if her husband hadn't died not long after. No coronary for me, only panic attacks. I kept a paper bag in my briefcase and huffed into it when they came on. Eventually they stopped.

When Donna and I remarried there was an older love, kinder and more reserved. There were none of the money arguments that bedevil many young couples who are just starting out; I had done well in the ad biz, and Donna was the superintendent of one of the biggest school districts in southern Maine. On the evening I saw her in that bar, she was in Providence for a New England conference of school adminis-trators. Her yearly salary wasn't as big as mine, but it was generous. We both had 401k's. Our financial needs were met.

The sex was satisfactory, although without a lot of fireworks (except maybe for that first time after our long—ha-ha—layoff). She had her house, I had mine, and that was how we lived. The commute wasn't a big problem. It turned out that we'd been living just seventy miles apart for all those in-between years. We weren't together all the time, and that was okay. We didn't need to be. When we were, it was like being with a good friend that you just happened to sleep with. We worked at the relationship in a way that couples just starting out don't need to do, because they have that wind beneath their wings. Older couples, especially those with a terrible darkness in their past that they need to avoid, have to flap. That's what we did.

Donna took early retirement, and in 2010 we became a one-house couple: mine, in Newburyport. It was her decision. At first I thought it was because she wanted more together time, and I was right about that. Just not why she felt more together time had become necessary. We spent a week getting her settled, then she asked one sunshiny October Saturday if I'd walk with her by the rock wall that divides my property from the Merrimack River. We held hands and kicked through the leaves, listening to the crackle and smelling that sweet cinnamon odor they get before they go limp and start to decay. It was a beautiful afternoon with big fat clouds sailing across a blue sky. I said it looked like she had lost weight. She said that was true. She said it was because she had cancer.

I was afraid that thinking about the buzzards tearing into Allie would keep me awake, so I went poking through Greg's double-sized med-icine cabinet (always a bit of a hypochondriac, my friend) and found an Ambien prescription with four left in the bottle. According to the label, this particular helping of sleep medicine had expired in May of 2018, but I thought what the hell and took a couple. Maybe they worked, maybe it was just the placebo effect, but I slept all night, and with no dreams.

I woke refreshed at seven the next morning and decided to make my regular walk, feeling I couldn't avoid the spot where Allie died for the rest of my stay. I put on shorts and sneakers and went downstairs to start the Keurig. Greg's driveway opens into a large courtyard on the side of the house. A window at the foot of the stairs looks out on this courtyard. I got two steps from the bottom of the stairs and froze, staring.

The stroller was out there.

I couldn't believe it. Couldn't quite take it in. I felt it had to be a trick of the shadows, only in that early morning light there *were* no shadows . . . except, that is, for the one thrown by the stroller. It was there. It was real. More than the object itself, the shadow proved it. Shadows don't exist unless there's something to make them.

After my initial brain-freeze, I was afraid. Someone, some mean person, had come here and left that stroller to freak me out. It worked. I *was* freaked out. I couldn't think who would have done such a thing, certainly not Officers Zane or Canavan. Mr. Ito had probably heard of Mrs. Bell's death—news travels fast in small communities—but he wasn't the practical joker type, and his son spent most of the time in Internet dreamland. There were no usual suspects, and in a way that didn't matter. What mattered was that someone had come to my house in what the pulp novelists call the dead of night.

Had I locked up? In my initial shock and fright (at first I wasn't even angry), I couldn't remember. I'm not sure I could have remembered my late wife's middle name just then, had I been asked. I rushed to the front door: locked. I went to the one that gave on the pool and the patio: locked. I went to the back door, which opens into the garage, and that one was locked, too. So at least no one had actually been inside, doing a midnight creep. It should have been a relief but it wasn't.

One of the cops must *have left that thing*, I thought. *Zane locked the garage and took the keys.*

There was logic there, but I just didn't believe it. Zane had seemed solid, dependable, far from dumb. Also, was a key to the garage really necessary? Probably not. The lock on the side door looked like the kind you could pop with a coathanger or credit card.

I went out to look at the stroller. I thought there might be a note of the sort that would be left behind in a creepy Grade C suspense movie: *You're next* and *Go back where you came from* both came to mind.

There was no note. There was something worse. Yellow shorts on one seat, red shorts on the other. Not the same ones as yesterday. And shirts draped across the backs, also not the same. I didn't want to touch those shirts and didn't have to in order to read what was on them: TWEEDLEDUM and TWEEDLEDEE. Twin shirts for sure, but the twins who had worn these were long dead.

What to do with the goddam stroller was the question, and a good one. Now that the reality of it being there was setting in, my first shock, closely followed by fear, was being replaced by curiosity and anger: what a shit way to start the morning. I had my cell phone in the pocket of my shorts. I called the County Sheriff's Department and asked for Officer P. Zane. The receptionist put me on hold, then came back and said Officer Zane was off-duty until the following Monday. I knew better than to ask for a cop's personal number, so instead asked the dispatcher to please tell him Victor Trenton had called, and would he please call back?

"I'll see what I can do," the woman said, a non-response that did nothing to ameliorate my shitty morning.

"You do that," I said, and ended the call.

Mr. Ito would also not be in until the following Monday, and I wasn't expecting any other company, but I had no intention of letting that stroller sit in the courtyard. I decided to push it back to Mrs. Bell's and return it to the garage. It was on my usual walk, after all, and I might be able to tell if some practical joker/mean person had forced the garage door. First, though, I took a couple of photos of the perambulator *in situ*, to show Zane. Assuming he was interested, that was. He might be less than happy that I'd moved the stroller from the courtyard where I found it, but was it evidence of a crime? Had Allie Bell been beaten to death with a perambulator, perforce? No. I was just returning it to where we'd put it.

I pushed it up the road under the simmering morning sun. Maybe the residual effects of the Ambien were still in my system, because once the fear had been dispelled by the pram's prosaic ordinariness (even the shorts and shirts were prosaic, the sort of clothing available in any Walmart or Amazon), I fell into a kind of daze. I suppose if I'd been in bed, or even lying on the sofa, I would have drifted off into sleep. But because I was walking on Rattlesnake Road, I just let my mind float on its own current.

Squeaky wheel or no squeaky wheel (*I really should oil it*, I thought), the stroller was easy to push, especially without any four-year-old boys to weigh it down. I did it with my left hand. With my right I touched the shirts hanging over the backs of the seats—first one, then the other. I didn't realize what I was doing until later.

I thought of the boys crossing the road and then fighting their way toward the beach through the undergrowth. Not angry about it, not using their little-boy cusswords if they got whapped in the face by a backswinging frond or when a jutting branch scraped an arm. Not angry, not impatient, not wishing they'd taken the boardwalk. They were deep in a shared fantasy—jungle explorers wearing newspaper hats their father had made them out of the *Tribune*'s Sunday color funnies. Somewhere ahead there might be a treasure chest left behind by pirates, or a gigantic ape like King Kong, a movie they had seen on *Tampa Matinee* at four o'clock, sitting crosslegged before the TV until their mom commandeered it for the *Nightly News* with Tom Brokaw.

They hear the rattling, low at first but getting louder and closer as they push heroically onward. At first they ignore it, then make the fatal mistake of dismissing it. Joe thinks it might be bees and they could find honey. Jake asks him how many times his brother would like to get stung and tells him not to be stupid. They are after treasure. Honey is not treasure. The rattling sound is coming from the left and the right. No problem! The way to the beach is straight ahead. They can already hear the waves and they will paddle their feet before digging in the sand for gold (and building a castle if the treasure hunt yields no results). They want to wade in the water because it's hot, a hot day like the one my little boy had to deal with. He had no water in which to paddle his feet, he was trapped in a hot car with his mommy because there was a monster outside. The monster wouldn't leave and the car wouldn't go.

They don't see the dip because it's masked by a tangle of bushes. Those bushes also hide a den of snakes—a rhumba of rattlers—that lives in its shade. Jake and Joe, side by side, could go around this overgrown clump of greenery, but that's not how brave explorers roll. Brave explorers go straight ahead, hacking away the greenery with invisible machetes.

That's what they do, and because they're walking side by side, they plunge into the dip together. And into the snakes. There are dozens of them. Some are still young—snakelets—and although they can bite, they cannot (contrary to popular belief) inject poison. But their bites are still painful, and most of the rattlers are adults in full protection mode. They shoot their diamond-shaped heads forward and sink their fangs deep.

The boys cry out—*ow* and *don't* and *what* and *that hurts*.

They are bitten multiple times on the ankles and calves. Joe goes to one knee. A snake strikes his thigh and wraps its body around his knee like a tourniquet. Jake struggles out of the brush-filled dip wearing snakes like ankle bracelets. That rattling sound fills the world. He tries to pull Joe to his feet and a snake sinks its fangs into the meat of his small palm as quick as winking. Joe is on his belly now, with snakes crawling all over him. He tries to protect his face, at least, and can't. He's bitten on his neck and cheeks, and when he turns his head in a futile effort to get away, on his nose and mouth. His face begins to swell.

Jake turns and begins to blunder back to the road and the Bell house on the other side, still wearing snakes around his ankles. One falls off. The other begins to twine its way up toward the leg of the boy's shorts, a rattlesnake barber pole. Why does he run, when the two of them have always done everything together? Is it because he knows his twin brother is already beyond help? No. Because he's in a blind panic? No—not even blind panic could cause him to abandon Joe. It's because he wants to get Daddy if he's still home, Mommy if Daddy isn't. It's not panic, it's a rescue mission. Jake pulls the snake off his leg and has a moment to see its beady assessing eyes before it buries its fangs in his wrist. He flings it away and tries to run but he can't run, the poison is coursing through him now, making his heart beat erratically, making it hard to breathe.

Joe is no longer screaming.

Jake's vision doubles, then triples. He can no longer even walk, so he tries to crawl. His hands are swelling up like cartoon gloves. He tries to say his brother's name and can't because his throat—

What brought me out of this vision was the clack and whine of the swing gate going up. The stroller I was pushing had broken the photo-electric beam that operates it. In my zombie state I'd walked far past Allie's driveway. I saw my right hand was still going back and forth, touching first one shirt (TWEEDLEDEE) and then the other (TWEEDLEDUM). I pulled it back as if it were touching something hot. The day was still relatively cool, but my face was wet with sweat and my tee-shirt was dark with it. I had only been walking (at least I thought so; couldn't remember for sure), but I was breathing fast, as if at the end of a two-hundred-yard dash.

I pulled the stroller back and the swing gate went down. I asked myself what had just happened, but thought I knew. The other members of my team at the agency would have laughed—except maybe for Cathy Wilkin, who had an imagination that stretched further than taglines for toilet bowl cleaner—but I had no other way to explain it. I had seen movies and at least one TV documentary where so-called clairvoyants were called in by the police to help locate the bodies of people who were presumed dead. As bloodhounds are given an article of clothing to get the scent they're supposed to follow, the psychics were given articles that were deemed important to the person they were supposed to locate. Mostly the results had been bullshit, but in a few cases it had worked. Or seemed to.

It was the shirts. Touching the shirts. And the part about Tad? Those were my own memories intruding on whatever vibe I'd been getting from those shirts. My son finding his way into my strange state of seeing wasn't surprising. He had died at about the same age as the Bell twins, and at close to the same time. Triplets instead of twins. Tragedy calling to tragedy.

As I turned the stroller and started back, the vividness of my vision started to fade. I began to question the idea that I'd had an authentic psychic experience. It wasn't as though I didn't know what happened to the Bell twins, after all; maybe my mind had just added some details, like the concealed dip they'd fallen into. It might not have happened that way at all. Plus, there was no denying that I'd been in an extremely suggestible state because of the pram showing up as it had.

That I *couldn't* explain.

I ducked under the yellow tape and pushed the stroller up the curving driveway to the Bell house. *Squeak, squeak, squeak.* The garage's side door was standing open, swinging lazily back and forth in a light breeze. There were no splinters above or beneath the lock plate, and none on the door itself. It could have been loided with a credit card, but it hadn't been forced.

I studied the doorknobs, both outside and inside. There was a keyhole in the middle of the outside knob, which Officer Zane had used to lock the door. You didn't need a key to lock the inside. There was a button in the middle of that knob and all you had to do was push it.

The solution is simple, I thought. *It was the twins. It was Jacob and Joseph. They just turned the inside knob. The button would pop out and the door would open. Easy as winking. Then they pushed the stroller down to my place, Jake on one side and Joe on the other.*

Sure. And if you believed that, you'd believe we won in Vietnam, the moon landing was faked, the horror-stricken parents at Sandy Hook were crisis actors, and 9/11 was an inside job.

And yet the garage door *was* open.

And the stroller *had* turned up at my house, a quarter of a mile away.

My phone rang. I jumped. It was Officer P. Zane. The receptionist at the Sheriff's Department had come through after all.

"Hello, Mr. Trenton, what can I do you for?" He sounded more relaxed today, and much more Southern. Probably because it was his day off and he was in civilian mode.

"I'm at the Bell house," I said, and told him why. I hardly need to add that I left out the part about my vision of the boys falling into the camouflaged snakepit.

There was a moment of silence when I finished. Then he said, "Go ahead and put that stroller back in the garage, why don't you?" He sounded unsurprised and not very concerned. Of course *he* hadn't had a vision of snakes crawling all over Joe Bell as he shrieked. "Somebody played a practical joke on you. Teenagers most likely, sneaking up Rattlesnake Road to see where the crazy lady died. She kind of had that reputation in Palm Village."

"You really think that's what it was?"

"What else could it be?"

Ghosts, I thought. *Ghost children.* But I wasn't going to say it. I didn't even like thinking it. "Maybe you're right. They must have popped the lock with a credit card or driver's license, though. There's no sign of damage."

"Sure. Nothing to popping a lock like that."

"Easy as winking."

He chuckled. "Got that right. Just put the stroller back and close the door. Deceased lady's keys are at the substation. Andy Pelley will pick em up. You remember who I'm talking about?"

"Sure. Super Gramp."

He laughed. "Right, but don't call him that to his face. Anyway, he got his judge friend to sign that Exigent Circumstances widget so he can go in and do a search for next of kin and local contacts. Andy's a sharp old bird. If anyone's been in there, he'll know. We at least have to find someone who'll take responsibility for the lady's remains."

Remains, I thought, watching the door swing back and forth in the breeze. What a word. "I guess she can't just stay in the morgue, can she?"

"We don't even have one. She's at the Perdomo Funeral Home on the Tamiami. Listen, since you're there and the garage is open, would you mind going inside and see if the lady's car got vandalized in any way? Punctured tires, broken windows, cracked windshield? Because we'd have to take that a little more serious."

"Happy to. Sorry to interrupt you on your day off."

"Don't you worry. I've had my breakfast and now I'm just sitting out back and reading the paper. Call me if anything's wrong with the car. If there is, I'll inform Andy. And Mr. Trenton?"

"Why don't you make it Vic?"

"Okay, Vic. If you feel like the kids who took that stroller down to Mr. Ackerman's house might do it again—the sort of kids who pull shit like that ain't what you'd call creative—you can roll it back and put it in your garage."

"I think I'll leave it here."

"Fair enough. You have a good day, now."

As I rolled the pram into the garage, rocking up the front end to get it over the jamb, I realized I hadn't told Zane about the shorts and shirts, either.

The garage wasn't air conditioned, and I began to sweat almost as soon as I was through the door. Other than needing a trip through the nearest car wash—the sides and windshield were crusted with salt—Allie's Chevy Cruze looked okay. I found myself staring at the empty car seats in the back (of *course* they were empty) and made myself look away. There were a number of cardboard cartons stacked along the back wall. Neatly lettered in Magic Marker on each was *THE Js.*

My mother had a saying, *Only snooping is lower than gossip,* but my father liked to tease her with another one: *Curiosity killed the cat, but satisfaction brought him back.*

I opened one of the boxes and saw board jigsaw puzzles, the kind with sturdy pieces in the shapes of animals. I opened another and found picture books: Dr. Seuss, Richard Scarry, the Berenstain Bears. Several more contained clothes, including shorts and paired tee-shirts with various cute twin-isms on them. So this was where the shorts and shirts on the stroller had come from. The question I had was whether or not a prankster would have known how Allie placed those things on the stroller, like a child dressing invisible dolls. Officer Zane would have said yeah, word gets around. I wasn't so sure.

Grief sleeps but doesn't die. At least not until the griever does. This was a lesson I re-learned when I opened the last carton. It was filled with toys. Matchbox cars, Playstix, *Star Wars* figures, a folded Candy Land game, and a dozen plastic dinosaurs.

Our son had Matchbox cars and toy dinosaurs. Loved them.

My eyes stung and my hands weren't quite steady as I closed up the carton. I wanted to get out of this hot, still garage. And maybe off Rattlesnake Key, too. I had come to finish grieving for my wife and all the years we'd foolishly wasted apart, not to re-open the long-healed wound of my boy's terrible death. Certainly not to have psychic flashes of the *Inside View* type. I thought I'd give it another two or three days to be sure, and if I felt the same I'd call Greg, thank him, and tell Mr. Ito to keep an eye on the place. Then I'd head back to Massachusetts, where it was hot in August but not *insanely* hot.

On the way out, I saw some tools—a hammer, a screwdriver, a couple of wrenches—on a shelf to the left of the door. There was also an old-fashioned oil can, the kind with a metal base you pump with your fingers and a long nozzle that reminded me a little of Allie Bell's snake pole. I decided that even though I had no intention of pushing the pram back to Greg's house, I could at least oil that squeaky wheel. If there was any oil left in the can, that was.

I picked it up and saw there was something else on the shelf. It was a file folder with *JAKE AND JOE* written on it. And, in bigger letters: *SAVE THIS!*

I flipped it open and saw two paper hats made out of the Sunday color funnies. I forgot all about oiling the squeaky wheel, and I didn't want to touch those homemade hats. Touching them might bring on another vision. In that hot garage, the idea didn't seem silly but all too plausible.

I shut the garage door and went home. When I got there I turned on my phone and searched for *Tampa Matinee*. I didn't want to do it, but I'd found the hats, so I did. Siri brought me to a nostalgia site created by a former employer of WTVT, Tampa's CBS affiliate since back in the day. There was a list of local programs from the fifties to the nineties. A puppet show in the morning. A teen dance party on Saturday afternoons. And *Tampa Matinee*, an afternoon movie that ran from four to six each weekday afternoon until 1988. Once upon a time, only three years after my son died, Joe and Jake had sat crosslegged in front of the TV, watching King Kong clinging to the top of the Empire State Building.

I had no doubt of it.

We had ten years after remarrying. Nine of them, before the cancer came back, were good. The last year . . . well, we tried to make it good, and for the first six months we mostly succeeded. Then the pain started to ramp up, going from serious to very serious to the kind where you can think of nothing else. Donna was brave about it; that lady had no shortage of guts. Once she faced a rabid St. Bernard with nothing but a baseball bat. With the cancer burning through her she had no weapon except for her own will, but for a long time that was enough. Near the end she was little more than a shadow of the woman I'd taken to bed that night in Providence, but to me her beauty remained.

She wanted to die at home and I honored her wish. We had a day nurse and a part-time night nurse, but I mostly took care of her myself. I fed her, and when she could no longer make it to the bathroom, I changed her. I wanted to do those things because of all the missed years.

There was a tree behind our house that split apart—maybe because of a lightning strike—and then grew back together, leaving a heart-shaped hole. That was us. If the metaphor seems overly sentimental, deal with it. I'm telling the truth as I understand it. As I felt it.

Some people have worse luck. We did our best with what we were given.

I lay in bed staring up at the slowly turning blades of the overhead fan. I was thinking of the stroller with the squeaky wheel, and the newspaper hats, and the toy dinosaurs. But mostly I thought of the night Donna died, which was a memory I had avoided. Now it seemed somehow necessary. There was a nor'easter with heavy snow blowing and drifting in a forty-mile-an-hour wind. The night nurse called from Lewiston at three that afternoon and canceled. The roads, she said, were impassable. The lights flickered several times but hadn't gone out, which was good. I wasn't sure what I'd do if they did. Donna had been switched from OxyContin tablets to a morphine pump in late December. It stood sentinel by her bed, and it ran on electricity. Donna was sleeping. It was cold in our bedroom—the furnace couldn't keep up with that howling January wind—but her thin cheeks were wet with sweat and what remained of her once thick hair clung to the fragile curve of her skull.

I knew she was close to the end, and so did her oncologist; he had taken the limiter off the morphine pump and now its little light always glowed green. He gave me the obligatory warning that too much would kill her, but didn't seem overly concerned. Why would he? The cancer had eaten most of her already, and was now gobbling the leftovers. I sat beside her as I had for most of the time during the last three weeks. I watched her eyes moving back and forth under her bruised-looking lids as she dreamed her dying dreams. There was a bag inside the pump, I reasoned, and maybe if the power went out I could get a screwdriver from the basement and—

Her eyes opened. I asked how she was doing, how bad the pain was.

"Not bad," she said. Then: "He wanted to see the ducks."

"Who did, honey?"

"Tad. He said he wanted to see the ducks. I think it was the last thing he said to me. What ducks, do you think?"

"I don't know."

"Do you remember any ducks? Maybe the time we took him to the Rumford Petting Zoo?"

I didn't remember ever taking him there. "Yeah, that's probably it. I think—"

She looked past me. Her face brightened. "Oh my God! You're all grown up! Look how *tall* you are!"

I turned my head. No one there, of course, but I knew who she was seeing. The wind gusted, shrieking around the eaves and throwing snow against the shuttered bedroom window so hard that it sounded like gravel. The lights dimmed, then came back, but somewhere a door crashed open.

"*You wouldn't BREATHE!*" Donna screamed.

I went gooseflesh from head to toe. I think my hair stood up. I'm not sure, but I really think it did. I wouldn't have believed she still had the strength to scream, but she always surprised me. Right to the end she surprised me. The wind was in the house now, a burglar eager to turn the place upside down. I could feel it rushing under the closed bedroom door. Something in the living room fell and broke.

"*BREATHE, Tad! BREATHE!*"

Something else fell over. A chair, maybe.

Donna had somehow managed to get up on her elbows, supported by upper arms not much thicker than pencils. Now she smiled and lay back down. "All right," she said. "I will. Yes."

It was like listening to one end of a phone conversation.

"Yes. Okay. Good. Thank God you are. What?" She nodded. "I will."

She closed her eyes, still smiling. I left the room to shut the front door, where there was already a fantail of snow almost an inch deep. When I came back, my wife was dead. You may scoff at the idea that our son came to escort her out of this life, and you are welcome to. I, on the other hand, once heard my little boy's voice coming from his closet while he was dying a dozen miles away.

I never told anyone about that, not even Donna.

*   *   *

These memories circled and circled. They were buzzards, they were rattlesnakes. They pecked, stung, wouldn't let me go. Around midnight I took two more of Greg's expired Ambien, lay back down, and waited for them to work. Still thinking of how Donna saw Tad grown to manhood as she passed out of the world. That her life ended in such a way should have had a calming effect on me, but it didn't. The memory of her deathbed kept connecting to the vision I'd had of the boys falling into the snakepit and coming back to reality to discover my hand going back and forth between TWEEDLEDUM and TWEEDLEDEE. Feeling their leavings. Their *remains*.

I thought, *What if I saw them the way Donna saw Tad at the end? What if I actually saw them? Allie did; I know she did.*

Seeing Tad had comforted Donna as she crossed the border from life to death. Would those boys comfort me? I didn't think so. Their comforter was gone. I was a stranger. I was . . . what? What was I to them?

I didn't want to know. Didn't want to be *haunted* by them, and the idea that it might be happening . . . that was what was keeping me awake.

I was just beginning to drift off when I heard the rhythmic squeaking. It started all at once and there was no way I could pretend it was the overhead fan in Greg's living room; it was coming from the en suite bathroom of this very bedroom.

Squeak and *squeak* and *squeak*.

I was terrified as a person can only be when they're alone in a house at the end of a mostly deserted road. But if Donna could face down a rabid St. Bernard with nothing but a baseball bat in defense of her son, surely I could look into the bathroom. It even crossed my mind, as I turned on the night table lamp and got out of bed, that I was imagining that sound. Hadn't I read somewhere that Ambien can cause hallucinations?

I walked to the left of the bathroom door and stood there against the wall, biting my lip. I turned the knob and pushed the door open. Now the squeaking was louder than ever. It was a big bathroom.

Someone was pushing that stroller around in there, back and forth, back and forth.

I reached around the jamb, terribly afraid—I think we always are in such situations—that a hand would close over mine. I found the light switch, fumbled with it for an agonizing length of time that was probably only two or three seconds, and flicked it up. The overheads were fluorescents, nice and bright. In most cases, light is a reliable dispeller of night terrors. Not this time. I still couldn't see into the bathroom from where I was standing, but on the wall opposite I could see a large shadow going back and forth. It was too amorphous for me to be sure it was that goddamned stroller, but I knew it was. And were the boys pushing it?

How else could it have gotten here?

Boys, I tried to say, but all that came out was a dry whisper. I cleared my throat and tried again. "Boys, you're not wanted here. You're not welcome here."

I realized I was speaking a bastardized version of the Monster Words, with which I had once comforted my little boy.

"It's my bathroom, not yours. It's my house, not yours. Go back to where you came from."

And where would that be? In two child-sized coffins under the earth of Palmetto Grove Cemetery? Were their rotting bodies—their rotting *remains*—pushing that stroller maniacally back and forth? Were pieces of their dead flesh falling off onto the floor?

Squeak and *squeak* and *squeak*.

The shadow on the wall.

Gathering every last ounce of my courage, I stepped away from the wall and went through the door. The squeaking stopped. The abandoned stroller was standing in front of the glass shower stall. Now there were two pairs of black pants draped over the seats and two black coats draped over the backs. Those were burial suits, meant to be worn forever.

While I stared at the pram, frozen by the horror of this thing that had no earthly way to be there, a rattling replaced the pram's squeaky wheel. It was low at first, as if coming from a distance, but rising until it was the sound of dry bones being shaken in a dozen gourds.

I had been looking at the shower stall. Now I looked at Greg's fancy clawfoot tub, which was long and deep. It was filled to the brim with rattlesnakes. As I watched, one small, supplicating hand rose from the twisting mass, that bathtub rhumba, and stretched out to me.

I fled.

It was the stroller that brought me back to myself.

It was standing in the middle of the flagstone courtyard, just as it had before . . . only now its shadow was being thrown by a three-quarter moon instead of morning light. I have no memory of running downstairs, wearing only the gym shorts I slept in, or out the patio door. I know I must have come that way because I found it standing open when I went back in.

I left the stroller where it was.

I went back upstairs, dreading every step, telling myself it had been a dream (except for the stroller outside; its presence was undeniable), knowing it hadn't been. Not a vision, either. It had been a *visitation*. The only thing that kept me from spending the rest of the night in my rental car with the doors locked was my clear sense that the visitation was over. The house was empty again except for me. Soon, I told myself, it would be *entirely* empty. I had no intention of staying on Rattlesnake Key when I had a perfectly good house to go back to in Newburyport. The only ghost there was the memory of my dead wife.

The bathroom was empty, as I'd known it would be. There were no rattlesnakes in the tub and no wheel-tracks on the faux marble floor. I went to the gallery and looked down on the courtyard, hoping the stroller would be gone, too. No such luck. It stood there in the moonlight, as real as roses.

But at least it was outside.

I went back to bed, and believe it or not, I slept.

The stroller was still there in the morning, this time with identical white shorts on the seats. Only when I got closer I saw they weren't completely identical after all. There were red pinstripes running down the legs of one and blue down the other. The shirts bore identical crows, one named HECKLE and one named JEKYLL. I had no intention of rolling it back down to Allie Bell's house. After a long career in the advertising business, I knew an exercise in futility when I encountered one. I put it in my garage instead.

You might ask if it all seemed like a dream in the bright light of morning—with the exception of the restless stroller, that is. The answer is simple: it did not. I had heard the squeaking and seen the moving shadow as the twins pelted their pram furiously back and forth in that bathroom, which was almost the size of a modest apartment's living room. I had seen the tub filled with snakes.

I waited until nine o'clock to call Delta Airlines. A recorded voice advised me that all reservation agents were currently busy and invited me to hold. I did, at least until a version of "Stairway to Heaven" by the One Hundred Comatose Strings came on, then gave up and went to American. Same thing. JetBlue, ditto. Southwest had a flight to Cleveland on Thursday, no connecting flight scheduled to Boston, but that might change, the agent told me. It was hard to tell. Thanks to the Coronavirus, everything was crazy.

I booked the flight to Cleveland, thinking if no connecting flight materialized I could rent a car, drive to Boston, and Uber to New-buryport. By then it was nine-thirty. I was very aware of the stroller sitting out in my garage. It was like having a hot stone in my pocket.

I went to the Hertz site on my phone and was put on terminal hold. Same with Avis and Enterprise. An agent answered the phone at Budget, checked his computer, and told me they had no oneway rental cars available in Cleveland. That left Amtrak and the bus lines, but by then I was frustrated and tired of holding the phone to my ear. I kept thinking of the stroller, the shirts, the child-sized black burial suits. The light of a hot August day should have helped. It didn't. The more my options closed off, the more I wanted—needed—to get out of Greg's house and away from Allie Bell's down the road. What had felt like a place to recover near the serenity of the Gulf now felt like a prison.

I got a cup of coffee, paced around the kitchen, and tried to think of what I should do, but it was hard to think of anything but the stroller (*squeak*) and the matching shirts (*squeak*) and the black burial suits (*squeak*). The coffins had also been matching. White, with gold handles. I knew this.

I drank the coffee black and another penny dropped: the nighttime visitation might be over but the haunting was still going on.

Thursday. I concentrated on that. I had a flight at least as far as Cleveland on Thursday. Three days from now.

Get off the Key until then. Do that much, at least. Can you?

At first I thought I could. Easy as winking. I grabbed my phone, found Barry's Resort Hotel in Palm Village, and called. Surely they would have a room where I could stay for three nights; hadn't I seen on the news that few people were traveling this summer? Why, the place would probably welcome me (*squeak*) with open arms!

What I got was a recorded message short and to the point: "Thank you for calling Barry's Resort Hotel. We are closed until further notice."

I called Holiday Inn Express in Venice and was told they were open but taking no new guests. Motel 6 in Sarasota didn't answer at all. As a last resort (little pun there—*squeak!*) I called the Days Inn in Bradenton. Yes, I was told, they had rooms. Yes, I could reserve one providing I passed a temperature check and wore a mask. I took the room, although Bradenton was forty miles away and two counties over. Then I went outside to try and clear my head before packing. I could have gone through the garage, but chose the patio door instead. I didn't want to look at the stroller, let alone oil the squeaky wheel. The twins might not like it.

I was standing by the pool when an F-150 pickup truck, blinding in the summer sun, came down the driveway and pulled up in the courtyard, exactly where I'd found the goddam stroller both times. The man who got out was wearing a tropical shirt with parrots on it, very large khaki shorts, and a straw sunhat of the type only lifelong residents of Florida's Gulf Coast can seem to get away with. He had a seamed, suntanned face and a really huge walrus mustache. He saw me and waved.

I went down the steps from the patio to the courtyard, already holding out my hand. I was glad to see him. It broke the repeating loop in my head. I think seeing anyone would have done it, but I was pretty sure I knew who this was: Super Gramp.

Instead of taking my hand, he offered his elbow. I gave it a bump, thinking this was now the new normal. "Andy Pelley. And you're Mr. Trenton."

"Right."

"Don't have the Covid, Mr. Trenton?"

"No. Do you?"

"Clean as a whistle, as far as I know."

I was grinning like a fool, and why? Because I was happy to see him. So happy to not be thinking about black suits and white coffins and squeaky wheels. "You know who you look like?"

"Oh boy, do I ever. Get it all the time." Then, with a smile below the mustache and a twinkle in his eye, he did a passable Wilford Brimley imitation. "Quaker Oats! It's the right thing to do!"

I laughed giddily. "Perfect! Nailed it!" Babbling. Couldn't help it. "That was a seriously good campaign, and I should know, because—"

"Because you used to be in advertising." He was still smiling, but I had been wrong about the twinkle in those blue eyes. It was actually a look of assessment. A cop look. "You handled the Sharp Cereals account, didn't you?"

"A long time ago," I said, thinking: *He's looked me up online. Investigated me. Why, I don't know. Unless he thinks I—*

"Got a few questions for you, Mr. Trenton. Maybe we could go inside? Awful hot out here. Guess the cold front's gone the way of the blue suede shoe."

"Of course. And really, make it Vic."

"Vic, Vic, got it."

I meant to take him up the steps to the patio, but he was already headed for the garage. He stopped when he saw the stroller.

"Huh. Preston Zane told me you returned that to Mrs. Bell's garage."

"I did. Someone brought it back. Again." I wanted to resume babbling, telling him I didn't know why, had no idea why the stroller was following me around, following me like a bad smell (if a bad smell could squeak, that was), but the assessing look was back in his sun-crinkled eyes and I made myself stop.

"Huh. Two nights in a row. Wow."

His eyes saying how unlikely that was, asking me if I was lying, asking if I had a reason to lie, something to hide. I wasn't lying, but I certainly did have something to hide. Because I didn't want to be dismissed as a crazy person. Or even considered as someone who'd had something to do with Allie Bell's death, the fabled "person of interest." But that was ridiculous. Wasn't it?

"Why don't we go inside and grab some air conditioning, Vic?"

"Fine. I made coffee, if you—"

"Nope, goes right through me these days. But I wouldn't mind a glass of cold water. Maybe even with an ice cube in it. You're really not sick, are you? Because you look a little pale."

"I'm not." Not the way *he* thought.

Pelley took no chances. He took a mask out of his voluminous shorts and put it on as soon as we were inside. I got him icewater and poured myself more coffee. I thought about donning my own mask and decided not to. I wanted him to see my whole face. We sat at the kitchen table. Each time he sipped his water he pulled the mask down, then returned it to its place. The mustache made it bulge.

"I understand you found Mrs. Bell. Must have been a shock."

"It was." The sense of relief at having company—another human being in the Haunted Mansion—was being replaced by caution. This guy might be in what Canavan had called the 10-42 Club, but Zane was right; he was sharp. I thought I was in for an interrogation rather than a courtesy stop-by.

"Happy to tell you what happened, how I found her, but since I've got you here, I'm curious about something."

"Are you, now?" Those eyes on mine. There were smile lines radiating out from their corners, but they weren't currently at work.

"Officer Zane told me you've been around here for a long time."

"Donkey's years," he said, sipping his water, wiping at his mustache with one big farmer's hand, then returning the mask to its place.

"I know about the rattlesnakes that killed Mrs. Bell's twins. What I'm curious about is how the posse got rid of them. Do you know?"

"Oh, you bet." For the first time he seemed to relax. "Should, since I was in on that snake hunt. Every cop in the county who didn't have the duty was in on it, plus plenty more guys and even a few gals. Must have been a hundred of us. Maybe more. A regular island party, except no one was having fun. Was a hot day, a lot hotter than this one, but all of us were wearing boots, long pants, shirts with long sleeves, gloves, masks like the one I'm wearing now. And veils."

"Veils?"

"Some were beekeepers' veils, some were made of that stuff—tulle, maybe—ladies wear on their Sunday hats. At least they did in the old days. Because, y'see—" Leaning forward, staring me in the eye, and looking more like Wilford Brimley than ever. "Y'see, a snake'll sometimes rear up. If it's scared enough, that is. Spray that poison instead of injecting it. If it gets in your eyes . . ." He waved his hand. "Short trip to your brain. Goodnight and good luck." And then, with no pause: "I see your midnight visitor brought back Mrs. Bell's snake pole, too."

He meant to catch me off-guard, and he succeeded. "What?"

"Saw it in the garage, leaning against the back wall." His gaze never leaving mine, waiting for my eyes to shift away, or any other tell. I held my eyes steady, but I blinked. Couldn't help it.

"You must have missed that."

"I . . . did. I guess . . ." I didn't know how to finish, so I just shrugged.

"Recognized it right away by the little silver ring on the handle. Lady went just about everywhere with it, at least on the Key. Many folks along Rattlesnake Road and over the swing bridge in the Village knew it, too."

"And the stroller," I said.

"Yeah, she liked to push the stroller. Talking to it sometimes. Talking to those gone boys of hers. I've seen her doing it myself."

"So did I."

He waited. I thought of saying *that stroller was in my bathroom last night and the dead twins were pushing it.*

"You asked about the snakes." He sipped his water and wiped his mustache with a cupped hand. Up went the mask. "The Great Snake

Drive of Eighty-Two or Eighty-Three. I'd have to look it up to be sure. Or maybe you already did, Vic?"

I shook my head.

"Well, those of us who didn't have snake poles had baseball bats, rug beaters, or tennis rackets. All kinds of things. To whack the brush with, you know. Also fishing nets. No shortage of nets on the Gulf. All the west coast keys are narrow, and this one's narrower than most. Gulf on one side, Calypso Bay on the other. Only six hundred yards across at its widest point and that's down by the swing bridge. This end, where the rattlers migrated to when all the building started down south, is about half that. From here you can see both the Gulf and the bay, right?"

"From the side yard, yes."

"This house wasn't even there then. Just palmettos and beach naupaka—the snakes loved that—and trash pines. Plus lots of bushes I don't even know the names of. We spread out in a line, from the Gulf to Calypso, and north we went, beating the bushes and dragging those nets and pounding on the ground. Snakes don't have much hearing, but they can feel vibrations. They knew we were coming. You could see the foliage shaking, especially the naupaka. Must have felt like an earthquake to em. And when we got toward the end of the Key, where the greenery ends, we could see em. Those suckers were *everywhere*. It was like the ground was moving. We couldn't believe it. And the *rattling*. I can hear it still."

"Like dry bones in a gourd."

He gave me a fixed look. "Right. How do you know that?"

"Seen them in the Franklin Park Zoo." I told this lie with a straight face. "That's in Boston. Also, you know, in nature programs."

"Well, it's a good description. Only you have to think of dozens of gourds, maybe hundreds, and a whole graveyard full of bones."

I thought of Greg's big bathtub. And one hand rising out of the writhing mass.

"Have you been to the north end of the Key, Vic?"

"I walked up there just the other day."

He nodded. "I haven't been there on foot since the snake hunt, but I've seen it plenty of times out fishing. The Key has changed a lot in the last forty years or so, been built up something terrible, but the north end is just the same now as it was then. A shell beach that looks like a great big lopsided triangle, am I right?"

"Just right," I said.

He nodded. The mask went down. A sip of water. The mask went up.

"That's where the snakes ended up, with no place to go except Daylight Pass. Backs to the water, you could say, except snakes are *all* back, aren't they? That half-acre of beach was covered with them. You couldn't see the shells at all, except every now and then for a split second or two as they moved around, shaking their tails. They were crawling all over each other, too. Enough poison in those snakes to kill half the people in Tampa, you would have said.

"We had a bunch of firemen from the Palm Village station and a bunch more from up Highway 41 in Nokomis. Big strapping fellows. Had to be, because they had twenty-gallon Smokechaser packs on their backs. What used to be called Indian pumps. Those things are made more for fighting brush fires, of which we have a lot, but they didn't hold water that day. They were filled with kerosene. When we had the snakes—most of em, folks found strays for months after—with nothing but water behind them, those boys sprayed them very good and proper. Then my old friend Jerry Gant, Palm Village Fire Chief, long gone, fired up a Bernzomatic propane torch and flung it. Those rattlers went up in a sheet of flame, and the stink—oh my God, it was terrible, and I could never get it out of my clothes. None of us could. Washing em didn't do any good. They had to be burned, like the snakes."

He sat quiet for a moment, eyes on his glass of water. He would return to the reason he'd come, but right now he wasn't here at all. He was seeing those burning rattlesnakes and smelling their stench as they writhed in the flames.

"Duma was still there back then, and some of the snakes swam for it. Maybe a few even made it, but most drowned. I don't know if you noticed there's a whirlpool where the water from the bay meets the water from the Gulf—"

"I've seen it."

"That whirlpool . . . that *eddy* . . . was stronger when Duma Key was still there, because the water came through with a lot more force.

I bet it's sixteen feet deep right there where the water spins, maybe more. Dug out the channel bed, you know. Plus the tide was low that day, which increases the spill from the bay. We saw snakes spinning in that eddy, some still on fire.

"And that, Vic, was the Great Snake Drive of Eighty-Whatever."

"Quite a story."

"Now you tell me one. About how you knew Alita Bell and how you found her."

"I didn't know her at all, and I only saw her twice. Alive, I mean. The second time she brought me oatmeal raisin cookies. We ate some at this very table. Had them with milk. I said hello to the twins."

"Did you, now?"

"Maybe it sounds crazy, but it didn't feel crazy. It felt like the polite thing to do. Because in all other ways she struck me as completely rational. In fact—" I frowned, trying to remember. "She said she knew they weren't there."

"Huh."

Hadn't she also said *and yet they are*? I thought so, but I couldn't quite remember. If she had, she was right. I knew that now for myself.

"And someone brought that stroller back. Not once, but twice."

"Yes."

"But you didn't see anyone."

"No."

"Didn't hear anyone."

"No."

"Didn't notice the motion lights going on, either? Because I know Ackerman had em put in."

"No."

"Didn't bring the snake pole back, either?"

"No."

"Tell me about how you found her."

I did, including the part about throwing a shell—maybe more than one, I had been upset and was no longer sure—to get the buzzards away from her body. "I told all that to Officers Zane and Canavan."

"I know you did. It's in their report. Except of course for the stroller turning up the second time. That's what you call new information."

"I can't help you with that. I was asleep."

"Huh." Down went the mask. He finished his water. Up went the mask. "Pete Ito says you're planning on staying until September, Mr. Trenton."

It wasn't lost on me that he'd spoken to Mr. Ito. Nor was it lost on me that he had reverted to my last name.

"Plans change. Finding a dead woman being pecked at by buzzards can do that to a person. I have a reservation at the Bradenton Days Inn tonight and a flight from Tampa to Cleveland on Thursday. Transportation the rest of the way to my home in Massachusetts is TBD. Things are pretty crazy in America just now."

Crazy. That word seemed to come out with more force than I intended.

"Crazy all over the world," Pelley said. "Why would you come down here in the summer, anyway? Most people don't, unless they've got free coupons from Disney World."

If he had talked to Pete Ito, I was sure he knew. Yes, this was an interrogation, all right. "My wife died recently. I've been trying to come to grips with it."

"And you . . . what? Feel like you've got it gripped pretty good just now?"

I looked at him dead on. He didn't look like Wilford Brimley to me anymore. He looked like a problem.

"What is this about, Deputy Pelley? Or should I call you Mr. Pelley? I understand you're retired."

"Semi. Not a detective these days, but a part-time deputy in good standing. And you need to cancel your flight plans." Was there a slight emphasis on the word *flight*? "I'm sure they'll take the charge off your credit card. Motel room, too. I guess you could go as far as Barry's over in the Village, but—"

"Barry's is closed. I tried it. What's—"

"But tell you what, I'd be more comfortable if you stayed right here until Mrs. Bell has been autopsied. Which is to say, Mr. Trenton, the County Sheriff's Department would be more comfortable."

"I'm not sure you could stop me."

"I wouldn't test that if I were you. Just a friendly piece of advice."

I heard it then, faint but audible: *Squeak* and *squeak* and *squeak*.

I told myself I didn't. Told myself it was ridiculous. Told myself I wasn't in a story called "The Tell-Tale Pram."

"Again, Mr. Pelley . . . *Deputy* Pelley . . . what's this about? You're acting like the woman was murdered and I'm a suspect."

Pelley was unperturbed. "Autopsy will most likely tell us how she died. Most likely that'll let you off the hook."

"I had no idea I was on one."

"As for what this is about—complicating matters, you could say—there's this. Found it on the kitchen table when I went in her house this morning at six o'clock."

He fiddled with his phone, then passed it over. He had taken a picture of a white business envelope. On it in neat cursive was *To Be Opened In Event Of My Death* and *Alita Marie Bell.*

"The envelope wasn't sealed, so I went ahead and opened it. Swipe to the next photo."

I did. The note that had been in the envelope was written in the same neat cursive. And the date at the top—

"This is the day after we had the milk and cookies!"

The squeaks were coming from below, in the garage. And as with the police in the Poe story, Pelley didn't seem to hear them. But he was an old guy, and maybe on the deaf side.

"Was it, now?"

"Yes, and some nice conversation." I wasn't going to tell him that Allie had sent Jake and Joe into Greg's study to play, and I'd later found the wicker basket of cat toys overturned. That was the *last* thing I was going to tell this sharp-eyed (but possibly dull-eared) man. Nor would I tell him that I had conversed, more or less, with the twins myself. *Hello, Jake. Hello, Joe, what do you know?*

It had been a harmless nod to an old lady's wistful fantasy. So I'd thought, but who knows when you open the door to a haunting? Or how?

"Go on and read the rest."

I did. It was brief and informal.

This is my last will and testament, revoking all previous wills. Which is silly, because in my case there are no others. I am sound of mind if a little less so in body I leave this house, my bank account at First Sun Trust, my investment account with Building the Future LLC, and all other worldly possessions to VICTOR TRENTON, currently living at 1567 Rattlesnake Road. My lawyer, who I didn't consult when I wrote this, is Nathan Rutherford in Palm Village.

Signed,
Alita Marie Bell

There was another signature below it, in a different hand: *Roberto M. Garcia, Witness.*

I forgot about the squeaking from the garage (or maybe it stopped). I read her death-letter—nothing else to call it—over again. A third time. Then I slid Pelley's phone back across the table, a little harder than I had to. He blocked it like a hockey puck with one tanned and wrinkled hand.

"That's crazy."

"You'd think so, wouldn't you?"

"I only met her twice. Three times, if you count finding her dead."

"No idea why she'd leave you everything?"

"No. And hey, that . . . that *note* . . . will never stand up in court. I'd say her relatives would go nuclear, but they won't have to because I won't contest it."

"Roberto Garcia owns Plant World. They did her groundskeeping."

"Yes, I've seen their trucks in her driveway."

"Bobby G has also been around here for donkey's years. If he says he saw her write that—and I have spoken to him and he says yeah, he did, although she held her hand over it when he signed so he didn't know what was in it—then I gotta believe it."

"Doesn't change anything." My words came out okay, but my whole face felt numb, as if I'd been shot up with Novocain. The oddest thing. "This lawyer will get in touch with her relatives, and—"

"I also talked to Nate Rutherford. Known him—"

"Donkey's years, I'm sure. You've been busy, Deputy Pelley."

YOU LIKE IT DARKER

"I get around," he said, and not without satisfaction. "He's been Mrs. Bell's lawyer for . . ." He seemed to consider *donkey's years* and decided it should be put to bed. ". . . for decades. He pretty much took over her affairs after Mrs. Bell's husband and boys died. She was what they call prostrate with grief. And you know what? He says she doesn't *have* any relatives."

"Everybody has relatives. Donna—my late wife—claimed that her family went back to Mary Stuart, also known as Mary, Queen of—"

"Queen of Scots, I did go to school once upon a time, Mr. Trenton, back when all the phones had dials and cars came without seatbelts. I asked Nate how much the lady's estate might total up to and he declined to say. But considering the property—bay to Gulf, very fine—I'd guess quite a tasty chunk of change."

I got up, rinsed my coffee cup, and filled it with water. Giving myself time to think. Also listening for the stroller, but that was quiet.

I came back to the table and sat down. "Are you seriously suggesting that I somehow coerced the lady into writing a jackleg will . . . and then . . . what? Killed her?"

The eyes, boring into mine. "I think *you* just suggested that, Mr. Trenton. But since you have . . . did you?"

"Good Christ, no! I talked to her twice! I indulged her little fantasy! Then I found her dead! Of a heart attack, most likely—she told me she had arrhythmia."

"No, I don't really believe that, which is why I'm not here asking you to make an official statement. But you see the position it puts me—the department—in, don't you? Lady makes out what they call a holograph will just before she dies, gets it witnessed up, and the man—the *stranger*—who finds her body also turns out to be the benny-fishie."

"She must have been crazy about more than just her kids," I muttered, and found myself thinking about that song Officer Zane had mentioned—"Delta Dawn."

"Maybe *sí*, maybe *no*. In any case the autopsy's probably going on as we speak. That'll tell us something. And you'll have to testify at the inquest, of course. That *will* be official."

My heart sank. "When?"

"Maybe not for a couple of weeks. It'll be by one of those computer video links. FaceTime, Zoom, I dunno. I can barely use this fancy phone."

I didn't believe that for a minute.

"In any case, it'd be good if you stuck around, Vic." Now my first name felt like a trap. "In fact, I have to insist. The way things are, with the Covid running wild, it would probably be safest for you to stay right here, buttoned up and masked in town. Don't you think?"

That might have been when I began to realize what Alita Bell had done, although it wouldn't coalesce until that evening.

Or maybe it hadn't been her. I thought of Donna on that last night. How she'd looked past me, her dying eyes growing bright one last time. *Oh my God*, she'd said. *You're all grown up!*

Children couldn't plot and plan. Adults, on the other hand . . .

"Vic?"

"Hmm?"

The smile lines at the corners of his eyes crinkled. "Kind of thought I'd lost you for a minute."

"No, I'm here. Just . . . processing."

"Yeah, it's a lot to process, isn't it? For me, too. Like one of those mystery novels. I think you better stick to your original plan. Stay until September. Take your walks in the morning or in the cool of the evening. Have a swim in the pool. We need to figure this out if we can."

"I'll think about it."

The smile lines disappeared. "Think hard, and while you're thinking, stay in-county." He rose and hitched at the belt of his shorts. "And now I think I've taken up enough of your time."

"I'll see you out."

"No need, I can find my way."

"I'll see you out," I repeated, and he raised his hands as if to say *have it your way*.

We went down the stairs to the garage. He paused partway and asked, with just the right combination of curiosity and sympathy, "How did your wife die, Vic?"

It was a normal enough question, no reason to believe he wanted to find out if there had been anything suspicious about it, but I had an idea that was in his mind. And not just in the back of it, either.

"Cancer," I said.

He went the rest of the way down the stairs. "Very sorry for your loss."

"Thank you. Will you be taking the stroller back to the Bell house? You could put it in the back of your truck." I wanted to be rid of it.

"Well, yes," he allowed, "I could. But what would be the point? It might just come back again, if this . . . prankster . . . is determined to have his little joke at your expense. We send a cruiser up Rattlesnake Road once or twice a night, but that still leaves a lot of dead time. And there are some officers down with Covid. Might be just as easy to leave it here."

He doesn't think there's any prankster, I thought. *He thinks it was me. Both times. He doesn't know why, but that's what he believes.*

"What about fingerprints?"

He scratched the back of his seamed and deeply tanned neck. "Yeah, could do, I've got a fingerprint kit in my truck, but that would mean taking transfers of any prints I made, and I might mess it up. Hands aren't as steady as they used to be."

I hadn't noticed that and didn't now.

He brightened. "You know what? I can at least dust those chrome bars and take some pictures with my phone if I find anything. No point trying the handgrips, they're rubber, and those little arms beside the seats are fabric. But those metal push-bars are, yeah, ideal for prints. Did Zane or Canavan touch it?"

"I'm not sure, but I think just me. And Allie Bell, of course."

He nodded. At this point we were still at the foot of the stairs. We hadn't gone out into the garage yet.

"So I could find two sets of prints—yours and Mrs. Bell's. Although unlikely. Most people would just use the rubber handgrips."

"I think I reached down and tilted the stroller up to get it over the doorjamb and into her garage. If I did, I could have wrapped my hands on those rods just below the grips. You might not find fingerprints, but there would be palmprints."

He nodded, and we went into Greg's garage. He headed outside to get his fingerprint kit, but I took his elbow to stop him. "Look," I said, and pointed at the stroller.

"What about it?"

"It's been moved. When I brought it in from the courtyard, I put it next to the driver's side of my car. Now it's on the passenger side."

So I *had* heard the squeaking.

"Can't remember for sure."

His frown—the vertical line between his brows so deep I couldn't see the bottom—told me he did remember but didn't want to believe it.

"Come on, Andy." I used his given name deliberately, an old ad conference trick I employed when arguments got heated. I wanted us to be in this together, if possible. "You've been a police officer long enough for observation to be a habit. That stroller was in the shade. Now it's on the other side of my car and in the sun."

He thought about it and shook his head. "Couldn't say for sure."

I wanted to make him admit it, wanted to tell him I'd heard that squeaky wheel when the pram had been moved even if he hadn't, wanted to shake the arm I was holding. Instead I let it go. It was hard, but I did it. Because I didn't want him to think I was crazy . . . and if he thought I was the one moving the stroller at night between the Bell house and Greg's, he was already halfway to drawing that conclusion. And there was Allie Bell's weird holograph will for him to think about, too. Did he really believe Allie and I were bare acquaintances who had only met twice? Would I have believed it?

I had an idea the questions were just beginning for me.

"I'll get my little kit," Pelley said. "Although I'm not hopeful."

He drove off in his pickup ten or fifteen minutes later, after reminding me again not to leave the county, saying it would be *a real bad idea*. He told me that he or one of the full-time county detectives would be in touch after the autopsy.

That was a long day. I tried to nap and couldn't. On several occasions I thought I heard the squeaky wheel and went down to the garage. The stroller hadn't moved. I wasn't surprised. I *had* heard it when Pelley was sitting at my kitchen table; that was real. Later on it was something else. *Imagination*, you would say, but it wasn't. Not exactly. I thought it was a form of teasing. You can believe that or not, but I felt sure of it.

No; I *knew*.

Once when I heard that squeaking (not real, but real in my head) and I went down to the garage, I thought I saw the shadows of snakes on the wall. I closed my eyes tight, then opened them. The shadows were gone. They hadn't been there, but they had been. Now there was only the stroller, sitting in the sunlight on the cement garage floor and casting its sane shadow.

Around noon, as I was eating a chicken salad sandwich, I thought of oiling that squeaky wheel after all—there was 3-In-One on the work-table in the second garage bay—and decided against it. I didn't like the idea of touching the stroller, but I could have; I wasn't hysterical or phobic about it. Only I remembered the old Aesop's fable about the mice that belled the cat. Why did they do that? Because they wanted to be able to hear it coming.

I felt the same about the stroller. Especially after Pelley dusted the chrome rods and found nothing—not even the random smudges and bits of dust he would have expected. "I think it's been wiped. By your *prankster*."

Looking right at me when he said it.

That evening I walked the length of Rattlesnake Key to the swing bridge. A long walk for an old man, but I had a lot to think about. I started by asking myself again if I was crazy. The answer was an emphatic no. The snakes in the tub and the waving hand could have been a stress-induced hallucination (I didn't believe it, but granted the possibility). The stroller in the bathroom, on the other hand, had been there. I'd only seen its shadow, but the sound of the squeaky wheel had been unmistakable. And when it was in the garage, it *had* moved. I'd heard it. I didn't think Pelley had, but he knew it was in a different place, although he didn't want to admit it to me (or probably to himself).

The swing bridge was a 24/7 deal. That night it was being manned by Jim Morrison ("*Not* of the Doors," he always liked to say), a guy who was probably older than either Pelley or me. We talked for awhile when I got there—the weather, the upcoming election, how Covid had emptied the baseball stadiums except for cardboard cutouts of make-believe people. Then I asked him about Mrs. Bell.

"You found her, right?" Jim said. We were outside his little booth, where he had a television, a beat-up easy chair, and a toilet cubicle. He was wearing his yellow high-visibility vest and his red cap with RATTLESNAKE KEY on the visor. A toothpick jutted from one corner of his seamed mouth.

"Yes."

"Poor lady. Poor old soul. She never got over losing those boys of hers. Pushed that stroller everywhere."

Which was a perfect lead-in for what I really wanted to ask. "Do you think she really believed the boys were in it?"

He scratched his stubbly chin as he thought it over. "Can't say for sure, but I think she did, at least some of the time. Maybe even most of the time. I think she made herself believe it. Which is a dangerous thing, in my opinion."

"Why do you say that?"

"Better to accept the dead, wear the scar, and move on."

I waited for him to say more, but he didn't.

"Were you in on the big snake hunt after they died? Andy Pelley told me about it."

"Oh yeah, I was there. To this day I can smell those rattlers as they burned. And do you know what? Sometimes I think I see em, especially around this time of day." He leaned over the rail and spit his toothpick into the Gulf of Mexico. "Dusk, you know. Real things seem thinner then, at least to me. My wife used to say I shoulda been a poet, with ideas like that. After the stars come out, I'm okay. I'll see plenty tonight. I'm on until twelve, then Patricia takes over."

"I wouldn't think you'd get many boats wanting to go through at this time of the year, especially at night."

"Oh, you'd be surprised. Lookit there." He pointed to the moon, which was just coming up and beating silver across the water. "Folks like a moonlight cruise. Makes em romantic. Dark of the moon's different, at least in summer. Then it's mostly Coast Guard boats. Or DEA. Those boys are always in a hurry. Like blaring their horns could make this old bridge open any faster."

We talked a little more and then I said I'd better be heading back.

"Yes," Jim said. "Long walk for a man getting on in years. But you'll have the moon to light your way."

I told him good evening and started back across the bridge.

"Vic?"

I turned back. He was leaning against his little booth, arms folded across his vest. "Two weeks after my wife died, I came down in the middle of the night for a glass of water and saw her sitting at the kitchen table, wearing her favorite nightgown. The kitchen light wasn't on, and the room was shadowy, but it was her, all right. I'd swear to it before God Almighty. Then I turned on the light, and . . ." He raised one loosely fisted hand and opened the fingers. "Gone."

"I heard my son after he died." It seemed perfectly right to give that up after what Jim had told me. "Speaking from the closet. And I'd swear to *that*."

He only nodded, wished me goodnight, and went back into his booth.

For the first mile of my walk home, maybe a little more, there were plenty of houses, first those of ordinary size but getting bigger and fancier as I went. There were lights in a few of them with cars parked in the shell driveways, but most of the houses were dark. Their owners would come back after Christmas and leave before Easter. Depending on the pandemic situation, of course.

Once I passed the swing gate at the north end of the Key, the few McMansions on this part of the island were hidden behind the rhododendrons and palmettos that closed in on both sides of the road. The only sounds were the crickets, the waves breaking on the Gulfside beach, a whippoorwill, and my own footfalls. By the time I reached the yellow police tape closing off Mrs. Bell's driveway, it was almost full dark. That three-quarter moon had risen enough to light my way, but it was still mostly blocked by the foliage that grows in Florida's hothouse climate.

As soon as I passed Allie's driveway, the squeaking started. It was thirty or forty feet behind me. My skin broke out in bumps. My tongue stuck to the roof of my mouth. I stopped, unable to walk, let alone run (not that with my creaky hips I could have run far, anyway). I understood what was happening. They had been waiting for me in their driveway. Waiting for me to pass so they could follow me back to Greg's. What I remember most about that first moment is how my eyes felt. Like they were swelling in their sockets. I remember thinking that if they popped I'd be blind.

The squeaking stopped.

Now I could hear another sound: my own heartbeat. Like a muffled drum. The whippoorwill had fallen silent. So had the crickets. A drop of cold sweat trickled slowly down from the hollow of my temple to the angle of my jaw. I took a step. It was hard. Then another. A little easier. A third, easier still. I began to walk again, but it was as if I were on stilts. I had gotten perhaps fifty feet closer to Greg's house when the squeaking started again. I stopped and the squeaking stopped. I started forward on my invisible stilts and the squeaking started. It was the stroller. The twins pushing the stroller. They started when I started and stopped when I stopped. They were grinning, I was sure of it. Because it was a fine joke on their new . . . new what? What, exactly, was I to them?

I was afraid I knew. Allie Bell had left me her house, money, and investments. But that wasn't all she had left me. Was it?

"Boys," I said. My voice was not my own. I was still facing forward and my voice was not my own. "Boys, go home. It's past your bedtime."

Nothing. I waited for cold hands to touch me. Or to see dozens of snakes weaving their way across the moonlit road. The snakes would be cold, too. Until they bit, that was. Once the poison was injected, the heat would begin. Spreading toward my heart.

No snakes. The snakes are gone. You could see them but they wouldn't be real.

I walked. The stroller followed. *Squeak* and *squeak* and *squeak*.

I stopped. The stroller stopped. I was close to Greg's house now, I could see the bulk of it against the sky, but that was no relief. They could come in. They *had* come in.

See us. See us. See us.

Roll us. Roll us. Roll us.

Dress us. Dress us. Dress us.

The thoughts were maddening, like one of those earworm songs that gets in your head and won't leave. "Delta Dawn," for instance. But I could stop them. I knew what would make them go away, at least temporarily.

They also knew.

See us. Roll us. Dress us.

I didn't dare turn around, but there was something I *could* do. If I dared. My phone was in the pocket of my shorts. I took it out, opened the camera app, and reversed the image so I was looking at my own terrified face, corpse-pale in the moonlight. I raised the phone over my shoulder so I could look behind me without actually turning my head. I tried to steady my hand. Hadn't realized it was shaking until then.

Jacob and Joseph weren't there and neither was the stroller . . . but their *shadows* were there. Two human shapes and the angular one of the double buggy their mother had pushed them around in. I can't say those disembodied shadows were worse than actually seeing them would have been, but they were terrible enough. I pushed the button to take a photograph with my thumb, sure it wouldn't work, but I heard the click.

See us. Roll us. Push us.

I closed the photo app and opened the voice memo.

See us, roll us, push us.

I thought those shadows were too long to be the shadows of four-year-old children and thought again of Donna at the end of her life: *You're all grown up! Look how* tall *you are!*

SEE US ROLL US PUSH US!

I started walking again. The squeaking followed me, close at first, then gradually falling behind. By the time I reached Greg's house it was gone, but the clamoring thoughts—not voices, *thoughts*—in my head were louder than ever. They were my thoughts, but I was being forced to think them.

The stroller was back in the courtyard. Of course it was, and casting the same angular shadow I'd seen on my phone. The shirts were still neatly draped over the seats; HECKLE on one and JEKYLL on the other. I knew how to quiet the storm in my head. I touched the backs of the seats. I touched the shirts. The clamoring, repetitive thoughts died. I pushed the stroller back into the garage, then stepped away from it, waiting. The thoughts didn't return. But they would, of course. Next time they would be louder and more insistent. Next time they would want more than my touch.

Next time they'd want to go for a ride.

I locked the doors—as if that would do any good—and turned on every light in the house. Then I sat at the kitchen table and looked at my phone. I had a missed call from Nathan Rutherford, but I had more pressing business than Allie Bell's lawyer. I looked at the picture I'd taken. It was a little blurred because my hand had never stopped shaking, but the shadows of the boys and the pram were there. Nothing was casting them. The road was empty. Next I opened the voice memo app and pushed play. For twenty seconds I heard the rhythmic squeaking of the pram's bad wheel. Then it faded away.

I thought about getting in touch with Andy Pelley, because I was sure he'd registered the different position of the stroller when our talk was over. He'd given me his card. I could email him the photo and the voice memo, but he'd reject both. He'd say the shadows were of the palmettos. He might know better, but that's what he would say. And the squeaky wheel? He'd think I did that myself, running the stroller back and forth in the garage while I recorded. He might not say so, but he would think so. He was a cop, not a ghost hunter.

But maybe that was okay. I had empiric proof for myself. I had already known what was happening was real, but the thought that it was all in my head had lingered in the background, even so.

I sat at the kitchen table with my palms pressed against my forehead, thinking. *Just a few missed beats of the old ticker*, Allie had said when I asked if she was okay, but suppose she had been a lot sicker than she claimed? And knew it? Suppose it wasn't just arrhythmia but congestive heart failure? Even cancer, one of those like glioblastoma that's a death warrant.

Suppose she was resigned to her own death but not to the deaths of her little boys? They had already died once, after all, but had come back. Or she had brought them back. And then . . .

"Suppose she met *me*," I said.

Yes, suppose.

I called Nathan Rutherford, introduced myself, and immediately cut to the chase: I had no interest in Allie Bell's estate.

I think his chuckle was more cynical than surprised. "Nevertheless, Mr. Trenton, you seem to have it."

"Ridiculous. Find her relatives."

"She claimed she had none. That after her husband died, and the little Js—that's what she called them—she was the last sprig on the family tree. It's the only reason that poor excuse for a will could ever stand up. Her estate is worth a good deal of money. Seven figures, perhaps even eight. She must have been taken with you, sir."

No, I thought, *I'm the one who was taken. But I don't intend to* stay *taken*.

"It's put me in a lousy position, Mr. Rutherford. I found her, and pending the autopsy I look like a man with a motive for killing her. You see that, right?"

"Did you have any reason to believe you were in line to inherit? Perhaps you saw that scrap of a will before Mrs. Bell's decease?"

"No, but Deputy Pelley told me the envelope it was in was unsealed. A county attorney who wanted to make a case could say I had access to it."

"Time will take care of this," Rutherford said. Which meant nothing. He had adopted a soothing voice he probably used on distraught clients. Those with money, at least, and it seemed that I now had a lot more than what was in my 401k. "If the will is unchallenged and goes through probate, you can do what you wish with the proceeds. Sell the house. Give the money away to worthy charities, should you decide to do so."

He didn't go on to say that charity begins at home, but his tone suggested it. I had had enough. He wanted to discuss the serpentine legal trail that lay ahead, but I had my own serpents to worry about. It was dark outside and I was scared. I thanked him and ended the call.

Had she made her will and then killed herself, with an overdose of Digoxin or sotalol?

No, I thought. *The little Js wouldn't like that. I could end up in the county jail, where* see us roll us dress us *would do no good. The verdict at the inquest will be accidental death, but in the meantime I'll be here . . . and* they'll *be here.*

"Because they want me to stay," I whispered.

I took a shower, put on a pair of gym shorts, closed the door to the en suite bathroom, and lay down on Greg Ackerman's big double bed. As a more-or-less swinging bachelor, he'd probably shared it with any number of honeys. My own honey was gone. In the ground. Like my son.

I crossed my arms over my chest in an unconscious gesture of protection and stared up at the ceiling. It hadn't been her, it had been them. *They* wanted me to stay. They wanted to work on me. They wanted me to take over from their mother, so they wouldn't have to go to wherever uneasy revenants go to. They liked it right here on Rattlesnake Key. Where—if I didn't want my head filled with tumbling and repetitive thoughts, if I didn't want to hear the stroller's squeaky wheel behind me—I would live in Allie's house. I would eat in Allie's kitchen and sleep in Allie's bed. I would push them in their stroller.

I would eventually come to see them.

I don't have to stay here, I thought. *I've got a rental car with a full tank of gas. I can get away. Away from* them. *I don't think the County Sheriff will issue a warrant for my arrest, although some judge might issue a bench warrant ordering me to come back pending the inquest . . . Rutherford would know, and I guess he's my lawyer now . . . but I'd fight it. And while the lawyers wrangled, Jake and Joe would be getting weaker. Because she's gone and I'm what they have.*

Yes. All true enough. And I *was* scared, you can believe that. There's a line from Scorsese's *Mean Streets* that's always resonated with me: "You don't fuck around with the infinite." But I was also angry. I had been put in a box I wasn't supposed to escape. Not by their mother—in my heart I was sure that Allie Bell hadn't been in on this—but by *a couple of kids. Dead* kids, in fact.

I had no secret weapon to fight them with, no cross or garlic to ward off vampires (which, if I was right, is sort of what they were), no rite of exorcism, but I had my *mind*, and I was too damn old to be pushed around by Bad and Badder.

If Allie hadn't built the box I was in, how could they have done it? Most little boys—I had one, remember—can hardly plan a trip to the bathroom.

I fell asleep thinking of Donna, minutes from her end: *You're all grown up! Look how tall you are!*

Squeak. Squeak. Squeak.

I didn't come awake in the dark at least, because I hadn't turned off the lights. This time the stroller's squeaky wheel wasn't coming from the en suite; it was further away. I thought it was in the part of the house Greg grandly called "the guest quarters." Those quarters consisted of a small living room on the ground floor and a spiral staircase leading up to a bedroom and attached bathroom on the second.

The stroller was in the guest bedroom. The real stroller might be still in the garage, but the ghostly one was also real, and so were the twins pushing it so maniacally back and forth.

The thoughts seeped back in. They were low at first but grew louder, as if an unseen hand was turning up the volume. *See us, roll us, dress us. See us, roll us, dress us! SEE US, ROLL US, DRESS US!*

I lay on my back, clutching my hands together on my chest, biting my lip, trying to make the thoughts—*their* thoughts, *my* thoughts—stop. I might as well have insisted that the sun not go down. I could still think other thoughts—how long that would last I didn't know—and there seemed to be only three courses of action I could pursue: lie here and go mad once those earworms swallowed everything; go down and touch the stroller in the garage, which would silence them for the time being; or confront the twins. That's what I decided to do.

I thought, *I won't be driven mad by children.*

And I thought, *roll us, roll us, push us, push us. We're yours, you're ours.*

I got off the bed and started down the upstairs gallery to the guest quarters. Halfway there the squeaking wheel stopped. I didn't, and the thoughts—*roll us, push us, dress us, we're yours, you're ours*—didn't, either. I didn't hesitate at the door, which was ajar. If I had stopped to think in the part of my mind that was still capable of independent thought, I would have turned tail and run. What was I going to do in there? I had no idea. Telling them to go home or get a spanking certainly wouldn't work.

What I saw froze me in place. The stroller was beached in the middle of the floor. Jacob and Joseph were in the guest bed. They were no longer children . . . yet they were. The bodies under the coverlet were long, the bodies of full-grown men, but the heads, although grotesquely swollen, were those of children. Rattlesnake poison had so bloated those heads that they had become pumpkins with Halloween faces. Their lips were black. Their foreheads, cheeks, and necks were stippled with snakebites. The eyes were sunken but hellishly alive and aware. They were grinning at me.

Bedtime story! Bedtime story! Bedti—

Then they were gone. The stroller was gone. One minute the twins were there, waiting for their bedtime story. At the next the room was empty. But the coverlet was turned down on both sides in neat tri-angles, and that bed had been perfectly made when I came here from Massachusetts. I had seen it for myself.

My legs were stilt legs again. I went into the room on them and looked at the bed where the boys had been. I didn't mean to sit on it but I did because my knees gave out. My heart was still thundering away and I could hear myself, as at a distance, gasping for breath.

This is how old men die, I thought. *When I'm found—probably by Pete Ito—the medical examiner would conclude it was a heart attack. They wouldn't know I had been scared to death by two dead men with the heads of children.*

Only the twins wouldn't like me to die, would they? Now that their mother was gone, I was their only link to the world in which they wanted to stay.

I reached out to touch a turned-down triangle of coverlet with each hand and knew they didn't like this bed. They had their own beds in the house down the road. *Good* beds. Their mother would have kept their room just the way it had been on the day they died, forty-some years ago. Those were the beds they liked, and when I lived there I would tuck them in at night and read them *Winnie-the-Pooh,* as I had to Tad. I certainly wouldn't read them Tad's Monster Words, because *they* were the monsters.

When I could get up, I walked slowly back down to the gallery to my own room. I might not sleep, but I didn't think I'd hear the stroller's squeaky wheel again that night. The visitation was over.

There was never a question of keeping the car in which my son had died. We wouldn't have kept it even if it hadn't been bashed at a dozen places by the dog trying to get in and get at them. A wrecker brought it back to our house. Donna refused to even look at that, either. I didn't blame her.

There was no junkyard in Castle Rock. The closest was Andretti's, in Gates Falls. I called them. They came, got the Pinto—the death car—and ran it through the crusher. What came out was a cube shot through with bright seams of glass—windows, taillights, headlights, windshield. I took a picture. Donna wouldn't look at it.

By then the arguments had started. She wanted me to go on her weekly pilgrimages to Harmony Hill, where Tad was buried. I refused that as she had refused to look at the crushed cube of the death car. I said Tad was at the house for me, and always would be. She said that sounded highflown and noble, but it wasn't true. She said I was afraid to go. Afraid I'd break down, and of course she was right. I imagine she saw it in my face every time she looked at me.

She was the one who moved out. I came back from a business trip to Boston and she was gone. There was a note. It said the usual things, you can probably guess: *Can't go on this way . . . start a new life . . . turn the page . . .* blah-blah-blah. The only really original thing was the line she'd scrawled under her name, perhaps as an afterthought: *I'm still in love with you and I hate you and I'm leaving before hate gets the upper hand.*

Probably I don't have to tell you I felt the same way about her.

Deputy Zane called me the next morning while I was spooning up Rice Chex—not enjoying them, just gassing up for the day. He said the autopsy had been completed. Alita Bell, wife to Henry, mother to Jacob and Joseph, had died of a heart attack.

"The ME said it was amazing she lived as long as she did. She had ninety per cent blockages, but that wasn't all. There was cardiac scarring, which means she'd suffered a number of previous heart attacks. Small ones, you know. He also said . . . well, never mind."

"No, go ahead. Please."

Zane cleared his throat. "He said even little heart attacks, ones you might not even feel, impair cognition. That could explain why she sometimes believed her children were still alive."

I thought of telling him that I *knew* her children were alive, or half-alive, and I'd never had a heart attack. I think I almost did tell him.

"Mr. Trenton? Vic?"

"Just thinking about that," I said. "Does this let me off the hook for the inquest?"

"Nope, you still have to be here for that. You found the body."

"But if it was a heart attack, pure and simple—"

"Oh, it was. But there won't be a toxicology report for another couple of days. Need to find out what was in her stomach. Just dotting *i*'s and crossing *t*'s, you know."

I thought it might be a little more. I thought Andy Pelley wanted to make sure that Allie Bell's last-minute legatee hadn't fed her something. Digoxin in her scrambled eggs at an early breakfast, perhaps. Meanwhile, Zane was talking and I had to ask him to rewind.

"I was saying there's a problem. Kinda unique. We've got a body, but no burial instructions. Andy Pelley says you might be on the hook for that."

"Wait, what? I'm supposed to plan a funeral?"

"Probably not a *funeral*," Zane said, sounding a trifle embarrassed. "Other than the bridge tenders and maybe Lloyd Sunderland—he lives on the other side of the bridge—I don't know who'd come."

I think her kids would, I thought. *Although no one would see them. Except, maybe, for their surrogate dad.*

"Vic? Mr. Trenton? Did I lose you?"

"Right here. I have the name of her lawyer. My lawyer now, I guess, at least until this gets straightened out. I better give him a call once it gets to business hours."

"That's a good idea. You do that. And have a good day."

As if.

I didn't want the rest of my cereal, which I hadn't been tasting any-way. I rinsed the bowl in the sink (*see us*) and put it in the dishwasher (*dress us*) and wondered what to do next. Like I didn't know.

Take us for a walk. Roll us!

I held out against the thoughts—partly *my* thoughts, that was the worst of it—until I got some clothes on, then gave up. I went out to the garage and grasped the handles of the stroller. I felt a sigh of relief, mine or theirs or both, I didn't know. The rat-run in my head ceased. I thought of rolling the pram down to the swing gate and knew it was a bad idea. Jacob and Joseph had already wedged their way into my consciousness. The more I did what they wanted, the easier it would be for them to control me.

What I had seen in the guest bedroom stayed with me: men's bod-ies, children's heads swollen with poison. They had grown in death; they had stayed the same. They had the will of men and the simple and selfish desires of small children. They were powerful, and that was bad. But they were also psychotic.

That said, that *accepted*, I could still feel a certain amount of sym-pathy. They had fallen among rattlesnakes. They had been stung to death by serpents. Who would not be driven insane by such an ending to life? And who would not want to come back and have the childhood that had been denied to them, even if that meant taking someone prisoner to do it?

I rolled the stroller back and forth across the concrete floor of the garage a few times, as if trying to lull colicky, cranky babies to sleep. I wondered if it could have been anyone and guessed it couldn't have been. I was perfect. A man alone, one suffering his own grief.

I let go of the handles and waited for *see us roll us dress us* to come back. It didn't. I left the garage, wanting to feel the warmth of the morning sun on my living face. I lifted my head and closed my eyes, seeing red as the blood in my eyelids lit up. I stood that way, as if in worship or meditation, hoping for a solution to a problem that was beyond existential. One I couldn't tell anyone about.

I'm supposed to see her into the ground because she has no one . . . on this side of the veil, at least. But am I not the same? My parents are dead, my older brother is dead, my wife is dead. Who will bury me? And what will those twins from hell do—supposing they get their way and I stay here, a male version of Delta Dawn—when I pass? Given my age and the actuarial tables, it won't be all that long. Will they shrivel and just fade away? I can bury Allie, but who will bury me?

I opened my eyes and saw Allie's snake pole lying on the court-yard cobbles, exactly where the stroller had been parked each time it returned. It crossed my mind that it might be another illusion, like the tub full of snakes, and knew it wasn't. This wasn't a vision or a visitation. Nor had the twins put it here. The stroller was their thing.

I picked it up. It was real, all right. The steel pole was warm in my hand. If it had lain out here much longer on the shadeless cobbles, it would have been almost too hot to handle. No one had been here, so who had taken it from the garage?

As I held it I realized my parents, brother, and wife weren't the only loved ones in my life who were dead. There was one more. One who had also died a terrible death at a young age.

"Tad?"

It should have sounded pathetic at best, crazy at worst: an old man speaking his long-dead son's name in the empty courtyard of an absurdly oversized house on a Florida key. It didn't, so I said it again.

"Tad, are you there?"

Nothing. Only the snake pole, which was undeniably real.

"Can you help me?"

There was that ramshackle gazebo at the end of Greg's boardwalk. I went out there with the snake pole over my shoulder, the way an old-time soldier might carry his rifle . . . and while the pole had no bayonet, it *did* have that wicked hook at the end. On the gazebo's floor were a few mold-streaked lifejackets that didn't look like they'd save anyone's life and an ancient boogie board decorated with a scattering of raccoon shit. I sat on the bench. It creaked beneath my weight. I didn't have to be Hercule Poirot to know Greg didn't spend much time out here by the beach; he had a Gulf Coast house worth six or eight million dollars, and this outpost looked like a forgotten privy somewhere in the wilds of Bossier Parish, Louisiana. But I hadn't come here to appreciate the architecture. I had come here to think.

Oh, but that was bullshit. I had come here to try and summon my dead son.

There were methods of summoning, assuming the dead hadn't drifted away to wherever they go when they lose interest in this world; I had looked some up on the Internet before coming out here. You could use a Ouija board, which I didn't have. You could use a mirror or candles, both of which I did . . . but after what I'd seen on my cell phone's screen last night, I didn't dare try it. There *were* spirits in Greg's house, but the ones I was sure of weren't friendly. So in the end I'd come out here to this uncared-for gazebo empty-handed. I sat and looked out at a beach unmarked by a single track and a Gulf unmarked by a single sail. In February or March, both the beach and the water would have been packed. In August there was only me.

Until I felt him.

Or someone.

Or just wishful thinking.

"Tad?"

Nothing.

"If you're there, kiddo, I could use a little help."

But he *wasn't* a kiddo, not anymore. Four decades had passed since Tad Trenton died in that hot car with the rabid St. Bernard patrolling the dooryard of a farmhouse as deserted as the north end of Rattlesnake Key. The dead could age. I had never considered the possibility, but knew it now.

But only if they wanted to. Allowed themselves to. It was apparently possible to both grow and not grow, a paradox that had produced the gruesome hybrids I'd seen in the guest room's double bed: man-things with the bloated heads of poisoned children.

"You don't owe me anything. I came too late. I know that. I admit that. Only . . ." I stopped. You'd think a man could say anything when he's alone, wouldn't you? Only I wasn't entirely sure I was. Nor was I sure what I wanted to say until I said it.

"I mourned you, Tad, but I let you go. In time, Donna did, too. That's not wrong, is it? Forgetting is what would be wrong. Holding on too tightly . . . I think that makes monsters."

I had the snake pole across my lap. "If you left this for me, I really could use a little help."

I waited. There was nothing. There was also something, either a presence or the hope of an old man who had been scared half to death and forced to remember old hurts. Every snake that ever bit him.

Then the thoughts came back, driving away whatever delicate thing might have come to visit me.

Dress us, roll us, see us. See us, dress us, roll us!

The kids wanted me. The kids who wanted to be *my* kids. And they were also *my* thoughts, that was the horror of it. Having your own mind turned against you is a gilt-edged invitation to insanity.

What interrupted them—partially, at least—was the honking of a horn. I turned and saw someone waving to me. Just a silhouette at the edge of the courtyard, but the shapes of the spindly legs beneath the baggy shorts were enough to tell me who my company was. I waved back, propped the snake pole against the gazebo's railing, and headed back along the boardwalk. Andy Pelley met me halfway.

"Good morning, Mr. Trenton."

"Vic, remember?"

"Vic, Vic, right. I was out this way and thought I'd drop by."

Bullshit you were, I thought. And I thought *roll us, dress us, see us, we're waiting for you.*

"What can I do for you?"

"I thought I'd fill you in on the autopsy."

"Officer Zane already called and told me."

I couldn't see if he frowned at that because of the way his bushy mustache held his mask away from his face, but his eyebrows—also bushy—drew together, so I think he did.

"Well, good. Good."

Bullshit you think it's good, I thought, and thought *roll us roll us you'll feel better you know you will.*

We walked back to the house. The boardwalk was too narrow for us to go side by side, so I led the way. The thoughts—*mine*, that I couldn't banish—were giving me a headache.

"Still waiting on the toxicology, of course."

We reached the end of the boardwalk and strolled across the court-yard past his truck, me still leading the way. He wasn't here just to tell me about the autopsy. I knew that and knew I needed a clear mind to deal with him.

"So Officer Zane said. Also that I'll still have to be at the inquest. Do you have something for me, Deputy? Because I was sitting out there, doing some thinking and trying to be peaceful. Meditation, you might call it."

"And I'll let you get back to it. Just a few questions, is all."

We went into the garage, where it was marginally cooler. I went to the stroller. As I neared it, the thoughts ramped up: *DRESS US! ROLL US! SEE US!*

For a moment I did seem to see them, not as monstrosities but as the children they'd been when they died. Just for a moment. When I gripped one of the stroller handles, they were gone . . . assuming they'd been there at all. And the maddening litany in my head ceased. I rolled the perambulator back and forth.

Just something to do with my hands, Andy. Think nothing of it.

"I looked you up a little," Andy said.

"I know you did."

"Terrible thing what happened to your own little boy. Just terrible."

"It was a long time ago. Andy, are you on this case? If there *is* a case? Were you assigned to it? Because somehow I doubt that."

"No, no," he said, raising his hands in a *perish the thought* gesture. "But you know how it is—you can take the man out of the cops, but you can't take the cop out of the man. Probably the same in your business. Advertising, wasn't it?"

"You know it was, and the answer is no. On the rare occasions when I watch network TV instead of streaming, I mute the ads. You really have no business here at all, do you?"

"Now, I wouldn't go that far. I just . . . man, I'm curious. This is a funny business. Meaning funny-peculiar, not funny-haha. You must see that."

Back and forth went the stroller, a few feet ahead, a few feet back. Soothing the kids, keeping them quiet.

"Why would she leave you everything? That gets me. And I bet you know."

That was true. I did.

"I don't."

"And why do you keep bringing that stroller back from her place? Because it's got to be you, doesn't it? No one else out here this time of year."

"Not me."

He sighed. "Talk to me, Vic. Why not? If her tox screen comes back negative, you got away with whatever you got away with."

So there it was. He thought I'd killed her.

"Help an old duffer out. It's just the two of us."

I didn't like this Wilford Brimley lookalike, who had interrupted me while I was trying something delicate. It probably wouldn't have worked, but that didn't make me feel any better about him, so I pretended to consider what he was asking for. I said, "Show me your phone."

Even the bulge of his mustache couldn't quite hide the smile on his mouth. I couldn't gauge the exact quality of that smile, but I'd be willing to bet it was of the *you got me, partner* variety. The phone came out of the baggy shorts, and yes, it was recording.

"Must have hit that by accident."

"I'm sure. Now turn it off."

He did so with no argument. "Now it really *is* just the two of us. So satisfy my curiosity."

"All right." I took a dramatic pause—the kind that usually worked with clients before you unveiled the ad campaign they'd come to see—and then led with two lies followed by the stone truth.

"I don't know why someone keeps bringing her stroller back. That's number one. I don't know why she left that crazy will. That's number two. And here's number three, Deputy Pelley: I didn't kill her. The inquest goes a long way toward proving she died of natural causes. The toxicology report will go the rest of the way."

I hoped it would. Hoped that the ghost twins hadn't somehow gotten into her head and compelled her to swallow a bunch of her heart meds so they could jump to a marginally more healthy host. You'd think a tox report showing she'd ingested too many pills would run counter to their best interests, and you would be right . . . but they were *children*.

"Now I think you should go." I stopped rolling the stroller. "And take this thing with you."

"I don't *want* it," he said, and seemed surprised at the vehemence in his own voice. He knew something was wrong with it, oh yes. He started out of the garage, then looked back. "I'm not done with you."

"Oh for God's sake, Andy, just do something else. Go fishing. Enjoy your retirement."

He went back to his truck, got in, revved the engine, and peeled out hard enough to leave a rubber tattoo on the courtyard pavers. I thought I might as well go back to the gazebo . . . at least until the earworms started up again.

Not really earworms. Snakes. Snakes in my head, two of them, and if I didn't do what they wanted, they'd inject their poison from sacs that never emptied.

In a way I didn't blame Pelley for his suspicions. Allie's lawyer, Rutherford, probably had some of his own. The whole thing was wrong. The most wrong thing of all was my current wretched position. What was unpleasant today would be terrible tonight. They were stronger at night. What had Jim the bridge keeper said? *Dusk, you know. Real things seem thinner then.*

It was true. And once night comes, the wall between real things and a whole other plane of existence can disappear completely. One thing seemed sure—any chance of contacting my dead son was gone. The old cop had broken the spell. Best to just sit for awhile, looking out at the Gulf. Try to get Pelley—*I'm not done with you*—out of my mind. Think about what to do while I still could think.

When I got to the gazebo I just stood there, looking in. Pelley wasn't the only one not done with me, it seemed. Tad—or someone—had made contact after all. The snake pole was no longer leaning against the railing. It was lying on the gazebo's floor. The litter of old lifejackets had been pushed aside. Scratched into one of the planks—by the sharp point of the snake pole's hook, I had no doubt—were two letters. A third had been started but left incomplete.

I looked at those letters and knew what I had to do. It had been staring me in the face all along. Jacob and Joseph—Heckle and Jekyll, Bad and Badder—weren't as all-powerful as they seemed. In the end they only had one link to the world of the living now that their mother was gone.

The two letters scrawled on the plank were PR. The one that had been started and then abandoned was the slanted bar of an A.

Pram.

If it could be all finished and done with when it's done, then it may as well be done quickly.

That was Macbeth's idea about such matters as this, and he was a thinking cat. I believed I might—*might*—be able to deal with my two hybrid harpies if I acted fast. If I didn't, and the thought-snakes burrowed deeper into my mind, I might end with only two choices: suicide or a life as their surrogate father. As their slave.

I went back to the house and into the garage, just ambling along: *look at me, not a care in the world.*

The thoughts started up at once. I no longer need to tell you what they were. I took hold of the stroller's handles and rolled it back and forth, listening to the hellish squeaking. If I couldn't get rid of them I'd oil that bad wheel. Of course I would. More! I'd drape different shirts over the backs of the chairs! Put different shorts on the seats! When I took up residence in the Bell house (which would become the Trenton house), I would talk to them. I would turn down their beds at night and read to them from *In the Night Kitchen, Sylvester and the Magic Pebble, Corduroy.* I would show them the pictures!

"How are you, boys?"

Good, good.

"Do you want to go for a ride?"

Yes, yes.

"All right, why don't we do that? I just need to take care of a couple of things. I'll be right back."

I went in the house and grabbed my phone off the kitchen table. I checked the county tide chart and liked what I saw. It was going out, and would be at dead low shortly after 11 AM. Soon.

I was still wearing my workout shorts and a tee-shirt with the arms cut off. I dropped the shirt on the floor, kicked off my sandals, and hurried upstairs. I put on a pair of jeans and a sweatshirt. I jammed on a Red Sox hat. I had no boots, but in the downstairs closet I found a pair of galoshes. They were Greg's, and too big for me, so I went back upstairs and put on three more pairs of socks to bulk up my feet. By the time I was back downstairs, I was sweating in spite of the air conditioning. Outside, in the August heat, I would be sweating even more.

Andy Pelley said they'd driven the snakes to the northern end of the Key, where those that didn't burn had drowned, but he had also said the line of beaters probably hadn't gotten all of them. I had no idea if the Js could call those that might be left. Maybe they couldn't, or maybe there weren't any at all after forty years, but I had dressed for snakes just in case. One thing I did know is that Florida is a reptile-friendly environment.

I looked under the sink and found a pair of rubber kitchen gloves. I yanked them on and went back out to the garage, pasting a big smile on my face. I'm sure if anyone had heard me talking to that empty stroller, they would have thought me as crazy as Allie Bell. But it was just me. And them, of course.

"Want to walk instead?" Trying to sound teasing. Trying to *sell the concept*, as we used to say. "Big boys like you can probably walk, right?"

No! Roll us, roll us!

"Will you be good if I take you on the beach?"

Yes! Roll us, roll us!

Then, chilling me all the way to my core:

Roll us on the beach, Daddy!

"Okay," I said, thinking *Only one boy ever had the right to call me that, you little shits.* "Here we go."

We cut across the courtyard in the hot August sunshine—*squeak* and *squeak* and *squeak*. I was sweating like a pig inside the sweatshirt already. I could feel it rolling down my sides to the waistband of my jeans. I pushed the stroller along the boardwalk, the slats rumbling under the wheels. Easy enough so far. The beach would be harder. I might get bogged down. I'd have to stay near the water, where the sand was packed and wet. That might work. It might not.

I rolled the pram through the gazebo. I picked up the snake pole on the way and placed it horizontally between the stroller's wide handles.

"Having fun, boys?"

Yes! Yes!

"Sure you don't want to get out and walk?" Please, no.

Roll us! Roll us!

"Okay, but hold on. Little bump here."

I eased the stroller down the single slumped step between the gazebo and the line of beach naupaka and seagrass. Then we were on the sand. I had the slope to help me as I pushed the stroller down to the harder pack at the edge of the water. The buckles of the galoshes jingled.

"Wheee!" I said. My face was running with sweat, but my mouth was dry. "Having fun, boys?"

Yes! Roll us!

I was beginning to be able to tell them apart. That was Joe. Jake was silent. I didn't like that.

"Jake? Having fun, big fella?"

Ye-es . . .

Didn't like the edge of doubt, either. Something else not to like— they were separating from me. Getting stronger. More there. Some of it was the stroller, but some of it was me. I had opened myself to them. I had to. There had been no choice.

I turned north and pushed the stroller. Little birds—the ones I called peeps—strutted ahead of us, then flew. The galoshes jingled and splashed. The wheels of the stroller threw up tiny rainbows in the thin water where the Gulf gave way to the land. The sand was firm but still harder to push through than on the planks of the boardwalk. Soon my breath was rasping in and out of my throat. I wasn't in bad shape, never drank to excess and never smoked at all, but I was in my seventies.

Jake: *Where are you taking us?*

"Oh, just for a little ride." I wanted to stop, take a rest, but I was afraid the wheels would get mired if I even slowed down. "You wanted to go for a roll, I'm taking you for a roll."

Jake: *I want to go back.*

That was more than doubt. That was suspicion. And Joe caught it from his brother just as I supposed he'd caught his brother's colds.

Joe: *Me too! I'm tired! The sun is too hot! We should have worn our hatties!*

"Just a little fur—" I began, and that was when the snakes began to come out of the naupaka and palmetto. Big ones, dozens of them, flooding down to the beach. I hesitated, but only for a second—any longer and the stroller would have been stuck. I pushed them through the snakes and they were gone. Like the ones in the tub.

Jake: *Back! Take us back! TAKE US BACK!*

Joe: *I don't liiike it here!* He started to cry. *I don't like the snakies!*

"We're treasure hunters." I was panting now. "Maybe we'll even see King Kong, like in the movie. How about that, you little rascals?"

Ahead I could see the triangle of heaped shells where Rattlesnake Key ended. Beyond it was Daylight Pass, with its eternal whirlpool. Andy said that eddy had dug the bed of the pass deep there. I didn't remember how deep, sixteen feet, maybe. But those heaped shells between me and the water were a problem. The stroller would get bogged down in them for sure, and crawling across them were a couple of snakes I didn't believe were illusions, or ghosts. They were too *there*. Leftovers from the great snake hunt? Newcomers? It didn't matter.

Jake, not begging but commanding: *Take us back! Take us back or you'll be sorry!*

I'm sorry already, I thought. I couldn't say it aloud; I didn't have enough breath left. My heart was running amok. I expected it to simply burst like an over-inflated balloon at any second.

To my horror, the twins were swimming into existence. Their men's bodies were too big for the stroller's double seats, but were in them, just the same. Their swollen children's heads turned to look at me, eyes black and malevolent, the red pepper of snakebites stippling their cheeks and foreheads. As if they were suffering from an apocalyptic case of chickenpox.

This pair of snakes was real, all right. Their bodies made a dry shushing sound as their sinuous S-curves spiraled through the shells. Their tails rattled—dry bones in a gourd.

Jake: *Bite 'im, bite 'im good!*

Joe: *Bite 'im, make him stop! Make him take us back!*

When they struck, it felt like BBs hitting the rubber galoshes. Or maybe hailstones. The stroller finally stuck fast, wheels-deep in shells. The men-children inside it were twisted around, staring at me, but it seemed they couldn't get out. At least not yet. One of the rattlers was gripping my right foot through the galosh, its head spiraling up. Because the stroller was stuck anyway—beached, so to speak—I let it go in favor of the snake pole. I plunged it down, hoping not to give myself a nasty gash but knowing I couldn't afford to hesitate. I caught a loop with the hook and flung the snake toward the water. The other struck at my left galosh. For one moment I saw its black eyes staring up at me and thought they were the same eyes as the ones looking at me from the stroller. Then I brought the hook down and speared it behind its triangular head. When I raised the snake pole I felt its tail thwap my shoulder, perhaps looking for a grip. It didn't find one. I flung it. For one moment it was a writhing scribble against the sky, then it was in the water.

The stroller was rocking back and forth as the things inside it—visible yet ephemeral—struggled to get out. They still couldn't. The stroller was their link to the world, and to me. I couldn't push it any further, so I dropped the snake pole and tipped it over. I heard them scream as they hit the shells, and then they were gone. By that I mean I could no longer

(*see us, see us*)

see them, but they were still there. I could hear Jake shrieking and Joe crying. Sobbing, really, as he had probably sobbed when he realized he was covered with rattlesnakes and his too-short life was ending. Those sounds made me sorry—I was sure my son had also cried while he and Donna were broiling in that Pinto—but that didn't stop me. I had to finish what I started, if I could.

Gasping, I dragged the stroller toward the pass. Toward the whirl-pool.

Jake: *No! No! You're supposed to take care of us! Roll us! Push us! Dress us! No!*

His brother only shrieked with terror.

I was twenty feet from the water's edge when flames burst up all around me. They weren't real, they had no heat, but I could smell kerosene. The stench was so strong it made me cough. The coughing turned into gagging. The blinding white heaps of shells were gone, replaced by a carpet of burning snakes. They weren't real, either, but I could hear the popcorn sound of their rattles bursting in the heat. They struck at me with heads that weren't there.

I reached the water. I could push the stroller in, but that wouldn't be good enough. They might be able to get the haunted thing out, just as they'd somehow managed to get it from the Bell house to Greg's. But I've been told that men or even women—*small* women—are sometimes able to lift cars off their trapped children. And once upon a time, a woman named Donna Trenton had fought a 150-pound St. Bernard with nothing but a baseball bat . . . and won. If she could do that, surely I could do this.

That stroller didn't weigh 150, but it might have gone 30. If the things had been in it, and if they'd also had actual weight, I never could have lifted it even to my waist. But they didn't. I hoisted it by the struts above the back wheels. I twisted my hips to the right, producing an audible creaking from my back. I turned the other way and slung the stroller like the world's clumsiest discus. It splashed down only five feet from the edge of the shell beach. Not far enough, but the current from Calypso Bay was running strong with the ebbing tide. The stroller, tilting this way and that, was pulled into the whirlpool. They were in it again. Maybe they had to be in it. I got one more look at those terrible faces before they were carried away. When the stroller came back around it was sinking, the seats underwater. Its occupants were gone. One of the shirts floated away, then the other. I heard a final shriek of anger in my head; that was Jake Bell, the stronger of the two. The next time the stroller came around on its watery carousel, only the handles were above water. The time after, it was gone except for a watery sunflash three or four feet down.

The flames were also gone. And the burning snakes. Only the stench of kerosene remained. A pair of blue shorts floated toward me. I picked up the snake pole, hooked them, and flung them out into the Gulf.

My back creaked again. I bent over, trying to soothe it. When I straightened up and looked across Daylight Pass, I saw a lot more than a few masses of floating green. Duma Key was there. It looked as real as the hand that had risen out of the tub of snakes, or the horrible hybrid beings lying in the guest room bed. I could see palm trees and a pink house standing on stilts. And I could see a man. He was tall, dressed in jeans and a plain white cotton shirt. He waved to me.

Oh my God, Donna said in the seconds before she died. *You're all grown up! Look how tall you are!*

I waved back. I think he smiled, but I can't be sure because by then my eyes were filled with tears, making liquid prisms that quadrupled the brightness of the sun. When I wiped them away, Duma Key was gone and so was he.

It took only ten minutes to roll the pram down to the end of the Key. Or maybe it was fifteen—I was a little too busy to check my watch. Returning to the gazebo and the boardwalk took me three quarters of an hour because my back kept seizing up. I undressed as I went, pulling off the gloves, peeling off the sweatshirt, kicking off the galoshes, sitting down on the sand long enough to pull off the jeans. Doing those things wasn't as painful as walking, but they hurt plenty. So did getting up after shucking the jeans, but I was lighter. And the horrible rat-run of thoughts in my mind was gone. For me that made the back pain—which continues to this day—a fair trade. I walked the rest of the way wearing only my shorts.

Back in the house I found Tylenol in Greg's medicine cabinet and took three. The pills didn't kill the pain, but at least muted it. I slept for four hours—dreamless, blessed sleep. When I woke up, my back was so stiff that I had to make a plan—Step A, Step B, Step C—to sit up, get off the bed, and on my feet. I took a hot shower and that helped some. I couldn't face using a towel, so I air-dried.

Downstairs—step by wincing step—I thought of calling Pelley, but I didn't want to talk to him. *No more than the fucking man in the fucking moon*, Donna would have said.

I called Zane instead. He asked how he could help me and I said I was calling to report a missing stroller. "Did someone from your department—Pelley, maybe—finally decide to come and pick it up?"

"Huh. I don't think so. Let me check and call you back."

Which he did, eventually, and told me no one from the County Sheriff's office had picked up the stroller. No reason to, really, he said.

"Whoever brought it up here twice must have finally taken it back to her place," I said.

He agreed. And that was where the matter of the haunted stroller ended.

May 2023

All that was almost three years ago. I'm back in Newburyport, and never want to visit the Sunshine State again. Even Georgia would be too close.

Alita Bell's tox screen showed nothing suspicious, which took me off the hook. Nathan Rutherford saw to Allie's burying. He and I attended the funeral. So did Zane and Canavan, an old party named Lloyd Sunderland (accompanied by his dog), and half a dozen swing bridge operators.

Andy Pelley also attended. At the reception, he came up to me as I waited my turn for a Dixie cup of punch. The smell of whiskey wafted from below his mustache. There was no mask to mute it. "I still think you got away with something, bub," he said, and headed for the door—not quite straight—before I could reply.

I testified at the Zoom inquest from Greg's house. There were no gotcha questions. In fact, the medical examiner gave me a strong attaboy for doing my best to keep the buzzards off the deceased until the proper authorities could arrive.

No relatives ever came out of the woodwork to challenge Alita Bell's scrap of a will. Said scrap's trip through probate was a long one, but by June of 2022, everything that was hers was mine. Incredible but true.

I put the Bell property up for sale, knowing no one would want the house, which was fairly run down in spite of Allie's reputed handy-woman skills. The land it stood on was a different matter. It sold in October of '22 for just shy of seven million dollars. Bay to Gulf, you know; prime real estate. Another McMansion will stand there soon enough. Allie's other assets totaled six million. After taxes and the other barnacles that attach to any large estate, that thirteen million total boiled down to 4.5. A nice little windfall, if you ignore the terrible children that were supposed to come with it.

I put half a million in my retirement fund—call it for services rendered and a back that will probably pain me until I die. The rest I gave to the All Faiths Food Bank in Sarasota, which was very happy—*over the fucking moon*, Donna would have said—to accept the money. The only other exception I made was the eight thousand dollars that went to Counselor Rutherford.

Allie's funeral expenses.

I stayed at Greg's house until after the inquest, when the matter of Alita Bell was officially closed. During that time there were no visions and no squeaky wheels to trouble me. Of course I still checked the courtyard and the garage for the stroller first thing each morning, even before putting the coffee on. It isn't just grief that leaves scars. Terror does, too. Especially supernatural terror.

But the twins were gone.

One day I asked Mr. Ito to show me the dip where Jacob and Joseph had come to grief on their fatal walk through the underbrush to the beach. He was willing enough, and after some casting about, we found it. In fact, Mr. Ito almost fell into it. Although it was hard to tell, being filled with naupaka and tangles of oxeye daisies so big they looked like mutants, I thought it was about as long as Greg's luxurious tub in the master bathroom, and almost as deep.

I had the keys to the Bell house, and I went in there just once. I was curious about the final thing—vision, hallucination, take your pick—I had experienced on the shell beach as I dragged the stroller toward the water: flames, a carpet of snakes, the stench of kerosene. The twins had died before the great snake hunt, so how could they have known about it?

The house was just as Allie left it when she took the ghost twins for their last roll (by her, anyway). There was a plate in the sink with a knife and fork laid across it. On the counter was a box of Wheaties with the bottom chewed out by some small, foraging critters. I forced myself to look into the boys' bedroom. I had thought she would have kept it as it had been during Jake's and Joe's short lives, and I was right. There were twin beds. The sheets and pillowcases were printed with cartoon dinosaurs. Tad had exactly the same set. This realization horrified and in some way comforted me at the same time.

I closed the door. On it, in colorful stick-on letters, was THE KINGDOM OF TWINS.

I didn't know what I was looking for, but I knew it when I found it. Henry Bell's study had also been kept as it was all those years before. Yellow legal pads were neatly stacked to the left of his IBM Selectric typewriter, folders to the right. On each side, like paperweights, were framed pictures: Joe on the legal pads, Jake on the folders. There was a picture of Allie, looking impossibly young and beautiful, on one wall.

On another wall were three framed black-and-white photographs of the great snake hunt. One showed men unloading trucks, putting on Smokechaser packs—called Indian pumps in those unenlightened days—and donning protective gear. Another showed men in a line, beating the underbrush as they drove the snakes north. The third showed the triangle of shell beach as thousands of snakes charred and died in the flames. I knew that Jake and Joe had haunted this house long before they had haunted mine. Perhaps Allie had even rolled them in here, and showed them the photographs.

See, boys? That's what happened to the bad snakies that hurt you!

I left. I was glad to go. I never went back.

Just one more thing.

Will Rogers said land is the one thing they're not making any more of, and in Florida land is gold, especially since the pandemic hit. And while they may not be making any more of it, reclamation isn't out of the question.

The county has begun talking about reclaiming Duma Key.

A consortium of real estate agents (including the one who sold Mrs. Bell's house for me) hired a remediation company to investigate the possibility. At a meeting attended by the county commissioners and chaired by the county administrator, several experts from Land

Gold, Inc. put on a PowerPoint lecture, complete with an idealized artist's conception of Duma risen from the deeps. It would be relatively easy and inexpensive, they said; just close Daylight Pass again, which would choke off the water's flow. A year or so of dredging, and there you have it.

They are discussing it as I write this. The environmentalists are raising holy hell, and I give money every other month to the Save Daylight Pass organization that has formed, but in the end it's going to happen, because in Florida—especially the parts where the rich tend to gravitate—money trumps everything. They will close the pass, and in the process they will surely find a certain rusty stroller. I'm sure that by then the awful things that inhabited it will be gone.

Almost sure.

If they're not, I hope they have no interest in me. Because if there ever comes a night when I hear that squeaky stroller wheel approaching, God help me.

God help me!

Thinking of John D. MacDonald

THE DREAMERS

I don't know what the universe means. I might have an idea. You might, too. Or not. All I can say to you is beware of dreams. They're dangerous. I found out.

I did two tours in Vietnam. Got out in June of '71. Nobody spit on me when I got off the plane in New York, and no one called me a baby killer. Of course no one thanked me for my service, either, so I guess that's a wash. This story—memoir? confession?—has nothing to do with Nam, except it does. It does. If I hadn't spent twenty-six months humping the boonies, I might have tried to stop Elgin when we saw the teeth. Not that I would have had much luck with that. The Gentleman Scientist meant to see it through, and in a way he did. But I could have walked away at least. I didn't because the young man who went to Vietnam wasn't the same young man who came back. That young man was empty. Emotions scrubbed. So what happened, happened. I don't hold myself responsible. He would have gone on regardless. I just know I stayed even when I knew we were edging past sanity. I suppose I wanted to wake myself up again. I suppose I did.

*   *   *

I went back to Maine and stayed with my mother for awhile in Skowhegan. She was doing all right. Assistant manager at George's Banana Stand, sounds like a roadside stall but it's a grocery store. She told me I'd changed and I said I know. She asked me what I was going to do for work and I said I'd find something in Portland. I said I'd do what I learned from Sissy and she said that sounded good. I think she was glad to see the back of me. I think I made her nervous. I asked her once if she missed my father or my stepfather. She said my father. Of Lester she said good riddance to bad rubbish.

I bought a used car and drove to Portland and applied for work at a place called Temp-O. The woman who took my application said, "I don't see where you went to school." She was Mrs. Frobisher.

"I didn't."

"Didn't what?"

"Go to school."

"You don't understand, young man. We hire stenographers here to fill in when someone is sick or quits. Some of our temps work in district court."

"Try me," I said.

"Do you know Gregg?"

"Yes. I learned from my sister. I was helping her with her homework, but I turned out to be better."

"Where is your sister working?"

"She died."

"I'm sorry to hear that." Mrs. Frobisher didn't sound sorry and I didn't blame her. People have problems enough coping with their own tragedies without taking on the tragedies of others. "How many words a minute?"

"Hundred and eighty."

She smiled. "Really."

"Really."

"I doubt it."

I said nothing. She handed me a pad and a #2 Eberhard Faber. "I'd like to see a hundred and eighty in action. That would be a treat."

I flipped open the pad. I thought of Sissy and me sitting in her room, she at her desk in a circle of lamplight, me on the bed. She said

I was better than her. She said how I picked it up like a dream, which was true. It was like picking up Vietnamese, also the Tay and Muong dialects. It's not a skill, just a knack. I could see words turning into pothooks and hangers. Thick strokes, thin strokes, curls. They marched across my mind in lockstep. You could ask me if I liked it and I'd say sometimes. The way a person likes breathing sometimes. Most of the time you just do it.

"Are you ready?"

"Born ready."

"We'll see about that." Then, very fast, "The quality of mercy is not strained it droppeth as the gentle rain from heaven upon the place beneath you can't just walk in off the street and say you can transcribe a hundred and eighty it is twice blessed both he who gives and he who takes. Now read that back to me."

I read it back to her without telling her she got the last part of Portia's speech a few words wrong. She just looked at me for a few seconds, then said, "I'll be goddamned."

I worked at Temp-O for the next ten months or so. We were losing in Vietnam. It didn't take a genius to see it. Sometimes people don't stop when they should. Saying that makes me think of Elgin. The Gentleman Scientist.

There were four of us when I started, then six, then down to three, then back up to six again. Temping was a high-turnover job. They were all women except for Pearson, a tall drink of water with a bald spot he tried to cover and eczema around his nose and the corners of his mouth. Around his mouth it looked like dried spit. Pearson was there when I came and there when I left. He could do maybe sixty words a minute. On a good day. If you went too fast he'd tell you to slow down, slow down. I know because sometimes when it was slow the bunch of us would race. Two minutes of TV ads. Dishwashing liquid. Toothpaste. Paper towels. Things women who watch daytime TV buy. I always won. After awhile Pearson wouldn't even try. He called it a childish game. I don't know why Mrs. Frobisher kept Pearson on. She wasn't fucking him or anything.

I think maybe he was like something you get used to overlooking, like a pile of Christmas cards on the hall table that are still there come Valentine's Day. He didn't like me. I didn't feel one way or the other about him, because that was how I rolled in '71 and '72. But it was Pearson who introduced me to Elgin. Or so you could say. He didn't mean to do it.

We'd come in around eight-thirty or nine and sit in the back room there on Exchange Street, drinking coffee and eating doughnuts and watching a little portable TV or reading. Sometimes having a race. There were usually two or three copies of the *Press Herald* and Pearson always had one of them, muttering away at the stories and rubbing at his eczema so it snowed down in flurries. Mrs. Frobisher would call for Anne or Diane or Stella if it was an ordinary job. I mostly got court if someone was out sick. I had to learn the stenograph and I had to wear a stenomask, but that was all right. I got sent to high-powered meetings sometimes where recording devices were *verboten*. Then it was just me and my pad. So far as I liked any job, I liked those. Sometimes I'd transcribe and then have to hand over my pad. That was all right. Sometimes I got tipped.

Pearson used to drop sections of the paper on the floor when he finished with them. Diane called that slutty behavior one day and Pearson told her that if she didn't like it she could just roll it small and stick it up her ass and a week or two later Diane left. Some days I would pick up the sections Pearson dropped and glance through them. The back room, which we called the bullpen, got boring when there were no jobs. The game shows and talk shows were tiresome. I always carried a paperback but this one day, the day I found out about Elgin (although I didn't know his name just then because it wasn't in the ad), the book I was reading didn't engage my attention. It was a warbook written by a man who didn't know anything about war.

It was the ad section I got hold of. Cars for sale by owner on one page and help wanted on the other. I cast my eye down the help wanteds, not exactly looking for another job, I was okay with Temp-O, just passing the time. The words *Gentleman Scientist* in boldface caught my eye. And the word *phlegmatic*. Not a word often seen in classified ads.

GENTLEMAN SCIENTIST wants assistant to aid in series of experiments. Stenographic expertise a must (60-80 wpm or better). Excellent wages upon receipt of excellent references. Confidentiality and phlegmatic temperament also a must.

There was a number. Curious to know who wanted a phlegmatic assistant, I called it. Passing the time. That was Thursday noon. On Saturday I drove seventy or so miles to Castle Rock in my used Ford and out Lake Road, which ended at Dark Score Lake. On the beach was a large stone house with a gated drive and a small stone house behind it where I came to live while in the employ of Elgin, the Gentleman Scientist. The house wasn't a mansion, but it was close. There was a Volkswagen Bug and a Mercedes in the driveway. The Bug had a Maine plate and a flower decal on the gas hatch and a bumper sticker saying STOP THE WAR. I recognized it. The Mercedes had a Massachusetts plate. I thought it must belong to the Gentleman Scientist, which turned out right. I never knew where Elgin's money came from. Maybe gentlemen don't tell. What I thought was that he inherited it because he had no job so far as I could tell except for gentleman science and called the not-quite-a-mansion his summer place. I don't know where the winter place was. Probably Boston or one of those outlying suburbs where the only Black or Asian faces you ever saw were pushing lawnmowers or serving lunch. I could have investigated these things, asked around town because town people have a way of knowing things and if you ask the right way they will always tell you, they want to tell you, nothing passes the time like gossip, and I did know the right way having grown up in a small town myself and elided my *r*'s as good Yankees do, but that wasn't "where I was at," as we used to say back then. I didn't care if it was Weston or Brookline or the Back Bay. I didn't even want the job or not want it. I wasn't sick or anything, but I wasn't a well man. You might understand that or you might not. Most nights I didn't get much sleep and darkness is full of long hours. Most nights I fought the war and the war won. It's an old story, I know. You can see it on television once a week.

I parked beside the Bug. A young woman came out carrying a briefcase in one hand and the steno pad in the other. She was dressed in a skirt suit. It was Diane, lately of Temp-O.

"Hello stranger," I said.

"Hello yourself. You must be the next one. I hope you have better luck."

"Didn't get it?"

"He said he'd call me. I know what that means. Is Pearson still there?"

"Yes."

"That fuck."

She got in the Bug and puttered away. I rang the bell. Elgin answered it. He was tall and thin with a lot of sweptback white hair like a concert pianist. He wore a white shirt and khaki pants with the crotch hanging down like he'd lost weight. He looked about forty-five. He asked me if I was William Davis. I said I was. He asked me if I had a steno pad. I said I had half a dozen in the backseat of my car.

"You better get one."

I got one, thinking it would be Mrs. Frobisher all over again. He took me inside to the living room, which felt like it still held the ghost of winter when the house was empty and the lake turned to ice. He asked me if I had brought my resume. I took out my wallet and showed him my honorable discharge and told him that was my resume. I didn't think he'd care about me pumping gas or working as a busboy in the Headless Woman after I graduated high school.

"Since I got out of the Army I've been working at an agency in Portland called Temp-O. Your last one worked there, too. You can call if you want. Ask for Mrs. Frobisher. She might even let me keep my job if she finds out I'm looking for another one."

"Why is that?"

"Because I'm the best she has."

"Do you really want this job? Because you seem, what's the word, lackadaisical."

"I wouldn't mind a change." That was true.

"What about the wages? Want to know about them? Or how long the job lasts?"

I shrugged.

"Rolling stone are you?"

"I don't know." That was also true.

"Tell me, Mr. Davis, can you spell *phlegmatic*?"

I spelled it.

He nodded. "Because the last one couldn't, even though she must have read it in my advertisement. I doubt if she even knew what it meant. She looked flighty to me. Was she, when you worked together?"

"I wouldn't want to say."

He smiled. Thin lips. Lines going down the sides of his mouth like you'd see on a ventriloquist's dummy. Hornrim specs. He didn't look like a scientist to me. He looked like he was trying to look like a scientist.

"Where did you serve? Vietnam?"

"Mostly."

"Did you kill anyone?"

"I don't talk about that."

"Get any medals?"

"I don't talk about that, either."

"Fair enough. When you say you're the best at Temp-O—I've seen a couple of others from there, not just Diane Bissonette—how many words a minute are we talking about?"

I told him.

"I'm going to test you on that. I have to. If you're the best, that's what I need. Stenography will be the only record. Almost the only record. There will be no audio recordings of my experiments. No motion picture film. There will be Polaroid photographs, which I will keep if I publish and destroy if I don't."

He waited for me to be curious, and I was, but not enough to ask. He would either tell me or he wouldn't. There was a stack of books on the coffee table. He picked up the top one and tested me from it. The book was *Man and His Symbols*. He spoke at a good pace, but not speeding along the way Mrs. Frobisher had. There was some technical jargon, like *activation-synthesis*, and some difficult names, like Aniela Jaffé and Brescia University, but I saw them correctly. That's what it is, a kind of seeing. I put them down, even though he stumbled over the name of Jaffé, pronouncing it Jaff. I read everything back to him.

421

"You are wasted at Temp-O," he said.

I had nothing to say to that.

"You would live here during the course of my experiments. In the guest house out back. Days off. Plenty of free time. Do you have any medical skills as a result of your service?"

"Some. I could set a bone and I could resuscitate someone. If they were fished out of the lake in time, that is. I don't suppose you'd have any need for sulfa packs here."

"How old are you?"

"Twenty-four."

"You look older."

"Sure."

"Were you by any chance at My Lai?"

"Before my time."

He picked up one of the books in the stack: *The Archetypes and the Collective Unconscious*. He picked up another called *Memories, Dreams, Reflections*. He hefted them. Seemed to weigh them in each hand, as if on a balance scale. "Do you know what these books have in common?"

"They're both by Carl Jung."

He raised his eyebrows. "You say his name correctly."

Better than you say Aniela Jaffé, I thought but didn't say.

"Don't suppose you speak German?"

"*Ein wenig*," I said, and held my thumb and forefinger apart.

He took up another volume from the stack. It was called *Gegenwart und Zukunft*. "This is my treasure. Rare, a first edition. *Present and Future*. I can't read it, but I can look at the pictures, and I've studied the graphs. Mathematics is a universal language, as I'm sure you're aware."

I wasn't because no language is universal. Numbers, like dogs, can be taught to do tricks. And the title of his first edition was actually *Presence and Future*. There is a world of difference between present and presence. A gulf. I didn't care about that, but the book under *Gegenwart und Zukunft* interested me. It was the only one not by Jung. It was *Beyond the Wall of Sleep*, by H.P. Lovecraft. A man I knew in the 'docks, a doorgunner, had a paperback copy. It burned up and so did he.

There was more talk. The wages he proposed were high enough for me to wonder if his experiments were strictly legal. He left me several opportunities to ask about them but I didn't. Finally he gave up teasing and asked me if I would like to hazard a guess about what his experiments would concern. I said dreams seemed likely.

"Yes, but I think I will keep the exact nature of my interest, the *thrust*, shall we say, to myself for the time being."

I hadn't asked about the *thrust*, another thing I didn't bother to point out. He took a photo of my discharge papers with his Polaroid camera, then offered me the job. "Of course you could keep working at Temp-O, but here you would be aiding me as I explore realms no psychologist, not even Jung, has visited. Virgin territory."

I said all right. He told me we would start in the middle of July and I said all right. He asked for my phone number and I gave it to him. I told him it was a roominghouse phone and down the hall. He asked if I had a girlfriend. I said no. He wore no wedding ring. I never saw any help. I cooked my own meals once I moved into the little guest house, or ate at one of the cafés in town. I don't know who cooked his grub. There was something timeless about Elgin, as if he had no past and no future. He had a present but no particular presence. He smoked but I never saw him take a drink. All he had was his obsession about dreams.

On the way out I said, "You want to go over the wall of sleep, don't you?"

He laughed at that. "No. I want to go under it."

He called me on July 1st and told me to give my two weeks' notice. I did. I didn't think Mrs. Frobisher would tell me to never mind two weeks, just take a walk (or roll it small), and she didn't. I was her best, and she wanted as much of me as she could get. He called me on July 8th and told me to move in when I finished work on the 14th. He said if I was living in a roominghouse I probably didn't have much. He was right about that. He said he had a task for me right away, a small one.

My last interaction at Temp-O was with Pearson. I told him he was an asshole. He had no reply. Possibly he agreed with the assessment. Possibly he thought I might strike him. I don't know. I drove around to the guest house and saw a keyring with two keys hanging down and a third stuck in the lock. Four rooms. Tidy. Warmer than the big house, probably because it was added later, after in-wall insulation became a thing. There was a fireplace in the living room and plenty of seasoned wood out back in a pile covered with a canvas tarp. I like a fireplace fire, always have. I didn't go around to the big house. I figured Elgin would see my car and know I was in. There was an intercom in the little galley kitchen and a fax machine beside it. I had never seen a home fax machine before, but I knew what it was, having seen a few in Vietnam HQs. On the kitchen table was what looked like a scrapbook. A note taped to it said *Familiarize yourself with these. You may want to take notes.*

I leafed through the book. I didn't take notes. My memory is good. There were twelve pages and twelve photographs under cellophane or maybe it was isinglass. Two were driver's license photos. Two were headshots. Six women and six men. They were all different ages. The youngest looked like a high schooler. Below the photographs were their names and occupations. Two were college students. Two were teachers probably on their summer break. One was retired. The rest were what are known as bluecollar workers by people who don't do bluecollar work, waitresses and store clerks, a carpenter and a long-haul truck driver.

There were eggs and bacon in the Frigidaire. I fried four eggs in bacon fat. There was a little deck on the side with a view of the lake. I ate there and looked at the water. When the sun was in the wedge between Mount Washington and Mount Jefferson and gold across the lake, I went in and went to bed. I slept better that night than I had in four years. Ten hours of thoughtless imageless darkness. It's what being dead must be like.

On Saturday morning I walked down to the lakeshore. There was a bench. Elgin was sitting on it and smoking. Same white shirt and same long-crotch khaki pants. Or maybe different ones. I never saw him wear anything else, as if they were a kind of uniform. He asked me to sit down with him. I did.

"Get settled in all right?"

"Yes."

He took out his wallet from his hip pocket and handed me a check. It was from The Dream Corporation LLC and made out to me. The sum was a thousand dollars.

"You can take it to the KeyBank in Castle Rock. That's where I have my accounts, both personal and corporate. You can open your own account, if you like."

"Can I just cash it?"

"Of course. Do you remember the first test subject in the book I left you?"

"Yes. Althea Gibson. A hairdresser. Looks to be about thirty."

"Good memory. Is it eidetic? Given your stenographic speed and your knowledge of Vietnamese, I think it might be."

So he had done some digging. Made some calls, as they say. "I suppose so. I picked up steno from my sister. Helping her study."

"And you were better at it."

"I guess I was but she landed rightside up. Got a job in Human Resources at Eastern Maine Medical. Better pay." He didn't need to know she died and I didn't want to tell him.

"You were a translator in Vietnam."

"Some of the time."

"Don't want to talk about it? That's fine. It's nice here, isn't it? Peaceful. Later in the day there will be picnickers. The whine of the boats is annoying, it goes on from Memorial Day to Labor Day, but the picnickers stay further down the beach."

"Your part is private."

"Yes. I like my privacy. Mr. Davis, I believe I am going to change the world."

"You mean the world's understanding of dreams."

"No. The *world*. If I am successful." He got up. "I'm going to send you a fax. Look it over. Mrs. Gibson will be here at two o'clock on Tuesday afternoon. I'm paying her to close her hairdressing shop. You will greet her and show her in. I will want to show you the set-up before. Say noon. In case she comes early."

"All right."

"Read the fax. If you have comments, use the intercom. Otherwise, you are off until Tuesday." He offered his hand. I stood up to shake with him. I was struck again by his timeless look. A kind of serenity. He believed he was going to change the world. He really believed it.

The fax shrieked in while I was making coffee. It was a release for his test subjects. I wondered again about the legality of this particular op. There were spaces for the test subject to print her or his name, address, and phone number. Below that it said that the undersigned had been informed and agreed to a light hypnotic drug being administered before the test run. It said the drug would wear off in six hours or less and that the test subject would feel fine. Since Elgin would be the one administering the drug and I wouldn't be on the hook if something went wrong, I had no comments. I will admit I was becoming a little more interested. I thought it was possible that Elgin was crazy. After Vietnam I had a nose for it. I went downtown and bought groceries. The bank was open until noon. I started an account and deposited the check, taking a hundred dollars in cash. There was nothing about waiting for the check to clear. So they knew he was good for it. I had lunch at the Castle Rock Diner, then went back to the guest house and took a nap. There were no dreams.

On Tuesday I went to the big house at noon. Elgin was waiting on the stoop. Inside on the left was the living room where he had looked at my discharge papers and showed me his books by Jung. On the right were double doors. He opened them. It used to be a dining room but was now where he meant to conduct his experiments. It had been partitioned in two by a wall that looked made of plywood. One half of the room was for his test subjects. There was a couch with the head lifted and the feet lowered, like a psychiatrist's couch. On one side of the couch was a Polaroid camera mounted on the tripod and pointed down. On the other side was a small table with a Blue Horse tablet open to the first blank page and a pen. So he expected his subjects to write notes, or thought they might, probably what they dreamed while the dreams were fresh. There were Bose speakers mounted on the walls. In the middle of the plywood wall facing the raised portion of the couch was a mirror and you'd have to be someone who never watched a cop show on TV not to know it was oneway glass. On Elgin's side of the wall was a desk and another Polaroid on a tripod, looking through the oneway glass and pointed at the couch. There was a microphone on the desk. There was a row of buttons. There were more speakers on the walls. There was a Philips stereo system with a record on the turntable. There was a chair by the oneway glass.

"That's for you," he said, pointing at the chair. "Your post, where you will sit and watch. Do you have a fresh pad?"

"Yes."

"You will take down everything I say. If Mrs. Gibson says anything, you'll hear it from the speakers on this side and take that down. If you don't understand what she says, often what a person says while asleep is unintelligible, draw a double line."

"If you had a tape recorder," I began, but he waved that off.

"I told you there will be no audio, no film. Only Polaroids. I control the sound system and both cameras from the desk."

"No audio, no film, roger that." There was also no medical equipment of any kind, no way to record the brainwaves of his subjects or REM sleep. It was crazy but the check hadn't bounced so I was okay with it. I saw no excitement on his face, could detect no nervousness. Just that serenity. He was going to change the world. He was five-by-five on that.

Althea Gibson showed up fifteen minutes early. She was one of the two who had sent Elgin a headshot, probably taken by a professional photographer who had used a ringlight to make her look a bit younger. She was about forty and on the portly side. I met her at her car and introduced myself as Mr. Elgin's assistant.

"I'm a little scared," she said while we walked to the house. "I hope I'll be all right. Will I be all right, Mr. Davis?"

"Sure," I said. "Easy as falling off a log."

They say truth is stranger than fiction, don't they. Here was a woman at the end of a country road that dead-ended at a private beach, talking to a man she had never met before, and had she met Elgin or only talked to him on the phone? She didn't think anything bad would happen to her even though she had been told she would be taking a drug described as a "light hypnotic." She didn't think that because bad things happened to other people, on the TV news. Was it lack of imagination that she had never thought about rape or a shallow grave or only the close horizon of her perception? That raises questions about what imagination and perception even are. Maybe I was thinking a certain way because I had seen certain things on the other side of the world, where bad things happened to people all the time, sometimes even to hairdressers.

"For eight hundred dollars, how could I refuse?" She lowered her voice and said, "Am I going to get high?"

"I really don't know. You're our first . . ." What? "Our first customer."

"You're not going to take advantage of me, are you?" Said in a joking way that meant she hoped she really was joking. "Or him?"

"Nothing of the sort," Elgin said, coming down the hall to greet her on the stoop. He had a little flat case like a recon officer's mapcase on a strap over one shoulder. "I'm safe as can be and so is Bill." He held out both of his hands and took both of hers and gave them a brief squeeze. "You are going to enjoy this. It's a promise."

I gave her the release form, which was probably about as legal as a three-dollar bill. She gave it a cursory skim, filled in the blanks at the top, signed at the bottom. She was living her life and did not believe it would end or even change. Blindness to possibility is either a blessing or a curse. You choose. He led her to the couch in the former dining room and took a beaker of clear liquid from his case. He pulled the rubber stopper and gave it to her. She took it gingerly, as if it might be hot.

"What is it?"

"A light hypnotic, as I told you. It will put you in a serene state, and from there it may lull you to sleep. There will be no side effects and no hangover. It's quite harmless."

She looked at the beaker, then made a toasting gesture at me and said "Over the teeth, over the gums, look out tummy, here it comes." She tossed it off easy as that, truth being stranger than fiction, then looked to Elgin. "I expected a kick but there wasn't one. Are you sure it wasn't just water?"

"*Mostly* water," he said with a smile. "You'll be back in your car and headed home to . . . where is it you live? Refresh me."

"North Windham."

"Back in your car and headed back to North Windham by four o'clock with a check for eight hundred dollars in your purse. In the meantime, relax and I'll tell you what I want you to do. It's quite simple." He took the beaker and returned the stopper and put it back in his little case where there was a loop to hold it. He took out the only other thing in the case. It was a picture of a small house in the woods. The house was painted red. It had a green door atop two stone steps and a brick chimney. He handed it to her.

"I'm going to play some music. Very soft and very calm. I want you to listen to it and look at this picture."

"Ooo, I'm feeling it now." She smiled. "It's like from smoking a doob. Mellow!"

"Look at the picture, Mrs. Gibson, and tell yourself you want to see what's inside that house."

I was writing all this down, G for Gibson and E for Elgin. Pothooks racing across the page of a virgin steno book. Doing what I was being paid to do.

"What *is* inside it?"

"That's up to you. Perhaps you will dream of going inside, then you can see for yourself. Will you try to do that?"

"If I don't dream of the inside of the house, do I still get to keep the eight hundred dollars?"

"Absolutely. Even if you just have a pleasant little nap."

"If I do go to sleep, will you wake me up by four?" She was starting to drift. "My neighbor is picking up my daughter at school, but I have to be back by six to make her . . . make her . . ."

"Make her supper?"

"Yes, her supper. Look at that green door! I would never paint a green door for a red house. Too Christmassy."

"Look at the picture."

"I *am*."

"Dream of the house. Try to go inside." A hypnotist's chant.

"All right."

429

I thought she was already under. I thought if Elgin asked her to bark like a dog she'd give it a try.

"Go inside and look around."

"All right."

"Go to the living room."

"All right."

"Not inside, just to the doorway."

"Do you want me to tell you what it looks like in the living room? The furniture or what kind of wallpaper? Things like that?"

"No, I want you to kneel down and look for a crack in the floor. Right there in the living room doorway."

"Will there be one?"

"I don't know, Mrs. Gibson. Althea. It's your dream. If there's a crack, put your fingers in it and lift up the living room floor."

She gave him a dreamy smile. "I can't lift up a *floor*, silly."

"Maybe you won't be able to but maybe you will. Things are possible in dreams that would otherwise not be."

"Like flying." The dreamy smile got bigger.

"Yes, like flying." He sounded a little impatient with that idea, although to me the idea of flying in dreams seemed as logical as anything else about them. According to Jung, dreams of flying indicated the core psyche's desire to break free of the expectations of others, or even more difficult, usually impossible, the expectations of the self.

"Lift up the floor. See what is beneath. If you remember when you wake up, write it down on the pad I've provided for you. I'll ask you a few questions. If you can't remember, that's all right. We'll be back soon, won't we, Bill?"

We left the patient half of the former dining room and went into the other half. I took my seat in front of the oneway glass with my pad on my knee. Elgin sat at the desk and pushed one of his buttons. The record turned, the tonearm went down, and the music started to play. It was Debussy. Elgin pushed another button and the music in our half of the experimental station stopped but I could still hear it in Mrs. Gibson's half. She was looking at the picture. She giggled and I wrote, not in Gregg but in plain, *G laughs at 2:14 PM.*

Time passed. Ten minutes by my watch. She studied the picture of the house with the close attention only those who are quite seriously stoned can attain. Little by little it began to sag in her hand. With the head of the couch facing us I could see the way her eyes slipped closed and then opened. Her lips, dressed in bright red, softened. Elgin was now standing next to me, bent forward with his hands on his knees. He looked like a bird colonel I knew over there in that other world watching through his binoculars as the F-100Ds of the 352nd came in low over Bien Hoa, pregnant with the firejelly they would drop in an orange curtain, burning a miscarriage in the belly of the green, turning part of the overstory to ash and skeleton palms. The men and women, too, them calling *nahn tu, nahn tu* to no one who could hear or care if they did.

The picture of the house settled to her belly. She was asleep. Elgin went back to the desk and turned off the music. He must also have turned up the sound in our part because I could hear her snoring, very lightly. He came back and resumed his former position. The Polaroids on timers flashed every thirty seconds or so, the one on our side and the one on the Gibson side. Each time they flashed a picture extruded with that catlike whirring sound they make and fell on the floor. I saw something three or four minutes after she fell asleep and leaned forward. I didn't believe it, the way you don't believe anything that runs contrary to the way things are supposed to be. But it was there. I rubbed a palm across my eyes and it was still there.

"Elgin. Her mouth."

"I see it."

Her lips were slipping apart and her teeth were rising between them. It was like watching something volcanic rising from the ocean, only there were no sharp points except I guess for the canines. Not fangs or animal teeth, they were her teeth, just longer and bigger. Her lips folded back revealing their pink lining. Her hands were jerking, flipping back and forth, fingers wiggling. The Polaroids flashed and whined. Two more times in there, two more in with us. The photos fell to the floor. Then the cameras were out of film. Her teeth began to retract. Her hands gave one more jerk, the fingers seeming to play an invisible piano. Then that stopped, too. Her lips closed but there

431

was a faint red ghost on her philtrum where the upper one had pressed a lipstick tattoo.

I looked at Elgin. He looked serene and didn't. I got a brief glimpse of what was underneath his serenity, the way a bank of clouds at the end of day may rift apart just enough and just long enough to see the bloodred glare of the setting sun. If I ever doubted the Gentleman Scientist was the Gentleman Mad Scientist, that was the end of that.

"Did you know what was going to happen?" I asked.

"No."

Twenty minutes later, at 2:58 PM, Mrs. Gibson began to stir. We went in and Elgin shook her all the way awake. She came from sleep with no inbetween muzziness, just stretched with her arms spread wide as if to embrace the whole world.

G: *That was wonderful. A wonderful nap.*

E: *Good. What did you dream? Do you remember?*

G: *Yes! I went inside. It was my grandfather's house! The same Seth Thomas clock in the front hall, what my sister and I used to call Grampa's tick-tock.*

E: *And the living room?*

G: *It was Grampa's, too. The same chairs, the same couch, slippery horsehair, the same table model TV with the vase on top. I can't believe I could remember it all. But you said you didn't care about that.*

E: *Did you try to lift the floor?*

G (after a long pause): *Yes . . . I got it a little way . . .*

E: *What did you see?*

G: *Darkness.*

E: *The cellar, then.*

G (after a long pause): *I don't think so. I put it down. The floor. It was heavy.*

E: *Anything else? When you lifted the floor?*

G: *There was a bad smell. A stink. (Long pause) Stench.*

That evening I went down to the beach and Elgin was on the bench and I sat down beside him.

"Did you transcribe your notes, William?" Clicking his lighter open and closed.

"I will tonight. What was in that beaker?"

"Nothing remarkable. Flurazepam. Not even a clinical dose. Very diluted."

"No drug would do what we saw."

"No. But it rendered her suggestible. I told her what to do and she did it. Accessed the reality beneath the dream, if you will. Assuming there is such a thing, reality being what it is. Or isn't."

"What it did to her teeth . . ."

"Yes." The serenity was back. "Remarkable, wouldn't you say? Proof. The Polaroids show it, in case you think we were sharing a hallucination."

"The idea never crossed my mind. What are you doing?"

"*Now* you ask."

"Yes. Now I ask."

"Have you considered existence, William? Really considered it? Because few people ever do."

"Considered it and seen the end of it."

"You mean in the war."

"Yes."

"But wars are human affairs. In relation to the universe, which encompasses all existence, including time both backward and forward, human wars mean no more than those you might see in an anthill with a magnifying glass. Earth is our anthill. The stars we see at night are just eternity's first inch. Someday telescopes, perhaps hurled into space as far as the moon or Mars or beyond, will show us galaxies beyond galaxies, nebulae hidden behind other nebulae, wonders unthoughtof, on and on to the edge of the universe, beyond which another universe may await. And consider the other end of that spectrum."

He laid his Zippo aside and bent over and picked up a fistful of beachsand and let it run through his fingers.

"Ten thousand tiny flecks of the earth in my fist, maybe twenty thousand or even fifty. Each one composed of a billion or trillion or a googleplex of atoms and protons, whirling their courses. What holds it all together? What is the binding force?"

"Do you have a theory?"

"No, but now I have a way to look. You saw it today. So did I. Suppose our dreams are a barrier between us and this neverending matrix of existence? That binding force? Suppose it's conscious? Suppose we could defeat that barrier not by trying to go through it but by looking under it, like a kid peeking under a circus tent to see the show going on inside?"

"Barriers are usually there for a reason."

He laughed as if I'd said something funny.

"Do you want to see God?"

"I want to see what's there. I may fail, but what we saw today makes me believe that success is possible. The floor of her dream was too heavy for her. I have eleven more test subjects. One of them may be stronger."

I should have left then.

We had two more subjects in July. One was a female carpenter named Melissa Grant. She dreamed of the house but couldn't get inside. The door was locked against her, she said. One was the owner of a bookstore in New Gloucester. He said his shop was probably going to go under but he wasn't ready to give up and eight hundred dollars would pay for another month's rent and a shipment of books few people would buy. He slept for two hours while Debussy played and said he didn't dream of the house at all but of his father, dead for twenty years. He said he dreamed they went fishing. Elgin gave him his check and sent him on his way. There was one more July appointment on our schedule, a man named Norman Bilson, but he never showed up.

On the 1st of August a man named Hiram Gaskill came to the house at the end of Lake Road. He was a construction worker who had been laid off. He kicked away his boots and took the couch. He said "Let's get to it" and drank down the contents of the beaker with no questions. He looked at the picture and at first I didn't think the drug was going to work on him, he was a big fellow, probably close on to two-seventy, but eventually he dropped off and began to snore. Elgin stood in his usual position beside me, bent forward vulturelike so his nose almost touched the glass and his breath fogged it. Nothing happened for almost an hour. Then the snoring stopped and still sleeping Gaskill groped for the pen resting on the open pad of Blue Horse paper. He wrote something on it without opening his eyes.

"Note that," Elgin said, but I already had, not in Gregg but in plain: *At 3:17 PM Gaskill writes for approx. 15 secs. Drops pen. Sleeping again now & snoring again.*

At 3:33 Gaskill awoke on his own and sat up and swung his legs off the couch. We went in and Elgin asked him what he had dreamed.

"Nothing. Sorry, Mr. Elgin. Do I still get the money?"

"Yes. That's all right. Are you sure you remember nothing?"

"No, but it was a good nap."

I was looking at the pad of paper and asked him if he'd served.

"No, sir, I did not. Went to the physical and they said I had high blood. Take pills for it now."

Elgin looked at the pad and what was written there. When Gaskill was gone in his old pickup truck, leaving a blue cloud of exhaust for the wind to fritter away, Elgin tapped the single line which had been neatly printed even though the man running the pen had his eyes closed. That look of excitement, of *triumph*, was in his face.

"This isn't his writing. Nothing like it."

He laid down Gaskill's release form beside the tablet. The name and address on the form were in the hand of someone who wrote seldom and found it laborious. Although we had background on Elgin's subjects no more than Elgin had actual scientific equipment to test his subjects with, Gaskill's laborious printing suggested to me a man who had only completed as much schooling as the state of Maine required, and that unwillingly except perhaps for the shop courses. The printing on the pad was neat and precise, although there were no diacritical marks over the words where they should have been and the spelling was not correct. It was as if Gaskill had been writing what he heard. Taking dictation like any steno would do. Which raised the question of who had been giving it.

"Vietnamese? It is, isn't it. It's why you asked if he served."

"Yes."

Of course it was. *Mat trang da day cua ma guy.*

"What does it say?"

"It says the moon is full of demons."

That evening when I went down to the water, Elgin was on the bench, again smoking. The water was gray as slate. There were no boats on it. The sky was crowded with thunderheads coming in from the west. I sat down. Without looking at me, Elgin said, "That message was meant for you."

Of course it was.

"He knew you were in Vietnam. More. He knew you knew the language."

"Something knew."

Lightning hit the water a mile out, electrocuting whatever fish happened to be near the surface. They would float in and feed the gulls. The rain would come soon. The hills on the far side of Dark Score had disappeared behind a gray membrane that would soon descend on our side.

"It could be time to stop. Something on the other side of your barrier is saying don't fuck with me."

He shook his head without looking away from the coming rain. "Not at all. We're on the verge. I feel it. I know it." Now he turned. "Please don't leave me, William. I need your skills more than ever. If I publish, I will need your raw notes, not just the photos and the transcriptions. And you are a witness."

Not just a witness. It had been me that Gaskill, or whatever came into Gaskill, had singled out. Not Elgin. The Gentleman Scientist was fooling with something dangerous and knew it but either wasn't willing to stop or couldn't and in the end those things come to the same. I *could* stop which made me a fool to go on, but there was another factor. Something had happened to me. I had grown curious. It was welcome and dreadful in equal measure. It was a feeling and in my world those had been in short supply. You see a man with his legs gone and his face sliding off even as he screams in agony, you see his teeth on his shirt like a barbaric necklace and know you were standing where he got it only seconds before and it stuns your feelings the way hitting a rabbit with a junk of firewood will stun it and lay it out flat on the ground, sides heaving but eyes far away, and when those feelings start to return you see the possibility that your humanity isn't as gone as you thought it was.

"I'll stay."

"Thank you, William." He reached out and squeezed my shoulder. "Thank you."

The rain came, mixed with hailstones that stung like bees. He went back to the big house and I went back to the small one. Hail rattled on the windows. The wind. I dreamed that night of a hollow moon filled with demons eating each other alive. Eating themselves alive like the worm ouroboros. I could see the red house below the hollow moon. The green door.

We saw two more before the end came. The sixth, a woman named Annette Crosby, screamed herself awake. When she calmed down she said she dreamed of the red house and opening the green door and then remembered nothing except for darkness and wind and a foul odor and a bodiless voice that spoke a word that sounded like *tantullah* or *tamtusha*. It filled her with horror. She said she would not dream of that house again for another eight hundred dollars. Or eight thousand. But she took Elgin's check. Why not? She earned it.

Then came Burt Devereaux, a teacher of mathematics at Saint Dominic Academy in Lewiston. He filled in the form and before signing asked Elgin several questions, more than the others had, about the "light hypnotic" he would have to take. Elgin answered these questions to Devereaux's satisfaction. He signed the form, took his place on the couch, and quaffed the beaker of clear liquid. I took my seat before the oneway glass with my pad on my knee. Elgin sat behind the desk and started the music. In the testing room Mr. Devereaux was studying the picture of the red house with the green door. Eventually his eyes began to slip closed and the picture began to sag in his hand. It was like every one of our other test runs until it wasn't.

*   *   *

437

I was in my chair. Elgin was in his place beside me. Ten minutes passed. Eyes closed, Devereaux reached for the pad and the pen resting on the upturned page, then dropped his hand. It began to clench and unclench. The other hand rose up, hesitated, then moved swiftly. I wrote in plain *3:29 PM, Dev raises right hand & makes a fist & hits self in cheek.*

"He's trying to wake himself up," I said.

Devereaux began to shiver all over like a man suffering a fit of ague. His legs jittered and scissored. His back arched. His midsection rose from the couch and thumped down and rose again. His feet tapdanced and he began to make a sound, *mump-mump-mump*, as if his lips were spitstuck and he was trying to get them open to articulate.

"We need to wake him up."

"Wait."

"Jesus, Elgin."

"Wait."

The Polaroids flashed. Their cunning inbred motors whirred. Pictures fluttered to the floor in our part and his part, already starting to develop. His eyelids began to bulge until the eyes beneath must have swelled almost to the size of golfballs as if from an infusion of hydrostatic fluid. The lids didn't open naturally but split apart. Devereaux's eyes had been gray. The eyes which continued to protrude from their sockets were dead black. They grew like tumors out of his face. Elgin's hand was clamped on my shoulder but I barely felt it. Neither of us asked what was happening, not because we couldn't believe it but because we could. We might as well have been witnessing a locomotive emerging from a fireplace. Devereaux screamed and his eyeballs split and fine tendrils wavered up like dandelion filaments only black. There was no breeze to blow them, but they bent toward the oneway glass, as if sensing us.

"Oh my God." Elgin.

The Polaroids flashed. The black tendrils separated from the black orbs that had given them birth and drifted toward us, at first in a small cloud but beginning to melt and disappear as they came.

"I need them!" Elgin shouted. "I *need* them! Proof! Proof!"

He started for the door. I grabbed him and held him back. He struggled but I was stronger. I wasn't going to let him go in there, not because I cared for him enough to save him from himself but because I didn't want him to open that door and let any of them out.

The split black eyeballs began to retract toward Devereaux's face like a film run in reverse. He said *mump-mump-mump.* The crotch of his pants darkened as his bladder let go. The split black eyeballs healed themselves, first there was a seam and then that was gone and they were smooth again, only bulging from his face in small knobs like those you sometimes see on an old tree. Then they pulled back in and his eyes closed and Devereaux gave a galvanic twist at the waist and fell on the floor. Elgin's white shirt ripped as he tore free of my grasp. He was out the door and around the partition and in the other half. He knelt and got his arms around Devereaux's shoulders.

"Help me, William! Help me!"

If Devereaux was dead, this would be partly on me and even in my shock I knew it. Saying I was a witness rather than an accomplice wouldn't fly. So I went around the partition and into the test room and asked Elgin if he was breathing.

He leaned forward, then winced back. "Yes, but his breath is *foul.*"

It wasn't only his breath that was foul. His sphincter had let go. I looked around. Not all the black tendrils were gone. Some of whatever Devereaux had brought back from the red house when he picked up the living room floor, perhaps flying up at him from the darkness and infecting him with one indrawn breath, was still floating in the far corner of the room under one of the speakers. I watched them. If they moved toward us I intended to flee and let the Gentleman Scientist fend for himself. This was his experiment, after all. Yet even then in those endless moments I thought of far stars beyond the reach of any telescope and the fuming interiors of a hundred thousand grains of sand and knew it was also my experiment. I hadn't left. I could have but I hadn't. I had felt the returning tingle of something approximating a normal human being, whatever that is and assuming there is such a thing. Like a limb that has been slept on and fallen asleep and begins to awake. On the hook, we used to say in the boondocks. Or FIDO. Fuck it, drive on.

"We need to get him out of here." I pointed to the black tendrils. They were stirring lightly, restlessly. I think they were watching us.

"I need a sample."

"You need to think about how you would look in a jail suit. Help me."

We lifted him, Elgin taking his ankles and me taking the rest of him. We got him out the door and across the hall and into the living room. We laid him on the floor with drool running from both sides of his mouth. I went back and shut the double doors to the former dining room, shutting in those black things from the other place, the place under the floor, unless they could waft under the doorjamb and in with us. I hoped the rest of them would just disappear. If Elgin wanted to fuck with them, that was on him. I was done.

But first there was the matter of Devereaux. I told Elgin to help me sit him up so what was left of him wouldn't choke. We lifted his top half, Elgin on one side, me on the other, our hands meeting and clasping behind Devereaux's back. Blackish-red tears ran from the corners of his eyes. Blood and something else. I didn't want to know what the something else was. I slapped his cheek and bent to the ear on my side and told him to wake up, snap out of it, afraid of what his eyes would look like if he did.

His eyes opened. They were bloodshot and gray as they had been but empty of understanding. Elgin snapped his fingers in front of his face and nothing changed. I darted my fingers at his eyes and nothing changed. He was a breathing mansized doll.

"Oh my God, will he come back?"

"I don't know. Will he? You're the scientist."

Elgin raised one of Devereaux's hands. It only hung there until he put it down again.

"We'll give it an hour," he said.

We gave it two. Most of the black tendrils were gone by then but there were yet a few and Elgin donned nitrile gloves and a facemask from one of his desk drawers and collected them in a plastic bag. I tried to stop him but he wouldn't listen. I thought they might melt away in his hand but they didn't. One of them curled around his gloved forefinger and he had to detach it by scraping along the inside of the bag.

"You're a fool to mess with those things," I said, and he repeated "Proof."

It wasn't good to be chained to him as I now was. The teacher of mathematics had become a drooling mannequin who showed no signs of coming back and I had to deal with that, not for Elgin but for myself. At least the former teacher and present idiot wasn't married with children.

I thought I am on the hook.

I thought Fuck it. Drive on.

"Did you give him the check?"

"What? No. I always keep the check until after the run is complete and they're ready to go home. You know that."

"Burn it. He never came. Like the other one. Bilson."

What a way to wake up to the world.

I got his keys out of a pissdamp pocket. We got him out to his car carrying him like a sack of laundry that's still wet and heavy and put him in the passenger seat. He leaned forward and put his forehead on the Chevy's dashboard as if praying to Allah. I told Elgin to push him back and I fastened the seatbelt. Not all cars had them but this one did. It was a three-point harness, the kind with a chest strap, and that held him more or less upright, although his head was down with his chin on his chest. I thought that was all right, anybody who saw him might think he was asleep. One of those black filaments came out of his nose and floated toward me but Elgin was still wearing his nitrile gloves. He snatched it out of the air and blew it away. I wondered if there were more inside Devereaux.

"What are you going to do with him?"

"I don't know."

I got in the Chevy and drove away back down Lake Road. I looked in the rearview mirror and saw Elgin standing in his driveway and watching.

I drove with the windows open and the air conditioner on full. I was wearing a pair of Elgin's nitrile gloves, had been since I got in the car. Twice more black things came out of his nose and once from his gaping mouth but the moving air took them out the passenger window. I drove in the direction of Lewiston-Auburn but had no intention of going that far. I knew where he lived, his Minot Avenue address had been on the release form, but there was no way I was going to drive him into the Twin Cities, not with still having to get him over into the driver's seat. I needed a quiet place to do that.

I was on Route 119 in Waterford when I came to the Wolf Claw rest area. In the heat of the day no one was there. I parked under the trees and went around to the passenger side and opened the door and unclipped the seatbelt and Devereaux went leaning forward until his forehead was resting on the dashboard again. I wished I had asked the Gentleman Scientist for one of his masks, but what good would covering my mouth and nose do? The black filaments had come out of Devereaux's eyes; they could just as easily go into mine. I would just have to hope they were all gone. I hadn't seen any for the last ten miles or so but they might have come out and flown away through the open window while I was watching the road.

I tilted him toward me and caught him and pulled him out of the car and dragged him around the hood. He was wearing loafers and one of them came off. His blank eyes stared raptly into the sun. I got him behind the wheel but it took time and wasn't easy. I hadn't expected it to be. He was breathing but dead inside and I knew from Nam that dead people are heavier. They shouldn't be but they are. Gravity is greedy for the dead and wants them in the ground. Just my opinion but others share it.

He tilted forward again and I grabbed him by the backhair and pulled him up before his forehead could hit the horn. I fastened his seatbelt and his head sank until his chin was on his chest. I thought that was all right. I hoped no one would come until I got the righteous fuck out of there. I put the keys in the ignition and closed the door and started down Route 119. I had walked about a quarter of a mile before I remembered the shoe and went back. Somebody will be there by now, I thought, someone who looked in the open window of the Chevy with the St. Dom's sticker on the bumper and said hey mister wake up and hey mister are you all right and by the way mister what are those black things coming out of your nose?

But no one was there. I picked up the loafer and opened the driver's door again and put it on his foot. Then I brushed out the tracks going around the front of the car, the ones his heels had made, and set off walking again. About five miles down the road, my shadow now starting to drag out long behind me, I came to a combination general store and gas station with a phonebooth on the side. I had enough change in my pocket so I didn't have to go into the store where someone might see and remember me. That probably would have been all right but by then I was thinking like a thief or a murderer. I called Elgin, wanting a ride. Elgin didn't answer and I had come alive enough to feel scared. I had a plan now, one that might get me and the Gentleman Scientist in the clear, but plans change. I kept thinking of him saying proof, proof. I kept thinking he was crazy and then I thought of how I knew that. I knew it all along but said fuck it and drove on.

I turned back the other way, my shadow now drawing out longer and longer before me rather than behind. A car came and I stuck out my thumb. It passed me by. So did the next one but then came a pickup that slowed and stopped. The man driving had a weathered red face under a gray brushcut.

"How far you going?"

"Castle Rock. It's where my father lives."

"Well hop in. Did you serve? You got that look about you and you're the right age for the current fuckadiddle."

"Yes, sir, I did."

"So did I. About ten thousand years ago. Semper fi if you like it and semper fi if you don't."

He let out the clutch with a jerk and talked about Korea and asked me what about those peaceniks. I said that's right. He said ship them all out there to Haight-Fucksberry and I said that's right. He offered me a beer from behind the seat. I took it and when he said "Take another, sojer" I did. Half an hour later he pulled over to the curb of Main Street in the Rock.

"We're going to beat those gook sonsofbitches."

"Yes, sir."

"Take care of yourself, son."

"That's the plan."

Off he went. By then it was evening and more thunderheads building up in the west. I walked the six miles out to Lake Road. By the time I got there the rain was beating its way across the lake again. Lightning flashed. Thunder rolled. The smell of ozone in the air like an unburned burning. My car was still parked next to Elgin's Mercedes. I went inside. He hadn't turned on the lights and the hall was a bowl of shadows.

"Elgin?"

I got no answer. The living room was empty, the books knocked over. *Beyond the Wall of Sleep* was faceup. On the coffee table was a glass ashtray, a pack of Winstons, and his Zippo. I took the Zippo and put it in my pocket. I went to the former dining room, thought about going into the room with the couch, fortunately thought better of it. I went into the room with the desk instead and sat in my chair and looked through the oneway glass. What was left of Elgin the Gentleman Scientist was on the couch. Polaroids scattered all around. The beaker shattered among the photographs. His head was in what looked like a black sack. Some of the photographs, those that were faceup, showed it forming over his sleeping face. The picture of the red house with the green door was also on the floor and so was the plastic bag into which he had put his samples. Now the bag was empty. The black sack on his head was made of those filaments. It sucked in and out from what was left of his mouth as he breathed. I thought about him telling me of endless universes both out there and below our very feet. I thought of a face sliding down a man's skull. I thought of a helicopter on fire sinking into the very sea of napalm it had created. I thought of putting Devereaux's shoe back on his foot. I thought of all the unknown and unknowable nether creations that might exist beneath a barrier of dreams. I thought that yes, plans change. Elgin could no longer get out of this but maybe I still could.

Some of the black filaments saw me and rose from the black bag and crossed the room and plastered themselves on the glass. More came. And more. I watched as they squirmed around until they made my name: WILLIAM DAVIS.

*   *   *

There was a gas stove in the kitchen. I turned on all the burners and blew out the blue gas flowers one by one. I turned on the oven and opened the oven door. A pilot light came on in there and I blew that out, too. As I created this nascent gasbomb I looked constantly over my shoulder for the black filaments. I was in *sự kinh hãi.* Terror. I was in *rùng rợn.* Horror. I closed the windows. I closed the doors. I went around to the guest house and gathered up my belongings in my dufflebag and one suitcase. I put them in the trunk of my car. Then I went back to the stoop and waited, clicking the top of the lighter up and down. Lightning panfried the lake and thunder rolled. After about ten minutes the rain started, at first just pattering down, the storm's foreplay. I opened the door. The gas was a stench. I flicked the Zippo and got a flame and tossed it and ran for my car. I got there and had just decided nothing was going to happen when the kitchen exploded. The rain came in a deluge as I drove away. In my rearview I saw the house burning like a candle under a black sky cut with lightning. There were houses and summer cottages on Lake Road but no one was out in the storm and if anyone was looking out a window they would have seen nothing but an amorphous car-shaped blob behind headlights. I drove out of Castle Rock and into Harlow. The rain slackened, then stopped. In my rearview mirror, just before the sun sank behind the mountains in New Hampshire, I saw a rainbow. Then the sun was gone and the rainbow clicked off like a neon sign. I stayed the night at a motel in Gates Falls and drove to Portland the next morning, to the roominghouse where I had been living when I worked at Temp-O. There was a rooms for rent sign in the front window. I rang the bell and Mrs. Blake answered.

"You again."

"Yes. Sign says you've got a room."

"That's right, but not your room. It's on the third floor and there's no air conditioning."

"Is it cheaper than the one on the second?"

"No."

"I'll take it."

*   *   *

445

The next day I went back to Temp-O and got rehired. I had no plans to spend very long working for Mrs. Frobisher, but I wanted to have a job when the cops came. Pearson was in the break room. So was Diane. There was a talk show on the TV. Diane gave me a crooked little smile and said, "Once more into the breach, dear friends." Pearson was reading the paper, sections piled up around his shoes. He took one look at me and raised the paper again.

"So you came back," I said to Diane.

"So did you. Didn't work out at Elgin's house?"

"It did for awhile, then didn't. He started getting strange when his experiments didn't work out."

"And here we are. All roads lead to Temp-O."

Mrs. Frobisher came in. "Who wants a depo at Brune and Cathcart?" She didn't wait for an answer, just pointed to a new woman I didn't know. "You, Janelle. Chop-chop."

Pearson was done with the local section of the paper so I picked it up. On the bottom of page 1B was a story headlined CASTLE ROCK MAN DIES IN GAS EXPLOSION AT DARK SCORE LAKE. It said the case was being investigated as an accident or possible suicide. It said that because of heavy rain, the fire hadn't spread.

I said, "Holy shit, my last boss is dead," and showed Diane the story.

"Bad luck for him, good luck for you." She read the story. "Was he suicidal?"

I had to think that over. "I don't know."

The next day I had court. When I went back to the roominghouse, two cops were waiting for me in the parlor. One was in uniform, the other was a detective. They introduced themselves and asked how long I had worked for Elgin. I told them about a month. I told them what I had told Diane, that Elgin started to get dinky-dau when his experiments hadn't been panning out, so I left. Yes, I had been living in the guest house but moved out when I quit the job. No, I hadn't been there when his house blew up. They asked me if I knew a man named Burton Devereaux. I said I knew the name, it had been on Elgin's list of test subjects, but not the man. I had never seen him. The detective gave me his card and asked me to call him if I thought of anything. I said I would. I asked if the detective thought Elgin had killed himself.

"Would that surprise you, Mr. Davis?"

"Not a lot."

"He turned on the gas stove and we found a melted chunk of lighter on what was left of the kitchen floor, so what do you think?"

What I thought was a smart detective might have wondered if they found the remains of the Zippo in the kitchen, how Elgin could be on his subjects' couch in the dining room. But I guess he wasn't that smart.

I worked at Temp-O until September, then quit and drove to Nebraska. No reason for Nebraska, it was just where I went. I got temporary work on a farm, one of those big agribusiness spreads, and the foreman kept me on after the harvest season passed. I'm here now. It's snowing a blizzard. I-80 is shut down. I sit at this desk thinking of galaxies beyond galaxies. In a little while I will close this notebook and turn out the lights and go to bed. The sound of the wind will lull me off to sleep. Sometimes I dream of the boondocks and men screaming in fire. Sometimes women screaming in fire. Children. *Nahn tu*, they cry. *Nahn tu, nahn tu.* Those are the good dreams. You might not believe it but it's true. In the bad dreams I am standing outside a red house with a green door. If I tried that door, it would open. I know this and know one day I will go in and kneel at the living room doorway. *Nahn tu*, I will cry, *nahn tu*, but when this final dream comes there will be no mercy. Not for me.

Thinking of Cormac McCarthy and Evangeline Walton

THE ANSWER MAN

1

Phil Parker had the great good fortune—or great ill luck—to meet the Answer Man three times during his life. On the first of these occasions, in 1937, he was twenty-five, engaged to be married, and the possessor of a law degree on which the ink had almost dried. He was also caught on the horns of a dilemma so fierce that his eyes watered each time he thought of it.

Nonetheless, it had to be thought about, and resolved in one way or the other. To that end, he left his apartment in Boston and came up to the small New Hampshire town of Curry, where his parents owned a summer home. Here he planned to spend a decision-making weekend. He sat on the deck overlooking the lake with a sixpack of beer on Friday night. He thought about his dilemma, slept on it, woke up on Saturday morning with a hangover and no decision made.

On Saturday night he sat on the deck overlooking the lake with a quart bottle of Old Tyme ginger ale. He woke up on Sunday morning with no decision made, but with no hangover—a plus, but not enough. When he got back to Boston that evening, Sally Ann would be waiting to find out what he had decided.

So he climbed into his old Chevrolet after breakfast and went motoring along New Hampshire back roads on a gorgeous, sunshiny October day. The trees were in full autumn flame, and Phil pulled over several times to admire various vistas. He reflected that there was no beauty like New England beauty at the end of the cycle.

As morning drew on toward noon, he scolded himself for dillydallying. Getting drunk on beer hadn't solved his problem, sipping ginger ale hadn't solved it, and mooning over fall foliage wouldn't do it, either. And yet he suspected that his absorption in the scenery was quite a bit more than communing with nature. It was either part of the solution or his mind's effort to squirm away from a decision that would—one way or the other—set himself and his fiancée on a lifetime course.

It's part of growing up, he told himself.

Yes, but the idea of choosing one single thing was abhorrent to him. He knew it had to be done, but that didn't mean he had to like it. Wasn't it a little like picking the prison cell you wanted to spend your sentence in? Your *life* sentence? That was silly and overblown . . . yet it wasn't.

His dilemma was simple and clear-cut, as most of the real ball-breakers are: where was he to practice law? Each choice was full of ramifications.

Phil's father was a senior partner in an old Boston law firm of the white shoe variety—Warwick, Lodge, Nestor, Parker, Allburton, and Frye. Sally Ann's father was a senior partner in the same firm. John Parker and Ted Allburton had been best friends since college. They had married less than a year apart, each serving as the other's best man. Phil Parker had been born in 1912, Sally Ann in 1914. They were playmates growing up, and maintained their liking for each other even during that difficult period in early adolescence when boys and girls tend to express a public disdain for the opposite sex, no matter what they may feel privately.

The parents on both sides might have been the least surprised people on earth when Phil and Sally Ann began to "keep company," as the saying was in those days, but neither couple quite dared to hope that their children's affection would survive four years of separation: Vassar for Sally Ann, Harvard for Phil. When it did, the parents were delighted, as were Phil and Sally Ann (of course). Love wasn't the problem. At least not directly, although love played a part (as it almost always does).

Curry was the problem, that small town near the Maine–New Hampshire state line where the Parkers and Allburtons had summer homes on adjoining lakefront lots.

Phil had been in love with Curry at least as long as he had been in love with Sally Ann, and now it seemed he might have to choose between them. He wanted to hang out his shingle in Curry, although it boasted only two thousand year-round residents. The downtown area, where Route 23 crossed Route 111, consisted of a restaurant, two gas stations, a hardware store, the A&P, and the town hall. There was no bar and no movie theater. For those amenities you had to go to North Conway, quite some distance away. There was an elementary school (in those days called a grammar), but no high school. Curry teens made their glum bus ride to Patten High, ten miles away.

There was also no lawyer in town. Phil could be the first. The Parkers and Allburtons thought he was crazy to even consider Curry. John Parker was hurt and angry that his son was thinking of not joining the firm, where his grandfather had been a senior partner back in the horse-and-buggy days. He also found it difficult to believe, he said, that a young man who had graduated *cum laude* from Harvard Law School would even consider practicing in the wilds of New Hampshire . . . which he called the *forgotten* wilds of New Hampshire (sometimes, after a cocktail or two, the *misbegotten* wilds).

"Your clients will be farmers suing each other over cows breaking down fences," John Parker said. "Your biggest cases will involve poaching or fender-benders on Route 23. You can't be serious." But the dismay on his face made it clear that he knew his son might be.

Ted Allburton was even angrier than his old friend. He had one special reason to be angry other than the ones John had already voiced to his son: Phil would not be committing a wanton act of destruction upon his future alone. He was planning to take a hostage, that hostage being his daughter.

When Phil persisted, Allburton had drawn a line in the dirt, one that was deep and harsh. "I'll forbid the marriage."

"Sir," Phil had replied, keeping his voice level and (he hoped) polite, "I love Sally Ann. She says she loves me. And she's of age."

"You mean she could marry you without my consent." Ted was a big, broad-shouldered man partial to suspenders (which he called braces). His blue eyes could be warm, but that day they'd been like flints. "That's true, she could. And I like you, Phil. Always have. But

451

if you were to do what you're considering, any marriage would take place without my blessing. And that, I believe, would make her very unhappy. In fact, I rather doubt she'll do it."

Phil had looked into those flinty eyes and understood Ted Allburton was understating the case. He was *sure* Sally Ann wouldn't do it.

Phil didn't know if she would or not, especially if Mr. Allburton decided against a cash dowry. Phil knew Sal understood what he wanted more clearly than their elders, who either wouldn't or couldn't understand at all, and he knew part of her wanted it, too. After all, she'd also grown up spending her summers and the occasional snowy and magical Christmas in Curry.

She was willing to listen when Phil told her that he believed Curry, and all of southern New Hampshire, was going to grow. "It'll be slow getting started," he had told her that summer, when he still had hopes of bringing his parents onboard with his tentative plan, if not the Allburtons. "The depression's not really going to end for another seven years or so . . . unless there really is a war. My dad thinks there will be, but I don't. The growth is going to start in the North Conway area and spread from there. By 1950 there'll be more highways. More highways mean more tourists, and more tourists mean more businesses. The new people will come from Massachusetts and New York, Sal, and they'll come by the thousands. *Tens* of thousands! To swim in clean lakes in the summer, to watch the leaves change in the fall, to ski in the winter. Your father thinks I'll live poor and die poor. I think he's wrong."

Unfortunately it wasn't 1950, or even 1945. It was 1937, and he hadn't been able to bring any of them around. He hadn't—not yet, anyway—dared to ask Sally to commit, which might mean turning her back on her family . . . or having them turn their backs on her. It seemed horribly unfair, but to leave her dangling on the horns of *his* dilemma was unfair, too. And so he had told her he was going to come up here, spend the weekend, and come to a decision. Either the firm on Commonwealth Avenue or the little wooden office behind the Curry town hall and next to the Sunoco. Boston or Curry. The lady or the tiger. And so far he had decided . . .

"Absolutely nothing," he muttered. "Gosh Almighty!"

He was on Route 111 now, and headed back toward the lake. His stomach was talking to him about lunch, but it was doing it in low and rather respectful tones, as if it was also abashed by his inability to decide.

His greatest wish was that he could make his father and mother understand that the firm was just not *right* for him, that he would be a square peg in a round hole. The fact that the firm had been right for his father and grandfather (not to mention the Hon. Theodore Allburton, Esq., and *his* father) did not make it right for him. He had tried in every way he could think of to express to them that he might be capable of doing perfectly adequate work at the double brownstone on Comm Ave and still feel desperately unhappy there. Would that unhappiness seep into his home life? It could, and probably would.

"Nonsense," his father had replied. "Once you get broken in, you'll love it. I did, and you will. A fresh challenge every day! No suits in small claims court over broken plows and stolen farm wagons!"

Broken in. What a phrase! It had haunted him through all this spring and summer. It was what you did with horses. Broke them in, worked them until they became nags, then shipped them off to the glue factory. He felt the metaphor, while melodramatic, was also realistic.

His mother, who at least sensed that his distress was real—a true thing—was kinder. "You won't know if the firm is right for you until you've tried it," she said, and that was the most reasonable and seductive reasoning put forward to him in favor of the firm. Because he knew himself.

He had been a very good student of the law. Not good enough to be brilliant, perhaps, but there was no shame in being very good. He wasn't much of a rebel, though, and neither was Sally Ann. If they had been, they wouldn't have been so deeply distressed at the idea of going against the wishes of their parents—they weren't still teenagers, for gosh sake!

If he went to work for the firm, Phil suspected he *would* find aspects of it challenging, and he suspected even more strongly that he would, in time, become *broken in*. His idea of being the first lawyer in a sleepy little town that might someday grow into an affluent large town, possibly even a small city, would recede. Slowly at first, then, as the first strands of gray appeared at his temples, more quickly. In five years it would seem more dream than desire. There would be children and a house to take care of, more hostages to fortune, and each year—hell, each month, each week, each goshdarn *day*—it would be more difficult to turn back.

A lifetime course.

He tried to imagine telling Sally Ann he had settled on Curry. His parents would help them get started (*probably*), even if the Allburtons wouldn't. He had some savings, and so did Sal (not much). It would be hard, but not impossible (perhaps). He suspected Ted Allburton was wrong about his daughter refusing to marry without his blessing, Phil dared to believe he knew Sal better than her father did in that respect, but what would a marriage lacking that blessing be like? Was it fair to either of them to start out with acrimony instead of support?

So his mind swung back and forth—town or city, lady or tiger—as he breasted one of the long hills on Route 111. A bright yellow sign, hand-painted, caught his eye. 2 MILES TO THE ANSWER MAN, it read. Phil grinned, then laughed out loud. *It would be nice if there really was such a guy*, he thought. *I could certainly use a few answers.*

He drove on and passed another sign soon enough. This one was electric blue. ANSWER MAN 1 MILE.

Phil topped another long rise and there, at the bottom of the downgrade, he saw a splash of bright red at the side of the road. As he drew closer he saw it was a large beach umbrella with hanging scalloped sides. There was a table beneath it. A man sat behind it in the shade. Phil thought the set-up looked like the lemonade stands you often passed in the summer. But those were hopeful little kids who had forgotten to add sugar to their puckery brew more often than not, and this wasn't summer but mid-autumn.

More curious than ever, Phil pulled over and got out of his jalopy. "Hello!"

"Hello yourself," the Answer Man responded, equably enough.

He looked to be about fifty. His thinning hair was salt-and-pepper. His face was lined but his eyes were bright and interested and unaided by specs. He wore a white shirt, plain gray slacks, and black shoes. His long-fingered hands were folded neatly on the surface of his table. A bag like a doctor's satchel rested by one foot. He looked like an intelligent fellow, and Phil got no sense of eccentricity about him. He in fact reminded Phil of the dozen or so mid-level and middle-aged lawyers in the firm: solid, respectable men who lacked that final increment of ability which would propel them to partner level. It was that very feeling of comfy corporate normality that made the man's appearance here beneath a bright red umbrella, sitting in the middle of nowhere in particular, so curious.

There was a folding wooden camp chair on the other side of the table. The client's chair, presumably. Three little signs had been set up in a row to face the Answer Man's prospective customers.

THE ANSWER MAN

read the sign in the middle.

$25 PER 5 MINUTES

read the sign on the left.

YOUR FIRST 2 ANSWERS FREE

read the sign on the right.

"What *is* this, exactly?" asked Phil.

The Answer Man fixed him with a look that was ironic but not unfriendly. "You look like a smart young man," he said. "A young man who has been to college, judging by the pennant I see on your car aerial. Harvard, no less! Ten thousand men of Harvard cry for victory today!"

"Right," Phil said, smiling. "For they know that over Eli, fair Harvard holds sway."

The Answer Man smiled back. "Such young fellows as yourself— and girls, and girls—are so used to asking questions that they don't even think about what they are asking. And, since business has been slow this morning, I'm going to do you a favor of not answering that question. Which still leaves you with two free ones, if you want them."

Phil thought that even if the guy had a few screws loose, what he said made perfect sense. He *had* asked a question to which the answer was obvious. For twenty-five bucks, this man would answer questions for five minutes. That was what was going on here. And that was all.

"Well, say—don't you think twenty-five smackers for five minutes' worth of answers is pretty steep? It's no wonder your biz has been on the slow side."

"Well, what is steep? No, don't answer that—you're not the Answer Man, I am. My rates vary according to my location and my prospective customers. I have charged a hundred dollars for five minutes, and on one storied occasion I charged a thousand. One thousand iron men! Yes! But I've also charged as little as a dime. You might say I charge what the traffic will bear. Answers aren't always painful, young man, but correct answers should never come cheap."

Phil opened his mouth to ask if the guy was serious, then closed it again. He could easily imagine the Answer Man saying *Yes I am, and that's your second free question.*

"How would I know the answers you gave me *would* be true and correct?"

"You wouldn't now, but in the course of time, you would," said the Answer Man. "And that's—"

"Two," Phil said. He was grinning widely, enjoying the game. He said, "How much 'course of time' are we talking about?" It was no sooner out than he clapped a hand over his mouth, but too late.

"It's been slow today, so I'm going to give you a third free one," the man behind the table said. "The answer: it varies. Which helps you get to the truth of my profession—if it's the truth you're seeking—not at all. Do you see what I mean about how easy it is to ask questions that don't aid understanding? It devalues the whole process of asking, doesn't it? Of *delving into* matters?"

The Answer Man leaned back in his chair, laced his fingers at the nape of his neck, and gazed at Phil. "I shouldn't be surprised at how unhelpful the questions of smart people can be, having been in this business for as long as I have, yet somehow I still am. It's *loose*. It's *lazy*. I have often wondered if smart people really understand what answers they seek in life. Perhaps they just cruise along on a magic carpet of ego, making assumptions that are often wrong. That's the only reason I can think of as to why they ask such impotent questions."

"Impotent! Really!"

The Answer Man went on as if he hadn't heard. "You asked me how you'd know if my answers were the correct ones. 'True and correct' is how you put it, which was quite nice. So I gave you one for free. If this were the pre-Christmas rush, I would have seen you back into your car and down the road two minutes ago."

The breeze gusted, flapping the scalloped edge of the red umbrella and ruffling the wings of the Answer Man's salt-and-pepper hair. He looked down the empty road with an expression of deep melancholy.

"Fall is a slow time for me, and October is the slowest month of all. I think more people are able to find answers on their own in the autumn."

He continued to look along the black ribbon of road winding its way into the blazing trees for a moment. Then his eyes cleared and he looked back at Phil again.

"Why didn't you just ask me something specific?"

Phil was caught by surprise. "I don't know what you mean."

"What you really wanted to know is if I'm a fake," the Answer Man said. "And if you had asked me what your mother's maiden name was, for example, or the name of your fifth-grade teacher, something I couldn't possibly know unless I am what I say I am, you could have found out." He shook his head. "People without your intellectual advantages usually ask exactly that sort of question. People *with* them—people with a Harvard education, let us say—hardly ever do. It goes back to what I said. Smart people labor under a dual disadvantage: they don't know the answers they need, and they don't know what questions to ask. Education doesn't inculcate mental discipline. You'd think it would, but it's often just the opposite."

"Okay," Phil said (nettled). "What *is* my mother's maiden name?"

"Sorry," the Answer Man said, and tapped the sign that said $25 PER 5 MINUTES. "For that you need to pay."

"You crooked me!" Phil exclaimed humorously. He didn't *feel* humorous; he felt exasperated. With both of them.

"Not at all," the Answer Man replied equably. "You crooked yourself."

Phil was about to remonstrate, then didn't. He could see the man's point. This was a kind of intellectual three-card monte.

"It's been interesting, sir, but twenty-five dollars is a little high for a fellow not long out of college and thinking of starting his own business, so I better get back on the road. It's been fun passing the time of day with you."

As he started away, Phil thought—no, he was sure—that the man sitting beneath the red umbrella would say, *Business being so slow and all, maybe I could give you five minutes for twenty dollars. Hell, I'll make it fifteen. Fifteen simoleons and you can set your mind to rest about all sorts of things.* And when that happened, Phil decided, he was going to pay right up and sit right down. The man was obviously a charlatan, and a screwtip in the bargain, but what the hey. He had a twenty, a ten, and two fives in his wallet. Even with a splurge here, that was more than enough to buy a tank of ethyl for the old jalop' and a good lunch at a roadside restaurant. Phil thought that even hearing the questions—spoken right out loud instead of just knocking around in his head—might go a good way toward solving his problem.

The self-styled Answer Man was right about one thing, Phil thought; getting good answers was mostly a matter of asking good questions.

But all the Answer Man said was, "You drive safe, now."

Phil walked to his car, crossed around the slightly dented front fender, and looked back. He still expected the Answer Man to offer him a cut rate, but the Answer Man seemed to have dismissed Phil entirely—he was looking over toward Vermont, humming and using a small twig to clean beneath his nails.

He intends to let me go, Phil thought, nettled all over again. *Well be damned to him, that's just what I'm going to do.*

He opened the driver's door of his Chevy, hesitated, then closed it again. He took out his wallet. He removed the twenty and one of the fives.

Just hearing the questions out loud, he thought again. *And I don't have to tell anyone that I stooped to paying a fortune teller during a depression.*

Also, it might be worth twenty-five dollars just to see the smug son of a buck groping around and making excuses when Phil *did* ask him for his mother's maiden name.

"Change your mind?" The Answer Man tucked his nail-cleaning twig into the breast pocket of his shirt and picked up his satchel.

Phil smiled and held out his money. "For the next five minutes, *I'm* the one asking the questions."

The Answer Man laughed and pointed a finger at Phil. "Good one, my friend. I *like* you. But before I take your money, there's one rule we need to get straight."

Oh, here it comes, Phil thought. *The hole he intends to wriggle through.*

From his bag, the Answer Man removed what looked like an old-fashioned Big Ben alarm clock. When he set it on the table, Phil saw it was actually a giant-sized stopwatch, with numbers running from 5 to 0.

"I am not a psychiatrist or a counselor. Nor am I a fortune teller, although I'm sure that's what you're thinking. Here's the point: don't try asking me any questions with *should I* in them. No *should I* this, no *should I* that. I answer questions, but I'm not going to solve your problems."

Phil, who had planned to ask the fellow if he should join the firm or open his own office in Curry, started to pull back his money. Then he thought, *If I can't couch my questions in a way that skirts his "should I" prohibition, what kind of a courtroom lawyer will I make?*

"I'm in," Phil said, and handed over his money. Into the Answer Man's bag it went.

"I can't keep calling you son, son. Perhaps you'll give me your name."

"Phil."

"Phil what?"

Phil smiled craftily. "Just Phil. I think that's all you need, considering we're not going to be together long."

"All right, Just Phil. Give me a sec to wind this sucker up. And I see you're wearing your own timepiece, looks like a very fine Bulova, so if you care to check it against mine, feel free."

"Oh, I will," Phil said. "I intend to get my money's worth."

"And so you shall." The Answer Man wound his oversized stopwatch with a clackety-clack sound very similar to the clock Phil had kept by his bedside during his undergraduate years. "Are you ready?"

"Yes." Phil sat down in the client's chair. "But if you can't answer my first question, I'll have my money back double-quick. You'll either give it to me willingly, or I'll take it by force."

"That sounds positively brutal!" the Answer Man said . . . but he laughed when he said it. "I'll ask again: are you ready?"

"Yes."

"So we begin." The Answer Man clicked a lever on the back of his clock, and it began to tick.

"*Your* suggestion: what's my mother's maiden name?"

The Answer Man didn't hesitate. "Sporan."

Phil's mouth dropped open. "How in the *hell* do you know that?"

"I don't want to waste time you've paid for, Phil, but I have to point out that you've asked another question to which you know the answer. I know because I am, ta-da, the Answer Man."

Phil felt like he had been tagged by a right hook. He actually shook his head to clear it. The ticking of the Answer Man's big stopwatch was very loud. The hand was approaching the 4.

"What's my girl's name?"

"Sally Ann Allburton." No hesitation at all.

Phil began to be afraid. He told himself not to be, it was a fine October day, and he was both younger and no doubt stronger than the man on the other side of the table. It must be a trick, had to be, but that didn't make it any less eerie.

"Tempus is fugiting, Phil."

He shook his head again. "Okay. I'm trying to decide if I should—"

The Answer Man wagged a finger at him. "What did I tell you about that word?"

Phil tried to put his thoughts in order. *Mock court*, he thought. *Think of it as mock court. He's the judge. There's been an objection to your line of questioning. How do you get around it?*

"Can you answer questions about future events?"

The Answer Man rolled his eyes. "We've already established that, have we not? I said you'd know if my answers were true and correct *in the course of time*. Such an answer presupposes knowledge of the future. For me there is no future and no past. Everything is happening now."

460

What old-lady-séance bullshit, Phil thought. Meanwhile, the black hand on the big stopwatch was almost to 3.

"Will Sally Ann agree to marry me when I propose?"

"Yes."

"Will we live in Curry? The town down the road?"

"Yes."

The big black hand on the stopwatch reached 3, then passed it.

"Will we be happy?"

"A broad question, and one to which you should also know the answer even at your young age. There will be ups, there will be downs. There will be agreements and there will be arguments. But on measure, yes—the two of you will be happy."

He somehow knew my mother's maiden name, Phil thought. *And Sally's. The rest is just carny fortune teller guesswork. But why? For a measly twenty-five dollars?*

"Tempus still fugits," said the Answer Man.

The ticking of the oversized stopwatch seemed louder than ever. The hand was past 3 and closing the gap on 2. Phil had no sane reason to be relieved by what the Answer Man was telling him, because it was what he wanted to hear, wasn't it? And hadn't he already made his decision about Curry? Wasn't all that "horns of a dilemma" stuff so much self-dramatization? And as for Sal . . . didn't he pretty much know she would marry him even if he did make moving to rural New Hampshire part of the deal? Not for absolute sure, not a hundred per cent, but ninety?

Abruptly he changed direction. "Tell me where my father was born. If you can."

Again the Answer Man did not hesitate. "He was actually born while at sea, on a ship called the *Marybelle*."

Phil again felt like he had been socked in the jaw. It was an old family story, much treasured and often told. Grandfather and Grandmother had been returning to America after a pilgrimage to London, where their parents had been born and lived their early lives. Gram had insisted on making the trip even though she was eight months pregnant by the time they returned. There was a storm. Grandmother's seasickness was so violent it triggered her labor. There was a doctor onboard, and he delivered the infant. No one expected baby John to live, but—wrapped in cotton batting and fed from an eyedropper—he had. And thus, Philip Yeager Parker, Harvard Law School graduate, became possible.

He started to ask again how the man on the other side of the table— hands still neatly folded—could know such a thing, then didn't. The reply would be the same: *Because I am the Answer Man.*

Questions crammed his mind like a panicked crowd trying to escape a burning building. The stopwatch hand reached 2 and passed it. The ticking seemed louder than ever.

The Answer Man waited, hands folded.

"Will Curry prosper the way I think it will?" Phil blurted.

"Yes."

What else? What else?

"Sally's father . . . and her mother, I suppose . . . will they come around to us?"

"Yes. In time."

"How long?"

The Answer Man seemed to calculate briefly as the single hand on his clock reached 1. He said, "Seven years."

Phil's heart sank. Seven years was a lifetime. He could tell himself the Answer Man had plucked that number out of thin air, but he no longer believed it.

"Your time grows short, Just Phil."

He could see that for himself, but he couldn't think of another question except *how long will I live* and the concomitant question, *how long will Sally Ann live.* Did he want to know either of those things? He did not.

But he didn't want to waste his remaining forty or fifty seconds, so he asked the only thing that came to mind. "My father says there's going to be a war. I say there won't be. Which of us is right?"

"He is."

"Will America be in it?"

"Yes."

"How long before we're in it?"

"Four years and two months."

He was down to twenty seconds now, maybe a little more.

"Will *I* be in it?"

"Yes."

"Will I be hurt?"

"No."

But that wasn't the right question. It left a loophole.

"Will I be killed?"

The big stopwatch reached zero and went off with a *BRRRANG* sound. The Answer Man silenced it.

"You asked that question just before the alarm, so I'll answer. No, Just Phil, you will not be killed."

Phil sat back in his chair and let out a breath. "I don't know how you did that, sir, but it was very intense. I have to believe it was a shuck and jive, you must have known I was coming, got some background, but you certainly earned your twenty-five smacks."

The Answer Man only smiled.

"But *I* didn't know exactly where I was going or what road I was going to take . . . so how could *you*?"

No reply. Of course not. His five minutes were up.

"You know what? I feel . . . weird. Swimmy."

The world seemed to be going away. The Answer Man was still sitting at his table, but he appeared to be withdrawing. As if on rails. Grayness began to encroach on Phil's field of vision. He raised his hands to his eyes to clear them, and gray became black.

When Phil came to, he was behind the wheel of his Chevrolet, parked on the shoulder of Route 111. His watch said it was 1:20. *I passed out. First time in my life, but don't they say there's a first time for everything?*

Passed out, yes. Pulled over first, thank God, and turned off the engine. Probably from hunger. He'd had six bottles of beer on Friday night, and he supposed there were calories and at least some nourishment in beer, but he hadn't had much to eat yesterday or today, so it made a degree of sense. But when you passed out—as opposed to being asleep—did you have dreams? Because he'd had a doozy.

He could remember every detail: the scalloped red umbrella, the big stopwatch (or maybe you called that sort of thing a stopclock), the Answer Man's salt-and-pepper hair. He could remember every question and every answer.

It was no dream.

"Yes," he said aloud. "Yes it was. Had to be. He knew Mother's maiden name and where Father was born in the dream because *I* knew those things."

He got out of his car and walked slowly to where the Answer Man had been. The table was gone, the chairs were gone, but he could see marks in the soft earth where they had been. The grayness started to come back and he slapped himself hard, first on one cheek and then on the other. Then he kicked at the dirt until the marks were gone.

"This never happened," he told the empty road and the blazing trees. He said it again: *"This never happened."*

He got back behind the wheel, started his engine, and pulled onto the highway. He decided he wouldn't tell Sally Ann about passing out; it would worry her, and she would probably insist that he see a doctor. It was just hunger, that was all. Hunger and the most vivid dream he'd ever had. Two hamburgs, a Coca-Cola, and a piece of apple pie would put him right, and he was pretty sure there was a greasy spoon in Ossipee, not five miles down the road.

One good thing had come from his odd roadside fugue. No, actually two things. He would tell her he meant to hang out his shingle in the little town of Curry. Would she still give him her hand in marriage?

Parents be damned.

Phil Parker and Sally Ann Allburton were married in Boston's Old South Church on April 29th, 1938. Ted Allburton walked his daughter down the aisle. This walk, which he had at first refused to make, was a result of his wife's diplomacy and his daughter's gentle supplications. Once he was able to think about Sal's impending nuptials calmly, Mr. Allburton realized there was another reason to make that short walk: business. John Parker was a senior partner in the firm. Ted heartily disapproved of Phil's decision to throw away a bright future in a hick farming community, but there was the firm to think of. In the years ahead there must be no friction between the partners. So he did his duty, but he did it with a set, unsmiling face. As he watched the ceremony, two old sayings came to Ted Allburton's mind.

Youth must be served was one.

Marry in haste, repent at leisure was the other.

There was no honeymoon. Phil's parents had reluctantly opened his trust fund, thirty thousand dollars, and he was anxious not to waste it. A week after the ceremony, he opened the little office next to the Sunoco station. The sign on the door—painted by his new bride— read PHILIP Y. PARKER, ATTORNEY AT LAW. On his desk was a telephone and an appointment book full of blank pages. They did not stay blank for long. On the very afternoon he opened for business, a farmer named Regis Toomey walked in. He was wearing bib overalls and a straw hat. He was everything Phil's father had predicted. Toomey offered to take off his muddy boots and Phil told him not to bother.

"I'm thinking you came by that mud honorably. Sit down and tell me why you're here."

Toomey sat. He took off his straw hat and placed it on his lap. "How much do you charge?" It came out Yankee: *Chaaage.*

"Fifty per cent of what I get for you. If I get nothing, twenty-five dollars." He hadn't forgotten the Answer Man's little sign, and he, Phil, hoped to have answers for all sorts of people. Starting with this man.

"Sounds fair," said Toomey. "Here's what. The bank wants to foreclose me and auction off the farm." *Faaam.* "But I've got a paper . . ." He brought it out of the front pocket of his biballs and passed it across the desk. ". . . says I've got ninety days' grace. Bank fella says that's null and void if I didn't make the last payment."

"Did you?"

"All but ten dollars. The wife went groceryin', don'tcha see, and that left me short."

Phil could hardly believe it. "Are you saying the bank wants to take your farm because of a ten-dollar shortfall?"

"Bank fella says so. Says they can auction it off, but I'm guessin' they already have a buyer lined up."

"We'll see about that," Phil said.

"I don't have twenty-five dollars just about now, Lawyer Parker."

Sally Ann came out of the other room with a pot of coffee. She was wearing a dark blue dress and a pinafore of a slightly lighter shade. Her face, free of makeup, shone. Her blond hair was pulled back. Toomey was struck dumb.

"We'll take your case, Mr. Toomey," she said. "And because it's our first, no charge no matter the outcome. Isn't that right, Philip?"

"Absolutely," Phil said, although he had been looking forward to that twenty-five bucks. "What's the bank fella's name?"

"Mr. Lathrop," Toomey said, and grimaced like a man who's bitten into something sour. "First Bank. He's the chief loan officer, and in charge of mortgages."

Phil presented himself at the First Bank of New Hampshire that very afternoon, and enquired of Mr. Lathrop if his bosses would enjoy a story in the *Union Leader* about a cruel bank that took a farmer's property in the depths of a depression over a measly ten dollars.

After discussion, some of it fairly warm, Mr. Lathrop saw the light.

"I'm tempted to take you to court anyway," Phil said pleasantly. "Unfair business practices . . . pain and suffering . . . financial deception . . ."

"That's outrageous," Mr. Lathrop said. "You'd never win."

"Perhaps not, but the bank would lose either way. I think five hundred dollars paid into Mr. Toomey's account would close this matter to the mutual satisfaction of both parties."

Lathrop groused, but the money was paid. Toomey offered to fork over half, but Phil—with Sally Ann's concurrence—refused. He did take twenty-five dollars when Toomey insisted, thinking of the Answer Man as he did it.

The news spread, both in Curry and the surrounding towns. Phil discovered several banks were using the same short-payment fiddle to foreclose on farms. In one case, a farmer in neighboring Hancock came up twenty dollars short three months before his mortgage would have been paid off. His farm was foreclosed and then sold to a construction company for twelve thousand dollars. Phil took that one to court and got eight thousand back for the farmer. Not full value, but better than nothing, and the press coverage was gold.

By 1939 his little office had been refurbished—new shingles and a fresh coat of paint. Like Sally Ann's face, it shone. When the Sunoco station went bust, Phil bought it and added an associate just out of law school. Sally Ann picked out a secretary (smart but elderly and plain) who doubled as a receptionist to help him winnow his cases.

By 1941 his business was in the black. The future looked bright. Then, four years and two months after Phil's encounter with the man sitting under a red umbrella by the side of the road, the Japanese attacked Pearl Harbor.

Not long before their wedding, Sally Ann Allburton took Phil by the hand and led him out onto the back lawn of the Allburton house in Wellesley. They sat on a bench by the goldfish pond, where a skim of ice had melted only recently. Her color was high and she wouldn't look him in the face, but she was determined to say what was on her mind. Phil thought that on that afternoon she had never looked more like her father.

"You need to lay in a supply of French letters," she said, looking fixedly down at their linked hands. "Do you know what I'm talking about?"

"Yes," Phil said. He had also heard them called English caps and, as an undergrad, naughty bags. He had worn such a thing exactly once, on a trip to a house of ill repute in Providence. It was an expedition that still filled him with shame. "But why? Don't you want—"

"Children? Of course I want children, but not until I'm sure I won't have to come begging to my parents—or you to yours—to help us out. My father would love that, and he'd put conditions on it. Strings to draw you away from what you really want to do. I can't have that. I won't have that."

She snatched a quick glance at him, reading his emotional temperature, then looked back down at their linked hands again. "There is a thing for women, it's called a diaphragm, but if I ask Dr. Grayson, he'll tell my parents."

"A doctor is enjoined from such behavior," Phil said.

"He would do it, just the same. So . . . French letters. Do you agree?"

He thought about asking her how she even knew about such things and decided he didn't want to know; some questions should not be answered. "I agree."

Now she did look at him. "And you must buy them in Portland, or Fryeburg, or North Conway. Far from Curry. Because people talk."

Phil burst out laughing. "You are a sly one!"

"I am when I have to be," she said.

His business prospered, and several times he and Sally Ann discussed throwing the French letters away, but in those first years Phil was working farmers' hours, dawn to dusk, often in court, often on the road, and the idea of adding a kiddie seemed more like a burden than a blessing.

Then, December 7th.

"I'm going to enlist," he told Sally Ann that night. They had been listening to the radio all day.

"You could get a deferment, you know. You're almost thirty."

"I don't want a deferment."

"No," she said, and took his hand. "Of course you don't. If you did, I'd love you less. Those dirty, sneaking Japs! Also . . ."

"Also what?"

Her answer made him realize—as with the business about buying his French letters far from Curry—just how much her father's child she was. "Also it would look bad. Business would suffer. You might be called a coward. Just come back to me, Phil. Promise."

Phil remembered what the Answer Man had told him under the red umbrella that day in October: not killed, not injured. He had no business believing such a thing, not all these years later . . . but he did. "I promise. I absolutely do."

She put her arms around his neck. "Then come to bed. And never mind the damn rubber. I want to feel you in me."

Nine weeks later, Phil sat in a Parris Island Quonset hut, sweating and aching in every muscle. He was reading a letter from Sally Ann. She was pregnant.

* * *

On the morning of February 18th, 1944, Lieutenant Philip Parker led his contingent of the 22nd Marines ashore on the atoll of Eniwetok. The Navy had subjected the Japanese to three days of bombardment, and intelligence said the enemy forces were thin on the ground. Unlike most of Naval intelligence, this turned out to be true. On the other hand, nobody had bothered to tell the gyrenes about the steep sand dunes they would have to climb after the Higgins boats grounded. The Japs were waiting for them, but they were armed with rifles instead of the dreaded Nambu light machine guns. Phil lost six of his thirty-six, two killed and four wounded, only one seriously. By the time they reached the top of the dunes, the Japs had melted into the thick brush.

The 22nd Marines swept west, meeting only scattered resistance. One of Phil's men was shot in the shoulder; another fell into a hole and broke his leg. Those were his only casualties after the landing.

"Walk in the park," Sergeant Myers said.

When they reached the ocean on the far side of the atoll, Phil got a walkie-talkie message from the jackleg Marine HQ that had been set up on the other side of the dunes that had caused them the worst casualties. They could still hear scattered fire from the south, but that was dying out even as they ate a noon meal. *A picnic lunch at the seashore,* Phil thought. *Who knew war could be so pleasant?*

"What's the word, Loot?" Myers asked when Phil holstered the walkie.

"Johnny Walker says the island is secure," Phil said. He was speaking of Colonel John T. Walker, who was bossing this little farrago along with his fellow colonel, Russell Ayers.

"It don't sound secure," said Private First Class Molocky. He nodded toward the south.

But by 1500, the shooting had fizzled away to nothing. Phil waited for orders, got none, posted three guards at the edge of the overgrowth, and told the rest of the men they could fall out until further notice. At 2000 hours they were told to pack up and head back east, where they would reconnect with the main landing force. There was grumbling about having to trek back through the thick underbrush when it would soon be dark, but orders wuz orders and they saddled up. After Private Frankland broke his leg in another hole and Private Gordon nearly put out an eye running into a tree, Phil radioed HQ and asked permission to camp for the night because the terrain was difficult.

"Fucking difficult is right," said Private First Class Molocky.

Permission was granted. They camped under their netting, but plenty of mosquitos still got in.

"At least the ground's dry," Myers said. "I've had trench foot, and it's not for sissies."

Phil fell asleep to the sound of his men slapping and Private Frankland—he with the broken leg—moaning. He awoke just before dawn, aware that shapes were moving north of their little encampment through the gloom. Hundreds of shapes. He found out later that Eniwetok was riddled with spider holes. Frankland had probably broken his leg in one of them; a Japanese infantryman might have been at the bottom, looking up, as Rangell and Sergeant Myers pulled him out of it.

Myers now put a hand on Phil's shoulder and murmured, "Not a word, not a sound. They might miss us. I think—"

That was when one of the Marines coughed. Conflicting lights crisscrossed the gray morning—grayer still under the canopy—and picked out the humped shapes swaddled in mosquito netting. The firing began. Six Marines were slaughtered in their sleep. Eight more were wounded. Only one Marine got off a shot. Myers had his arm around Phil; Phil had an arm around Myers. They listened to bullets whicker overhead, and several thumped the ground around them. Then there was a harsh command in Japanese—*zenpo, zenpo* it sounded like—and the Nips moved on, running and crashing through the brush.

"They're counterattacking," Phil said. "That's the only reason I can think of why they didn't finish us off."

"HQ being their objective?" Myers asked.

"Got to be. Come on. You, me, anybody else who's not wounded."

"You're crazy," Myers said. His teeth shone as his lips parted in a grin. "I like it."

Phil counted only six men who chased after the Japanese; there might have been one or two more. Now the firing started up again ahead of them, first sporadic, then constant. Grenades crumped, and Phil heard the chatter of the dreaded Nambu. It was joined by other machine guns. Three? Four?

The remaining Marines in Phil's contingent burst out of the over-growth and saw the far side of the dunes that had given them so much trouble the day before. It was covered with Japanese soldiers headed for the lightly defended HQ, but Phil's men were behind them.

A portly Jap—perhaps the only overweight Jap in the whole army, Phil thought later—had fallen slightly behind his comrades. He was carrying a Nambu light machine gun and was festooned with belts of ammunition. Slightly ahead of him was another, thinner machine-gunner.

Phil drew his knife and ran at the portly soldier, feeling that if he could get that machine gun, he could do a fair amount of damage. Maybe a lot. He plunged the knife into the nape of the Jap's neck. It was his first kill, but in the heat of the moment that hardly registered. The Jap shrieked and fell forward. The skinny machine-gunner ahead of him turned, raising his weapon.

"*Loot! Drop! Drop!*" Myers screamed.

Phil didn't, because in that moment he thought of the Answer Man. *Will I be hurt?* he had asked. The Answer Man said no, but then Phil realized he'd asked the wrong question. He had asked the right one just before his five minutes ran out. *Will I be killed?* And the answer: *No, Just Phil, you will not be killed.*

In that moment on Eniwetok, he believed it. Perhaps because the Answer Man had known his mother's maiden name and where his father had been born. Perhaps because he had no other choice. The skinny Jap opened fire with his Nambu. Phil was aware of Myers staggering backward in a spray of blood. Destry and Molocky fell on either side of him. He heard bullets whip by on both sides of his head. He was aware of tugs at his pants and shirt, as if he were being nipped by a playful puppy. He would later count over a dozen holes in his clothing, but not a single bullet hit him or even grazed him.

He opened fire, raking the appropriated Nambu from left to right, knocking down Japanese soldiers like Kewpie dolls. Others turned, momentarily shocked to stillness by this unexpected attack from their rear, then opened fire. Bullets struck the sand in front of Phil, cover-ing the toes of his boots. More ripped at his clothes. He was aware at least two of his men were firing back. He pulled another ammo belt from the dead Jap at his feet and opened fire again, unaware of the twenty-pound weight of the Nambu, unaware that it was heating up, unaware that he was screaming.

Now the Americans were returning fire from the other side of the dune; Phil could tell by the sound of the carbines. He advanced, still firing. He walked over dead Jap soldiers. The Nambu jammed. He threw it aside, bent, and a bullet whanged his helmet off his head and sent it flying. Phil hardly noticed. He picked up another machine gun and began firing again.

He became aware that Myers was beside him again, half of his face awash with blood, a piece of his scalp dangling and swinging as he walked. *"Yaah, sons of bitches!"* he screamed. *"Yaah, you sons of bitches, welcome to America!"*

That was so crazy Phil began to laugh. He was still laughing when they crested the dune. He threw the Nambu aside and raised both arms. *"Marines! Marines! Don't shoot! Marines!"*

The counterattack—such as it was—ended. Sergeant Rick Myers was awarded a Silver Star (he said he would rather have had his right eye back). Lieutenant Philip Parker was one of 473 Medal of Honor recipients during the Second World War, and although unwounded, his war was over. A photographer took a picture of his bullet-riddled shirt with the sun shining through the holes, and it made all the papers back home in what combat Marines called "the world." He was an authentic hero, and would spend the rest of his service in America, making speeches and selling War Bonds.

Ted Allburton embraced him and called him a warrior. Called him *son*. Phil thought, *This man is ridiculous*. But he hugged back willingly enough, knowing when a hatchet was being buried.

He met his son, now nearly three years old.

Sometimes at night, lying wakeful beside his sleeping wife, Phil thought of the skinny Japanese soldier, the one who had heard his compatriot's dying scream. He saw the skinny soldier turn. He saw the skinny soldier's wide brown eyes beneath his field cap, a scar in the shape of a fishhook beside one of them. Something the skinny soldier might have gotten as a child. He saw the skinny soldier open fire. He

remembered the sound the bullets made as they whispered around him. He thought of how some of those passing slugs had tugged playfully at his clothes, as if they weren't pellets of death, or worse, bringers of lifelong injury. He thought of how sure he'd been of his survival because of the Answer Man's—call it what it was—his prophecy. And on those nights he wondered if the man under the red umbrella had seen the future . . . or made it. To this question Phil found no answer.

2

On his War Bonds rounds, which consisted of speaking engagements in the New England states and sometimes New York as well, Phil had the chance to talk with many soldiers who had served, and heard many stories of difficult homecomings. One ex-Marine put it very succinctly. "At first, after four years apart, we were strangers sleeping together." Phil and Sally Ann were spared this awkward phase, possibly—probably—because they had grown up together from childhood. The physical love between them came naturally. Once, at the moment of their mutual climax, Sally Ann said, "Oh, my *heero*," and they both collapsed with the giggles.

Jacob was shy of him at first, clinging to his mother and looking with fearful eyes at the tall man who had come into their lives. When Phil tried to hold him, the boy struggled to be put down, sometimes crying. He would toddle to his mother, grasp her leg, and stare at the stranger he was supposed to call Daddy.

One evening while Jake was sitting between his mother's feet and playing with his blocks, Phil sat down across from him and rolled him a tennis ball. He expected nothing, and was delighted when Jake rolled it back. Back and forth went the ball. Sally Ann put down her book to watch. Phil gave the ball a low bounce. Jake put out his hands and caught it. When Phil laughed, Jake laughed with him. After that it was all right between them. Better than all right. Phil loved everything about his son—his blue eyes, his fine brown hair, his sturdy body. Most of all he loved the little boy's potential. He couldn't see the man Jake might become and didn't want to. *Let it be a surprise*, he thought.

There came an evening late in that year of 1944 when Jake refused to let Sal pick him up and carry him to bed. "Want Daddy," he said. It might not have been the best night of Phil's life, but he couldn't think of a better one.

Will Curry prosper the way I think it will? he'd asked on that long-ago day that seemed like a dream (although he still remembered each question asked and each reply given). The Answer Man had told him it would, and he was right about that, as well. Partly because of his fame as a Medal of Honor–winning Marine, but mostly because he asked a fair price for his services and because he was good at his job ("a clevah bastid," the locals said), Phil Parker had more clients than he could handle in the years after the war.

The associate he'd added in 1939 was killed in a bombing raid over Hamburg, so Phil added a new fellow, then a second, then—at Sal's urging—a young woman. That caused some disgruntled talk among Curry's old Yankees, but by 1950, there were new people in town with new ideas and new money. A shopping center was built in the neighboring town of Patten; Phil and his associates did the legal work and made a good profit. In Curry, the five-room grammar was replaced by a spanking new eight-room elementary school. Phil bought the old building for a song, and it became his new office: Phil Parker & Associates. The Allburtons came often to visit with their daughter, their grandson . . . and, of course, with the war hero. Phil was quite sure Ted had come to believe he had always supported his son-in-law's prescient decision to move to Curry, which was booming.

Phil was able to put aside any old animosity he might have held onto concerning his father-in-law because of Ted's fierce and unconditional love for Jake. On the boy's sixth birthday, Ted gave him a little baseball glove and played underhanded toss with the boy in the backyard until it was almost too dark to see and Sally Ann had to tell them both to come in and eat supper.

No matter the press of work, Phil always tried to get home before dark in order to have a catch with his son. By the time Jake was eight, they were standing thirty feet apart, then forty, and throwing overhand.

"Bring it, Dad!" Jake would cry. "Really steam it in!"

Phil wouldn't throw even close to as hard as he could have, not to a boy of eight, but he increased the speed of his throws little by little. On spring and summer weekends, the two of them would sit together listening to the Red Sox on the radio. Sometimes all three of them.

One November day, after they had been out throwing the baseball in two inches of snow, Sally Ann took Phil aside. "Did you play ball as a kid? Because I don't remember that you did."

Phil shook his head. "Pick-up games after school, sometimes, but not often. I could field, but I couldn't hit worth a damn. The guys used to call me Whiffer Parker."

"I never played sports, either, but Jake . . . is he good, or is it just my imagination and a mother's pride?"

"He's good. I can't wait to take him to his first Sox game."

That happened in 1950. They sat in the bleachers, Phil on one side, Ted on the other, the boy between them, staring at the green outfield grass of Fenway Park, eyes wide, mouth agape, his bag of popcorn forgotten on his lap.

Ted leaned over and said, "Someday maybe you'll be out there, Jake."

Jake looked up at his granddad and smiled. "I know I will," he said.

On an unseasonably warm October day in 1951, Phil visited the new Western Auto store in North Conway and drove back home along Route 111 with a present for the whole family in the trunk: a Zenith television set, the Regent model with the porthole screen. He also bought rabbit ears, but with an antenna they might be able to get the Boston stations. He was thinking Jake would go out of his mind with happiness at the prospect of actually watching *Range Rider* instead of listening to it on the radio.

There was something else on his mind as well, potentially more important than the new TV. He'd had a conversation that morning with a man named Blaylock Atherton, who happened to be the Republican in charge of the New Hampshire state senate. A real mover and shaker was Senator Atherton, and it had been an interesting conversation

STEPHEN KING

indeed. Phil was thinking of the discussion he'd have with Sally Ann about that when he passed a bright yellow sign planted on a stick by the side of the road. The message, 2 MILES TO THE ANSWER MAN, brought back brilliant memories.

Can't be him, not after all these years, Phil thought. But in his heart he knew it was.

Just past the Curry town line he passed another sign, this one in electric blue, announcing that the Answer Man was a mile ahead. Phil breasted the hill at the edge of town. Two hundred yards ahead he saw the red umbrella. This time the Answer Man had set up shop in a large clearing not far from the new elementary school. It was where the Curry Volunteer Fire Station would stand in a year or so.

Heart thumping, new TV and Blaylock Atherton forgotten, Phil pulled off the road and got out. His Chevrolet jalopy was long gone. He slammed the door of his new Buick and for a moment just stood there, amazed by what he saw. More like thunderstruck.

Phil had aged; the Answer Man hadn't. He looked exactly the same as he had on that October day fourteen years ago. His thinning hair was no thinner now. His eyes were the same bright blue. White shirt, gray slacks, black shoes—all just as before. His long-fingered hands were folded on his table just as before. Only the signs flanking the one proclaiming him the Answer Man had changed. The one on the left read $50 PER 3 MINUTES. The one on the right read YOUR FIRST ANSWER FREE.

I guess even magic isn't immune to inflation, Phil thought. Meanwhile, the Answer Man was looking at him with lively interest.

"Do I know you?" he asked, then chuckled. "Don't answer that! You're not the Answer Man, I am. Just let me think." Like a creature in a fairy tale, he laid his finger to one side of his nose. "I've got it. You're Just Phil. You wanted to know if your girl would marry you, although you knew she would, and if you'd come to live in this little village, although you knew that, too."

"They were impotent questions," Phil said.

"Yes, they were. They were indeed. Sit down, Just Phil. If, that is, you'd like to do some business. If not, you are of course free to go on your way. Freedom is what makes America great, or so they say."

A bell rang loudly not far away. The doors of the new elementary school flew open. Yelling kids carrying book satchels and lunch boxes fled out the doors as if from an explosion. One of them was undoubtedly his son, although in the general scrum Phil couldn't pick him out; there were lots of boys wearing Red Sox caps. Two school buses were ready to take in those who lived more than a mile away.

Phil sat down in the client's chair. He started to ask if this strange roadside salesman was human or some sort of supernatural being, but he must have learned at least a few things between twenty-five and thirty-nine, because he shut his mouth before he could waste his free question. Of course the Answer Man wasn't a human being. No man looked exactly the same after fourteen years, and no man could have known that he would survive close-range machine-gun fire on Eniwetok.

What he said instead was, "Your price seems to have gone up."

"For certain people," the Answer Man said.

"So you knew I was coming."

The Answer Man smiled. "You are trying to get information by making statements. I'm hep to that trick."

I'll just bet you are, Phil thought. *A real hep cat.*

Children were walking past the site of the future fire station now, and although kids were curious by nature, the few who looked at the vacant lot looked away without interest.

"They don't see us, do they?"

"Another question to which you know the answer, my friend. Of course they don't. Reality has folds, and we're currently in one of them. That's your free question. If you want to ask others, you have to pay. And in case you were wondering, I don't take checks."

Feeling like a man in a dream, Phil took his wallet out of his hip pocket. In it were three twenties and a ten (there was also a C-note for emergencies, tucked in behind his driver's license). He gave the ten and two of the twenties to the Answer Man, who made them disappear. He picked up his little bag—same bag—and took out the same oversized stopwatch. This time the numbers only went from 0 to 3, but there was the same ratcheting sound as he wound it up.

"I hope you're ready, Just Phil."

He thought he was. There weren't any dilemmas this time, he was perfectly happy with the current course of his life, but he supposed men and women were always curious about the future.

"I'm ready. Let's go."

The Answer Man's reply was just as it had been on that day in 1937. "So we begin." He clicked the lever on the back of his big clock. It began to tick and the single hand started its journey from 3 to 2.

Phil thought of his conversation with Blaylock Atherton—not a proposal but a possibility. A trial balloon.

"If I'm asked, should I run—"

The Answer Man raised an admonitory finger. "Have you forgotten what I told you about that word? I am the Answer Man, not your agony aunt."

Phil hadn't forgotten, exactly; he had just gotten used to asking questions that didn't advance matters. Impotent questions, in fact.

"All right, here's my question. Will I run for the U.S. Senate?"

"No."

"No?"

"The answer won't change just because you ask the question again. In the meantime, tempus is fugiting."

"Is it because Sal won't want me to run?"

"No." The single hand on the clock passed 2.

"Is Atherton going to offer the chance to someone else?"

"Yes."

"Bastard," Phil said, but was it really a disappointment? Yes, but not a big one. He had his law practice, and it still engaged him. Nor was he crazy about leaving New Hampshire for Washington DC; he was a country mouse and supposed he always would be.

As he had fourteen years ago, Phil changed direction. "Will Sal and Jake like the TV?"

"Yes." A brief smile flicked across the Answer Man's face.

Having thought of Jake, another question occurred to Phil. It was out of his mouth before he realized he might not want to know the answer.

"Will my son play pro baseball?"

"No."

The hand on the clock passed 1 and headed for zero.

"Any pro sport?"

"No."

This was more disappointing than hearing he wouldn't be asked to run for the Senate, but was it surprising? It wasn't. Sports were a pyramid, and only those who were almost divinely talented reached the top.

"College ball?" Surely that would be in Jacob's grasp.

"No."

Like a gambler on a losing streak who keeps throwing good money after bad, Phil asked, "High school ball? Surely—"

"No."

Phil stared at the Answer Man, mystified and starting to be worried. Starting to be scared, actually. *Don't ask*, he thought, and one of his mother's favorite sayings occurred to him: *Peep not at a keyhole, lest ye be vexed.*

The hand on the Answer Man's clock reached zero and gave out its hoarse *BRRRANG* sound just before Phil asked his last question: "Is my son okay?"

"I can't answer that, sorry. You were just a bit late, Just Phil."

"I was?"

No answer. Of course not. His time was up.

"I suppose I was. All right, I'll go again. I can do that, can't I?" No answer, so Phil answered for himself. "I can, of course I can. The sign says *per* three minutes." He bent and slipped the hundred out from behind his license. "Just let me . . . okay, here it is . . ."

He lifted his head and saw the sign now read $200 PER 3 MINUTES and NO FREE ANSWERS.

"Wait," he said. "That isn't what it said. You crooked me."

As before—or almost—the Answer Man said, "Perhaps you crooked yourself."

And—as before—the Answer Man seemed to be withdrawing, as if on rails. The grayness started to come. Phil fought it with no success.

He came to behind the wheel of the Buick, hearing a tapping on the passenger side window. "Dad? Dad, wake up!"

He looked around, at first not sure where he was. Or when. Then he saw his son peering in at him. His friend Harry Washburn was with him, both wearing identical Red Sox caps. That slotted Phil into place. Not 1937 but 1951. Not a young man with the ink still wet on his law degree but a war vet who was important enough in this part of New Hampshire to be considered a viable candidate for the U.S. Senate. A husband. A father.

He leaned over and opened the door. "Hey, kiddo. I must have dozed off."

Jake wasn't interested in that. "We missed the bus because we were playing pepper behind the school. Can we have a ride home?"

"What would you have done if I hadn't been here?"

"Walked, accourse," Jake said. "Or hooked a ride from Missus Keene. She's nice."

"Pretty, too," Harry said.

"Well, hop in. I got something in North Conway you boys might like."

"Really?" Jake got in front. Harry got in back. "What?"

"You'll see." Phil looked at the spot where the Answer Man's table and umbrella had been. He looked in his wallet and saw the C-note, folded small behind his driver's license. Unless the whole thing had been a dream—and he knew it hadn't been—he supposed the Answer Man must have put it back. *Or maybe I put it back myself.*

He drove home.

The TV was a great success. The rabbit ears would only pull in WMUR out of Manchester (the picture sometimes—well, often—obscured by snow flurries), but once Phil put up the antenna, the Parkers could indeed get two Boston stations, WNAC and WHDH.

Phil and Sal enjoyed evening shows like *The Red Skelton Hour* and *Schlitz Playhouse*, but Jake did more than enjoy the television; he embraced it with the all-in fervor of a first love. He watched *Weekday Matinee* after school, where the same old movie played all week long. He watched *Jack and Pat's Country Jamboree*. He watched *Boston Blackie*. He watched ads for Camel cigarettes and Bab-O cleanser. On Saturday he and his friends gathered as if in church to watch *Crusader Rabbit*, *The Little Rascals*, and thousands of old cartoons.

Sally Ann was first amused, then uneasy. "He's addicted to that thing," she said, with no idea this parental cry would be repeated for generations to come. "He *never* plays catch with you when you come home anymore, just wants to watch some junky old Hopalong Cassidy movie he's seen four times already."

Jake actually did want to have a catch sometimes, or hit behind the garage when Phil slow-pitched to him, but these occasions were rarer than they had been. In the pre-TV days, Jake would have been waiting for his dad on the front stoop with his glove on and his bat propped beside him.

The truth was Phil didn't mind his son's loss of interest as much as Sal did. When the Answer Man told him that Jake wouldn't play organized ball—no, not even in high school—his mind had first jumped (as any parent's would) to dire possibilities. Now it seemed the reason was more prosaic: Jake was just losing interest in baseball, as Phil himself had lost interest in learning to play the piano when he was about Jake's age.

Inspired by shows like *The Lone Ranger* and *Wild Bill Hickok*, Jake started to write his own Western stories. Each came with an exclamation mark and bore titles like "Gundown at Laramie!" and "Shoot-Out at Dead Man's Canyon!" They were lurid but not half-bad . . . at least in the opinion of the author's father. Perhaps someday he would be a writer instead of an outfielder for the Boston Red Sox. Phil thought that would be a fine thing.

Blaylock Atherton called one evening and asked if Phil had thought any more about running for the Senate, perhaps not this time but what about '56? Phil said he was considering it. He told Atherton that Sally Ann wasn't crazy about the idea, but said she would support him if that was his decision.

"Well, don't consider too long," Atherton said. "In politics we have to think ahead. Tempus fugit, you know."

"So I've heard," Phil said.

One Saturday morning in February of 1952, Harry Washburn came into Phil's closet of a home study, where Phil was going over depositions for an upcoming trial. He was alarmed to see a streak of blood on one of Harry's freckled cheeks and more on his hands.

"Did you hurt yourself, Harry?"

"It's not mine," Harry said. "Jake has a nosebleed and it won't stop. He got blood all over his Roy Rogers shirt. Top to bottom."

Phil thought that had to be an exaggeration until he saw for himself. On the Zenith's round screen Annie Oakley was shooting it out with a bad guy, but none of the four or five little boys was paying attention to anything but Jake. His favorite shirt—his Saturday morning cowboy-watching shirt—was indeed soaked with blood. So was the lap of his jeans.

Jake looked at his father and said, "It won't stop." His voice was clogged and nasal.

Phil told the other boys to watch the show, everything was fine, five-by-five. He kept his voice level, but the amount of blood he was looking at scared him badly. He took Jake into the kitchen, made him sit down and tilt his head back, then filled a dishcloth with ice cubes and pressed it to the top of the boy's nose. "Hold it there, Jake-O. It'll stop."

Sally Ann breezed in from a trip to the IGA, saw Jake's blood-soaked shirt, and drew in breath to scream. Phil shook his head at her and she didn't. Kneeling beside him, she asked what had happened. "Did one of your friends punch you in the nose playing cowboys?"

"No, it just started. There's blood on the floor but I didn't get any on your blue rug, at least."

"I gotted it on me, too," Sammy Dillon said. He and Harry had come into the kitchen. The other boys were standing behind them. "But I warshed it off."

"That's good, Sammy," Sally Ann said. "I think you and the rest of the guys had better go home now."

They went willingly enough, only pausing at the kitchen door to get a final look at their gore-spattered friend. When they were gone, Sally Ann leaned over their son and whispered to Phil. "I don't think it's stopping."

"It will," Phil said.

It didn't. It slowed from the original shirt-soaking gusher, but continued to seep. The Parkers' local doc was on vacation, so they took him to the hospital in North Conway, where Richmond, the on-call MD, peered up Jake's nose with a little light and nodded. "We'll fix that in a jiff, young man. Mother and Dad are going to wait outside while we do our biz."

Sal wanted to stay, but Phil, having an idea of what the fix would entail, took her by the arm and escorted her firmly out into the waiting room and closed the door. Which did no good at all, because when his nose was cauterized, Jake's howls filled the small hospital from end to end. Phil and Sally Ann clutched each other, both of them shedding tears, waiting for it to be over. Eventually it was . . . and wasn't.

Dr. Richmond came out with one lapel of his white coat dotted with Jake's blood. He smiled and said, "Brave kid. That's no fun. Can I talk to your parents a minute, Jacob?"

He took them into the exam room. "Have you seen the bruising?"

"Sure, a couple on his arms," Phil said. "He's a boy, Dr. Richmond. He probably got them climbing trees or something."

"On his chest, as well. Scrapper, is he?"

"No, not really," Phil said. "He and his friends sometimes tussle, but it's all in fun."

"I want to do a blood test," Dr. Richmond said. "Just crossing *t*'s, you know—"

"Oh my God," Sally Ann said. Later she would tell Phil that she knew, right then she knew.

"Check his white count and his platelets. Rule out anything serious."

"Doc, it was just a nosebleed," Phil said.

"Bring him back in, Phil," Sally Ann said. She had a white look around her eyes and mouth that Phil became very familiar with over the next year or so.

Phil brought Jake back into the exam room, and once he had been assured that a blood-draw would be a walk in the park compared to having his nose cauterized, Jake rolled up his sleeve and took the needle stoically.

A week later their family doctor called and told them he was sorry to be the bearer of bad news, but it looked like Jake had acute lymphocytic leukemia.

Their sturdy son went downhill fast. Eight months into what was then called "the wasting disease," Jake had a remission that gave his parents several weeks of cruel hope. Then came the crash. Jacob Theodore Parker died in Portsmouth Regional Hospital on March 23rd, 1953, at the age of ten.

Sal laid her head on her husband's shoulder during most of Jake's closing ceremony. She cried. Phil did not. His tears had all been used up during Jake's last hospital stay. Sal had hoped for another remission right to the end—prayed for it—but Phil knew Jake was going down. The Answer Man had as much as told him so.

Later that day he asked himself if he had smelled gin on her breath at the funeral. If he did, it would hardly have been worth noticing. The Parkers were part of the Booze and Cigarettes generation. Sally Ann had been enjoying light cocktails with her mother and father and their friends since she was sixteen, and there were always cocktails waiting when Phil came home. Two before dinner was the usual. Sometimes Phil would have a can or two of beer while they watched TV. Sal would have another gin and tonic. It was only later that Phil looked back and realized that one G&T in the evening had progressed to two and sometimes three. But she was always up at six, making Jake's school lunch and breakfast for the three of them. It was also the generation of Females Cook, Males Eat.

He *did* notice at the reception after the graveside ceremony. There was no way not to. Sal was in the kitchen, telling Mrs. Keene a story about Jake losing his first tooth, how she had looped one end of a thread around that troublesome wiggler and tied the other to the knob of his bedroom door.

"When I slammed the door, that tooth flew right out!" Sal said, only tooth came out *toof*, and Phil saw Mrs. Keene—the pretty one, Harry had said on the day Phil met the Answer Man for the second time—easing back from her, a step at a time. Easing back from her breath. Sal matched her step for step, commencing a second story. She had a pony glass in one hand, tilting slowly so what was in it slopped on the floor.

Phil took her by the arm and told her his folks wanted to see her (they didn't). Sal came willingly enough, but looked back over her shoulder to say, "That toof just *flew*! Gosh, what a sight!"

Mrs. Keene gave Phil a commiserating smile. It was the first of many.

He got Sal as far as the doorway to the living room before her knees buckled. The glass dropped from her hand. He caught it and had a memory, momentary but oh God so brilliant, of catching a return throw from Jake behind the garage. He got her through the groups of people in the living room, by then supporting almost all of her weight. His mother gave him a look and nodded: *Get her out of here.* Phil nodded back.

There was no point trying to take her upstairs, so he half-carried her into the guest room and laid her down among the coats of the mourners. She began to snore immediately. When Phil came back, he told folks that Sal was overcome with grief and felt she couldn't see people, at least for awhile. There were sympathetic nods and more murmurs of condolence—God, so many condolences that Phil found himself wishing someone would crack a dirty joke about the farmer's daughter—but he was pretty sure there were people (Mrs. Keene for one, his mom for another) who knew it wasn't just grief that had overcome his wife.

It was the first lie he told about her drinking, but not the last.

Phil suggested they might try to have another baby. Sal agreed with a kind of listless, what-does-it-matter lack of interest. Sometimes he wanted to grasp her by the shoulders—hard enough to hurt, to leave bruises, to get *through* to her—and tell her that she wasn't the only one who'd lost a child. He didn't. He kept his anger to himself, knowing what she'd say: *You have your work. I have nothing.*

But she did. She had her Gilbey's Gin and her Kool cigarettes. Two packs a day. She kept them in a little alligator case that looked like a change purse. She became pregnant in 1954. He suggested she quit smoking. She suggested he should keep his advice, however well-meant, to himself. She miscarried in her fourth month.

"No more of that," she told him from her bed in North Conway Hospital. "I'm forty. Too old to have a baby."

So it was back to the French letters, but on New Year's Eve of 1956, Phil realized he still had three rubbers left in a box of a dozen he'd purchased in North Conway not long after Easter. Sally Ann was willing enough to lift her nightgown and take him into herself, but when he looked at her and saw her looking at the ceiling, he knew she was just waiting for him to spend and get off her. This was not conducive to intimacy.

Only once, in 1957, did Phil tackle her about the drinking. He told her that if she had to go to one of those drying-out spas to quit or at least cut down, he had found a good one in Boca Raton, far enough from New Hampshire that no one would know. He could say she was visiting friends. He could even say they were separating, if that was what she wanted, but she had to stop.

She looked at him, his now overweight wife with the bad complexion and the dull eyes and the clumpy hair. He found her eyes especially fascinating. There were no depths there.

"Why?" she said.

On the evening of November 8th, 1960, Phil came home to an empty house. There was a note on the kitchen counter that said, *Dinner in oven. I have gone to GD to watch election results come in. S.*

There was no invitation for Phil to join her, and he had never cared much for the Green Door in North Conway, anyway. Once, around the time he and Sal were married, it had been quite a nice bar. Now it was a dive.

According to the police report, Mrs. Parker left the Green Door at approximately 12:40 AM on the morning of November 9th, shortly after Kennedy had been declared the winner. The bartender cut her off at eleven but allowed her to stay and watch the returns.

Coming home on Route 16, driving at a high rate of speed, her little Renault Dauphine veered off the road and struck a bridge abutment. Death was instantaneous. The postmortem reported a blood alcohol level of .39. Upon hearing the news that his daughter was dead, Ted

Allburton suffered a heart attack. After five days in intensive care, he died. The back-to-back funerals almost made Phil wish he were back on Eniwetok.

Three weeks after the death of his wife, Phil drove to the Curry Volunteer Fire Station, where there had once been a vacant lot. It was late, and the fire station was dark. Between the red-painted double doors was a manger scene: Jesus, Mary, Joseph, wise men, assorted animals. The manger was—to the best of Phil's memory—the exact place where a red umbrella had once shaded the Answer Man's little table.

"Come here and talk to me," Phil said to the windy darkness. From the pocket of his overcoat he took a roll of bills. "I've got eight hundred here, maybe even a thousand, and I've got a few questions. Number one is this—was it an accident, or did she kill herself?"

Nothing. Just the empty lot, the empty fire station, a cold east wind, and a bunch of stupid plaster statuary lit by a hidden electric bulb.

"Number two is *why*. Why me? I know that sounds like self-pity, and I'm sure it is, but I'm honestly curious. That fucking dummocks friend of Jake's, Harry Washburn, is still alive, he's a plumber's apprentice down in Somersworth. Sammy Dillon is alive, too, so why not my boy? If Jake was alive, Sally would be alive, right? So tell me. I guess I don't even want to know why me after all, I want to know why *at all*? Come on, fella. Get out here, wind up your clock, and take my money."

Nothing. Of course.

"You were never there at all, were you? You were just a figment of my fucking imagination, so fuck you and fuck me and fuck the whole fucking world."

Phil spent the following three years in a daze of dysthymic depression. He did his work, always showed up for court on time, won some cases, lost others, didn't much care either way. Sometimes he dreamed of the Answer Man, and in some of these dreams he leaped across the table, knocked the ticking stopclock to the ground, and locked his hands around the Answer Man's neck. But the Answer Man always faded away to nothing, like smoke. Because really, that was what he had to be, wasn't he? Just smoke.

That period of his life ended with the Burned Woman. Her name was Christine Lacasse, but Phil always thought of her as the Burned Woman.

One day in the early spring of 1964, his secretary came into his office looking pale and distraught. Phil thought there were tears in Marie's eyes, but wasn't sure until she wiped one away with the heel of her hand. Phil asked if she was all right.

"Yes, but there's a woman here to see you, and I wanted to warn you before I sent her in. She's been burned, and badly. Her face . . . Phil, her face is *terrible*."

"What does she want?"

"She says she wants to sue the New England Freedom Corporation for five million dollars."

Phil smiled. "That would be a trick, wouldn't it?"

New England Freedom did business in the six states stretching from Presque Isle to Providence. They had grown into one of the biggest development companies in the northland during postwar years that Phil supposed were now over. They built housing developments, shopping centers, industrial centers, even prisons.

"You better send her in, Marie. Thanks for preparing me."

Not that anything could truly prepare him for the woman who shuffled in on two canes. From the left side of her face, Phil guessed she might be in her late forties or early fifties. The right side of her face was buried in a landslide of flesh that had melted and then hardened. The hand gripping the cane on that side was a claw. She saw his expression and the left side of her mouth pulled up in a smile that showed the few teeth remaining to her.

"Pretty, ain't I?" she said. Her voice was as harsh as a crow's caw. Phil guessed she had inhaled the fire that had burned her and scorched her vocal cords. He supposed she was lucky to be able to speak at all.

Phil had no intention of responding to a question that had to be rhetorical, or downright sarcastic. "Sit down, Miss Lacasse, and tell me what I can do for you."

"It's Missus. I'm a widow-woman, don't you know. As to what you can do for me, you can sue the shit out of NEF." She pronounced it

Neff. "Five million, not a penny more or a penny less. Not that you will, I'd bet a cracker. I've been to half a dozen other lawyers, including Feld and Pillsbury in Portland, and not one of em will have anything to do with me or my case. NEF's too big for em. Can I have a glass of water before you kick me out?"

He buzzed Marie and asked her to bring Mrs. Lacasse a glass of water. Meanwhile, the Burned Woman was fumbling with her good hand in a little pack cinched around her waist. She brought out a bottle of pills, and thrust them across Phil's desk.

"Open these for me, would ya? I can do it meself, but it hurts like a bugger. I want two. No, three."

Phil opened the brown bottle, shook out three pills, handed them across to her, and re-capped the bottle. Marie came in with the water and Lacasse swallowed the pills. "It's the morph, don'tcha know. For pain. Talking hurts. Well, everything hurts, but it's the talking that's the worst. Eating ain't no fun, either. Doctor says these pills'll kill me in a year or three. I said they won't kill me until I get my case in court. I'm fixed on that, Lawyer Parker.

"Ah, they're starting to work. Good. I'd take another but then I'd get sloppy, start puttin' things in the wrong order."

"Tell me how I can help," Phil said.

She threw back her head and gave a witch's cackle. He saw that part of her neck had run down into her shoulder. "Help me sue the shit out of those fuckers, that's how you can help." And with that, she told her tale.

Christine Lacasse had lived with her husband and five children in Morrow Estates, a NEF-built community in the town of Albany, just south of North Conway. The lights in their house kept fizzing on and off, and sometimes smoke drifted out of the electrical sockets. Ronald Lacasse was a long-haul truck driver, making good money, but gone much of the time. Christine Lacasse did ladies' hair at home, and her driers and blowers were always shorting out. One day the electrical panels in the utility rooms of their four-house bloc caught fire and they had no power for almost a week. Christine, not yet the Burned Woman, talked to the Estates superintendent, who merely shrugged and blamed New Hampshire Power and Light.

"I knew better than that," she told Phil, sipping at her water. "I didn't fall off a haytruck yesterday. A power surge wouldn't cause the electric panels of four houses to catch afire. The fuses would blow first. Other blocs of houses in Morrow Estates had problems with their lights and their electric heat, but nothing like ours."

When she got no satisfaction from the super, she called NEF's Portsmouth office, spoke to a functionary there, and got the runaround. She investigated the corporation bigwigs at the North Conway library, found the number for NEF's Boston HQ, called them, and asked to speak to the president. No, she was told, he was far too busy to speak to a housewife from East Overshoe, New Hampshire. She got another functionary instead, probably one with a better salary and better suits than the Portsmouth functionary. She told the Boston fella that sometimes when the power was flickering the wall in her little home salon got hot, and she could hear a buzzing, like there were wasps in there. She said she could smell a kind of frying. The functionary told her that she was probably using hair driers and blowers with a voltage too high for the electrical system. Mrs. Lacasse enquired if his mother had had any kids who lived, and hung up.

That Christmas, NEF put up Christmas lights all over Morrow Estates. "The Corporation did that?" Phil asked. "Not the Homeowners Association in the Estates?"

"Didn't have no Homeowners Association," she told Phil. "Nothing like that. Everyone got a flier from NEF in their mailbox after Thanksgiving. Said they were doing it *in the spirit of the season.*"

"Just out of the goodness of their hearts," Phil said, scribbling on his legal pad.

The Burned Woman gave her witch's cackle and pointed one deformed, half-melted finger at him. "I like you. You'll kick me out like all the others, but I like you. And none of the others wrote down anything I said."

"Do you still have that flier?"

"Mine burned up, but I've got a pile of other ones just like it."

"I'll want one. No, I want all of them. Tell me about the fire."

She said her husband was home that Christmas. The presents were under the tree. Two nights before the holiday, with the kids all tucked up in their beds (dreams of sugarplums optional), their house and the Duffys' house next door caught fire. Christine was wakened by screams from outside. The house was full of smoke, but she saw no flames. What she saw out the bedroom window was Rona Duffy, her next-door neighbor, rolling around in the snow, trying to put out her flaming nightgown.

"That house of theirs was burnin' like a birthday candle. I shook Ronald awake and told him to get the kids out, but he never did. By then I was out of door and throwing snow over Rona." Mrs. Lacasse added matter-of-factly, "She died. Her two kids were with her ex-husband in Rutland, lucky for them. Mine weren't so lucky. I don't know what happened to them. I think the smoke must have gotten to Ronnie before he could get to them. I went back in to do it myself and half the goddam living room ceiling fell on me. Lawyer Parker, that house went up six licks to the dozen. I crawled out, on fire. And you know what happened during the year I was in the hospital?"

"They played beanbag with the blame until that old beanbag disappeared," Phil said. "Is that about right?"

The twisted finger pointed at him again. She gave another cackle. Phil thought it was the way the damned in hell must laugh.

"NEF said it was the fault of the company that did the wiring. The company that did the wiring said the state had inspected both the Christmas lights and the original wiring specifications, so it was the state's fault. The state said the specs weren't the same as the actual wiring in the houses still standin' and the engineering firm must have cheated to save money. The engineering company said they took their orders from New England Freedom Corp. And do you know what New England Freedom Corp said?"

"Sue us if you don't like it," Phil said.

"Sue us if you don't like it is exactly right. A big old corporation against a woman who looks like a chicken that got left in the oven too long. Okay, I said, I'll see you in court. They did offer me a settlement, forty thousand dollars, and I turned em down. I want five million, one for each of my children, fourteen to three years old. They can have my husband for free, he should have got em out. Now is it time for me to go?"

For the first time since Sal died—maybe for the first time since Jake died—Phil felt a stirring of real interest. Also outrage. He liked the idea of going against a heavyweight corporation. Not for the money, although his piece of five million would be considerable. Not for the publicity, because he had all the business he could handle . . . or wanted to handle. It was something else. It was a chance to get his hands around a neck that wouldn't fade away like smoke.

"No," Phil said. "It's not time for you to go."

Phil pursued New England Freedom relentlessly for the next five years. His father disapproved, saying Phil had a Don Quixote complex and accusing him of letting his other cases slide. Phil said that was probably true but pointed out that he no longer had to save up to send his son to Harvard, and John—Old John, by then—never said another word about the case. Ted Allburton's widow said she understood and was with him a hundred per cent. "You're doing it because you can't sue the cancer that took Jakey," she said.

Phil didn't disagree—there might have been an element of truth in what she said—but he was really doing it because he couldn't get the Answer Man out of his mind. Sometimes when he couldn't sleep, he'd tell himself he was being foolish; the Answer Man wasn't responsible for his misfortunes or for those of the Burned Woman. All that was true, but something else was, as well: when he really *needed* answers, the man with the red umbrella was gone. And, like Mrs. Lacasse, he had to hold *somebody* responsible.

He got NEF into Boston District Court shortly before Mrs. Lacasse came down with pneumonia. He won. NEF appealed, as Phil and Christine had known they would, but she did have that one conditional victory before the pneumonia took her off in the fall of 1967. By then Phil had seen her wasting away almost by the day and knew, just as he'd known with Jake, that the writing was on the wall. He added Ronald Lacasse's brother to the case. Tim Lacasse had none of the Burned Woman's thirst for revenge, none of her fervor; he told Phil to go at it, knock himself out, and followed the case from his home in North Carolina. He refused to pay any fees, but would be happy to take some money if it fell out of the sky, wafted down south from Boston or New Hampshire. The Burned Woman left no estate. Phil continued anyway, paying expenses out of his own pocket. Twice NEF offered to settle, first for three hundred thousand dollars, then for eight hundred thousand. The publicity was making them *très* uncomfortable. Tim Lacasse urged Phil (via long distance) to take the money. Phil refused. He wanted the whole five million, because it was what Mrs. Lacasse had wanted. A million for each child. There were delays. There were continuances. NEF lost in the First Circuit and appealed yet again, but when the Supreme Court refused to hear their case, they ran out of road. The final bill for the Christmas lights—the straw that broke the camel's back—and the shitty wiring Phil proved was standard NEF policy (focusing on other developments the corporation had built) was 7.4 million dollars awarded to Plaintiff Tim Lacasse. Plus considerable court costs. NEF, initially unable to believe it could not outlast a country lawyer from East Overshoe, could have saved almost two and a half million dollars by giving up.

Tim Lacasse threatened to sue when Phil informed him they would be splitting the award right down the middle. "Go right ahead," Phil said. "Your three-point-seven will melt like snow in April."

Tim Lacasse finally agreed to the split, and on a day in 1970, Phil hung a framed picture on his office wall, where he would see it first thing every day. The picture showed Ronald and Christine Lacasse on their wedding day. He was beefy and grinning. In her white wedding gown, Christine looked drop-dead gorgeous.

Below the photograph were six words in capitals Phil had carefully lettered himself.

ALWAYS REMEMBER OTHERS HAVE IT WORSE

Following the final adjudication of the suit against New England Freedom—a case that made him something of a star in legal circles—Phil could have had all the work he wanted. He eased up on the throttle instead, and because he was now financially comfortable, he began to take a greater number of *pro bono* cases. In 1978, fourteen years before the Innocence Project was founded, he got a new trial, and eventually freedom, for a man who had served twelve years of a life sentence in New Hampshire State Prison.

There was a hole in his life where Jake and Sal had been, of course. Legal work couldn't fill it, so he became more active in the community. He served as a trustee for the Curry Public Library and inaugurated the first Curry Book Festival. He did PSAs on the New Hampshire TV channels for the annual statewide blood drive. He worked one evening a week at the North Conway food bank (because others have it worse) and one evening a week at Harvest Hills, the animal shelter across the state line in Fryeburg. In 1979 he got a beagle puppy there. Frank went with him everywhere for the next fourteen years, riding shotgun.

He did not remarry, but he had a lady friend down the road in Moultonborough who he visited from time to time. Her name was Sarah Coombes. He did her legal work and paid off the mortgage on her house. He and Frank didn't always spend the night, but Sarah kept a bag of Gaines-Burgers in her pantry for those times when they did. These visits grew rarer as the years passed; Phil was more likely to go home when the day was finished and microwave whatever his housekeeper and woman of general work left for him. Sometimes—not always, but sometimes—he was struck by the emptiness of the house. On those occasions he'd call Frank to his side and scratch him behind the ears, and tell him that others had it worse.

The one community job he refused was co-coaching the Curry Little League team. That was just too close to home for Just Phil.

So the time passed, so the story was told. For the most part, it was good time. There were scars, but not disfiguring ones, and what were scars, after all, but wounds that had healed?

He picked up a limp and began to walk with a cane. Marie retired. He began to suffer arthritis in his hands, feet, and hips. Marie died. He announced his retirement and the town (Curry was now on the verge of becoming a small city) threw him one hell of a party. He was given many presents, including a plaque proclaiming him CURRY'S #1 CITIZEN. Several speeches were made, culminating in Phil's address to a gathering that almost filled the auditorium of the new high school.

It was a modest address, it was witty, and most of all it was short. He needed to piss like a racehorse.

Frank the beagle died peacefully in the fall of 1993. Phil buried him in the backyard, digging the hole with his own hands, although his joints squalled in protest at every shovelful. When the grave was filled and patted down and re-sodded, he gave a funeral oration, also short. "I loved you, old boy. Still do." That was the year Phil turned eighty-one.

In 1995, he began to suffer migraines for the first time in his life. He went to see Dr. Barlow, who he still thought of as the New Doc, although Phil had been seeing him for checkups and arthritis for ten years. Barlow asked him if he was having double vision with the headaches. Phil said he was, and admitted that sometimes he found himself in different parts of the house when the headaches eased up, without remembering how he got there. Dr. Barlow sent him to Portsmouth for an MRI.

"Not such good news," said the New Doc after examining the results. "It's a brain tumor." Then, as if congratulating him: "Quite rare in a man your age."

Barlow recommended a neurologist at Mass General. Because Phil no longer drove except around town, he hired a young fellow named Logan Phipps to chauffeur him. Logan talked a great deal about his family, his friends, his girl, the weather, his part-time job, his desire to go back to school. Other things, as well. It all went in one of Phil's less than acute ears and out the other, but he nodded along. It came to him on that ride that you began to separate from life. It wasn't a big deal. It was like tearing a supermarket coupon slowly but steadily along a perforation.

The neurologist examined Phil and examined the scans of Phil's elderly brain. He told Phil he could operate and take that nasty brain tumor right out, which made Phil think of an old song where a girl proclaimed she was going to wash that man right out of her hair. Sal frequently sang it in the shower, sometimes while she was washing her own hair, which Phil never took personally. When Phil asked the neurologist what the odds were that he would wake up from that operation—and as himself—the neuro guy told him fifty-fifty. Phil said he was sorry, but at his age those odds weren't good enough.

"Your headaches may be quite bad before . . ." The neuro guy shrugged, not quite wanting to say *before the end*.

"Others have it worse," Phil said.

3

On a windy October day in the fall of 1995, Phil slid behind the wheel of his car for the last time. Not a Chevrolet jalopy or a Buick these days but a Cadillac Seville equipped with all the bells and whistles. "I hope to Christ I don't kill anybody, Frank," he said to the dog that wasn't there. He was headache free for the time being, but a coldness—sort of a *distantness*—had begun to inhabit his fingers and toes.

He drove through town at twenty miles an hour, increasing his speed to thirty when he left downtown. Several cars swerved around him, horns blaring. "Eat shit and die," Phil told each of them. "Bark if you agree, Frank."

On Route 111 the traffic thinned away to almost nothing, and was he surprised when he passed the bright yellow sign reading 2 MILES TO THE ANSWER MAN? He was not. Why else was he risking his life and the lives of anyone he happened to meet going the other way? Nor did he believe it was the spreading black rot in his brain sending out false information. He came to the next one soon after: bright blue, ANSWER MAN 1 MILE. And there, just over a rise on the outskirts of Curry Township, was the table and the bright red umbrella. Phil pulled over and turned off the engine. He grabbed his cane and struggled out from behind the wheel.

"You stay there, Frank. This won't take long."

Was he surprised to see the Answer Man looked just the same? Same bright eyes, same thinning hair, same clothes? He was not. There was just one change Phil could see, although it was hard to be sure with his vision doubling and sometimes trebling. There was only a single sign on the Answer Man's table. It read

ALL ANSWERS FREE

He sat down in the client's chair with a grunt and a grimace. "You're just the same."

"So are you, Just Phil."

Phil laughed. "Pull the other one, why don't you?" A stupid question, he supposed, but why not? Today all the answers were free.

"It's true. Inside, you are just the same."

"If you say so, but I have my doubts. Have you still got your big clock in your bag?"

"Yes, but today I won't need it."

"Freebie Friday, is it?"

The Answer Man smiled. "It's Tuesday, Just Phil."

"I know that. It was an impotent question. Are you familiar with those?"

"I'm familiar with *every* kind of question. What's yours?"

Phil decided he no longer wanted to ask *why me*; it was, the Answer Man would have said, another impotent question. It was him because he *was* him. There was no other reason. Nor was he curious about how long he would live. He might see the snow fly, but it was a sure thing he wasn't going to be around for the spring melt. There was only one thing he was curious about.

"Do we go on? After we die, do we go on?"

"Yes."

The grayness started to come, closing in around them very slowly. At the same time, the Answer Man began to recede. Also very slowly. Phil didn't mind. There was no headache, that was a relief, and the foliage—what he could still see of it—was very beautiful. In fall the trees burned so bright at the end of the cycle. And since all the answers were free . . .

"Is it heaven we go to? Is it hell? Is it reincarnation? Are we still ourselves? Do we remember? Will I see my wife and son? Will it be good? Will it be awful? Are there dreams? Is there sorrow or joy or any emotion?"

The Answer Man, almost lost in the gray, said: "Yes."

*   *   *

Phil came around behind the wheel of his Cadillac, surprised to find he wasn't dead. He felt okay for the time being; actually pretty good. No headache, no pain in his hands or feet. He started the engine.

"Do you think I can get us back home in one piece, Frank? And without killing someone? Bark once for yes, twice for no."

Frank barked once, so it was yes.

It was yes.

For Jonathan Leonard

AFTERWORD

One day while I was taking my morning walk, listening to the Jeff Healey Band playing "Highway 49" and thinking of nothing but how cool that slide guitar solo is, I saw two green plastic figures wearing red caps. They were flanking the road and bore the warning SLOW! CHILDREN AT PLAY. The story "Rattlesnakes" came into my mind, fully blown. The only thing I didn't know in that moment of conception was that an old friend from *Cujo*, a novel I'd written long ago, would be the main character.

That's how it works for me sometimes—a story will arrive fully formed, just waiting for the right trigger to declare itself. It's a very cool thing. I rarely know the details (the elderly cop in "Rattlesnakes," Andy Pelley, came out of nowhere), or how the stories are supposed to finish up; part of the joy, for me, at least, is in the discovery. Why this process works, or how it works, is a complete mystery to me.

"Danny Coughlin's Bad Dream" was like that. One day, while getting dressed with nothing on my mind but a bowl of cereal and taking my dog for a walk, I thought, "What would happen if a man had a single psychic flash? A dream that showed him where a body was buried? Would anyone believe him, or would they think he was the killer?" That was while I was putting on my shirt. By the time I was pulling on my jeans, I was thinking about an obsessive cop, sort of like Inspector Javert in *Les Misérables*, hounding my protagonist.

The rest of the story fell into place. I didn't know my cop—Jalbert instead of Javert—would have a counting obsession; he started doing it pretty much on his own. I simply followed that particular thread. Does that make me a storyteller or a stenographer, like William Davis in "The Dreamers"? Maybe it's both.

Am I curious about the process? Since it's played a big part in my life, of course I am. I've written about writers in my fiction, and I've written about the *act* of writing in nonfiction, but I still don't understand it. I don't even understand why people need stories, or why I—among many others—feel the need to write them. All I know is that the exhilaration of leaving ordinary day-to-day life behind and bonding with people who don't exist seems to be a part of almost every life. Imagination is hungry, and needs to be fed. And sometimes—again like William Davis in "The Dreamers"—I actually see the words even before I write them. The first paragraphs of "Red Screen" and "Finn" existed weeks and months before I actually put them down. I could see every period and comma. Does that put me *on the spectrum*, as they say? Maybe, even probably, but who gives a shit? Storytelling has entertained me and others over a number of years, and that makes me happy.

As to why so many of my stories are about dark matters . . . that's another subject. Must I apologize for my material? I think not. Francisco Goya did an etching which showed himself surrounded by fantastical creatures as he dozed, and called it *The Sleep of Reason Produces Monsters*. I have always thought such sleep, and such monsters, are a necessary component of sanity. (Check out the first line of Shirley Jackson's *The Haunting of Hill House*—she says it well.) Horror stories are best appreciated by those who are compassionate and empathetic. A paradox, but a true one. I believe it is the unimaginative among us, those incapable of appreciating the dark side of make-believe, who have been responsible for most of the world's woes. In stories of the supernatural and paranormal, I have tried especially hard to show the real world as it is, and to tell the truth about the America I know and love. Some of those truths are ugly, but as the poem says, scars become beauty marks when there is love.

Most of these stories are quite new, and the longest of them have never been published. I don't need to delve into the provenance of most;

that would amount to no more than a tiresome recitation of where I was when each idea presented itself. If I could even remember, that is.

The only other one worth mentioning is "The Answer Man." My nephew, Jon Leonard, dug around in my old stuff, a lot of it unfinished and long forgotten. He made a photocopy of one particular six-page fragment with a note attached, saying it was too good not to finish. I read it and thought he was right. Those first pages were written when I was thirty. I finished it when I was seventy-five. While working on it, I had the oddest sense of calling into a canyon of time and listening for the echo to come back. Does that even make sense? I don't know. I just know it's how I felt.

I have been called prolific, which Constant Readers of my work consider a good thing and critics of it sometimes consider a bad one. I never meant to be; I never meant not to be. I have done what was given to me to do, and mostly it's been a joy to me. The only drawback, call it the fly in the ointment (or the fatal flaw, if you want to be hifalutin), is that the execution has never—no, not one single time—been as splendid as the original concept. The only two times I even came close to getting it all were in two prison stories: *The Green Mile* and "Rita Hayworth and Shawshank Redemption." All the others fell short of what I wanted for them. Even with long novels such as *It*, *The Stand*, and *Under the Dome*, I finished with the sense that a better writer would have done a better job. Still, on measure I'm proud of what I've done. And I'm proud of my short fiction, probably because they have always been hard for me.

I can't begin to name all the editors who worked on them and made them better, but I can thank Julie Eugley, for digging out literally dozens of old stories, most of which were terrible, a couple of which begged to be finished. I can also thank Jon Leonard, who brought the long-forgotten "Answer Man" story to my attention. I can thank both of my sons for collaborating with me and bringing their own unique talents to bear. Joe has collaborated with me on two stories, "Throttle" and "In the Tall Grass." Owen collaborated with me on *Sleeping Beauties*, one of my all-time favorite novels. I can thank my other collaborators, Stewart O'Nan, Richard Chizmar, and the late Peter Straub. To work with other writers is always a risk, but in each case I reaped great rewards.

AFTERWORD

I have to thank my long-time editor, Nan Graham, and Liz Darhan-soff, my agent. She stepped into the late Chuck Verrill's place and took a weight off my shoulders. Thanks are due to Robin Furth, my tireless researcher and my friend. Thanks most of all to my wife, Tabitha, who keeps me grounded. She can be both sweet and tart, sometimes in the same breath, but she's always whip-smart. It was she who suggested that I needed to say more about Danny Coughlin's brother and pointed out I had more work to do about Covid in "Rattlesnakes."

Great thanks to you, dear readers, for allowing me to inhabit your imaginations and your nerve-endings. You like it darker? Fine. So do I, and that makes me your soul brother.

PS: The first line of *The Haunting of Hill House* is as follows: "No live organism can continue for long to exist sanely under conditions of absolute reality; even larks and katydids are supposed, by some, to dream."

PPS: The Leonard Cohen song from which I got the title of this book is "You Want It Darker." Apologies for changing the verb.

April 23, 2023